FURIOUS HEAVEN

FURIOUS HEAVEN

KATE ELLIOTT

TOR

Tor Publishing Group

NEW YORK

FURIOUS HEAVEN

Copyright © 2023 by Katrina Elliott

A Tor Book
Published by Tom Doherty Associates / Tor Publishing Group
120 Broadway
New York, NY 10271

www.tor-forge.com

Tor® is a registered trademark of Macmillan Publishing Group, LLC.

The Library of Congress Cataloging-in-Publication Data
is available upon request.

ISBN 978-1-250-86700-1 (hardcover)
ISBN 978-1-250-86701-8 (ebook)

Our books may be purchased in bulk for promotional, educational, or business use. Please contact your local bookseller or the Macmillan Corporate and Premium Sales Department at 1-800-221-7945, extension 5442, or by email at MacmillanSpecialMarkets@macmillan.com.

First Edition: 2023

Printed in the United States of America

0 9 8 7 6 5 4 3 2 1

There is but one true sun, and each of us
casts nothing more than her reflected glory.

FURIOUS HEAVEN

1

Never Say the Wily Persephone Can't Take the Triceratops by the Horns in a Crisis

The heart of Lady Chaos is a knot, which some call binding fate while others thought it nothing more than luck's capricious cull. Or call, if destiny has any power. Philosophers debate these questions now and have debated them for untold years. Do humans live in harmony with fate? Or do they suffer powerless in life as fate's demands adhere to a set pattern? *We are the spears cast at the furious heaven.*

"That we are spears means we have been loosed from the hands of those who brought us into the world. It doesn't mean we are forever bound to the trajectory they choose for us," says Sun Shān, heir to the throne of the Republic of Chaonia. "Fate is not just the command of heaven. It is also a matter of strategy."

She pauses with perfect timing and flattering intensity to survey us, her loyal Companions.

We sit on cushions beneath the red gazebo. In the night courtyard a lamp shines, casting a golden aura over the outdoor hearth, the troughs of flowers, and the expanse of pavement where we drill morning and afternoon. The sounds of washing-up drift in from the kitchen, which opens off the courtyard. I would far rather be on mess duty than trying to hold my own in this cutthroat crowd.

Three of her loyal Companions are paying close attention to the long-winded discussion of the *Sayings of the Elder Sages*, which is the sort of evening entertainment a meticulously educated princess like Sun and her royal-academy-trained intimates naturally love best. Since I am neither meticulous nor royal academy trained, I am picking my way through platters of five-spice pumpkin seeds, lightly salted edamame, and the particularly delicious red bean buns.

"Is that what 'spears' means?" counters the Honorable James Samtarras, tugging on the obnoxious flatcap he always wears, although I couldn't tell you if he sleeps in it. "Trajectories? Commands? Strategies?"

Sun gives him one of her put-up-or-shut-up stares. "Did you have an interpretation to offer, or are you just sticking spokes in the wheel of discussion?"

"Spokes," I mutter under my breath as I toy with another bun. Two is usually my limit, but I feel I can make an exception for a third given how long this discussion on knots, fates, and destinies has ground on and the likelihood it will continue to grind for another hour at least.

James doesn't hear me because, like the others, he is really into these debates. "The passage refers to the ancient Argosies that fled the Celestial Empire's fall. The spears are a reference to the physical ships. Get it?"

Sun flicks her fingers as if to swat away a fly. "That's the hill you want to die on, James?"

"Sometimes the literal explanation is the best one," retorts James.

The Honorable Alika Vata plucks a sour chord from his ukulele, punctuating the musical commentary with the handsomely mocking smile he reserves for James and anyone else who annoys him, like me.

Sun nods. "Alika is correct. That line of debate can only run a short distance before it hits a locked gate. Why use a metaphor if you can just say ships?"

"I like facts," says James, "and facts can be awfully difficult to determine one hundred generations after the *fact*."

"Ooo, good one," I offer sarcastically, but the others ignore my spirited sally.

James is on a roll. "I can't help that poets and philosophers feel obliged to gild the lily with myth-making and fancy metaphors that everyone praises as great intellect. It's unnecessary obfuscation of what is more plausibly explained in concrete terms."

Alika plucks a fresh tune from his ukulele. "'I could while away the hours, if I only had a mind.'"

"It's not 'if I only had a mind.' It's 'if I only had a brain.' Respect the ancient classics. Be accurate!" James slaps Alika's leg with his cap, then flaps it in the air so vigorously he almost hits the fourth Companion, the Honorable Hestia Hope.

Hetty, of course, is the one who has been reading aloud to us from the "Reflection" that is this week's philosophy assignment.

"Dear James, I pray you, calm your cap and mind," says Hetty with the quiet dignity and sly pinch of mischief she fully inhabits. Her lips part in an inviting way that draws Sun's gaze for a caught breath, although Hetty never looks at her, not once.

I politely look away from their adorable if perilous little interaction as Alika continues singing of riddles and oceans.

James, Alika, and Hetty have been with Sun for years. She knows their foibles and their strengths. She relies on them absolutely. Which is why all my warning klaxons blare when the princess turns her attention to me, her newest Companion. That diamond-drill mind of hers is always going, which means her Companions need to be on their game all the time. If there is anything I am not, it is on my game all the time.

"Perse, what do you think?"

My suddenly nerveless fingers drop the bun as I blink. "What do *I* think?"

"*Do* you think, is the question we are all asking ourselves," remarks James, because he can't help himself.

Never say I can't take the triceratops by the horns in a crisis. I snatch James's cap out of his hand, leap up, and sprint away. James yelps and scrambles after me, but he's not anything as quick as I am and utterly lacks my impressive ability to alter trajectory and dodge.

Alika raises his voice with a new verse. "'Her head all full of stuffin' . . .'"

Sun leans back on an elbow, amused by Alika's twanging melody, James's outraged shouts, and my bold bid to avoid the question. But we all know I've only put off the inevitable by a few minutes before I have to pay the piper and admit that I did not, in fact, do the reading, whereas James certainly did and is just being contrary.

Shadow and light shift behind the rice-paper screens of the bodyguard's office. It once belonged to Sun's faithful bodyguard and military tutor Octavian. He was murdered in front of our very eyes six weeks ago. Sun burns a stick of incense every day in his honor.

A screen slides aside. Colonel Isis Samtarras emerges, holding an unrolled tablet in her right hand. "Princess, I have last week's training scores."

"Saved by the bell!" With a triumphant grin I toss the cap at James and trot back to the gazebo, not remotely out of breath.

"You might not say so, Honored Persephone, once you see the scores," remarks Isis as she offers the tablet to Sun. Her teacup pteranodon, Wing, perches on her shoulder, watching me as if wondering if I'm small enough to be a snack.

A roll-call assembly request from Sun pings onto our rings, the private network that allows Sun to share shielded communications within her trusted inner circle.

WEEKLY SCORES. NOW.

We four Companions are already here, of course.

Wiping damp hands on towels, Candace and Tiana emerge together from the kitchen. The two are a study in contrast. Battle-fan-wielding

Candace grew up on military ships as the child of dead soldiers, herself destined to be a soldier. Glamorous, beautiful, accomplished Tiana graduated top of her class from Vogue Academy. Like Isis, they are Companions'-companions, the cee-cees who attend to us Companions as we tend to our Sun.

In an alcove set into the wall beside the courtyard's entry gate stand two of the other three current ring-wearers. Marine Ensign Solomon Iosefa Solomon and Ensign Jade Kim are anomalies, temporary additions to Sun's inner circle even though they are neither Companions nor cee-cees. They're my fault.

During my tumultuous entry into Sun's orbit, I led the princess and her retinue to the Central Defense Cadet Academy, where I took my training. I drafted my CeDCA classmates into the battle that followed. Having noticed their effectiveness, Sun kept these two instead of releasing them into the fleet with the rest of our graduating cohort. Solomon and Jade move forward with the cautious respect of citizens who aren't sure how much longer they'll be allowed to remain in the palace.

Sun hands back the tablet. "Isis, you announce the scores."

Isis has the smile of a basilisk eager to turn her victims to stone. "This week, as I'm always fascinated to say, the lowest aggregated score combining physical training, marksmanship, military science, operations and management, philosophy and the arts, fleet history, and field exercises again can be presented to the Honorable James."

He smiles without shame and waves his cap as if he is in the cheer section of a rugby game. "You're welcome," he calls to me.

From the edge of the gazebo, Solomon snorts derisively.

I shoot him a killing look. "Fuck you, Solomon."

"Weak ass, Perse," Solomon replies with the equanimity of someone who knows he has one of the higher scores.

"The Honorable James has anticipated me," says Isis, referring to James with the familiarity of a legendary relative who has known a young person for the entirety of their short and uninteresting life. "The Honorable Persephone does indeed have the second-lowest aggregated score. James, she edged you out because of her superior physical fitness, which is in the top three. A significant accomplishment that nevertheless does not offset her deficiencies."

Jade Kim opens their mouth to make a cutting remark but when Sun casts a sharp look that way, the ensign closes perfect cherry lips with prim innocence and settles for shading a picturesque sneer in my direction.

Ignoring the byplay, Isis goes on. "Third-lowest this week, I'm surprised to say, is—"

The ringing of the entry-gate bell interrupts her. Its triple chime fades into silence, followed by a five-tone phrase signaling the arrival of the queen-marshal her very own self.

Just the Two of Us

Sun kept a carefully vetted staff to minimize the intrusions of either of her strong-minded parents into what few spaces of her life belonged solely to her. Her high secretary hurried toward the gate, but it opened before Nisaba got there, its lock overridden by the superior authority of the queen-marshal.

Eirene strode in with her usual decisive energy, the proverbial allosaurus in a china shop. She had been off-planet tending to the aftermath of the Molossia battle, leaving Sun as nominal regent. Now she had returned. She came attended by three of her seven Companions, individuals of her age who had supported her climb to power.

Sun was already on her feet with her own Companions. The queen-marshal paused to look them over with the menacing glint of her obsidian eye, the reminder of a battlefield injury from early in her reign.

"Sun! Why do you still only have four Companions? You ought to have seven."

Sun lifted her chin as if to bring the fight back at her opponent. "Colonel Isis is bringing in the Honorable Razin Nazir for an interview tomorrow. She was three years ahead of me at the royal academy."

"I know who she is and where she was. She's Qìngzhī Bō's niece, so it ties him to you. A politically astute choice." The queen-marshal noted Solomon's presence in the manner of an experienced soldier making sure she has identified the presence of every person in a space. Her gaze lingered too long on Ensign Jade Kim before she returned her attention to Sun. "Who are these two, again?"

"Ensigns from CeDCA who performed with distinction in the recent battles."

"I see." Eirene's preferred mode was to intimidate and then attack. "I will speak with you in private. Just the two of us."

She walked away, thus requiring Sun to follow. High Secretary Nisaba settled Eirene's Companions under the gazebo on cushions. Candace and

Tiana emerged from the kitchen with platters of food and drink. The polite chatter of Companions young and older faded as Sun passed through her suite's audience hall.

Eirene was waiting for her in the private reception room. She had stationed herself on the balcony that overlooked the palace's Memory Garden of the Celestial Empire. As always she wore an unadorned on-duty uniform. She left the art and display of fashion and its accoutrements to her consorts.

Before her daughter could speak to formally welcome her back to the palace, Eirene raised a hand for silence. Her gaze shifted past Sun, who turned. Tiana appeared in a rustle of glowing silk and graceful manners to set a tray of drinks and tapas on a side table.

"May your constant duties be met with needful refreshment, Your Pacific and Never Indolent Highness." With a respectful but not subservient bow she retreated, leaving the queen-marshal and her heir alone.

"Keep your eye on that one," said Eirene.

"It's contractually illegal for the employer or employer's employer to have sexual contact with a cee-cee."

"That's not what I meant, although I'm fascinated that's the first thing that came to your mind," said Eirene with a laugh that made Sun's cheeks burn. "Your libido has been the subject of much discussion between your father and me."

Sun restrained a scream of frustration by clenching her fingers together. Once again, her mother had unbalanced her and placed herself in the dominant position.

"Yes, Sun, we talk about you, as parents do. But not recently, since he has taken himself into unknown territories with his scientists and Gatoi test subjects. I just learned you arranged a mothballed Titan-class ship for him without consulting me. The *Keoe*, I've come to learn. Next time, consult me first."

"There was a lot going on, such as the battles we were fighting and winning."

"That's no excuse, and you can take that as a warning." Eirene walked over to the side table and ate a deep-fried sesame ball with the savoring consideration of a gourmand. When she finished, she said, "You employ a good cook. Anyway, I'm not here to discuss João's situation."

"All right." Sun pinged a connection via her ring network, opening a one-way voice channel so Hetty would hear everything. Knowing Hetty was listening might help her keep her temper in check, as much as she loathed the monotony of prudence.

"You've proven yourself to my satisfaction. In time"—Eirene wagged a finger at Sun, which was as playful as she ever got with her daughter—

"and assuming you survive and I meet my end as all must do if they are not one of the Celestial Immortals, you'll become queen-marshal. To prepare for that day, are you ready to take an official military command in the fleet?"

Of course she was ready! What a question! But Sun kept her voice cool. "Yes."

"That's all you have to say?"

"I've proven myself. Is there something more I'm meant to say?"

"Nothing more." Eirene's smile was a knife that would stab you in the gut while she was praising you to your face. Rumor had it that, early in her reign, she'd eliminated three political opponents in exactly that fashion. "Come with me. I have something to show you."

The Wily Persephone Is Long Beyond Blushing

My best friend and I stand side by side with our backs against a wall. The queen-marshal's august Companions mingle with the others beneath the gazebo where we were just discussing the *Sayings of the Elder Sages* as you do when you come of age in the hothouse of the palace. Which I did not, although I was supposed to.

This failing is why I retreat the instant the queen-marshal's Companions stride into the courtyard: to get out of the line of fire. They're older and so confident, radiating a war-hardened sheen of success. To James, Alika, Hetty, and the veteran Isis they are familiar figures. Marshal the Honorable Precious Jīn, who spearheaded the Eighth Battle of Kanesh from a shattered cruiser. Marshal the Honorable Nà Bō, who survived a crash landing at the Battle of the Esplanade. Marshal the Honorable Grace Nazir, who never met a Phene soldier he didn't kill. They greet their younger counterparts with the in-jokes and sociable asides of people who have rubbed elbows and shared platters all their lives.

I'm the outsider here, even if I was born into one of the Core Houses just as they all were. Honorables whose purpose is to honor the republic through service.

Solomon, on the other hand, stands with his back to the wall as if he is on sentry duty at the citizen academy where he and I met. His height and bulk reassure me. We've patched up our falling-out. Together we're stronger than ever before, like the song says.

"This is daunting," he remarks in a low voice. The others interact in the way of people who belong to the same club and have never had a moment's doubt about their right to be there. "I never thought I would meet Companions face-to-face."

"Maybe they'll just talk to the people they already know. I can hope."

"Don't they know you?"

"They knew Perseus, so they know *who* I am. But they don't know me, do they? Not the real me, only the girl-from-Lee-House me." I cross my arms like barriers that can make me feel less conspicuous. I'm almost sorry I told Tiana to go after Sun with a tea tray.

Meanwhile, Jade Kim is on the move.

Like Solomon, Jade is not an honorable from a Core House. Unlike Solomon, Jade doesn't hang out with their back to the wall unless it's in a dark closet with their latest hot squeeze, not that I would know anything about that. Jade begins circling in like a hungry carnosaur with eyes for the tempting morsels that the rest of us would call connections with the most important people in the republic.

Solomon looks along my line of sight. His body stiffens and his breathing gets sharper. He hates Jade too, just for different reasons. Of course Jade smoothly insinuates themself into the conversation by gliding up alongside Candace as she delivers a tray of fluted glasses filled with sparkling wine. Those kissable lips drop a few words to Isis, who is standing next to Grace Nazir. Who could fail to notice the glossy dynamism of Jade's features? The muscled shoulders and supple hands? The half-tilted smile and the lying warmth of those drowsy brown eyes?

Solomon nudges me. "Holy hells, stop staring. I thought you were over Jade."

"Someone should kill that social-climbing parasite. Would you look at that?"

Water flows downhill along the path of least resistance. Jade Kim flows toward those most vulnerable to a slick combination of beauty and brilliance. Beneath the gazebo where we were so recently discussing fate and destiny, Jade pivots to chatting up the older Companions with the serious suck-up look that fooled our teachers at the academy. Sure, the teachers admired Jade's top scores, but it was the performative humility that snagged them.

Sun's Companions are harder marks than CeDCA's teachers or Eirene's bosom buddies. James ignores Jade while Alika smolders with indignation at the intrusion. Hetty glances around the courtyard until she spots me and Solomon up against the wall. Her mouth twists with amusement and a wink of sympathy. She tilts her head to invite me over, but I gesture a no. No fucking way am I wading into that poison swamp where Jade Kim will, I guarantee, find a way to put me down in front of Eirene's closest friends.

"Give it up," says Solomon.

"You give it up. You hate Jade too."

"Yeah, but that's because Jade insulted my family. I'm not the one who—"

"Shut up! It was my first year."

"And your second year, and your fourth year."

I'd blush but I'm long beyond blushing. "I didn't think you knew about those other times. It was a momentary weakness."

"You are just one momentary weakness after the next."

I would frown threateningly at him and even kick his boot but my thoughts drift to my last kiss.

Memory is a nag. I close my eyes as if that will block out the image of Zizou's blindfolded face. How arousing is it that we couldn't touch unless he was blindfolded? My fingers twitch as I think of how my arms embraced him; the texture of his hair on my skin; the solid line of his jaw; the touch of his lips to mine, hesitant at first as he too is astonished by the intensity of this mutual feeling, and then . . .

The scent of sandalwood makes my nose itch. Zizou did not wear perfume. I rub my nose with the back of a hand and open my eyes to see my cee-cee walking up to us holding a tray of warm egg tarts.

Ti offers a tart to Solomon as she flicks her gaze sideways in a message to me.

"Did you hear anything?" I whisper.

"No. The queen-marshal saw me coming before I got close enough to overhear. I couldn't think of a way to loiter without being obvious."

"So we don't know why she called Sun away."

"She *is* her mother."

I shudder.

"Not all mothers are like yours." She glances toward the lively gathering under the gazebo and back to me. "Walk over with me."

"No way."

Solomon says to Ti, "Are you going to try to convince her to go?"

"Not worth the effort." Ti shrugs eloquently.

He chuckles. "You've got her number, that's for sure."

Ti sighs, hands me the tray as if I'm the cee-cee and not her, and taps Solomon on his beefy forearm. "Solomon, it's important you not act like part of the furniture."

"Why is it important? I'm very comfortable here by the wall."

"Because you represent provisional citizens. You stand in for their importance to the republic. For their competence to serve and their worthiness to be given full rights and privileges. You need to act as if you are a full citizen with all that implies. Which means you can be introduced to the queen-marshal's Companions. You can speak to them with dignity and honor. If not for yourself, then do it for your family and all the other families and clans who live in the twilight legal limbo that is provisional citizenship—"

"All right, all right." He nudges me with an elbow. "Is she always like this?"

"Yes," I say, even though I've only known Ti for six weeks. "And no, I'm staying here with my wall. I love my wall. Let them come to my wall if they're so eager to make my acquaintance. If I go over there they'll murmur pointless regrets about poor dead Percy and afterward praise the eight-times-worthy war hero Resh and tell me how much I look like her and I can't take it. I just can't."

Ti takes the tray from my hands with the smile of a benevolently patient ancestor. "Come with me, Solomon."

Who wouldn't go with the most glamorous person in the room? Me, that's who. My wall keeps me in the shadow, cool and safe. With arms folded I watch Ti sail in like a festival barge adorned in miraculous lights, not that she's wearing lights. Jade has the looks and the arrogance. The Handsome Alika, past winner of Idol Faire, has the looks and the stage presence. But Tiana graduated top of her class at Vogue Academy. She knows how to command attention without seeming to. Heads turn her way. Suddenly everyone wants an egg tart in order to bask in her smile.

Solomon lumbers behind with the shyness that occasionally cracks his veneer of solidity. Isis immediately brings him to the attention of the older Companions. Colonel Isis Samtarras is a veteran of Eirene's campaigns too, even though she now works as James's cee-cee. She's commanded marines all her life, and she can spot the worth of a big, strong, fast, smart, hardworking, and dedicated young man from hardscrabble circumstances who at the academy kept his head down, worked hard, and scored high without ever once boasting about it.

My shoulders start to relax. Maybe I'll get through this unscathed after all. What could Sun and her mother have to talk about that they haven't already talked about before? How long could it possibly take?

4

She Alone of All Chaonia

To reach Fleet Strategic Command a person had to have the highest level of military clearance. With that clearance, an individual could descend via one of five security elevators or enter by a reinforced tunnel that linked FSC to Battle Reserve Command buried deep in the western mountains one hundred klicks away. The queen-marshal had direct access via stairs that connected the war room in her private quarters in the aboveground part of the palace to the underground nerve center of Chaonia's military.

Eirene's retinal scan and blood trace unlocked an airlock that let onto the stairs. Two spatharioi snapped to attention as the queen-marshal entered and gave them a curt nod. Sun admired the patience of palace guards, the whole of their duty to stand at the top of an enclosed stairwell that might be used once or twice a day at most, or not at all for weeks on end when Eirene was out on campaign.

She virtually clipped their ID bars into her network to find their names. "Sergeant Saif Yíng Alargos. Lance Corporal Sukja Rèn Alcotai."

Their faces brightened. "Your Highness."

Eirene had charged on without waiting. Sun scrambled to catch up. They descended three long flights to a second airlock guarded by a second pair of spatharioi, both corporals whom Sun also greeted by name.

The airlock opened onto an underground foyer. Anyone entering via stairs, elevators, or tunnel had to cross the foyer as through a shooting gallery to the entry barrier. This metal-and-ceramic gate was decorated with an image of the five-headed scylla native to Chaonia Prime's oceans. Instead of waiting to be admitted by the security stationed on the other side of the gate, Eirene placed a hand on the barrier.

"Eirene Shān, queen-marshal of the Republic of Chaonia."

The gate opened to her touch, she alone of all Chaonia able to open any door, any airlock, any shield. Sun followed her through a secure set of airlocks and into a cavernous chamber. Since Chaonia was on a wartime footing, soldiers stationed at consoles did not rise as Eirene entered.

Machines hummed. The light of screens painted a glow on faces intent on their tasks. The night watch was a quiet time if there were no immediate crises. In the aftermath of the battles at Molossia and Troia, both the republic and the empire had defaulted to "retrench and wait" mode, but of course Chaonia had limited knowledge of what was really going on in the Phene Empire and it would take weeks for news to trickle out.

At the center of the cavern a transparent dome sealed in a large strategos table. Here the location of every asset in the republic was marked, tracked, approved, and deployed. A colonel and a chief attended the table at all times. They stepped away to leave the queen-marshal and her heir alone beneath the dome. Eirene tuned the dome to become opaque.

A three-dimensional virtual map appeared above. It displayed the local belt of stars through which humanity had spread after the ancient Argosy fleets discovered Landfall, a system with an inhabitable planet. Each star system was marked with the symbol of the confederation to which it was politically aligned: a sunburst for the Republic of Chaonia, a double helix for the Phene Empire, a lotus for the systems collectively associated as the Yele League. There were other designations for other coalitions, as well as for the modern Argosy fleets and the nomadic banner fleets known as Gatoi, but at the moment these weren't the focus of military operations.

For six generations Chaonia had been beleaguered by the Yele League or subject to the Phene Empire. Eirene had changed all that. Now the Yele were yoked by a treaty, leaving Chaonian fleets free to fight the empire.

The queen-marshal removed a disk from a pocket tucked into the sleeve of her uniform. Setting it onto the table she turned the red glimmer of her obsidian eye upon it and, with a hidden code, opened its secrets. Lights sparked to indicate the three founding systems of the republic: Chaonia, Molossia, and Thesprotis.

Eirene expanded the view of Molossia System, scene of the recent monumental battle. "The damage the Phene inflicted sets back our fleet readiness by years."

"If I were the Phene, I'd make my move now while we're most vulnerable."

"That's the thinking of certain of my marshals. Qīngzhī recommends retreat from our forward footholds in the Hatti territories. He argues we should consolidate our gains by establishing a static and permanent frontier at Troia System."

"Marshal Qīngzhī wants us to abandon Aspera, Maras Shantiya, Hatti, Tarsa, Kaska, Na Iri, *and* Kanesh too?" Each star system sparked with a brighter light as Sun spoke their names. "After all the people who died to liberate them from the Phene? All the resources we expended in order to get control of beacons surrounding Karnos? Are you considering it?"

"Of course I'm not considering it. I'm going to stay on the schedule I set in motion years ago. And do you know why?"

Eirene's love of lecturing included treating her daughter as if she were the queen-marshal's student, and of course in most political and philosophical ways Sun was. Sun had learned never to interrupt. Half of successful tactics was knowing not to expend your effort to no benefit. Eirene zoomed the map to enlarge and focus the current-to-the-day configuration of the biggest prize of all: Karnos System and its eleven planets. Seven of these planets had beacons anchored to them like moons.

"Because Karnos used to be an independent territory with its own dynastic lineage, it still functions as a buffering frontier between us and the central imperial systems of the Phene. You may find my pedagogy annoying," she added with a quirk of one eyebrow as she studied her daughter's expression, "but drill is the heart of discipline. Why is Karnos such an effective buffer, given that it has seven beacons? The presence of six functional beacons out of those seven ought to make it a porous and difficult-to-defend system."

"Because only two of the beacons lead directly from Karnos into the heart of imperial space. That makes it a bottleneck."

The planets spun through the next year of their orbits around the Karnos star until Eirene paused them. "Twenty years ago I identified a local-to-Karnos window when the configuration of the planets and their beacons in Karnos System would favor an attack into Karnos through the Na Iri and Tarsa beacons. Why is that?"

Sun used a laser stylus to indicate the different beacons. "At this time and in this alignment the two beacons that link directly into imperial space—Sleepless and Windworn—will be disadvantageously positioned. If we attack into Karnos System via the Tarsa and Na Iri Beacons, then any reinforcement forces the Phene send into Karnos via Sleepless and Windworn will be separated by greater distances from each other than our fleets will be from each other. So our forces can coordinate more rapidly than theirs can."

"Very good."

"That's all very well, but nothing we can do will counter the communications advantage the Phene have."

"It's true. But physical distances remain the same for their ships as for ours. Once we are all in the same system, their Riders give them a much less disproportionate comms advantage. And it burdens them with the need to get the Riders out of harm's way." She indicated each beacon in Karnos System, named according to the system it linked to: Tarsa, Na Iri, Windworn, Sleepless, Aspera, Hellion Terminus, and the seventh, the dead one, whose paired system no one knew. "That's why this configuration is a rare chance I intend to take advantage of forty-two republic weeks from now. Some have argued it's too big a risk because it's too short a time frame for such a massive undertaking considering the losses we took. But I say it remains our best opportunity to take Karnos."

"Isn't the bigger risk that the Phene attack us sooner than we can attack them?"

"Maybe. But a good marshal knows when to sit tight. The Phene have so many more resources and population than we do that they'll think we can't bounce back after the damage we suffered. We were hit hard, it's true. But our shipyards, industrial parks, and training camps are working longer hours, more efficiently than ever. Combined with our better training and stronger unit cohesion, we have reserves of toughness the Phene lack. Chaonians don't dither. And despite Baron Voy's cowardly flight, and perhaps partly because of it, we maintain a substantial contingent of allied Yele League ships. Like the Larissan Centaur Division and the heavy frigate division. Neither of which were damaged in the battle."

Although lacking an obsidian eye, Sun did possess a laser stylus embedded in her ring, which she used to indicate Karnos Prime. One of three rocky planets in the goldilocks zone, it was the main center of the system's population.

"How do you mean to deal with the planet defense system and ground installations on Karnos Prime? The Phene could keep our forces stuck for years fighting over each patch of dirt."

Her mother had a smug smile that she only trotted out in private. It wasn't that Eirene was a modest or humble person; she was perfectly happy to rub her victories into the faces of her enemies. But she knew better than to tip her hand in front of people who might use foreknowledge against her.

"That's what clandestine operations and secret allies are for." She popped the disk out of the table and handed it to Sun. "Memorize everything on this. It opens to your retinal scan and voice only. It will erase itself if anyone else tries to access it. Do you have any questions?"

Sun bit back irritation at it having taken so long for her mother to trust her with the full military intelligence an heir ought to have. Octavian had trained her in a hard school. *Don't let your temper control you.* She had her mother's trust now. *Start as you mean to go on.*

"What happened to the Rider I captured on Tjeker? I've asked, but no one seems to know."

"Ah." Eirene's gaze lit up, as if she had forgotten her daughter had personally captured one of the Phene ruling class, the first Chaonian ever to do so. Perhaps she had. It would be exactly like her. "A good question. Let's go see."

5

Eirene's Companions Aren't Impressed by the Wily Persephone's Trivial Point Scoring

Voices speak at the entry gate to the heir's courtyard, more arrivals. A premonition of disaster whirls through my mind. I push away from the wall with a glance toward the kitchen door, wondering if I can make an excuse to go there. A toilet break! We all need those!

My first step in that direction comes too late.

Everyone turns toward the gate as another of Eirene's Companions walks in, my distant cousin the Honorable Marduk Lee. That's not so bad until I notice he is not alone. A pregnant pause settles upon the gathering as the pregnant consort of Queen-Marshal Eirene makes a stately entrance, solicitously escorted by Marduk. Consort the Honorable Manea Lee is halfway through her pregnancy. She's not waddling yet, but the gown she wears is cut to emphasize the curve of her growing belly.

There's an entire layer of politics involved in her marriage to and pregnancy by Eirene. For one thing, it reminds everyone at court and all citizens of the republic that Princess Sun's father is an untrustworthy foreigner while Manea is a good Chaonian girl who will give birth to a wholly Chaonian child. What else Manea is has been kept a secret, maybe even from her.

The Companions greet her kindly but with the patronizing smiles of hard-assed people who find her youth and gentle bearing to be not quite worthy of their full respect. I can't blame them. I grew up with Manea in Lee House: her and me and Percy and Resh the four acknowledged children of the three sisters in the governing line. Manea was the compliant one, blandly sweet. What she thought of me I never knew because she never let on and we were never close.

So I'm taken by surprise when she moves deftly through the greetings and cuts across the courtyard to my wall. Her long hair is dyed a pale pinkish white. She's taller than I am. People might not notice how much we look alike because of her plumper cheeks and curvier build, and because she sports the current fashion among those who follow Vogue trends of painting one side of her face. Today a curling explosion of waves of golden joy gives visual expression to her pleasure at having her beloved return to her side.

"Persephone," she says with an inviting smile, as if we are old friends. She squeezes my hands with more strength than I expect from uncalloused fingers. Her soft eyes melt winningly as she addresses me. "We've not had a chance to spend any time together since you were brought into Sun's household. Perseus's death was a shock. He was always very kind to me, you know."

"Percy was always kind." I don't add: kinder than I've ever been.

She smiles graciously. "I miss him. Now you're here in the palace, I'm hoping we can spend more time together. You'll be busy, of course. Sun's Companions must have a beast of a schedule. I can guess how it is for you, and I sympathize."

I blink, too puzzled by this assault to know how to act. "How what is for me?"

She lowers her voice. Everyone is looking our way, waiting for drama to drop. "It's got to be difficult to return to court after you ran away. I know my mother and your mother pretend otherwise, give out another story. I also know how hard Resh's death hit you. Maybe even why you felt you had to hide at the citizens' academy. We weren't close as children, but maybe we can be cousins now? You're all the close kin I have left besides my mother and Uncle Marduk. And your mother, of course, but Aunt Aisa is not an individual one can confide in."

"Or trust," I mutter.

She squeezes my hand. "You've had the worst of that."

So prudently spoken. So genuine. So sweet.

"Also . . ." She leans closer, looking at me through half-lowered eyelids like a helpless hatchling. "Where's Eirene? I don't want to ask the others because then they'll know she didn't tell me where she was going. They're kind of jerks about how well they know her and what they've all accomplished together and how I'm just the budding flower that's taken her current fancy."

Even I am not immune to people asking for help so flagrantly, with a shimmer of unshed tears in their eyes. "She and Sun went off for a private meeting."

"Ah. Well then." She releases one of my hands but not the other. "Please come keep me company. They're condescending to me, to be honest. I was hoping you'd stand beside me."

I believe her, which is possibly the worst part.

"All right."

We walk over together. Solomon looks honestly confounded.

Ti glides up and says, "Honorable Manea, may I be first to congratulate you on this winning ensemble. I'm impressed by its layers of meaning, and how well the colors work together."

Manea presses a hand to her chest with a smile made piquant by a delicate blush. "My thanks. I followed you in the final examination competition at Vogue Academy. I'm honored by such complimentary words from an adept of your accomplishments."

"My praise is honestly meant. Is there anything you need? Drink? Food?"

"I've been drinking goji juice."

"I'll get you some right away, Honored Consort." She heads for the kitchen, leaving me to face the onslaught alone.

"Perseus's death was so sudden," says Marduk Lee by way of greeting. "And his cee-cee, too. Shocking business."

After everyone has said their piece about my twin's unfortunate demise, Precious Jīn says, as if on cue, "You look so much like your eight-times-worthy sister."

"May I live up to her stellar example," I reply with creditable calm.

Before the reminiscences can start about Ereshkigal's sacrifice with all its gory details, Manea indicates the tablet unrolled on the table.

"Goodness, did we interrupt you while you were studying the ancient classics? Isn't this the 'Reflections on the Decree of Destiny'? 'We are the spears cast at the furious heaven.' So many discussions Persephone and I had with our tutor Kadmos. He made us memorize the whole thing. 'Do humans live in harmony with fate? Or do they suffer powerless in life as fate's demands adhere to a set pattern?' Are we bound to the trajectories of those who set us in motion? Are the spears merely a reference to the physical ships of the Argosy fleets on which we escaped the broken land? Those are in the first half. What else?"

She pauses to leave me an opening.

Jade Kim has never been shy about grabbing the spotlight when they believe it will benefit their status, and they aren't shy now as they grab my line. "In the next part of the 'Reflections,' it is said the spears represent anger. The loyal citizens and subjects had lived faithfully and obediently for their part. Yet they had been punished alongside the leaders, when it was the leaders who allowed the imperial gardens to wither. The leaders who did nothing as the blood of innocent and dutiful alike became corrupted because they thought the plague would not touch them. Thus, according to the sages, the spears can be interpreted as the anger of a population betrayed by both rulers and gods."

"Thanks for the timely lecture, Ensign." I use Jade's rank to remind everyone that I'm an Ensign the Honorable as well as a Companion, not a mere citizen ensign.

My pettiness does not intimidate Jade. "As if you had any idea, since I remember the scores you got in philosophy class." The murmur is a shot across the bow, accompanied by the tremor of a sneer.

"That was the other philosophy class," I reply. "I'm surprised you forgot how I aced the one on the *Sayings of the Elder Sages*. As Consort the Honorable Manea reminds me, I can still recite the entire scroll by heart. Anyone game to hear it? It only takes two hours."

Jade flushes with anger. My heart swells to ten times its previous size with smackdown satisfaction. Alika's mouth curls into a smirk, and Hetty hides a smile behind a hand. James gives a sideways tug to his cap as a salute to my wicked counterpunch. Solomon sighs because he's already figured out Eirene's Companions aren't impressed by my trivial point scoring.

Marduk Lee has the instincts of a typical Lee House scion, every one of whom fights dirty. He settles onto a divan and by doing so invites all to sit. All except me. "Eirene might be some time. I think it's a wonderful idea for you young people to focus on your elders while we wait. Go ahead, Persephone. We're all listening."

My mind goes blank and my skin goes cold. Where in the hells is Sun, and how soon is she going to get back here?

6

A Janus Face, Peering in Both Directions

The queen-marshal and her heir made their way past banks of consoles to a back wall. They took an elevator deeper into the bedrock. The lift opened onto an underground level known in whispers as "the Nineteenth Hell."

Airlocks and a gate sealed off a klick-long corridor. High-security rooms held military prisoners, although officially no one in here existed. There were three conventions of war. The third was that enemy soldiers and spacers taken prisoner could not be tortured or killed in custody. Since this level was not part of the Ministry of War, prisoners held in its cells were not formally in custody. Even so, Eirene rarely allowed military prisoners to be imprisoned here. As she often said, a strong military can hold to civilized conventions because it doesn't need savagery to succeed; it needs discipline and training.

Because the level was not a military installation, no one in the Guard or the Fleet worked down here, only civilians wearing white coats. The individual in charge was one of Eirene's Companions, the Honorable Norioghene Hope. She was tall for a Chaonian, wearing a white lab coat and blue gloves. She greeted the queen-marshal with a tap of forearms.

"Here you are, Eirene. When I heard you were back I was expecting you to come by sooner. I suppose you had to entertain the lovely Manea first."

"Needs must," said Eirene with the softening that gentled her usually belligerent expression when the subject of her young consort arose.

Norioghene wasn't one to make a lewd joke. She politely turned to Sun. "Princess Sun, peace be upon you."

"And upon you peace, Honored Norioghene."

"Where is the Rider?" Eirene said.

"This way." Norioghene led them along the passage. As they walked she glanced at Sun. "All the scans we've been doing remind me of the time I did a complete scan of your neural system to see if there was any inherited network from your father's side. You have some vestigial structures but you are not neurologically enhanced like other Gatoi. You won't remember. You were only three."

"I've seen the scans," said Sun. "Only children born on the wheelships develop the full neural network."

"I'd love a chance to study the wheelships and figure how and why that neural system develops in Gatoi soldiers."

Sun glanced at her mother, unsure of how much the Honorable Norioghene knew about Prince João's work with banner soldiers.

Eirene ignored the comment. "What can you tell me about the Rider?"

Norioghene's grin sparked with ghoulish excitement. "Remarkable and mysterious. In here."

An unmarked door opened into a chamber with guards, and thence through an airlock into a laboratory and surgical suite populated by monitors, worktables, and on-duty white coats. The coats came forward to be introduced to the queen-marshal and her heir. Anyone working down here had the highest security clearance. All were honorables from the various Core Houses.

After greeting them, Sun walked to a clear wall. Red lights flashed above an airlock entryway. Inside the chamber two individuals in vac suits were taking notes on either side of a transparent stasis pod. Eirene and Norioghene came up beside Sun.

"It's a vacuum chamber," said Norioghene. "The presence of a vacuum tells the stasis pod to stay in stasis rather than to open, because it thinks it's in space. We don't know how much awareness a Rider has if their physical body is unconscious or in stasis. We follow strict protocols to avoid a Rider spying on us or even hearing our voices or seeing our faces."

The figure inside the pod was a human of forty or fifty years of age. She had four arms on a somewhat elongated torso and a second face on the back of her head. The eyes and mouth and nostrils of the riding face were more like slits, as if someone had sketched a face on skin stretched over the back of a skull.

Norioghene was gushing enthusiastically to Eirene. "We've done multiple scans at different times of the day. The brain has subtle but anomalous structures when compared to normal brains, and even compared to the brains of imperial Phene with their larger cerebellum. However there's nothing we can pinpoint as the source of their ability to communicate with other Riders. We suspect the differences embedded in a Rider brain don't become fully apparent unless the brain is actively riding. We'd expect to see different regions light up. With the body in stasis it's impossible to get an accurate look at what is going on when a Rider is in active communication with other Riders."

"Have you woken the subject?" Eirene asked.

"Not yet. I advise against it because of the risk of suicide. That's not a chance we should be willing to take."

"Have you opened up her skull yet?" Eirene asked.

"You do realize that cutting into the skull of a prisoner if there's no medical indication would constitute torture," said Sun.

"I do realize," said Eirene so dryly that Sun felt her ears wither with the rebuke.

Norioghene said, "We can't open her skull without taking her out of the stasis pod. Once she's out of stasis, even if under sedation or unconscious, we don't know what level of communication she can manage without us knowing it's happening. She might be able to overhear everything we're saying and doing. If so, then every Rider would know. The Rider Council would have proof of torture. You see all the complications that would ensue."

"We're already at war with them," said Eirene. "But I take your point. It could create complications with our allies."

"What about trying to talk to the Rider Council through her?" Sun asked.

Eirene gave a caustic laugh, not quite mockery and not quite disdain, but close enough that Sun's cheeks heated with annoyance. "The Rider Council will have nothing to say to us. To them we are upstarts pawing through the rubbish like junkyard hatchlings."

A mirror placed on the wall reflected an image of the woman's ordinary face, relaxed in slumber. A janus face, peering in both directions.

"Think of what it would mean to have Riders of our own," said Sun. "We could coordinate an attack into the heart of the empire."

"We need not break ourselves against that behemoth," Eirene scoffed. "Their Council and syndicates may be reactionary, fractious, and hidebound, but they're still a hundred times more populous and a thousand times wealthier. Once we take Karnos we'll control a significant percentage of trade between the empire and the Yele League. That puts us in a powerful position no one expected us to be in twenty-five years ago. Not even me."

"We did it," said Norioghene, who had been with Eirene from the beginning.

"Don't say so before the outcome rests in our hands," Eirene snapped.

Norioghene gestured with a sign against ill fortune. "I didn't mean Karnos. I meant stabilizing Chaonia at our moment of greatest vulnerability, when we were falling apart after your brother's death. I mean gaining enough leverage and strength to force the Yele League into a treaty on our terms. I mean pushing the Phene and the Hesjan cartels out of Kanesh to give us access to Karnos and the Hatti regions. Your accomplishments are one of a kind. They'll never be outdone by any marshal or any ruler. Not now. Not ever."

"That's probably correct." Eirene contemplated the slack body and its seemingly unconscious faces. Her expression of heady triumph took on a calculating eye. "Sun's right, though. What if we had Riders of our own? It would make administering our new domains a cursed sight more efficient."

Norioghene shot her a look. "You've got some terrible thought percolating in your devious mind." The words were said with admiration, not as criticism.

"Maybe I do," said Eirene. "I need to think on it some more. For now, continue your passive scans and analyses. Do you have any theories on how riding works?"

The queen-marshal and her Companion walked away to a table. Sun remained at the wall.

Not now. Not ever.

Eirene had accomplished what everyone said was impossible, but that didn't mean what Norioghene thought it did. It only meant the impossible was achievable for the person who refused to set limits for themselves.

The Phene had built an empire with their Riders. A commander could do a lot with such an advantage. If she had Riders under her control, she would know instantly no matter how far apart they were what was happening where other Riders were. With a properly placed spy, for example, she could know what was going on right now in the heart of the enemy.

7

The Enemy of My Enemy Is My Friend

Long ago in the autocratic theocracy of Mishirru, scientists and laborers joined forces to form syndicates through which they demanded better working conditions as well as the right to alter their bodies. Persecuted by the unbending hierarchs, the beleaguered movement pooled resources and fled into an unexplored region of the local belt. All those later known as imperial Phene trace their descent from the 101 fleets that escaped Mishirru.

Once the earliest beacon routes were set into place by the engineers of the Apsaras Convergence, the syndicates established a loose philosophical union of administrative Exchanges, communication centers known as Unity Halls, and religious basilicas reaching across linked systems. This decentralized union of self-governing local entities endured for many generations, until the collapse in which at least a third of the beacons stopped working and the Convergence's home world was cut off from the rest of the local belt.

The collapse changed everything. It made empire possible.

Empire was why Lieutenant Apama At Sabao was standing on the portico of Grand Unity Hall on Anchor Prime. The domed hall rose at South Cliff, one end of a dam-like artificial ridge. Founders Exchange stood two klicks away at North Point. On the western side of the ridge, the city of Melo stretched across the flats toward distant hills. On the eastern side lay the glittering shallows of an endorheic sea studded with crumbling tuft pillars, known as Fair Water. Midway along the ridge's processional way, a bridge extended over the water to an artificial island where the founders had built a glass-walled basilica.

Apama could scarcely have ended up farther away from her humble birthplace on a rundown habitat in a distant system situated at the back-assed behind of the Phene Empire. At any moment she expected one of the four soldiers who flanked her, the proud Incorruptibles in their shining white dress uniforms and magnificently crested duty helmets, to turn to her and blurt out, "How dare a slimy shell from the dregs of Tranquility Harbor walk on these exalted heights?"

Of course none of them did. None of them would, because they knew who she was about to become.

At the sound of a bell she turned. Wind tugged at the calf-length cape she wore fastened to the shoulders of her parade dress uniform.

She'd worn her formal parade cape only once before, on the day she'd graduated from lancer academy. She shut her eyes against a stab of anger. She wanted to be with her unit, where she belonged, not here where she had no desire to be. How cruel to force a soldier to abandon comrades in the middle of battle. Memory assaulted her in a vivid flashback. A lancer shorn in half, its pilots still attached by umbilicals, spinning past her position in the silence of space among the rest of the debris. Her pulse thundered in her ears.

The bell chimed again with the call to meeting.

"Lieutenant At Sabao! Salutations!" cried a too-loud and unpleasantly familiar voice.

The Incorruptibles stiffened but did not intercede as a man wearing a foreign military uniform approached with the rangy stride of a person at ease with action and, of course, with himself. He had only two arms, particularly noticeable when he pressed his palms together as a greeting, but it was his hearty smile that annoyed her.

"What a fortunate chance brings us together again!"

"Admiral Manu," she said politely and without an answering smile. She did not salute. He was Yele so she need not acknowledge him as her superior officer.

"Perhaps we can enter Unity Hall together, Apama. May I call you Apama? I feel after what we survived in tandem we have long since passed the gates of formality."

"I prefer Lieutenant."

Did the lips of the Incorruptibles twitch with amusement? She hoped so.

"A palpable hit!" Nothing could dent the admiral's relentless cheer. "Accompany me, Lieutenant. You can explain the intricacies of Unity Hall and the empire's formal synod proceedings. The workings of its inner circle remain a mystery to outsiders. Does the Rider Council rule the Exchange or merely advise it? Do the syndicate bosses vote in Council proceedings or merely observe and then carry out Council orders via the Exchange?"

She started walking because the doors into the hall would close at the fourth bell and she was required to be inside when they did. Manu kept pace beside her. He was as tall as she was, longer in the leg, so he didn't have to scramble to keep up as people who weren't imperial Phene often did because they were usually shorter.

"I can't help you with the niceties of protocol, Admiral. I've never been inside a Unity Hall. Growing up we saw delayed broadcasts like everyone else." She'd been speaking Yele as a courtesy and now switched languages. "But everyone will be speaking in Phenish."

"I'm serviceable in Phenish," he replied in the same language, punctuating the words with a big, broad, self-satisfied grin.

Of course he was.

"You've been employed by syndicates before this?"

"Indeed I have. Once that cursed Eirene crushed the Yele League under her boot, many of us had no choice but to seek our fortunes elsewhere. The reward has been well worth it."

"What reward have you received, Admiral?"

"Why, your delightful company, Lieutenant." He took the liberty of patting her on the upper arm. She didn't slap his hand away only because the action would be visible to people eager to report any déclassé behavior to the one who'd brought her here.

"Lieutenant, are you all right? You flinched."

"Dust in my eye."

They reached the open doors as the third bell chimed. The doors let onto a curved vestibule adorned with festive chandeliers. Bright tiers of curtains depicted the migration fleets on which the founders of the syndical territories of yore had fled the despised autocracy of Mishirru.

"Manu! There you are!" A Yele man of about Manu's age hailed them, then approached with a bland smile that turned into a razor when he spotted Apama. "Here you are with *young* Lieutenant At Sabao, Manu. How like you."

Manu's frown made Apama feel in charity with the newcomer. That was how you started a skirmish! Get in the first blow!

The man pressed palms together in formal greeting. "We met before, Lieutenant. Perhaps you do not recall. I am Aloysius Pan, Baron Voy."

"I do recall. You are one of the consorts of Queen-Marshal Eirene of the Republic of Chaonia."

"That is correct."

"You are Yele and yet allied yourself to your old enemies in Chaonia."

"I married her as part of a nonaggression treaty forced on the Yele League by Eirene. People see her as a belligerent fighter, but her most successful strategic moves have been made through what she calls negotiation."

"So you are a successful strategic move?"

"I like to think so even if not everyone would agree," he said with a grin.

Manu rolled his eyes.

She hadn't qualified as a lancer pilot by being timid. Now she had a chance to test if her new status gave her scope to play a bigger game. "If that's so, it seems strange you fled your position as consort and treaty-sealer. Then again, how could a mere lancer pilot like me know what dwells in the minds of you Yele with your endless and intricate parsing of grammar and logic? What constitutes negotiation and success? Which better options may have presented themselves? Didn't you say something about that when we met before?"

The baron laughed heartily. He even threw his head back a little, as actors did to show how greatly entertained and affably good-natured they were. It was superb.

"You are a lancer, indeed, Lieutenant. Locked and loaded. If you will forgive the metaphor. It seems a bit crass given the empire's recent losses. You were at the battle of Molossia System, were you not?"

Manu said, "That's really enough, Aloysius. This isn't the place for your self-aggrandizing theater. I still don't trust you're not a spy sent into Phene space by Eirene. It's exactly the sort of plan Eirene would relish."

The baron cocked a look at the other man. "The independence and well-being of the Yele League is no laughing matter, even if a jest here or there may leaven our sorrow at being crushed for so many years under Eirene's boot. Now, Lieutenant. May I introduce you to seven Yele patriots? They're eager to meet you."

Which meant the news had already spread. Why else would they want to meet a mere lancer pilot? Among the group—all men—she could not help but look twice at a man about Manu's age dressed in the white robes of a religious order. He was lean-faced and handsome in a polished, even challenging manner. What she and her friends in their adolescent days would have called "hot dad."

Baron Voy missed nothing. Gesturing toward the waiting Yele, he said to Apama, "I can introduce you to that most interesting of specimens, a seer of Iros."

"The seers are hardly Yele patriots," said Manu. "I would scarcely call them Yele at all. But you'd say the enemy of my enemy is my friend, would you not, Aloysius?"

"You would know, since you taught the rest of us that phrase when you ran begging to the Phene for the military post you'd lost among your own people."

Manu stiffened, hands clenching. Voy smiled his blandest smile.

When caught in the middle of someone else's firefight, usually the most prudent course was to retire as quickly as possible.

"My apologies, Baron, but I need to get to my seat."

"No pardon required, Lieutenant. I've just gotten the news I'm to be an envoy for the Yele League here in the empire, so I hope to have an opportunity to speak at more length another time."

As she walked away, Manu kept pace even though she had absolutely not invited him along. He said, "Voy's a complete fraud, the most opportune of opportunists. He must see you as his new mark."

"I liked him," said Apama, deadpan.

"Oh. Ah! I see." Manu chuckled. "You are teasing me, are you not? Clever girl."

He moved to touch her shoulder.

She stepped out of reach, and exactly then, as if in collusion to ruin her day entirely, the fourth bell rang. "I have to go."

She broke into a run but the doors into the circular auditorium were already closing, too far away to reach in time.

A Synod, Begun Without Preamble

The door into the auditorium was held open by an Incorruptible long enough for her to slip inside. How fortunate, she might have said, but it wasn't luck. She paused to assay her surroundings.

Banks of tiered seats surrounded a circular central stage that was covered by a transparent half sphere like an upside-down bowl. The top level of the auditorium had no seats, the standing-room-only balcony crowded with foreign legations. The Yele group jostled their way up to the railing. Baron Voy was chatting with Hot Dad as if they were old friends, and maybe they were or maybe the baron was just that good at being a diplomat. Admiral Manu pushed his way into the group. He effusively greeted the men wearing the slate gray of the Yele fleet and the forest green of the Yele army. Spotting her, he raised a hand to get her attention.

She looked away and hurried down an aisle to the seat she'd been assigned. The auditorium was full except for one square of sixteen where three civilians sat amid thirteen empty seats: a stout man wearing the sash of the Oreella Syndicate; an adolescent glassy-eyed with nerves; a tidily dressed older woman wearing a batik head scarf. The auntie smiled kindly and indicated a seat next to the youth.

Inside the sphere, sixteen chairs with low backs were set in a circle, placed so the person seated in them would face out toward the auditorium. As the lights in the auditorium dimmed, the round stage sank out of view.

No one spoke, not even a whisper. As the gathered assembly waited for the stage to return, the traditional four-minute "procession of history" played along the walls for all to see.

Long ago a plague of corrupted blood ravaged the Celestial Empire, the lost home of humanity. Argosy fleets fled the carnage, carrying hundreds of millions of desperate refugees. After generations of travel, living and dying on the ships, the last group of surviving fleets still in contact stumbled onto Landfall. From this miraculous base they explored neighboring star systems and thus founded the venerable queendom of Mishirru, the true inheritors of the Celestial Empire, or so its holy rulers claimed. From here humans spread to establish new planetary homes across a star-rich region colloquially called "the local belt."

The Phene had started as a labor and science syndicate in Mishirru. Scientists and laborers had worked together to adapt the human body, through genengineering, to a widening variety of planetary environments and to life and labor in space habitats and long-haul vessels. Protective exoskeletons had their uses. Extreme temperature tolerance had its uses. Four arms had their uses. These adaptations gave humans more tools to survive and prosper.

But the religious authorities on Mishirru had condemned, outlawed, and cruelly persecuted the syndicates. In a series of migratory waves the Phene, as the rebels now called themselves, fled farther into the local belt to discover more habitable systems and create their own union of worlds.

Right now in the Unity Halls of Anchor, Auger, and Axiom Systems, the Rider Council met in a synod. Those allowed physical entry to each of the three auditoriums could witness in person as a treasured mark of distinction. The billions who lived on one of the Triple A Prime planets would watch the speeches in real time. Those in the three main star systems would view the proceedings at a varying string of lag times depending on how far they were from the Prime planet. When the synod finished, recordings would be taken by courier ship down the beacon routes to the farthest outposts of all the far-flung worlds of the empire. Any locale where a Rider was stationed or accompanying a fleet could hear an immediate report if the Rider chose to share what they had witnessed. Isolated Phene systems that had fallen off the beacon routes because of the collapse might get the news months or years later from an Argosy ship plying knnu trade routes.

As the "procession of history" faded, the stage rose, bringing with it four individuals dressed in dark blue attire. Each was seated in a chair with gazes fixed outward onto the auditorium. Shadowy simulacrums of twelve other individuals wavered into view to fill the other twelve seats. Distances involved between interstellar systems were too great for these to be actual images of people seated in those chairs at this moment in the other two Unity Halls. They were recordings projected for the benefit of people watching in real time in Anchor System, a reminder of the unity of purpose at the heart of the empire.

Apama's mouth went dry as she examined one in particular of the four Riders physically seated in Anchor's Unity Hall. She had reluctantly to admit she could see her resemblance to him in his square chin and the striking profile of his aquiline nose. But this man, the embodied half of the Rider, the one whose genes she shared, was not the one who had ripped her out of her life. He had a second face on the back of his hairless skull, a sketch of a face with thin lips, flat nose, and narrow eyes. The riding face was awake, alert, and intent.

The eldest of the physically present Riders stood. A large, imposing woman, she raised a speaking whip with her upper right hand to instantly gather the audience's attention. Her ordinary face spoke to the auditorium in a gravelly alto.

"Here present on Anchor System I name the four Riders Kubaba, Zakurru, Neferure, and Manishtusu."

After these words, her ordinary lips closed and her ordinary face fell into a slack repose. Now her riding face spoke to her peers listening across the empire.

"I, Kubaba, Speaker for the Rider Council, begin this synod without preamble," she said in a harsh, whispery voice. "The debacle of the attack on Molossia embarrasses us all. The Styraconyx Syndicate in its rash campaign failed our empire. Tanarctus's fleet did its best to stem the gushing wound but could not patch what was a foolish endeavor to begin with. The Styraconyx Syndicate has been censured for its reckless and self-aggrandizing stunt that caused such a devastating loss of life and ships. Those who supported and enabled the disastrous gambit should be criticized as well. This is not innovation. It is irresponsibility. We must stick with the strategies that have served us in times past."

When she lowered her speaking whip, silence followed. Riders on Axiom and Auger would be replying. None of the Riders here on Anchor repeated what was being said elsewhere by their comrades. The administrators, officers, and notables honored with seats in the Unity Halls would have to wait for the official release of the collated proceedings.

Finally, the man who named himself Apama's sire stood. He raised his speaking whip with an exasperated flick, and it was his riding face who spoke.

"I, Zakurru, speak. These are not times past. Kubaba, you and your faction on the Council treat the matter of Chaonia as if they are the same weak and ill-managed republic they were thirty Anchor years ago. They have changed, as have their tactics. We must change if we mean to defeat their belligerent and effective queen-marshal. You have seen it with my eyes. You have seen it with the eyes of Anchi."

"Anchi got herself captured by the Chaonians!" hissed Kubaba, interrupting with a snap of her whip. "She is a disgrace to us all and to the code we live and die by!"

The youngest Rider jumped to his feet. He didn't look much older than Apama. "I, Manishtusu, speak! I protest this criticism of Anchi."

Zakurru gave Manishtusu a nod. The young man sat, setting his whip across his thighs. His ordinary eyes were tight with anger. If there was an argument going on in the other Unity Halls, it was carried out on Anchor in eerie silence, just the slow play of sunlight through baffles set in the dome.

Apama's sire spoke again in his high-handed way, as if he was continually astonished when people did not automatically do what he wanted.

"We must be bold in the manner of the far-sighted first Council, the Young Tailors of Anshan of cherished memory. Am I really required to remind you that in the wake of the fall of the Apsaras Convergence and the beacon collapse, it was they who began to stitch together an empire from the many scattered pattern pieces? While meanwhile the syndicate bosses of those days counseled caution and inaction—those strategies that served us in times past—because they feared change? If we wish to recover our greatness then we must act without fear of change, as did the Young Tailors eight hundred years ago. Therefore I call for a vote by the Council, we sixteen seated in public assembly before the eyes of the members of the empire, whom we serve. I call for a vote to institute amendments proposed by our comrade Baragesi, whose steadiness and wisdom is honored among us."

Kubaba hissed. "Shame! Shame! These amendments make a mockery of our traditions!" She gestured with her whip toward the seats where Apama and the other three individuals sat separated from the rest of the auditorium. "Don't think I don't know what this is about. Flaunting your unsanctioned bastards and illegal lovers before a law-abiding, virtuous public."

As every gaze in the hall turned their way, the adolescent whimpered nervously, the stout man flushed, starting to sweat, and the auntie fussed with her gloves. Apama sat straight, as befit a lancer.

Kubaba went on with her tirade. "We Riders must have no entanglements. Must favor no one. Not our birth kin. Not those to whom we might grant undue favor out of affection or a sense of debt. That is why we remove our heirs from their birth families. That is why we do not allow entourages and households, only the Incorruptibles. That is why it is forbidden of Riders to marry, form families, and beget children who can be recorded as legal kin in the imperial census. We on the Council must make decisions unmoved by personal or familial preferment. Yet *now* you wish to change that. *Now* all that is to be cast aside for exactly the petty, personal reasons our predecessors warned us against."

Kubaba's riding face fixed its gaze across the distance to stare at Apama. But Apama knew she had done nothing wrong. She lifted her chin in a silent rejoinder. Let people remark on her profile. Let them see the resemblance. She'd never wanted or asked for this, but by Arthas she would not cower in the face of bullying.

Kubaba rudely pointed toward Apama with her whip. "Zakurru, I suppose you intend to become Speaker in my place. And ally this pretty youth to some syndicate boss in exchange for a hidden benefit."

Her sire's ordinary face twitched, a tic of the eye, a spasm of the cheek, but it was his riding face who hissed a retort. "You see your own reflection in this mirror, Kubaba. You have held the Speaker's whip for too many years because you are unwilling to let go of your power. Your thinking has become ossified just like that of Mishirru's hierocracy. Under your leadership we have lost battle after battle to Eirene. Your failures are why the syndicates feel they must take huge risks against the Chaonian fleets."

He paused to let the accusations sink in. Some idiot in the balcony section whispered excitedly, "That's told her!" and was shushed.

Zakurru's smile held a whetted edge, eager to draw more blood. "As for me, I want only the best for the empire. I stand in support of Baragesi. It is Baragesi who calls you to account for your timid leadership and lack of decisiveness. It is Baragesi who bids for Speaker. I call for a vote. I call for a vote. Three times I call for a vote."

He raised his whip, or at least, the body he rode raised the whip. Manishtusu raised his whip. Kubaba kept her whip pressed crosswise over her thighs, fingers clenched, although of course her riding face could not see what the body did on its other side. But she knew, because Riders knew. They could control the physical body of the individual they rode. They were not companions but mutations, or symbionts, or maybe they were just a weird quantum parasite.

The fourth Rider, Neferure, was a middle-aged woman of somber demeanor and carefully neutral expression. She had not spoken and did not move as the vote was called.

Kubaba's riding face gave a rictus grin of triumph, seeing two whips raised and two down. What the other councils looked like, only the Riders could know.

She said, "Eight for and eight against. A tie means the vote does not pass. The synod closes as it began with no amendments and with me remaining as Speaker . . ." She broke off.

Neferure raised her whip.

For a split second the hall seemed void of air, unable to transmit sound. Then a flood of astounded gasps and frantic whispers swept around the auditorium. Neferure's ordinary face glanced toward the section where Apama sat. With a squeak of nerves, the adolescent reached out and grasped Apama's lower left hand between their two rights.

Apama leaned a shoulder against theirs. "Shh. It's all right."

Tears rolled down the youth's pale cheeks.

Kubaba's faces tightened in matched fury.

Zakurru brandished his speaking whip until the murmuring quieted. With a final squeak of a shifted shoe, silence fell, weighty and expectant. Apama felt the events as a pressure wave in the wake of a ship whose ripples would spill on endlessly, tipping and turning the vessels running behind.

His thin smile held triumph. "Mindful of those who witness today, I repeat the words of Baragesi, spoken at the Unity Hall on Axiom Prime just now. 'The amendments pass. The whip of Speaker passes from Kubaba to Baragesi. I, Baragesi, will serve with humility, loyalty, and a truthful heart. This synod closes.'"

The lights on the stage changed. The twelve projections vanished. Only the four who physically attended remained in the circle. Kubaba sat with whip gripped in tense hands. Neferure's gaze stayed fixed on the youth seated next to Apama, while Manishtusu kept his riding gaze on Zakurru, waiting for a signal.

A worm of doubt wriggled in her thoughts. What if she hadn't truly earned her place at the coveted lancer academy? What if she hadn't truly earned her berth on the *Strong Bull*? What if her sire had been pulling strings all along to give her preferment that she didn't deserve except that his seed had impregnated her mother? And how had *that* deed happened? Why had her mother hidden the truth from her? Had Rana been ashamed? Commanded to remain silent? Had she hoped to keep Apama's paternity a secret from the Council, as if she had feared Zakurru would one day seek to claim the child he was never meant to acknowledge?

The questions whirled in her head like the spinning evasive maneuvers of a lancer. But she was used to the gyre. It didn't make her dizzy. It just made her want to get in the killing shot, if only she could figure out what battle she was fighting.

A bell signaled the end of the synod. Zakurru and his two allies walked through the sphere's curve as through a shimmering and insubstantial curtain. Kubaba remained on the platform as it descended into the bowels of Unity Hall, where only Riders and Incorruptibles could walk.

Zakurru led the other two up an aisle, his ordinary face leading. Apama rose because she did not like to face danger from a position of passivity. The other three rose with her. In the packed auditorium no one spoke, everyone rapt with shock. The traditions of the empire had been overturned.

Neferure entered their section first. The adolescent burst into tears. The Rider embraced the youth with the tenderness of a parent who understands their child, who has known them for some time.

Manishtusu clasped loving hands with the stout man. "My heart," he murmured. They both beamed, sweetly in love.

"That was well done," said the aunt, addressing Zakurru with remarkable calm. "I am glad I was here to witness it on Baragesi's account."

"We Riders have lived with these artificial restrictions for too long," replied Zakurru before turning to Apama. "Daughter, I acknowledge you in the sight of the empire, as I have long wished to do. Walk with me to the basilica to give thanks."

She had her priorities too! "Will I be allowed to return to duty on the *Strong Bull* once they return to imperial space?"

"It will be many months before we know which ships survived the retreat. Your duty now is to attend me, as I have already stated. Is that clear?"

She knew when to withdraw in order to fight again another day. So she gave a quick check to make sure all the buttons and bows on her uniform were properly placed and her half cape draping correctly. She clasped her lowers behind her back with her uppers free and took her place beside him.

As they walked up the steps of the aisle toward the exit, people pressed forward from the seats to greet them. No one touched Riders. It simply wasn't done. As a sign of respectful distance everyone clasped both pairs of hands behind them.

As a pilot in training and junior officer she had taken this deferential stance in the presence of higher-ranking officers and senior officials. Now syndicate bosses wearing the colored sashes that identified their affiliations and associated trades deferred to her, eager to be introduced. Even if they did not like the outcome of the synod they could gauge which way the winds of power were blowing. High officials paid their respects with ingratiating smiles. Military officers who outranked her must halt before her Rider sire and thus before her as if she were their superior in the chain of command. She hoped her lancer's insignia won them over. Her name falling from so many powerful lips was a heady brew to consume. It made her giddy even as she distrusted it. What was in this for Zakurru? There had to be something more, something she wasn't aware of.

At last they made their way out of the auditorium's packed vestibule. Accompanied by a smaller group of Zakurru's trusted associates, they strode along the floating concourse toward the bridge. Apama was not required to speak, although a man who introduced himself as the leader of the Angursa Syndicate made polite small talk with her before it was his turn to pay respects to the Rider. Finally they reached the bridge that led across the water to the gothic glass splendor of the magnificent basilica. Incorruptibles fell into step before and behind to make it clear the others had to remain on the ridge. All except one.

"So you have accomplished it, Zakurru. I knew you would."

Could the man never speak in a normal tone?

The Rider's faces smiled in a synergy that made her shudder. "Manu, join us."

They headed across the span. Admiral Manu wormed his way between them so he might speak to the Rider while casting Apama broad looks meant to be confiding and warm.

"Can you assure me of command? If I'd been in charge, the outcome at Molossia would have been a triumph for us instead of a disaster."

"Not quite a disaster. We badly damaged Chaonia's fleet and their production capacity. It will take them years to rebuild."

"They have other shipyards and industrial parks. They have an entire population enlisted in Eirene's war effort as well as resources in the systems they've stolen from the empire. Mark my words, in one year she'll attack Karnos."

"Chaonia can't recover so quickly."

"I've been right in all the advice I've given you so far, haven't I?"

Zakurru's riding face closed its eyes, talking to someone worlds away. They walked the rest of the way in silence. The sun beat down, and the wind was hot and humid. When they reached the end of the bridge and the steps up to the basilica's entrance, the riding eyes snapped open. They did not have pupils and irises like human eyes. They were a dark screen tuned to unfathomable frequencies.

"We value your expertise, Manu," he said. "You will get your command when the time is right."

"And my reward?" Manu asked with a sidelong glance at Apama that made her lean away from him.

"That too. Now." He gestured for the Incorruptibles to block the open doors. "I wish for a private moment within the basilica with my *daughter*." His smile had a cruelly satisfied tinge. The victory in the Council had given him pleasure not just because he had won but because he had seen Kubaba lose.

Apama followed him into the vestibule, an enclosed porch whose glass doors let onto the lofty nave beyond. No one was in the nave that she could see. To her surprise a man waited in the vestibule, having been allowed in by the Incorruptibles. He wore the white robes of a religious order. Although he had only two arms, his distinguished good looks made him instantly recognizable as Hot Dad. Seen from this close, his eyes gleamed with an odd sheen, making her remember a random rumor from her school days: blind to visual light, the seers of Iros saw heat and lies.

The seer pressed palms together. "Your Eminence, thank you for agreeing to meet."

"Dispense with such antiquated hierarchical terms," said Zakurru. "You are Kiran Seth, a seer of the Order of Iros. You were with Anchi when she was captured."

"I was. I regret my order was unable to secure her safety."

"I regret it also, considering all the assurances the Prime of your order made to the Council. Be that as it may, we went to a great deal of trouble to get you here to Anchor. What is it you want?"

"I bring a proposal that will end your war with the Republic of Chaonia."

Zakurru's body crossed all four arms, a gesture of such insulting skepticism that Apama was surprised Hot Dad didn't protest. But the seer wasn't imperial Phene, so how would he know?

"The Chaonian antipathy for the empire is strong and of long standing. How exactly do the seers mean to bake this pie in the sky?"

"By eliminating Sun Shān."

"According to Aloysius Voy, you tried to eliminate her once already, and failed."

"A miss is not a failure. Surrender is the only failure."

"A tidy if meaningless aphorism. How does your proposal help us? Sun is barely more than a child. Queen-Marshal Eirene is our biggest problem. She's proven herself to be shrewd, brutal, canny, relentless, and patient. And she's not yet fifty."

"Eirene is exceedingly popular in Chaonia. Her internal enemies are either dead or locked up. The weakness of Chaonia is their hereditary system of rulership. Factions simmer under the surface, waiting for their chance to boil. As seers, we take the long view. As befits descendants of the ancient Argosies, we launch our purpose onto the raft of time, knowing we have the patience to see it through to a distant end."

"Yes, yes, that's all pleasingly philosophical, but what is your plan?"

"We can use our influence among the factions to place the heirship into the hands of an eligible person more accommodating to the empire."

"And of course more accommodating to the seers of Iros," remarked Zakurru with a flicker of his eye slits.

"Of course," agreed the seer. "It will benefit us all."

"It won't benefit Sun Shān."

The seer shrugged. "The history of Chaonia is riven with violent succession disputes. She will join numerous other scions of the royal house who lost their bid for power and vanish as another meaningless shard into the broken Archives at the Gyre."

Not to Her Taste as a Rallying Cry

As she waited for her mother, Sun's attention caught on a private hallway set off to one side. The passage ran about ten meters and ended in a sealed balcony overlooking a large chamber.

A strip of ceiling lights illuminated a rolled-up mattress, a divan, a stool, cushions, a set of shelves secured to the wall, and a large rug. The chamber held two occupants. One was a woman a bit older than Sun, heavyset, with short black hair and the pallid complexion of an individual who hasn't been outdoors in a long time. She was seated cross-legged on the rug in front of a mat marked with shapes, the kind of thing a small child would play on to learn rectangle, square, and circle. A teacher sat opposite, trying to convince her to place blocks onto a matching shape on the mat.

Sun studied their interaction for a while, the teacher's air of extreme patience as with an oppositional child, the woman's unvoiced frustration whenever the teacher would place a block where the woman did not want it to go. They had reached an impasse. Sun unsealed the balcony's entry door, which dropped a temporary staircase down, and descended. The woman did not react because she was busy snatching all the blocks off the mat and piling them in front of herself.

"Your Highness!" The teacher jumped to her feet.

"You are?"

"The Honorable Merci Bō."

"Related to Governor Hakan Bō?"

"Yes, Your Highness."

"May I try?"

The teacher blanched as she glanced toward the one-way view bubble of the balcony and back at Sun. "She can't communicate, Your Highness."

"Why is that?" Sun studied the focused way in which the seated woman arranged the blocks.

"Beacon sickness, Your Highness."

Sun crouched on the other side of the mat. "You're looking at the shapes," she remarked to Merci. "She's looking at the shadow and light."

At the words "shadow and light" the woman's gaze lifted as if she had just then realized a third person was present. Her eyes had neither iris nor pupil, and no whites. Neither were they a sheen-like screen of artificially implanted eyes hooked to a brain's neurons, like the eyes of a seer. Hers bore an oddly luminous and yet opaque surface that reminded Sun of beacons, as if eyes weren't windows onto a soul but into a void.

"I'll go first, if I may." When the woman did not object, Sun placed a shape so it was bisected by a shadow, half of it in light.

With a brilliantly unexpected grin, the woman answered by tucking a shape next to the one Sun had laid down, also bisected. Trading off turns, they created a new pattern determined by the shadows cast by the arrangement of the overhead lighting.

"Do you have a name I can call you?" Sun asked.

"Teacher calls me Metis." Her tone was halting.

"After our great-grandmother, Queen-Marshal Metis. I'm your cousin, Sun."

The name won her another glance. "I don't like this place."

"Why is that?"

"It has no sun to make lines. I was in a different place before. There was sun. The light changed. Here it is always the same light. Is Uncle Kiran to visit?"

Uncle Kiran! "Does he visit often?"

"He is not ashamed of me. But he hasn't visited me here yet."

Whew. Any doubts Sun might have entertained about Persephone's account of her cousin's imprisonment vanished. Careful not to stare directly into Metis's oddly colored eyes, Sun smiled warmly. "I'll make sure you get sunlight. Also, I will ask about Uncle Kiran and come back to tell you. If you don't mind me visiting again."

The opaque gaze darted to Sun's face and away. Then Metis handed Sun a block in the shape of the eight-rayed sunburst, the symbol of the Republic of Chaonia.

"I never noticed that about the shadow!" exclaimed the teacher.

"Now you know," said Sun.

Briefly she considered a stronger remark, but Merci Bō wasn't worth the effort. She climbed back up the stairs to find her mother watching from the balcony with an amused expression on her face.

"That was enlightening," said Eirene. "Her handlers can barely get any sense out of her."

"I expect they keep trying to force their own pattern of mind onto hers rather than recognizing she has her own. So Uncle Nèzhā really did have an illegitimate child by Moira Lee. According to Persephone, Metis was held in secrecy at Lee House for years. That seems harsh for a potential heir to the throne."

"Moira wanted no trouble. She just wanted the child to exist in peace."

"Then why did you move her out of Lee House and into your high-security prison? Is it to do with Kiran Seth?"

Eirene's gaze sharpened. "What do you mean?"

"Metis mentioned him. Persephone told me Moira said Kiran is the only person who could coax fragments of sense out of Metis."

"Persephone Lee tells you a lot."

"She *is* one of my Companions."

Eirene laughed. "Thereby you see the value of Companions. I'm sorry I had to kick out Moira from my inner circle because she is very dear to me, but I admit Marduk has the more pragmatic temper, valuable for a Companion."

"True. Marduk didn't insult my father to his face the way Moira did."

"What?"

"Nothing."

Nothing was ever *nothing* to Eirene. "Moira's no fan of the Gatoi. Or João."

"Or me," said Sun, willing to push this line of attack.

Eirene shook a finger at her. "Don't annoy me. You're the one standing next to me. Not Metis, poor girl. Lest you yammer at me about Manea being pregnant, as your father has done once too often, a child can't rule as queen-marshal."

Best to sidestep that land mine. "Does the lovely Manea know she has a half sibling through her mother?"

"Manea is the one who suggested I transfer Metis here for her own safety now we know Kiran is a traitor and might have secret accomplices still in Lee House. You should keep an eye on Persephone Lee. According to reports, her father favored her over his other children."

Sun glanced down the hallway but they remained alone. "Kiran's not really her father though, is he?"

Red flickered in the depths of Eirene's obsidian eye. "Speak of that again, and I will destroy you, Sun. Now. I'm done here. And so are you."

As they climbed the stairs out of Fleet Strategic Command, Sun said, "Have the Phene still made no offer for the Rider?"

"I've received no diplomatic delegations from the Phene. But I don't expect it with hostilities at such a pitch. They'll accept the loss. What is it their soldiers say? 'We are all destined for death.' Which is true enough in the philosophical and biological sense, but not to my taste as a rallying cry."

"Are you going to leave the Rider in stasis? It seems wasteful."

Eirene halted. They were halfway up the stairs, equidistant from the guards below and above. "Do you think I should have the Rider cut open after all?"

"I do not."

"Not as bloodthirsty as I had thought." Eirene's smile had an edge of disdain, the way she always probed for weakness.

"It has nothing to do with bloodthirstiness. Experimenting on prisoners is dishonorable. Also, it would be foolish to flout convention in a way that would hurt our soldiers and spacers if they're captured. And for what? We can't know if dissection or experimentation would teach us anything useful about Riders. Or useful enough."

Eirene leaned against the metal railing. "What would be useful enough?"

From a young age, Sun had learned to keep secrets from her mother when she'd realized her mother admired her brilliant daughter but distrusted João's influence.

"Having Riders of our own." She watched her mother's expression for any hint that her mother suspected, but Eirene took the statement at face value.

"I think it unlikely we can trust a captured Rider to work with us." Her gaze shifted to the wall, a glimmer of red tracing her gaze. "If there was any evidence the janus mutation is inheritable, I'd get her pregnant."

"Forced pregnancy is a war crime."

"It is, and for good reason, but I'd do it if I thought it would work. There's no evidence the mutation is inheritable. As far as anyone knows it appears at random among the imperial Phene. Like identical twins among all human populations."

Was Eirene dangling the answer in front of her, to see if she'd bite? She bit.

"You could clone her."

Eirene laughed, the sound echoing in the stairwell. She crossed her arms. "Cloning is illegal in the Republic of Chaonia. You know that."

"So do you. Yet your beloved young consort Manea—"

"That's enough!" Mother and daughter stared at each other. "I have few choices of heir, and none as capable as you. But that doesn't mean I can't or won't change my mind at any time about supporting you if you piss me off again like you did at my wedding banquet."

"I'm not trying to undercut Manea. I'm saying Manea and Persephone are clones of the same individual. Yet neither of us have turned them over to the Ministry of Rites and Culture as we are legally mandated to do."

Eirene nodded with grudging respect. "How did you work that out?"

"The governorship of Lee House was inherited by Nona Lee, eldest of three sisters. When she died almost thirty years ago, the governorship passed to Moira. Afterward, Moira and Aisa between them gave birth to three girls who everyone says look an awful lot alike."

"That happens in families."

"Skip forward to now. A source known only to you delivers banner soldiers captured behind Phene lines to my father for his work. One of those prisoners tries to kill both Persephone and Manea due to what appears to be an engineered hallucination program in his neural network. The Phene have no reason to target two young women. So it must mean they believe Nona is alive."

"Why would the Phene care about Nona?" Eirene wasn't going to make this easy.

"What if the empire hates Nona because they believe she is a war criminal responsible for the massacre of thousands of civilian Phene at a refugee camp? The very operation in which, the official history tells us, she died fighting insurgents. Was it actually a massacre of innocent civilians?"

"It happened during my brother's reign. Those comms records became corrupted and can no longer be accessed."

Sun was not about to reveal the extent of James's hacking capabilities.

"If the Phene believe it was a massacre, and that the chief perpetrator was allowed to escape justice, then you can see why they might try a different path to get rid of her. It would also suggest they think she's the source capturing banner soldiers behind their lines. If so, she's likely operating in or around Hellion Terminus. Which as you certainly know is one beacon drop out from Karnos System. If you know she's alive and where she is, then you've taken no action to bring her in for trial. Some would say that makes you complicit in her war crime. If it happened the way the Phene say it did."

"War is a dirty business. You'd do well to listen carefully to what I'm about to say." Once launched, Eirene's rapid-fire speeches could not be interrupted except by fire or hull breach and, in one famous incident, not even then. "Enjoy the gripping tales of the final days of the Celestial Empire. Thrill to the noble battles and heroic honor of the emperor's last heir as she fought the plague of corrupted blood to save her people. But don't believe what we do doesn't soil our hands no matter how righteous our claim. I know what I want, and what price I'm willing to pay to get it. Because I'm both smart and wise, I will use negotiation, bribery, treachery, and sedition when I can to lighten the load. It's a cursed waste to train up good soldiers but recklessly throw them away when you could be cannier about how you deploy your options."

She tapped fingers on the railing, turning over arguments.

"The idea of cloning a Rider has indeed crossed my mind. However, contact with an exile based in hostile territory takes time and risk I'm not willing to expend at this juncture with so much else on the line. Karnos first. Then we shall see."

So Nona Lee *was* alive, and still loyal to Chaonia.

"That makes sense," Sun said.

Eirene studied her with a lifted eyebrow, the speculative gaze of a soldier who has survived numerous engagements because they are never quite taken by surprise. "I don't think you've learned obedience, but you have learned prudence. To reward you for your part in the battle of Molossia, I'm giving you a special assignment."

"A special assignment?" A jolt surged through Sun, the rush strong enough to flush her cheeks. She gripped the railing and lifted up on her toes.

"In your capacity as my heir, you will tour the forward fleets in Na Iri, Kaska, Tarsa, Hatti, Maras Shantiya, and Kanesh. To see and to be seen. The trip should take about thirty-eight weeks."

"So when I return, it will almost be time for the attack on Karnos."

"That is correct. Which leads me to my final point. We are not immune to death. Not me and not you. Our Companions are our shields, the inner circle we trust absolutely. They will follow us into the worst carnage, will report any threat to our persons, will advise and protect us, fight beside us, stand guard over us when we are most vulnerable. They are more important to us than consorts or lovers, which is why we who rule must never sully the exalted bond of loyalty and trust with something as ephemeral as sex."

She paused, that twenty-kiloton stare trying to break through Sun's wall.

Sun returned the gaze without flinching. It was different for her and Hetty, even if people might not understand why. "I learned by watching you and my father together about the danger of playing favorites, with or without sex."

"There's the knife! I respect that you never let anyone bully you, not even me."

Eirene began climbing again, throwing words over her shoulder.

"A queen-marshal has seven Companions because our Companions are our conduit to each of the Core Houses. The support of the Houses can make or break a queen-marshal. I have asked the governors of Jīn, Bō, and Nazir Houses to send candidates to the palace for you to choose from before you depart. In fact, Hakan Bō already recommended someone."

A pause in her speech, if not her stair-climbing, invited Sun's acquiescence.

"The Honorable Merci Bō, perhaps?"

"Why, yes. She already works in the palace. In fact, you just met her."

"I wasn't impressed."

"A queen-marshal can shape rough clay to her purpose."

"Is that what you did with me?"

Eirene laughed.

Sun said, "What about the other two?"

Eirene slammed to a halt and rounded on her daughter, looming a step above her. "Did your father put you up to this little ambush?"

That hadn't at all been the reaction Sun expected.

Eirene went on in a rush. "All by himself he's a drama worthy of Channel Idol. There's nothing to discuss about my other possible heirs. They're safely put away out of reach."

"I was asking if Nazir House and Jīn House had sent candidates," Sun said as calmly as she could as a hot surge of suspicion swelled. Why in the hells was her mother still fixed on the issue of heirs if she was content with Sun as her successor? "More out of curiosity than anything, because I can choose my own Companions."

"But will you?" Eirene retorted with her usual speed at adapting, as if she hadn't just mistaken Sun's query for a different one. "Would you even have replaced Perseus Lee if his family hadn't thrust his twin sister on you at a moment when you couldn't say no? That being said, I'd be delighted if you decided to replace Persephone with a different Lee House Companion. Marduk has several sons."

"I'm keeping Persephone. And I'm not done talking about Kiran Seth."

"What about him? He fled like the spy and traitor he proved to be."

"He murdered Octavian."

"You have no proof."

"Proof was deleted. Persephone saw it with her own eyes."

"Moira tells me Persephone was always a liar as a child."

They were nearing the top of the stairs but Sun would never be ready to let this go. "Kiran was welcomed into Lee House. He lived there for over twenty-five years. He was allowed to become an administrator in the Ministry of Security, Punishment, and Corrections, with fingers in every security pie. I'd think you'd want Lee House's governor to pay some price for that degree of fuckup."

Eirene leaned forward, seeming to grow a size larger out of sheer intimidation. "Don't insult my consort."

Sun did not back down. "This isn't to do with Manea. Enjoy her all you wish. She is certainly more charming and pliant than my father, even I would be first to admit that. It's her *mother* who let it happen—"

"Leave Moira out of this!"

"Kiran murdered Octavian. I can't believe you're just letting this go."

"Leave the seers of Iros to me." Her indulgent humor wholly evaporated, Eirene had reverted to her harsh, crusty mode.

Sun would never let this go. "The seers were implicated in Phene smuggling operations. They had a hand in the Phene raid on this very planet. The seat of our government. Wasn't that raid an insult to Chaonian pride?"

"Part of being queen-marshal is balancing competing factions. I need the allied Yele fleets for the attack on Karnos. I don't need the Yele to be offended by some clumsy probe up their self-righteous, puckered asses. Do you understand me?"

Sun understood all right. Fists pressed against thighs she said, curtly, "Yes."

They climbed the rest of the way without speaking, through the airlock, and along the dim walkways of the palace courtyards, all the way back to Sun's reception room, as if they had never gone on this unexpected expedition.

Once in the room, Eirene ate another sesame ball and drank a glass of the mint-and-honey tea, now cool. "Perfectly sweetened. We'll talk at length next week before you depart. No need to see me out."

The queen-marshal left, leaving Sun and her tumultuous heart to take a seat in the dark room. She sipped at the tea, which was, in fact, perfectly sweetened. Her mind launched onto the complex map of what she knew and what she'd learned. The seers of Iros. The Yele connection. The dead war criminal Nona Lee being alive and likely acting as Eirene's go-between with secret allies in Karnos. Nona's illegal cloning.

Sun's own secrets. Those she shared with her father. Those she shared only with the other half of her soul.

A whisper of footfalls caught her hearing.

Hetty walked into the room holding a decorative lantern to guide her steps. Its diffuse light illuminated the dearest face whose steadiness could enclose even the lightning-struck tumult of Sun's splintering thoughts. Hetty's steps passed from wood floor to dense rug. She knelt beside Sun's chair and set down the lantern. For a precious eternity she rested the back of a hand against Sun's cheek. Wind sighed through the bamboo and cypress in the royal garden bathed in night beyond the balcony railing. A hanging chime tinkled like distant laughter. The rolling murmur of an ever-flowing stream sang of a thousand-year journey across the vast ocean of space powered by the engine of constancy and hope.

The warmth of that touch calmed the thunderous clamor of Sun's unquiet heart. She leaned against it, pressed a kiss onto Hetty's skin that smelled as if it had been washed in nectar of orange blossoms. From there it was easy enough to turn a little more—always she needed only to turn a little more into Hetty's embrace, forbidden by custom but irresistible in the moment. Hetty understood her well enough to make no overtures, merely to hold, the pressure of her breasts and thighs against Sun's body both promise and memory. Yet was it not a weakness to give way? Wasn't physical desire a form of obliteration, catching its victims in a strong current that would drag them to their deaths?

"Ha! Ha!" cried James loudly from the audience hall, a sound meant to carry.

Hetty untangled herself and rose with a flushed face and tender smile. Together they walked into the audience hall with its checkerboard wooden floor and pillars carved with the faces and forms of mythical beasts. Alika, James, and Persephone had gathered at the base of the dais.

James looked up. "Did you know Persephone can recite the entirety of the 'Reflections on the Decree of Destiny'? It takes two hours! Not even Alika can do that."

"I could if I decided to," said Alika, hands twitching on his ukulele.

"Here I thought you weren't paying attention earlier." Sun ignored the formal chair placed on the dais and sat on the lower step, the others seated around her.

"I *wasn't* paying attention," admitted Persephone. "Philosophy sends me to sleep. I'm more of a jog-around-the-block-looking-for-trouble kind of person."

"You're about to get your chance." Sun bent forward. They leaned in, pulled to the intensity of her expression. "We're going to find Kiran Seth de Lee and put him on trial for Octavian's murder."

Hetty said, "Dear Sun, you were forbidden from this quest."

"I'm not letting Octavian's killer get away with it."

Persephone raised both hands, palms up. "Hetty just said the queen-marshal expressly forbade you from investigating anything about my father."

"Do you have a question? Or have you just not yet figured out how I work?"

"You work by pissing off the queen-marshal?"

"If you know his home hermitage, start by visiting there."

"Me? Why me?"

"He's *your* father," Alika said with a curl of the lip.

Persephone slapped her forehead with the heel of a hand. "How could I have forgotten? The man who hated my mother for all the years they were married, not that I blame him, and who barely had time for me. It flew right out of my mind. Go figure."

Sun went on. "If there's no trace of his whereabouts there, you can expand the search to the cardinal hermitage on Yele Prime, although that might draw official attention. Still, an inquiry from his concerned daughter will seem unexceptional."

"No, it won't. I was one of your Companions when the Tjeker raid went down. It'll seem suspicious."

"Which some of us are still wondering about," remarked Alika to his ukulele. "How your father got out of the basilica with you the only witness to claim you hadn't helped him."

"What is wrong with you?" Persephone demanded. "I was being choked out by Zizou."

James snickered. "Your type of kink, eh?"

Persephone snatched his cap off his head and smacked him with it.

"Are you flirting with James?" Sun asked mildly. Hetty hid a smile behind a hand. Alika plucked a dissonant chord.

Persephone said, "The hells! He is so not my type. No offense, James."

"Believe me, none taken. I can think of no worse disaster." He retrieved the cap and tugged it back over his curls as they both laughed.

Sun gave each a quick once-over, gauging their tempers and their postures. Those two were fine, although Persephone and Alika had never warmed up to each other, which might become a problem later. "Tracing his history will give us insight into where he might be and also what he might intend to do in the future. Take your time and don't overlook any stray detail. You shouldn't go alone. Take Jade Kim."

Persephone toppled backward, hands over her face. "No fucking way. Give me Solomon."

"You can take Solomon too."

"I meant instead of Jade."

"I know what you meant. My order stands. As for you, James—"

"Ugh," said James. "Don't hurt me. I didn't do it."

"I want a full accounting of my cousin Jiàn's movements and visitors for the last ten years. Suspicious contacts. Odd messages. You know the routine."

"That should be easy given he's been confined to Pelasgia Terce since his affectionate aunt Eirene set aside his claim as her brother's heir in favor of elevating herself. But surely you don't really think he's a threat to you. He has no backing at court."

"That we know of. Also track down the Alabaster Argosy's last known port of call. Find Lady Sirena's child and contact him on my behalf. I want to open up personal communications, one sibling to another."

Alika twanged a heartfelt chord.

James grinned. "Tracking down an Argosy is a challenge I like. What's your game?"

"No game. I'm deadly serious about making it clear to myself whether the other heirs are potential allies or rivals."

"But—" said Persephone.

"But—" said Alika.

"Dear Sun—" said Hetty.

"This isn't under discussion." She gave each Companion a hard look. "Get it done."

10

Interlude in Bustling Argos

Working at Channel Idol has been Beau's dream since childhood despite his family telling him over and over that he should be a scholar and not a hack. How many times did they ask him why even get an impressive university degree from Yele if he is just going to waste it writing personality puff pieces and covering the ridiculous nonsense that is the yearly Idol Faire competition? But he loves Idol Faire. The hyperbole and breathless coverage can be ridiculous, sure. But people who scorn the competition ignore the skill and charisma of those who take part.

Channel Idol isn't just puff and nonsense. It's politics at the deepest level. Whose story will be remembered? What events will limn the narrative? Who are the players on the stage of history?

What people think they know and what they remember aren't an accident. History gets torn and shredded. It gets lost or thrown out or twisted to create a different image depending on who is telling the story and how much of the story is left to tell.

Think of the Celestial Empire, a place lost both in location and also to a past four thousand years gone. How do you reconstruct a world from the fragmented remains of damaged and defective archives? Are the stories told about the Celestial Empire a true if partial recounting of that ancient history, as most people believe? Or is the truth shattered and slippery and thus hard to grasp? It's all about what remains are scooped to the surface and who is allowed to assemble a picture from the shards.

If he plays his tiles right, he can work his way into production. Then he'll be able to influence how the citizens of the Republic of Chaonia and the natives of the Yele League view the events of these tumultuous days. How their descendants remember them. That's all he's ever wanted: to make a mark with his perspective. To see his byline splashed across the shoreline of history where the water of incident is always churning.

Is that a good metaphor? *The shoreline of history. The water of incident.*

Mmm. Maybe too stretched. Beau hunches over his tablet. It's an arduous commute from the shabby room he rents in an outlying neighborhood to the center of bustling Argos, but he uses the time on the train to get a jump on his day's work.

The first half of the commute runs aboveground and offers a stunning view of the wind-capped bay, the distant islands belonging to the seven Core Houses, and the eight mirrored sails of the palace. The palace compound is joined to the mainland by the light-studded arches of Petitioners Bridge. Someday soon he'll walk across the bridge to visit Victory Hall and the Temple of Celestial Peace. So far he's been too busy. In his first month here, he hasn't had a single day off.

He switches lines at the transportation hub known as the Wheelhouse. Two more stops bring him to Idol Square. He jostles upward into the glass pyramid that rises at the center of the square. Crowds flood out through its four glittering gates. Tourists and school groups head west for the entrance to Idol Park while employees head east across the plaza toward the massive headquarters building.

Today's peak-rated montages play inside augmented-reality banners, each fixed to one of many pillars around the square. Most of the montages focus on yesterday's 100-day anniversary of the birth of the child of Queen-Marshal Eirene and her lovely young consort, Manea Lee. The formal naming of young Princess Inanna at the Temple of Celestial Peace. A feast attended by House governors, court officials, and high-ranking military officers not out in the field. Recipes so citizens can make similar dishes for themselves. An "at home" montage of the devoted couple followed by a formal reception for favored citizens in the audience hall. Vogue Academy fashionistas analyze the flora, fauna, and color symbology of each of Manea Lee's five outfits. The queen-marshal wears a military uniform in all public appearances. She might be called away at any moment if the relentless Phene invade again.

In the main lobby all the screens are running the streaming Channel Idol daily feed. An update on Princess Sun's popular tour of the fleet segues into a jaunty sidebar on the Handsome Alika's impromptu concerts for intrepid marines at isolated duty stations and weary shipyard workers grateful for the heir's visit to the industrial yards. Today's farm report highlights a tenacious collective expanding the verge of sedge, horsetail, and sego lily on the salt flats of Molossia Prime. Farmers grimed with sweat stand in noble profile against a stalwart blue sky. Twin moons hang palely visible above the horizon as the characters for TOGETHER WE WIN scroll across the heavens.

Beau enters the elevator in step with a young woman who stares at the visuals with a wistful look as she adjusts her cane.

"You all right?" he asks, vaguely recognizing her face.

"I'm still adjusting to the gravity differential." She indicates her cane, then notes his gaze shift to the image of wind blowing over the salt flats. "And a bit of homesickness. I'm from Molossia Prime."

He tracks her image into the Channel Idol employee network and gets a match on a virtual screen just beyond his left eye. "Vida, isn't it?"

"That's right. Vida Borja Almaynilad. I'm sorry I don't remember your name."

"I'm in the history division. Beau Qiáng."

She tilts slightly away as if he has taken on an unpleasant odor. "You're an honorable?"

"Oh, no, no, my family line is just a minor branch of Bō House. We're not palace honorables, we're just back-door honorables." He pauses, waiting for a laugh.

She stares at him with furrowed brow. What was he thinking? She doesn't know what to make of his joke. To a citizen, all honorables probably look alike.

"I didn't go to the royal academy or anything," he says, hoping to smooth things over. Sometimes the best tactic is to keep talking in a wave of sound until they stop hearing whatever was bothering them a moment before. "In fact my special interest is the growth of the community journalist program. They claim that's why they hired me. But it might just be my good looks. Haha!" He grins, because he does not have the kind of good looks that catapult a person into the top tier of performers on Idol Faire.

She fidgets at the necklace she wears, opening its rose-shaped pendant. Inside is an engraving of three stylized women, some citizen folk religion, no doubt. He snaps a surreptitious photo and files it away to identify later.

She says in a cool voice, "I was a community journalist intern at the Maynilad bureau for three years before I got the promotion here."

"Wait, wait." He shakes a finger at her. "You put together that popular montage of the Maynilad-based stick-fighting club that came in seventeenth last year."

Her smile brightens as her cheeks grow rosy with pride. "It was so heavily viewed it won me this promotion. It's my first time on Chaonia Prime."

"No wonder the gravity is getting to you."

The elevator door opens. The community journalist program takes up an entire floor, divided into branch lines according to project and division. It turns out she's headed to the canteen. CJs receive one free meal a day, and no one in the program except supervisors gets paid enough to skip it. His praise of her montage has eased her discomfort enough that she doesn't object as he walks with her to the canteen. Part of his goal as historian is to get insight into the perspective of community journalists and those they represent. He can't let this chance pass.

He quizzes her as they eat today's fare, a bowl of noodles sprinkled with soy sauce, seaweed flakes, and sesame oil. Her wariness softens as she talks about her big dream of someday becoming one of the lead writers on *Legendary Narratives from the Celestial Empire*.

"What do you think of Argos?" he asks.

"As crowded as Maynilad, and more expensive. You been here long?"

"I started last month. I was teaching on Larissa Prime. Getting hired here was my big break."

The five-minute warning pings into everyone's network. They make polite farewells and head off to their separate divisions. On his own credit limit, he checks out the engraving from the pendant: Mayari, Hanan, and Tala, three goddesses thought to have been worshipped in the Celestial Empire. Something to pursue later.

At 0800 the desks turn on.

Coverage of the conflict with the Phene Empire is, obviously, the biggest branch of Channel Idol, but Idol Faire is the ratings winner. Last year broke all records when Princess Sun and her Companions unexpectedly entered the competition. That's his whole point, isn't it? The way to reach people, to influence their view of history and current events, is to find them where they are, not to confine debate to abstract discussions one hour a week on channel 4's *Hundred Philosophers' Hour.*

With the new season's Faire scheduled to start in four weeks, everyone is prepping retrospectives, deep dives, archival breakouts, and montages meant to highlight what ordinary citizens love best in the thrilling contest. What are they obsessing about from last year's Faire? Sun's fearless leadership at the industrial park when she rallied a company of brave citizen cadets to fight against the raid by Phene special forces? Her lightning-swift comprehension of the battle lines drawn in Molossia System when a Phene fleet slid out of deep space via knnu drive to target orbital command centers and shipyards so as to wreck Chaonian readiness for war? The Handsome Alika's rallying song lyrics "Wherever you stand, be the soul of that place?" Sun and her mother, the glorious queen-marshal, presiding together over the funeral pyres of Autumn West? Sun brought courage and sacrifice into a competition meant as a salve of entertainment. Chaonians ate it up.

Beau has his own obsession. He hacks a virtual path along the fading trail of a captured Gatoi soldier who acted as Princess Sun's bodyguard for a brief period chronologically situated in and around the wedding festivities of Eirene and Manea, which took place a year ago, right before the start of last season's Idol Faire.

He tells himself it's the mystery of the soldier's abrupt appearance and unrecorded disappearance that consumes him, but really it's the way the Gatoi moves as a honed weapon with a killing edge, and that one clip of his innocent smile. It's not that Beau has a crush on him or anything—that would be ridiculous—but that he can't let things alone once the claws of his mind have hooked into a problem.

Who is the mysterious soldier? Where did he come from? Does he have a familial relationship to Sun's father, Prince João? The prince is a member of the Royal clan of the Gatoi. His marriage to Eirene as her second consort was a scandal, given that most Gatoi are mercenaries in the employ of the empire.

No official footage of the young soldier exists on Channel Idol. He doesn't show up in any of the official Idol images of "Sun and her Companions" that accompanied their race up the Faire charts in last year's final five days. Beau has tweaked a facial recognition fishing program with an algorithm specially crafted to seek out traces of the neural tattoos woven into all Gatoi. This network can be seen as a shimmering pattern just below the skin. The neuro-enhancers make the Gatoi faster, stronger, and less sensitive to pain, and combine with their rigid code of honor to create deadly soldiers. Yet he can't get that sweet smile out of his head because it's so incongruous, not savage or grim at all, like going to the bakery and discovering the cinnamon roll has murdered you.

Beau has excavated deep into the twitch and recovered images, GIFs, flashpoints, and background shots. Here the soldier is moving through the background within a panning shot of the Point Panic Sports Garden during the republic-wide wedding festivities. He's wearing a nondescript hoodie but his face appears in snatches in thirty-eight shared citizen remembrances. The people who uploaded the clips probably don't even know he's there. If anyone from the palace is flagged in those clips it is Sun or Alika.

For example, inside a train, in the background of a clip of a girl excitedly talking about how she and her friend won a round of doubles pīng pāng qiú, a glamorous cee-cee offers the soldier a bun to eat, and he flinches as if food startles him. It's in a later clip, gacked out of the mob scene that formed at the Wheelhouse as fans chased the Handsome Alika, that the soldier smiles. Soon after, he vanishes from the record and is not seen again.

What Beau discovered on his first full day at the job is that his historian's clearance gives him access to government archives not available in the common twitch. Time stamps track him back to the shoreline at Point Panic, where a view from one of the city-wide security cameras shows Sun facing the young man, speaking to him. He says, to the princess, "My battle name is Zizou."

Beau's not sure what "battle name" means—he's not a Gatoi scholar and has flagged the term for later research—but Zizou is not a name known in the Republic of Chaonia. Why would it be? He's not Chaonian. He's a child of the nomadic tribes called Gatoi who roam the wilderness of space on their wheelships.

He tracks the algorithm back from the shoreline exchange. Sun and her people reach Point Panic on boats from Lee House's island fortress. Before that they can be found at the wedding banquet for Eirene and Manea, hosted in the celebration hall of Lee House. That's where Zizou first appears.

There's got to be a reason he's hard to find in the record. It's never wise to poke your nose in where there's evidence of censorship, yet Beau keeps circling back to a disjointed and fractured collection of images and clips that seem to have happened in the hall where the wedding banquet was hosted at Lee House. Officially the banquet involved toasts, feasting, music and poetry, and citizen dance ensembles. But in the last three days he's discovered shards of a puzzling incident which he watches over and over, trying to piece together what it means.

Zizou appears at the banquet as if out of nowhere. He is dressed in loose trousers and wears no shirt. The neural pattern on his lean, muscular torso is like the writhing of furious snakes. It's beautiful and scary. But what's scarier is that in the middle of the banquet he attacks two people, though from this angle Beau can't quite tell who. Each time, just before the attack, his neural network flares so brightly it smears the view like a flash of lightning, and then he charges like a wound-up spring forcibly uncoiled. No clip is more than three seconds long, artifacts broken off from a scrubbing program.

This morning the algorithm digs deeper, like a mole cricket seeking sustenance. It dredges up references to an old military incident, the destruction of a refugee camp on the moon of Tjeker about thirty years ago at the command of the Honorable Nona Lee. Beau leans forward, feeling a flare of excitement like smelling a hint of smoke that will lead him to fire.

A shadow falls across his desk. "The Honorable Beau Qiáng. Please identify yourself."

He jerks upright.

His supervisor stands three paces to the left, so it's not her shadow that's darkened his desk. It's a bland-faced bureaucrat dressed in the quail-badged garb of a human resources fourth-tier minister. Something about the position of their hands against their tunic, as if they're one breath away from grabbing a weapon, sends a shiver of warning down his neck.

He plays innocent. "I am Beau Qiáng."

His supervisor stares at the floor.

The minister speaks in a voice loud enough to carry across the open room with its rows of desks. "My apologies for interrupting your work. There's an irregularity with your housing allowance, probably in your favor. I've been asked to sort it out. I have an opening now in my schedule, if you don't mind."

He doesn't have a housing allowance. That's why he has to commute an hour each way from a shabby room in an outlying district. With two taps he shunts his searches into the virtual trash, blacks out his desk, and drinks the last of his now lukewarm tea. The supervisor abandons him at the elevator.

In silence he and the minister descend past the lobby into the basement. He virtually scrolls through all his paperwork, but he's always thorough and there was nothing amiss. He got this gig fair and square on the basis of his degree, his experience, and a testimonial from his uncle who taught at the royal academy for a few years and is a member at the same exclusive teahouse as the honorable who is head of Channel Idol.

On Basement Level 2 they leave the elevator, walk along a corridor past closed doors, and enter a key-coded room that houses another elevator. The door into the corridor locks behind them, gleaming red. The buzz of a scan wraps over them. It blinks green and the elevator doors open.

This isn't the way to HR.

The minister indicates that Beau shall enter the elevator.

His mind races with wild thoughts. Should he break and run, like that scene in the historical drama *Year of the Deceptive Lizard* where a defiant and parkour-proficient journalist escapes from collaborators working with the Phene military who have overrun Chaonia Prime?

He isn't hiding anything! He's done nothing wrong. He's an upright and loyal honorable of the republic who completed five years of mandatory service, was matriculated at university, and now works to benefit Chaonia.

He enters the elevator. The doors close, leaving the minister behind.

There are no controls inside, nothing he can do as he descends. Shielding has cut off his access to the network. The elevator opens into an entry hall where four gendarmes wait behind a barrier. They wear the emerald tree badge of Lee House. Each of the seven Core Houses controls one of the seven ministries. Lee House runs the Ministry of Security, Punishment, and Corrections.

Punishment. Oh shit. It's hard to swallow. *What did I do?*

Two gendarmes escort him through a door to a rail track siding. A private rail car awaits. They sit on either side, the three of them alone in a vehicle built to seat twelve. The car accelerates through dark tunnels.

The gendarmes don't speak. He tries once to start a conversation about the latest parkour league standings based on his uncle's advice to build a relationship however one can. They don't tell him to shut up but they don't respond either, just stare straight ahead, so he gives up and watches light strips flash past.

The vehicle slows to a stop at a tiny station with triple security gates. They hand him over to another pair of gendarmes, who walk him down another featureless corridor. This is not looking good. By now he's sure he's stepped in some very deep rubbish. With his network cut off there's no way anyone can trace him.

At the end of the corridor a double door opens into a surprisingly pleasant office decorated tastefully with a red rug and three artful calligraphy scrolls. The far wall is transparent and looks onto an underwater reef teeming with brightly colored fish, undulating feather stars, and huge coiled ammonites. This fascinating vista cannot hold Beau's attention, not when he recognizes the elegant, middle-aged woman behind the desk with her short black hair and gold and black qípáo.

The woman indicates a chair. He sits. They are alone in the room.

"Do you know who I am?" the woman says.

"You're Moira Lee, governor of Lee House. Minister in charge of Security, Punishment, and Corrections."

That the woman shows no annoyance or impatience is probably the most disturbing thing about her. "Answer my questions truthfully and we'll see."

"We'll see what?" He realizes he's offended. "On what grounds have you detained me?"

"I did not invite questions from you." She has a balls-freezing tone. "I've reviewed your records. You were born and grew up in Olynthus System. You graduated with honors from the University of Yele. Rare for a Chaonian citizen to gain admittance at such a prestigious institution, but your father's father was born in the Yele League, and your mother's brother was educated and later taught at that institution as well as teaching at the royal academy here for five years at the specific request of Queen-Marshal Eirene. You had a faculty position at the Larissa Institute of Technology and Dialectic. I find it strange you jettisoned a distinguished sinecure to take a poorly paid position at Channel Idol. Who are you working for?"

"I serve the Republic of Chaonia. And, of course, I serve truth and objectivity."

Moira Lee's lips twitch with disdain. She pulls a virtual cube up from the desk and, inside it, plays a speeded-up string of the clips and images of the Gatoi soldier that he so laboriously collected.

"I repeat: Who is this for?"

Beau blushes. It is so embarrassing to see the images strung together. What was he thinking? He'd mocked his sister for crushing on the

Handsome Alika during his star turn in Idol Faire two years ago. But he has to admit it looks bad. That is, right up until he suddenly wonders if he's holding the wrong end of this stick.

What if it isn't battle name Zizou who Moira Lee cares about? What if it is *something else* he's stumbled on, adjacent to that sweet smile? This is a precipice, and he is dangling on the edge of a fatal fall.

"Governor, I just thought he was hot. You see the prestigious degrees and the faculty honors. What you can't know is I've been dreaming all my life of working for Channel Idol. Despite my respectable family mocking me for my childish yearning."

Moira Lee has been watching his face the whole time, maybe with her own algorithms or maybe with long years of interrogation experience. She blinks to engage a link in her network, and says to the air, "I need a cell made ready."

"What am I being charged with?" Fear surges into anger as he leans forward. After all, he's not a hapless unknown to be shut away without consequences. "My family will ask questions."

The governor peremptorily gestures *Silence* as the door opens. Queen-Marshal Eirene strides in. Beau's mouth drops open as Eirene comes around behind the desk to tap forearms with Moira. The queen-marshal turns her gaze onto him. She has one limpid brown eye; the other is an orb of obsidian, armed with a laser, that replaced the eye she lost in battle. A tiara of optical fiber laces around her short hair.

It's breathtaking to be in the same room as the woman whose remarkable deeds lifted the Republic of Chaonia out of defeat and annexation and built it into a powerhouse military that now controls the Yele League and the fractious Hesjan cartels. The fleet she commissioned and designed has pushed into once-independent territories held for over a hundred years by the mighty Phene Empire. She looks as if she's ready to wrestle the entire empire and its Riders Council right here on the red rug, if they're brave enough to meet her. Which they probably aren't.

Her gaze is cold and her manner blunt. "An honorable with a prestigious university degree, yet you work in Channel Idol's community journalism division?"

"There are important stories Channel Idol can tell with dignity and not just as racy entertainment that sounds like propaganda."

"Channel Idol *is* propaganda. My propaganda."

"It can be more than catering to the needs of today, Your Highness. How do you want history to remember you? You needn't leave it up to chance."

Eirene examines the cube of data and then Beau. "Really, Moira? Your solution is to bury this audacious person in prison?"

"His lineage isn't important enough to—"

"That's not what I mean. This isn't about lineage."

"We can't risk what he may have guessed."

"Yes, yes, of course he can't be allowed to run around without restraint. But he's done us a favor. Now we know to look for this vector of contamination. Chaonia can't waste a single pair of hands in our coming fight. Especially not a clever individual like this one. I can use him."

She pins Beau with a look. Behind her, beyond the glass, a big shark glides past on its ruthless, regal patrol.

"I'm assigning you to the chamberlain's office, in the archives division. You will be given the rank of formal palace historian. You'll work on behalf of Channel Idol, and of course posterity. It's possible that if you were to slowly and not too obviously turn your attention to the affairs of Princess Sun, you might even chance to meet that striking young savage Gatoi in the company of Prince João. The prince is scheduled to return to the palace for my anniversary celebration next month. Your formal essays and official chronicles will be cleared by my office and given their own prominent stream on Channel Idol. Of course you'll report to me personally any particular insights you might glean, especially with respect to the retinue of Sun. Do you understand?"

"Yes, Your Highness," he chokes out.

This ought to be a great honor, yet instinct grips him with a presentiment of disaster. It's like looking through a prophetic telescope and seeing not a luminous living star but the ragged, remnant outlines of a dying one.

11

Hunger Unfulfilled

The shuttle skimmed low across the waters of the Iridescent Sea on Kanesh Prime. Sun sat behind the pilot, studying the approach to the worlds-famous Esplanade. Twenty years ago a grueling weeks-long battle had consolidated Chaonia's control over Kanesh System, which gave access to a strategically crucial beacon route into the Hatti territories and thus to Karnos System.

The twenty-klick-long white-sand beach and raised promenade of the Esplanade were still littered with wreckage. A sunk ferry had become a sea wall. Downed Phene gunships lurked in the shallows like half-submerged leviathans. Burned-out Chaonian lighters carrying Republican Guards had been left where they'd crashed, pilgrimage sites for family members.

Three grand, fortified buildings overlooked the strand. What had been a Unity Hall under Phene rule flew Chaonia's sunburst banner as its seat of military governance. The former Phene Exchange now housed a re-formed Kanesh parliament, which met under the benevolent oversight of Eirene's longest-serving Companion, Tiger Marshal Tomyris Vata.

Sun's attention fixed on the third compound. Once a massive fortified embankment and the Phene military headquarters, it remained in a state of staggering ruin. Fitted with walkways, the edifice stood as tomb and monument to the heroic soldiers and spacers who had paid for Chaonia's victory with their lives.

"Princess Sun, I must object," said Crane Marshal Zàofù from the seat beside her. He spoke in his usual tendentious drawl, not unlike James when he was being pedantic. The whole family had that annoying tendency, perhaps because they were all exceptionally good at what they did and accustomed to having their skill and status recognized. "I have received numerous reports of a large protest gathered at the Monument to Fallen Heroes. Chatter that there may be an attempt to murder you. It would be prudent to confine your visit to the offices."

It was exactly the sort of thing she expected him to say to her.

"Your concern is noted, Marshal. However, I will be lighting incense and making an offering at the monument. You may accompany me, or remain in the offices of Marshal Tomyris. I would never insist that a venerable elder be subject to the grueling schedule of a young person like myself."

Hetty, who was seated behind Sun, tapped her shoulder in warning, but Sun had kept her tone scrupulously polite. She hadn't asked Zàofù to accompany her on this detour to the Esplanade. He didn't have to be here with his tiresome lectures. But after she'd completed her extensive tour of the fleets in the Hatti region, he'd invited himself along since they were both headed back to Chaonia Prime for the forthcoming celebration. He'd known her all her life, and could not help but treat her as the child he'd watched grow up. The heir to the republic wasn't going to allow a few local malcontents to keep her from honoring the dead and carrying out what she had determined to be Octavian's final wish.

The marshal made no further objection as they landed in a secure courtyard beside a sunburst flag. Tomyris was waiting as Sun disembarked. Older even than Zàofù, she was as durable as ironwood and knew Kanesh System better than any Chaonian alive.

"Princess Sun. Let us take tea with my general staff, so you can re-acquaint yourself with them. Then we will go to the monument."

"You're accompanying me?" Sun asked.

"With your goodwill, I would indeed accompany you."

"Isn't there some trouble afoot?" Zàofù said.

"Everyone knows the princess is coming, that is correct. A vocal crowd has gathered. I'd call it a slip-up by military intelligence if I hadn't seen Channel Idol's constant reports on your tour."

"Nothing classified," said Sun as she paced the elder into a fine chamber, overlooking the sparkling sea, where the general staff waited. "It keeps Phene spies busy without giving away anything they don't already know."

An hour was spent amid Tomyris's staff. Sun enjoyed the challenge of measuring the people she met: Who was stationed here because they weren't fit for the front lines? Who was recovering from injuries behind the lines, preparing to go back to the front? Who was ambitious and competent and headed up? Who was mediocre and over-whelmed and headed toward the reserves? Who waxed starry-eyed upon meeting Alika? Who did Hetty find smart enough to talk to about logistics and supply? She logged notes for later reference.

They took a wheeled vehicle along an underground tunnel and ascended via elevator. The doors opened onto a balcony overlooking the mourners' plaza, an open space divided into levels that funneled visitors to a curved viewing platform overlooking the eighteen acres of blasted and burned-out ruins. Seeing their party, a seething crowd of perhaps five thousand restless Kanesh citizens erupted into jeers and hisses.

"Your Highness, shall I have the Guard move in?" Tomyris asked.

"No need." Sun nodded at Alika.

He already had his ukulele tuned and ready, and the means to in-sinuate his dedicated Channel Idol feed into the plaza's display pillars. With the distinctive hair flip he'd made recognizable in his winning run on Idol Faire, he launched into a sequence of songs from Kanesh's history. A classic revenge poem set to music about a cheating lover, "Five Ways to Run," the refrain a reference to a time before the beacon collapse when all five of Kanesh's beacons were functional instead of only three. A medley from the epic tragedy, *The Curse of Eel Gulf,* about an ill-fated squadron of Kanesh frigates stuck in the middle of a war they had no part of.

The crowd quieted, too respectful to shout over his bravura rendition.

As he finished, Sun stepped into weighted seconds of heavy silence before the listeners caught their breath.

"Citizens of Kanesh, you still remember how you were collateral damage in the war between the Yele League and the Phene Empire. Like Chaonia, you went through a period in your history when you were used and discarded. Your cherished institutions were torn up by your conquerors and cast into ruins. Both Yele and Phene set oligarchs of their choosing to rule over you and enrich themselves in defiance of your ancient traditions. I am here to salute your indigenous parliament, reopened by my mother Eirene after the Phene shut it down one hundred years ago. I am here to salute your industry in rebuilding time and again, as we in Chaonia have been forced to do. We share this history. This determination. We are people of lofty purpose, as the poet sang."

She stepped back as Alika strummed the opening cadence of a song Octavian had often sung for Sun. A somber and yet hopeful melody the sergeant major had learned in the back alleys and night markets of Kanesh, the battlefield that had caused him to turn away from war and become the bodyguard of a seven-year-old princess.

"Seek for what you have lost, the smile of hope, the kiss of friendship, the sun that rises with a new light each day."

While Alika played, she, Hetty, and Candace took a set of stairs and a private bridge to the viewing platform. Chaonian marines stood at attention as an honor guard alongside local militia wearing parliament colors of red and green. The marines kept their gazes forward while the locals looked curiously at her as she walked past. One young Kaneshian in uniform went so far as to take a step out of line to stare before he was pulled back by the militiaman beside him.

The altar was a block of shattered concrete left as it had fallen. Sun lit a candle and a stick of incense and intoned the hymn for the honored dead in a low voice, for herself, because Alika was still singing to keep the crowd busy. Just as she reached into her jacket to retrieve Octavian's medals, instinct warned her. A militiaman lunged toward her, a blade glinting in his hand as he thrust.

Hetty leaped to place herself between Sun and the attacker.

Sun shoved her to get her out of the way, but the man toppled sideways before he reached them. Gurgling, he hit the ground. A battle fan stuck out of his neck, courtesy of Candace. The cee-cee raced to grab the person who had stepped out of line earlier; the attacker was the one who had yanked the other guard back. She fought them to their knees. Opening another battle fan, she looked toward Sun for an order to cut his throat. Sun shook her head. Marines swarmed forward to surround

Sun while the rest boxed in the militia, looking ready to murder the shocked locals.

"Hold your positions," she said as she pinged Alika. GET ATTENTION AWAY FROM ME.

Without missing a beat, and in a perfect segue, Alika broke into the verse he was singing. "We have a fainter. Please, my friends, step aside for medical. Otherwise stay where you are. Join me in the chorus. 'After the fall our hearts lifted. Our voices embraced those we had lost.'"

Sun tugged on Hetty's arm, pulling her up too hard because her pulse was racing. How dare someone come so close to murdering a beloved person standing next to her? Not again. She would not allow it.

Hetty was out of breath, cheeks flushed. "I am all right. Pray let me go. Let go."

It took Sun several breaths before she could relax her hand enough to release Hetty. She was so angry that she had to turn her back on the person she trusted most lest she rage at her beloved for doing what she was supposed to do.

The attacker sprawled lifeless a mere two steps away. A ceramic blade rested beyond motionless fingers. She used her boot to roll the man over, revealing a youthful face smeared with blood. Her vision checked for respiration and pulse but Candace's fans were lethal, and he'd bled out fast.

The officer in charge hustled up. "Your Highness!"

"I'm fine," she said, to forestall useless questions or attempts to take the blame. "Take all the militia into custody but do it quietly. Don't telegraph. Get this one out on a stretcher as if he's the fainter. Take your time. I need five more minutes."

On the lower plaza the crowd was singing along with arms raised, swaying back and forth like the kelp the fourth verse praised at length within a catalog of invaluable species that had made the millennium-long journey from the Celestial Empire alongside humanity.

Sun returned to the altar. This time she was able to place Octavian's medals in an offering bowl. *The dead deserve them more than I do,* he had told her once, reflecting on his time fighting in Kanesh. Survival was its own burden, and she would honor it. Sunlight glinted on burnished surfaces. She hadn't seen the medals often because he only wore them when required for formal parade dress. He had guarded her. Guided her from childhood into adulthood: *Don't let your temper control you.* Trained her to understand what mattered most: loyalty, skill, and honor.

Keep the target in mind.

Tomyris appeared, flanked by officers.

"Your Highness! Under my watch! I tender my resignation."

"I refuse it. Kanesh is crucial as we move forward. No one knows Kanesh better than you do. You will remain here on duty, to serve the republic. Think of it as an ambush on our part to draw out the dangerous elements."

"Your Highness." She acquiesced, but the attempt on the princess's life had clearly rattled her.

"I must go if I'm to reach Chaonia in time for the queen-marshal's celebration. I'll leave the Honorable Alika with you to trace the man's movements and provenance. Send me a full accounting."

"Sixth Fleet, arriving." Zàofù was rung on board the *Boukephalas* after her.

She waited beside Captain Tan as the crane marshal arrived on the quarterdeck past the line of ceremonial sideboys. The spacers and marines standing at attention had gotten used to Sun. She knew all their names, and made sure to take one meal every day on the mess deck with a different table of enlisted. By their wide eyes and reverent expressions she could tell none had ever been this close to Zàofù, whose exploits were almost as legendary as those of the queen-marshal.

As the courtesy due his age and eminence, she had cleared out of the flag suite. Captain Tan escorted the marshal and his adjutants on their way while Sun and Hetty took a separate passage toward a guest suite on the same deck. Any other marshal hitching a ride on her flagship would have been assigned to a guest suite, but Sun was not about to explain to her mother that she had parked the venerable Zàofù in the second-best cabin.

The passage snaked a long way around the central compartment. As they walked Sun fixed her hands behind her back, glaring at the deck because she couldn't bear to look at Hetty.

"You're angry, Sun. But I did what I must. I'm no Companion if I let you die."

"It's not that," Sun said, even though that was exactly the nub of it. That she wanted Hetty among her intimate circle, and yet in doing so placed her beloved at risk.

"I would be nowhere else. You know it's true."

"I do know."

The big battle cruiser had been poised and ready for its beacon drop. They hadn't even made it to the suite when comms chimed.

"Two minutes. Take all weigh off the ship."

Sun hooked her feet through a stability rail. The gravity cut. She floated off the deck. Hetty's hand caught hers as she began to drift away in the direction the ship was going. Their fingers twined together, a promise, a binding.

There was no one else in the passageway, only blank bulkheads and closed hatches. Sun gave a tug, pulling Hetty in even though she knew she ought not, here where anyone could walk into view. But it was too late to turn back now as Hetty fell into her with her laughing eyes and parted lips.

The transition bell rang. The ship rolled once, and rolled Sun with it. Hetty's tender mouth touched hers, as if all the universe had compressed to this one ecstatic pressure. Rose petals and balm. A rich, sharp heat.

Everything vanished as they slid past the beacon's aura. No breath. No light. Only a void of hunger unfulfilled, the augury of the oblivion that is failure.

The ship dropped out of the beacon and entered Troia System with engines firing and gravity realigned. Their feet thumped onto the deck.

Hetty laughed, cheeks flushed with a delicate rosy blush. She shook her hand out of Sun's grasp because like every good Companion she guarded Sun's reputation and status as vigilantly as she guarded Sun's life. So must it be. The strictures and customs of the palace ruled Sun because she wasn't her mother's only possible heir, she was merely the best. No use pushing where there was no benefit to breaking rules.

They reached the guest suite and went inside to be greeted by her senior factotum.

"Your Highness, is there anything you require?" Eleuterio asked.

She raised a hand to forestall further questions as a secure packet dropped into her network. According to the time stamp it had been waiting in-system for five Troia Prime days. It was a message from her father.

A moment later her ring buzzed with a message from James.

INCOMING ON A COURIER FROM MOLOSSIA. ETA 237
    MINUTES.

"Eleuterio, dinner in an hour. I'll take it privately with Hetty. Arrange a formal breakfast with the crane marshal and his staff tomorrow. That's all."

He withdrew to the suite's galley and staff rooms.

When necessary Sun's father communicated with her by encrypted text-only messages, but if allowed a courier's bandwidth he preferred to send a visual message. She unzipped it. An image of her father spun into existence. He stood on a tasteful carpet against a backdrop of distinguished wallpaper embossed with golden scallops.

The message began with five seconds of silence. Prince João was a handsome man who used his good looks and curated style to make an impression on people he needed to influence or overawe. He was also a Royal of the Gatoi, which meant his skin was underlaid by a softly gleaming neural network like silver threads of a tattoo across his face and skin. For this message he wore a high-collared lab coat, unbuttoned, over a red tailored shirt and pale gold trousers. The lab coat indicated his current enterprise with its secret experiments on banner soldiers. The red and gold was a reminder of his daughter's military capacity as heir. He had been obsessed since she was young with using dress to remind the worlds who Sun was meant to become. The otherwise bland lab coat had embroidery down its arms: butterflies flitting along a vine that bore not grapes but endless knots, eight on each sleeve.

Hetty grinned. In her light but tuneful voice, she sang softly, "I see by his outfit that he's bringing good news."

The holographic João spoke.

All that I have done for my people I have done a thousandfold for you, my unconquerable Sun. Meanwhile, a rumor has reached me that Lady Sirena might be dead. That gives an opening for you to make your own relationship with the Alabaster Argosy. Even to contact your half sibling without your mother's knowledge. See if there's benefit or danger there. Don't speak of this to anyone and don't try to reach me again. I will see you at the anniversary festival when I present the results of the lab's work to your mother.

The image winked out.

"He's succeeded," Sun said, gaze narrowing. "That opens up a number of possibilities with regard to shifting alliances and what the banners may choose to do. How like my father to anticipate that I'd already thought of reaching out to my half sibling."

"I wonder what news James will bring of this."

"We'll soon find out."

They ate a light dinner, after which Sun settled at a desk to go over High Secretary Nisaba's official record of the last forty weeks. She annotated it with her own observations on ship readiness, promising young officers, and her thoughts on the composition of auxiliary task forces. Hetty worked through the registry of supply. Sun had just begun reviewing Nisaba's account of her meeting with the oligarchs-in-exile from Karnos System, who were eager for Chaonian support, when a new message pinged into her ring network.

Alika's ukulele appeared. INCOMING 28 MINUTES.

"That was fast," said Sun.

She called for a tray of freshly brewed tea and newly baked desserts. James and Alika arrived on board at almost the same time and came jostling into the suite with a light punch to each other's shoulder. Isis and Candace, following behind, greeted each other with more formality.

"I have news!" said Alika in the same tone he had accepted his win on Idol Faire.

"Wait! I haven't secured this suite!" cried James. Repeatedly slapping his leg with his cap in a state of high excitement, he walked a circuit of the compartment to scan. "All right. Go ahead, Alika."

"What about your news?"

"Idol Faire winners first."

"You're also an Idol Faire winner. In a way. As part of our group, obviously, but in technical and factual terms you still count."

James's eyes had a feverish brightness. For once he didn't succumb to the desire to squabble. "Of course I do. Go ahead."

"No, no, you go ahead."

"Enough," said Sun, having enjoyed their byplay for about two seconds. "Alika, you got here fast. Report."

Whatever Alika's flaws, he absolutely obeyed her. "Once the corpse arrived at the hospital the situation was easily exposed. He was wearing cosmetic lenses to disguise that he was a seer of Iros."

Sun rose up on her toes and, with an effort, settled back down. Her heart burned with eagerness, the desire for revenge served hot. "And?"

"There is a hermitage on Kanesh Prime. The leadership claimed the suspect was never there. There's no obvious evidence he was. Marshal Tomyris will send along a full accounting when she's excavated all their records."

"Evidence can be scrubbed," said Sun.

"It can be, but her quartermaster was able to trace the suspect's entry stamp into Kanesh System to one hundred and forty-eight days ago on a freighter whose registry is the designate Libertalia in the Trinity Coalition."

"An independent operator, in other words."

"One paying protection money to the Trinity. Once we started looking in that direction, his trail was easy to uncover. He met up with members of the Evergreen, an interdicted Kanesh faction calling for return to Phene rule. They have some kind of an in with discontented factions inside the Esplanade militia. They're probably part of the umbrella of groups that got the protest going. Still, it wasn't as hostile of a crowd as it could have been. Easier to sway than I'd feared."

Sun shook her head. "The territories conquered by the Phene in the last hundred or so years aren't big fans of the Phene. There's no reason for them to like us either, but as they say, two hands are lighter than four. What else?"

"I have the body in tow, in stasis for forensics. Marshal Tomyris will send along a further report after her full investigation, but there was no need for me or the body to stay behind for that."

"Well done. I knew I could count on you, Alika."

She held his gaze for one extra beat, like the slap of a drum in punctuation. As a performer he desired and even needed such cadences, so she offered them. Once he nodded an acknowledgment she turned her attention to James. "Well? You have news."

James looked ready to leap out of his skin for the sheer thrill of finding out what would happen to his meat popsicle when it was no longer held together by his epidermis.

Was Persephone's exaggerated way of speaking rubbing off on her? She smiled slightly. It had never been her way to mimic others, but that didn't mean she couldn't enjoy the quirks and gifts that made them the right Companions for her. She slid a glance toward Hetty, who stood off to one side, overlooked and underestimated and absolutely drinking it all in and filing it all away. Hetty looked a question in her direction.

"You have the floor, James," Sun added as she turned back to him.

"So I do. Alika, may I have a portentous chord?"

"I only have pretentious chords left for you."

"I'm waiting," said Sun.

James gave her his best "what, me?" look as he tugged his cap to a jaunty angle. The pause was him at his most infuriating, meant to provoke. She said nothing. He broke first, bouncing with excitement.

"The data I gathered on Jiàn's visitors and trading partners is inconclusive. I could undertake other angles of investigation, if you want that. However . . ."

He slid a pin out from a sheath woven into the skin of his left forearm. She took it, an object two centimeters long and possible to snap in half if need be to destroy the physical evidence. Her ring network was private enough for most communication. It could not be breached by Chaonian military or security because the technology came from Prince João, not from the queen-marshal.

James had borrowed the pin trick from the Phene, who preferred physical equipment because it could be walled off securely. Chaonia loved its network, anchored by the ubiquitous Channel Idol, whose tendrils of surveillance reached everywhere. But not to a physical pin unreadable by the cloud. She had a node hidden under a fingernail.

She slipped in the pin, feeling first a pressure against her nail and then a sting up her nerves.

The message popped up beyond the edge of her network as seemingly random code debris barnacled onto an anodyne request for a palace audience, a communication her high secretary would normally handle. Characters arrayed on a rhombus faced each other with a message of respect and honor for the reputation of the opposite one. In the center, a time stamp, a location stamp, the characters for Odrysa System, and a name. Soaring Shān.

She studied it, then looked at his grinning face. "I didn't expect a response like this. But this likely means Alabaster Argosy is headed for Odrysa System, which means my mother will already have wind of it. We need to get there before she does."

12

Introducing the Valiant One

The wreck hung in space, cold and dead amid an accumulation of dust. Ensign the Honorable Makinde Bō's initial sensor sweep detected no heat, no particle drift, nothing. Kind of like the career he'd hoped for, scuppered and set adrift.

"Who would be raiding out here?" he remarked to the duty crew. Including himself as officer of the watch there were three, although the bridge of a picket ship normally took a complement of seven. "Or trading out here? There's no one to trade with and nowhere to go."

"A hit job by one of the cartels?" suggested Comms Petty Officer First Class Sayre Guī Alsura as she exchanged a glance with Chief Sharru'ukin Jī Allygos, who sat at the helm.

Makinde shook his head. "The cartels *protect* shipping."

"As long as you pay them, Ensign. Don't they teach that at the royal academy?"

Makinde stiffened as he considered cutting retorts, but with a controlled exhale he decided an enlisted assigned to a lowly patrol circuit at the ass end of nowhere could not possibly be deliberately insulting an honorable of Bō House, even if she didn't know who his grandmother was. Anyway, as data flowed in, the boxy formation that might have held cargo containers flattened out to become the smooth, sleek lines of a warship.

He grunted with adrenaline-charged surprise. "Holy hells. It's not one of ours. Chief, send in a hornet. Alsura, sound general quarters."

Again the spacer and the chief exchanged a glance. Makinde was the youngest on the *Sunbird* by twenty years. Veteran reservists bearing the scars of war hadn't felt any need to be welcoming when a high-ranking honorable fresh out of the royal academy had been tossed into their tight-knit crew. But they obeyed.

A light blinked green, the picket ship gave an infinitesimal shudder, and the outside cameras picked up a visual of a three-lobed hornet-class drone speeding away toward the hulk.

After the alarm sounded, Guī Alsura spoke into the 1MC. "General quarters. General quarters. All hands, man your battle stations. Proceed up and forward to starboard, down and aft to port. Set condition one throughout the ship. Reason for general quarters, unknown contact on sensors."

The alarm blared again. By now the hornet was too far away to track visually. Its heat trail left a wispy thread on the sensor display.

"Alsura, open a secure line to COSA to report a hostile."

The hatch whined, whirred, and finally lurched open. Commander Situri Rèn Alviasalaria wheeled herself onto the bridge, short hair standing up in a spiky mess and duty tunic rumpled as if she'd rolled straight out of her rack. She blinked sleep out of her eyes as she clicked through views of the sensor sweep. Her scarred lip curled as she glanced toward Makinde.

"Belay the comms to COSA. Proceed with a secondary sweep, Ensign." Then she addressed the other two. "I'll be back with tea. Carry on."

She wheeled herself out. The hatch shut behind her with a flatulent hiss. The seal needed repair but the fleet couldn't spare parts for a backwater picket ship that functioned well enough on spit and baling wire.

"*Tea?* Shouldn't this be immediately reported to COSA? Isn't that mandated procedure?"

Guī Alsura gave him a look. "Ensign, with respect, we all know you're a Core House scion"—she made the word sound like *brat*—"while the commander came up through the ranks the hard way with a stellar service record and the commendations to back it up. Feel free to report me for saying so, but we citizens have the right to speak our minds even to the queen-marshal."

Makinde was too surprised to object to this scolding. Of the forty-one members of the crew, Sayre Guī Alsura had been the only friendly in his long weeks aboard. Or maybe he only thought so because her gruff demeanor reminded him of his no-nonsense grandmother.

Like his grandmother she kept on talking, never one to stint on a good smackdown. "It's pretty clear an honorable like you must have offended someone very high up to get slapped down this hard into such a junk duty station."

She paused as if waiting to see if he would finally confide in them.

He would not.

With a sigh, she bent back over her console, fielding queries from elsewhere on the ship as the crew sought information. Jī Allygos was running a check through the weapons systems, which at best might hold off a space-suited carnotaur.

After confirming there was no other bogie within a ten-thousand-klick range, Makinde scanned back toward the planet they'd passed by a few hours ago. At that time he'd done a thorough scan of its abandoned orbital habitat and various bits of in-orbit debris, gutted ships, broken satellites, and long-empty zero-g factories. No trace of life or artificial energy had shown up then and he didn't expect any to show up now, but he was going to be thorough all over again.

Odrysa Sept was a terrestrial world with a sluggish white-and-pink cloud cover filled with toxins. Its massive beacon drew the eye, like a spiral moon gravitationally tethered to the planet.

In the first thousand years of post–Landfall settlement, all transportation between star systems in the local belt was controlled by Argosies with their knnu drives. After the Apsaras Convergence built the beacon routes the dynamic changed radically. Instead of a months- or years-long knnu passage, a ship could drop through a beacon and emerge an instant later from its linked beacon in another star system. In just this way, the other beacon in Odrysa System, which was anchored to Odrysa Prime, connected to Pselkis System. The route led back into the heart of the republic.

Eight hundred years ago, parts of the beacon network had collapsed for reasons no one understood. Many beacons had failed. This was one of those.

No ships would ever enter or exit this beacon again. An aura of garish colors shimmered inside its coil and spilled outward to create an undulating halo the little picket ship had carefully avoided. Whatever had killed the beacon had infected the previously habitable planet and its orbital habitat and factories as well. The loss of its second beacon had turned Odrysa System from a busy janus through-route into a terminus system, a dead end. Like his military career, which hadn't even gotten off the ground before it had died and been sent here to this tomb of a posting. Guī Alsura wasn't wrong, which was why he couldn't feel exercised over her plain speaking.

Nothing new appeared, because he'd done his sweep correctly the first time. He switched his view back to the hornet, clearing the last hundred klicks to the wreck.

"Oi. Hold on. Look here."

The other two clipped over.

"What are we looking at?" Guī Alsura asked in a calm tone at odds with the gravity of the situation.

"There's a blot inside the hull blocking normal background radiation." He indicated an area with an odd matte-black finish that seemed to be hanging inside the outlines of the big wreck. "It could be a shielded compartment. Here's a trickle of energy like leakage. Might be a battery on low power mode. Might be life support."

"You think people could be alive in there?"

"Both the Phene and the Yele have shields that can block heat signatures. So maybe?"

The chief made a noise, quickly stifled, but when Makinde looked his way, the man had hunched low over his console, face hidden. He was an old-timer whose jaw had been blown off during one of the queen-marshal's campaigns, which must mean he had a lot of bad memories.

"It is weird, though," Makinde went on. "Wouldn't there be a record of an enemy ship arriving through Pselkis Beacon, especially if it happened in the wake of last year's battle? Wouldn't we have been alerted that a hostile was in-system?"

The hornet pinged an alert. He tweaked the visual to grab an image of abrasions etched into the hull where a ship's registry number would usually be found. Then he dumped the image into an analysis program and let the hornet hover outside the ship while he awaited a result. He kept his gaze on the sensors, alert for any sign of an enemy sailing out of nowhere. Even so, his thoughts began to drift.

He should never have offended the governor of Bō House in the first place, but there was no point in mending the pen after the ankylosaurs were lost. Honestly it had felt so good to see that lewd worm cringe and blush in front of the entire assembled House. No one else was willing to call out the man, even knowing what he'd done.

Yet even after all the whispers of gratitude and encrypted messages of thanks, he was the one assigned to a backwater border system in retribution. Meanwhile every other member of his academy cohort had either fought in the battle of Molossia or would be fitting up for the long-awaited assault on Karnos System. News took so long to get here that the campaign would be over before he heard about it. Just his cursed luck.

The hatch clunked twice before scraping open. The commander

wheeled in with a tray of bulbs steaming with hot tea. "Sayre, get supply up here to look at that hatch again. I know this tub is old, and we get the refurbished repair kits, but this is ridiculous. What do we have to do to get—" She broke off as she registered the hornet's visual feed. "Ah, here we go."

"Shouldn't we wait for a registry number?" Makinde asked.

"With those abrasions, and given it's a Phene ship, we might never get one."

"How do you know it's a Phene ship? Looks like a Yele frigate. There are breakaway Yele factions allied with the Phene. Not to mention Yele-class ships used by Skuda marauders, Gatoi arrows, and independents like the Franklin Gang."

"Ensign, look at the hull. Those two sawed-off spurs are where the double-helix component of a Phene torch drive would have been attached. The question you should be asking is: Who has the capacity to remove a drive so cleanly without being in a shipyard? Chief, can you take the hornet in?"

The chief guided the hornet through an airlock passage that had been left open all the way into an inner staging compartment.

"Who leaves airlocks open to deliberately vent a compartment?" Makinde asked.

The commander didn't look up from the visual. "It could be attackers or defenders. Or an accident or a malfunction. Or an artifact of systems failure."

They watched the probe's cameras scan the inner compartment with its racks for vacuum suits and a stacked complement of the hover chariots the Phene used for ground combat.

Annoyed that he'd missed the helix drive, Makinde said, "A Phene destroyer can't land in atmosphere, so it's odd they have chariots. The only explanation is they were intended to be transferred to an accompanying gunship. Phene gunships can dock with this specific configuration of airlock but are limited to in-system travel because they're not big enough for beacon drives."

"Thank you for the academy lesson, Ensign." The commander's dead-even tone fell like a scalding rebuke.

Makinde counted to ten in his head before adding, "I'm just saying, it might help us figure out where this destroyer came from and why it's here. It can't have been part of the recent attack on Molossia, because there was no ground attack involved."

"There *was* a ground attack in conjunction with the Molossia engagement."

"Oi. That's right. The raid on the industrial park on Chaonia Prime.

The one Princess Sun responded to before anyone else knew it was happening."

"That was some battle," agreed Guī Alsura, tone warming with approval. "Humble CeDCA citizen cadets holding their own against Phene special forces."

Was the comment meant as a slam at honorable royal academy graduates like him? He said, "The princess took command."

"An heir to be proud of. We're lucky to have her." Guī Alsura paused, then said, "You must have been at the royal academy with her."

He shrugged. "Sure, but she was three cohorts ahead of me so we only overlapped by one year. She has her own bodyguard and her own Companions. A junior scrub like me would never have gotten anywhere near her orbit."

The chief tapped his console to interrupt.

The hatch between the inner compartment and the passageway beyond already stood open, left that way just like the airlocks. The chief paused the drone at the rim of the hatch and had it extrude a camera filament through the opening for a scan of the corridor's length. Makinde found himself holding his breath as the view scanned aft and forward, not sure what carnage they would see. The bulkheads were intact, painted with elaborate images of feasting and hunting. Every hatch within view stood open, as if someone had decided to flush all atmosphere out of the ship. No sign of life. No wreckage or random drifting items.

The hornet took its time working a path aft along the corridor, poking extrusions into each compartment. Everything was shipshape, stowed tight, locked up: like they'd abandoned ship hoping to return. In a cabin, some joker had left an empty cup affixed to the fold-out desk and taped the left hand of a small figurine to the cup's handle as if the figurine had just finished drinking.

"What in the hells?" Makinde gave a startled laugh. The figurine depicted a winged individual with breast-hugging white body armor who held a caduceus staff in their right hand. "It looks like one of my little brother's toys."

"It's a figure of one of their saints," said the commander. "Which is some cursed kind of slops-bucket worship, if you ask me. All manner of rubbish cant about personal dedication and individual goals instead of veneration of the ancestors and respect for community."

"Sure, but think about having enough presence of mind to keep your sense of humor while your ship is dying around you," retorted Makinde.

"It was probably some loner of an ensign," said Guī Alsura with a dry look.

He grinned. "I'd absolutely do it if I had time before I asphyxiated."

Even the commander cracked an unexpected smile.

The chief's vocoder croaked in a harsh metallic monotone. "Anomaly ahead."

The hornet eased past illustrated scenes of stalwart work gangs enjoying picnics in lush gardens and of knights of the Celestial Empire hunting vicious packs of coelophysis. It nosed through a hatch, its camera making a sweep of a huge cavity carved out of the central decks of the ship. In this space floated a big object like a tumorous ovoid mass. In a way the mass was darker than the lightless interior. His eyes told him it was solid, but an instinct deep in his mind whispered it was liquid confined by a transparent outer skin. Its contents were moving in a way his suite of sensors could not quite register. Even seeing it through the step-back of the hornet's camera made him queasy.

"What is that?" he asked.

"That is the first smart question I've heard you ask since you came aboard," said the commander. "It's a knnu anchor. Have you never seen one before? Don't they do a unit at the royal academy on the mysterious history of Argosy technology?"

"A knnu anchor? Like a channel buoy and lighthouse combined? That kind of a knnu anchor?"

The chief's shoulders heaved. The man was *laughing* silently. Guī Alsura hid her mouth with a hand. The commander had the bland expression of an even-tempered person who has been done with your shit for a while but is only now letting the anvil drop. The truth hit like a kiloton of bricks.

"You let me run with general quarters and the whole sweep, knowing we'd find a hulk out here turned by Argosy tech into a knnu anchor? An anchor that's probably been here all along for . . . what? . . . Generations?"

"About three hundred years, yes," remarked the commander. How she kept up that mockingly deadpan expression he could not fathom. "An artifact, really. The last known record of an Argosy fleet arriving in Odrysa System is ninety-four Republic years ago during the reign of Queen-Marshal Metis. So it's not like there's much risk getting close up like this."

Makinde was still struggling with the surge of adrenaline. "You *knew*. You *pranked* me. On purpose."

The commander cleared her throat and with a wave of her hand signaled the others to politely look away. "Listen, Ensign, I get that no honorable wants to be stuck patrolling a heavens-forsaken terminus on an outdated dump of a picket ship. But we're here so the central systems don't get hit with a surprise attack. The pickets didn't do a good enough job a year ago in Molossia System, did they? Do you want to be them? Or do you want to make sure we don't miss a Phene invasion?"

"No, no. You misunderstand me. No need to apologize."

The chief cocked a startled gaze at him.

"I'm in *awe*. That was perfectly played. You didn't even plan it in advance. You just ran with it. I have so much respect for a good practical joke."

He began to laugh. After a moment, the others broke into laughter as well, a long-awaited release. He even had to wipe his eyes.

"The smile looks good on you, Ensign," said Guī Alsura. "You should try it again sometime."

He rubbed away his tears as he considered the *Sunbird*'s crew: Situri Rèn Alviasalaria, whose wheeled braces mostly hid the damage done to her legs in battle years ago. Sharru'ukin Jī Allygos, who preferred signing and messaging to speaking through the vocoder on his neck. Sayre Guī Alsura, who like so many in the reserves had interrupted retirement to take routine patrol and desk duty so younger people could go to the front lines. He'd been digging so hard into his own grievances that he hadn't given the respect due their loyal service.

"I guess I have been kind of a jerk," he said.

The chief shot him a look, then glanced at the commander, who looked at Guī Alsura, who said, "If you open up to people, they won't think you're stuck up."

"People think I'm stuck up?" He scratched at his shaved-short hair, stunned at this observation. His cohort couldn't get a party started without him and Dozer.

"What are they supposed to think when you're an honorable who won't talk to any of us citizens? Who hides in your cabin? Which you don't have to share because we're short-handed."

A solo cabin had been the only lucky break of this junkyard venture. He wondered if he would ever trust anyone on this ship enough to reveal Dozer.

"With respect, Ensign, I've got a clutch of grandchildren more or less your age, and you remind me——" Guī Alsura broke off as comms pinged, delivering a message.

"This is *Mocker*, headed your way. We identify you as *Sunbird*. Please acknowledge. Please acknowledge."

The commander scratched her head. "Pretty sure *Mocker* is a courier. What are they doing out here? Acknowledge receipt of their message and ask—"

She broke off as everyone's eyes turned to the hornet's feed. The mass began to glow with a sullen color, although it wasn't really a color; it was a translation of the hornet's feed into a visual fit for human comprehension.

Dozer's voice blurted into Makinde's ear on their personal link. BOSS. BOSS! DANGER! ALERT!

"Shit!" swore the commander. "Get us out of here. General quarters. All hands batten down. Seal your vac suits."

The alarm blared as faceplates hissed into place. Jī Allygos flipped the short-range thrusters and slammed the little ship with a series of bursts. The force shoved Makinde into the chair. Pressure squeezed his lungs.

The glow flashed, whiting out the hornet's feed. After a second, a brief image returned of the cavity's walls slewing past as the little drone tumbled. The view jerked sideways and went black. A pulse surged off the distant hulk, spiking all their sensors.

Finally they began to move away, picking up speed. The shock wave raced after them. One minute. Two.

"What happens when it hits us?" Makinde choked out.

No one answered. Maybe they didn't know. Or maybe they were veterans doing everything they could to secure and protect the ship with no time to answer pointless questions.

Four minutes. Eight. Sixteen. Thirty-two . . . thirty-three . . .

A massive jolt rattled Makinde's teeth. His head whacked back against his chair. The ship's torch drive shuddered and died before it could stabilize the vessel. Sensors snapped out but life support held as the ship rolled in a backward pitch through a slow-motion reverse tumble. With gravity loss, only the straps held them down. Tea bulbs floated, liquid sloshing inside.

BOSS?

DOZE, YOU OKAY?

FUN! THIS IS FUN! YOU OKAY? WE SHOULDNA BEEN SO
CLOSE.

The sensor array rerouted through emergency power and lit back up. Makinde's console displayed the pulse as it expanded away from them into space as a ripple of energy across the vast ocean of night.

The *Sunbird* reached a 180 in relation to where it had started and began to pitch back, bringing the main view around back toward the wreck.

"Holy hells. Will you look at that!" Guī Alsura said.

The central region of space was gone, replaced by an object so large Makinde couldn't make sense of its glittering lights and cliff-like wall until he realized space wasn't gone. Space had never left. A gigantic ship had appeared as if in an eyeblink, rather like a magician's hat trick but really just a perceptual artifact of knnu drives. The effect was hugely disconcerting and utterly terrifying. Makinde shifted in his chair to make sure he hadn't peed in his vac suit, which fortunately he had *not* even if he was damp around the crotch.

The ship was not alone, of course it wasn't. The thousand or so extra lights were smaller vessels. He'd never thought to see the pulse of a knnu entry with his own eyes.

Staring in wonderment and dismay, the commander breathed, "That's a Titan-class Argosy mothership and its entire tow chain. We are so fucked."

13

The Valiant One Finds His Voice

It took an hour to stabilize the ship under auxiliary power. By then a vessel had detached from the Titan, pushing a diplomatic code out in front: a request for permission to approach peacefully according to Treaty 31.7.2.14 Injunction 5.31 as agreed between Queen-Marshal Eirene Shān and the Consensus of Elders and the Sterling Senate of the Alabaster Argosy.

The commander gave an unfathomable grunt that made Makinde nervous. "I'll need an attaché to give me face. Ensign, you're assigned. Bring your symbiont."

"His *what?*" demanded Guī Alsura.

The chief's vocoder squawked as in surprise. The noise cut off as the chief gave him a hard stare.

Right on cue, Dozer's voice blurted into his inner ear. BOSS! I CAN DO IT! I'M READY TO GO!

Makinde's thoughts scrambled. He knew his mouth was gaping open in an expression surely comical to the others.

The commander slanted him a look. "Do you think I wasn't suspicious when your orders pinged into my box? A new-minted royal academy graduate with a decent academic and solid field trials record. Born into Bō House, cousin twice removed to the current governor. Descendent of a much-decorated maternal grandsire. Honorables of your stature go to the queen-marshal's escort fleet for a year or two of seasoning and maybe a mentorship before you get a transfer into the general fleet. So I asked myself, how did he get here? Who did he piss off?"

Makinde stiffened his shoulders, lifted his chin, and said nothing.

"My digging didn't turn up any legal trouble or reckless mischief beyond a couple of citations for public drunkenness. Which is apparently true of half the honorables at the royal academy. But it did turn up an unexpected wrinkle. Your maternal grandmother is a honcho."

"I'll be hells-cursed," remarked Guī Alsura.

The commander went on. "She was born into one of the richest Hesjan cartels. She married that decorated Bō House scion as part of a trade and revenues alliance negotiated by her brother, who was head honcho of their cartel at the time. So I did a quick scan of your cabin—"

"My cabin!"

The commander snorted. "You think you have privacy in the fleet? This isn't your beautiful Core House compound on an island on the bay off Argos. In republic space all low-mind AI are required to be registered to the military or one of the ministries. Anyone who acquires a low-mind AI is mandated to report it to the Ministry of Rites and Culture. That includes Hesjan bionic enhanced escorts. I'm surprised you were allowed to attend the royal academy with a bee in tow. But maybe not. Status and wealth buys most anything."

Citizens always said things like that. "Why didn't you write me up?"

"I'm shorthanded. I don't need to lose a crew member for the sake of a reg that doesn't do anything for readiness. Did your grandmother gift all of her children and grandchildren one of those things?"

"Every Hesjan child is sealed to a symbiont when they make one thousand days. She wasn't about to let anyone tell her she couldn't pass on the tradition to her own progeny. I'm one of three surviving grandchildren, so all of us, yes."

"All right, then. Sayre, I want you to go to the aft receiving airlock and make sure the comms link is working. Ha-rin will be checking the seals. Ensign, I want you there in formal palace dress uniform."

"Aye, aye, Captain," Makinde replied.

Guī Alsura and the chief shot him looks.

He grinned. "In all the serials about the Celestial Empire that's how military crew responds. I always wanted to try it."

To his delight, they all smiled. A tentative glow of acceptance infused his chest as he rose. "Dozer will be delighted."

"Dozer?" The commander cocked an eyebrow at him.

"Every bee has a name, Captain. Just as people do."

"Dozer it is. I want the symbiont to remain concealed for advanced surveillance and additional security. Can it manage that?"

"Ou can."

Picket ships were the cheap patrol vessels of the fleet, meant primarily for sentry duty. They had port and starboard guns, torpedoes fore and aft, and three decks. Each deck was more or less a single long passageway sealed into airtight sections by hatches, with compartments welded to either side. With everyone scrambling to repair the ship, no one was loitering.

"I have to see this," Guī Alsura said, tailing him. "I have a grandchild who is obsessed with *Old Honcho and Baby Bee*."

"That series is sixty years old, at least."

"Yeah, I watched it obsessively as a kid. The scamp might have picked up the habit from me."

"It was inspired by my grandmother's marriage, you know."

"I'll be pickled in the hell of brine. And here you are."

He didn't know how to take the comment, so he let it go.

The officer cabins clustered on the upper deck near the bridge. A picket ship usually had three ensigns, one for each watch, but these days there were never enough ensigns for the battle fleets so he had the cabin to himself. Guī Alsura stood back as he palmed the door panel from red to green. It slid open.

"Wait," he said into the cabin, because Dozer was an enthusiast.

Guī Alsura craned her neck, trying to get a look inside the cramped cabin with its three-tiered rack, lockers, and a folded-up table. "What . . . where . . ."

She yelped in surprise as Dozer, resting on the top rack and hearing an unknown voice, erupted outward in a welter of excitement.

VISITOR! VISITOR! CAN I SHAKE HANDS?

The symbiont flowed down the bulkhead to the deck in a confusion of limbs but stopped short of the threshold, mottled skin shading pink with eagerness.

Guī Alsura's mouth gaped as she raised a shaking arm to point. "The hells! How many tentacles does that thing have?"

"Eight arms, two tentacles. This is Dozer. Dozer, this is Sayre Guī Alsura."

She looked at him for permission, and he nodded. He was honestly staggered when she crouched and cautiously extended a hand to the threshold. Dozer mimicked the gesture, shifting an arm forward until its tip touched her fingers. She sucked in a breath as Dozer's pink color deepened.

Makinde had to take a couple of breaths to settle his racing heart. "The pink is excitement. Dozer has a social streak. The ship's been a lonely place. It's kind of you to reach out."

A second arm curled over to gently tap the back of her hand, an invitation to play. She cracked a smile. "I had no idea."

"No idea what?"

"I've only seen war bees and cargo bees. Dozer isn't anything like those."

"Dozer is a decapod, a common model for ship and habitat dwellers. Agile, strong, dexterous, and can squeeze through most any size gap."

"You want me to take it down, give it plenty of time to get in place?"

"With respect, among Hesjan it's considered discourteous to use 'it' for symbionts. My grandmother's clan uses 'ou' for theirs, so I follow that tradition."

"Thanks. You want me to take ou down? I'd love to."

Dozer was shifting colors with excitement.

"All right. Doze, pay attention to the petty officer." He indicated the carry bag left open at all times in case Dozer needed a comforting slow-down in an enclosed space. Dozer slithered into the bag, folding into a blob that neatly filled the bag's confines. Purple and yellow patches shaded the symbiont's flexible skin, the blend of colors signifying determination and caution. Makinde latched the bag and handed it over.

"I'll meet you in forty-three minutes."

"It takes you that long to dress?"

"Have you seen the formal palace dress uniform?"

"Do I in any way act or look like I've ever seen a formal palace dress uniform in the flesh? Old Honcho and Baby Bee, headed for their next adventure." She grinned and left, carrying the bag.

He went into his cabin and began the laborious process of dressing, made more difficult by the gravity cutting out and back in twice as the engineers tried to reroute to main power. So it took almost an hour before he headed out, eager to get a frontline engagement with the mysterious Argosy.

Adrenaline put a spring in his step. With repairs to make and an incoming unknown, the entire crew was hustling. Those moving through the passageways stopped to stare as he made his way below and aft. No one else on the *Sunbird* had a formal palace dress uniform with all its bells and whistles and bustles and bows, as the song went. Maybe his shipmates had never seen one up close.

One of the older fellows gave him a sly wink as he passed and said, "Got a hot date, Ensign?"

"It's either a hot date with an Argosy diplomat or a cold date with an airlock," he replied, to general laughter. It felt good to make people laugh instead of give him a side-eye and the cold shoulder. Maybe he shouldn't have stewed in his own resentment for so long. Maybe he could have lightened up.

The sealed doors at the aft receiving airlock had to be opened manually from inside. As he waited, fidgeting, his thoughts wandered. What if he hadn't decided to call out that corrupt abuser? He'd known nothing would happen to the reprobate. Any governor of a Core House was protected by the simple fact of their exalted status and political power. If he'd kept his mouth shut like everyone else did . . .

The door clunked open and he stepped over the threshold. Immediately he saw Dozer, busy with several arms inside a comms hub as a pair of techs stood on either side giving directions in cheerful voices. Doze had already made friends! Guī Alsura lifted a hand in greeting. Dozer blazed a bright joyful yellow but kept working, just like everyone else. As Makinde glanced around the compartment with its cobbled-together equipment repairs and redoubtable crew, he knew he'd rather be here with a clear conscience.

The commander had arrived before him. "Ensign, nice getup."

"That's what everyone says who doesn't have to wrestle into it."

Comms clicked over, and a voice from engineering announced, "We have the workaround ready, Captain. On your go-ahead."

"All brace."

Gravity cut. Makinde drifted in the direction of the bar he clutched. The thunk of an impact shuddered the little ship. The bulkheads gave a weird buzzing trill as his feet reoriented to the floor with an emphatic thud.

Engineering clicked back over. "The incoming shuttle is attached. Clearing airlock in fifteen minutes."

"Incoming shuttle here already?" Makinde asked. "I thought the ETA was one hundred thirty-one minutes."

"The situation has changed radically." The commander pressed a hand against her eyes, shielding her face for a few private breaths. Her shoulders heaved, as if she was working through some strong emotions. With a wry smile she lowered her hand. "We now have two Chaonian military vessels approaching our position. The *Mocker,* whose captain has offered us assistance. And the *Shadowfax* some hours behind."

"The queen-marshal's flagship? That *Shadowfax*?"

"That's right."

"Who just attached?"

"The utility shuttle from the *Mocker*. Which according to my fleet registry is a courier assigned to the escort group of the *Boukephalas*."

"The *Boukephalas*?"

"Yes, I found that odd, too. You're the most well-connected individual here, even if you did piss off somebody very high up. Any background I might need to know?"

"This has nothing to do with me!"

"That's not what I was asking. Any insight into our current situation?"

"Queen-Marshal Eirene's first marriage was to Lady Sirena from the Alabaster Argosy. If the *Shadowfax* is incoming, then this is likely a high-level diplomatic visit. The *Mocker* might be carrying a diplomatic team in advance of the queen-marshal."

"COSA did not apprise us of any expected diplomatic activity in the region. As a picket I would have been warned ahead of time, even if not the particulars."

When Dozer finished the repair and flowed over to him, everyone yelped at the movement, then laughed. He'd been wrong to keep ou hidden. His life on board could have been easier all along if he hadn't worn his grievances as a mask.

Lights went green. The commander stiffened as the airlocks cycled. The inner airlock opened as a double bell rang. A stocky young officer stepped into the compartment. Her gaze marked every person with a swift yet comprehensive scan, as if she were identifying targets before a barrage of fire.

In her wake two soldiers entered. They wore the silver shield badges of the elite royal marines. After them came a civilian wearing a formal robe embroidered with an ibis insignia to indicate her status as a palace secretary. The last individual to embark was a tall and attractive young woman with a familiar face, wearing one of the tailored vac suits available only to the highest-ranking individuals.

Finding his voice, he murmured, "Commander, that's Sun Shān."

The commander nodded reflexively toward the taller officer. "Commander Situri Rèn Alviasalaria, at your service. Welcome aboard the *Sunbird*, Your Highness."

"I'm Sun," said the shorter officer.

"Your Highness." The commander flushed a splotchy red. "Of course you are. I abjectly beg your pardon."

"It doesn't matter." She bent her head toward the secretary, who whispered in her ear, then turned back to the commander. "You received the Sunburst Medal for Heroic Conduct in rescuing one hundred spacers from a foundered ship during the Battle of Hatti Reach. You managed this feat despite grave injuries to your own legs, which you later lost to amputation. Chaonia is fortunate to have officers like you."

The commander's flush deepened. "Your Highness!"

"Your ship has taken damage from the knnu pulse. Captain Malik is loaning you a detachment of engineers and techs."

The airlock chimed again. Five vac-suited individuals came on board and immediately made their way out of the compartment onto the ship.

"You have tea service on board, I assume, Captain."

The commander cast a glance at Makinde. "Ensign, go to the galley and make sure everything is prepared properly according to palace protocol."

Sun followed the look, head tilting to the left as she studied him in his dress uniform. When her gaze fixed on his face he had the unexpected sensation of facing into a turbulent storm about to break over him. Its crash would obliterate him or loft him to wild heights before he plunged to a gruesome death. He grinned, never one to quail before a challenge.

Her gaze narrowed as she took in Dozer's presence, half wound up his right leg. "Who are you?"

"Makinde Bō."

"Bō House? You've got to be a recent graduate of the royal academy. How bad were your scores for you to get assigned to this duty?" She glanced at the commander, the techs, and the *Sunbird*'s three marines. "No offense intended to those of you engaged in this crucial home patrol."

Makinde felt defiant words rising, just like the other time. His mouth always got him into trouble. "My scores were as good as yours, Your Highness. You can check, because I did. It's all public record, unless they doctored your scores."

For a drawn-out interval he thought she'd blow.

She laughed. "Challenge accepted."

She caught the eye of her secretary, nodded with an unspoken command that surely presaged an unpleasant consequence, and turned back to the commander.

"Captain, have the tea service set up in the wardroom. I'm sure your steward can manage it correctly. No need for the ensign to be involved."

"Yes, Your Highness."

Ouch, thought Makinde as the princess lost interest in him. She asked each of the *Sunbird*'s marines their name, then went to the techs to observe, asking them questions in a comradely way as they detached the airbridge from the *Mocker*'s utility shuttle.

Eventually she returned to her secretary. She bent her head as the secretary spoke into her ear with the other woman listening. Makinde ran a finger between his uniform collar and his sweat-prickled neck. The officer was the Honorable Hestia Hope, whose diplomat father had died seven years ago in the anti-Chaonia riots on Yele Prime.

Makinde had been eleven and well remembered the uproar in Bō House when, in the aftermath, Queen-Marshal Eirene announced her intention to settle the conflict by marrying a Yele notable, an accomplished orator and diplomat named Aloysius Pan, Baron Voy. Eirene's pragmatic decision bought Yele cooperation, sweetened by generous donations to various branches of the many-winged Yele League archival projects and enforced by Eirene's military superiority. In the wake of her father's death, Hestia had been delivered to the palace to become one of the heir's trusted Companions. Good optics, Makinde's grandmother had told little-Mak at the time, words he'd never forgotten: *If you reward the people who have lost something precious then they will think you care about their sacrifice.*

Hestia Hope caught him looking at her. She had lovely eyes, her gaze inquisitive and weirdly calming.

BOSS? BOSS! THEY'RE LOOKING AT US! CAN I GREET THEM?

Makinde snapped a virtual command to keep Dozer still. His ears burned, and he straightened his shoulders a little more and also forgot to breathe because it seemed there was no more oxygen in the room.

"Really? That one?" Sun said in a tone of surprise as she looked at Makinde. "*You* are the cadet who stood up at a Bō House banquet and called out Hakan Bō for demanding sexual favors from provisional citizens in exchange for residency permits?"

No point in pretending not to know what she was talking about. The instant he'd opened his mouth at the banquet he'd torpedoed his aspirations, his career, his hopes and dreams, a self-inflicted wound. "I am that cadet. I didn't realize word got out. Bō House council made it clear no one was to speak about it."

"That took guts. You must have known you'd be punished."

Her praise took him off guard. "It just pisses me off when people keep covering for him because he's governor of Bō House and the highest official in charge of the Ministry of Revenue."

The commander whistled under her breath. Makinde hoped it was an admiring whistle but he couldn't be sure. Everyone knew ordinary citizens bore no love for the mobs of provisionals grasping for a hand up into the safety net granted to citizens. Even the techs had paused, trying not to stare.

Dozer twitched impatiently: New friends to greet! Interesting vac suit to analyze! So hard to stay still!

The princess exchanged a look with Hestia Hope, a message passed in a code he didn't know, dense with meaning, fraught with emotion. The Companion dipped her chin. Sun swung back to pin Makinde with her extraordinary gaze. He couldn't have moved even if he'd wanted to.

"I've accepted no Companion from Bō House because I don't trust that lewd worm Hakan Bō not to place a spy in my household," Sun said in a tangent he could not at first follow, not until she extended a hand, palm up, toward him. "Makinde Bō, are you up for being one of my Companions?"

He laughed in elated, astonished surprise. "Hells yes!"

14

No Longer to My Taste

Although Sun had not been looking for the infamous young Makinde Bō, she was delighted to find him. His scandalous conduct in publicly criticizing a powerful elder had been the talk of the palace, made all the more interesting because of the speed with which the youth had been disappeared. Now here he was, complete with a Hesjan symbiont.

But there was no time to consider the fortunate chance that had led her to run across him. She was braced, alert, but also insatiably curious. Would her sibling come? Or was something else going on, perhaps an attempt to discredit her with the queen-marshal hot on her heels?

"Spacebridge secured," said the primary tech. "Outer airlock cycling. Argosy personnel incoming."

The watch bell rang twice as the inner airlock cycled open. Two tall and exceedingly slender individuals wearing red vests over plaid kilts entered first, scanned the compartment, and stepped aside. Another pair entered behind them. Their uncovered and hairless arms and calves, and bare feet exposed by sandals, seemed indecent on shipboard. As well as cold. Thin gloves sheathed their hands.

One wore a knee-length silver vest, their only adornment a pair of earrings whose tow chain of tiny linked ships dangled halfway down their chest.

The other wore a long blue vest, but it was the pulsating gem-like rhombus set into their forehead that attracted Sun's attention. This individual met Sun's gaze with alert interest. The cast of eyes, the intensity of the scrutiny, the rhombus. Sun dipped her chin in acknowledgment, a message passed between strangers. Something more than strangers. A connection tugged deep in her bones. This was the one.

The commander said, "You are welcome aboard the *Sunbird*. I am Captain Situri Rèn Alviasalaria. I see by your colors that one of you is a wayfinder. You honor my humble picket ship with your presence, Navigator."

The blue-vested wayfinder pressed palms together in reply but it was the silver-garbed individual who spoke.

"Your courtesy is noted, Captain. I am called Bodashtart. As Communicator assigned to this mission, I speak on behalf of the Consensus of Elders and the Sterling Senate of the Alabaster Argosy. We acknowledge the treaty sealed twenty-five years ago between our senate and Queen-Marshal Eirene of the Republic of Chaonia. Are you the representative of the queen-marshal?"

The captain looked at Sun.

"I am Sun Shān, heir to the throne of the republic. I greet you in peace and amity. If you will accompany me to the wardroom, we will drink to health, prosperity, and good will."

The Communicator pressed the back of her right hand to her left palm. "As Communicator, I am obliged to meet exclusively with Queen-Marshal Eirene now that I know her vessel is soon to arrive. Thus I must decline your congenial invitation. However, if the courtesy of a quiet waiting place may be extended to the Navigator, that would be graciously accepted."

The Navigator's lips lifted in a slight smile that intrigued Sun. So far so good.

"Of course." Sun did not know much about the Argosies because they were so insular, but the wayfinder guilds held the highest status. Even a humble apprentice was like to royalty. But she had a feeling there was much more going on. "I'll leave the Honorable Hestia Hope to attend you, Communicator Bodashtart."

She gestured to the Navigator to accompany her. The Navigator signed a yes. Together they followed the captain to the wardroom.

The picket ship was held together by spit and baling wire, as the old saying went, but well maintained for all that. The wardroom boasted utilitarian metal tables and chairs padded with homemade cushions. A tray of sweet rice cakes and a pot of tea waited on the table, courtesy of a well-run galley. The captain retired, leaving Sun to examine a face leaner and longer than her own, with a narrow nose and emerald-green eyes. She saw no obvious resemblance beyond the texture of their black hair.

"I am Sun Shān," Sun said without preamble, "and you are my long-lost brother."

"Your sister," said the Navigator politely.

"Ah. My mistake. I was given incorrect information. What may I call you?"

"Soaring Shān would be my name in Chaonia."

Sun poured tea and set out the cups. The two young women faced each other across the table.

"Why did you contact me?" Soaring asked.

"I have been curious about you all my life. Wondering if the child born before me would be a rival or an ally. My existence changed the pattern of your life."

"Because La Sirena took me away from Chaonia when you were born?"

"Yes. People say it was because she feared harm would come to you as a potential heir to Queen-Marshal Eirene."

Soaring's brief smile had the allure of a pleasing scent enjoyed for a tempting moment before being lost on a wind. "Would it surprise you to learn I was never intended as a possible heir?"

Sun sat straight up, almost as a recoil. "Why have a child, then?"

"Ah. Truly, the politics of the Argosies are labyrinthine, to say the least."

Sun leaned forward. "I am all ears."

"As the Communicators say. All ears and mouth."

Sun smiled at this gently spoken witticism that might double as a dagger in the eye. Realizing that Soaring had not touched her drink or food, Sun sipped at her own tea—a little bitter but acceptable—and ate one of the chewy, sweet rice cakes.

Soaring lifted the cup to her lips, inhaled the tea's sharp scent, then sipped with proper discernment before setting the cup down.

"You have no reason to trust me, Sun. But I have for all my life felt a connection to a sister I was separated from before we had a chance to know each other. Such as I could with the long delays in communications, I have followed your life as an interested observer. I would be your ally, if you will take me as such. I am no soldier. Thus, I am no rival for a position as marshal."

"No. You are a Navigator, rarer and more valuable than a soldier. Why did you answer me? Why are you here now?"

Soaring drank more tea, composing herself to speak words she must have gone over many times in her thoughts.

"My Communicator Bodashtart was a longtime associate and intimate of my mother. They served together in the Communications Guild as a diplomat and negotiator before my mother's death."

So, her father had been right. How like him. "It happened so suddenly," Sun said politely.

Soaring contemplated her folded hands. Her eyelashes were long and had the quality of shading her dark eyes with a veil of mystery. "Her death brings me to you, because I have a humble request of you."

Sun poured another round of tea and settled herself to listen.

"My mother was born into the Ousoos Argosy. Do you know them?"

Sun leafed through the map of her mind. It took her longer than she'd have liked, but she found it. "They are the Argosy based out of the Trinity Coalition."

"That is correct. Well placed to enrich themselves through trade and communications brokering. As you may not know, to sustain genetic variation in their ship-bound populations, Argosies trade groups of young people at intervals. Sometimes such a change benefits those individuals. Sometimes they find themselves in an unpleasant situation. This latter was how it happened for my mother. She was born into Ousoos and traded to Alabaster. However, once in Alabaster Argosy she could not obtain a license to reproduce. When the Republic of Chaonia proposed an alliance with the Alabaster Argosy, the Consensus favored the alliance but no high-status Argosy individual could be found to agree to marry a dirt-sider." She paused, wincing. "No offense meant."

"No offense taken. At least we don't have four arms."

With a puzzled look, Soaring said, "The Phene do not use marriage as a seal of alliance with outsiders that I've ever heard."

"That's a good point," mused Sun.

Soaring went on. "As a Communicator, my mother was part of the diplomatic mission. She found a way to privately speak to your mother. They came to a secret agreement. My mother would marry her and live on Chaonia. In exchange Eirene would have a child with her."

"You!"

"Me!"

They shared an easy smile.

"The agreement stated Eirene would give up all political and legal rights to that child if and when she had another viable heir. Once you were born, my mother requested permission to return to the Argosy."

Sun nodded. "My mother's earliest needs were for shipping and transport on the frontiers of Chaonian territory. That's why she needed an alliance with an Argosy at that time. Later her need for the Argosy was no longer pressing."

"Exactly. Our mothers parted on good terms, but they parted definitively."

"What was your life like in the Argosy? Your status has not suffered, given you are a Navigator."

"That's not how guilds work. I was placed in the Wayfinders Guild because of my aptitude for maths and spatial orientation." Soaring took another sip of tea, then bent closer, lowering her voice. "I've always been a bit of an outsider, to be honest. It's a subtle claw, but one always digging into my flesh."

"I understand."

"My mother and Bodashtart protected me as well as they could. Then Maman died abruptly." She toyed with her empty cup, turning it around several times before realizing she was doing so and stopping. The furrowing of skin between her eyes told a story that Hetty would have read with ease. To Sun it looked like remembered pain, and it never seemed to her that it was worth holding on to pain if there was no answer to it, no response that could be made. But death had its own rules. She felt her own forehead tense with memories of Octavian: his life beside her, his death which she had been helpless to prevent. *Kiran Seth.*

"Are you all right?" Soaring asked.

It took her two tries to get the words out. "Grief is a beast."

"Yes, I suppose it is. It eats you up, and if you're fortunate eventually it spits you out much chewed up but still able to function." She busied herself pouring the third round of tea, eyes on her work as if she feared to see Sun's reaction. "To cut to the chase, when your message reached me, I decided to jump the gap and see what lies on the other side. Here I am."

Sun took the filled cup. "My thanks. But I'm puzzled at your arrival with the entire Argosy, if you are not a person of highest status."

Soaring lifted her gaze, chuckling. "As you are? The circumstance is easy to explain. The Elders were already preparing a diplomatic mission to Eirene. They want answers. The Phene Empire used interdicted knnu drives and Argosy wayfinders to guide the fleet that attacked Molossia System. Where they got the drives no Argosy knows, or will admit. Furthermore, no charter-abiding Argosy hires out wayfinders. In addition, it is specifically written into the Argosy charter that no wayfinder may pilot warships under any circumstance."

"That can't always have been true. Before the beacon routes were set into place, wars between systems could only have been conducted by fleets using knnu drives."

"That was a long time ago, when our ancestors were willing to commit any kind of atrocity. Including cutting off tow chains far between stars so the severed ships would slowly lose power and life support with no chance of rescue or reaching safe harbor. A barbaric age."

Sever a tow chain while under knnu drive. How could that be done? She made a note to research later.

Soaring went on. "Since no Argosy mission can move easily among the confederations to seek answers, the Elders will request the queen-marshal's help to find out who was suborned by the Phene. The diplomatic mission is Bodashtart's responsibility. I came because of your message. Because I wondered if I could make a new start with you."

It took Sun a moment to process the simple words because they were so astonishing. So filled with potential. "You want to leave the Argosy."

"I do."

"Will an Argosy allow one of their Navigators to leave?"

"As an adult, we enter a guild for the rest of our lives. Everything we are is through the guild, except one thing. Blood ties. If I petition to enter your household, they can't stop me."

"*My* household? Why would you want to join my household rather than my mother's? You are her eldest child."

"As you have reminded me. In fact, it was the first thing you said, was it not? Let me tell it straight, Sun. Listen to my words. I do not wish to challenge your mother's rule. I do not want your position as heir. If such a time comes, with respect to chance and the whims of Lady Chaos, that the rank of queen-marshal falls to you, I will support you."

"In Chaonia you'll be seen as a foreigner. That and your lack of military experience will disqualify you as a possible heir regardless. However, those who dislike me or want to cause trouble might treat you as my rival."

"If you cannot stomach my presence, I will retreat back to the Argosy. It is not a terrible life there. Just no longer to my taste."

Sun breathed in the scent of the tea they shared. Its subtleties were like crosscurrents blended to enhance each other rather than being at odds. She set down the cup. They fell well together. Just sitting here she was comfortable, not relaxed but rather engaged and delighted, fascinated and eager.

And yet.

"When you leave the Argosy, what happens to your wayfinding knowledge?"

Soaring sighed with a hint of regret. "How important is my knowledge to you, compared to my person?"

Sun laughed. People thought her calculating but it was sentiment that flooded her with waves of powerful emotion. She felt it now as an exhilarating lift. She had sensed a connection with her sister on first setting eyes on her, lightning coruscating across the heavens.

"Very well, big sister. It's done. You and I will present a unified front."

Soaring closed her eyes, pressing clenched hands against her chest as she breathed in and then out. Opening her eyes, she extended her right hand, palm toward Sun. When Sun hesitated, Soaring said, "The mirror of trust. Do you not have this custom?"

"We do not." Sun touched her sister's palm with her own, feeling the warmth and smoothness of the other woman's hand. Soaring had soft, uncalloused skin: not a soldier's hand. "What do you mean by trust?"

"We give into a person's keeping a piece of ourselves that they will hold safe."

"It's a lot to ask on such short acquaintance and knowing as little as I do about you." But Sun's heart and mind snapped with the bright heat of a decision made at quantum speed, more felt than analyzed. As the ancient sages proclaimed: Go big or go home. "You're on."

For breaths they held, palm-to-palm and face-to-face, looking into the other's eyes. What this sister-stranger saw in her eyes Sun could not know and wasn't concerned to guess. In her sister's face she saw a brass-like scaffolding in place of natural eyebrows. Pale veins linked this scaffolding to the gleaming rhombus set into the skin at the center of her forehead. Her brilliantly green irises were shot through with gold that might be natural coloration or an intricate architecture of technology known only to the Wayfinders Guild.

Soaring recited, "Let us be bound by trust, which cannot be seen, heard, smelled, touched, or tasted, but which exists beyond these bounds and ties together objects in motion as we are people in motion in the great span of the universe."

"Let us be bound by trust," echoed Sun, the words and their utterance sinking into her bones. The sensation of jumping in feetfirst without hesitation was one of the few things that could calm her racing mind. Anyway, this private understanding was a strong tile for her to hold in the game played among Chaonia's Core Houses as they jockeyed for position at Eirene's court. And Soaring hadn't said she *couldn't* use her wayfinding knowledge.

On a relieved exhalation, Soaring withdrew her palm. She cautiously tasted a rice cake, then finished it off with an appreciative smile. Sun ate a second slice to be companionable. It was very good, testament to its baker.

A ping dropped into Sun's network. "The flagship is within hailing distance. We'll take the shuttle over."

Soaring rose with a graceful smile. "What do you think the great Eirene will make of us together?"

"We'll soon find out."

On the quarterdeck of the *Shadowfax*, Eirene waited, accompanied by three Companions, the ship's captain, the ceremonial sideboys, and an honor guard of eight marines. She met Sun's look with a stare that promised a dressing-down later. Her gaze slammed to a halt on Soaring for a drawn-out breath. A tremor of her lips betrayed a deep-felt emotion but she buried it and with a genuine smile approached the Communicator.

"Bodashtart, peace be upon you."

"And upon you peace, Eirene."

To Sun's astonishment they raised hands for a greeting touch, palm-to-palm like old and trusted friends.

Lowering her hand, Bodashtart drew a rolled-up tablet from a sleeve and offered it to Eirene. "With a mournful heart I carry this news, and her last testament. I promised Sirena I would hand-deliver this to you, if you accept."

"Of course I accept." The austerity of Eirene's grim mouth and bleak eyes hit Sun hard. She had never seen her mother this stricken, not even at public funerals in honor of those who died in battle, when Eirene wore an appropriately somber face.

"With it, find our request for mutual aid," the Communicator added.

Eirene unrolled the tablet and skimmed its initial statement. Her eyes widened as she absorbed the information Sun had just learned. She studied Soaring before turning back to the Communicator. "This is the Navigator I'm to use to seek out the illegally employed guild members and the source of the illegally obtained knnu drives?"

"It is."

"I'd have thought your Elders would send a more experienced Navigator. This one is not even wearing mastery stripes."

"You'll understand the necessity when you've read the whole."

"Ah." A spark lit her gaze as her lips parted. Eirene was never slow to put together connections. It was one of the ways she'd raised the republic from the mire to the height: by never being caught flat-footed. She so forcefully did not look at Soaring that her Companions, ever attuned, gave the young Navigator curious glances.

"Will you take a meal with me, for old times' sake, my dear Bodashtart? Who knows when we will see each other again? Let Sirena's memory live briefly through what we say to each other about her life as together we remember the many fine meals we three shared."

Bodashtart placed crossed hands against her chest. "I am honored to accept, dear Eirene."

"Very good." Eirene rarely missed anything. The only new arrival she had not acknowledged was Makinde in the full glory of his formal palace dress uniform. She fixed her gaze on him now. The glare wasn't anger. It was her usual application of aggressive charm. "And who is this well-turned-out young honorable?"

"This is Makinde Bō, my newest Companion," said Sun.

He grinned nervously under the gleam of the queen-marshal's obsidian eye.

"Aren't you the disgraced one?" Eirene gave a curt laugh. "Sun, I see you are consistent in your choices. We'll see how they work out when you finally land in battle."

"I already did land in battle," said Sun tightly.

"This is the Royal's child, I take it," said the Communicator to Eirene in the manner of people who were once intimate friends and have immediately fallen back into easy familiarity after years apart. "She has the abrupt manner and prickly honor of the Gatoi."

"My thanks," said Sun stiffly. "I'll take that as a compliment."

Eirene settled a gaze on her heir that, like needles, started soft and then stung. "You and your people may return to the *Boukephalas*."

No use arguing. Sun gestured an order, but as Soaring started walking toward the airlock with her, Eirene raised a hand to stop her.

"Soaring stays with me. I promised her mother on my honor that should anything happen to her, I would take care of the child. So it shall be."

"I'm happy to take Soaring under my wing, Mother."

"You have not asked my permission."

Sun wrestled her anger down. This was not the place to snap.

Soaring took a step forward. "Gracious Queen, it is my preference as well, to have a sister at my side as I adjust to life in a new climate. With your kindly blessing, I would ask to be allowed to abide within Sun's household amid people of my own age cohort. You and I would still be close at hand to each other, would we not? For I would not wish to lose any chance to become acquainted with the woman of whom my mother spoke so highly."

"Prettily phrased. You must have gotten that from Bodashtart, certainly neither of your biological mothers. It makes no matter to me in which courtyard you choose to live in the palace. You can even have your own. All that matters, Sun, is that this person remains safe and secure, as I promised La Sirena on my honor. Do you understand me?"

"I do. That is also my intention."

"Is it? Interesting." Another time Eirene would have smiled her gnomic smile, amused at some layer of complexity Sun had not yet grasped. But not today. "Nevertheless, I require Soaring's attendance now. This is a private matter, not a diplomatic one. You did not know Sirena, Sun, so this has nothing to do with you."

Sun struggled constantly with storm-torn emotions when she contemplated her mother. Doubtless her mother had hatched some labyrinthine plan known only to her, whose mind twisted through snakes and ladders with a deviousness Sun admired, although she could never admit it lest she seem the lesser satellite to a greater luminary.

But she understood grief, and this was grief, however differently Eirene processed it. She could not bring herself to bow her head, not even to her parent, but she tipped her chin slightly to show she understood. Never acquiescence, never that.

Once back on the utility shuttle, Hetty clipped in next to her. "Your sister seems both pleasant and intriguing."

"You'll like her."

"Is that meant as threat or as promise?"

"Up to you."

Hetty's rich chuckle was its own promise, the sound a shiver of delight down Sun's spine. But this was not the place. Anyway, her thoughts had rushed onward.

"Who could act as go-between, between a rogue Argosy and the empire? What if it was the seers of Iros who negotiated the deal between the empire and whichever Argosy was involved in illegally loaning knnu drives and Navigators?" She rubbed a finger along her lower lip as her thoughts boiled. "We know there's something else going on with the seers. Something bigger than the devout religious order they're meant to be. I mean to discover what it is."

Nisaba had clipped into the opposite seat. The high secretary's prim mouth pressed tight. "The queen-marshal won't like that you've gone behind her back on the matter of Kiran Seth."

Sun held her gaze. "Your comment has been logged. But no one else at court is going to find out who placed a spy into my household. A spy whose actions resulted in the deaths of Percy, Duke, and Octavian." She shut her eyes, seeing Octavian's final convulsions; seeing the blood in the water as they'd fished out Percy's and Duke's remains.

Hetty rested a hand on her arm, sensing Sun's tangled whirlwind of grief and anger as a dangerous tempest blowing in.

Makinde and his multi-limbed drone hustled onto the shuttle. He'd already stowed his duffel in a locker, leaving the picket ship behind. With a grin he dropped down beside Sun as if she were his new best friend, and in a way she was.

He held up the hand with the ring she'd given him. "This is the best thing that's ever happened to me. I can't wait to see that lewd worm's face when he gets the news. Please let me be there to see his reaction with my own two eyes and Dozer to record it for posterity."

"Sure," said Sun, and let Hetty and Nisaba engage him in conversation. The hatch sealed and the departure countdown began.

She wrapped a finger around her own ring, the centerpiece of her private communications. Interstellar distances meant the ring network was only useful within a star system. Otherwise Sun, like everyone else, was dependent on fast courier ships bringing dispatches and news through beacons. What had Persephone found out? How soon would she know so she could begin planning a suitable response? A knife to the heart. A shot to the head.

15

In Which the Wily Persephone Wears Her Asshole Title Proudly

Someday I am going to punch that perfect specimen of youthful beauty and brilliance Jade Kim right in that too-gorgeous face, but that day is not today. Even if I had the chance I couldn't, because Ensign Kim's stellar marksmanship is the only thing shielding me from certain death.

Jade and I are pinned down in a walled courtyard that has three gates. The main gate faces north onto the street. A gate facing south leads into the entrance hall of an old hermitage repurposed as an administrative center. A service gate opens west onto an alley.

The shooters appeared without warning at the service gate just as I left the building. So, to be more precise, I am the one who is pinned down, because I am the one who was inside checking records while Jade stood sentry on the street beside our rented hover-cycles.

Fortunately, stone statues of pontificating seers rise on either side of the gates. A marble man with a painstakingly sculpted curly beard, box braids, and long robes caught the first blast of stinger fire, thus saving my life.

Unfortunately, I tripped on my attempt to run across the plaza past its fountain and benches and had to scramble back to hide behind the same stony philosopher. Now there's no chance I can sprint across the plaza without giving the shooters a clear line on me. Worse, I dropped my own stinger, which lies on the pavement out of reach. The only reason the shooters haven't charged in to slaughter me is because the good ensign has been laying down an efficient screen from behind a statue at the street gate.

Retreat is not an option. At my back, the gate into the interior has been closed and its entry panel winks red. *Locked.*

On Chaonia such a standoff would follow a predictable course. After an exchange of insults and boasts, some rude discussion of lineage, and a few crude jokes, I would have revealed I'm one of the heir's Companions. The gendarmes would have given way with pointed remarks about my lack of readiness for battle. I'd have left with nothing but my pride tarnished.

However, we are not on Chaonia or anywhere in the republic. We are on Yele Prime. Given the abrupt appearance of two armed people who began shooting before asking a single question, there's an excellent chance someone from the Order of Iros has gotten wind of my line of inquiry and isn't happy about it.

My ring pings in a message from Jade.

IN TEN SECONDS SPRINT FOR MY POSITION.

I can't verify, so I have to trust, which gripes me because I made that mistake with Jade Kim when I was a first year. Still, after finding nothing useful about my father in months of searching, I could never have expected that my low-key inquiries into the origin of Hetty's deceased cee-cee Navah would trigger this outsized response. We must have hit dirty dirty pay dirt.

Ten.

I bolt out from behind the statue and run flat out for the entry gate. A lance of heat sizzles past me as a loud pop bursts to my left. Smoke expands in an inky cloud to conceal me. I duck and roll in behind the other statue, the one Jade isn't using as cover, then kick open the gate. Well, it was already ajar.

We tumble out to the pair of hover-cycles we left leaning against the compound wall. A shot from inside sears past my ear and slams into the nearer hover-cycle with a lucky hit that melts its forward coil.

I leap onto the seat of the other cycle and grab the handlebars. Jade breaks my grip and sits down in front of me, shoving me back.

"I'll drive. Hold on."

No time to argue. The cycle lurches back, then launches skyward with a spin that forces me to wrap my arms around Jade's torso so I don't fall off as we precipitously lift. Two smoke bombs pop on the road below: more concealment. Jade releases a hornet programmed to mimic our cycle's sound. It should lead our pursuers a merry chase as it races toward the distant xeno-district where foreign workers congregate as they wait to get a work license.

Beyond the smoke we drop back to the pavement. Jade lowers the wheels and steers us at exactly one klick below the speed limit through the twisting back streets of this sleepy satellite town. We could be any young dating couple headed for a fun evening in the Glorious City.

When we reach the ramp onto the elevated speedway, Jade opens up the engine. I have to hold on a lot tighter around that lean, muscular torso as the cycle sheers up onto the expressway. My crash helmet is bumping against my back. Somehow Jade got theirs on. I close my eyes against the sting of the wind as we accelerate so there's nothing to do except hold on and wish I didn't keep having flashbacks to those heady days when I thought Jade Kim wasn't a top-grade jerk but rather the hottest cadet in CeDCA, the fish I'd landed, fancy me.

Some people never learn.

Hanging on for dear life as Jade guns the cycle and we race along the fast lane is one of the sexiest non-sexing things I've ever done, if not quite as memorable as kissing a blindfolded Zizou in the basilica on Tjeker. But since kissing counts as prelim to sexing, according to my extensive studies of this subject, it would be unfair to compare the two. Zizou was all coiled threat wrapped by disarming innocence.

My pulse races as my body remembers his lips and his arms. To calm myself I press a cheek against Jade's back. Tactical error. I feel muscles bunch and shift as Jade weaves through the traffic, careful to never quite violate the speed limits that will get us noticed while meanwhile not losing ground on our escape. Jade knows exactly how to skate the edge of the rules and win top cadet of the graduating class while doing so.

We aren't the only ones in a hurry. On Yele Prime, people are either in a hurry or they won't leave the café or park where they're engaged in an interminable debate on grammar or poetics. We hit a smooth stretch. I manage to wrestle my crash helmet on and clear the visor so I can scan for pursuit.

My gaze catches on our destination: the urban center known as the Glorious City, the most famous municipal zone on Yele Prime.

The Glorious City is a wonder of the worlds, a tiered confection like a huge urban mountain with four main terraced levels. Some say the core of the Glorious City is a Titan mothership set upright onto the earth, and that the city levels were built around it. Others say the founders carved the terraces out of a lonely mountain that rose in solitude on a featureless plain, or that its center is a pillar of metallic glass.

At the very top, the fourth and thus highest level, stands the Temple of Furious Heaven. With its spears and petals, it is said to be the most architecturally perfect building in the history of humankind. It looks good in the distance shining with mathematically exact proportions, but I'm not a student of architecture. This is my first visit to Yele Prime and I'm appalled at the inefficiency of their transportation network.

The bulk of the population lives in outlying districts linked to the central terraces by spokes. Transport that links the end clusters of each spoke to other outlying clusters is minimal, which means you have to go all the way in to the center and back out again to get anywhere.

It reminds me of the beacon map I had eighteen seconds to study on Tjeker before I had to hide it back between the leaves of an old book. It was remarkable that a physical map that had to be at least two thousand years old had survived. Creases had worn away images at the folds. The writing was faded, often illegible, and written in a script I didn't recognize. What I had recognized was the existence of a single central system with eleven beacons and eleven separate lines that did not connect with each other, only with the home system. Therefore the central hub had to be the home world of the Apsaras Convergence, She Who Bore Them All. Each of the eleven original beacon routes originated from her and returned to her. All traffic routed through her. Later the bottleneck was eased as the Apsaras engineers added multiple connecting routes to allow traffic between the original lines. After the collapse, when at least a third of the beacons died, She Who Bore Them All System vanished from the beacon map, no longer reachable. Not even by Argosies, so it is said.

In the wake of the collapse, Yele System was left as one of only two solar systems that has eleven beacons. The other is Anchor System, in the Phene Empire. Many of the systems who are members of the Yele League have to travel through Yele to get to the other League systems. It's a great way to control trade, monitor movement, and make yourself leader of the pack due to luck of the draw.

Worlds rule via access.

Jade shouts against the wind. "Hold me a little tighter and I'll think you're coming on to me."

"You wish."

"That's all you've got? I'm disappointed, baby."

I refrain from blurting out "I'm not your baby" because who wants to be the one stuck saying that hoary old cliché? For the hundredth time since this fact-finding operation commenced at 1000 this morning, I wish I'd brought Solomon instead of Jade. But I gave Solomon and Tiana a different task.

We exit off the speedway onto the lowest and largest tier of the city, known as Maker Terrace. Auto-carts piled with goods choke its narrow streets. Cycles and scooters beep horns as their riders push through intersections. Transit boardwalks glide past small-scale manufactories and shops where artisans ply their trades and crafters build and repair the necessaries of daily life. Every block has its own shrine tucked out of the way beyond a gate decorated with the symbols and colors of one of the holy avatars, some of whom I don't recognize because they aren't venerated in the republic.

We putt-putt through the crowds at an interminable pace. Even though the Yele supposedly don't have surveillance cameras every ten meters like Chaonia does, I'm glad the visors screen our faces.

Jade slides us into a rack at the wrong rental shop to take advantage of a quarrelsome customer who is monopolizing the attention of the proprietor. With an arm around my waist Jade swings me off the seat and around a corner. We pull off our crash helmets. Jade snatches mine from my hand, shoves both into a rubbish bin outside a busy paratha shop, and grabs my chin just as I hear the pitter-pat of footsteps approaching from around the corner.

I'm required to look up. I hate that gorgeous face. Jade grins with evil glee and kisses me just as a youth comes around the corner saying, "Did you see someone drop off a cycle . . . Oh."

Silence as they retreat back to the shop to sort out the mystery.

The unpleasant truth is that Jade does nothing if it can't be done well. The kiss pours heat straight down my spinal column until I'm flushed and panting as I push away.

"Let's go." My voice scrapes out hoarsely as I squeeze past the line snaking out of the paratha shop.

Some joker waiting in line whistles and says, to a friend, "Fuck me, there's a looker."

Jade knows how to deploy a wink to suggest you've just missed out on the biggest smashing burst of flavor in your whole tediously spiced life.

"You can turn off the spotlight, Ensign Kim. We don't want to be followed."

"You still get top marks in kissing."

"We aren't at the academy anymore. Let the competition go. We have a job."

"Which you messed up."

"I did not mess up."

"You didn't find Kiran Seth or any word of him."

"I found something better."

"Did you indeed?" Jade's tone turns sharp.

"Sun is going to pop a vein when she hears I've discovered a link between the seers and Navah. Not to mention that we got attacked the instant I opened up that line of inquiry."

"Navah?" Jade hates not knowing the answer, so answers immediately. "Oh. Hestia Hope's deceased cee-cee. You all say she was a spy. I never quite figured out how she died though."

I'm not about to tell him that Sun shot Navah and had James throw her overboard, still alive, for the scylla to feed on. Let Sun tell him herself, if she wants him to know. I glance back to see the cycle shop proprietor and the youthful assistant standing at the corner looking our way, so I grab Jade's hand. There are two doors immediately available, one an Eight Chapters School of Grammar and the other a shop selling religious goods and regalia. With Jade in tow I enter the shop past a meter-tall gilded statue of She Who Repairs the Sky holding a wrench and an Antikythera mechanism. The instant the door closes behind us, I shake off Jade's hand.

Inside it smells of incense. Shelves display bowls, bells, clappers, calligraphy scrolls quoting sage wisdom, prayer mats, candles, and replicas of icons. Jade fumes as I approach the stern elderly man who sits at a counter polishing a religious badge.

I press hands together in the Yele greeting, and ask him about the object. "That looks like a two-dimensional representation of a beacon coil."

"It is." He's neither smiling nor unfriendly as he sets the badge on the counter as an invitation for me to pick it up.

The badge's outer edge is just large enough to cover the palm of my hand. I examine both sides of its spiral with the greatest fascination, trying to read the tiny markings inscribed on its gleaming surface. "I never before saw a beacon coil used as a symbol to represent one of the holy avatars."

"Your accent tells me you come from out of system," he says, making our relative positions clear without rudely asking for more information than I'm willing to give. "These badges were popular among the Yele a thousand years ago during the height of the power of the Apsaras Convergence."

"This badge is a thousand years old?" I set it back on the counter, afraid I'm going to tarnish it.

"No, this is a replica from a heritage temple on Congress Moon. The temple was dedicated eighteen hundred years ago to She Who Bore Them All, who was venerated at that time as the progenitor of the Apsaras Convergence. Have you visited Entering the Waters Temple? It's popular on the tourist circuit."

"I have not! Tell me more."

"In the temple, the avatar is attended by a thousand divine messengers—"

"The apsaras," says Jade, because neither of us are paying attention to Ensign Kim and how can that travesty be allowed to continue?

The elder glances at Jade, then back to me and, when I don't react, goes on. "Each of the divine messengers attending She Who Bore Them All holds what historians call a beacon badge in their right hand."

"Representing the establishment of the beacon routes!" Excitement thrills through me as I wonder if there is any way I can make an excuse for our investigation to go to Congress Moon. I had taken the governmental moon off my list because the Iros hermitage there was shuttered thirty years ago after a shocking bribery scandal that rocked the League and soured the local reputation of the seers.

He smiles, seeing in me a fellow enthusiast. "It gets better. See here."

He shows me how a tiny latch allows the flat spiral coil to open and the hooked end in the center to pop out perpendicular.

"What is this?"

"Careful! It's very sharp. It's a blade."

I grew up in Lee House on the bay piloting boats, and I realize all at once what I'm seeing. "It's an emergency safety line cutter, hidden in the badge. Like you would have in your emergency kit on shipboard."

"That's right."

"It's clever, but why?"

"In truth, who knows? There's a great deal of debate."

"There would have to be, it being Yele," I remark.

His indulgent smile marks me as the provincial that I am. "I like the interpretation that it was a statement of liberation. Before the beacons were built and their routes established, all human voyaging was controlled and codified through the agency of the Argosies. To travel between star systems you had to attach yourself to an Argosy tow chain and thus to their oversight and rules. To be free . . ." He mimicked cutting.

"I've thought the very same thing myself! I didn't know there was an entire interpretive agenda and a whole temple dedicated to the idea!" I'm so delighted I clap my hands.

He nods. "That's why the safety line cutter is hidden in the design. The engineers of the Apsaras Convergence saw themselves as cutting people free from the control of the Argosies."

"This is the best thing I have ever seen in my life." Over by a shelf of incense, Jade mumbles a sarcastic aside, which I ignore. "How much?"

He names a price. I dig into my sleeve for coins. It's odd to handle physical tokens that act as currency. In Chaonia every transaction is registered and tracked in the government-run network, which means there's a seething underground market involving off-network exchange. That was the kind of thing Solomon's family was heavily involved in before Sun rewarded his clan for their help with a Titan-class ship, so they could go back to the space-faring knnu life that pirates kicked them out of forty or so years ago.

When I set the coins on the counter the shopkeeper gives me a complicated look, as if he is startled and a little embarrassed. After a moment he seems to come to a decision, and he gestures toward a shelf. "Please add a bundle of incense. It comes with the badge."

"Thank you!"

I know just what to get: a bundle of sandalwood incense sticks for Ti, her favorite scent. Then I think I should get something for Solomon too so he doesn't feel left out, but he never went to the temple the way the rest of us at CeDCA did, and I've never seen him light incense or meditate or drum, so it would be inappropriate and even awkward to bring him a gift from a practice he does not follow.

As I return to the counter with the incense the elder glances toward Jade, who stands with arms crossed and eyes rolled up to glare at the ceiling. I give a shrug as if to say, *What can you do with a jerk like that?* and the old man grins.

He again shows me the mechanism to open and close the badge before sliding it into a little silk pouch sewn to fit it exactly. The incense sticks he wraps in a scrap of cotton, which I drop in my coat pocket. Transaction complete.

In a low, confiding voice I say to my new ally, "Is there a back door? Got some friends out front I want to avoid. Romance troubles, if you see what I mean." I tilt my chin toward Jade, cause of all romantic ill in the worlds.

"The beautiful ones who know they're beautiful are the worst," he agrees in solidarity. He shows us out a rear door into an alley that runs along the backs of shops and past rubbish bins.

"Do you think I didn't hear that platitudinous little exchange?" Jade asks as we walk away.

"Oh, please. It worked."

"If only you were as adept at life-and-death firefights as you are at smarmy doublespeak."

"Yeah, yeah, I get it. Gloat all you want. You're a great shot and a great pilot and you can do maths super well and, I grant you, everything else really. Meanwhile, I'm a Companion while you're merely a citizen ensign who graduated from CeDCA. Which you had to attend because your grandparents got your branch of the lineage kicked out of Jīn House."

"Fuck you, you asshole," says Jade heatedly, finally losing the famous cool.

"Thank you! I wear my asshole title proudly!"

We make our way in antagonistic silence through the streets to one of the big ramps that link the levels. Amid hover-carts and mechanical mules we climb to the marketplace and garden terrace. Greenhouses and milpas are separated by blocks of bazaars with elaborate entry porticos, behind each of which a warren of lanes and alleys links the many stalls and shops.

The rendezvous is a modest but nevertheless expensive hostel where we've been staying in a narrow four-bunked space that's too close for comfort. Apparently Yele life is mostly lived outside their stuffy little homes, so it's assumed even foreigners like us won't do more than sleep in our cramped room. The hostel encompasses a cheerful courtyard with tables and chairs where folk sit in chattering groups drinking tea or wine or arrack. A few people throw double takes when they catch sight of the fabulous Jade, whose glower offers the sulky promise of a good hate-fuck. And I would know all about that.

Let them look. Ti sits in a corner half concealed by a potted kentia palm, reading from a tablet unrolled on her thighs. A twilight-blue tignon covers her hair, and she's wearing an unassuming ensemble of slacks, long sleeveless tunic, and a sash wrapping her waist. No one is paying attention to her because she knows how to mute the fire of her beauty. She glances up. Her high-octane smile is all I need to warm my cold, sullen heart. I stroll over and place the wrapped-up bundle of incense on the bench next to her.

She rolls up the tablet and slips it into her sleeve, then inhales with pleasure as she unrolls the cloth to expose the incense. "How lovely. Thank you!"

"It's hard to get Yele incense on Chaonia. Maybe I should have gotten more."

She spears me with a scolding gaze. "I hope you bargained. You have to bargain here or people won't respect you."

Oh shit. The shopkeeper probably threw in the incense out of pity.

"Sure." I wonder how much I overpaid as I immediately change the subject. "Did you get all our gear to the cutter?"

"We did. Solomon went over to the rugby café."

"Are you kidding me?" grouses Jade. "The asshole got us in trouble and we need to move fast."

Ti addresses Jade with polite formality. "Ensign Kim, the best concealment is not breaking an established routine. Solomon already told his club acquaintants he would be there today."

"It was stupid of him to join a rugby club when he knew we were only going to be here a few weeks at most."

"It makes us look ordinary. It's good cover for operatives."

"How do you know all this hanky-panky secret-agent stuff, anyway?" Jade asks.

"Being a good cee-cee is not unlike being a good spy," she says with one of her enigmatic smiles.

"Can we go now?" Trying and failing to one-up Tiana always makes Jade restless. Our emergency circumstances don't help. "The sooner we see the backside of Yele Prime the better."

"Give me a sec," I say as Jade stews attractively.

I crouch to write a brief report into the ring network, for Sun's eyes only, that will ping to her the instant we enter Chaonia System. I like to cover all eventualities.

ON A HUNCH FOLLOWED UP TO SEE IF ANY INTERSECTION OF NA-VAH WITH SEERS. FOUND PAY DIRT IN HERMITAGE RECORDS. A YELE LEAGUE FOREIGN WORKER LICENSE IN NAVAH'S NAME WAS SIGNED OVER AND APPROVED FOR HERMITAGE EMPLOYMENT BY A CLERK OF THE OCULI. HER PLACE OF BIRTH IS LISTED AS PELASGIA TERCE. SCANNED IMAGE AND LOCATION STAMP ATTACHED.

I hop up. "I'm done. If we're all shot dead and our corpses returned as per diplomatic treaty, this will still give Sun the evidence she needs to move forward."

"You're cheerful," notes Jade suspiciously.

"I've linked Navah to the fucking Oculi, the sister association to the seers of Iros. And to Pelasgia Terce. How fine is that?"

"I know who the Oculi are," says Jade pissily.

"I'm too hot," I remark to Ti as we stroll out like any group of friends who aren't in a hurry and don't have the authorities on their tail.

"I'll remind you next time Isis calls the weekly scores and you come in second to last again," she says sweetly.

Every bazaar sports a lane of cafés for conversation, argument, concerts, and slams. People speechify, play, recite, sing, compose, debate, pedant, and all around display their chops everywhere they have a chance to do so. It's the Yele way: I know, and I want you to know I know.

It takes ten minutes to walk to the café. The establishment is full because it's a game day. People who can't make it to a stadium like to watch in boisterous crowds. Solomon has taken a place off to one side, on the edge of the friendly amateur club he's played with a dozen times while we've been here. Even though the game is close and it's five minutes from the end and everyone is screaming with excitement, he spots us immediately. We work our way over to him.

Before I can speak, Jade breaks in. "We have to get moving *now*."

"Who put you in charge?" says Solomon, keeping his voice low but pulling his height so he looms.

"Let it go," I say, because the only person who hates Jade Kim more than I do is Solomon, and the big difference between Solomon and me with regard to Jade Kim is that Solomon never has bad taste in crushes. "It'll draw less attention if we leave using the crowd flow as cover. A few more minutes won't matter."

How wrong I am.

Solomon hands me his glass of flower wine. I've just taken a sip when white-clad, visor-shielded constables burst into the café. People jump up and lock arms, looking ready for a scrum. As the constables shove through the crowd, disrupting people's view of the final moments of the game, everyone starts flinging creative insults at them for having the temerity to interrupt. The constables ignore them, moving in on their target.

Solomon gives me a look.

"Stand down," I say, correctly interpreting his silent offer to inflict mayhem.

A surly officer stalks up to me. "Are you Persephone Lee, of Chaonia?"

"The Honorable Persephone Lee? Yes, I am." Maybe I did sneak away to attend the citizens' academy, my bid to break from my family. But I know exactly how to put on the one thing Jade Kim will never have over me: the absolute assurance that I belong to and was raised in one of the Core Houses of the Republic of Chaonia and thus am destined to rule over citizens, provisionals, ethnics, foreigners, and any barbaroi that get in the way. Especially now that Queen-Marshal Eirene of Chaonia to all intents and purposes holds the Yele League under her boot. "What does this interruption mean, pray tell? We are watching the game."

"I'd like to arrest you and your compatriots for false representation of your travel status as well as for illegally searching private records at multiple government offices and hermitage heritage sites, *and* besides all that for assault at Timoteo Hermitage against two constables." The angry twitch of his lips betrays he is not my newest friend. "But I can't arrest you, because of your antiquated aristocratic system of status and governance and the immunity from prosecution it grants you. So you're being deported back to Chaonia as of this hour. Consider this a diplomatic incident."

16

In Which Even the Wily Persephone Knows Enough to Keep Her Mouth Shut

Queen-Marshal Eirene didn't salvage the Republic of Chaonia from its nadir and build it into a force to be reckoned with by taking half measures. She sits in a chair in her office, one elbow propped on the chair's left arm and her right arm cocked out with fist set aggressively on her hip. I stand before her at attention, Tiana behind me. Befitting their citizen status, Solomon and Jade wait by the door, flanked by a pair of marines with the deadly bored look of veterans forced to babysit disgraced young honorables.

"Persephone Lee, you are a troublemaker."

I am dead certain I can hear the sarcastic roll of Jade Kim's eyes from ten meters away.

"It is absolutely outrageous for you to flout my authority and go behind my back on such a sensitive manner." Eirene dwells so long on my humble self that my hands begin to twitch as if I have a stain on my face or a rip in my clothes even though I know Ti made sure I was perfectly turned out in a pressed fleet uniform when we were decanted from the diplomatic cutter that hauled us back to Chaonia Prime.

"If it were up to me, I'd remand you to the Krinides mines. But it would upset Manea, who is unaccountably attached to you." Eirene glances at a hologram on her desk that shows her beloved consort holding their chubby-cheeked baby. The image captures my lovely cousin smiling with all the adoring charm of a young woman who has met the powerful ruler of her dreams and had her youthful infatuation unexpectedly reciprocated. "So, then. Moira wanted you back. She'll get you back. You're her trouble to deal with now. You have one hour to get out of the palace. If you're still in Argos tomorrow, I'll personally see you arrested and put on a one-way trip to the Krinides Labor Intake Center."

Tiana shifts her foot to put pressure on my heel as if she thinks I'm going to blurt out something stupid, but even I know enough to keep my mouth shut when Eirene is on a tear. As if she noticed the slight movement, the queen-marshal looks past me. Her gaze dwells longer than I'd like on Tiana, who is splendidly turned out in a pale yellow gown accented with a translucent chiffon overdress.

Finally her eyes flick toward Jade with a flare of interest. She has a reputation for enjoying her pleasures, and those who don't know Jade always think they've stumbled on a hidden cache of honey. But Eirene never allows pleasure to get in the way of winning her wars.

"Ensign Kim and Ensign Solomon, I've seen your CeDCA records. It's a heady drink for citizens like yourselves to get caught up in the palace, so I assign no blame to you for the insubordination of Persephone Lee. But let me assure you, I'm the top of this chain of command. You've been given new assignments. Ensign Solomon, you'll be headed to the Aspera front to join the Thirty-Second Marines. Ensign Kim, you'll be embarking on the *Shadowfax* as a junior comms officer."

"You honor me, Your Highness," says Jade, always the suck-up.

Solomon gives me a grimace of helpless solidarity but there's nothing I can do, and anyway it's exactly the assignment he wanted, straight into the steel of the war.

He and Jade are escorted out of the chamber. The door slides shut, followed by a moment of silence.

Eirene raises both hands, palms up, in a gesture both sardonic and impatient. "Well? I'm done. Go!"

My ring pings at the same time as Tiana blinks, which means she's gotten the same message from Sun.

INCOMING.

The door chimes.

"Enter," barks Eirene.

The door slides halfway open and a woman wearing the ibis badge of a high secretary sticks her head in. "Your Highness, Princess Sun has requested an audience."

Sun pushes past the woman and strides in without invitation.

"What took you so long?" Eirene's so mad she's not shouting. My skin creeps with a rush of breath-bated alarm, or maybe it would be better to say terror.

Sun brakes to a halt on the other side of the strategos table that stands like a vast oval lake of black glass in the middle of the chamber.

James, Alika, and Hetty stand in a row behind her in formal palace garb with elbow-length capelets over their fleet uniforms. Behind them stands the newest Companion, Razin Nazir, and some fresh-faced kid with such an inappropriate grin on his face that I'd like to congratulate his insouciance.

Eirene rises aggressively, chin jutted out, finger pointing. "Sun, I did not give you permission to send your people to Yele Prime. Bad enough you stuck your nose into Argosy business, but that gambit worked out for me. This time you have caused serious trouble with your reckless interference right when I need Yele cooperation the most. The League has formally complained that your Companion violated our nonaggression treaty. There was a firefight in their Glorious City at a culturally sensitive heritage site. You've gone too far this time."

"*I've* gone too far?" When Sun is this well launched all I can do is grit my teeth and brace for explosions. "The seers of Iros made an alliance with our enemies, the Phene Empire. Are you defending *them* against me?"

"A faction within the Iros order made that deal, not the entire order."

"A big enough faction that the head of the order was involved and killed himself rather than be captured by me," retorts Sun.

"His death and the action on Tjeker don't implicate the entire order, much less the Yele League. If you're about to remind *me* that the famous Admiral Manu has gone over to fight with the Phene, let me remind *you* that he had one big victory twenty years ago. When the League refused to grant him command of their navy he promptly sold his services first to the Trinity Coalition and then to the Phene."

"I'm not talking about the League or Admiral Manu. The seers of Iros were behind the murder attempts against *me*. Attempts which resulted in the deaths of my bodyguard, one of my Companions, and his cee-cee. There was a fresh assassination attempt on Kanesh, which Marshal Tomyris witnessed. Now I have evidence that Hetty's cee-cee Navah was in their employ all along. In fact—"

"It's time for you to stop." Eirene's obsidian eye swirls with streaks of red.

"In *fact*," Sun went on, "I have confirmation that Navah comes from Pelasgia System. Which makes me wonder if my cousin Jiàn has been working with the seers of Iros to undermine your choice of heir. Then they would put in place an heir more to their liking who is beholden to them. One like Jiàn."

Eirene makes a *go ahead* gesture to her high secretary, who steps backward into the entry to allow the door to shut. Her voice lowers but not in a gentle way. "You're not telling me anything I don't already suspect."

"You suspect your nephew is in contact with factions from the Yele League?"

"Nézhā's boy is ambitious enough to think he deserved to be named queen-marshal even though he was three years old when his father died. A three-year-old can't command the fleet. Unfortunately he's not smart enough to see he's being used by Chaonia's enemies."

"You knew Navah was an agent of Jiàn?"

"An accusation that she was a spy isn't proof. She came to the palace from Yele Prime with Hestia Hope. Are you suspicious of Hestia too?" It's a rhetorical question, left hanging between them for several fraught breaths before Eirene launches a new fusillade. "Bring me unassailable proof, and we'll talk. Meanwhile, I don't need trouble with the Yele on the eve of our attack on Karnos when a quarter of my fleet will be made up of League and allied forces like the Larissan Centaur Division. Have I not made my position clear?"

"You did," Sun mutters ungraciously. She is fuming, because even she has to admit Eirene has the upper hand through being correct. "But if the seers are working against you, aren't you worried about your newborn child?"

"Of course I am." We all look at the hologram image of brightly garbed Manea and the dumpling in her arms. "That's why I don't let them know how much I know. Now you've broken the doors open with your blunt-force instrument, and insulted the League at the same time. I had everything under control."

"Under control! Octavian, Percy, and Duke are dead."

"I haven't forgotten the assault on my authority that their deaths represent." She looks at me, and her organic eye narrows with calculated skepticism. "Odd that you keep the daughter of Kiran Seth so close beside you, Sun."

I can't keep it bottled up anymore. "My mother was involved too. She covered for him."

"Aisa Lee was a willing dupe, an unstable and malleable personality unable to see beyond her own arm's reach. She should never have been allowed to marry a seer of Iros, especially not one as conniving and ambitious as Kiran. If anything, I fault her elder sister—Nona, I mean—for allowing such an imprudent marriage to be sealed."

I have opinions about my vanished aunt! I open my mouth.

Sun says, in a cool tone, "Perse, that's enough."

I close my mouth. No one else moves. We are become statues, frozen within the orbit of a deadly obsidian eye.

"That's right, it is enough," Eirene agrees. "I have allies to placate, a campaign to finalize, and a festival to arrange. Sun, you need to get your household in order."

She scans the chamber as if committing each of Sun's Companions to memory.

The Handsome Alika, looking almost naked without his ukulele.

James hasn't fussed once with his cap.

Hetty looks demure but never cowed, her hooded gaze resting on Sun rather than on the queen-marshal.

Razin is hard for me to get a handle on. She's got a stolid face and wears a bland expression. Ti dug through her royal academy record to find it equally bland and stolid: no demerits, no awards. Yet her hair cut long on the right and short on the left suggests there's more to her than robotic obedience.

The new kid looks about sixteen. Who in the Eighteen Hells is he?

"I'll have Moira recommend a new Companion for Lee House."

"I'm keeping Persephone," says Sun in her flattest tone, which means she's livid but still in control.

"We'll see about that," says Eirene. "You also lack a Companion from Jīn House. I'll have Precious send over her nephew."

Sun's chin lifts. She doesn't hide a triumphant smile. "I have a Companion from Jīn House."

Eirene arches an eyebrow. "Who might that be, pray tell?"

"The Kim clan is a branch line of Jīn House one generation removed. They lost an internal dispute within the House. In retaliation they were removed from the House lineage rolls and remanded to the rank of citizen. It's in my power to restore the clan to full lineage membership. I've done so. Thereby on those grounds I assign the Honorable Jade Kim as my seventh and final Companion."

"Fucking hells," I mutter.

Eirene laughs, piqued by Sun's counterpunch. "We'll see about that."

She taps her ear. One minute later the door opens. Her high secretary escorts in a smooth-looking Jade Kim, whose anxiety I can read in the gaze that darts toward Eirene, then Sun, and then me, as if trying to figure out who holds the knife.

The queen-marshal speaks first. "Ensign Kim, I've arranged for you to be assigned to the *Shadowfax* as a junior comms officer."

"Yes, Your Highness. Your trust in me is a great honor."

"It is. Your stellar record at CeDCA speaks for itself. However, I am informed you have been offered a place as Sun's Companion, from Jīn House. Is that true?"

Surprise flares those honeysuckle eyes.

"Your Highness," says Jade with an astute display of not taking sides.

"One or the other," says Eirene in a tone that suggests any fool would know whom to please at this juncture in their brilliant but as yet virgin career.

Jade is no fool. Also not a virgin. But what Eirene doesn't understand is that although Jade Kim is obviously a backstabbing, ambitious competitor who worked relentlessly to graduate top of the class, there's another factor at work: the aspirations of the disgraced Kim clan rest on the shoulders of the child they named Jade.

Ensign Kim steps sideways into formation with us. "I am honored to be taken into the intimate circle of Princess Sun's Companions."

"Are you sure about this choice?" Eirene asks with what appears to be genuine curiosity. "My imprimatur guarantees fast advancement through the ranks."

"Advancement for me, Your Highness. And I am grateful. But my clan's well-being and future prospects outweigh my own personal ambitions."

With a huge effort I manage not to retch out loud.

Eirene accepts the words at face value. "Very well. I can't fault you for loyalty to your family, which certainly exceeds that of *some* in this room." She nods at me just in case I didn't realize she had to get in a final stab.

Nothing enlivens Sun's day more than throwing a spanner into the works when she's sure it will result in an outcome she wants, no matter the rest of us. But by the shocked looks on the other Companions' faces, not one expected this method and timing of attack. Not even Hetty.

Eirene doesn't look as surprised as the rest of us do. She addresses Sun. "Jin House won't like it, but that's not my maze to untangle. As for you, Jade Kim, for your flouting of my authority you, like Persephone Lee, will be exiled from court on my order as queen-marshal of the Republic of Chaonia. How you handle your duties as Companions is your needle to thread since you can't companion the heir while in exile, can you?"

Sun takes a step forward. "Ensign Kim was not a Companion at the time of the mission and could not have refused my order. Exile is too harsh a punishment."

"Don't argue with me, Sun. Be content I'm not exiling you, too. Now get out."

17

A Crawling Sense of Dread

From Apama's room the view through floor-to-ceiling windows faced east across Fair Water. On cloudless days, the rim of the rising sun breaching the horizon refracted through the glass of Anchor Prime's grand basilica on its island amid the waters. The flash always woke Apama. Before anything else, she prayed.

"Revered Arthas, give me the strength to do my duty. Give me the means to protect my honored mother and keep her far away from this place."

She swung out of bed and changed into her workout gear. The living quarters for the Riders were carved into the ridge that separated the sea from the city. The four-level bunker kept the Riders secure and isolated. She went down a level to the gymnasium, which adjoined the windowless core where the creche and its children were sheltered. This early she saw only the ever-present Incorruptibles on guard at stair-wells and elevators. She greeted them by names she'd taken care to learn. Although no one smiled—it wasn't done—she liked to think they regarded her with respect.

After a hard workout and a double session on the flight simulator she'd asked to have installed, she hurried back to her sire's suite. In her room she showered and changed into a uniform specially tailored to absorb her skin excretions.

When the second bell rang, the door that led from her room into the parlor of Zakurru's apartments unlocked and opened. The spacious parlor had a magnificent view through its east-facing glass wall over the sea to the Sunrise Mountains.

The parlor was more simply furnished than normally fashionable in the empire. Its walls were painted a drab off-white and the two divans upholstered in a muted rosewater pink. A shelf displayed four blue vases, each darker than the last. The only spot of disorder was the writing table with a hodgepodge of ink bottles and paper strewn across its surface.

Fresh rolls, congee, and sliced fruit waited on the table in the dining alcove. She stood behind her chair until the door into her sire's private rooms opened and he entered. He walked in the normal way, ordinary face leading. After he had selected from the platters, she dished up for herself and sat.

"Good morning, Uncle." She was careful to address the man as a separate individual, not as a mere vehicle for his Rider. After almost a year he still had not offered his name. "I see you're working on a new syllabary. Or is that an alphabet? I haven't seen those characters before."

His gaze flickered toward the desk before fixing on her with a flare of interest. Her breath caught in her throat. It was so hard to get him to talk to her.

Uncle said, "Our archivists are working to decipher a recently excavated writing system. It was found on one of the abandoned hulks in the Gyre."

"When did our archivists get ahold of a hulk from the Gyre? And why?"

"That's not important. The point is, this could be a writing system brought all the way from the Celestial Empire or perhaps one devised on the thousand-year journey before they discovered Landfall." He broke off.

His eyes flickered with a nystagmus Apama had come to recognize as communication? overload? override? The Rider giving orders or taking control.

Even after an Anchor year living among Riders she could not figure out how the connection between the two faces worked. Did they take turns using the brain? Share it along parallel pathways? Or, as she suspected but could not explain, were Riders entangled in a single brain across a deeper quantum level? How else could they communicate across the vast distances of space instantaneously? She knew better than to ask. There was no chance they'd share such information.

The riding face opened its eyes.

"Good morning, Zakurru," she said politely.

"Apama. I have received excellent reports of your behavior at the marine permaculture working group yesterday. As always, you asked intelligent questions, listened attentively, and took pains to greet every person in attendance. Tico Mn Abarca de Batillipes informed me he was pleased by your interest in the development of new anti-infection medicinals for battle injuries."

"Doesn't the Batillipes Syndicate hope to receive a substantial government contract to manufacture pharmaceuticals from kelp derivatives? No wonder he's praising me to you."

"You are cynical."

"Lancer pilots train to observe conditions on the field."

"Explain."

"People tell you what they think you want to hear."

"The Council does not punish people for speaking truth to power.

We are not autocrats like the hierocracy of Mishirru or the tyrant of Chaonia."

"It's not that you punish people for speaking their minds. But it isn't as if everyone in the empire has access to the perquisites Riders and syndicate leaders get. Every child is taught that virtuous people labor for the good of all. That we are all the same. But we aren't all the same."

"Go on," said the Rider, gaze drilling into her.

How many other Riders were paying attention and listening in? All could see and hear what any saw and heard. The children too, who had to be taught how to be rulers. That's why they had to be separated at birth from their original families, so they served only the empire. But it also meant they became so separated from everyday lives that they never fully understood the empire they served. In a way, she was speaking to all who were listening. That too was a form of power. Of responsibility.

"When I was a girl I never imagined I'd have a chance to leave Tranquility Harbor. I never figured I'd see one of the Triple As in person. Mine wasn't the only family who couldn't afford to travel down the beacon routes. We made do with virtual tours sponsored by the syndicates at the local Unity Hall. Famous landmarks would be highlighted as backdrops in the festival processions. Have you even been to a public procession?"

The slits of Zakurru's eyes narrowed. His lipless mouth closed.

Uncle speared a slice of carambola.

She hadn't qualified as a lancer pilot by being afraid to push the limit.

"The syndicate presidents and high-level officials all talk to each other. Know each other. Do favors for each other. Hand each other opportunities. Those opportunities don't go to people living and working in the Tranquility Harbors of the empire. Yet here I am, catapulted into their midst solely because of an accident of birth."

Uncle set down his spoon and, reaching back without turning, wrapped fingers around Apama's wrist as a metal cuff would shackle.

"No accident," Zakurru said in his whispery voice before he released her.

Best to fix her gaze on the half-eaten congee, to eat slowly to disguise a crawling sense of dread. Because that was the creepiest thing of all: thinking she might be the product not of a love match that had to be hidden or a sincere yearning for ordinary family life, but of a deliberate, years-long campaign to alter the balance of power on the Rider Council. Had she really won her flight academy place on merit? Her assignment to the *Strong Bull*? Rider Kubaba wasn't wrong: favoritism betrayed the Founders' intention and philosophy.

After breakfast she accompanied her sire to the Council's administrative chambers on the uppermost level, just beneath Unity Hall. Usually they went to his workroom, where she would receive a briefing on the tasks he wished her to accomplish on her daily rounds at the Exchange. Instead Zakurru led her to the envoys' hall.

Baron Voy stood as they entered one of the conference rooms.

"Rider Zakurru, thank you for agreeing to meet on such short notice." He turned his genial smile on her. "Apama At Sabao, is it not? Delighted that our paths have crossed again."

"Likewise, Baron," she said, glad it was him and not Admiral Manu. "I thought you returned to Yele Prime."

Tight lines at his eyes dimmed his smile's brightness. "So I did. I'm honored you have recalled I made the journey. The League has sent me back with their decision. Alas, the news I bring is not what I might have wished it to be. Rider Zakurru, shall we begin or are we waiting for anyone else?"

"We may begin," said Zakurru. "Apama, take a seat."

The door opened and Kubaba bustled in. Her ordinary face and person could have been that of any auntie in the kitchen with the authority to smack you on the hand with her spoon when you reached for a treat you weren't meant to have. Her riding face was awake, gleefully malicious.

"Given that I have requested to be physically present at any meeting with Yele envoys, I am sure it is a simple oversight on your part, Zakurru, that I discovered quite by chance that Baron Voy is here."

"We can begin," Zakurru said, more to any unseen Riders than to her. He sat in a chair that allowed his riding face to address Baron Voy while Uncle stared at the wall's elaborate painting depicting the Procession of Smiles.

As Apama pulled out a chair, Kubaba turned her riding gaze that way. "Lieutenant, you are not in the diplomatic corps to assume for yourself a seat at this table."

Apama glanced at Zakurru. He gestured an *at ease*. She said, "Yes, ma'am," and settled into parade rest. The baron took note of the exchange without remarking on it.

"What news do you bring us from the League, Baron?" Zakurru asked.

If the baron was surprised by this abrupt entry into the business at hand with no pleasantries and no coffee or pastries to soften the transition, he gave no sign. "I used all my considerable persuasive powers to argue for the League to break their treaty with Eirene and declare neutrality. Unfortunately the best I could manage was to keep them arguing for days. In the end my proposal was voted down."

"What argument won the day?" asked Kubaba.

"The majority claim that Eirene has kept her word to us while history reminds us the Phene have not. Many in the League still view the empire as the villain of the Battle of Eel Gulf. It will take some time to overcome their reluctance."

"Do you believe you can overcome their reluctance?" Kubaba asked.

"With patience. If I am afforded the time and your continued support."

Zakurru broke in. "Do you not have the support of the seers of Iros?"

The baron's smile melded regret and cynicism. "I have been warned off them."

"I told you they were untrustworthy," said Kubaba in a tone meant to offend.

Zakurru retorted, "Their representative offered us a deal that would go a long way to removing the threat Chaonia poses. What answer to that, Baron? It was you who introduced me to Kiran Seth as a potential ally."

The baron shrugged amiably. "My information was out of date. The seers have fallen out of favor with the leading factions in the League. They're seen as militant, uncooperative, and untrustworthy. They're of no use to you now."

"There was an attempt on Sun Shān's life in Kanesh System," Zakurru said.

"A failed attempt that resulted in the closing of the local hermitage, so I'm told. Knowing Eirene, as I do, I expect she will soon ban all hermitages and seers from Chaonian-controlled territory, using the attack as her excuse."

"Eirene has other heirs, people who would support a treaty with the Phene."

"Yes, yes, so the seers say, but it's all talk if there's no action."

"What action have you managed, Baron Voy?" Kubaba asked tartly. "I'm unclear on what you bring to the exchange now that the League has voted against you."

He smiled. "I bring continuity and a deep knowledge of the queen-marshal's palace. Winning over the League is not the work of a day. Many who voted to hold to the treaty with Chaonia see Eirene for the threat she is. But they fear her more than they hate her. A patient approach with the League is the best option." He paused in a way Apama recognized as a shift to a new and equally touchy subject. "I did not see Admiral Manu listed on the registry of current occupants in the Yele housing district."

Zakurru nodded. "He has been sent in an advisory capacity to look over the situation in Karnos System. Have you some comment on military matters, Baron?"

The man's chuckle was a masterpiece of modesty. "Military matters lie beyond my purview. I was just wondering because, from what I gathered, Eirene has not sent any of the Yele fleets home. She might just be holding on to them to show she can, a show of strength toward the League. Perhaps the Rider Council has more up-to-date intelligence of her troop movements."

For once Zakurru and Kubaba shared a look, a glance from one riding face to the other. Was it like looking into a mirror to see yourself through another's eyes?

Zakurru said, "The Rider Council thanks you for your efforts, Baron. Please make yourself at home on Anchor Prime as our honored guest."

The baron had a thousand smiles, each calibrated to a subtle nuance. "I understand," he agreed before turning to address Apama. "Lieutenant, I hear you are often seen in the evenings at cantinas and lounges and izakayas along the ridgeway terraces. Perhaps our paths may cross at Antikythera Terrace this evening?"

"Alas, I've scheduled the flight simulator for this evening."

Zakurru broke in. "Apama will be taking entertainment with her colleagues from the Exchange. Will you not, my daughter?"

Her face burned as she clasped her hands in the gesture of gratified obedience. Clearly he had an errand for her to run, away from the prying gaze of Kubaba and her faction of Riders. But it was fine. She had trained for this. Let him use her. She could be content knowing her mother resided untouched and at peace on Tranquility Harbor.

18

A Lancer Coasting on Momentum

Apama cleared four security barriers to emerge into daylight onto the portico of Grand Unity Hall. After admiring the view east across Fair Water and west across the metropolis, she walked north on the processional way. Stone beasts representing legendary animals of the Celestial Empire lined either side of the promenade. As she passed each one she tapped a hand to her chest as to a trusted friend because the dreadnoughts of the fleet were named after these mythical beasts: Noble Griffin, Resolute Basilisk, Strong Bull, Steadfast Lion, Stalking Horse, and many more.

The imposing bulk of the Founders Exchange marked the oldest administrative building on Anchor Prime. The first shiploads that arrived on the planet built a round hall for the settlers to exchange skills, knowledge, and labor. She slipped into her reserved seat in the main hall.

The assembly stood for the Trade Oath and the traditional opening song, "This Is the Final Struggle." Afterward, the proceedings broke into committees, task groups, field work, and the unglamorous but crucial efforts plied by civil servants at their desks. Her sire had pet projects he expected her to signal his interest in by showing up at their committee proceedings. The Rider Council was meant to be above personal vendetta or favor, yet he assigned her to cultivate specific supporters and to keep a wary eye on certain syndicates.

Since Apama was required to be here, she intended to learn everything she could. Partly because that was in her nature, but also because she hoped if she pleased her sire, then he would forget Rana At Sabao. Apama had long shied away from thinking about the circumstances that could have brought Rana's child into the world. It seemed disrespectful to speculate. Only now did she understand why her mother had never spoken about the past.

What bothered her most was that Zakurru did not speak of nor ask questions about her mother. The one time Apama had asked if she could write to her he had not answered. His silence struck her as so ominous she did not broach the subject again, not even to ask that her mother be told her daughter was alive. Even after a year there remained hope that some ships might yet turn up at Hellion Terminus, so casualties had not yet been formally announced. Stoic patience was a popular theme in epic dramas like *The Fortunate Eye* and *Spilling Over the Cataract of Redemption*. Her mother would be patient while Apama played the role of good child in the same way she had trained to become a lancer pilot: by relentless study, practice, and drill.

At the end of the Exchange's six-bell workday she locked herself in a private washroom. She stripped off her uniform and turned it inside out to run a quick-clean booster over it that she carried in her work case. Then she wiped down her skin and joints with a towel. An application of anti-mucus and a neutral perfume would carry her through an evening out.

Finally she was ready to brave the gauntlet. In the morning no one had time to chat. In the afternoon the representatives, clerks, officials, and stewards were like birds released to peck at grains strewn across the processional way. Over time a pattern had developed: the same people accosted her by the same statues.

By the Steadfast Lion, a glib Eschiniscus resource scientist who eternally hoped for favors. "Lieutenant At Sabao! You promised to have supper with my committee. What date would be best for you?"

This unctuous rep was not one of Zakurru's targets. "Let me check my schedule and get back to you. I was disappointed when last week's presentation didn't include figures on the bioavailability of nutrients in the soil samples from Picket Terce."

By the Indomitable Ram, a hearty syndicate inspector responsible for asteroid mining concessions. "Lieutenant! Lovely to see you again. We didn't have enough time at the session on recent advances in water extraction. Comrades and I are getting together at Borobudur Terrace after the seventh bell. We'd be honored to host you."

"My thanks, Inspector. I can't tonight, but send a recording of the proceedings to Zakurru's staff. The Rider has a particular concern about resupply of military fleets."

"I'm honored by your interest! I'll have it sent on at once."

By the Thundering Rhinoceros, the friendly Angursa high admiral Paulo Kr Manalon de Angursa. In the aftermath of the disgraceful defeat of the Styraconyx and Tanarctus Fleets, he was positioning himself for the post of central fleet commander. Today a glamorous young person accompanied him.

"Apama! I hope it's all right for me to call you Apama."

"You've shown me kindness from the first, so I'd be pleased."

Kr Manalon glowed with the confidence of a newly elevated power broker. "Then please call me Paulo. Uncle Paulo, if you're more comfortable with that. I'm delighted to have this chance to introduce you to my child Bartholomew. You and he have a great deal in common."

Bartholomew was dressed in a flowing garment reminiscent of the Festival of Fours, with one red, one blue, one green, and one saffron-yellow sleeve. Feathers ornamented his hair. He had the skill to wear his looks and fashionable clothing with grace. The tight line of his smile suggested a more complicated story.

Apama nodded politely at him before addressing Paulo. "What might that be?"

"Oh. Ah! You're both interested in piloting. Isn't that right, Bar?"

She caught the way he trod on his son's fashionably shod foot.

Bartholomew spoke with the measured cadence of a memorized speech. "You fought nobly at the battle of Molossia, Lieutenant. The Rider Council must be proud of your courage, as are we all."

"My thanks."

More foot pressure produced a pained flare of his kohl-lined eyes. A bright smile popped like the flash of a rising sun refracted through glass. "Friends and I are going to the Antikythera Terrace for drinks. You'd be welcome to join us."

Baron Voy had mentioned Antikythera Terrace.

"I'd be delighted. Thank you."

"You young radicals enjoy your evening," said the high admiral with the benign expression of a person getting exactly what he's been promised. "I release you from my tedious presence. Go and have fun!"

Fun fun fun. Maybe if she pretended she was back in the mess hall of the *Strong Bull* with her fellow lancers joking and laughing, just one of the squadron, not a pawn pushed onto a gaming board she wanted no part of.

From the rim of the promenade the view over the city was magnificent, and the wind not too bad today. The western-facing slope of the ridge was terraced with rice fields, gardens, and eating and drinking establishments. The setting sun poured light over the terraces' glorious colors.

Apama paused to let her companion choose whether to descend via one of the wide stairways or by escalator. His perfume suggested an exhilarating bloom of flowers in the heat of spring, the promise of a sensual beginning. Not subtle.

"Please, call me Bar." The young man rested a gloved upper hand on Apama's upper forearm. Apama politely bent both elbows, and he slipped a delicately gloved lower hand into the crook of Apama's lower elbow, a gesture of intimacy.

Well.

They started down the steps. Tripods set on every fourth stair burned myrtle, for honesty.

"Apama means youngest one, doesn't it? Do you have a lot of siblings and cousins?"

"No. I'm the last of an extended clan."

"The last?"

"My mother's entire extended family was killed in the big industrial accident at Tranquility Harbor."

"I'm sorry. When was that?"

The cataclysm that had devastated Rana's life and killed tens of thousands of people didn't even register as a blip on the screen of this Triple A heritage seed. "Before I was born. That's what made me the last. I guess my mom liked the symbolism of the name. Like a sprout in a scorched field. Something to be cherished."

Apama felt the sting of a tragedy which to Bar probably had the same impact as hearing a sad song: how lovely your pain. She altered vector.

"But that was a long time ago. How about you?"

His peach-colored lips gave a twitch of emotion, quickly suppressed. "What do you know about the recent history of the Kr Manalon family?"

"Nothing, except Uncle Paulo is angling for central fleet command. Wait. Wasn't your family forced into exile because of a syndicate dispute that got ugly?"

"Yes, but he was cleared of all charges. Our family was repatriated eight years ago."

"Ah. So what are your plans?"

A too-casual shrug shook off the question. "I come from a traditional family. First child to the fleet, second to the trades, third to the legion of science and security, and fourth to the hearth, which is me. I will enter the leadership queue for the Angursa Syndicate."

"You don't sound excited at the prospect."

"You're in the fleet. What do you think?"

"What do you wish you could do?"

"Fight for the empire, of course! We are all destined for death."

"The shine of glory reflected through the universe is hard to resist. But keeping the empire running is part of the fight."

"Easy for a lancer pilot to say." His tone bore a wistful envy that made Apama feel the full force of her twenty-four years as if she were the most aged of relics, even though he couldn't be more than a year or two younger. "But never mind me. That's just a childish dream of mine, as I'm sure an experienced lancer pilot like you understands. Anyway. You've been kept too busy, I'm told."

Who had told him that? Apama wondered.

"I'd be delighted to introduce you to all the best-connected young people. We know where all the fun is to be had. For example, I'm a member of a well-regarded processional troupe that would be ecstatic if you wanted to join us for any of the processions. You only need to know the basic steps, and who doesn't? The upcoming Procession of Smiles, for example. You'd be perfect as one of the . . ."

An exquisitely stubborn clutch of boredom squeezed at Apama's chest. The flight simulator would have been a hundred times better than this conversation, but fortunately they reached the entrance to Antikythera Terrace. The sprawling multi-level establishment was laid out as a map of the known inhabited star systems. The systems were cunningly linked by stairs or lanes or tunnels and by twisting links made by escher ramps to suggest the ways beacon routes connected distant star systems as if they were closer to each other than to their physical neighbors. Each system had its own cozy seating area with "local" drinks, delicacies, and entertainment available. Off to the north Apama caught a glimpse of a pillared outcrop with a seating area on top, the terminus of the route called Tranquility for its end station. A sign hovering over the gantry-crane-themed bar blinked *Tranquility Harbor.*

Bar towed her into the hanging garden taverna of Anchor System amid a swirling gleam of spinning globes representing the star and its planets. He displayed Apama as a prize to his cohort of young politicos drinking sparkling wine. Apama smiled and nodded, and nodded and smiled, and only four times heard a whisper of "shell" behind her back and once a laugh on the word "slimy." She didn't bother to skewer the speakers with a well-placed javelin of her gaze like a promise of political death for those who sneered at her. They weren't worth it.

She drifted like a lancer coasting on momentum. A craft could sail on a single shove as long as it didn't hit debris. Bar and his friends drifted with her because they dared not remain behind as she walked over bridges or swirled through escher ramps from one "system" gathering place to the next.

From Anchor it was a straight shot through four systems to Karnos System. It seemed forever ago she'd followed this route carrying orders to an unknown posting. From Karnos she'd dropped into Hellion Terminus where the ill-fated Styraconyx Fleet had left on its bold assault against the Republic of Chaonia. The Hellion lounge had a garish neon décor as a reminder of the dead beacon's weird aura that she had accidentally flown through on that practice shoot where she'd gained her nickname. That had been something. She missed the camaraderie. But as she looked around she knew she could not succumb to nostalgia for her ship and shipmates. She had a mission.

"Bar, isn't there a way from here to the Yele Prime lounge?"

"Yes! It's my favorite secret path."

"Secret path?"

"After the Chaonians took over Kanesh System and cut off our best trade route to Yele."

"The one via short knnu hop through Eel Gulf?"

"That's right. Since then we have had to funnel trade and diplomacy through the Trinity Coalition. Have you been?"

"To the Trinity Coalition? No."

He laughed charmingly. "No, I meant to the dangerous criminal bars that represent the Trinity Coalition here on the terrace."

Still on Apama's arm and with his cohort trailing at his heels like escort ships scurrying after a splendid dreadnought, he pushed through a curtain of beads. A dimly lit tunnel, meant to represent a knnu passage, took them into an ax-throwing parlor where laughter was punctuated with the thunks of blades hitting targets. A whirl of doors, meant to simulate a beacon, dropped them into an art bar illuminated only by honeycomb-shaped lanterns where dancers writhed seductively to a hypnotic beat. From here they filed through another simulated knnu passage, a claustrophobic tunnel barely illuminated with pale blue lights that winked on and off like desperate messages from forgotten castaways. A flight of steps took them into a bar where lotus-shaped tables floated beneath a naga's sheltering hood. Beyond this lay a quiet room where people meditated. A flight of steps led to a working studio where all the lamps were shaped as skulls. Here they spun the edge of an escher ramp to land in a big brash bar with a slam stage and debate pods. It was loud with voices talking all at once, the way folks from Yele liked it.

Bartholomew was acquainted with an unexpected number of Yele expats. He grazed through their ranks trading passages from poetic classics like code words in a cipher Apama didn't know. His Yele was excellent, and his education not Phene standard. He was in his element, trading complex quips and elegantly shading an individual who had muttered "shell" in his hearing. Observing him play this game was more entertaining than she had thought it would be. But she had her own work to do. Her boredom sloughed off as she went on the hunt, arrowing in on an unknown target, phrases bursting in the air around her like shrapnel.

". . . that traitor left Congress to reenlist with the Larissans who fight for Chaonia . . ."

". . . Ablaut? Of course, and lenition in some cases . . ."

". . . he can give a speech, but it shouldn't surprise anyone that Voy's resolution failed. Too many in Congress fear Eirene's displeasure."

She identified the speaker as a man wearing the ivory robes of a holy order. He stood beside a door painted with a staring eye and was speaking to someone whose face she couldn't see. The slant of light fell pleasingly on his distinguished good looks. It was Hot Dad.

She edged sideways along a row of marble columns until she was sure Bar had lost track of her, then walked over.

"Your Holiness, I believe we met briefly about a year ago. I am Lieutenant Apama At Sabao."

"I know who you are." His voice had a silky texture that turned sharp when he addressed his companion. "Were you just leaving?"

"I was, Your Holiness!" said that hapless individual, offering Apama a polite gesture before scuttling off.

Kiran Seth was not a man to cross.

"Are you in league with Baron Voy?" she asked, dispensing with pleasantries since she knew Bar might be looking for her so she didn't have much time.

"He and I are not allies, but some of our goals align. I'm given to understand the Rider Council has been warned that the seers have lost favor within the League and are considered a poisoned brew not to be sipped."

She nodded, then wondered if he could see her nod and said, "What is it you wish to say to me, Your Holiness?"

"I understand the Rider Council's reluctance to engage with what must seem like a disgraced and thus ineffective Order. But we seers can get the Phene the things they need while the League's majority does nothing but appease Eirene."

"The attempt to kill Eirene's heir on Kanesh failed."

"Risks bring failure as well as success."

"What success can the seers bring to the empire?"

"The key to Chaonia's coming assault on Karnos."

"The military estimates it will take five years for Eirene to build back her fleet from the Molossia attack."

"I know Eirene better than the Phene military do. She'll be softening her path into Karnos Prime by negotiating with the dispossessed dynasts."

"Weren't they replaced by a Phene governor a hundred years ago?"

"Families don't just give up on the hope of power. Native insurgents will support Eirene on the ground by blowing up Phene bases and ambushing troops. In exchange she'll restore the dynasts to power. Get me passage to Karnos, and I'll track down the war criminal Nona Lee and hand her over to the Council."

"Nona Lee? The architect of the Tjeker massacre? She's dead."

"She is not dead. She's in exile and still working with the queen-marshal. Who do you think has been working as Eirene's agent with the dynasts?"

"What do you mean?"

"For years Nona Lee has been smuggling weapons and machinery between the Trinity Coalition and Hellion Terminus and thereby getting it into the hands of the locals in Karnos. She's even kidnapped Gatoi auxiliaries and sent them to Chaonia."

"Why would she do that?"

"To protect herself. Your own military has been trying to capture her for years. They engineered a handful of Gatoi specifically to target her, partly because of her smuggling operations but mostly because the Chaonians never punished her for her crime on Tjeker. Did you not know?"

"I'm a lancer pilot, not an intelligence officer."

"Yet Rider Zakurru trusts you enough to send you as his go-between to me. My Oculi sisters do not make mistakes. Nona Lee was recently spotted on Karnos Prime. I have every reason to believe she is there in advance of Eirene's coming attack. Get me to Karnos, and I'll dispose of her in return for Council support."

Now she would find out what the seers really wanted. "What kind of support?"

"To start with, I need use of an arrow of Gatoi soldiers. Two arrows, if I can get them. Four would be better—"

The ribbon on her collar vibrated with a message marked urgent from her sire. She checked the band on her wrist. PROCEED TO THE BASILICA.

She bit back a curse. Just as she locked on target, she got jerked out of line. And why now, so suddenly, when her sire had sent her here to begin with?

"I have to go, Your Holiness. I'll pass on your message and your request."

"As you wish." He wasn't a smiler. Maybe smiles would make him look less hot.

She made her way back to the main space. Bar had drifted into a scrum of people by the slam stage. It was a relief to have an excuse to not say goodbye.

She hurried up a set of stairs that exited on the processional way. Red glazed the western horizon while stars shone in the east. Twilight had brought with it an eerie cessation of wind. She crossed the bridge that spanned the gap between the ridge and the basilica. Sparks of luminescence rippled through the shallows as slow waves rolled in as if they carried the deepest questions of existence on each swell.

Why had her sire summoned her? Why to the basilica, of all places? She prayed at the altar of Saint Arthas most evenings, partly because the ritual soothed her but also because he never entered the basilica except on formal occasions. He had told her months ago that Riders did not dedicate themselves to a saint. They did not follow the path of worship but rather the equations of the universe in the hope of wisely stewarding the great union entrusted to them by their forebears.

Incorruptibles waited at the basilica's doors to let her through.

Every basilica had the same layout. A vestibule. A long, high, vaulted nave with eight alcoves on each side, always in the same order with altars to the sixteen saints. The apse at the far end represented truth, objectivity, and the ultimate end of all living systems in entropy and death.

The basilica's walls, piers, and spires were woven of a glass-ceramic blend. The last of a rose-red sunlight poured like a river of oily blood along the floor of the nave. She walked past paired alcoves, one to her right and one to her left. Nearest the door, the altars dedicated to Saint Hrothgar the Near-Dweller and Saint Cygna the Revealer, known as the guardians.

A basilica was meant to be open perpetually as a vessel of hope and survival, but right now it was so quiet that as she walked she heard the *tick tick* of one of her bootlaces, come undone. She didn't like the way solitude crept like a monster at her back. Usually there were other worshippers.

The two alcoves closest to the apse belonged on the right to the twins, who give succor from anguish and pain, and on the left to Arthas the Cursebearer, he who took on the curse so humanity could escape the plague of corrupted blood.

Pushing past a curtain of beads she entered the alcove devoted to Saint Arthas. Its altar stood in the shape of a mighty blade set upright. A person stood to one side, hands folded contemplatively as she regarded the icy blue of the massive sword and the wreathed candles set before it. At the sound of Apama's footfalls she looked up.

Apama's chest squeezed. She forced out a breath. *"Mom?"*

"Oh, my precious girl. I feared you might be dead."

Choked by tears, Apama flung herself forward. The saints understood human frailty and need. It was why people were encouraged to dedicate their lives to a path through which to discipline themselves as they struggled with the vicissitudes of life. The saints watched over you, schooled you, lifted you up, granted you peace.

Her mother wrapped her arms around Apama's body. Rana's exoskeleton—what some called a shell—wasn't a skeleton of bone but a thin exterior shell something like a skin suit. Rather than being an exosuit you pulled on or off, it grew on an individual because of a genengineered adaptation. An exo wasn't rigidly hard like wood or stone or metal, but it wasn't soft either. It was reassuring, not easy to penetrate, a shield against radiation and debris and, in the early days of the Phene expansion, against bullets and blasters and blades. Within this metaphorical shield her mother had persevered despite the tragedy that had ripped away her entire extended kin group. Had raised her daughter, nurtured her, held her close, and believed in her. Had set aside her own dreams until Apama was old enough that she could take care of herself while her mother went to night school to complete medic's training.

Had gotten pregnant by a Rider.

Apama squirmed in her mother's powerful grasp. "Why did you never tell me?"

"Tell you what?" said her mother evasively.

Apama broke away. "Didn't you see the recording of the synod?"

"What synod? There's been no news of a synod. Not out by T-Harbor, anyway."

"Why are you here, if not because of the synod?"

"I was summoned by imperial order."

The words hit like javelin fire. "Oh shit."

"Apama! Be respectful in this holy place."

"We need to go right now."

The curtain rustled as he stepped partway through. With his simple clothing and his ordinary face, the front of him framed by long strings of shimmering beads, he appeared as any ordinary man.

Rana stiffened. "I was told that once I left the service I need never see any of you again."

The man's expression flickered with a quiver that might have been distaste or dismay. The emotion was the flutter of a moth passing in and out of an aura of dim light on a murky night: gone so fast it might have been a trick of the eye.

The Rider took a step forward, strings of beads rustling down behind him. He turned so his riding face watched them, less gentle than a saint's taxing gaze and more demanding. "Do you remember me, Rana?"

"I was told that once I left the service I need never see any of you again," she repeated.

"You are the only one who had the courage to look my brethren in the eye. That's what intrigued me. That's why I sought you out."

"I agreed to work in the service because I was expressly promised I need never see any of the clients again. That the law prohibited all contact afterward."

"A separation forced upon us by old rules. Those rules no longer restrain us. Now we can be a happy family together, reunited at last, as I have long desired."

Some claimed people with exoskeletons were emotionless, because it was hard to read them without the supple quirks of a soft-skinned face. But Apama could read her mother perfectly well in the flare of her eyes and the curling of her left hand. Rana had closed the book on a past she wanted to forget, but the story had fallen open to reveal a poisonous centipede crawling out of a wound she'd thought sealed.

"What if I don't desire it?" Rana said.

He had the courtesy not to smile. "You'll want to, for your daughter's sake."

Apama broke in. "Mom, you don't have to—!"

"Enough, Apama." She drew Apama close, placing herself between her daughter and the man. "I will do what I must. So will you."

19

Yet Again the Wily Persephone Wonders Why She Does Not Just Keep Her Mouth Shut

The aircar lands at the Lee House estate in Pleasant Vistas Province and deposits me at a tiny aerodrome. With my duffel bumping on my back and Tiana at my side, I plod across a windy runway toward the rear entrance to the main house.

Tiana surveys the cluster of buildings: the main house, its outbuildings and warehouses, the winery complex, workshops, and villages, whose red-tile roofs and greenhouse gardens nestle in the distance amid vineyards, fields of rice, millet, and sorghum, and orchards of haw and plum. Rows of windbreak trees create hedge-like walls partitioning the land and settlements.

She whistles. "This is some setup. How many people live here?"

"I don't know. It'll be in the census."

"Are the villagers citizens or House retainers?"

"House retainers *are* citizens."

"But they are bound by contractual obligations to House service for generations."

"Something like that." It's not a topic that grabs my attention. I shade my eyes to get a better look at the person approaching from the back portico. To my surprise, I recognize my old tutor, Abdul-Lee Kadmos Rèn Aljiu. I greet him with the respectful bow of student to teacher.

"Honored Persephone. Citizen Tiana." His smile has the sweetness of grapes ripened beneath a rich summer sun. "Welcome home."

"Did you get exiled here too?" I ask as a pair of house servants comes up to take our duffels. When Ti does not relinquish hers I keep hold of mine and wave them off.

"I was born here, Honored Persephone."

Of course he was, I recall belatedly, not that I am going to admit I forgot. "I meant, why are you here now? Everyone else is in town for the big celebration."

"I asked permission to become the new teacher for the estate. It was always my hope to retire here while I still have teaching years left in me. I have family here. Sisters and cousins. Their children, and their children."

Of course he does.

"Consort the Honorable Manea gave her blessing to my petition," he adds.

"Did she?"

"She brings Princess Inanna here every few weeks. She thinks of this estate as a safehold from the hothouse that is the palace."

Old memories crawl along my shoulders as the training grounds come into view: the playground fitness circuit, the pool for laps, the stinger maze, the wǔshù arena, the target range, the path into the hills for endurance running. I remember the citizen children, some of whom were surely Kadmos's young relatives, who lined up behind Percy and me when we were all seven and began the republic-wide mandated education that includes martial exercise. Manea floats through those days in my mind too but she's vague, half seen, my cousin who I didn't have much time for. I wonder if she resented me and Percy for leaving her out, or if she was content to be left alone.

Ti's hand flutters against my arm, a check-in to test my mood.

"I'm all right," I say. "When I was little we kids spent half the year here. Percy and I were in the thick of it, always together." My murdered twin.

"I'm sorry, Perse. That's hard."

"I don't know. I miss him. But he left home when we were eleven and I don't know who he became after that."

"I also meant getting thrown out of court like you just did."

"Nah. I'm not upset to be exiled in exchange for getting Sun the evidence. I'd do it again in a heartbeat. Especially since Sun said she's keeping me as a Companion. That means she plans to get me back into court. I just need to be patient. So the big question is, what is Sun going to do now?"

"Why wouldn't the queen-marshal have done something about her nephew before this if she suspects he's in touch with factions from the Yele League?"

"The story goes that Eirene was very close to her older brothers. That she promised Nézhā before he went off to fight that if he died she would shield his young child from palace intrigue." I shrug. "Who knows? She could name Jiàn as her heir at any moment and cut out Sun. But he hasn't proved himself capable of command. Or maybe it's better to say he hasn't been allowed to do so. Which makes you think, doesn't it? What a classic Eirene move. She kept her promise to her brother without putting her plans to choose her own successor at significant risk. That's what I call a schemer!"

Ti laughs, as I hoped she would.

Kadmos accompanies us to the children's wing of the main house. The bedrooms cluster along a central gathering hall furnished with couches and table tennis, floor space for exercise on stormy days, and a ceiling high enough for badminton. A wall of windows overlooks the agricultural land and beyond to the golden cliffs of Aspiring Heights Province in the far distance, a one-thousand-meter precipice whose geology we learned about when we were young.

The room where my sister the eight-times-worthy hero Ereshkigal slept as a child is festooned with gold ribbons and white mourning wreaths, even after all these years. Its door stands open with a gilded rope barring the threshold. Ti stands beside me as I press my hands together in greeting to the empty space that once held my beloved big sister. Resh kept a simple room with a neatly made bed, a five-headed scylla lamp, a writing desk and gear, and a shelf with a basket of shuttlecocks, her favorite pīng pāng qiú paddle, and three glass jars of marbles. She could sort those marbles into varying sets for hours. She always said sorting calmed her.

Kadmos takes Ti to the side wing where attendants sleep. I pass Manea's old quarters, whose door is shut. Percy's room has a white ribbon strung across its open door. Inside it looks exactly as it did when he left at the age of eleven to become Sun's Companion. My room sits adjacent to his with a crawl door linking them; we thought that was cool when we were small. The bed in my room is the same three-quarter-size one I had as a kid. Fortunately I hit my growth spurt early and then stalled out like a train whose brake valves got flipped. Maybe the staff would have exchanged the bed if they'd had more notice, or maybe they had time and just chose not to on Aunt Moira's order. It's the kind of petty shit she'd savor.

I sling my duffel onto a chair beside the black network table where I used to follow Chaonia Prime's trains as they sped around the globe, and design transportation systems that met no standard of feasibility except in my childish mind. With a quick call-up I ascertain what I suspected: the network here on the estate has been censored so I can't tap into anything except a curated feed of Channel Idol and the estate's local administrative web.

Inside my academy duffel nestles a cloth bag in which I carried a change of clothes and five items I took from home when I ran away at the age of sixteen to become a humble citizen cadet at CeDCA. I set to one side the antique tonfa, which twist together to become a stinger, and the tuning fork Resh gave me when she left for the fleet. From a velvet pouch I pull out Resh's memorial tablet, which I stole from Lee House all those years ago. Before leaving Lee House this trip I grabbed some of Resh's favorite red bean cakes from the kitchen. Ti and I ate all but one on the way here. I set the last one beside the tablet on an altar tray placed in a tiny alcove. Sitting back on my heels I settle my hands on my thighs and calm my mind with recitation.

The traditional characters with their blessing gleam up at me. What would my life have been like if Resh had lived? Would I be here now? Did her death set me on this path? Is fate a command from heaven? Or a matter of strategy?

A brisk clip-clop beat catches my ear. I mutter a curse under my breath. No one else walks in that staccato way, determined to be heard. I should have known she'd be here, secured at our isolated estate where she can't get into trouble. Aunt Moira hadn't warned me, her shiv of revenge. With fumbling hands I shove the memorial tablet back into my duffel and turn to face the inevitable.

"Persephone? Is it possible you arrived without greeting your old mother first?"

Perfectly coifed and beautifully turned out in the vogue-est of current fashion, my mother sweeps into my private room without asking permission to enter. She engulfs me in an unwanted hug as she bursts into dramatic sobbing. As always, there are no actual tears, so my shoulder stays dry.

"I didn't know you were here," I blurt out, and immediately wonder why I do not just keep my mouth shut.

"Of course you knew! Why does everyone lie to me so casually? Do you expect me to believe Moira didn't mention how cruelly I've been treated?"

"You covered for your husband so he could murder the princess's bodyguard!" I try to escape her grip but she clutches harder.

"I did no such thing! Even if I had, how could I have known there was anything except normal riot projectiles in his gun? It's remarkable how people get away with these accusations! But never mind that. What about you?" She holds me at arm's length, her fingers tightening like vises as her eyes bore into my face. "What news do you have of your father?"

"Why would I have news of him?"

"You saw him last!"

I can't deny it. "He fled while I was unconscious."

"Fled! He was falsely accused! Why didn't you rescue him? Support him! Your own father! Have you no filial duty toward your parents? But no, I suppose you never did." Her gaze falls upon the hapless duffel with its CeDCA logo. "Moira says you meant to humiliate us by attending the citizens' academy, but maybe you had a deeper scheme. It has worked well for you, has it not? Perseus dead. You snuggled up to Princess Sun and all without the least regard for your father's fate. Or my state of mind. Abandoned by everyone!"

"He was trying to help a Rider escape!"

"He did no such thing! That's a vicious rumor put about by Eirene. She never liked him."

"I thought it was Moira who never liked him," I thoughtlessly retort.

"Moira envied me, and was secretly in love with him." She leans confidingly toward me. "Now! Tell me the truth! What was done with your father?"

A horrible swell of ugly emotion rages through me. In an instant I'll be shredded by its torrent. Tears burn at my eyes, and I will be damned to the Eighteen Hells if I will let my mother see me cry. I step out of her grasp.

Her expression goes still, as if her emotions have congealed to make a mask.

"Everyone knows in the palace, don't they? Eirene knows where Kiran is but Moira won't tell me. My own sister won't discuss the palace goings-on or the governance of Lee House with me, as if she thinks I'm a traitor!" With a sly shift of expression, she leans closer. "Where did Sun send you? To Yele? Did Eirene force Kiran to return to Yele?"

"Where are you getting your information if Aunt Moira isn't telling you?"

A crooked smile lifts her mouth. "Wouldn't you like to know!"

I wouldn't like to know but I ought to find out. So I deflect, hoping she'll take the bait and tell me more than she intends. "Rumor has it Father is still at large."

"Don't ally yourself to rumor. The seers are innocent of wrongdoing."

"I was on Tjeker when the raid went down. The seers were aiding the Phene."

"People will say anything! Eirene uses Channel Idol to lie for her!"

Since this is technically true, just not true in this instance, I don't refute it. "The seers were disgraced years ago in a bribery scandal where they were meant to be objective mediators."

"Fabrications! Envy! Hearsay! Eirene always hated the seers most of all, that's what your father confided to me in private. He only trusted me, you see. He said I was the most intelligent of the sisters, no matter what people said. Eirene knew Kiran saw through her. She could bend the weak-hearted Yele League to her will, but the seers resisted her because they see heat and lies. She even turned Moira against him, even though Moira adored him when he first came home with me."

"Moira was against the marriage."

"Of course she was! Just because *she* couldn't keep any partner for more than a year because of her ugly temperament, she didn't want *me* to have a desirable spouse." She reels onward. "Even one smile from Moira toward Kiran was enough to decide Eirene to rid herself of him. That jealous harpy has been waiting for her chance to ruin my life."

Eirene's interest in ruining Aisa Lee's life must rank about as high as her interest in which fashionable shoes Aisa wears. My mother's demands and extremes ripped like flood tides and storm winds in and out of my life as a child. I thought they were normal. It wasn't until I left home that I learned otherwise.

I'm not responsible for her. Maybe that's why Resh chose the sacrificial path she did: because she thought that somehow she was. It's time to be done with this.

"Mother, your husband betrayed Chaonia. He abandoned you the instant he had no more use for you."

"Snake! Ungrateful child!"

Footfalls ring from the hall.

Tiana appears at the threshold like a celestial messenger. "Your Honor, I offer my humble greetings . . ."

My mother pushes past her and strides away across the hall, her heels clicking in snaps of rage. I join Ti at the door and we watch in tense silence. When my mother vanishes into the passage that leads to the other wing, Ti gives me a wide-eyed look and says, "Whoof. That was something."

My hands are cold and my core ablaze. "I need to go for a run. You want to come? The trails are great here."

"How long of a run?" She's familiar with my needs now that she's been my cee-cee for almost a year.

"A short one. Ten klicks."

She gestures toward the view through the hall, looking over the pool terrace and the exercise fields beyond. "That pool looks very inviting."

"I'll get a guard to go with me. You swim."

I run to flush out adrenaline that has nowhere else to go. The guard who accompanies me is an easygoing veteran who served his ten years in the Kanesh campaign and returned to his home village with a re-built shoulder and blown-off ear. He's a fourth cousin of Kadmos. After mentioning he's glad to have such a highly qualified teacher in the area, he shuts up and lets me pound the trails.

When I return I shower, then dress in the clothing Ti has laid out. She checks me out thoroughly, aware my mother will try to find any least detail to criticize. Ti is going to eat in the attendants' hall to start getting to know people and make a good impression. I'm resigned to an unpleasant meal.

But when I reach the entry portico to the summer dining hall, I find myself alone. Everyone else in Lee House has stayed in Argos to attend the great festival celebrating Eirene's reign. Only my mother has been banished, because even though Aunt Moira erased the clip of Father shooting Octavian the day of the wedding banquet, Moira and Eirene know Aisa at best looked the other way and at worst was in on the plan. They've chosen to confine her in internal exile because they don't intend to prosecute her. Lee House can't be exposed to that sort of scandalous publicity. It's not unlike Eirene's treatment of her nephew: out of sight, out of mind.

I wait thirty minutes at the table because I don't want to endure Mother's complaints that I'm rude for starting without her. She never arrives. Her epic sulks can last for days.

Eating alone is a staggering relief. As I savor the meal, I can't help but wonder what it would be like to have a mother I could confide in and enjoy being with.

A Sudden Change of Subject

The flash of the rising sun refracted through the glass of the basilica woke Apama. She bolted upright, dragged on leggings and a workout singlet, and slapped her palm against the pressure latch of the door that led from her bedroom into the parlor of her sire's suite. She'd gone through this exact routine every morning at dawn for the last four days, ever since her mother had arrived on Anchor Prime.

The door did not open. It wouldn't open until the second bell.

Stress made her sweat with the pungent blend of perspiration and citronella peculiar to people with exoskeletons, and to people like her whose birth caul had been removed in infancy and therefore could never harden into an exoskeleton. Even so, her glistening skin and weeping glands would always give her away, no matter how she treated herself with two showers a day and carefully curated dosages of anti-cholinergics. She grabbed a handkerchief to wipe her forehead, the caul spurs at her collarbone, and the moist creases of her four elbows. Her mother had long ago shown her how to sew absorbent patches into her clothing, but mostly her mother had repeated, over and over, "This is an adaptive part of your physiology, Apama. People who mock or name-call are the ones who should be ashamed."

Staring at the closed door Apama blinked back a cruel thought: But then why had her mother had her daughter's caul excised?

She checked her wristband: 112 minutes until the second bell. She went to the gym and, after a workout, wrapped an exhausting turn through the flight simulator's most challenging level.

When the second bell rang and the door into Zakurru's private suite opened, she was ready and waiting in her uniform. She strode through to find her mother seated in the dining alcove, gaze serene as she looked out the window onto the shining waters. It was the first time they'd been alone since her mother's arrival.

"Hey, Mom. Hey." She bent to give Rana an emotional squeeze.

"I'm all right, Apama. Just as I was yesterday and the day before and the day before that."

Apama looked toward the other door, which to her relief stayed closed. The writing table bore its usual messy surface, such a contrast to the spare furnishings and perfect order of the rest of the spacious parlor.

"We can eat without waiting for him," said Rana.

"Are you sure?"

Her mother's gaze flashed up with a tightening of her eyes that came and went as quickly as sunlight clipping the curl of a wave. "I have my limits. Waiting to eat is one of them."

Apama indicated the unused plates on the side table next to fried long bread, ginger-and-cinnamon-scented congee, fruit, and her mother's favorite salty tofu and pickled mustard greens. "And yet you're not eating."

Rana playfully tapped the handle of her spoon against Apama's forearm. "I make an exception of waiting for you out of long habit."

"Oh, Mom."

"Dish up. You're too thin. You're not eating enough."

They ate in silence. Rana seemed to be savoring the view over the sea. As a little girl Apama had childishly boasted that her mother was the prettiest mom in all of Tranquility Harbor, and it might even have been true. But only now did she contemplate what it would have meant for a vulnerable youth to have lost her entire extended family at the edge of seventeen in a massive industrial accident that devastated the surrounding area for years afterward. Kinship lines were your security and your legitimacy.

Her mother shifted her gaze to Apama. "Just say it."

"Are you—? Did you—?" She covered her face with her upper hands. She could not force the words "are you having sex with him" out of her mouth.

"My dear girl, I am truly all right. I've dealt with worse."

Apama churned, her thoughts twisting through endless gyrations.

Rana sighed. "Back at that time I was required to sign a binding nondisclosure agreement. Had I spoken of my work in the service, they would have taken you away."

"What is 'the service'? You were never a member of the sex workers guild."

"I was not a member of the Campaspe Guild, that's right. Nothing so aboveboard and licensed as that. 'The service' is what we called it because we couldn't call it anything that might give away what it really was."

"What was it?"

"I was seventeen. I had no one to sponsor me into a guild or pay entrance fees to a syndicate or help me meet the educational standards for the fleet because I could not afford school. I was living in the ruins scavenging through garbage to eat."

Apama shut her eyes, wishing she had asked before. But Rana never encouraged questions about those days, and maybe Apama hadn't really wanted to know.

"People like the girl I was get placed in restructuring. They get sent to one of the marginal systems on a syndicate contract. I would have lived in contract barracks, probably on an orbital habitat plagued by toxins or on a planet or moon without breathable air. My wages would have been garnished to pay for my travel, lodging, board, water, and air before I received anything for myself. Then I got a mysterious offer. Serve four years in a secret posting in lieu of basic military service, and I'd receive a deed to a flat, a nest egg, and an entry chit to any apprentice school of my choosing. I said yes."

"Did you know it would involve having . . ." Apama pulled fingers across her forehead as if trying to rub away the thoughts that crowded into her mind with disgusting rapidity. ". . . sex with Riders?"

Rana had a way of pouching her upper lip—the most supple part of her face—that always made Apama laugh. It was her sardonic face. "They were cautious about what they told us, sure. But they were careful to make sure we were well treated. They created a whole bureaucratic fake trail to account for our whereabouts."

"It's so weird, Mom."

"Yes, it means every Rider alive who wanted to see me naked did."

"I can't."

Rana's chin quivered.

"Are you *laughing*?" Apama demanded.

"Your face! It's just sex, Apama. Riders are human. They have bodies. Or share bodies."

"Were you having sex with the Rider or the, uh, the embodied person?"

"I never quite figured it out. It depended on the individual and which part of them wanted sex or if they both did."

"Ugh, Mom."

"I didn't think prudery about sex was allowed in the military. I've been meaning to ask, do you have any lovers or interested alliances you've been meaning to tell me about? What about that lancer pilot Gail you mentioned? I hope he survived and that I get to meet him someday. Or Bartholomew Kr Manalon? He's got great conversation and a posh sense of style. You know what grandchildren would mean to the survival of the Sabao clan."

Apama crossed both her uppers and lowers.

Rana cleared her throat. "If you're not going to eat that tofu then give it over."

Apama shoved the bowl across the table, but respectfully, with her upper right.

Rana ate efficiently and almost mechanically, someone who had trained herself not to gorge at speed. After she wiped the last juices from the bowl with a roll, she stared past Apama out onto the landscape. Maybe it wasn't the sea and sky she was seeing but those long-ago days. She spoke in a distanced cadence.

"I learned a lot of things that most people don't know. For example, when Riders come of age they are assigned first as roamers in order to learn the entire network of Phene space. To see it with their ordinary eyes. They're young, fresh out of the restrictions of the Unity Hall living quarters. Adventurous. Anxious. Eager. Sexual. Their bodies need tending just as anyone's do."

"That's fair, I guess."

"They are in fact people too," said Rana wryly. "After they finish their roaming they are assigned to one-year postings at a sequence of strategically crucial systems. So service pods like the one I was at are set up at places like Tranquility. Usually there are four of us service workers to a pod, something for most tastes. We serve any roamers who come through. If need be, we serve the Rider stationed in the area."

Apama looked at her own untouched congee. She'd lost her appetite.

"I knew what I was getting in for. I could have said no."

"It wasn't much of a choice."

"The accident killed tens of thousands and scarred more. It worked out for me in the end."

Apama crept her fingers over the table to brush at her mother's, wanting the reassurance.

"I have you. I have dear friends, a network of trusted colleagues. I got a medic's license that would have been out of reach for me otherwise. I love my work. I'm not complaining."

"What about *him*? How did *he* happen?"

"This was during the first years of Queen-Marshal Eirene's rule, when her position was unstable. Tranquility has strategic significance for the empire."

"The forgotten 'back door' to Hesjan, Hatti, and Chaonian space."

"All sex jokes aside, which I'll spare your tender military ears, it meant our pod had a lot of roamers come through. That's how I came to his attention."

"Because he was creepily watching you have sex with other Riders. Oh holy blood, Mom, he even said so in the basilica. He said you were the only one who had the courage to look Riders in the eye. That he sought you out because of it."

"I do believe Zakurru developed an obsession with me before we met."

After a while the depths of her story became numbing. Maybe Rana's pragmatic approach was the right one. Just another specialty within sex work. The Campaspe Guild was one of the original sixteen trade unions registered within the Phene Exchange.

No. This felt different, like having a collar around your neck that someone else could tighten.

"And the law was supposed to prohibit all contact afterward," Apama said.

"It did. Until this recent synod."

"See, that's what bothers me." Apama leaned toward her mother, table rim pressing into her ribs. "How did he know about me? Was he there when I was born?"

"No. He had been transferred on by then."

"But he could have found out whatever he wanted about us. He could violate the agreement as long as the Rider Council didn't catch him at it."

"I suppose he could."

All her lancer scores tasted like ashes. He'd put her on the *Strong Bull* to get her close to him on the long road to Molossia.

"Mom, why did you excise my caul?"

Rana sat back, an upper hand raised with palm facing outward as if to ward off a blow. "That's a sudden change of subject."

Apama waited.

"I know that sulky set of lips all too well." Rana relaxed as she placed her hand back on the table next to its left-side pair. "You'll sit stubbornly in the chair the rest of the day if I don't answer."

"You told me you aren't ashamed of having an exoskeleton."

"I'm not. But it made me vulnerable. The restructuring committee would have sent me to a radiation-heavy undesirable environment. Resistance to radiation is a blessing and a curse in that way, isn't it? So you're right, Apama. I was offered a bad choice or a less bad choice. That isn't much of a choice. I wanted to spare you what I had to go through." Her sharp "huh" was more of a laugh than a gasp. "I never realized how hard it was to have to hold it all in. All the things I couldn't talk about. Things people don't know because they're kept secret."

"What I don't get is why there aren't sex worker Incorruptibles, if Riders need sex. Incorruptibles already pledge their entire lives to the Rider Council."

"Which is exactly why Incorruptibles are restricted to administration and military. Riders rule objectively because they don't have families to favor."

"Except they did. They do. Here I sit. And here you sit. Are you glad to be here, Mom? Are you going to live with him as his spouse? For the rest of your life? Or until he gets tired of you? Isn't this one of those bad choice versus a less bad choice situations? Like if you don't want to be here, but you can't say no?"

Rana tapped a finger to her lips as her gaze flicked toward the door. With a click, and the faintly heard whine of a mechanism, it opened.

Uncle was smiling as he entered.

Smiling.

Apama had never seen him smile. Everyone back home said she had her mom's eyes and smile, and maybe it was true or maybe it was just them being nice about her lack of a birth certificate with the names of both parents, a shameful mark of questionable status although no one outright used the word "bastard," a terrible insult worse than slimy shell. She had inherited his skin tone, darker than her mother's complexion. His jawline, nose, the long-fingered shape of his hands. Only her mother's more oval face, her eyes, and her exoskeleton had bred into her daughter.

He paused at the side table. "Rana, may I get you more salty tofu?"

"No, thank you, Dasa, but I appreciate the offer."

Dasa. The name exploded like a shell burst in Apama's head. Had her mom always known the name he'd refused to tell to the child he'd sired?

He turned his back to them as he dished up a plate for himself. Zakurru's face was lively, more intense than usual, and he was smiling too, lipless mouth stretched more broadly than she'd ever seen it. A chill crawled all over her skin. She planted her feet flat on the floor and braced herself in the chair. If her mom could deal with this, then so must she.

In his eerie whisper Zakurru said, "We will go to Cipari Terrace for a supper with Paulo Kr Manalon and Bahala Rn Maki. Bahala is the Angursa Syndicate president. I haven't introduced you to her yet, Rana." His gaze shifted to Apama. "Young Bartholomew will be there."

Under the table, her mother stepped on her foot, hard, not unlike the way Kr Manalon had stepped on his child's foot the day Apama met Bar.

"Yes, that would be lovely," Apama said stiffly.

21

A Confused Moment of Luxuriant Well-Being

What a day in festival-clad Argos! For the industrious among us—that's those of you listening now, because you're up and about your business before the first bell!—Channel Idol is here to keep you company for every second of today's historic events as we commence a week's spectacular festivities to celebrate our beloved Eirene as she completes twenty-four years as queen-marshal and embarks on another twenty-four!

The gratingly cheerful voice of Channel Idol woke the Honorable Hestia Hope. She blinked off the audio to merciful silence. After a confused moment of luxuriant well-being, she realized she was still wrapped in the arms of the woman she loved. The weight of a bent knee on her thigh. A cheek resting on her shoulder, breath a brush of warmth on her neck. The pleasing fragrance Sun gave off, maybe just pheromones but more attractive than any perfume.

However gratifying, it was odd to wake like this. Sun never slept overnight in Hetty's bed. Sun rarely slept the entire night through, ever.

Hetty opened her eyes to see Sun awake and gazing at the shadowed ceiling as if it contained a battle she was replaying in her mind. There was just enough dawn light coming through the latticework windows to reveal the implacable stare, the determined set of lips, the ambition in the way her chin jutted toward the heavens. The gravity of her, that held Hetty close. Sun was more than people understood, Hetty knew that, and it was her hoard to cherish. She shifted to kiss Sun's mouth, her lips dry from the heat and from the wine they'd drunk too much of last night at a palace banquet in honor of Eirene.

Sun was already sliding out of the embrace, out of the bed, moving fast. "There's been a change of plan."

"Oh. I see now. Your father must be here."

The downward twist of Sun's mouth was all the answer Hetty needed. No wonder Sun had lingered in the bed to hold on for a while longer. The prospect of seeing her father after almost a year apart would make even the indomitable Sun get tense.

Hetty watched her stride naked to the chair where she'd tossed a silk robe last night. Like her mother, Sun had a stocky, tough build honed by training. Her hair was cropped short, revealing the muscular lines of her neck and shoulders. Because she had a Yele father, Hetty liked to think of herself as having a refined sensibility, but she had to admit Sun had a great ass, round, tight, and . . . Well. Enough of that.

Sun vanished through the secret door that linked their suites. Hetty got dressed in a faded blue qípáo and went to the kitchen. Within minutes the cook had a bowl of noodles for her. A feed was playing in a corner, spilling images within a waterfall of virtual fireworks: The nobly posed figure of Queen-Marshal Eirene. The character for "mountain," festooned in chrysanthemums. A volley of flaming spears pouring toward the stars. Volume a whisper in the background, words like wind chasing at the edge of her hearing. Footsteps approaching. Sun, a brisk beat she would recognize anywhere because she had fallen into step alongside her years ago.

Sun wore a laborer's kit with a knit cap pulled over her short hair. She was reviewing instructions with Isis as she grabbed two rice balls and a cup of bean broth. James and Makinde entered behind her, James pontificating as he loved to do.

"It's easy to explain, Mak. Sun likes to get out into the markets early on a festival day to get a sense of the crowd. Citizens are proud to rub shoulders with the heir in the shops. Gives them a story to tell their grandchildren."

"It's Makinde."

"Sure it is, but you're the baby of the group, so Mak makes more sense. Don't fight destiny, my friend. Be happy I don't call you Mak-mak."

Makinde had one of those faces that told you everything. For example, was it worth it to punch an obnoxious scion of the most influential military clan in Chaonia? Hetty enjoyed watching the struggle in the twitch of his lips and the flare of his eyes.

"You know," Makinde remarked as if at random, "first year of academy when we scrubs earned our first liberty, we went out drinking in Neon District. All this time I'd been getting a lot of hazing for my grandmother and my symbiont. Somebody slipped something into my drink, I guess, because I woke up on a cold dawn in a cold alley, hung over and dumped and lacking my gloves." His voice dropped to an ominous whisper that made everyone perk up. "My favorite gloves."

"And?" Sun asked, his narration having grabbed her attention.

"Dozer tracked them down, hidden in the locker of a Vata House cadet. That's when the other cadets stopped harassing me for being a Hesjan bastard. That, and a well-aimed punch to that loser's glass jaw."

James grinned. "Colonel Isis had a look at your scores from the academy. She'd make you odds-on favorite for beating me to a pulp. But my big brother won't like it."

Makinde's cocky expression stiffened as he considered the reputation of the infamous Anas Samtarras. Then he laughed, mock-saluted James, and accepted a bowl of noodles from the cook. Only when he turned to sit at the table did Hetty notice the decapod folded up like a knapsack against his back.

Sun tapped her foot, looking toward the door. Lagging behind, and later than any Companion would ever have dared to be, came Princess Soaring. The Navigator wore similar garb to Sun but with a sports headband tied around her forehead as if to keep her hair back but actually to hide the rhombus. Her slender height and the gravity braces around her ankles revealed her to be from off-planet, but that didn't mean she wanted to advertise she was a Navigator. She greeted everyone profusely, an Argosy custom Sun suffered impatiently but did not cut short because people were still eating. Armies marched on their stomachs.

Hetty loved breakfast, the gathering of equals, the reminder that she had a family and wasn't isolated and alone with one father dead and the other as good as dead, lost to the worlds. Their presence and their chatter filled her up like sweetest honey, warmed under the heat of Sun. Let people think her bland, or besotted. She didn't care. She knew where she belonged.

"Your Highness, Secretary Nisaba gave me a list of cee-cee candidates to vet," Isis was saying. "Let me know when you and your Companions want to go over it. Candace and Tiana have been exemplary but it's a lot of extra work for them now you have a full complement of Companions and not enough cee-cees."

"I have a candidate for my cee-cee," put in Makinde.

"After the festival," Sun said. "Anything else?"

"Everyone's whereabouts are accounted for. Razin will hold down the fort here."

"Let's go."

Sun had once privately joked that she knew the central district of Argos as well as she knew Hetty's body, if a body had architecture, if it could be mapped with pedestrian streets, swift bike lanes, broad cargo alleys, slideways, bridges, and tunnels. This lacework connected the neighborhoods that marked the core settlement of the first inhabitants on Chaonia Prime when it was a frontier world two thousand years ago.

They ducked into back-alley bakeries and hole-in-the-wall candy shops brimming with festival delicacies: candied coconut ribbons and sweet potato and kumquat, sugar-sprinkled kringler, fortune cakes warm from the ovens whose crust crunched beneath meltingly sweet pineapple jam, cakes with the characters for longevity and victory and strength molded on top and the insides filled with nut paste or red bean or durian.

Hetty sampled one too many rich delicacies and had to stop, feeling vaguely nauseated. Sun ate sparingly from a bag of baked seeds as she chatted in a familiar way with shopkeepers and householders out buying last minute for their midday banquet. An uncle who'd fought at Kanesh showed off his prosthetic foot. A woman boasted about her cousins who'd set up shop on an orbital habitat at Hatti Prime now that it was under Chaonian control. A shop window displayed an image of a recently graduated local citizen cadet posted to their first duty station in the fleet. People praised Eirene's deft and aggressive maneuvering. Her willingness to fight had brought prosperity to the republic: What are words compared to spear-won land? The one who acts will outlast the idle. Having spent so much of her childhood among the hair-splitting sophists of a Yele university community, Hetty adored the fierceness with which these everyday citizens praised their queen-marshal and the powerful military she had built.

Pillars sang out the second bell as Channel Idol ramped up its coverage.

Those who fight together win together! Here in Argos the crowd already stands eight ranks deep at Harmony Plaza, waiting for the triumphal procession. Meet the lucky citizens allowed to line Petitioners Bridge and cheer our glorious queen-marshal up close and personal as she crosses the water eight hours from now. Don't miss our live coverage starting at the sixth bell. And now, the farm report brings us a special treat as a venerable delegation from the Yele Institute of Agronomics tours a prize-winning ube collective in the company of Satet Nazir, governor of Nazir House and Minister for Agriculture.

Sun led them through a residential district so old it still had its original three-story row houses. The buildings crammed together cheek by jowl, sagging with age and yet like old comrades holding each other up.

In the deepest heart of the neighborhood stood a barricaded compound at the terminus end of a walled lane. Its bronze gate was streaked with a green patina. Life-size statues of threshold guardians stood watch on either side of the gate, one carrying a spear and the other a club.

"What is this place?" Makinde whispered as if waiting for the guardians to descend from their alcoves and smite them for trespassing.

James leaned against him as a brother might, relaxed while pushing deliberately into his space. "This is the Heart Temple of the Divine and Pacific Lotus Queen, She Who Preserves and Delivers Voyagers. It's the first temple built in Chaonia System, nineteen hundred years ago."

"I thought that was Dodona."

"Dodona is the first temple built in what is now the Republic of Chaonia, but it's on Molossia. Did you sleep through history classes? Have you really never been here? My family walks the labyrinth once a year."

"My grandmother never brought me, which means I've never been here. She doesn't follow that religious path."

Isis turned to them. "You two stay here, but do me a favor and keep your eyes open and your mouths shut."

"What are we guarding against?" Makinde asked.

James gave his cap a dramatic downward tug. "We guard against the unexpected! Also, foreign agents pretending to be journalists and festivalgoers."

Hetty gave Makinde what she hoped was a sympathetic smile, but he was examining the deserted lane as if for the ghosts of malevolent spies. Sun had already opened the wicket gate to enter.

The gate let onto a footbridge that crossed a moat. Water rippled lazily against a steep inner wall two stories high and topped with spikes.

Canopies of flowering trees could be seen beyond the wall. Isis remained on the bridge.

Where the bridge ended on a stone landing stood another closed gate, this one set deep into a thick retaining wall. The gate's burnished wood was inlaid with a twelve-sided knot. Soaring looked to Sun for permission. When Sun nodded, Soaring traced the plaiting, which was woven so as to have neither beginning nor end.

"In the great span of heaven we are always leaving and always home. The first Argosy to seed this soil must have planted this Journey Temple here."

"So the accounts tell us," said Sun. "Let's go in."

A temple gate was always unlocked. Soaring opened it a meter and slipped in, but Hetty caught Sun's elbow and gave her a look.

"Are you so sure this is a good idea?"

"I brought her here to introduce her to my father without the whole palace looking on and listening in," said Sun with the peevish edge that crept out when she thought someone was objecting to what she wanted to do.

"Can you be sure he'll see her as no threat?"

Sun's expression darkened with a surge of temper. "I didn't think *you* would doubt my judgment!"

She shook her arm out of Hetty's grasp and went in, dragging the gate shut behind her. Hetty was shaken by Sun's tone. By the gesture of closing the door. She wanted to say it wasn't Sun she doubted, but Prince João, but it was too late. Once Sun had made a decision it was always too late to stop her from plunging into the fray. Probably that was why Hetty had said nothing earlier, stalled for choice.

Move! Move! she scolded herself. Too like her scholar father, unable to pause the cycling natter of uneasy thoughts. It was why she liked systems, information she could comb through and set into order. The work soothed the part of her that spun like galaxies in a slow continual whirl. The weight of Sun's surety pulled her forward when otherwise she would have stagnated at anchor.

She set a hand on the latch just as a *tap tap tap* sounded as if from the inside of the retaining wall. A crack opened to reveal a narrow passage, out of which stepped the queen-marshal her very own self.

"Ah, so I'm not too late." Eirene's spiky smile was a javelin ready to launch. She grasped Hetty's arm in an unshakeable hold. "How are things with you, dear Hestia? I still mourn your father. Hasan, I mean. He and I got into so much mischief when we were young. I know your other father has retired to a hermitage. Do you hear from him often?"

Hetty was too startled to answer. Had João invited Eirene without telling Sun? Or had she invited herself? Was this going to be some kind of big blowup?

"Compsognathus got your tongue? You're not scared of me, are you?"

The accusation jolted words onto her tongue. "My father spoke of you in glowing terms. So I am minded to believe that you possess a softer heart than you let on."

"Do you? Ha! Let me give you this advice, then. Sun benefits by your presence because you moderate her worse impulses. Don't get a big head and ruin it as Moira did by believing the attention of a royal lover places you above the customs of court."

Hetty prided herself on her ability to stay calm. She had nothing to be ashamed of. "In truth, Your Highness, I have no such wish."

"We never think we do, until the great ruddy sac of golden eggs hangs within our reach. And I speak from experience. Let's enter, shall we?"

Eirene shoved open the gate and walked through, hauling Hetty with her. Beyond the gate and inside the circular retaining wall lay the temple. Its meditative labyrinth was an unbroken spiral path folded multiple times back on itself to create a long winding walk to a hidden center. High ceramic walls too high to see over hedged the pathway so it wasn't possible to see anything of the walkway from the gate except the entrance arch and a first short stretch of path that vanished into a sharp left turn. The walls also acted as a sonic baffle. Not a sound could be heard, not even the strident life of the city in the distance, as if they'd left Argos behind and fallen through into a liminal space like the gap between beacons.

Eirene led Hetty to the basin with its ever-flowing water set next to the entrance arch. They rinsed their hands as they recited the prayer for a safe journey. Jasmine and wisteria draped the arch. The air hummed with the buzz of insects. The scent of flowers weighed like dreams on Hetty's eyes. Night. A lingering kiss.

Eirene's voice broke up her straying thoughts. "Don't get distracted."

Again she took hold of Hetty's elbow. They passed under the arch of flowers and paced the first stretch to the first turn. Just around the ninety-degree bend stood Sun with Soaring behind her, looking confused.

"I thought I heard your voice," Sun said to her mother. "Did he tell you I was meeting him here?"

"Really, Sun, you have an exaggerated notion of your father's amplitude. I have my own sources of information. Shall we go?"

Sun stepped to one side, indicating that the queen-marshal should, as appropriate, precede her onto the path. Hetty had walked the labyrinth often over the years. She loved its calming properties, and she also knew it took a good ten minutes at a moderate pace to reach the center but many more if you took your time as the original Argosies had in their generations-long journey from the Celestial Empire of ancient memory. Soaring glanced between mother and daughter and prudently chose to fall into line behind Eirene.

As Eirene and Soaring set out, Sun did not move. Her mouth was set with an annoyance tempered by a sheen of victorious gloating. She had something in mind that she hadn't shared with Hetty.

Eirene did not look back to see if Sun was following. She and Soaring vanished along the gentle curve of the path. There would be hairpin turns and curved stretches growing shorter and shorter as the spiral tightened.

Sun stepped back to where the first straight stretch of path ended against a blank wall at the ninety-degree leftward angle. She knelt, ran a finger along the base of the wall, grasped something out of sight, and clicked it. The wall cracked to reveal a slender opening that let onto another short straight stretch. It was the last bit of the long path, and it speared directly into the center of the maze. Hetty felt her mouth gape. She'd had no idea this shortcut existed.

Sun said, "I know you enjoy the practice of walking the labyrinth to measure life's long journey, but I don't have the time. Are you coming with me, or following my mother?"

Hetty stepped through with her. The wall clicked seamlessly shut behind. Ten minutes away along loops and hairpin turns, Eirene would still be walking. Sun strode a brisk fifteen seconds to a central plaza, a shallow, bowl-like depression meant to represent the holy lotus. At the center lay a circular reflection pool ringed by benches.

Here sat Prince João, legs crossed, holding a baton with a gloved hand. His deep purple sherwani was cut on a bias and adorned with intricately carved chrysanthemum buttons. The bland-seeming beige color of his trousers and shoes served to set off the elaborate floral damask. His hair was shorter than the last time Hetty had seen it, and his beard a little longer. His smile was the same, which was to say a complex and challenging mix of parental love and princely calculation.

"Sun," he said, expecting her to come to him.

She nodded at his bodyguard, standing on the other side of the reflecting pool with a clear view of the entrance. Hetty was surprised to see Zizou rather than the prince's longtime head of security, Colonel Evans. João never ever did anything for no reason, so there was something afoot. Some scheme in the prince's mind.

Sun bent to kiss her father's cheeks, first left then right, as it was the custom on the Gatoi wheelships for youth to salute their elders in this way. Sun loved her father, and he also frustrated her with his overprotectiveness and sometimes exhausting demands. Hetty could see the wings of these complicated emotions fluttering in the subtle ways Sun reacted: the tilt of her head, her hesitation before she sat beside her father, the way she leaned toward him as toward warmth. Her sigh as she braced herself, and her smile when he took her hand and pressed it affectionately.

Hetty had never butted heads with either of her fathers; the diplomat had the skill of listening and the scholar the gift of silence. They had cherished her without any expectation but that she be content with who she was. Now they were both taken from her, one by death and the other by a profound depression and his retreat into the hermitage. It hurt to see Sun and her father, not that she blamed them or wished them ill, but that the wound in her heart bled afresh knowing she had no hand to touch, no words to hear. Rather than deal with a grief still raw and weeping after five years, it was easier to face the reunion as if she saw it through Sun's eyes and heart.

His Smile Was Balm, or It Was Poison

"Mother is coming," Sun said irritably.

Her announcement did not rattle her father's cool. "Of course she is."

"I meant to introduce you to Soaring alone."

"It's not the kind of thing your mother would let pass. Haven't I taught you better?"

Before she could reply to this condescending attack, he gestured elegantly to acknowledge Hetty's presence. He was the master of distraction. Hetty offered the prince a polite bow and prudently walked around the benches to greet Zizou with friendly chatter. The prince's gaze drifted after her.

Like all Gatoi, whether those who lived out their lives on nomadic wheelships or those sent from the wheelships to become mercenaries, both Zizou's and João's bodies were threaded with neural enhancers. These neural patterns appeared to the naked eye like shimmering tattoos just under the skin; no two Gatoi had the same pattern any more than any two individuals had the same fingerprints. The enhancement gave them speed, endurance, strength, and healing beyond that of most humans.

Her father said in a low voice, "His innocent face is quite at odds with his lethal training. Elegance with precision. He makes a good bodyguard for that reason, Sun, which is why I'm handing him back to you. Since you have not replaced Octavian."

"No one can replace Octavian."

"That's not my point. You need a bodyguard."

"That's the purpose of my Companions."

He sighed the way he would when she was younger and hadn't worn the right colors to match his outfits. "Of course it is, but they are also representatives of their Houses. They bring ambitions and connections with them. Look at Moira Lee or her cousin Marduk. Don't believe any of those you surround yourself with are but blank slates without goals of their own. Not even Hestia Hope. Which reminds me."

Here it came, some objection, some demand, an expectation that she ought to agree to whatever he was about to propose. "I was delighted to read the report you sent me on Soaring. What a brilliant stroke to contact her in secret and build a personal alliance. She'll be a valuable partner for you."

"Oh."

"Oh?" He studied her face in the way he had of seeing past her shields and baffles. "You feared I would disapprove or see Soaring as a rival."

Since she had, she refused to admit it. "You'll like her."

"Will I?"

"For one thing, she has a sense of style."

He chuckled. She always felt a swell of satisfaction when she could amuse him. Tapping the baton against a leg, he rose. "Why wait here, then? Let's walk back along the path and surprise them."

He set off. Like every Royal of the Gatoi he had training in both soldiering and diplomacy and had served in his youth as an acolyte of Lady Chaos. It was the latter training that influenced him the most. Sun signed to Hetty and Zizou to remain where they were and hurried after him. He smiled as she fell in beside him. They turned left into the curving pattern of path, walking briskly rather than meditatively. She had so many questions about the work he'd been doing and about the Titan-class ship she'd arranged so he could supervise that work away from her mother's scrutiny, and she wanted answers. He gave her a warning look as he raised a hand to touch an ear.

Footsteps. Voices. She glanced at him, not sure what to expect or how he would proceed and knowing better than to stand in his way when it came to him and her mother. They came around a tight bend and into view of a long curved stretch. Approaching them along the path, the queen-marshal and Soaring walked side by side, engaged in relaxed conversation. Eirene had the ability to bring people into her orbit with ease. She knew who she was, and never needed to pound that knowledge into those around her, because they knew, too.

The queen-marshal looked up with the smug smile of a person who cannot be ambushed. Her gait shortened, brisk with anticipation as she looked her second consort up and down.

"I do like your beard at that length," she said by way of greeting. "More to hold on to."

"So you always say."

"So you always claim. What do you have for me that I can't get elsewhere, João?"

He had a smile he only used on Eirene, as polished as a well-cared-for blade. "Before we proceed with business, let me greet Soaring as I would any long-lost daughter come home at last."

Sun halted as the prince glided forward with both arms extended to take Soaring's hands in his own. A coil of frustration burned in Sun's belly. She had set up this meeting so she could bring her father together with her new sibling without interference. But her mother could never not stick her oar in, not when it came to the politics of the palace. Eirene had outflanked her.

Galling.

She waited as the three of them bent together in the very Channel Idol image of a loving family group. Soaring looked a little over-whelmed by the attention of two such powerful personalities, but the truce wouldn't last long, and indeed it did not.

In her most hectoring style, Eirene said, "You'll leave Soaring alone, João. None of your tricks or schemes."

"I will treat Soaring as my own."

Eirene laughed curtly. "What, you see some benefit in her? No doubt, her being a Navigator. I'm glad you admit she's no threat to Sun's status as heir. Now, enough of this sentimental family reunion. What do you have for me? You promised results."

"Do I ever not give you results, Eirene? Can you name one time?"

"Stop it."

"That's not what you usually say. But here, have my baton."

Eirene accepted the baton with a smirk that, had she been among her Companions, would have been accompanied by a crude joke. "What can this accomplish that I don't already know about?"

He began walking back toward the center, Eirene beside him grilling him with questions and both ignoring the two young women following at their heels.

Soaring glanced at Sun with a startled question in her gaze.

Sun murmured, "They're always like this. Pretend you don't notice. They're not giving the performance for our benefit, if that helps."

"It does if by that you mean I need not involve myself."

"Best to stay clear."

Soaring nudged her with an elbow in answer, a gesture between intimates that made Sun feel unreasonably pleased. "What means the baton?"

"Do the Argosies know about banner soldiers?"

"They are mercenaries hired from the Gatoi clans. The Phene Empire uses them as auxiliaries because Gatoi would rather die than surrender or retreat."

"It turns out that the main reason they fight so fiercely is Phene scientists have learned to tune—to leash—the neural networks all Gatoi are born with."

"So their fighting to the death is a form of compulsion?"

"That's right. The Phene value the banner soldiers only as fodder to be chewed up to create openings so their own soldiers will take less damage and fewer casualties. The baton is like a tuning fork a Phene officer can use to impose actions through neural patterning."

Ahead, João was speaking. Gloating, really. ". . . we have devised a key by which the leash can be destabilized, leaving banner soldiers free of external neural coercion. It's slow, one person at a time, but completely effective. It restores dignity to people who've had that dignity stripped from them by this appalling procedure."

"Surely the Phene can devise another pathway to control?"

"They can, but it will take time. And they will have to realize they have lost control of the banner soldiers in order to know they need to do something about it. This method will work for now."

"Good." Eirene studied the baton from João as they emerged into the center of the labyrinth, the lotus heart of all existence. She pointed it at Zizou, fiddled with the controls. When he did not react but rather looked quizzically at her, she nodded with satisfaction and handed the baton back to João. "How many batons can be produced and how quickly?"

Soaring nudged Sun. "Is that a banner soldier? How cute is he! He looks so incredibly noble, and stoic, and . . . and *fit*. Are there stratum rules? Is he allowed to speak to me?"

Infatuation was such a waste of time. Sun sent Soaring over to Hetty, but before she could insert herself into her parents' discussion,

Eirene looked skyward. The *chutter chutter chutter* of a Hummingbird grew in volume.

"Enough of this delightful breakthrough. I have to go and prepare, and so do you all. I will see you in a few hours." She strode to the opening in the lotus's heart, then paused and turned back, looking daggers at João while pointing at Zizou. "And by the way, that one is not to enter the palace, not today and not ever. It's not that I'm shocked you'd bring him. Provocation is exactly your style. I'm surprised at the baldness of this move. I expect you of all people to show a little more sophistication in your jockeying for position. For the heavens' sake, trust me to have common sense about the security of the republic and Chaonia's need for a competent adult heir. Do you understand me, João? Will you stop playing these games with me, of all people?"

"Eirene—"

"It was a rhetorical question. Soaring! Hestia! You two will accompany me to the palace. Sun, you can make your own way back with or without your father."

Then she was gone, like a fireball vanishing down a passage. Soaring and Hetty scrambled after with apologetic looks. No matter. Eirene had a petty side; it was part of what made her seem human and approachable instead of a towering monolith who had single-handedly saved Chaonia, leaving nothing for her daughter to accomplish except preside over a republic whose stability Eirene had secured. Not now, not ever, so people like Norioghene would say.

But Sun wasn't one to dwell. Not much, anyway. She turned to her father, who wore the bland face that meant he was annoyed. "Did the lab figure out how to take the engineered hallucination off Zizou?"

"That's a much deeper and more complex problem we've not been able to crack. Yet. You'll regret taking that Lee girl on, mark my words."

"Maybe, but that's neither here nor there. I can't imagine why you brought Zizou to Argos when you know he'll attack Manea if he so much as catches a glimpse of her. It seems rash. Even for you."

That her father was calculating and bloody-minded she knew. She just wasn't quite sure how far he was willing to go.

"I'm not worried about Manea and her child supplanting me," she added.

His smile was balm, or it was poison. Usually it was impossible to tell the difference. "My dear child, neither am I."

The Valiant One Gets Blood on His Hands

Despite his five years at the royal academy, Makinde had never gotten used to the exquisitely boring protocols of public events. That was probably the reason he had lost his cool at the Bō House banquet and loudly called out Governor Hakan Bō in front of everyone: the sheer tedium. He was always surprised more people didn't break under the assault of hours of self-aggrandizing orations delivered in pompous monotones.

He checked the time. Sun and her Companions, excepting Persephone Lee and Jade Kim, had been standing on Petitioners Bridge for seventy-one minutes.

Here on the mainland side of the bridge, the approach slab was a gently sloped ramp shaped like an unfolded fan that funneled people onto the narrower deck of the bridge. Thousands crowded onto the plaza, awaiting the procession from the palace. The crowd of citizens was held in place by a rope barrier. Foreign dignitaries observed from the tiered seating of temporary open-air stands. On the opposite side of the ramp a stage had been erected for musicians. Mixed in among them was the Honorable Alika, whose smoldering frown was attracting more attention than the silk-and-bamboo ensemble currently playing.

James bumped a shoulder against Makinde. Hells, he was annoying. "That's Alika's grouchy face. Do you think he is offended by the string players or just mad he only got to play one song and that was an hour ago?"

"Don't you like Alika?"

James slapped his flatcap against his thigh. "No one likes Alika. He's too handsome, too famous, and he always gets the highest score on our weekly ranking."

"Higher than Sun? She allows people to outscore her?"

"You don't understand Sun yet, do you, Mak?"

"It's Makinde, not Mak." He closed a hand into a fist.

James cleared his throat. "The point is that Sun expects us to work as hard as she does. If that means we are better than her at some things, then she'll use our skills to her ends. I haven't figured out what your skillset is yet except your drone—"

"Ou's name is Dozer." The symbiont had folded up portmanteau style next to Makinde's left boot, both tentacles lifted skyward and twitching as they took in visuals, sound, heat, and other ambient information.

"—and your mouthiness. I tracked down a recording of that banquet where you went off on Hakan Bō. An impressive piece of coal-raking!"

Makinde had no intention of going over the episode ever again. "Is the queen-marshal always this late?"

"She's never late. She'll be exactly on time. That's why we all have to line up so early." He tugged his cap onto his curly hair. "Oi. Here we go."

The ensemble crescendoed to a dramatic final cadence. The drummers raised their sticks. Alika stepped forward, causing shrieks of excitement to explode throughout the crowd. He strummed an opening cadence. Gongs and drums pounded to life in a military rhythm.

Citizens lined either side of the bridge's long deck, which stretched from the mainland over to the palace. Makinde could not yet see the queen-marshal or her Companions, who would be escorting her, but a ripple of excitement advanced through the crowd as Eirene made her way across, accepting their accolades and cheers. His heart beat faster as the drums rumbled and the percussionists swayed and danced. Even Alika looked like he'd gotten into the swing of it, though Makinde could not make out the ukulele above the boom of drumming.

To his own right, Hestia Hope stood in gracious stillness as if she attended celebratory festivals every day. Sensing his gaze, she tilted her head enough to catch his eye and give him a reassuring nod. Then she looked beyond him, past James and the always-silent Razin to where Sun stood beside Prince Consort João.

Living as he now did in the princess's court, Makinde had his suspicions but no proof, and for sure he was not going to say anything about what wasn't his business. He expected Sun to feel Hetty's gaze on her and look their way, as often happened when people had a "thing" going, but Sun was staring hot-eyed at a group of dignitaries opposite, the assembled governors of the Core Houses.

There stood Hakan Bō preening in his long embroidered robe and contrasting sash. The old butthead hadn't even noticed Makinde. He'd never personally met any of the other governors, but they had faces familiar from Channel Idol's programs *Your Government at Work!* and *Minister's Portfolio*. The spry elder who led Nazir House, her hair white and her eyes as clouded as a gas giant. Vata House's rugby-playing leader draped in a magnificent ankle-length embroidered shawl. The pinch-mouthed governor of Jīn, her festival tunic gaudily decorated with replicas of coinage used in the Celestial Empire. The portly Hope

House senior whispered an aside to the tall, lean governor of Samtarras House. The infamous security chief Moira Lee stood at the edge of the group, arms crossed and expression stormy as she turned her head to angrily address an individual crowding up behind her.

Hetty canted forward enough to speak across Makinde. "James. *James*. Do you see her? Aisa Lee."

"I'll be hanged and quartered. So it is."

Makinde put his oar in. "I heard she was given indefinite internal exile at the Lee House estate. Why would she be here?"

"It could be a face-saving measure for Moira Lee," said James. "Or a favor for Consort Manea. Hard for Eirene to deny her darling anything when it's of such little importance. Maybe she wants Aisa to be reminded of her power, smack her in the face with it after the business with Kiran Seth. Eirene can be petty like that."

The drums crashed. Pipes took up a howling refrain. Alika stopped playing and stepped back, looking at his ring. Makinde checked his own network as a tremor buzzed on his right index finger.

BE ALERT Sun warned.

Shouts of acclamation washed like a wave through the citizens lining the bridge. Eirene strode into view. Every Channel Idol wasp swiveled to train its camera on her. She walked about ten paces ahead of her Companions, the battle-hardened veterans she had bound into a tight circle around her. Each carried a spear, symbol of their status as her most trusted advisors, confidantes, and personal guard.

The embroidered sleeves of Eirene's red-and-gold dress uniform shimmered. A hip-length cape fluttered from her shoulders. She wore at her side an antique sword and scabbard, a rare artifact from the Celestial Empire carried by ancient emperors. It was audacious to place herself among that august company, but the gleam of her obsidian eye reminded all present how she had thrown herself into the front line on behalf of Chaonia. How all her enemies had fallen in defeat before her.

Movement caught his eye.

A woman pushed past the governors and stormed toward the queen-marshal, shouting, "This is for Kiran!"

One moment the celebratory drums and cymbals.

The next, the woman rammed hard into the side of a surprised Eirene, as if she were trying to body-block the procession.

Sun shouted, "With me!"

The queen-marshal's knees buckled. Makinde ran after the princess, followed by Razin, James, and Hetty. The woman spun away and headed back across the bridge, dodging around Eirene's stunned Companions as they rushed toward their fallen leader. By the time Makinde got there the queen-marshal was flat on her back.

Someone cried, "Murder!"

A great roar lifted as everyone within sight began to shout and scream.

James yelled, "Sun, get back to us. There might be others."

Makinde staggered to a halt in the scrum. Razin punched his shoulder to get his attention. It was impossible to hear as emergency sirens started to blast. He looked up to see Alika shoving past on the trail of the attacker. Together he and Razin raced after Alika.

Aisa Lee had lost herself in the confused tangle of citizens swarming the deck as they tried to figure out what had happened. Makinde and Razin followed Alika easily because he'd grabbed one of the Companions' spears. Its iron point bobbed above the crowd. With ruthless elbows and kicks and by their conjoined efforts they forced a passage through until they reached the palace end of the bridge.

The palace forecourt offered benches beneath arbors for people to wait for their turn in the public audience hall. Farther along the rim of the palace island, each Core House was allowed a private pier by which ministers and honorables could reach the palace by boat from islands farther out in the bay.

There ran the perpetrator, faster than he'd expected, given her court finery. As soon as he shoved free of the crowd, Alika sprinted flat-out after her. He began to close the gap, with Makinde and Razin keeping pace behind, but even as fit and young as they were they weren't close enough. She would reach a pier and its waiting boat before they could catch her. And them without stingers, since ranged weapons were banned for the festival.

"Doze, cut her off on the Lee House pier."

He flung portmanteau'd Dozer into the water. The symbiont unfolded in a flash and sped away beneath the water.

Alarms blared as the clamor of voices and the horns of emergency vehicles rose into the heavens in an unholy confusion.

Was the queen-marshal dead?

He had no time to think. Just as he and Razin reached the Lee House pier, their quarry reached her escape boat. She'd secured it with a single loop, easy to cast off. She was going to get away.

As she braced to jump onto the boat, Dozer exploded out of the water in a flurry of spray and limbs. He wasn't heavy but his arms tangling around her ankles tripped her. She kicked Dozer away and scrambled back to her feet, but the break to her momentum allowed Alika to reach her.

As Makinde shouted, "Oi!" and Razin put on a final burst of speed, Alika stabbed down right under her ribs once, twice, and then knelt, grabbed the dagger out of her spasming hand as she tried to cut him, and slit her throat. Then he jumped to his feet and stood straddling her body like a colossus athwart the ruins it has caused, nobly browed and unrepentant.

Blood spilled in streams across the wet boards of the pier. Shocker. Shocker.

Makinde had participated in the family washings of an uncle and cousin who'd died in the wars, had prayed beside his grandfather's corpse all night, had scattered incense on the dead at funeral pyres. He'd seen death, but this scalded him, brought him up staggering and panting.

"What in the hells? Shouldn't we have taken her into custody? For trial?"

Razin signed to him: *Be prudent. Back off.*

Most people knew the Handsome Alika's Idol Faire persona as a mischievous vagabond with a heart full of wounds and yet a laugh in his eyes. When Alika looked up at Makinde, his eyes held no heart-rending wounds or softening laughter, only a harsh stare.

"She's a traitor to Chaonia. She deserved nothing more."

24

In Which the Wily Persephone Is About to Make a Brilliant Rejoinder

Only now, with Mother gone and me the sole honorable in residence at the estate, do I realize how tightly I've been wound for years. The weight of her constant drama. The expectations of my father, who it turns out was a foreign agent trying to undermine the republic. The pressure of Lee House internal politics. The demands on us children to perform in lockstep with the needs of the clan. Even the strict routine of CeDCA succeeded by the relentless training Sun expects of her household.

For the last thirty-six hours I have done nothing but sleep, eat, drink, run, dance to whatever melodies Ti and I feel like putting on, and relax poolside. Sprawled on a chaise lounge under a transparent UV awning, I bask in filtered sun and watch Ti swim laps. She's wearing a swim cap, a bikini top, and knee-length swim tights. She strokes past with an efficient crawl. Her breathing is easy, her head and spine relaxed, her arm action smooth and fluid rather than choppy and stiff like mine. Her form is definitely better than mine.

I smirk at my own joke as my gaze follows the sexy flash of her legs, but out of respect for Ti I shut down this train of thought immediately. Not only does she work for me, but over the year we've been Companion and cee-cee I've come to value her friendship as a treasure.

The heat nuzzles my face. My eyelids droop as I imagine wandering the paths of the Pleasure Garden with its fragrant wisteria maze and tunnels of golden chain where I might stumble upon an attractive and welcoming gardener stripped to the waist under the hot, hot sun. But when I turn a corner I find Zizou staring right at me as the neural patterns in his skin flare with a blinding light and he lunges to fasten his hands around my throat . . .

Water splashes me in the face. Spluttering, I sit up. Ti floats at the pool's edge, arms propped up on the tiled deck. She's got that Vogue-Academy-is-judging-you look.

"What?" I demand, rubbing water out of my eyes and Zizou's memory out of my heart. I'll never see him again, not if Prince João's scientists can't scrub the engineered hallucination out of his brain that impels him to attack me or any other clone of Nona Lee.

"I know that young gardener is attractive but they are an employee of Lee House. I would be remiss in my duty as your cee-cee if I did not point out that sexual relations between people of unequal station— especially when one works for the family of the other—are unethical. And also gross."

So much for relaxing. "I am not having sex with them!"

"But you're thinking about it. And they're dazzled by you. You must not encourage it to go any farther."

"If you must know, I was trying to think about the gardener but my mind threw Zizou in my face instead. Or at my throat, anyway." I draw my knees up to my chest and wrap my arms around them. A tingle of old pain nooses my throat, my flesh's physical remembrance of his hands wrapping my neck.

Ti has a way of looking at me that mingles amusement spiced with a tincture of aggravation. "Why do I feel sure him trying to choke you to death is part of his allure?"

I'm about to make a brilliant rejoinder when our rings buzz.

RETURN TO THE PALACE

Ti and I exchange a look. We both blink through into Channel Idol, which is streaming celebratory scenes from street-side Argos.

Ti says, "Look at the food stalls in the background. See the white-bait? That's not available this time of year. They're recycling old footage."

"Shit. You're right." I ping Hetty, figuring Sun is too busy. INFO?

Hetty doesn't answer. Neither do James, Alika, Razin, or the new boy, Makinde.

Fuck.

The ring vibrates again. COLLECT JADE AT THESE COORDINATES.

Silence to my next barrage of inquiries.

A gust of wind scallops waves across the pool. A feathery tendril of golden chain swirls out of the garden and lands on my thigh, curled into a diadem like an omen, but an omen for what I couldn't say. Not that I believe in omens.

"This is bad, isn't it?" Ti asks. "What about Solomon? He has a ring."

I ping him but get nothing. "He's probably out-system on his way to Aspera. No one in Argos is answering."

The ring buzzes with a personal message from Jade Kim.

I WILL BE READY FOR PICKUP IN 38 MINUTES. DON'T DELAY.

"Fuck you," I mutter as I jump to my feet.

Ti drips out of the pool and grabs a towel. With a piercing whistle she grabs the attention of the house staff, who hustle because she makes allies. In twenty-three minutes we and our duffels embark on the estate's secondary aircar, a grumpy old Shearwater. The rest of our gear will be sent after. My hair is still wet. Moisture dampens my uniform collar.

"Peace be upon you, welcome, and please be seated, no, not there, in the other seat, thank you, I have weight distribution restrictions because of faulty stabilizers." The aircar's voice has ground down over its years of service into a resigned drawl.

I blink in the coordinates.

Lights shimmer on the control bank. A noise clicks like the tsk-tsk of a disappointed auntie.

"This aircar has never set down in a district like *that,* I am sure. Are you certain these coordinates are correct, Honored Persephone?"

As much as I would like to leave Jade Kim high and dry, I have to answer. "I'm sure. Thank you for your service."

The ramp groans up.

Ti mouths, silently, *Is this ship for real?*

"Old retainer," I say aloud. I'm not worried about hurting the ship's feelings because they don't have any, only a sheen of personality that reflects the character of the people who have spent the most time inside them.

"Now that I think about it," I say to Ti as we bank upward, headed toward our cruising altitude, "this aircar would have been new before my mother was born. So it was probably mostly in service to the notorious Eileithiyia Lee."

"Why notorious?"

"Lee House used to hold the portfolio of the Ministry of Agriculture. Eileithiyia wrested the Ministry of Security, Punishment, and Corrections out of the hands of Nazir House and forced them to take Agriculture."

"Agriculture is the most important ministry of all!"

"Says the granddaughter of kalo farmers. Eileithiyia wanted power."

"She was your grandmother?"

"No. Second cousin to my grandfather. When she was mortally wounded in battle he ripped the power from her branch of the family. That was about seventy years ago. It's how his daughters came to be the governors, Nona first and now Moira."

"Cutthroat!"

"You asked for this."

She shakes her head. We both know why she took the job as Companion's companion, with all the dangers and benefits it entails. Times like now, when she's not dressing for public appearances, she wears a locket, a gift from her parents, to remind her of her younger brother, the boy they are all protecting.

I ping Sun's ring network again. Silence. Channel Idol plays festival music alongside sweeping scenes of flying banners, a joyous parade, and soldiers marching in formation at planet-side training camps intercut with proud spacers queueing to board ships docked to orbital stations. Our ETA is fifty-three minutes.

Ti pulls a box out of her duffel. "Draughts, mah-jongg, Go, Ayò, or wayfinder?"

"Let's go over Isis's training protocol again," I say.

I'm a pragmatic person, not a dreamer, not an idealist, not a spiritualist who believes the universe breathes and we breathe with it. Even the whispers I hear during a beacon drop are surely just an artifact of the system. But my gut tells me we're on the edge of a precipice.

25

You Have to Do What It Takes and Not Flinch

The orderly scene on the plaza had collapsed into absolute chaos: shoving, hollering, alarms, whistles as gendarmes struggled to impose control on the frantic crowd, most of whom could not see what had happened. Not knowing made the panic worse.

James and Hetty stuck next to Sun like burrs. She shouted to be heard over the commotion. "Hetty, go to the chamberlain's office. Make sure all communication gets routed through Nisaba before it goes to any marshal or governor."

Hetty's diplomat father had come up through the chamberlain's service so she knew the office well. She left at a run.

"James, go to FSC. I'll be there in person as soon as I assess the situation here."

He gave his cap a tug and raced after Hetty.

Spatharioi formed a tight circle around the fallen queen-marshal. As Sun pushed up to their ranks, she saw her father try to squeeze past in the company of a palace medic, but the palace guards turned him back after letting the medic through.

"Make way!" she commanded as she came up to the line.

They did not break ranks. Commendable discipline but not to be tolerated. Any sign of hesitation in taking orders from her damaged her position. She identified a captain bearing the facial jewels of a Larissan but wearing a Chaonian red-and-gold dress uniform with a palace sunburst sewn to her tunic.

"Captain, let me through."

"My orders . . ." The officer faltered. The minute twitches in her expression revealed the officer calculating the situation and her place in it: if the queen-marshal survived versus if the queen-marshal was already dead and a battle for power erupted. She broke the circle to open a way in. "Yes, Your Highness."

"Prince João will accompany me. As senior consort present, he has the right and the duty to escort the queen-marshal to the medical pavilion."

"Yes, Your Highness."

"Your name?"

"Captain Qulan Yeh."

"Go after the Honorable Alika Vata. If there is a murder weapon, collect it in a sterile container and report to my secretary."

The captain's eyes widened as she realized she had just altered the trajectory of her career. "Yes, Your Highness."

Sun slipped through the gap in the security chain.

Her father grasped at her arm as he followed her. "I want you to take Colonel Evans as bodyguard. You're in danger as long as the situation is fluid."

"I am aware, which is why we must move quickly. My Companions will prove their worth. Colonel Evans stays with you."

Eirene's Companions had formed up around the bloodied body, which lay utterly still in a puddle of cape splashed onto the deck of the bridge. Norioghene Hope knelt beside Eirene, flanked by two palace medics. Amid the storm and chaos the rest of the queen-marshal's Companions stood with the staggered expressions of people who know they have failed.

She pinged Alika. His reply lit her ring network. DEAD. I HAVE A KNIFE.

STAY WITH THE BODY. GIVE KNIFE TO CAPTAIN QULAN YEH.
RAZIN. MAKINDE. TO ME.

"Incoming. Incoming."

In a deafening clutter that drowned out the crowd's noise, the palace medevac descended, an armored Hummingbird emblazoned with the sunburst. The Companions made room as a physician barked out orders. All the medical personnel wore masks and gloves as they got the queen-marshal onto a gurney and rolled her into a lifepod in the medevac. The lights on the lifepod immediately blinked code red.

The physician looked up at Precious Jin and spoke two words. Sun couldn't hear over the sirens and the frantic tempest of voices all hammering at once, but she could read the physician's lips because she had not forgotten how her bodyguard Octavian had died or who had killed him.

Late bloomer.

A stab wound, even to the heart, ought to be survivable at the speed and delivery of Chaonia's most advanced battlefield medicine. But a knife contaminated with a dark tech that infects and pulverizes the lungs and heart would kill in minutes with no chance of revival.

Precious signaled to the other Companions to wait for the next vehicle while she and the physician got on the medevac. As the aircar took off, wailing sirens announced the arrival of palace carriages approaching across the bridge.

City gendarmes had begun herding the crowds off the bridge and out of the plaza. The chaotic seething frenzy of frightened people began slowly to congeal into the vaunted discipline Eirene had built as the watchword of the republic. People keened and wept, and held on to each other, but they formed lines for an orderly withdrawal. The wasps that should have been hovering to record Eirene's triumphant celebration had all been killed by an electronic burst, fallen to the ground in a metallic hail now crunching beneath people's feet.

Eirene was dead. The savior of Chaonia was *dead*.

Sun had never known any world except that ruled by her mother. No queen-marshal could possibly follow Eirene, and yet one must. She checked Channel Idol to find a montage of festival scenes proceeding as if nothing had happened.

Everything had happened. In one moment, her life had been sliced in two. Who she was before, and who she would become as long as she did not hesitate.

She needed all her Companions, so she pinged Perse and Jade and did a quick check of their ETA. So much to accomplish. No time to waste.

Three carriages rolled up: eight-seaters, each with an attendant at the controls. The governors pushed forward like fans at an Alika concert, clamoring for a seat, while the Companions demanded the first carriage as their right as Eirene's intimates.

Eight spatharioi got in her way. "Your Highness, Captain Yeh ordered us to shadow you."

"Very good. Hold a perimeter at eight meters back."

She worked her way over to Marduk Lee. Just as he was about to step into a carriage, she tapped his arm. He swung around into a defensive stance, then gritted his teeth and straightened.

"Don't surprise me like that."

"Come with me." She tipped her chin toward the third carriage, where his cousin Moira Lee had found a seat with the other governors. His eyes narrowed as he looked toward Moira. Good.

He gestured to the other Companions that they should go on, but the carriage he watched go was not the one with the Companions or the one with the governors, but the one that conveyed the two consorts. Her father appeared shaken but calm. Collapsed across three seats lay a sobbing Manea Lee being comforted by a palace chamberlain while a nurse held the baby.

Sun headed out at a jog, Marduk matching her pace as they wove in and out through the surging confusion of the crowd.

She said, "Did Moira ever tell you who murdered Octavian?"

"A strange thing to ask me at this catastrophic moment, but I'll bite.

I didn't realize he'd been murdered. I thought he died in the battle of Molossia. He didn't?"

"He was murdered by a late bloomer."

"A late bloomer! Who had a late bloomer? How did Aisa Lee get one, that's what I want to know!"

"Octavian was shot with a late bloomer by Kiran when my Companions and I fled the wedding banquet at Lee House last year."

"Bloody hells," he muttered. "Why would he shoot Octavian?"

"He was trying to kill me."

"Ah."

"I guess Moira never told you."

"I'm in the palace. She's governor of Lee House. She does as she wishes." The tightness of his mouth changed, complicating the tremors of despair and shame that chased across his face. Was he resentful? Angry? Or just impatient for Sun to get to the point when he had failed to protect his queen-marshal and would have to remember the disgrace and dishonor of her death for the rest of his life?

They jogged the next twenty meters in silence, the spatharioi carefully keeping their distance. Clusters of citizens streamed past in the opposite direction, crying or talking or stumbling in shocked muteness as they struggled to process the terrible event. No one glanced at Sun or Marduk, who wore the same fleet uniforms of any Core House officer, as Eirene always had.

As Sun and Marduk pounded down the ramp of the bridge onto the plaza that fronted the palace, Razin and Makinde appeared, running toward her. Beyond them Alika stood by a boat on one of the piers, surrounded by more spatharioi. She signed her Companions to lag behind with the guards as she and Marduk started up the processional stairs. Spatharioi swarmed everywhere, forming a cordon of control. The lack of wasps was eerie, but it also meant no one could overhear, not out in the open like this.

She said, "I need governors I can trust."

Marduk shot her a glance. "Be plain."

"Moira Lee was rude to my father. She insulted my lineage. And she's made two plays for the future of the throne. I don't trust her. But Lee House needs a governor. So where does that leave me with regard to Lee House?"

"You tell me."

They reached the grand portico. He halted, crossing his arms. His eyes were already shadowed, exhausted, haunted.

"Moira doesn't trust you either," Sun added, "or she'd have told you the truth about Octavian and Kiran. I'm surprised Eirene didn't tell you."

He looked toward the entrance into the public audience hall, with its eight-tiered lintel and sunburst reliefs. "Those two go back a long way."

Everyone knew he was Eirene's second choice to be her Companion from Lee House, that she'd only taken him when Moira had been forced to leave the palace.

"Didn't anyone in Lee House argue that Aisa could be a threat? That at the very least she covered for Kiran by telling people he was confined to his rooms when he was actually out on the walls shooting at me? No one suggested she should be locked away instead of carted off to a luxurious exile like a disobedient child?"

"We didn't know, for one. And who would ever think of Aisa as a threat? She's like an overgrown and less endearing toddler stamping around in a tantrum when she can't get her way. She never accomplished a thing in her life. Well, not until today."

He winced, rubbing at his eyes. When Sun said nothing, he went on.

"I don't know a single person in Lee House who wasn't shocked when Kiran fled. He wasn't warm or likable, but he did his job effectively, and he was the only one who could keep her under control. She was obsessed with her belief he was in love with her. Anyway, after he ran, Aisa looked like nothing more than Kiran's dupe. Exile was punishment enough. We should have been told she was a potential hotspot. Everything would be different if we'd known." Bitterness flooded his tone. He blamed himself, but he also wanted someone else to blame.

"You understand my situation. If Moira remains governor of Lee House, then I can't trust Lee House and I can't trust the Ministry of Security, Protection, and Punishment."

She spoke the words evenly, not threateningly. Even so he took a step back, lowering his hands to hover close to the ceremonial sword Companions wore on formal occasions. A long look gave him the lay of the ground: Razin and Makinde standing on alert ten paces away, spatharioi another ten beyond them with more guards surrounding the palace complex, the plaza and bridge emptied of people by the gendarmes. A tumultuous noise rising out of Argos as the news spread in the oldest manner known to humankind: mouth-to-mouth and face-to-face.

"Why are you telling me this, Sun?"

But he knew. She could see it in the avaricious glint of his gaze. She answered the rhetorical question anyway. It was part of the ritual of succession.

"Persephone Lee has been taken out of the running because she is one of my Companions. If Moira were gone, that means the governorship of Lee House would pass to a different cousin branch. Your branch, perhaps."

"You're offering the governorship to me. On what conditions?"

"You understand on what conditions, Honored Marduk."

He clipped his chin down to examine, for two breaths, the pavement beneath his feet. Its molded sunbursts echoed those carved onto the lintels and friezes, the radiance of Chaonia above and below, their great heritage and proud tradition of independence and strength. You have to do what it takes and not flinch.

He puffed out a brusque exhalation between his lips, then lifted his dark gaze to hers. "I have a condition of my own."

"Do you?" She was glad of it. Octavian had taught her that people who gave way to ambition too easily were prone to sloppiness.

"After the period of mourning, I want Manea returned to Lee House, under my wing, alive and well."

"Manea?"

"Don't act naïve, Sun. João is the most ruthless person I know."

"I'd have said my mother is more ruthless, but I take your point. I'm asking why you want her."

"Would it surprise you to hear I am fond of my niece? She's a delightful, warm, and compassionate young woman."

"That's true." Sun had wanted to dislike Manea for the insult the marriage had given to her father, and to herself, but it was difficult to dislike a person who was an unfailingly good listener.

"Unlike her cousins Ereshkigal and Persephone, Manea did not scorn my boys and the other Lee cousins as not worthy of their august attention. She showed kindness to everyone. I had nothing to do with Moira pushing her at Eirene. But I'm not surprised Eirene fell in love with her."

"Do you think Manea genuinely loves my mother?"

"You saw them together. What do you think?" When Sun did not answer he went on. "She wouldn't be the first innocent, gentle soul to become infatuated with an older person whose power and status gives them an irresistible radiance."

"It's difficult for me to think of anyone raised in Lee House as innocent or gentle."

"Manea has no Shān blood. Of herself, she can't be in line for the throne and is therefore no threat to you." He scrubbed at his eyes, wiping away tears. "You have the capacity to become a fit queen-marshal if you're not dead within a month. But I have my price for support, and that's it."

It was less than she had been ready to accept. "Very well. On the honor of my ancestors, I pledge this, as long as we both fulfill our part."

"On the honor of my ancestors."

She nodded.

He paused for so long she thought he was about to speak again, but his shoulders heaved with a tremor of grief and he strode away into the palace.

Razin and Makinde ran up at once.

"You two are my bodyguards for the rest of today. Use that squad of spatharioi as backup, but keep an eye on them, too, until we're sure of their loyalty."

Razin nodded, waiting for further orders.

"Is the queen-marshal dead?" Makinde asked in the blurt-it-all-out way he had.

"Yes."

"What do we do?" Makinde was so cursedly young that for an instant Sun doubted the wisdom of taking him on. Then she recalled the outraged look on Hakan Bō's face, and that alone was worth it. Keep them off-balance. Don't hesitate. *Move.*

"We take charge. First of all we're going to Fleet Strategic Command."

26

Not That the Wily Persephone Would Know Anything About That

Ti and I have reviewed parts one and two of the protocol by the time the aircar begins a steep descent. The view from the window reveals a mining zone established over a thousand years ago, back when beleaguered colonists weren't particular about how they got what they wanted. Barren slag heaps and oily lakes paint the hilly landscape in eerie colors. Reclamation and remediation work pushes into the strip-mined region, native scrub forest rewilding in the outer rings, and elsewhere hardy sego lily for feed and switchgrass for biofuel.

We pass over a rail line and drop to the military airfield at the edge of industrial district Karmanion. It's no longer gushing pollutants without restriction but it's no picnic either, a huge diseased rectangle of grim residential towers, factory blocks, and klick after klick of ore-processing plants. No one lives here except people who have no other choice of work or who were sent here by one of the ministries to serve out a debt claim. Dust spatters the aircar's viewing window as we land a short distance from a metal-gray terminal. The Shearwater's air-quality warning light pips twice and slides from green to yellow.

"Zut alors!" says Ti. "I thought Tjeker was down-ticket."

"I wouldn't admit to being from here, that's for sure," I remark as I unbuckle.

I saunter to the top of the ramp in my clean uniform and observe with all the glee of Team Petty as Jade Kim walks from the terminal across a pitted tarmac through the dust-laden wind to reach us. Their pristine pressed uniform is streaked with red dust and black soot by the time Jade climbs the ramp. I stand there, secure in knowing Jade knows I know: why they left off their third name, the usual al-location designation required for citizens but not for honorables. We thought it was an excess of social-climbing rigor, clinging to the cliff's edge of having once been a recognized branch line of Jīn House. But what if it was just embarrassment?

A smear of dirt smudges Jade's nose but unfortunately does nothing to damage those sultry looks. At the academy Jade outranked me by having a higher cohort ranking. However, among the Companions, I've been around a full year, while Jade is not only new but was lifted out of their branch line's disgrace to an unexpected honor.

"Does your family still live here?" I ask. "Did Jīn House refuse to accommodate them to a new domicile even though Sun elevated you—"

"Fuck off, asshole," says Jade, striding past me into the interior.

The Shearwater says, "Peace be upon you, welcome, and please be seated in the left forward seat. Don't touch the dials. While your identification matrix indicates you possess a superior pilot's qualification, I do not allow manual piloting except by qualified Lee House scions. We depart in forty-five seconds. Please buckle up."

I scramble to my seat while the ramp groans as it closes.

"Peace be upon you, Honored Jade," says Tiana in her politest Vogue tone, clipped and tidy.

"Peace be upon you, Citizen Tiana."

Jade removes a paper book from their duffel before stowing it, and straps in. The aircar rises steeply. The industrial wasteland and its staggering grimness recede from view. Jade ostentatiously opens the book so as to display its title: *Statutes and Regulations for Nautical Traffic, Beacon Passage, and Planetary Transit.* What a swot.

The moment we reach cruising altitude and without looking up from the page, Jade says, "Tiana, I'd like a ginger beer."

"That's a fascinating thing to know, Honored Jade," Ti says as if with honey melting off her tongue. "But I'm not your cee-cee to serve you."

Jade's gaze flashes up. Anger? Respect? A test? I have no idea.

"Oh, that's right." I tag team. "You don't have a cee-cee. Hasn't Jīn House hired one for you? Or are they still arguing about your status?"

To my surprise Jade smiles as if I've made a misstep, and I admit it wouldn't be the first time. Instead of a cutting retort, they go back to reading. The alluring shape of those striking features distracts me: pale pink lips, a straight nose, a strong chin, and bold eyebrows. Jade has added fashionable chrome-red streaks to the military cut of their black hair, a privilege of Companions. The color brings into relief a shimmering gold eyeliner meant to set off the rich glamour of brown eyes that more than one haplessly love-struck cadet drowned in, prior to choking to death on the realization that Jade Kim measures every interaction as part of the stairstep up the ladder of promotion. Not that I would know anything about that.

Ti pings through the protocol rubric to remind me we haven't finished. When I look her way, she gives a curt shake of her head as if to say *Get a grip.*

Because I'm an asshole, I ask, "Ti, could you get me a ginger beer?"

Jade doesn't even look up as Ti goes along with my petty status signaling and hands me a soothing beverage. Once again I trawl through Channel Idol and the wider net, but the whole thing is weirdly bland, as if a shallow fake got dropped into place. I've got a bad feeling about this.

She Alone of All Chaonia

To enter Fleet Strategic Command one had to have the highest level of military clearance. Sun's retinal and blood trace unlocked the emergency stairs. She raced down with Razin and Makinde behind. They reached the heavily guarded underground foyer at the same time as Marshal Zàofù, who had descended via elevator. James was already there, of course. He waylaid his father to give Sun the extra seconds she needed to reach the entry barrier first and place both hands on the security wall and its retina scan. A pinprick stabbed her left little finger for a DNA sample.

She said, aloud, for the voice match, "Sun Shān of Shān House. Heir to—"

Broke off.

A flush of heat burned through her. Her ears got hot, and her chest grew tight as if all the air in her lungs were being compressed into an impermeable layer whose armor could not be breached. Marshals, officers, and spatharioi all turned to look first at her and then at Zàofù, Eirene's most senior marshal, veteran of thirty years of war. He crossed the foyer and held out the command tiara that only the queen-marshal wore. He must have taken it off Eirene's head himself. No one else would have dared. It was delicate-looking, three wires woven into a glittering lacework headband, and for such a powerful tool it weighed barely anything as she took it from him and set it on her own head.

Pressing both hands to the barrier, she spoke again. "Sun Shān of Shān House. Queen-Marshal of the Republic of Chaonia."

The rule of succession had always been simple: a queen-marshal must be battle trained, battle worthy, and ready to lead. The program sought out Eirene, whose rule was being challenged by Sun's request. A flood of information coursed through Sun's network as a pathway leading to the medical unit.

Confirmed: Deceased.

Trigger succession.

Her vision went white and for at least one minute or ten minutes—hard to keep track when her entire world was being rearranged—she stood vulnerable except for James, Razin, and Makinde. A fierce reconstruction hammered through her military codes as it built a temporary scaffolding and shield for the expansion of her access to the full capacity necessary for the queen-marshal.

The program released her. The blast of blinding light faded to wiggles and spots in her field of view. Sweat soaked her armpits. Until this moment she hadn't been sure her mother trusted her enough to allow the succession to proceed.

The barrier opened to her touch, she alone of all Chaonia able to open any door, any airlock, any shield. She entered the pulsing nerve center of Chaonia's military. Everyone in the great humming cavern looked to see if it was Eirene. *Dead* weighed in her mind, too heavy to shift. No time to pause.

She walked to the central strategos table.

"Lock down all outgoing beacon traffic until we've secured comms."

"Done, Your Highness," said the senior comms officer on duty, voice hoarse.

She addressed the cameras she knew were everywhere. "Let my words be recorded and sent by courier to the fleets. I am Sun, daughter of Eirene. Honorables and citizens, my eight-times-worthy mother and your most faithful and fierce queen-marshal, the savior of Chaonia, is dead. Eirene is dead. With the acclamation of the fleets and the consent of the assembly, I take command as queen-marshal of the Republic of Chaonia according to the decree and desire of my predecessor."

An hour later she and her Companions convened in her compound. Captain Yeh waited in Nisaba's office. She rose from a bench as Sun entered.

"Where is the knife?" Sun asked the high secretary.

"Colonel Isis took it to forensics."

"And my mother?"

"Her body has been removed from medical and placed on a temporary bier in the queen-marshal's private audience hall. Afterward it will be moved to Victory Hall."

The words fell like a rainstorm on ocean's horizon: seen but not felt. *Her body.*

Keep moving. "Take charge of my mother's comms team immediately. I want them under your wing and all their connections vetted by James. The ones you and James clear will form the nucleus of a new palace comms bureau."

"Already in progress, Your Highness."

Sun addressed Captain Yeh. "You may return to your post in the spatharioi. If you prefer, you may receive a new assignment, in my headquarters or elsewhere."

"Your Highness! I request reassignment to my original division."

Sun gave Yeh a sharp, approving look. People who could think on their feet were invaluable. The tiny jewels embedded along the line of Yeh's jaw revealed the captain as a native of Larissa System, a territory lying on the route between Chaonia and Yele which, as an important strategic asset, Eirene had assimilated early in her reign.

"You come from one of the Centaur Divisions?"

"I do, Your Highness. I had command of a heavy frigate."

"Did you request this ceremonial position at the palace?"

"I did not, Your Highness."

"Had you trouble with your ship?"

"I did not, Your Highness. My ship met all its requirements with top ratings. We fought with honor in the battle of Molossia."

"Then why were you kicked upstairs to the spatharioi?"

For the first time the captain hesitated, as a junior command-line officer must always do when dealing with chain of command issues.

"I need an answer."

Yeh spoke with reluctance. "Internal politics, Your Highness. I came up from the citizen ranks, not the elite core."

"If this checks out, I'll send you back to your ship. If you prove your competence, I'll put you in command of a squadron."

"Your Highness! The honor is mine!"

"Nisaba, have the household ready to proceed to the audience hall in thirty minutes. I will need complete privacy while I consult with my father."

"Yes, Your Highness."

Sun left the secretary's office and strode across the courtyard. Hetty waited under the gazebo's shade, still in her red-and-gold ceremonial uniform. She cast Sun an interrogatory look—*Do you want me to come with you?*—to which Sun shook her head and kept going.

Each consort had their own compound, rooms set around a private courtyard within the consorts' quarter of the palace. As the adult child of a consort, Sun had her own compound connected to her father's. Since he had been absent from the palace for almost a year, the gilded gate linking the two suites hadn't yet been unlocked, as it was when they were both in residence. Just hours ago she would have had to make a request and wait for permission from Colonel Evans to clear. Now she need only speak her name, press a hand against the sensor, and let it read her retina. The lock chunked decisively. She stepped through to let it close behind her and, as a courtesy, pinged her father and waited in the access alleyway.

Within moments Colonel Evans trotted into view, a battle-scarred banner soldier of unflappable demeanor. "Your Highness. The prince is expecting you."

"It seems you had a productive voyage with my father aboard the *Keoe*," Sun said as she accompanied the colonel, whom she'd known for years.

"Your Highness, we among the banners will not forget how you helped make it possible to free our chained and leashed brethren. Please allow me to offer my deepest condolences. We are all shocked by the sudden nature of this event."

Dead. How could her mother, the towering colossus, be dead? The word was too large. The impact too severe. Most importantly, if she did not take charge, then someone else would.

She heard voices. Who was her father talking to?

Colonel Evans led her across the main courtyard where a banner soldier stood guard and through an arcade to the intimate garden where João entertained the few friends he had ever made in the palace. The colonel halted by the last pillar of the arcade, leaving Sun to thread her way on a narrow path that zigzagged through a thick ring of rustling bamboo. Impossible to sneak up in this dense vegetation.

Zizou stood like a statue at the last turning, where the path opened onto an oval patio. He tapped his chest, acknowledging her presence. Had he been here all along, against her mother's express command? It was the sort of thing her father reveled in doing. Well, it scarcely mattered now.

"—and I did not have a chance to get to know her for myself—"

She emerged into a jewel-like scene. An awning strung tight to shield a rose-colored divan from the sun's glare. Glasses set on a transparent oval that covered an unlit fire pit. Prince João somehow already in white mourning garb, speaking intently to a shaken, tear-stained Soaring. Who was, Sun noted, also wearing white. They looked comfortable together, her father holding one of Soaring's hands between his own and nodding as she spoke in a ragged murmur. Sun lost track of the words as a strange disconnection wrenched through her.

It had always been just her and her father, she the focus of his attention. Yet here he was bending his shrewd gaze on another as if Soaring had been beside him all along and dressed exactly in the manner he would have wished.

He glanced up at her, not rising. Soaring saw her too and she got to her feet as Sun hastened over.

He said, "You should be in mourning garb. What will people think?"

Soaring said, "Father, has she not had the entire republic in her hands? Surely it was more important she saw to the security of Chaonia before taking the time to change her clothes."

She was already calling him *Father*?

Soaring caught Sun's eye and gave her a nod. "But let me go and leave you two to discuss matters of state, to which I cannot be privy. Nor would I wish to be. I'll ask one of your factotums to lay out appropriate garb so it will be ready for you later."

She paused long enough to give João a warning look as if they already understood each other well enough to be on such a footing. Then she turned to Sun and offered the gesture of trust, palm-to-palm. "We belong to the heavens, and to the heavens we return."

Her sad smile was meant to reassure. In the silence after she left, Sun heard her exchange words with Zizou, then the rustling of bamboo as she worked her way out of the courtyard.

"Sit. My neck hurts from staring up at you." Her father's peevish tone meant he knew Soaring was right but wouldn't admit it.

She sat, snagged the third glass, and downed its contents in one slug. The alcohol hit in a heady rush that, a few breaths later, steadied her galloping mind.

"*Have* you taken the reins?" he demanded.

She gave him a scathing look that made him chuckle.

He added, "As I said earlier, I'll attach Zizou to you."

"As I said earlier, I can't take him. He'll try to kill Persephone."

"Replace her with a better Lee House Companion."

"No."

"Her mother murdered your mother. That doesn't bother you?"

"She's not her mother."

"Her father is a foreign agent inserted into the highest levels of Chaonian society, who tried to murder you, murdered Octavian, and instigated Eirene's assassination."

"The latter is likely but not proven. Kiran fled a year ago. Why wait so long to act?"

"Maybe it took this long to get the message to Aisa?"

"Moira controls Aisa's comms."

"Maybe Moira was in on it. Manea has a healthy child. You need to look to your own security. I'm telling you, Sun. The seers won't stop trying to kill you. And they won't be the only ones. Persephone Lee is a plant."

"I am not going to talk about her any more with you, Father, with all respect. I came to tell you I took command of FSC and the chamberlain's office. As you see, I wear the command tiara. Except for the formal acclamation of the fleet and the assembly, I am queen-marshal."

He raised his glass in toast and took a long swallow. The gesture settled a restless churning in her heart. Her mother was dead. This moment was what her father had prepared her for. His life, meeting its stated goal. His child on the throne, with all that meant to Chaonia and to him.

Setting down the glass, he said, "You need to marry as soon as possible."

She stiffened. "I don't have time. I'm leaving for Molossia in three days to commence the countdown to the Karnos Campaign."

"What about the proper funeral rites and ceremonies?"

"Hetty is sorting out the palace communications division. Channel Idol will agree to have this year's Idol Faire dedicated to Eirene's memory. I'll request the competition's launch ceremony be moved up to coincide with my departure."

"Before you rush off into battle you need an heir, Sun."

"Ah. Funny how I so well remember what we were taught about Chaonia's turbulent history. Every new queen-marshal sat and waited for nine months before showing their mettle on the battlefield."

With a flick of his fingers he brought up a holographic map of the Republic of Chaonia from the tabletop. Each system was labeled according to its resources and population. The beacon routes were traced with silver lines like rail tracks. He tapped Pelasgia System and opened it up to display its terminus beacon, single habitable moon, resource-heavy asteroid belt, and a dwarf star.

"Your cousin Jiàn is a capable young man."

"Really? I've only met him twice, when we were children. Are you visiting him in secret, Father?"

"What sort of father would I be if I didn't keep my eye on threats to my child? One way to neutralize him would be for you to marry him."

"Now is not the time," she said stiffly.

"Now was not the time for Eirene to die, and yet, here we are."

He wiped the virtual map from the air, replacing it with an ancestral family tree of the Shān lineage. Eirene, her three brothers who had each been queen-marshal until each was killed in battle, their father, their father's sister, and then her great-grandmother Metis and great-great-grandfather Yǔ of blessed memory, and so on into the distant history of the republic. Tapping the icon for Sun, he drew a bloom of light around her, around her cousin Jiàn, and after that around three other individuals.

"Soaring hasn't the support to challenge you, but you might offer her as consort to someone whose support you need."

Sun crossed her arms. "She's more useful to me as a Navigator. And I'd never force her to marry."

"You say that now, but you'll come to understand the usefulness of diplomatic alliances." He flicked away Soaring's image and enlarged that of the mysterious prisoner. "Moira Lee's child by Nézhā—"

"Metis."

"—hidden beneath Lee House for twenty-five years because unfit to rule."

Another swipe closed the hazy form. He opened a recent Channel Idol 3-D image of the infant princess, the dumpling of Chaonia, as she was popularly called. "And then, of course, we have Inanna. Look at that sweet, darling face. Wholly Chaonian, as Moira reminds everyone at every opportunity."

He leaned back on the divan, crossing his legs, his gaze on the baby's image like the lick of flame across oil waiting to explode.

Sun said, "Leave Manea alone."

He closed his hand into a fist to close the map and looked at her with his flintiest stare. "What could you possibly mean by that?"

"I can't leave you as regent in my absence because you aren't Chaonian, so I'm appointing Marduk Lee."

"Marduk?"

"Is there a different person you have in mind? Who you'd trust more?"

"In what capacity will Marduk be able to act as regent? He's not even senior-most of Eirene's Companions."

"As governor of Lee House."

How rare it was to render her father speechless. She savored the moment as his gaze drifted from her face to follow the twists of the knot-work tile of the pavement, a two-dimensional replica of the four-dimensional maze of Lady Chaos, she who bore them all in the primordial ocean of creation. Perhaps he was tracing the convoluted set of decisions and agreements that would have brought Sun to make this statement.

He looked up with a disconcertingly bland expression. "Very well."

"That's not like you, Father. You hate Manea."

"No one hates Consort the Honorable Manea Lee. She is a delightful and guileless confection, as amiable as she is pliable."

"I'm serious. I made a deal with Marduk. You understand me."

"I do."

"Manea will need to remain in the palace for the thirty days of mourning, as will you. Marduk's support is crucial."

"He's not the one whose support you need. Look to Zàofù."

"I'll make certain of his support. For that, we need to go to the audience hall and pay our respects to my mother."

He rose languidly. "Whether following Kiran's bidding or her own twisted grudge, Aisa Lee did us a great service."

What a thing to say, and yet he was exactly the person to say it.

"You're an adult, Sun. You've proven yourself three times over. The truth is, sooner rather than later Eirene would have decided you were a threat. Mark my words, she would have taken action to rid herself of you. We'll never know if she was behind Kiran's attempt on your life, will we?"

"You can't possibly think . . ." She trailed off, remembering how her mother had threatened her at the wedding banquet.

"She kept Jiàn alive all this time. Eirene never takes—*took*—any action from sentiment. But that's water under the bridge. You're queen-marshal. Don't let them take it away from you."

"Do you think I will?"

"Not the child I raised."

A Queasy Nausea Stirs in the Wily Persephone's Chest

We reach Argos on the sea. The city extends north and south along the coast. Tendrils of sprawl snake inland through river valleys to the interior plains. The windows go dark, cutting off our view as we spiral down to land at the palace.

As soon as the landing chime rings I grab my duffel and get down the ramp before Jade. As expected, the aircar has set down on the restricted airstrip that serves the palace's residential wing. But it isn't Sun or any of my fellow Companions who greet me at the arrivals pavilion. It's my aunt Moira, looking as shattered as if she's been punctured and hollowed out. Two Lee House security flank her but they slump like defeated soldiers.

She totters forward as if to find support in my arms. "Persephone! Thank the holy heavens you're finally here."

I step out of reach. "What happened?"

"They won't let me in. They've barred me from the palace. You have to find Manea. Get her and the baby out of there before that monster murders them too!"

My cousin Manea? Her baby? What monster? *Murder?*

Jade strides past, headed for the gate to the residential wing. There are spatharioi everywhere, far more than usual. I suddenly realize Jade has known all along what happened. I'm the one not smart enough to figure out how to get around the network block. When Jade reaches the gate, the spatharioi direct them to the corridor that leads to the queen-marshal's residence.

"What happened?" I demand of my aunt.

"Your mother . . . stabbed . . . she just lunged . . . I couldn't stop her . . ." Moira shrieks like her heart is being torn from her chest. "My dearest Eirene!"

She breaks into racking sobs.

Realization sparks through my flesh like electrical current. I stagger, catch myself on Ti's arm. Holy fucks. Is Eirene *dead*? Did my mother kill her?

From the other side of the open gate Jade casts a knowing look my way. That smile is as mean as a bag of venomous centipedes. Then Jade walks on, out of sight. For ten breaths I'm too stunned to move. As I stand there, my mind reeling through my final conversation with my mother, the buzz of an aircar nears. A shiny Swallow-class lands as

gently as
security pil

I leap back
to her. "Find Su

Ti grabs my w

Like a swarm of
chin up, and swallow
people she knows, peop
queasy nausea stirs in my

Their captain speaks. "B
you, Moira Lee, must surrend
of complicity with the murder
accomplice, Aisa Lee."

Tiana presses a hand against my
whispers.

I cannot shift my feet. If Sun called
killed, then at least I'll know she turned o
Is that satisfaction? I don't know. I just kn
won't run and I won't beg.

The guards grasp Aunt Moira's arms and ha
low. She shouts over her shoulder with a desperat
heard from the woman who has ruled diligently and
as head of Lee House all my short life.

"I beg you, Persephone. Find Manea. Save your cou
nocent child. I beg you—"

The ramp closes, cutting off her cries.

A disciplined stamp of footfalls catches my ear. A file of s
jogs out of the gate onto the landing site. I stiffen, thinking they
for me, but they run past and go out the far gate to deal with some
or someone else.

Fuck.

I collect my scattered thoughts and adrenaline-racked flesh. With
my duffel slung over my left shoulder and bumping on my butt I walk
at a measured pace toward the gate into the palace. What will happen?
My mouth goes dry and my palms sweat. Tiana sticks with me, thank
the heavens. I don't think I could walk up to that threshold alone.

We are waved through by the spatharioi as if nothing has happened.
As if they didn't just witness Governor Moira Lee's downfall. The punishment for treason is death.

"Whose hand caused this?" Ti murmurs in my ear.

Moira's sobbing, the way she begged me with her last words to rescue Manea: it drags on me like chains pulling me to the bottom of a

a lying kiss. The ramp sighs down. A phalanx of D

out and head straight for me. "Get through the gate," I say

shoving Tiana behind me.

n."

ist. "They're not here for you."

swift raptors they surround Moira. She straightens,

s her tears as she stares at each guard in turn,

le she promoted. None will meet her eye. A

chest.

r order of the Lee House council of elders,

yourself into our custody, on the charge

us act perpetrated by your sister and

back. "Get through the gate," she

me back in order to have me

me at the first opportunity. I

ow I'll not turn coward. I

l her toward the Swal-

ion I've never before

with an iron hand

sin and her in-

patharioi

e here

hing

the baby,

baby into a space

ess you're making a state-

eirs. But in that case, why arrest

on her private strategos table. Her vivid features
luster, drained by death. Bloody patches dry on her cer-
al robe where she was stabbed. Her Companions group around
ner with the look of people who know they have failed catastrophically:
Precious Jīn and Grace Nazir stand at either end of the ovoid table,
holding spears in the guise of dour angelic guardians. Norioghene
Hope and Nà Bō kneel before the makeshift bier, their backs to me.
Marshal Tomyris will still be in Kanesh System; she can't have heard
yet. But where is Marduk Lee?

Zàofù Samtarras stands facing the door as if to confront implacable destiny should it try to enter uninvited again. To his left stands Sun, flanked at her back by James, Hetty, Alika, Razin, and Makinde. Jade hurries to get in line next to Makinde. It's only when I belatedly step into place after Alika and before Razin that I realize I'm wrong: Sun isn't standing to Zàofù's left. He is standing to her right, and by this gesture indicates to everyone present that he intends to honor Eirene's choice of heir.

Prince João stands to Sun's left, already in fashionable mourning garb. That was fast. Beside him stands Soaring, who is also wearing white as if the prince dressed her to match him. Her presence here suggests she is either firmly in Sun's camp or under constant surveillance. Since I have never exchanged words with her because my exile happened too fast, I have no idea. The other two potential claimants to the throne are conspicuously absent, because one lives in a prison and the other in confinement in a star system at the edge of Chaonian territory.

Sun flicks a nod to acknowledge my entrance. Alika takes a half step away, as if he fears I'll contaminate him by association. Hetty nods gravely at me. James has his hand turned palm up and is looking at some virtual construction cupped there that I can't see.

I tip my head toward Razin, who is reliable. She signs, *She was waiting for you. Gesture of trust.*

I sign, *My mother?*

Yes.

My brain spins into high gear, constructing scenarios, but I ruthlessly dial them back as Sun signals to a court attendant at the door. The governors enter first to file past the body, the final test so all the high officials can be assured Eirene is truly dead. That's when I see Marduk Lee standing with the other governors.

Wow. I did not see that coming.

After the governors come the high marshals and high ministers, then marshals and ministers and palace officers. We Companions stand in perfect stillness as they shuffle past. Some sob; others are ashen or trembling. A few look angrily at me, but if Sun doubted my loyalty she would not have brought me back. Her trust armors me.

I keep darting glances toward Manea where she sprawls prone on the floor, felled by grief. Moira's words still ring in my ears.

But of course Prince João is a bereaved consort too. Drying tears streak his face with the delicacy of a staged illustration. He remains theatrically posed as he receives the murmured condolences of the court. It's impossible not to feel in my body the moment he shot me in the underground lab with a paralyzing blast from a stinger. Remembering his implacable hostility toward me, the hapless Lee House scion he'd never before met, it's hard not to be troubled by the speed with which Aunt Moira was cut off, ostracized, and arrested.

That's when I notice how, at every pause when he has no one to acknowledge, João looks toward Manea. How his hooded gaze lifts to make a cold, thorough study of the baby who is both Eirene's only fully Chaonian child and her only heir untainted by any admixture of incapacitating illness or foreign ancestry.

What Was She, in Their Eyes?

Seeing her formidable mother dead on the ground soaked in her own blood had never played a part in Sun's vision of the future. The shock of it had disrupted every cell of her universe, had thrown her systems into contradiction and wild disarray. Yet, here she sat in her mother's chair with Crane Marshal Zàofù on her right and her high secretary on her left.

Her Companions stood at her back. Six governors, the three palace chamberlains in charge of protocol, security, and ritual, and the other two highest-ranking marshals present on-planet took the other seats. Marduk Lee had arrived at the last moment, to the surprise of the governors. A crowd of thirty or forty marshals, ministers, officials, and the Argos gendarme commissar lined the walls. Eirene's personal staff and her Companions remained in seclusion with the body.

The body.

Something deep in her shook. Grief? Opportunity?

"Chamberlain, what is the protocol for announcing the death of the queen-marshal?"

Chamberlain the Honorable Uzoma Hope was old enough to have been in service during the deaths of all three of Eirene's brothers and her father as well. He spoke in a quavering voice appropriate to the gravity of the situation. "We have placed Channel Idol on lockdown until the palace is ready to announce."

"What is the palace waiting for?" Sun's words weren't a demand but a question.

He glanced at the other chamberlains, who looked nervously toward the marshals and governors. All of these crucial people were her mother's age or older, veterans of thirty years of constant war. They had built Chaonia's current state of military dominance according to the plan of its towering architect, Eirene.

"I see," said Sun. "It's the question of succession and my readiness."

The palace's intrigues ran as deep as the Ocean of Sorrows. The Core Houses jockeyed for status the same way competitors scrambled to win Idol Faire. Over the years Eirene had ruthlessly pruned the daughter branches of the seven Core Houses to rid herself of those who would not support her to the degree she demanded. She had raised as Companions and marshals the best of her officers and friends, and they followed her with the loyalty of people who trust in success.

Sun was not Eirene. Nor did she intend to try to be. So be it. This was her first true command, a battle she intended to win.

"As acknowledged heir, I am now queen-marshal. Chamberlain, commence the mourning protocol according to the proper ritual. Governors, return to your Houses and prepare for the funeral pyre tomorrow."

Hakan Bō rose in his blustering style. "The governor of Lee House is absent. Should we not wait until she arrives to continue this council?"

Marduk Lee lifted a cold gaze to Hakan. "Lee House has convened an internal tribunal into the events leading to Eirene's murder by a prominent member of our own House who was meant to be secluded in exile. Do you challenge my authority to sit here as representative of Lee House?"

Hakan took a tour of the expressions of the other governors. No one backed him up. He said, huffily, "I do not. Let it stand that I remarked upon Moira Lee's absence."

At the back of the room, a man wearing the badge of Channel Idol's palace division cleared his throat audibly. "Your Highness, if I may speak?"

"You are?" she asked.

"Beau Qiáng, Your Highness. Palace communications and chronicles."

"Did you have a question?"

"More of a comment, Your Highness. About the acclamation of the fleet."

"I recorded a message at FSC. Once we allow traffic through the beacons, couriers will be dispatched to the fleets in all locations."

"If it hasn't been sent yet, perhaps I might review it with you. Or assist in recording a follow-up, perhaps staged alongside the bier to emphasize continuity of rule. If you wish to control the message, start at the beginning."

His brazenness surprised her but she respected audacity if accompanied by competence. For the last two years, making her way onto the stage of public image, she had relied on Alika. That had been fine when she'd been heir. But surrounded as she was by elders who would second-guess her every decision, she needed Alika beside her in his military capacity as a loyal subordinate.

"Very well. Nisaba will get you a desk and we'll meet later. Are there other questions?"

She leaned forward to set them on edge, as if they weren't already on edge. Her posture, the heat of her gaze, the way she braced herself as one who is ready to leap into action: this too was her message. *Don't impede me.*

No one spoke.

She said, "Once the palace rites are sung and our glorious queen-marshal's ashes are given to the waves, we continue on schedule to attack Karnos System."

Zàofù spoke at last. She'd been waiting for him to object. "Your Highness, under the circumstances we must consider a delay."

"We cannot delay. The Rider Council will learn of my mother's death sooner than we imagine. The Phene will take advantage of Chaonian discord and confusion to attack into the territories we control."

"That's all speculation," said Zàofù.

"Every campaign is speculation. Regardless, Eirene's attack on Karnos has been planned for years to coincide with an opportune window of beacon alignment."

She stood, forcing everyone seated to stand. Officials and governors shifted restlessly, these powerful individuals who in concert with the indomitable and cunning Eirene had dragged the republic out of tottering weakness into the bright heaven of strength. They had lived through those days, fought through them, sacrificed and won.

What was she, in their eyes? A child grasping at a gleaming spear someone else had forged. Maybe they were waiting for her to beg for their permission. That would never happen. But as much as it galled, she needed Zàofù's imprimatur.

"I don't intend to waste my mother's life work. Marshal, is Chaonia not ready?"

He drew himself up with the pride for which he was famous, the man who had walked the road alongside Eirene. It was his plan too. His work, his blood, his sweat. His readiness the others doubted, in doubting Sun.

"Of course Chaonia is ready, Your Highness."

Thus was her position sealed. "I will address the republic at twenty-one hundred tonight, from Victory Hall. Dismissed."

A Dispatch from the Enemy

Another morning overlooking Flat Water and the basilica. Apama never skipped breakfast, because it was the one time of day she could be sure of having an entire hour with her mother. Even if they usually had to share it with the Rider.

Rana had the gift of glib chat. "I don't know if you recall Chona. She's the person I met at the Medics Guild the other day. We really hit it off. And do you know what, Apama?"

"I don't know what, but I know you're gonna tell me."

It was their old joke, and they both grinned. Apama studied her mother every day for signs of a crack in her cheerful armor, but she hadn't seen it yet, even with her sire always looming, lurking, possessive. In love. Or something.

Rana waved her spoon as she liked to do, including Dasa in the gesture. He was at the side table filling his plate and admiring Rana while Zakurru had perforce to stare over the sea.

"She said there's a new replica of Vigil Keep in the Eleventh District. She's on the governing council. It's not open to the public yet but she said she'd be happy to get us early-bird entry. We could make it an overnight and take a side trip to the Auric Falls, which we've talked about so many times! How about Second-day next? The Exchange doesn't meet that day."

Rana meant the words for Apama but Uncle smiled with sudden interest. "The Falls are very pleasant this time of year. One can go swimming."

"That sounds lovely, Dasa," said Rana. "I was thinking, hoping even, maybe a trip for just Apama and me. It's a cozy old tradition for the two of us."

Uncle turned so stiffly that Apama realized Zakurru had taken control. He had something to say in his silken whisper. "An overnight trip is out of the question."

"What harm in it?" Uncle muttered, turning his head jerkily as if against Zakurru's will.

Abruptly he set his plate down on the table and, with a strange bodily shudder, froze in place. His eyes flickered, moving up and down.

A hot, ugly anger coursed through Apama, as fierce as a shock wave. Maybe they were arguing. Maybe they would tear themselves apart in an internal cataclysm, and her mom would be free and Apama could return to the fleet where she belonged. How good would that be?

But the eye movements were the nystagmus that signaled messages flowing between Riders. Dasa jerked around like a puppet on a string and strode to the writing desk to drop onto the cushion. He yanked an unmarked sheet of paper in front of him, uncapped a bottle of ink, and began writing characters with fast strokes, working at speed as if taking dictation.

Zakurru's face was visible from where she and her mother sat at the table. At first Apama thought his flicking horizontal side-to-side eye movements were a continuation of the nystagmus, but then she realized he was reading something seen through the eyes of another Rider. Uncle was writing on paper what the Rider was reading. He was able to copy incredibly quickly because he used both upper hands, writing from the center out to each edge, simply copying characters.

Afterward, using only his left upper, he wrote out the text in Phenish letters directly below the ideograms, pausing now and again as he thought through how to rephrase the wording out of Yele into Phenish. A bell began to ring, its high chime ringing the call to synod. She looked at her mother, who turned all four hands palms up in the gesture that in their home meant "I have no fucking idea."

Dasa set down the pen and stood with paper in hand.

Zakurru said, "Apama, come with me. Rana, remain here."

Outside his quarters a quartet of Incorruptibles escorted him into an unmarked elevator she had thought reserved for domestic Incorruptibles going about their duties. Instead of ascending to Unity Hall above, the elevator descended beyond what she had thought the lowest floor.

The doors opened into a heavily shielded series of compartments along a passageway that resembled nothing as much as a spaceship buried deep in the ground. A double airlock admitted them into a large, bowl-shaped chamber carved out of bedrock. Overhead shone a virtual representation of the Phene Empire highlighted within beacon space. Below, four concentric rings of tables housed what Apama immediately recognized as a war council. Admirals and high-ranking administrators were rushing in and taking seats at the lower two tiers of tables.

Her sire strode down steps to a ring of seats at the center reserved for Riders. The Incorruptibles shunted Apama to the upper ring of tables. She stood with lower hands resting on the back of a chair, waiting for an order to sit.

Above, the virtual map shimmered beneath the great curve of the ceiling. Star systems gleamed with different colors and relative sizes dependent not on their actual astronomical class but according to their status within the empire: inhabited systems, resource systems, central imperial provinces in contrast to outlying provinces that had been conquered and absorbed later like Mishirru and Karnos. The Hatti region was shown as contested because most of its systems were currently under the military control of the Chaonians. Beacon routes were marked by silver lines. Other stars shone as pinpricks, present for the sake of accuracy.

Every military ship, command post, and training center carried a version of this three-dimensional map. Here in the secure operations chamber the map had an additional set of lights: it tracked where each and every Rider was. Clusters at each of the Triple A Unity Halls at Anchor, Auger, and Axiom marked the presence of children and elders. Otherwise Riders had a station posting on one of the major systems, were attached to a fleet, or roamed.

The map made it clear how rare Riders genuinely were: several hundred at the most in a multi-system empire carrying a population of tens of billions.

An officer appeared to her right, colonel's pips bright under the artificial light. "Lieutenant, no one of your rank is allowed here. I'll need to see your clearance."

An Incorruptible took a step forward. "Colonel, this is Rider Zakurru's daughter."

"How nice. A desk posting, I assume." A sneer glimmered but did not fully sharpen as the colonel looked over Apama's uniform. His gaze halted on the wings on the collar. His chin came up. "Lancer?"

"Yes, ma'am. I fought with the Styraconyx Fleet at Molossia. The *Strong Bull.*"

"Oh. Well." The colonel's tone lost its edge of mockery, and he gave a curt nod of respect. "It's good to see council members putting their own forward."

"Firstborn to the fleet," said Apama with the deadpan tone she'd perfected during her years of training.

"May all your siblings serve unity. Carry on, Lieutenant." The officer strode off to the third tier of tables.

All your siblings.

A numb horror washed through her as the words sank in. Rana wasn't post-menopause. She could have more children. What if that had been Zakurru's intention all along? Or Dasa's wish, if he was allowed to have wishes and desires. A sick certainty clenched like a stone in her stomach. It wasn't Apama he had wanted. It had been Rana all

along, and Apama merely the bait he'd dangled to gain Rana's cooperation. She clutched the back of the chair, sweat stinging at her joints.

Two Riders arrived in wheelchairs. The Riders sat. The officers and
administrators sat. Apama sank into her chair as stragglers hurried in.

Horribly, one was Admiral Manu. Of course he sat next to her even
though there were multiple empty seats farther away.

"You'll be assigned to my command at Karnos," he said, bending
his big grin her way as if she'd be as glad to hear the news as he was to
deliver it.

"You've been assigned to command the fleets in Karnos?"

"It's not official yet, but Zakurru, Paulo Kr Manalon, and I have a
handshake deal. I get the command, and the Angursa Syndicate provides my main fleet alongside a squadron of Incorruptible ships."

"When did you return?"

"Yesterday. It's an unbelievable opportunity for us."

For *us*?

He leaned closer as she stiffened. "I requested the *Strong Bull* to be
assigned as my flagship."

The name hit like a broadside, speech scraped from her throat as
flashes of memory filled her mind. The ship shuddering under a series
of wrenching impacts. Cold sorbet melting on her tongue. Groans from
Renay and Ana in their cabin as Delfina polluted the recycled air with
an unforgivable pun.

She raked together words out of the scatter of her thoughts. "I hadn't
heard any of the Styraconyx Fleet had arrived safely back yet."

"The first ships began arriving in Hellion Terminus a few months
ago. The *Strong Bull*'s beacon drive needs a refit and recalibration but
it is otherwise serviceable. By the way, the news is still classified but all
that is about to become moot." He bent a concerned look on her as he
leaned yet closer until his shoulder was a finger's-breadth away from
hers. "Didn't Zakurru tell you?"

She edged away. The lights dimmed. A watch bell chimed to announce the opening of an emergency synod.

"Here we go," murmured Manu. To her relief he shifted back into
his own seat, no longer pressing into her physical space.

The center ring of seats was situated in the same configuration as
Unity Hall. The Riders sat with their bodies facing outward toward
the tiers while the riding faces looked inward at each other and all the
other Riders in the empire. There were Riders in the seats she'd met
during her time at Anchor and two she'd never seen before. Zakurru
didn't socialize with other Riders, and he mostly kept her away from
them.

Furthermore, after the change in Council leadership the leaders of the victorious faction had been careful to spread themselves out so as never to be physically present in the same place at the same time. The precaution made her wonder if Kubaba and her faction would stoop to something as brutal as assassination. At the synod where they'd taken control, their leader Baragesi had been on Axiom. He'd chosen not to visit Anchor in the interim, so she hadn't met him, only seen recorded holographic projections like the one that now shimmered into view of a broad-shouldered man holding the Speaker's whip.

Zakurru stood to repeat Baragesi's words for the assembly.

"I, Baragesi, begin this synod with preamble. A dispatch filed by an agent of the Council has been delivered at courier speed to our colleague Maka on Yele Prime. Maka read it in the sight of all. Zakurru's Dasa has copied the original and translated it into Phenish orthography for those not fluent in Yele. This dispatch will now be projected at each of your seats. Read it. We will then open proceedings."

The tabletops illuminated a written dispatch in Dasa's precise if hurried calligraphy. The hall went silent except for the slow *whish-whoo* cycle of the chamber's respiratory system as everyone started to read.

The festival culminated in a grand procession. This vain parade was meant to display Queen-Marshal Eirene's complete dominance of her republic, its noble houses and citizens, and the foreign collaborators she calls guest friends, as well as those she has required to become her allies.

To begin with, Eirene made offerings of the greatest magnificence at the Temple of Celestial Peace on behalf of the ancestors. Afterward, she paraded in grandeur across the span known as Petitioners Bridge. Crowned by a golden halo, she strode ahead of her Companions and by this means indicated to everyone in attendance and all those watching, and those who would see the festival via recording later, that she had no need of the protection of guards. Such was her degree of authority, preeminence, and pride.

As the sages say, We are all destined for death.

One among that company, an eminent honorable named Aisa Lee, had cause to resent with consuming bitterness the queen-marshal, because she blamed her for the loss of her husband who was, she claimed, unjustly accused of being a traitor to Chaonia. Having stationed a boat next to Petitioners Bridge, she hid a knife on her person and placed herself within the ranks of the nobly born. When she saw Eirene walking separate from the rest, Aisa rushed forward and drove her blade into the queen-marshal's heart. As Eirene fell lifeless to the ground, the attacker ran for the nearby dock.

Eirene's Companions rushed to the corpse while young bodyguards loyal to the heir raced in pursuit of the killer. They struck down the murderer before she could get on the boat. Thus the one who killed Eirene was herself sacri-ficed in the cause of her revenge.

This, then, encompasses the end of Eirene's reign.

Queen-Marshal Eirene was dead? Was this some kind of a joke? Manu smiled slightly as he rested his chin on steepled hands. He looked like a man anticipating even better news.

Zakurru raised his speaking whip. "Eirene is dead. Now that she is dispatched, the rest will fall back in disorder. Chaonia is finished."

"Nonsense!" Kubaba lumbered to her feet with a slash of her whip. "There is an heir."

Zakurru's disdain for his rival tightened his shoulders. "Eirene was a formidable person. Sun Shān is barely more than a child. Untested and immature. What is Chaonia, after all? A jumped-up rag doll propelled forward by a belligerent leader. Against our numbers and resources they cannot prevail. To that end, it is time for us to discuss what we do next. I call upon Paulo Kr Manalon de Angursa, who the Council intends to appoint as high syndicate admiral for the duration of our next campaign."

He pointed his whip at the Angursa admiral. Discontented mur-murs swept through the seats as Paulo stood.

Unlike Manu, he displayed no unseemly gloating, only the serious face of a person who understands the stakes. "The honor is mine."

"Bought and paid for," remarked the Batillipes high admiral as if to the person in the next seat but loud enough that everyone could hear.

Paulo ignored the heckler. He spoke in a measured, sonorous tone. "Eirene's court will be in disarray for some time. With the blessing of the saints, we have been granted a fortuitous opportunity. As a first step, we will ask every syndicate to send a fleet to Karnos System as soon as possible. While they gather, our strategic command will for-mulate a plan to retake all of Aspera, the entire Hatti region, Kanesh, and ultimately honored Troia."

Manu jumped to his feet, hand raised in the style of Yele orators. "If I may address the war council, I speak as someone who has just returned from Karnos System with the most up-to-date observations of the situation there."

"We have Riders in-system," said the Tanarctus high admiral acidly.

"Yes, but they aren't me. There must be no delay, no lackadaisical assembly of ships. We must take immediate defensive measures in Kar-nos System against the likelihood of an imminent assault."

"But Eirene is dead," objected an admiral wearing Oreella's whirl-wind icon.

Batillipes chimed in with their big voice that was always easy to hear. "Chaonia can't yet have rebuilt from their losses at Molossia. Despite the other failures of the Styraconyx campaign, it succeeded in pounding their shipyards and ships. Yet perhaps our dear Paulo would know more about that, since he has spent more time in Chaonia than any of the rest of us."

Eschiniscus's admiral got to her feet, leaning on a cane. "That's uncalled-for, Javier. Paulo's right to return was recognized and embraced by the Council. It isn't your place to keep sniping, even if you are mad he wouldn't agree to that bad trade deal your syndicate offered to Angursa."

Apama watched with interest as Kubaba looked toward Zakurru as if expecting him to shut down these side arguments, but her sire did nothing.

Paulo sighed as if he had just realized how much pushback he was going to get in his new role and was swiftly recalibrating to find a way to create consensus. "I agree that it is important to recognize the limits of Chaonia's capacity to rearm. But we must also take into account their resolve to do so."

Manu broke in as if he couldn't bear to wait any longer. "I don't put any feat past the republic, and nor should any of us. The Chaonians have superior discipline and cohesion, whatever their numbers. In addition, Eirene's allies make up an unknown percentage of her force."

"That is certainly true with regard to the Yele League," agreed Paulo, thus reminding the chamber where Manu was from.

"This is immaterial," said Batillipes. "We hold too strong a defensive position in Karnos System."

"Not strong enough." Manu's objection came as fast as the counterstrike he'd made famous in his big victory. "My considered opinion is that an attack will come within an eight-day window that opens in fourteen days. That's all the time we have to prepare. Fourteen days."

"Impossible!"

"It's too soon!"

"Even if it were the plan, who will lead them?"

Laughter from many, but at least half the officers present bent to study virtual orreries on their tabletops. So did Apama, and she immediately saw how the alignment of planets and beacons offered an advantage to the Chaonians, should they choose to attack within that window.

"You're asking the wrong question. Chaonia has capable, experienced, and victorious admirals who can still bring the fight to us." Manu bulldozed on with the confidence of a man who knows he is right. "Current defensive strength in Karnos is considerable but it might not be strong enough to hold against an all-out assault, even if we move the dreadnoughts into Karnos."

"What do you propose?" Paulo asked, as if he and Manu had prepared this dance between them.

Manu waited until everyone was looking expectantly at him. "The best defense will be to place mines."

Everyone looked at each other with confounded expressions.

He went on. "We place mines across the arrival vectors of the three beacons that link to the neighboring systems currently under Chaonian control."

The words shocked the entire chamber into a horrified silence. Apama expected her sire to banish Manu for the effrontery of the suggestion, yet none of the Riders interrupted as he kept speaking. Maybe it was because he was right, if all you counted was a binary win-loss column and not the ethics or economics of the option.

"If mines are laid in a dense half sphere around each beacon, then any ship that drops through will enter the minefield, no matter what exit vector it takes. The Na Iri, Tarsa, and Aspera Beacons can be fully mined within four to five days, before our reinforcements arrive. What is the use of having a communications advantage with the Riders if you don't use it?"

Batillipes sputtered with indignation. "Absolutely not! A mined beacon entry isn't a weapon shot at the enemy. It hurts everyone. It hurts our trade and our people most of all."

Manu was undaunted, of course. "Let me state this simple fact again. If we mine the arrival vectors, then the Chaonians can't attack Karnos at all. That gives us time and space to formulate a campaign on our own timetable."

Tanarctus stood at the same time as Oreella's admiral. Apama wasn't sure who would give way first, until Batillipes rose and the other two sat.

"Such a course of action will harm our syndicates grievously!" Batillipes punctuated his booming voice with the aggressive shaking of his lower hands as if scolding an ignorant child. "We have a substantial population of imperial Phene still living in the Hatti territories. Do you mean to cut them off from their own people? You might as well burn down their homes and crops and say it is for their own good!"

"It halts Chaonian aggression if they can't enter Karnos," repeated Manu in the tone of a man who can't believe his interlocutor refuses to accept the truth.

"My syndicate won't be a party to such an outrageous and immoral course of action!" proclaimed Tanarctus.

"Nor will mine!" cried Oreella.

A spontaneous outburst of applause met these statements. Many of the admirals and ministers and officers began to whisper with great agitation among themselves, glancing toward the Riders, then at Paulo as if he were meant to do something, and then at Manu, shaking their heads. Angry. Suspicious.

Mining a beacon arrival vector was dishonorable as well as counter-productive. Beacons belonged to no confederation, they had no loyalty, they were tools, not weapons. Any ship with a beacon drive and a living human on board could drop through. All people who used beacons must maintain and protect them at all costs, because any harm done to a beacon route harmed everyone.

"Mines don't hurt beacons," said Paulo, entering the fray. "It is a temporary measure to guard against Chaonian aggression in the short term while we prepare."

Batillipes shot back. "I have to wonder what benefit you see it in for yourself, my dear friend Paulo. Do you intend to be placed in charge of Karnos System in recompense for your efforts? Angursa lost a lot of influence during your exile, although I must say you've done remarkably well in reestablishing yourself."

"I support the empire, as do we all," said Paulo with unflappable dignity.

Batillipes smirked. "It isn't your loyalty I question. It's your . . . what shall we say? . . . your appetite for influence and prestige and wealth. And what of your new ally? Perhaps Admiral Manu hopes to receive a syndicate and fleet of his own, given how little he came to us with? Or perhaps he hopes for some more tempting reward?"

Zakurru snapped up his whip. Everyone shut up. All sat.

"The Council has listened to the debate. Now we will make our final judgment on the matter."

The Riders present turned their thoughts inward, listening to words spoken far away. No one in the chamber talked or even whispered, but people shifted in their seats or moved hands restlessly as they waited. Apama realized she was sweating, palms hot. She dabbed at her face with a handkerchief, hoping that her uniform wouldn't soak through at the joints, hoping no one was looking at her. For once even Manu was intent on the Council's circle, not on her.

At length Zakurru spoke. "These are the words of Speaker Baragesi. 'Queen-Marshal Sun will be bound up with the confusion of succession. High Admiral Paulo Kr Manalon de Angursa will proceed with coordinating an emergency assembly of syndicate fleets in Karnos System. Urgency is the measure of the day. Once news reaches Chaonia of a fleet buildup in Karnos, she'll not wish to meet us head on. We will develop the next stage of our campaign once the fleets are assembled, with a view to retaking the Hatti region first of all. You all know your responsibilities. Convene at your stations. This synod closes.'"

With lower hands clasped in her lap and uppers braced on the table, Apama watched Dasa stride up the steps toward her with the energy of a man greatly excited by his new prospects. What did Zakurru want? But he wasn't coming to talk to her.

Manu rose to greet the Rider. "What authority am I to be given? You promised me command of the Karnos System."

Zakurru said, "I promised you *a* command in the Karnos System. This I will deliver, an Incorruptibles task group with the *Thunderbolt in Hand* as flagship."

"What authority am I to be given?" Manu repeated.

"You'll have authority over your task group. You'll work in concert with an Angursa Fleet as well as with all other syndicate fleets posted there."

"In Yele, we assign a sole war commander. Not this endless arguing."

"This is not Yele, Admiral. Theory is delightful, but it must be backed up by results. I have supported you thus far, and given you this opportunity. However, once in Karnos, it will be up to you to convince Baragesi of your ability to succeed."

"Then how about this? Let my task group also be assigned authority over Hellion Terminus. That way I can oversee the reintegration of the returned ships from the Styraconyx Fleet, who know me and my capabilities."

"As I said, take it up with Baragesi. You'll need his support to expand the ambit of your command."

To Apama's surprise, Manu neither bristled nor sputtered. "The opportunity is all I ask for. I can do the rest."

Apama finally found her feet and stood. "What about me?"

"You'll get your wish, Apama," said her sire.

"Reassignment to the *Strong Bull*?"

"Return to the front lines. You're being assigned as the Rider Council's attaché to Admiral Manu's command."

With a smile, the admiral rested a hand too intimately on her lower right arm. "Just as I'd asked."

She took a step away so he had to let go.

Her sire tapped her on the shoulder with his whip. "Like your mother, you know your duty, Apama. I expect you to do your duty."

31

It's the Familiarity of Their Backside That's Caught the Wily Persephone's Eye

On the forecourt of the Temple of Celestial Peace, we seven Companions flank Queen-Marshal Sun. Her new title sticks in my mouth. In my head she's still the heir, a gleaming star ringed with the invisible chains imposed on her by Eirene's preeminence.

Times change. Circumstances alter.

The highest officials of the court stand on the steps leading onto the temple's portico. Chamberlains wearing phoenix badges open the central gate. Sun leads the way into this holiest of precincts. The outer courtyard serves as a reminder of the generations-long journey out of the Celestial Empire from which we all descend, a place lost to the mists of time. Our passage takes forty steps instead of forty generations.

We pass between threshold guardians and into the Temple of Celestial Peace. The air is heavy with incense. An altar takes up the entirety of the far wall. Eight giant statues of the Celestial Emperor in her most common avatars gaze upon us as we approach.

As a courtesy Sun walks to the feet of She Who Bore Them All, with her braided headdress studded with stars and an infant cradled in each arm. It's always prudent to visit her first, even in Chaonia. Lighting a stick of sandalwood incense, Sun sets it before the seated deity, then walks to the largest statue in the hall, towering even above the others.

In Chaonia, a Temple of Celestial Peace is dedicated to She Who Rises as the Sun, on whose chest beams the eight-pointed sunburst. Sun kneels before the shining warrior who led her people through the darkness, blood, and ashes of a fallen world to a safe harbor. Sun would never bow her head but she presses her hands together and her lips move in words I can't hear. I'm pretty sure Sun's father named her in honor of this avatar of the Celestial Emperor.

There are no Channel Idol wasps evident, because it is grossly disrespectful to treat a temple as a stage. But all the high officials, governors, and marshals witness by crowding onto the temple's balcony. Tasteful images will be woven into whatever message Sun and her new historian decide to broadcast.

While Sun prays, the other Companions move along the altar to make offerings to their preferred avatars. Tiana glides up to hand me a necklace braided of my sister's favorite jade orchids.

I whisper, "Where did you get this?"

She leans close. "Everything is for sale if you know where to look."

"Everything but my dignity," I joke, to which she replies with a side-eye worthy of a basilisk.

She lights incense to the Holy One Who Eases Misfortune with their gentle eyes and healing hands. I offer the necklace of orchids to She Who Voyages on the Winds of Furious Heaven in honor of my sister's sacrifice. I'm not much of a believer but I like staying connected to Resh because she was dutiful in her observance. Even so, I finish a truncated prayer cycle quickly, give a bow to each of the other avatars, and then, bored, stroll through the echoing hall.

The hall proper is populated by human-sized statues of the thirteen exalted officials and gracious courtiers who tend the divine palace, each accompanied by an offering table. Necklaces woven from flowers and leaves drape the statues. Through the open doors I hear the distant hum of a large assembly gathered in Victory Hall.

Alone of the Companions, Hetty chooses to make her offering not to an avatar of the Celestial Emperor but to one of the humble officials. She pours oil onto the altar of the loyal Charioteer who never left the side of her beloved She Who Rises as the Sun as they braved the fiery storm.

I sidle over as she lights a stick of incense. She is aware of me but does not look up from her prayer until she finishes every single word the prescribed number of repetitions. How like her. Then she gives me an arched eyebrow in silent query.

I whisper. "I know we all pretend we don't see it. And I get that James and Alika don't worry that if Sun is sleeping with you she might favor you over them."

"Is this a thing you worry on?"

"Me? Nah. I'm too late to this party to compete. And we all know I'm never going to be high scorer. But Jade Kim will kick hard if they think by kicking they can crawl over you into a higher position."

Hetty's smile is guarded. "What prompts this warning, dear Persephone?"

"Ugh, when you call me by my full name I know you're letting me know I'm treading on your toes. But I like you, and I don't like or trust Jade. It's one thing for an ambitious climber to look the other way about things in the palace that aren't supposed to be happening when Sun is heir. But we have entered unknown territory with a lot more at stake. That's all. Eyes open."

A slight movement by the statue of a randomly gracious courtier catches my attention. A person partially obscured by the statue is standing with their face turned toward the wall. It's the familiarity of their backside that's caught my eye. I never forget a handsome pair of shoulders, much less a trim set of hips and a shapely butt. I stiffen, trapped between the adrenaline rush of flight and the spark of remembered heat. When Hetty glances that way there's no one to be seen; either I imagined the figure or he's stepped out of sight behind the statue.

"Excuse me," I murmur as I head that way like a javelin loosed. Never say I won't walk recklessly into danger just because of a kiss.

My footfalls clip softly on the ceramic floor as I walk up beside the statue, a blessed courtier with half-furled wings who carries a star in the shape of a disk inscribed with writing. I can't for the life of me recall their blessed name because I was a bad student and a worse temple-goer.

Zizou has stationed himself between the statue and the wall. His chin comes up, yet he does not turn.

In a low voice I say, "What are you doing here?"

His breathing tightens. "Honey-tongued Persephone. I pray you, do not get into my line of sight."

"I thought you got the leash taken off your neural systems."

"The leash imposed on banner soldiers under the command of the Phene, yes. But not the engineered hallucination."

I take a step back, my anxious retreat halted by the courtier's wing. After a few calming breaths I try again. "Then why did Sun allow you to enter the temple?"

"Sight is not the only sensation we humans use to explore what interests us," he says in a tone that scalds me to my toes as it accelerates my heart rate. He adds, "My hearing is also excellent."

Daringly I touch the small of his back. He inhales sharply. The impulse washes over me the way it always does: I cannot resist the agitation of desire's violence. Its perturbation is balm to my restless, dissatisfied heart. One step is all it takes for me to close the gap between us, for me to press my lips to the back of his neck, to taste the sting of him. Risk is so sweet.

"There's a storage room beyond the wine cellar that's completely blacked out, no light at all when the fixtures are turned off," I whisper into his hair as if into the heady perfume of a whirlwind.

He has not moved, as if my touch has frozen him. I swear I hear him lick his lips, but I wonder if I've pushed too hard.

He says, "The Royal is departing the temple. You have to go."

I glance over my shoulder into the hall. Sun is headed toward the big doors. "Will I see you on the *Boukephalas*?"

A shake of the head. A tendril of black hair tickles my knuckles. "I've been assigned to the prince and will remain here on palace duty.

The Royal has chosen you over me, Honored Persephone. She can give no greater compliment."

He takes a step toward the wall, leaving my hand hanging in the empty air. The tincture of sandalwood drifts into my nose as Ti hurries up.

"What are you doing over here with the courtier in charge of examinations? They don't strike me as your kind of avatar . . . Oh!" She stops, although nothing can truly fluster her. "Zizou, peace be upon you." After a brief silence she adds, "The customary reply is, 'and upon you, peace.'"

"And upon you, peace, grace-bearing Tiana."

"Come along," she says briskly, hooking my elbow with a hand. "My apologies, but Sun will be meeting the envoys next, so you need to get in formation."

As we walk away I don't look back lest I surprise him looking at me and be turned into a shade the hard way. At the door Sun checks to make sure we are all assembled: James, Alika, and Hetty to my right and Razin, Makinde, and Jade to my left. I'm in the middle. What a cozy place to be.

Eirene was one to walk amid the crowd of her palace officials but Sun leaves the temple first and in the lead. Her mother was murdered in public in front of our eyes while doing exactly this, but no one would know it from the way Sun boldly advances into Victory Hall, as vulnerable as the front rank of any attack. For once I pay close attention as she greets her father, seated in a stately chair, and stations herself beside him and next to the pillar representing Queen-Marshal Inanna, the founder of the republic.

Sun and the historian cooked up the sequence and positioning of events. Envoys and ambassadors from various confederations and independencies have been parked for two hours in Victory Hall to await the arrival of the new queen-marshal. Each delegation is escorted forward to pay their respects.

Chaonia didn't have many friends thirty years ago, but now members of the Larissan Senate and the Parliament of Kanesh declare their continued hope for lasting comity. Representatives from Hesjan cartels pledge good faith. A new ambassador from the Yele League pontificates too long on the honorable tradition of fighting together against the Phene threat, but Sun takes it in stride, listening intently. I let the words slide past as I study the waiting envoys: gaily dressed representatives from the Hatti region, which was so recently conquered by Eirene; a crowned and robed dynast from Karnos; another Royal of the Gatoi, reminder that Prince João has for years been advocating for greater cooperation with the wheelships and their clans. That's why he has worked so hard to free Phene-controlled banner soldiers from the leash.

My gaze slams up against the unexpected sight of an emissary from ancient Mishirru. Once an independent queendom, holy Mishirru is now just another conquered province of the Phene Empire. This elderly and strikingly beautiful woman carries herself with the greatest dignity, and wears gold and white. She shifts to look right at me, across the gap. Her dark gaze makes me as dizzy as if I've fallen into a mill and am being ground into a new form. I sway, blinking.

Hetty catches my arm. "Are you all right?"

"I'm fine, I'm fine, I'm fine," I say as I straighten back up. "What's an envoy from Mishirru doing here?"

"There's no such envoy here. What do you mean?"

When I search again I no longer see the old woman. I rub my eyes.

A delegation of Skuda strut forward, making a big show with their peaked hats and spangled waistcoats. They aren't allies or guest friends. I suspect they are the equivalent of scouts, checking out the new game in town.

"Fear not, you are welcome in Chaonia," says Sun. "Friendship with our republic will benefit your tribes."

"What would we fear? We live in the shadow of Jade Skirt." They smile amiably. "Out at the terminus end of beacon space, there's not much to fear except a beacon shutting down."

They are the last of the envoys. As they depart the hall Sun mutters, "Big talkers, those Skuda."

Prince João rises, moving to take his place with various notables from the consorts' wing. The envoys leave the hall for the grand portico. The palace officials, the marshals, and the governors follow. For once we Companions precede Sun out of Victory Hall to the portico. The great plaza lies beyond, packed with military personnel, all the way out along Petitioners Bridge. Seething masses of citizens crowd the mainland plaza and the shoreline as far as I can see.

At the top of the processional stairs overlooking the great plaza, Eirene rests on a funeral bier atop a lattice of sandalwood. Her arms are crossed over her torso. Her face is slack in death, and her obsidian eye has faded to a lifeless black.

Normally the funeral speech is made first and the body burned afterward. At Sun's signal, a chamberlain wraps the last piece of mourning cloth to cover Eirene's face. Sun pours a vial of oil onto her mother's corpse. She touches flame to the shroud and steps back. It's primed to go fast. Flames leap clean and hot as we retreat a few steps. The smell of sandalwood rises.

Every voice lifts in the Hymn of Leaving. All of Argos is singing.

Crossing the ocean of stars we leave our home behind us.
We are the spears cast at the furious heaven
And we will burn one by one into ashes
As with the last sparks we vanish.
This memory we carry to our own death which awaits us
And from which none of us will return.
Do not forget. Goodbye forever.

The bier is also a furnace. Its jaws open and the wrapped corpse is lowered within as the bier closes over it. In a few hours, all that will be left is ashes.

Sun moves forward into the full glare of sunlight. Wasps hover to carry her voice as far afield as the entire planet in this moment, the solar system with a delay, and outward by courier through beacons to the rest of the inhabited systems, to orbital stations, to the far-flung ships of the fleet, to the final outpost of the republic.

I have known Sun for a year and it's only now I realize I never knew her. The person I thought I saw this whole time was occluded. She shines as she addresses the republic not with fierceness but with absolute conviction.

"This is not a day any of us expected to come so soon. Yet here we are. There is much I could say about my mother but you lived every hour and every day with her as she raised Chaonia from the vanquished to the victor. What are we to do now with her legacy? Do we turn our backs on what she built? *We do not!*

"The Phene Empire thinks we will back down. They believe they can easily overcome us and take back what they think belongs to them but which we proved belongs to us. They're big. They're rich. Yet we defeated their fleets at Kanesh, at Maras Shantiya, at Kaska, at Tarsa, at Na Iri. At Molossia itself. They are not our match in fighting spirit and physical strength! They fight for their syndicates, all grappling with each other for preeminence. We fight as one people. We fight as Chaonia!

"We each of us are Captain the Honorable Ereshkigal Lee, who sacrificed her life to save the Second Fleet. We each of us are Chief Alejandro Bu Alargos, who led his unarmed gulls against the merciless weaponry of Phene gunships. We each of us are Commander Situri

Rèn Alviasalaria, who rescued one hundred spacers from a foundered ship despite grave injuries to her own legs.

"I have fought with you. I have taken wounds I am proud to have suffered. I will always risk myself as you risk yourselves. No other honorable course lies before the queen-marshal of this republic.

"This we can promise each other: what we have started will not end with Eirene. We are the spears cast at the furious heaven. Feast this evening. Tomorrow, we launch."

32

Interlude on a Phene Ship in Aspera System

Specialist Leandro Mo Monnier rubs his bleary eyes and checks the clock on his duty console. Surely an hour has passed since the last time he looked, but in fact it has only been eleven minutes. An agonizing ninety-eight minutes of his watch remain. He cannot keep his eyes open. This watch schedule of six on six off is brutal, and the *Glancing Blow* has another seven Anchor days left on this round of sentry duty.

He yawns just as the ship's commanding officer appears to his right.

"Looks like you need this." With a sympathetic nod, Lieutenant First Class Odette Ne Gage sets down a tumbler. The aroma of freshly brewed coffee hits Le like a shot of hope. By the sharp aniseed scent, it's got to be from her own private stash of barako.

"Thank you, ma'am." He gulps down too much too fast and burns his tongue but the jolt is worth it.

The commander moves on to bring coffee to the other five people on the bridge: the officer on watch, comms, weapons, engineering, and the second sensor station. It's quiet, lights dim, ventilation purring. It's not even that it's night cycle. It's like this all the time. The ship runs as dark as possible, shielded by heat baffles and tucked into a stable field of debris left over from the famous Battle of Aspera Drift.

They're posted in Aspera System as an early-warning tool for the Phene task group that guards the Karnos Beacon. The Phene-controlled beacon is anchored to a barren atmosphere-stripped planet some wit named Rocky. The other beacon in Aspera System, the one that links Aspera to Troia System, is anchored to the fifth planet. Since the fifth planet is currently occluded by the sun, the task group can't track ship movements. That's why, on a regular schedule, a sentry nestles into the debris that's collected at the second planet's L4. From here the sentry can see the fifth planet as a pinprick of light. They're too far away to plot

Chaonian ship movements around the Troia Beacon and in the outer reaches of Aspera System, but that's not their purpose.

The lieutenant returns to look over Leandro's shoulder at the display. Just like last watch there is nothing to see except a slow slide of planets on their long orbits and the stellar flare and storm tracker, currently normal levels. Rocky has two big orbital habitats and a dome complex planet-side, but the main population center in Aspera System is on the third planet, which has no beacon anchored to it and thus avoided the worst impact of the battles for control of the system.

He murmurs, "Ma'am, do you think it's true the queen-marshal was murdered?"

"We've received multiple confirming reports that she's dead."

"What will happen? Will the Chaonians withdraw?"

Ne Gage opens a link that gives them a closer look at the Karnos Beacon and their task group. Phene ships have transponders to alert other Phene ships they are friendlies. They see the ships where they would have been minutes ago. A courier ship keeps pace with the beacon spiral, ready to drop out of Aspera and into Karnos at a moment's notice with a code-red message. Gunships and a pack of destroyers cycle a steady patrol around a stalwart old dreadnought, the *Grappling Minotaur*.

"Hard to know," she muses. "The Chaonians locked down beacon traffic right away, so we're not getting news except what their military wants us to hear. With Eirene dead, they might just call the whole thing off. Even if they do attack, we're not going to see action here in Aspera."

"You don't think so?"

"Their main fleets were already massed in Tarsa and Na Iri. Since they control both those systems in their entirety they can attack into Karnos without warning. Why would you attack through Aspera, past a dreadnought, when you'll be giving away the only surprise you can have if you don't have Riders?"

"Because Aspera is the most direct and fastest route from Chaonia to Karnos. It's just three hops. Chaonia to Molossia to Troia to Aspera to Karnos. Wait, that's four."

"It seems reckless," says the lieutenant with a shake of her head. "Queen-Marshal Eirene may be a lot of things, but she's not—I mean, she wasn't—reckless. Her marshals are just like her. Relentless but measured."

Leandro isn't sure if you can be relentless and measured at the same time, but he knows what the commander is trying to say. Eirene is infamous, but she was effective, and it's shocking that she's gone. Shocking, but fortunate for the empire.

"Do you think we'll be able to take back Aspera? Troia? Even Kanesh? My aunt died at Kanesh."

The commander nods. "My uncle, too. He was in command of the destroyer *Hard Tackle*."

His aunt had worked her way up to specialist, like Leandro, but then again they aren't Triple A heritage seeds like the lieutenant, who is about the same age he is. But he can't complain. He's had worse ship captains, and Ne Gage is clear-headed and friendly without being awkwardly familiar. She gets that picket duty is stressful, so she's always checking on the crew's state of readiness and mental health.

In fact, she says now, "And your aunt?"

"She was a specialist, like me, but a ground pounder. Artillery. My mom—her sister—said she was always blowing things up as a kid so I guess it was inevitable. Not her dying, I mean. She died on the Esplanade."

"We are all destined for death. You have any syndicate ties? You're from . . . Windworn, right?"

"That's right, ma'am." She's got an impressive memory for names and places.

"I think Styraconyx and Angursa have halls there?"

"Yes. Though when I was home on leave six months ago the Styraconyx hall had closed. Rumor had it Oreella was in the process of a hostile takeover of their syndicate ties. I guess the Molossia defeat really did a number on Styraconyx's influence."

"Wouldn't be the first time a syndicate's fortunes fell after an overreach." She gets a faraway look on her face and scratches at her chin with her upper right hand as if contemplating the deadly plunge of her most hated rival.

"You think the Molossia gambit was an overreach?" he asks curiously.

She shrugs, suddenly cautious. "Not my circus, not my monkeys."

"You say that a lot. What is a monkey, anyway?"

"It's a kind of wrench. You use it to build the arena and seats of a syndicate's traveling sports and games concession. No circus ever came through Windworn?"

"Not where I grew up. But my people lived way out. Five hundred klicks from the nearest city. Not enough people to fill an arena, I'll tell you that . . ."

He breaks off.

One reason he's good at his specialty is that he grew up on a mostly uninhabited plateau where you learned early to read minor signs of change in the sky and on the ground that warned of a toxic blow coming on. He stiffens before his brain consciously registers what he's seeing.

"MoMo?" Her tone sharpens as she uses his nickname.

He taps frequency and light changes to alter the view, digging after what he doesn't quite know. There it is, at the far range of the sensors. The lick of torch drives.

"Captain, there's movement. Calculating lag and numbers."

She says to the other sensor station, "Chief, what do you have?"

"I don't have anything, ma'am, just the same view as always . . . Hold on."

The silence stretches into eternity as Leandro and the chief dive into the console readings. The lieutenant hustles over to the captain's chair, where the officer on watch gives way. They both bend over the readouts.

A sentry is an early-warning system. If they break radio silence they give away their position. If it's just a routine Chaonian patrol sweep, a poke and prod to try to get a rise out of the Phene's beacon garrison fleet, then they have to keep their head down and let the *Grappling Minotaur* and her escorts take care of it.

Growing up, he'd known what that prickle in the air meant, the tickling shift of the constant wind, the way the color of the sky changed subtly but with menace.

The chief says, "Routine poke and prod, ma'am."

"I disagree," says Leandro. "They're using the occlusion to hide a big fleet coming at speed. Look at the radiation spectrum and how hot they're burning. There are at least three heavy cruisers. That's not normal. There's the twitch of an anomaly in octant five, which might be a second fleet approaching along a different vector."

Everyone on the bridge looks toward him, then at the captain.

The chief says, reluctantly, "Yes, ma'am. The signs could be interpreted that way. I can't confirm. They're still too far out."

"Closing fast," says Leandro.

The officer on watch, a know-it-all young ensign, says, "Chaonians are rigid about tradition, everyone knows that. They observe a ten-day mourning period followed by a one-hundred-day mourning period. It's nowhere near up yet. They won't dare offend their ancestors by attacking."

The lieutenant chews on her lower lip as she stares at the readouts.

As ship captain, it's her call. Her responsibility. She records the coordinates into a packet.

"Send the message. Full steam ahead. We're going to run."

The signal with its packet bounces off a transmitter and amplifier hidden on a trojan several thousand klicks away but it won't take the enemy long to track back to their position. The engines take too many agonizing minutes to fully fire up from cold rest. The commander takes the helm as they nudge out from their hiding place. Once clear of the dense inner zone of the debris field, they have a clear shot to the task group. But it's a long way. As they accelerate, Leandro keeps an eye on the Chaonians.

"We have pursuit," he says.

No one speaks. The *Glancing Blow* is a gunship modified for stealth, sensors, and speed, sure, but it can't outrun a Chaonian fast frigate. Their task is to warn.

Survival is optional.

33

However Amiable He Seemed

Apama startled awake to a quad tap on her cabin door. It took her a moment to remember she wasn't in the confines of a rack but had her own private cabin with a sink and a desk. The ship's logo was painted on the door: a thunderbolt in the hand of an unseen power.

Four taps sounded again. She'd only gotten off duty three and a half hours ago. What was up? She rolled to her feet, flipped the latch, and swung the narrow door inward. Admiral Manu stood in the dimly lit passageway, left forearm propped by the upper hinges, lounging like a person who has all the time in the world to tell you what he's sure you want to hear. Belatedly she realized she was wearing her usual sleeping gear: skimpy, lightweight cotton shorts and a knit tank cut with one long armhole for both arms on each side of her torso. The admiral's eyes widened as he gave her a swift once-over.

He smiled in a way that made her neck prickle. "Were you expecting someone, Apama?"

"It's Lieutenant." She glanced at her berth, wondering if she should grab her blanket and wrap it around her body, but that would let him know he'd rattled her.

He said nothing, because his gaze had followed hers to the rumpled bed.

"May I help you, Admiral?" She glanced at the clock. By ship standard it was the middle of the night watch. "I'm not on duty."

"You know, Lieutenant, I didn't come here to say this but I can offer you a better deal than the Angursa Syndicate."

"What?"

"They've been trawling that young socialite Bartholomew in front of you. An alliance with a syndicate confines you inside a higher fence. That's not what you want."

Her ears burned with a rage she could not show to a superior officer, even if he was only a foreigner who'd been granted military powers through a Council remit and not the regular chain of promotion. "I was promised a return to lancer duty."

"You were promised a return to the front. After I sort out the Karnos situation we'll have time to talk about your father's wishes and what's most advantageous for you. But alas, there's no time for this. Be in the conference room in fifteen minutes."

"You could have sent that order over comms."

His gaze lingered on the topography of the thin fabric over her chest. Finally he turned away, but paused and said over his shoulder, "Yes, I could have."

She shut the door, wishing she could slam it, not that slamming did any good. After stifling a yawn, she downed a cup of lukewarm coffee, brushed her teeth with her lower right while with her uppers she spritzed a little oil on her short cap of hair and rubbed it through with her fingers, and dressed in her duty uniform. Her flight suit hung unused in the locker. She touched it for luck, a habit she'd started the day she boarded the heavy cruiser in Anchor System and now couldn't shake.

In the passageway she had to give way to two different syndicate admirals who had clearly just arrived via shuttle from other ships. Definitely unusual. The flag entrance brought her into the Combat Information Center.

A virtual map filled the airspace in the compartment's dome-like ceiling. The *Thunderbolt in Hand* had arrived in Sleepless System nineteen watch hours earlier. They were one beacon drop away from Karnos.

Sleepless was a janus system. One beacon linked directly to Karnos and the other to Anchor via Sandbank, Haymarket, and Cut Stone Systems. A clean, fast shot into the heart of the empire, which is why Sleepless had long served as the leading edge of the old frontier of imperial space. That was before the empire had absorbed Karnos, the Hatti region, Kanesh, Troia, and even for a while the Republic of Chaonia.

Sleepless still retained a fortress edge. Its in-system fleet presence was geared to defense, anchored by four older-class dreadnoughts.

Currently, three dreadnoughts waited within hailing distance of the *Thunderbolt in Hand* as the big ships, their escorts, and Manu's fleet approached the Karnos Beacon. A conference would have easily been convened via comms. How had he managed to convince the high command to use his flagship's CIC conference room for an in-person meeting?

The conference room shared a wall with CIC, up steps and with a long window overlooking the command center. Manu kept the shared wall transparent. She wasn't sure if it was because he liked to keep an eye on the comings and goings in CIC as he held meetings, or because he liked people to see him holding meetings.

Today, to her surprise, the wall was tuned opaque. A pair of Incorruptibles stood guard at the door. The presence of the Incorruptibles meant a Rider had come on board. Her jaw tensed. Her sire would be looking through their eyes.

Breathe.

The Incorruptibles inclined their heads to let her know she could go directly in. It was like having a brand seared onto your forehead: *Belongs to the Rider Council, handle with performative care.* The door slid aside. At the conference room's long table an intense but muted discussion was taking place as preamble to a formal meeting.

Paulo was present, as well as syndicate admirals from Tanarctus, Oreella, and Eschiniscus. Three brigadiers had seats at the table, which meant ground forces were expected to come into play. For once, Admiral Manu was not sitting in the end chair. That was reserved for the Rider.

Seeing her enter, the Rider stood. He was a big man with big shoulders and a big manner and a big smile. For an instant she forgot she was looking at a Rider's half-formed face because his had such a full gleam of existence, nothing like her sire's prim, whispery, and menacing presence.

"Apama At Sabao. Zakurru's daughter. May I call you Apama? I'm Baragesi."

The high officers at the table and the adjutants seated on a ring of benches against the walls all stared as Baragesi walked the length of the room to greet her. The Rider set a hand to her shoulder, a disconcerting shift into her intimate space. Manu stared in consternation as if someone else was trying to steal his toy and he could not interfere. Eyebrows rose among the onlookers.

Baragesi whispered for her ears only, "Excuse the informality, but I'm delighted to meet you, Apama. It's odd for me to know more of you than you of me, if you'll forgive me. Not much I can do about it, heh."

He turned to present his front to her. His other face, his ordinary face, regarded her with a faintly embarrassed smile on features marked by the rugged looks of an active outdoorsman who gets a lot of sun. His other face said to her, "I am Gil. I'm also pleased to meet you, although I have not seen you before or even heard much about you. You know how it is."

Apama was so shaken both by the courtesy, and the glimpse of self-deprecating humor, that she thought her legs were going to give way and she'd collapse onto the deck in a humiliating heap. Gil tucked an upper hand under her upper elbow so as not to assume too much intimacy as he caught her weight and steadied her.

She got her balance back. "I'm all right," she murmured.

He released her just as the door opened to admit the assertive Batillipes admiral accompanied by an admiral wearing the badge of Apochela Syndicate. This was a lot of brass present in one small room.

She made her way to a place left open on the bench behind Manu. He shot her a dark look that she pretended not to see. The colonels on either side gave her side-eye as she said "Ma'am" to each. The moment every butt touched a seat, Manu stood, but he had to wait for the Rider's go-ahead.

"We are listening, Admiral Manu," said Baragesi. The atmosphere intensified as Riders throughout the Phene Empire shifted their attention through their comrade.

"You'll all have the news," said Manu.

That Eirene was dead? That was old news. His next words made her stiffen with a lancer pilot's instinct for trouble coming fast.

"Four hours ago, a courier ship dropped through Aspera Beacon into Karnos System. Their message was heard one hundred and forty-seven minutes later by the fleet Rider stationed at Tarsa Beacon. Baragesi immediately relayed the news to me and asked that we meet in person. I contacted all of you, who have gathered now."

He paused for their nods, then went on portentously. "A Chaonian fleet in Aspera System is approaching its Karnos Beacon with intent to attack. We have perhaps thirty hours before a Chaonian vanguard could enter Karnos System via the Aspera Beacon."

"The *Grappling Minotaur* defends that beacon," said the Batillipes admiral, always the first to object. "It outweighs anything the Chaonians can throw at it."

"The Styraconyx Fleet did not have good luck with its dreadnoughts at Molossia," said Manu. "A big ship alone isn't enough to defeat their tactics. I recommend we send immediate reinforcements into Aspera System to strengthen the beacon defense task group."

Tanarctus asked, "Is there news from Tarsa or Na Iri Beacons?"

Baragesi shuttered his eyes as he communicated with Riders stationed in Karnos System. "No movement. Nothing coming through."

"Are there no Riders in Na Iri or Tarsa Systems?" Manu asked.

Baragesi said, "We withdrew all forward sentry Riders stationed in those systems when it became impossible for them to do their jobs. Since we have no military ships remaining and control no orbital stations by which to measure the movements of the Chaonian fleets, they can't report on what they can't observe."

"So does that mean the empire has no Riders left anywhere in Chaonian territory?" asked Manu with a meaningful look around the table.

"Except our sister Anchi."

Silence met these words as everyone reflected on the Rider who had been captured in Troia and remained a prisoner of war.

"So when it comes to Tarsa, Na Iri, and Aspera, your fleets have the same limited comms ability that the Chaonians do when it comes to knowing what is going on with enemy fleet movements," said Manu. "That's my point. Aspera is your bellwether."

Tanarctus said, "This Aspera attack is a feint. They want us to panic and send reinforcements through Aspera Beacon. Then their fleets will attack via Tarsa and Na Iri against our depleted strength."

"What if it isn't a feint?" said Paulo. "Can we afford to take that chance?"

"A feint is a classic Eirene maneuver. I've fought her before, even if you haven't, my dear Paulo," said Batillipes.

Tanarctus and Oreella chimed in with agreement. Eschiniscus and Apochela defended Paulo's position, arguing for a more aggressive response.

As the discussion swept back and forth and sideways, Apama watched Gil's face in profile as he faced the wall with its mural depicting the Procession of Bells. He wasn't studying the elaborate details of the painting. His eyes slid in and out of the nystagmus she recognized as Rider communications. Baragesi was holding his own council session. How did they keep their voices separate? What was it like to be inside that network of minds?

Manu broke in. "We can churn this bug butter for hours without making any progress. The Aspera attack is not a feint. Have none of you learned the lessons of the Molossia engagement? Eirene is no longer queen-marshal. Sun has a bolder, blunter style. This is a frontal assault we're meant to think is a feint. They want us to keep our defense separated at the other beacons while she smashes through."

Objections rose in a flood of outrage and disagreement.

Tanarctus's voice rose above the rest with the experienced bellow of a man who has presided over many a syndicate circus. "Ridiculous. It would be sheer recklessness for a military without Riders to try to coordinate this kind of narrowly effective timeline between three star systems. Who would risk that?"

"Sun would risk it," said Paulo abruptly. "It's exactly what the girl I knew would do were she to command the Chaonian fleet. The more I think this over, the more I agree with Manu that we are looking at their main attack via Aspera. There are four dreadnoughts here in Sleepless. We should move three into Karnos System immediately together with all our fleets."

No.

No.

No.

The Batillipes faction was unyielding, and with the brigadiers voting in their favor, they held a majority of the military votes. Sun was too young. It was too soon after Eirene's death. No one could consolidate power that fast in the notoriously cutthroat Chaonian political sphere.

One point they kept coming back to: Who would attack across a boundary that would put you immediately in a worse tactical position? There was too great a risk that your attack would be overwhelmed and obliterated before reinforcements could reach you.

The pragmatic side of Apama agreed with them, but the lancer pilot in her kept spinning back to the idea of a surprise attack from an unexpected angle. Still, she had no input, no authority, nothing to say. Watching the dynamic of the contentious discussion play out had its own fascination. Even if Manu was right, the high admirals were imperial Phene while he was an exile working among people not his own. He could not command syndicate fleets. He was dependent on the Rider Council's support, and Paulo, too, was arguing from a position of weakness as he worked to lift his syndicate back to its former prominence. Had the Council elevated these two precisely because they had more control over them? An interesting question. The Rider Council ruled the empire, but the syndicates held all the local and regional power bases and the labor resources they represented.

In the end a majority of admirals voted to hold the dreadnoughts in reserve in Sleepless System, under Angursa command, while maintaining the current defensive disposition of the fleet currently in Karnos, focused on the Tarsa and Na Iri Beacons. Manu and the Incorruptible task force would drop through into Karnos System, accompanied by an additional squadron of Angursa ships, and he would assess circumstances on arrival. The meeting ended in a flood of chatter and complaint as the admirals left to return to their ships. Paulo spoke quietly with the Rider before departing, face somber. Manu remained with his two adjutants and Apama.

"This is a mistake," he said to Baragesi when they were alone. "What is the point of giving me a strategic command if the Council won't require the syndicates to obey my orders?"

"Do you wish to retire, Admiral?"

"And be succeeded by whom? I don't doubt Phene courage, mind you."

"Just our effectiveness?"

"I'm finding the high command to be short-sighted. Stuck in the battles they fought a generation ago."

"Against you?"

"I beat you."

"You did, which is why the Council has welcomed you."

"You'd do better to welcome my ideas."

"One battle is not a war. A war is waged through attrition and endurance. We have more ships, more people, and more resources. The Chaonians will overreach. That will be the end of their ambitions. Now, I mean to return to the command ship. Apama will come with me."

"What?" Manu's outrage was glorious to witness. He set an arm akimbo. It was always so odd to see such a coarse gesture stunted by the lack of four arms whose many varied positions could convey much more nuanced degrees of rudeness. "Lieutenant At Sabao was assigned as *my* adjutant."

Baragesi remained untouched by Manu's indignation. "So she was. But as there is no immediate military purpose for her to remain on the *Thunderbolt in Hand,* I am removing her to the *Virtuous Heart.*"

Not even Manu could countermand the order of the Speaker for the Rider Council of the Phene Empire. He stood at attention but fuming on all cylinders, if Apama was any judge of the tension in his lips and the anger in his eyes.

"Admiral, see you on the other side," she said politely.

"We are all destined for death," he replied in the formal manner.

She followed Baragesi out, an odd experience in itself, because Gil walked two steps ahead of her to leave her tête-à-tête with Baragesi's face.

Baragesi winked—*winked!*—as they made their way to her cabin. When she opened the door he said, "I could have sent an attendant to fetch your things but I thought you would want to collect them yourself."

She packed quickly because she knew exactly where everything was stowed and how to layer it into her kit with maximum efficiency. Using the activity as cover, she spoke without looking at him.

"Why would you think that about me?"

"You act with discretion and duty, but in your own way you challenge the well-trodden path. You speak your mind in a refreshing way."

"Do you all spy on each other?"

"Ouch. We try not to. We have our own courtesies among ourselves. We live in a peculiar state. It's inexplicable to anyone not a Rider. It's inexplicable even to my friend Gil, who suffers my presence stoically."

"You're not half so bad as some of the others," said Gil with a chuckle.

"Hush, you yammerer," said Baragesi good-naturedly.

Apama thought of how her sire and Dasa seemed more like contenders fighting over a shared scrap of land than like the symbiotic partners Baragesi and Gil seemed at first acquaintance to be. Were Riders symbionts or parasites?

She sealed her kit and hoisted the strap over her left shoulder.

With the *T-Hand* readying for battle stations as the ship prepared for a beacon-drop into Karnos System, people were moving about the passageways. When personnel saw the Incorruptibles, then her, then the Rider, they swiftly stepped back against a bulkhead with lower arms at their sides and upper arms crossed, hands to opposite shoulders, in a gesture of respect. Some looked spooked and worried, eyes averted. Others looked on in awe. As a girl she'd never thought she'd see a Rider in person, and yet here she was walking with the head of the Rider Council.

Why couldn't Baragesi have been her sire instead of Zakurru?

Even as the thought seared through her, she cast it away. What did she really know about Baragesi except that he had flawlessly executed a power play to upend the old Council leadership? That he had installed his faction as the majority, with himself as its de facto leader? He was not a genial uncle, however amiable he seemed.

Yet as she heard him greet the people they passed with heartening phrases, she couldn't shake the feeling that he wouldn't have manipulated a young lancer pilot's duty station in order to drag her into his orbit. That he wouldn't have used a young pilot as bait to lure a woman who didn't want him into a situation where she could not say no. Why had Zakurru sent Apama with Manu if not as a similar lure? But what was in it for her sire, since it was already in Manu's interest to ally with the empire?

In Hangar 4 they boarded a courier built for speed, all engines and maneuverability. Instead of taking the single cabin to isolate himself, as Zakurru would have done, Baragesi strapped in alongside Apama in the tight quarters of the passenger hold with its sixteen seats. They were the only passengers.

The soldiers took seats by the airlock. The courier departed the hangar. Watching the screen, Apama admired the powerful lines of the heavy cruiser as it receded. The image collapsed into a pinprick among a cloud of torch drives, one light among many. The courier accelerated for the Karnos Beacon, a palely glowing spiral growing larger and larger as they approached.

Gil turned his head so Baragesi could speak. "We live in a different world from that of a year ago. One, I hope, with a return to the ideals of our founding syndicates."

"What do you mean?"

"I mean you, Apama. You and the other family members."

She worried for her mother, and yet in her gut she suspected her mother had a degree of safety that even she lacked: Zakurru's ego. How might she phrase dangerously critical thoughts when she knew any Rider could hear her?

"Wasn't Kubaba right? Riders relinquished clan and family ties so they could never be accused of nepotism. Syndicates built the empire, but they're also rife with favoritism. Maybe everyone was an idealist in the early days. But what have I ever done to earn the chance to speak to you, and to have you speak to me as if I am an equal?"

"We in the empire are all equals. This core belief drove our founders out of Mishirru's rigid hierocracy. That has been my point all along."

"I was given a berth on the *Strong Bull* before I'd earned it the way other lancer pilots had. How is that equality?"

"We humans have hierarchal tendencies, it's true. We will always struggle with the gap between the ideal and the real, the good and the imperfect. In this case I mean equality for those we ride. Gil, here, for example." An arm gestured toward the front of his body, whose expression she could not see. "Is his life mine to consume? I use 'he' as my pronoun as a courtesy to Gil. Gender means little enough to me but it matters to him. Is it right for me to take away from him a chance to experience the joy and warmth of a family of his own? To be acquainted with his womb parent and sire? Is it right to steal that connection from him for the sake of an objectivity that's impossible to achieve, despite Kubaba's claims?"

"Rider children are raised in creches. You're your own family."

"An inadequate solution, I think you'll agree."

"I don't know. I was never allowed inside the creche. Those children are guarded like treasure."

"All children are treasure, Apama. If you don't know that now, then perhaps you will discover it one day when you have children of your own. Which reminds me."

Comms chimed. "Five minutes to transition. Taking all weigh off the ship."

The gravity cut. Her body pressed against the straps. She desperately wished she weren't trapped for this conversation, because she knew where it was going. He and Zakurru were allies. She must never forget that.

"The Angursa Syndicate is dangling one of their young ones in front of you."

"Bartholomew."

"It's a limiting offer, Apama."

"For me, or for the Council?"

He chuckled. She couldn't see how Gil reacted, only the soft features of the riding face. It hadn't occurred to her that Riders could have personalities. Had she thought them less than human?

"Advantages accrue to both. Young Bartholomew is a delightful confection, and more canny than his affectations may make him seem. But Paulo Kr Manalon has a taint about him because of his past. He's not fully trusted, yet Angursa does control a substantial fleet and resources and labor. An alliance with Angursa offers the Council nothing it doesn't already have, which is his need for our support to reassert Angursa's prominence. However, an alliance with Admiral Manu brings the Yele League into a true accord with us."

"How does it do that? Admiral Manu is in exile from the League."

"Once we defeat Chaonia, the Yele League will gladly tear up their treaty with the republic in favor of a new one with us. Baron Voy. The seers of Iros. Admiral Manu. They all weave that connection more tightly, through various factions who will eventually outnumber the other Yele factions. The Yele don't have strong syndicate ties as we do. That's why they're fractious and easy to defeat."

"And Manu defeated a Phene fleet."

"As he is ever reminding everyone."

"That's why you want to keep him on your side, so he won't be the one fighting against you when the time comes. Keep your friends close and your enemies closer."

"That's right. The Yele exiled him because they feared his popularity. Nevertheless, the Chaonians remain a greater threat. Even after we defeat this stunt of an attack on Karnos, the Chaonians will try to bury their sharp little teeth into our hides, however tough our skin may be.

Obviously we can't pledge a Rider to the Yele League to sweeten an alliance and show we have placed our own skin in the game."

"But you could send me, daughter of a prominent member of the Council, tied to a victorious Manu. What do you think the League will offer in return?"

"A more sympathetic ruler on the throne of Chaonia. Isn't that what we all want? Peace from Chaonia's aggression?"

Why did they keep piling this burden on her? "I want to go back to the *Strong Bull*."

"Ah." An ambivalent expression, but she heard it as *You were never going back.*

The transition alert chimed. The ship rolled.

They dropped into the gap, a void both infinite and minute. Whispers chased in her head as if someone were seated behind her, murmuring secrets.

". . . a lover on the *Strong Bull*? . . . why has that supervisory in Mishirru been accused of graft by the local torchbearer? . . . an Asmu envoy wishes to hand over a janus-child in accordance with the Fallen Angels Treaty, quite unexpected since we've had no official contact beyond the Asmu frontier in five Anchor years . . ."

The courier dropped into Karnos space.

"Transition complete," said comms.

The viewscreen fuzzed out and went white. An agonizing 108 seconds ticked past before the screen reformatted with the status of fleets, the relative position of planets and beacons, and a spectacular view of the icy blue-gray glare of Karnos Oct, which the display informed her was locally known as Mausoleum.

She'd been through Karnos System on her way to the *Strong Bull*. Since that passage, her life had changed beyond anything she had ever imagined for herself. There was no going back to those innocent days. She was fully in the Council's grip now, and they had no intention of letting her go.

The Valiant One Has One Job

As Sun's official liaison to the Sixth Fleet, Makinde had been given a seat in the command center on Crane Marshal Zàofù's flagship. Next to him sat a Lieutenant Commander Zahrah Yún Albalasagun. She had a skin graft across her cheek that gave her the distinguished look of a soldier who has had part of their face blown off and not only survived but kept fighting. It was the Chaonian way: be flat-out tougher than the enemy.

"Five minutes to transition," comms announced.

She looked him up and down. "You sure you're a graduate? You look fifteen."

"I'm actually forty years old, sir. I just could never get rid of this baby fat."

She snorted a laugh that made the people around them look their way, everyone except the crane marshal on the strategos dais with his bushy eyebrows drawn tight like a fuzzy caterpillar. Zàofù was the kind of august personage who never cracked a smile. "You can't have fought at Molossia. You must have still been in the royal academy. Nursery school, maybe. You seen any action at all?"

"A harrowing patrol in Odrysa System in a picket ship on its last legs. We had to eat cold rations for six months."

"Brutal."

"We were the first responders when the Argosy fleet arrived bringing Princess Soaring to the queen-marshal-who-was."

Now he had her interest!

"Really? What I wouldn't give to see a Titan-class ship and its tow chain arrive!"

"The pulse of the arrival knocked out our drive, no lie."

"You get to go on board?"

"I did not. Maybe someday."

The transition bell chimed. The *Red Hare* dropped out of Tarsa System and, before he could worry about taking a breath, back into Karnos System.

Yún Albalasagun said, "Good luck," sealed her helmet, and headed off.

A visual of Karnos System played overhead. Here they were, racing out of a beacon anchored to a smoky-colored ice giant with pretty rings and a bunch of moons. Points of light marked Phene ships. So many lights. He was seeing the past through a lag, so it was just in his imagination that he saw the Phene ships gathering their feet under them as they made ready to charge with shields raised and spears lowered.

Makinde had one job. He pinged Sun. SIXTH AND NINTH IN KARNOS.

Battle stations klaxons blared. A ping dropped in from Razin, assigned as Seventh Fleet liaison under the command of Crane Marshal Qìngzhī Bō at Na Iri System.

SEVENTH AND SECOND HAVE ARRIVED IN KARNOS SYSTEM.

Incredible timing, considering their coordination was a shipboard clock set to Argos Mean Time.

Sun would not yet have dropped into Karnos, letting the veteran fleets engage the bulk of the enemy at Tarsa and Na Iri Beacons. It was a good plan as long as the Phene believed the attack in Aspera was a feint.

"Incoming. All hands brace for shock."

Makinde was no expert on tactics, not yet anyway, but at the royal academy they were all drilled in the basics. The Phene reacted with a practiced expertise. From long range, volleys of missiles and heavy artillery fire poured out of their assault cruisers. A line of resilient Yele-style frigates and the sleeker, punishing Phene destroyers formed up to meet the Chaonians head-to-head. While they brawled, light cruisers and missile boats harassed the flanks of the Chaonian line. Lancers lurked in the gaps, waiting to pick at any scratch and exploit where they could.

It was a battle-tested formation that had allowed the Phene to conquer large swathes of the local belt. Thirty years ago, it would have been a battle at long range which the Chaonians couldn't have hoped to win. Eirene had changed all that, and Zàofù had been there with her every step of the way.

The venerable marshal spoke to his ships as if their captains were riding alongside, in a calm, almost monotone voice that seemed immune to the chaos and violence swirling around them. "Battleships to the front. Hold your position. Do not give way."

A big boom, and they were in the thick of it, hammered by Phene assault cruisers. Makinde's hands itched. He hated sitting here with nothing more to do while the battle raged.

Comms crackled. "Marshal, we are taking heavy damage. We are outgunned. Permission to give ground to draw them in."

"Very well," said Zàofù. "Maintain formation." Then to another voice, "Flanking squadrons advance, draw them into a melee."

The *Red Hare* shuddered. Alarms blared on life-support consoles, immediately muted. Over comms a windy hoot betrayed a breach.

A calm voice reported, "Hull breach on Hangar 3—" Cut off.

Yún Albalasagun's voice on comms: "This is the damage control assistant from DCC, repair parties respond to hull breach on Deck 3!"

A loud pop. A shudder rang through the ship, followed by silence for fifteen endless seconds. Comms rerouted. Damage reports poured in from across the fleet.

The ring buzzed. I'M HERE.

"Marshal, Sun is in-system," announced Makinde, knowing it would take a minute for comms to route the official message.

A cheer burst from the *Red Hare*'s bridge crew. The audacious plan had worked.

"Earlier than I expected." The old man was unflappable. "The local Aspera Beacon defense won't be able to hold her off, so she should be able to support our flank soon."

If by *soon* he meant twenty or forty or eighty hours. Makinde hadn't done the calculations, and he wasn't about to ask. He just hoped the old battleship would still be in one piece by then.

The crane marshal went on. "Chief, do you have information on fleet movements elsewhere in-system?"

The chief looked up from their console. "We still have no access to Phene-controlled satellite intel."

"No word from the operatives on Karnos Prime who are supposed to link us into those systems?"

"Not yet."

Makinde said, "I'll get on it, Marshal."

As the *Red Hare* shuddered under relentless attack, Makinde collated intel from the four fleets. Dozer's enhanced processing capacities helped him calculate telemetry and comms lag as he tried to get a sense of the battle playing out across the system. Karnos Sext, anchoring Aspera Beacon, sat a bit separated from the other beacons in the current alignment. Karnos Terce, anchoring the Na Iri Beacon, and Karnos Quince, anchoring Tarsa Beacon, were at perihelion in relationship to each other. Deci and Sept anchored the beacons that led into imperial Phene space, Sleepless and Windworn, and were in relative terms close to each other but at aphelion compared to Terce and Quince. Karnos Duodeci, anchoring the Hellion Terminus Beacon, was off on its own, not really in play. Karnos Oct was likewise about as far from the others as it could be, but since the planet anchored a dead beacon, its orbital shipyards and mining colony wouldn't matter for this engagement.

An orderly swung past with stim bulbs, tea, and protein. Makinde's mouth was dry and he wasn't hungry but he knew he had to eat. It was strange how a battle could drag on and on even as each moment seemed like clutching the edge of a cliff. The Sixth and Ninth Fleets barely clung to the octant surrounding Karnos Quince. The marshal had forbidden even an injured ship from retreating through the beacon, lest other captains and crews give way to doubt. Multiple ships had already been hulked and abandoned with grim losses, and more were barely holding on with all power to shields. It seemed as if a hundred hours had already passed.

But something in the battle had changed. The division of Chaonian battleships that had taken the brunt of the first volleys had carefully withdrawn, pulling the heavier Phene ships after them. Eager for the glory of sinking those old monitors and cracking the Chaonian line, the lighter Phene warships had closed in, only to be drawn into close-range battle by Chaonian fast frigates and allied corvettes. That careful initial formation of Phene ships had fallen into disarray in the face of the resilience and discipline of the Chaonians. Now the Phene light missile ships had come in too close to the Chaonian assault frigates, and thus all their advantages of superior range and mobility were wasted. What must have seemed to the Phene at the beginning like a perfect rout of the Chaonians had become a battle of attrition that could go on for days.

The chief broke in. "Hold on, Marshal. Getting a burst of intel from the *Boukephalas*. A large Incorruptibles fleet is approaching Aspera Beacon. Not clear where it came from but it must have anticipated the queen-marshal's attack."

Zàofù's brief scowl suggested his worst-case scenario had come true, as he had warned. "She's got heavy weather ahead of her. We'll have to press our attack so these fleets can't reinforce the ships attacking Sun's fleet. Tell Captain Yeh to bring up her Centaur Division. We keep up the pressure here until Sun breaks through or retreats back to Aspera. It's what Eirene would expect from us. I see no reason we should hold to a different standard for her heir."

A Command Politely Framed as a Request

The *Virtuous Heart* was a command ship, built to maximize communications and sensors. An escort of Incorruptibles assault cruisers and pugnacious destroyers protected it, together with a task group of tankers, haulers, and transports, the worker ships of the great Phene fleets. Staffed entirely by Incorruptibles, its passageways reminded Apama of the corridors beneath Unity Hall because they felt less military and more communal. The discipline of focused work was the same. Galleys battened down as cooks prepared foods for battle stations. An infirmary shielded in the center of the ship readied for intake.

She accompanied Baragesi to a double-airlocked internal security barrier that led into a core compartment. An Incorruptible wearing a steward's bars ushered them into a reception area with desks and couches. An adolescent Rider sat with her ordinary face scanning information from a screen while her riding face mouthed words and numbers that evidently matched what her other face was reading. The girl broke off and rose with a twinned smile.

"Uncle! A Chaonian task force has broken through at Aspera! The fleet under *Thunderbolt in Hand* will intercept them in a few hours." The smile flattened, and she blushed. "Not that you don't already know," she muttered as if to herselves.

He gave her an avuncular nod. "Admiral Manu's fleet will take care of them. I've brought someone to meet you."

Seeing Apama, the girl ducked her head shyly. She looked so young and gawky. "Oh! You're the lancer pilot."

Of course the girl already knew her. "That's right. I'm Apama At Sabao."

The girl pressed her upper hands to her cheeks, took in a breath as if this was the most remarkable thing ever to happen to her, and lowered her hands. "I'm Giolla. Tadukhipa has a quiet voice so I'll introduce her to you on her behalf."

She turned her head so Apama could see her riding face, with its eyes like shards of infinity and its mouth an almost indistinct line.

Apama had no idea how the young ones were raised, except in creches among their own kind, but the girl's awkward politeness was endearing. "My greetings to you, Giolla. Tadukhipa. Please call me Apama."

The girl pressed her hands together excitedly at this modest offer of intimacy. "Thank you, Apama! Uncle Baragesi says I can apply to get a pilot's license when I'm older."

"All in good time," said Baragesi to the girl. "Back to monitoring. Things will start moving fast."

The girl flushed, looking chagrined.

He said, "You're doing well, Tadukhipa, and you too, Giolla. You'd never know this is your apprentice assignment." He smiled encouragingly before informally gesturing toward an internal door with his lower right. "Apama, if you will."

It was a command politely framed as a request. Baragesi led her into a secondary room fitted with two four-person lifepods and an air seal: an emergency escape hatch. In this empty space he paused, the two of them alone.

"I brought you here to meet others like you."

"What do you mean?" Without meaning to, she brushed one of her elbows where she could always feel a stub of the caul removed so long ago.

"Gil's family."

"Gil's? Not yours too, Baragesi?" She regretted the words the instant they left her mouth but it was too late to un-say them.

He opened all four hands, palms upward. "I am just here for the ride. My concerns are not with the flesh, although some among my brethren do concern themselves with the flesh. Perhaps too much."

Ouch. Silence was prudence. She folded her hands and waited.

"May I ask of you a kindness, to greet these as kinsfolk. You and they are alike in having been cast into an ambivalent position."

"Of course."

She couldn't help but be curious as the door opened. The suite beyond was decorated in the bold colors of an airy mountain scene. An old man was seated on a divan reading to a child of eight or ten years of age, tucked affectionately against his side. Apama saw the child's resemblance to Gil immediately: the bronze-brown hair color was distinctive.

"Here you are, son," said the old man with a smile.

"Daddy! Daddy!" The child hopped off the divan and ran over to the Rider, who embraced him with the enthusiasm of a devoted parent. Baragesi closed his eyes as if to allow Gil privacy.

The old man rose with the assistance of a cane, a gesture of respect toward Apama's perceived status that she saw too late. She hurried over.

"My apologies for making you stand, Uncle. I'm Apama At Sabao."

"Not at all. The effort is good for my health, else I'd lounge all day long and lose what remains of the strength in my legs. I'm Gil's sire. Jejomar Os Cook. We call this rascal Banoy."

It was strange to hear a Rider associated with one of the diaspora fleet names, yet it also served to remind her that Riders were born into every and any part of the population of imperial Phene. Stranger still, Os Cook had only two arms. He was a stunt, a throwback to the distant past before the flowering of Phene genengineering.

"Yes," he said with a good-natured smile as he watched her take in his arms.

"I'm so sorry, how rude of me," she said with a flush of shame. Baragesi and Gil had not made a single comment about severed cauls.

"Please, don't apologize. There's a slight statistical correlation for those with the rare two-armed condition among imperial Phene to produce Riders. Did you know?"

"I did not."

"Here I am to tell you." His bantering tone and lively expression reminded her of her mom.

He rang a hand bell. A splendidly vibrant woman appeared from a farther room. She pulled a nursing shield over her chest with her uppers as with her lowers she balanced a baby on a hip.

"What is it . . . Oh! Gil! You've arrived already, darling, and with the guest you promised. Please, join us. I'm Tamira Zr Guerrero. You must be Apama At Sabao. Please call me Tamira. May I take the liberty of calling you Apama?"

"My thanks, Tamira," said Apama, feeling overwhelmed as by a pleasantly warm salt wave rushing over her.

The woman offered Gil a dignified kiss to the cheek, greeted Baragesi separately, then called out, "Aunt Pilar! We have a delightful visitor!"

A second door opened to reveal the old woman who had been at the synod. She was Jejomar's sister, it turned out. Soon Apama found herself seated at a table, being offered an array of sweets: sticky rice cake, dishes of halo halo, dried mango. Gil acted like any ordinary man relaxing with family. Baragesi seemed asleep, features slack.

Giolla Tadukhipa did not come inside. When Apama asked, Tamira said, "She's on duty. Aunt Pilar will take her a plate later. Tell us more about yourself, Apama. If you don't mind, I mean."

"I saw you at Anchor," said Aunt Pilar. "Where did you go after that? Back to a lancer squadron?"

"Are you a lancer pilot?" asked the boy with breathy awe.

"I am, but at the moment it seems I'm a functionary getting to know how the administration of the empire works."

Banoy bounced in his seat. "There's a full squadron of lancers on board! Do you think they'll let you fly one?"

"Not by myself. It takes eight hands to launch a lancer."

"Could you take me? I have a pilot's license on the game *Bold Lancer*."

"You're not quite tall enough, but soon."

"Have you been at Anchor all this time?" asked Aunt Pilar. "Working the Exchange? I did that for a few years when I was young like you but it's hard work and long hours."

"Anyone special waiting for you there?" asked Tamira with a knowing wink.

Uncle said, "You ever eat at Lola Pinang's Lugawan, on Katipunan Boulevard by the flower market? No one makes lugaw like Lola Pinang does." He smacked his lips with pleasure at the memory.

It was exactly like the neighborhood where she'd grown up. She'd only had her mother, but everyone else lived in a network of kinship and knew everyone's business and everyone's whereabouts, an unending discussion that went on day and night, the gossip that binds. Orphans they might have been, but she and her mother had been wrapped tightly into the life of their district in a way she'd missed bitterly during her years at flight school.

All of them went quiet as Gil's eyes began the telltale nystagmus. He rose. Baragesi had returned, alert and in charge.

The riding face said, "Apama, attend me. Aunt, prepare in case of emergency."

Apama barely had time to give a nod to the worried company before she followed him out. In the reception room, Tadukhipa swiveled as they entered.

"I need you to remain here with the others," he said.

"But I can—"

"No. You will remain here under Code Five."

The steward appeared. "May I assist you, Eminence?"

"Emergency lockdown, Heitor. Coordinate with the other family suites."

"Of course."

Outside, a new pair of Incorruptibles stood guard. "Eminence?"

"Remain here in case of emergency measures." Gil strode on.

She hurried after. "Baragesi, what is happening?"

"I need you to get a lockdown code at the infirmary. You're to avoid capture at all costs as an asset that may be vulnerable to Chaonian retribution."

"Retribution?"

"There is some concern about how Chaonians might treat prisoners known to be important to the Rider Council. Not that we are likely to find ourselves in that position, but we prepare for the worst."

He took a breath, prelude to saying more, just as the comms system crackled to life. "All alert. All alert. Battle stations."

As they reached the hatch letting into CIC, an adjutant swung it open. Several officers came jogging down the passageway to enter behind them before the hatch was dogged. The cavernous space had multiple levels like balconies circling a dome. It seemed as vast as a basilica even though she knew it was a trick of the compartment's shape and the ship's lighter-than-Anchor gravity. The shifting colors of the big virtual display smeared out and in as it adjusted to an avalanche of new information immediately superseded by new information.

A voice erupted from a console: Admiral Manu sounding fed up but calm. "We're looking at exactly the scenario I warned against. Baragesi, contact the Rider in Sleepless and have Paulo send through the dreadnoughts immediately. We must stop the attack at Aspera Beacon. I'm headed there."

Baragesi went directly into a ready room tucked like an egg behind a balcony. A Rider circle was placed in the middle of the space. He sat in one of the chairs. Two indistinct figures shimmered in and out of focus—two Riders in-system—while the other chairs remained empty except as a symbol. As they spoke silently, she looked back out the open door at the virtual display. A lancer pilot had the skill of separating sparks of light and threads of movement. Quickly she sorted the main sorties and confrontations going on in real time with variable lags.

Astoundingly, an aggressive fleet had entered Karnos System via the well-guarded Aspera Beacon and in timed coordination with attacks via Na Iri and Tarsa Beacons. How dared the Chaonians try it? To coordinate across light-years without Riders was reckless beyond belief.

A lieutenant colonel came to the ready room door. "Lieutenant At Sabao?"

"Ma'am."

"Come with me."

The image of one of the in-system Riders scattered in a burst of static. She sucked in a breath, fearing the ship the Rider was on had been destroyed. More likely it was a comms interruption. Ships didn't blow up in one big burst. They died hard and slow and ugly. As static crackled across the circle, Baragesi didn't look at her. The officer was walking away, so she scrambled after.

There was a secondary infirmary in an adjoining compartment. An Incorruptible physician waited in the intake room beside an IV chair. "Please, have a seat. The microscopic marker in this vial is cued to override fleet lockdown systems."

"Wait. You're giving me some kind of physiological marker that allows me access to all fleet systems?"

The physician glanced at the officer, a shared look whose implications she couldn't parse. "Usually reserved for Riders."

She opened her mouth, meaning to say something, but her parted lips soundlessly held an *Oh* and she gave up and shut her mouth.

"Lower left just below the elbow," said the physician. She rolled up her sleeve. "We're compressing a seventy-two-hour load into twenty-four. That's the highest rate a body can endure. I've added an anesthetic so you will sleep for the duration."

"I'd rather stay awake."

"No, you wouldn't. Brace yourself."

"Yes, ma'am, I'm used to it," she said stoutly.

"Lancer pilots," said the physician in a dour tone, as if he'd dealt with too many.

She settled into the IV chair, resting her lower left on a pad. The officer caught her eye and courteously offered her a sympathetic smile. The needle pricked a vein. For a few breaths everything was fine. Then a million fiery microscopic ants burned an angry hot column up her arm. She broke out in a sweat. Her nubs leaked, dammit, so embarrassing as moisture oozed from beneath the pads she laboriously sewed into all her garments, creating stains at all her joints. That was the least of it, really. The walls began to sway and slowly spin.

Still holding her gaze, the officer said, "Is it true you were on the *Strong Bull* for the Molossia campaign?"

"Word gets around, ei. Wish I was back on . . . I'm going to throw up."

The physician stuck a bowl in front of her. She retched into it until there was nothing left of the delicacies she'd eaten with Gil's family. In a weird way the vomiting distracted her from the dizziness and the ghastly burn of the marker through her veins. A prickling blaze of agony raced through her body until she wished she could turn inside out and eject fluid everywhere.

When she stopped heaving, the physician handed her a glass with ice chips to suck on. "All normal reactions. Don't fight it."

Lancer pilots always fought, but the drugs won. She passed out.

Instinct Grabbed Her by the Throat

There were two universal rules of fleet war.

Don't fire on lifepods.

Keep beacon coils out of the direct trajectory of an attack.

Sun knew how to use obstacles that hindered others to work to her advantage. While still in Aspera System she swung her attacking force around the beacon in order to attack parallel to its coil. Her missed volleys sped into space rather than into the beacon. Not that beacons were fragile—far from it—but no one dared take the risk.

The Phene had expected an old-model dreadnought and its escort fleet to be an effective blocking force. But they had never been much good at a close fight, especially against Eirene's new tactics. After clearing out the dreadnought with a rapid-strike force of Tulpar-class battle cruisers, the *Boukephalas* led a phalanx of heavy cruisers with their deep shields straight down the drop and into Karnos System.

Because only one ship at a time could drop through a beacon, the path itself forced offensive attacks into a vulnerable column. That made defense strong. Conversely, a beacon's presence limited the amount of heavy fire a defender could bring to bear for the first few thousand klicks. No one shot toward ships as they emerged, because that meant shooting *at* the beacon. This gap was all she needed to force a crossing and get ships in formation. Directly behind her squadron came Angharad Black on the *Rakhsh*, commanding a company of heavy cruisers loaded with defensive power.

The instant she and the ship dropped through and entered Karnos System, messages appeared in the ring network from Makinde and Razin, confirmed minutes later by comms from Crane Marshal Zàofù and Crane Marshal Qìngzhī. Their fleets had engaged hours ago at the Tarsa and Na Iri Beacons. The battle was on across three fronts. No sign of dreadnoughts. Where were they?

Together she and Angharad smashed into the local beacon defense fleet. The heavy cruisers absorbed flight after flight of Phene weapons fire as they galloped toward the enemy, driving through in a wedge so the enemy risked hitting their own ships opposite if they fired on the intruders. The Tulpars followed, with the firepower that the heavy cruisers lacked, savaging the lightly armored Phene ships as they passed. The pounding from Phene missiles was relentless but slackened quickly, and she did not give way. As always, she muted the streaming casualty report. The cost of victory had to be set aside while the battle was being fought.

Behind, a third squadron dropped through, followed at speed by a fourth, no room for error as each individual ship cleared the beacon with barely a klick before and behind, running in a column tighter than anything Eirene had dared attempt.

Reports from the fleets streamed in with the expected lag. According to their comms, so far the Phene fleets assigned to defend the Tarsa and Na Iri Beacons had not broken formation to converge on Sun's attack, which meant Zàofù's and Qìngzhī's attacks were doing their job. It took extra time for her sensors to get intel across these distances, and even then the information was hours old and not as detailed as she'd like. She had hoped to have access to the Phene military network of sensors and arrays that would give her a commanding overview of the solar system, but the insurgents on Karnos Prime hadn't come through. Maybe James could have managed it but she'd sent him on a different mission.

Her mind raced through solutions that could have been taken if Eirene had thought through options to create a jury-rigged strategos system. Local agents could fasten spy bots onto orbital habitats. Work-aday spacecraft like miners, surveyors, and haulers could carry long-range wasps attached to their exteriors. Everything could be put in place and set to come online at drop time. She should have thought of it before this battle, but even if she had, there wouldn't have been time to implement it.

"Fifth squadron through," reported Lieutenant Ruiz at comms. "The Honorable Captain Alika Vata in command."

She pinged a query to Makinde and Razin.

HOLDING, both replied within seconds. Makinde added an editorial. GETTING HAMMERED BUT THE OLD GUY IS SOME KIND OF HARD-ASS LEGEND, I'LL TELL YOU. EPIC.

For an instant she wondered how things would have fallen out if Zàofù had not chosen to support her. He could still change his mind. But she set those thoughts aside. No distractions, only the battle now unfolding.

Captain Tan said, "Your Highness, an Incorruptibles fleet is moving in fast toward our position. They are led by an assault cruiser identified as the *Thunderbolt in Hand*. They outnumber and outgun us. At their current trajectory they will engage before our entire fleet has dropped through."

So. One enemy commander had anticipated her attack, not believ-ing it to be a classic Eirene feint. It grated that a sharp military mind had seen through her, realized the other attacks were the feints, not hers. But the Phene weren't fools, even if their military strategies and tactics were often predictable. She would push back this unexpected enemy and stick with the plan.

"Angharad, with me. We need to do as much damage as possible while the other squadrons head to Karnos Prime."

The *Boukephalas* surged forward surrounded by its escorts, burning hot and fearless as shields got pounded by the dogged defense force, those still able to fight. A fast frigate spun out of control as its drive and stabi-lizers were pulverized. Its attacker went silent minutes later, penetrated fore-to-aft by the main battery of a Tulpar and venting atmosphere and debris out of gaping wounds. Captain Black accelerated alongside as they sped toward the Incorruptibles fleet and its big assault cruiser. In her mind's eye Sun could already see the escort of destroyers lighting with a battery of weapons fire. But not yet. They were still too far away. And no dreadnoughts. Whoever was in command of the Incorruptibles, or the syndicate fleets, they'd elected to prioritize thrust over durability.

A fresh sheaf of data pinged in from Hetty at a console on the other side of the bridge. With James absent, Hetty was the one combing through the onslaught of information and telemetry for crucial items to bring to Sun's attention.

OPS HAS IDENTIFIED A PHENE COMMAND SHIP

"A command ship?" Eirene had never captured a command ship.

INTERCEPTED CHATTER SUGGESTS THE SPEAKER IS ON
    BOARD

Sun's hands tightened on the railing of the dais. Eirene had never personally confronted the most powerful individual in the empire. "Coordinates?"

Numbers dropped into her stream. The command ship was attended by a swarm of auxiliary vessels. Assault cruisers and heavy frigates gave escort.

"Speaker Baragesi himself." Sun's spirit swelled as with a blaze of light. Instinct grabbed her by the throat. "That's our target."

Captain Tan replied with his usual measured recitation of facts. "Your Highness, that's tens of hours away. Such an attack will delay our reinforcement of Sixth and Ninth."

"Tell Zàofù to hold his position. Relay to Captain Black that the approaching Incorruptibles fleet lacks heavy ships. She'll meet it head on. My squadron is going to break through and pursue the enemy command ship. We may never get this chance again."

"Your Highness, I am obliged to advise that such a course will separate this ship and its escorts from the rest of the fleets. We'll expose ourselves in a deeply vulnerable situation for what would not prove a decisive blow."

"Cutting off the head of their most recently elected leader will prove decisive. We're going after the Speaker. Full speed ahead."

The Wily Persephone Has Her Reputation as One of the Queen-Marshal's Hard-Ass Companions to Think Of

Solomon and I are sitting side by side on a bench in the spinward hangar of the fast frigate *Suvannamacha*. My hands are clenched in my lap as I practice breathing to calm my rattled nerves. He sits with perfect straight posture and feet flat on the deck, in full vacuum kit except for his helmet, ready for his part in the engagement.

"No shit here we are about to drop out of Aspera and straight into a titanic battle," I say, my voice not as squeaky as I fear it will be.

"You better get up on the bridge. Isn't that where you're supposed to be? Liaison for the queen-marshal to the squadron leader?"

Every time I think about Sun I still want to call her "Princess" because it annoyed her so much when I did. Eighteen days ago my mother murdered Eirene on Petitioners Bridge but it feels like it happened yesterday and also like it happened years ago, ancient history, water under the bridge, unmoored from Lee House with my line now attached to the ship of Sun.

"Do you think this is a suicide run?" I whisper. "Isn't it a little crazy?"

"For Sun to punch through a guarded beacon knowing the enemy defense on the other side will have warning that she's coming? Sure. But they'll think it's a feint, so it'll lessen their ability to confront her while also throwing them off their guard. It's brilliant. As long as we win."

I blow out a long exhalation, meant to be cleansing like we were taught at the academy.

Solomon says, "You sound like a leaking vent. You better go, Perse."

I want to give him a big, sloppy hug but there are five boarding parties of suited-up marines waiting in the hangar and I have my reputation as one of the queen-marshal's hard-ass Companions to think of. Instead, I jump to my feet and brush together my hands like I'm dusting the sticky residue of anxiety off my skin.

"Don't fuck this up, Solomon." He gives me a look, and I hastily add, "I mean, just get through it. You've never boarded a hostile before."

He punches my arm. Even as a playful gesture it staggers me two steps to the left.

"Get out of here, weak ass," he answers.

I give a nod to Colonel Wallace, who's in command of the marines, and exit the hangar into a passageway. The fastest route to the bridge is not the route I take. I detour down three decks to pass the galley with its hushed buzz of activity.

The distances of space mean battles are fought in brief pummeling impacts separated by long exhausting waits. We've been on board the *Suvannamacha* for four days and Ti is already in tight with the galley crew. I pause in the open hatch to watch her joking as she seals tumblers of tea and packs them with stim bulbs and protein-and-carb spikes into mesh bags, so they can get handed out to crew. She's dressed in a drab jumpsuit and with her hair in a tidy bun sans decoration, appropriate for the situation. I don't know where she gets the courage to walk clear-eyed as a noncombatant into the battle zone but here she is.

She glances up as if she's heard a whisper on the air, not that I said her name. Her gaze turns toward the hatch across twenty meters of worktables. Catching my eye, she nods decisively or reassuringly, or both. Then she gets back to work, the reminder that I need to return to where Sun expects me to be.

Comms blares. Transition in fifteen minutes.

I break into a trot, dodging the few crew members on their way somewhere; everyone else is at battle stations, like I should be, but of course I am a Companion and that gives me special responsibility but also enough leeway to glide onto the bridge with no one to stop me or remark on how long it took me to take a supposed trip to the head.

The fast frigate under the command of Captain the Honorable Gayathri Vata has the efficient focus of a crew honed during the years Eirene reshaped the Chaonian military. We're the last wave, the re-arguard of Sun's personal fleet. Sun with the vanguard has long since dropped through, straight on 'til morning. Given that I don't have anything to do except relay her orders to Captain Vata, I feel like a decorative cushion. Beacon engineering seems a long way away from where I am now.

We enter the combat zone around the Karnos Beacon as the last squadron in Sun's fleet still in the Aspera System, making ready to drop through. Captain Vata stands on the fast frigate's strategos dais. A visual of Aspera System is zoomed in to display the dregs of the battle that has raged for the last twenty or thirty hours as the Phene tried so desperately to stop Sun from reaching the beacon.

"Fire at will," says the captain, broadcasting to her squadron. She doesn't glance my way now that Sun is no longer in Aspera but light-years away. I have nothing she needs. I admire her calm command and the way she looks like she's been here before, which she has, since I checked her records and she fought at the Battle of Aspera Drift. Our shields throw off the detritus of the engagement and a late railgun attack from the few surviving Phene destroyers. One of our corvettes takes a brutal hit near its stern engine compartments and spins away. We're jolted constantly as we surge toward the beacon. The smell of smoke burns in my eyes, wafting through the ventilation system from distant decks where something very bad has happened.

Weapons says, "Captain, target of opportunity. An enemy picket ship. Want me to take it out?"

"Not worth wasting a javelin on a picket ship. Alert Aspera Drift reserve."

A warning bell chimes. "Transition in five minutes. Take all weigh off the ship."

I'm already hooked in so I bump against my console's harness. My hair rises like cilia beating against the air currents.

My thoughts cycle round to the other Companions. Razin and Makinde, who like me are posted to relay messages. Fine, they're new. Hetty with Sun. James off on a mission and Alika with his own squadron command, fair enough since they've been with Sun longest. But how did Jade rate their own unit command with the Second Battalion under Marshal the Honorable Nà Bō, assigned to attack ground installations on Karnos Prime? Where did that honor and responsibility come from? What am I, pureed algae?

The transition bell rings. The ship rolls. The last thing I see in the strategos display is an image of the hulked dreadnought drifting like a blot of crashed dreams against a backdrop of shining stars and broken hostiles. The *Suvannamacha* falls into the beacon's aura and we drop out of Aspera System.

No one knows how the Apsaras Convergence built the beacons or how the beacons work. Probably no one will ever know. The secret died when the Convergence collapsed, taking whole sections of the network with it as well as knowledge of the location of the Apsaras home world.

Each beacon has only one other beacon linked to it, thus creating the routes we know as the beacon network. Leave Karnos through the Aspera Beacon and you'll end up in Aspera. Leave Aspera through the Karnos Beacon and you'll end up in Karnos. A patrol ship on a routine schedule might trawl back and forth through that one set of paired beacons for the entirety of its deployment. But if it flew to the fifth planet of Aspera System to the Troia Beacon, then it would drop into Troia System.

For most people a beacon transit means falling through an infinite instant of nothingness. You're in one place, then you're nowhere in a measureless void without air or time or substance, and then you're an unfathomable distance away from where you started, emerging from the aura of the linked beacon.

There's something more inside a beacon transit. I know, because I see the ghost of a network deep in the heart of the nothingness. If I wanted to use a metaphor, I'd say the void has a nervous system that shimmers like barely tangible threads of silvery light. Ships slide like droplets along these traceries.

When we enter a beacon, are we falling in and downward, or falling out and upward? Is there direction inside a beacon or is there only passage? Were the engineers of the Convergence able to connect their beacons to a quantum scaffolding that can't be measured, only transited?

A breath of cold spills like half-heard voices across my eyes and ears. Lips touch the inside of my mind in an icy kiss that stalls my sluggish thoughts.

Connect. Connect. Connect.

The universe reappears as we drop into Karnos System. Sweat pours down my face as my pulse races. A klaxon blares.

"Incoming missiles at—"

A string of numbers flashes. The virtual 3-D display projected above the strategos dais fuzzes out as old data drops out and new data takes form. I wasn't joking when I spoke to Solomon earlier. We've fallen into the heart of a titanic battle, smashing straight toward clusters of enemy ships spread all over every octant for thousands and millions of klicks. Divots identify the local Phene beacon defense force, now mostly routed or disabled. So who are we still fighting?

Captain Vata says, "Evasive maneuvers."

She is slotting, measuring, marking, and tracking a few seconds ahead of the visual display the rest of us see, pulling in telemetry shared by other ships. The battle has shifted vector. Our squadrons are grappling with a big Incorruptibles fleet with a lot of flack and fire focused around the famous Captain Black and her *Rakhsh* at the heart of the impact. How did an Incorruptibles fleet get here so fast? They can't have been waiting for us. They couldn't have known. Where is Sun? She can't be . . .

My ring buzzes, shattering my attention. PERSEPHONE

I forgot my one task. I ping: EIGHTH SQUADRON IN KARNOS SYSTEM.

INCOMING. Sun's curt, which means she's focused.

"Instructions from the queen-marshal incoming," I say out loud, proud of how well I've done my duty, but comms already has Sun on the channel. Her voice rings out, tight with excitement without loss of coherence. Absolute certainty.

"*Suvannamacha,* I am in pursuit of a fast courier which has detached from the Phene command ship. I believe the courier conveys the Speaker of the Rider Council. Capture the command ship by any means necessary. Is that understood?"

"Affirmative, Your Highness," says the captain.

Shipboard comms light up as word travels throughout the ship. Decks away, Solomon and his unit are hearing the news. He'll get what he's always claimed he wants: boarding action.

38

The Veins and Arteries of Its Complex Astrionics

A massive jolt flung Apama awake, crashing her into the chair's left arms. Entirely disoriented. The room was empty. No, there was the physician, having stumbled against the bulkhead, rubbing his head. She found the clock on the wall. Twenty-two hours had passed.

"What was that?" she croaked, throat sore. "That was big. Are we under attack?"

Comms rang. "Incoming. Incoming. All hands—"

Boom.

It wasn't a sound as much as a shock, as if the big command ship had been injected with a marker hypersonically racing through the veins and arteries of its complex astrionics. Lights flickered but did not go out. The air flow switched off to uneasy silence, like the ship holding its breath, then wheezed asthmatically back on as the ship's klaxon blared.

The physician spoke while looking at a screen monitoring casualty reports, red dots popping into view as injuries were logged into the system. "Don't move until the light blinks green, because you need the entire dosage or it won't take. If there's no one available, pull out the IV on your own and stick this plaster on."

The passageway hatch opened and gurneys rolled in bearing four wounded spacers—two unconscious without obvious injuries, one bleeding from the nose, mouth, and ears, and the fourth moaning, with a horribly twisted broken leg. They vanished into the neighboring surgery ward.

"Ma'am, I can help at this duty station. I have a basic medic's certificate."

"Lieutenant, you're being given a level of access reserved for Riders. Your duty station is to evacuate the family quarters if it comes to that."

He tapped his heart, then followed the wounded. Slowly her dizziness stabilized, then faded. Only one hundred and eleven minutes to go. She hated being stuck in the infirmary with no command screens. It was better to be out there, exposed, but at least to have a view of the chaos. How had the Chaonians gotten here so fast and blown past the command ship's escort vessels?

She slipped her tablet from a uniform pocket and began studying a schematic for the *Virtuous Heart*.

Time and pages ticked past. It was chaos in and out of the infirmary, everyone ignoring her. That cursed IV would not blink green.

During a seventeen-minute lull in the constant jolts and tremors, the physician checked in to tell Apama that Baragesi had been injured badly enough to lose consciousness. That was scary. The Speaker had been bundled onto a courier and sent at emergency retreat toward Windworn Beacon. Riders must never be risked. Better to die than to lose a Rider. With two of the *Virtuous Heart*'s torch drives off line and life support wheezing on auxiliary power, an orderly evacuation of the wounded had started onto hospital transports bellied alongside. The medics directed gurneys.

Last to leave, the physician came over and studied the IV's measuring chamber. "You're almost there. We've lost thirty percent of drive capacity but Helm thinks we can reach Windworn Beacon and drop through before the enemy catches up. Stick it out, Lieutenant, but stay alert. We are all destined for death."

"We are all destined for death," she echoed.

Again he tapped his heart as if she were a Rider, and went out, sealing the hatch. She hadn't earned that heart-tap, or his loyalty. It went against the foundational tenets of Unity for her to be given a place she hadn't earned through merit. Yet stuck here in this IV chair, unable to pilot, she felt a stab of regret, missing the complex minefield of Anchor's syndicate politics. She missed Bartholomew's hand tucked into her elbow, the charming smile and alluring perfume, even if it was just for show. Missed her mom. That was the worst. Was Mom trapped, coerced, resigned, or relieved? Apama had had to leave Tranquility Harbor to understand how hard her mom had worked to shield her daughter from the hardships of their life. That hadn't changed, had it?

The medical screen was tuned to a general stations channel with a stream of fragmented chatter and reports. Evacuation proceeding. Emergency repairs. Lancers rolled into their launch tubes. All this was taking place on the outer skin far from the heart of the ship.

A chime rang four times, startling her. Neither hatch opened. The IV light was blinking green as its panel flashed: *Intake complete.*

She gritted her teeth and yanked. The needle came out with a gush of blood that brought tears to her eyes. She pressed plaster to the wound. Blood smeared her fingers and without thinking she licked it off as if it were the last smears of festival custard. Ugh. She was rattled. Breathe.

Cautiously she stood. The room juddered and she wasn't sure if the ship had been hit again or if the marker was messing with her balance.

The hatch into CIC blinked red: *No admittance.* Whoever was inside had sealed up. Had the command core been breached? Had Baragesi survived evacuation and gotten to the safety of Windworn System?

She found the emergency locker. It held a medic's kit, four breathing masks, and a pouch to stuff them in.

The ship shuddered again. A barely audible but grinding roar vibrated in the bulkheads. Not good. Again she glanced toward CIC but knew better than to breach an airtight seal in circumstances like this. She tugged a mask across nose and mouth and braved the passageway.

An acrid breeze hissed as air vented somewhere it wasn't supposed to go. The mask displayed oxygen levels: the passageway was still breathable at 19.2 percent oxygen but it was trending down and a mix of other gases were starting to build, making her eyes sting. Fail-safes breached. Containment limited. After scanning through her memory of the schematic, she headed left.

Four doors down she entered a spacious wardroom with adjoining galley, eerily empty. The galley's roll-down wall was open. The cooks had been getting ready to offer a mid-watch snack on the food line and hadn't had time to close up. She dodged between tables and through a swinging gate into the galley. An oven ticked off time. Freshly baked pandesal sat on trays on the counter. Stacks of savory suman cooled on a platter. She tugged off the mask and inhaled the heavenly scent of fresh bread. With the instinct of a girl who'd grown up on the hard side of town, she grabbed a roll and stuffed the warm bread into her mouth. Mmm. Ube.

A clunk sounded at the closed door she'd just entered through. She ducked behind the long counter. Slipping the tablet out with sticky fingers, she checked the schematic. Yes! There was a second smaller exit door set into a recess in the galley and thus not visible from the wardroom. The door was reinforced but also double-hung so the upper half could be opened and food passed through into a wardroom on the other side. If she could get out that door she could seal it behind her. The other wardroom served Incorruptibles who had duty both in the Rider residential core and in the command core.

Boarding parties would be searching for access to the residential core, but it was the hardest compartment in the ship to break into. If she could get to the living quarters, she could get to the Rider hangar and snag a lancer if there was one left on board. She was not getting captured.

A shattering pop brought her head around. The door was shoved open. In the glossy metal wall of the counter opposite her she watched the shimmering reflection of a weapon barrel easing in to make a scan of the room. A helmeted figure wearing a Chaonian marine battlesuit slid inside, crouched behind a table, and with a display of strength tipped the table forward to create a defensive position. Another barrel sighted around the open door.

A boarding party.

It wasn't worth grabbing a kitchen knife, however tempting it was to think of herself as a blade-skilled kalista out of the ancient past.

A marine behind the table spoke in Common Yele, his tone steady and firm, no battle shakes or squeaky adrenaline rush. "We know you're in there, behind the counter. I can see movement reflected in a reflection. Stand up, slowly, hands raised." He added in horribly mangled Phenish, "Comrade, please be to surrender your respectable person. No chance for to run. The slow is your movement."

What cursed rotten luck.

The intruders were about fifteen meters, five tables, and the galley window away, and she was three meters from an escape route. Lancer pilots knew how to run scenarios fast.

In Yele, she replied, "I am standing up. I am unarmed. I am a cook."

She led with her uppers, two hands first, then slowly raised her lowers as high as they would go, but keeping her body and head down.

From the door, a marine cracked, "Every time you think it's ordinary and then that second set of hands, so creepy."

"Enough," cut in the marine behind the table. Then, calling to her, "Stand all the way up. Slow."

Slowly she rose, stretching her arms out, her lowers parallel to the floor, her uppers angled as if reaching for the heavens. Three long backward and sideways steps would get her to the recess, if she could create an opening.

"Fuck, I didn't know there were sexy ones," said the door wit.

"Shut the fuck up! Show respect!" snapped the first marine. Then to Apama, "Sorry, Lieutenant. You're not a cook. I see by your wing tips that you are a lancer."

"You've done your homework, Ensign. I'm impressed."

"Sure you are. Jí. Rèn. Clear the next room. Garcia, with me." He had a scope he was tweaking to get a view below the tables and chairs in the wardroom, looking for additional crew. "How is it you speak Yele, Lieutenant?"

Get them to relax by creating common ground. Good tactics on his part, but she could match him.

"Learned it in school." She'd taken it as her easy class, a break from the grueling flying, tech, and maths schedule, but she wasn't about to tell him that. "So I could watch that show . . . 'Turbulence.'"

"*Turbulence*? I don't know it." The scope's camera swung away from her and toward a glint in the far corner of the wardroom. She took the opportunity to study the counter's rim and the control panel stretched along it, identified a button labeled *Shutter*. If she could close the galley window . . .

"Idol Faire," she said as her memory caught up to the words she was looking for. "There was a song, 'Turbulence.' A good-looking man with a tiny guitar."

The wit behind the door snorted. "The Handsome Alika gets around. Don't you know him, Ensign?"

"You know the singer?" She laughed, because it was too absurd. It was ridiculous. Wasn't the Handsome Alika a soldier too, an officer even? An honorable aristocrat, that's what they called people born into the highest levels of their hierarchical system. Best buddies with the heir to the throne, who was now the throne. "Is he here? He's so cute. Can I meet him?"

Door Wit cackled.

The ensign said, drily, "If you ever meet him, the shine will wear off fast."

"Thank you for the warning. A shame it would be for this fresh pandesal and suman to go to waste. You marines are hungry? Share it out with your squad." She reached for the platter with her lower left.

The scope jerked to a halt and the marine turned toward her, his dark, squarish face a floating presence behind the battlesuit's faceplate. "Keep all your hands raised, Lieutenant."

"Apologies." She skimmed her fingers over the control panel on her roundabout way back up, pressing *Shutter* and then *Gate Lock*. A click of the entry gate. A whine from the window lintel over the food line.

"What's that?" The ensign fixed his gun sight on her.

The metal sheet of the shutter began to roll down. She dropped and scuttled for the recess. Stinger blasts pumped heat above her head. As the shutter lowered into the line of fire, shots peppered its opaque shield with a sound like festival confetti popping open. The shutter clicked into place, giving her precious seconds.

"Stop firing, Garcia!" shouted the ensign from the other side. "Cover me."

She pressed her hands to the panel that controlled the locked door into the Incorruptibles wardroom. It was now or never for the marker to work.

Revered Arthas! The panel clicked to green and the upper half of the door unsealed just as a weight slammed into the locked gate and, with a crash, broke its hinges. She squeezed through the half-open door, dogged it behind her, and locked it. Fuck those boarders. Her pulse sped at high gear, and her mind was clear.

The Incorruptibles wardroom was small, two tables with four chairs each. Most importantly it offered entry into the secure residential core. Thank Arthas that the Chaonians hadn't yet gotten into the inner ring. Looking down at her sticky hand, she realized she was holding suman she'd grabbed without realizing. She stuffed it in her mouth rather than toss it aside.

Hammering pounded on the door, followed by the thump of shots fired as they tried to break the lock. She crossed the little wardroom to a hatch that let onto a double-sealed security airlock. The controls gave way before her as if she herself were a Rider. It was a heady brew for the instant she enjoyed it, before the door behind her started heating as in a blast furnace. What on earth were those idiots doing in a ship with gear like that? She exited the wardroom through a breaching chamber, sealed it, cycled through a security airlock and through another breaching chamber, and sealed the final door, sweating and triumphant.

A gun barrel pressed against her back.

39

Another Firefly Risen

She raised all four hands and spoke in Phenish.

"I'm unarmed. It's a breach of conventions of war to kill unarmed people."

The pressure of the barrel vanished. "Lieutenant At Sabao? Thank the saints! Can you help us?"

She turned to face the Incorruptibles who had escorted her and Baragesi onto the ship. Asim and Wymond. They stood in a staging room, guns laid out alongside flash grenades, survival packs, and a disrupter spear.

She patted the exit hatch. "There are Chaonian marines trying to break through."

Gray-haired Asim tipped open a control panel and tapped in a sequence. "This code floods the secure airlock with acid."

"I guess we're not going back that way." She heaved, lungs feeling heavy.

"You'll want to put your mask back on. We're leaking atmosphere."

She followed them into a passageway that she recognized. She had passed this mural with Baragesi: the Angel of Industry with four wings that lift all souls to a better life, and in her hands an auger, a balance scales, a wrench, and a hypodermic needle.

"Their initial attack damaged our dedicated launch tube, so the family lifepods can't reach space," said the much younger Wymond. "Our brethren had to evacuate Rider Baragesi directly from CIC command shaft."

"Did his family not get out with him?"

"They did not."

She hurried into the living suite. It wasn't the sight of Gil's stranded family that jolted her to a halt. It was the person they surrounded.

The girl stood in a pose reminiscent of Saint Zee of the Wild: stoic and proud in the face of danger coming at her, knowing she is always its target.

Asim said, softly, "As you see, Lieutenant, Rider Tadukhipa is still on board."

The Incorruptibles would kill the girl rather than allow her to be captured.

Breathe. Consider all options.

"Do you still have comms? Is the *Thunderbolt in Hand* still in-system?"

"We no longer have comms. Last we heard, Admiral Manu's fleet was under heavy weather at Aspera Beacon."

She'd have to do this on her own. "Is access to the secure hangar open?"

"Yes, Lieutenant. But the courier is gone."

"Are any escort lancers left on board?"

A glance flashed between the three Incorruptibles in a wordless shared understanding. "I will find out," said the steward, and stepped into the next room.

Apama turned to Gil's father. "Uncle, I can't promise anything if you and your family remain here, but I can't get you all out."

"We are all destined for death." He looked at each of the others in turn. Each nodded, last the boy with his solemn eyes. "If you get Rider Tadukhipa out of here, then we can accept our fates with equanimity."

"Use the toilet right now," Apama said to the girl. "You need to change into any kind of tight underlayer you have. Bring a tablet and a tightly rolled-up change of clothes, nothing fancy. You'll want spare skivvies."

"Can I bring my teddy-rex?" She looked young enough at that moment to still cling to a favorite plush toy.

"Of course. Hurry."

The girl bolted into the sleeping rooms, Aunt Pilar following.

Apama's kit bag was still resting behind a table where she'd slung it earlier. She yanked out her flight suit, stripped down to her skivvies, and pulled on first the absorbent body sleeve and then the flight suit over it as the boy watched with big eyes. She grabbed a thermal jump-suit, a utility knife, the toiletries bag, and her personal tablet. The rest of her possessions, such as they were, would have to be cast onto the winds of fortune. So be it.

Apama offered the assembled family a tight smile meant to be reassuring but which felt as false as hope. "Anyone have a knit cap? A hoodie?"

"I do!" said the boy brightly. He ran into the sleeping rooms and returned with a garish knit cap and a midnight blue hoodie printed with the beaked mask of Saint Eileen. The steward returned and gave Apama a curt affirmative nod.

A plan was sliding into place.

"You can get us to the secure hangar?" Apama asked the two soldiers.

"We will see the Rider into the lancer, or die in her defense."

They would probably die anyway. She checked the room's clock. Too much time ticking. The boarding parties would eventually cut through into the secure ring. Then the gig would be up. She crossed to the lavatory, rapped four times firmly on the door, and counted under her breath to give herself focus so she didn't spiral into stress cycle over what she could not control.

Just as she subvocalized sixteen—good fortune!—the door opened. Giolla hurried out, looking distressed but properly dressed in skintight running gear. The girl was all lank and bone, no baby fat unfortunately. Tadukhipa's wiry little face was pinched up as at a bad smell.

"She's worried because in a flight suit she won't be able to here-see," said Giolla indignantly. "There's no—"

"No lancer suit is tailored for a Rider," Apama cut her off. "Let's go."

The boy had taken advantage of the time to grab a plushie T. rex with stubby arms whose colorful feathery coat had been rubbed raw and faded from years of cuddling. He shoved it into the Rider's arms.

"Smart thinking, Banoy," Apama said, and he beamed.

All pressed hands to hearts. Giolla wiped away a tear. Apama hadn't even known Riders cried. Well, Riders couldn't; they had no tear ducts. What she hadn't known was that any allowed their ridden bodies to cry or show emotion.

Jejomar walked to an alcove inset into the bulkhead. Its eight shelves displayed glass-blown figures representing the sixteen saints, with Saint

Arthas and the twins on the top shelf and the others paired all the way down as in any basilica.

"May the saints walk with you and give you strength."

She was about to tell him there wasn't time for prayer when Asim said, "Rider Tadukhipa, if you will open the door."

The girl placed her body in the inset, sideways, right shoulder facing the shelves and left shoulder the room. An energy field shimmered into visibility, reading both faces on a locked circuit. A basso click sounded. A shielded door opened onto a ladder descending into darkness. Motion lights popped on as Wymond started down first. Apama followed, the girl behind her, clinging to her plushie. The door shut as soon as Asim was through. The ladder descended twenty rungs to a tube. At the base of the ladder rested a sealed four-person pod ready to skim to the hangar, which if she read the schematic correctly was about one klick away. Asim waved them onto a walkway that ran alongside the track.

"The secure hangar is sealed, but their boarding parties will be scanning for any signature, like the engine vibration of that pod."

"Can you run?" Apama asked the girl.

In the dim light Giolla's stare looked vaguely threatening. "I'm the champion thousand-meter runner of my cohort."

"All right, then! Let's see what you've got."

The girl grinned, fear briefly taking flight at this challenge. Wymond took the lead, but Giolla set the pace. She had an easy, ground-eating lope with her long legs, and the gravity was a bit lighter on ships than on any of the Triple A planets. They made it to the far end of the tube in a brisk three and a half minutes, chased by echoes and shudders all the way. Was the Phene crew fighting the boarding party or surrendering? Which choice would buy more time to get the Rider off the command ship without giving away that the girl was still here, the asset the Chaonians most wanted to get their greedy hands on?

Wymond waved at Apama to stay back before exiting through an airlock. Two agonizingly long minutes later . . . so hard to wait when you were used to action . . . he popped back into view. "All clear."

They emerged into a compact hangar. The footprint of the courier was all that was left of the ship that had spirited away Baragesi. Someone would get a demotion for leaving Tadukhipa behind, but this wasn't a time for blame. She had to act.

Eight lancers had gone with the courier, leaving eight. As the young Rider walked out flush-faced and nervous, the pilots saluted her with hands to hearts.

Two pilots had been chosen to give up their lancer. One graciously helped the girl into a flight suit. The other looked Apama up and down, then said abruptly, "You know Gail, don't you? Gale Force. He mentioned you. Ice, isn't it?"

"When did you see Gail?" Apama demanded.

"The *Strong Bull* is under repairs at Hellion Terminus. He came through Karnos with some of the other lancers on their way to Axiom to get new assignments."

She sucked in a harsh breath. "Any chance you know if Splash, Cricket, and Deadstick were with them?"

The lancer nodded. "I remember them. Nothing but bad jokes, those three."

Stricken by the emotion of the moment, Apama gripped the pilot's lower right with her own. "I owe you for this, Lieutenant."

"That's Greensleeves, to you. And my lesser half, Fry-baby." She nodded toward the other pilot, who grinned. "Now listen. This sweetheart has one glitch, a spinward hitch at sixteen degrees. You'll get the hang of it. Get that girl home."

"We are all destined for death."

Even as she spoke the words she knew it was the other lancers who would throw their lives onto the bonfire of duty. The sacrifice grated. But she hadn't the luxury of hating herself. She had to survive before she could do that.

Fry-baby was sealing the Rider into the life-support membrane, showing her where to place her palms for activation. Apama saluted the remaining Incorruptibles, hand to heart, then climbed into the rhombus-shaped lancer, strapping into her side of the back-to-back flight chairs. An icon representing Saint Laranthir stared at Apama from where it had been stuck on the control panel.

"Are you *kidding* me? I have to share this cockpit with that smug face and green goatee?" Apama demanded, looking up at Greensleeves.

"'I've seen more of the world than most,'" retorted the woman with a laugh. "You've got the duty-ridden look of an Arthas devotee. Tell me I'm right."

"Gail told you that."

The pilot gave her the two-finger "salute" as deck crew sealed up the lancer.

At her back the girl whispered, "Does it hurt to die?"

"It depends," said Apama. "The hardest thing I need from you, Tadukhipa . . . Giolla . . . saints alive . . . Can I call you Teegee for short? Would that be insulting?"

"I like Teegee," she said shyly, carefully trying out the syllables as if they were red-hot rebellion. A second voice, barely audible, whispered, "tee gee" like an echo.

"All right, Teegee. Set four palms where he showed you."

A dreadnought like the *Strong Bull* had launch tubes for its lancers; they launched without open hangar doors. The command ship had tumblers instead of tubes to allow the lancers to roll out alongside the courier as it took off. It was disorienting and took a fair bit of skill to avoid hitting the ship's exterior if you overcompensated, but a good lancer pilot—and you had to be good to get command ship duty—used the tumble to spin out into escort position at increased speed.

The hangar doors parted onto a forbidding void shot through with debris. Pinprick lights of battle swirled so far in the distance it might well be the souls of the newly departed, each another firefly risen into the holy dance. She rolled out first, as per the plan, and tucked herself against the ship as the rest of the squadron spun outward toward the enemy. A lancer exploded in a direct hit from a ship she couldn't see. The sight speared into her heart. But shock, anger, guilt twisted away as she spun into the trail of the dying lancer and used its cover to leap outward into the shadow of a chunk of debris kicked from an unknown vessel. Chaff adrift in the ocean of stars.

At Apama's back, unseen but softly heard, the girl was trying to squeeze back the fear weeping out of her.

"This your first time in a lancer?" Apama asked in the joking tone her old lancer-mate Splash would have used. Now that she held the controls, her nerves spilled away toward the stars, leaving her focused, alert, ready.

Teegee choked on a sob that was also a laugh. "No, no, at least a hundred times I've been. Now what?"

"Hang on."

Poison in Her Belly

Windworn Beacon pulsed on the screen as if mocking her, an open gate through which the Speaker of the Rider Council had fled on a fast courier as into the night. Frustration burned like poison in her belly. Why the Phene had withheld their powerful dreadnoughts from this battle Sun could not know, but she was certain at least one of the massive warships waited on the other side. To drop the limping *Boukephalas* with a mere seven battleworthy escort ships through a beacon into its attack range would be suicidal.

About one hundred klicks from the spiral eye of the beacon, a pair of lancers traced a slow infinity figure of eight as if their pilots were dead and had locked them into a loop. These two vessels were the only survivors of the eight who had escorted the courier. Lancers had only torch drives; they could not drop through a beacon on their own, so they'd been left behind.

"Captain, hail those lancers and offer honorable surrender. Any access to Phene relays and sensors?" She looked around for James, expecting to see him hunched over a console, his flatcap stuck straight on his head. No, he was missing. She'd sent him elsewhere.

The captain chewed on a stim stick. "Not yet, Your Highness. Their network is unusual. Our engineers would love to capture a cooperative imperial engineer."

Sun studied the lagging telemetry of the battle as it spiraled outward into skirmishes throughout the system. Phene squadrons fought their way toward Windworn and Sleepless Beacons or ran for the outer asteroid belt and distant Karnos Duodeci, with Chaonians and their allies in dogged pursuit. Fleet reports dumped into her network. Hetty pinged in a preliminary casualty report. The *Boukephalas* began taking on wounded from hulked frigates and corvettes of her own squadron, which had taken a terrible beating.

A headache burned under her brows. Her neck was stiff, and the thigh injury she'd taken a year ago in the battle of Molossia System ached. When she glanced down at her leg, she was surprised to see blood staining the fabric of her uniform. How had that happened? She closed her hand around the stim bulb she'd been sucking on, only to find it empty. She had no memory of draining it, no taste or moisture in her mouth. She'd won the victory she'd sought, but it lacked the coup de grâce she desired. It just wasn't satisfying to have lost Speaker Baragesi. She'd been so close.

Her Companions pinged in.

Alika: THUNDERBOLT IN HAND AND REMNANT FORCES HAVE RETIRED THROUGH THE HELLION BEACON. AWAITING ORDERS.

Why retreat to a terminus system, that was the question.

Razin: NINTH FLEET STAGING A LANDING ON KARNOS PRIME. SEVENTH HAS OPERATIONAL CONTROL OF NA IRI BEACON AND NEIGHBORING OCTANTS. SHALL WE PURSUE?
Makinde: ZÀOFÙ PURSUING PHENE FORCES.

Jade: KARNOS PRIME GROUND INSTALLATIONS SECURED IN HEAVY FIGHTING. MARSHAL NÀ BŌ DECEASED.

Sun whistled low, feeling the blow as in her gut. To lose such a decorated, experienced officer, and one of Eirene's Companions to boot, was a staggering hit.

Jade added: AFTER THE DEATHS OF MULTIPLE OFFICERS I PERSONALLY COMMANDED THE ASSAULT THAT FREED THE BESIEGED CITADEL AND ITS LOCAL ALLIES FROM PHENE CONTROL.

At her console, Hetty rolled her eyes, having received the same message. Sun had taken a chance placing Jade Kim into a formal command role so soon, but she trusted her gut. She trusted that Jade's ambition was perforce tied to *her* success. And she just plain liked people who got results.

"Very good," said Sun, checking her telemetry. "Sixth Fleet push through into Sleepless. Second Fleet into Windworn. Alika, Jade, return to me. Pull Twelfth Fleet up from Aspera for pursuit into Hellion Terminus. We keep pushing."

Nothing from James, but he wasn't in-system and thus out of range.

Last of all, Persephone: VIRTUOUS HEART UNDER CHAONIAN CONTROL.

"We captured the command ship?" Sun laughed as the bridge crew cheered and applauded. "Hetty, send a courier to Aspera System. Have the *Shadowfax* brought through as a backup flagship while repairs are made here. While we wait, let's dine where no Chaonian boots have set foot ever before. Take us to the *Virtuous Heart*."

41

The Mundane Horror

For tens of hours Apama skimmed debris, outward spin by spin, to put distance and signal-blocking flotsam between her and the dogged Chaonian fleet. Eventually she got far enough away to risk a dash toward a retreating Phene squadron as it closed in on Sleepless Beacon. If she could get aboard a light cruiser, she and Teegee would drop with the ragged remnant into Phene-controlled space. Done. Safe.

Just as she pinged an anonymous identity-ask toward the squadron, a volley of Chaonian javelins blinked into the telemetry en route toward the ships. Her query was pinged back from the beleaguered command. They weren't braking for a mere lancer. We are all destined for death.

As she was running a quick calculation to determine whether there was any point in trying to catch them, a point of light materialized out of the Sleepless beacon. A Phene fast courier dropped in and blared an all-hands blast to Phene vessels in Karnos System. Coded in military cipher, it would be untranslatable to the Chaonians.

KEEP CLEAR. BEACON MINED. KEEP CLEAR. BEACON MINED.

The girl said, "Wait, is that rod supposed to break off our lancer?"

A weight chunked against the hull. External cameras caught a piece of comms array rebounding off the lancer's hull. Teegee squeaked, seeing the image but not knowing what it meant. Probably she feared the fighter was breaking apart. But lancers were sturdy little beasts. They had to be.

Telemetry flared and vanished. Popped back in but Apama immediately saw it was a saved view, no longer real time because there was no sign of the fast courier.

Dammit.

She clipped through to the fallback comms, waited an agonizing ten seconds. A person could be dead ten times over in that span.

Telemetry blanked out but comms came back, the ciphered message on loop.

KEEP CLEAR. BEACON MINED. KEEP CLEAR. BEACON MINED.

Telemetry resurfaced, fighting a lag. The Phene squadron she was following had been on a tight course toward the beacon coil, ships rolling into the column formation needed to drop through one by one in close order. The destroyer in the lead altered course, putting on a blast of speed to move out and around the beacon instead of dropping through. They were staying in-system.

For three breaths—you could be dead three times—she stared, trying to figure out what had gone wrong. What was she missing? Had the waiting and hiding frayed her nerves to the bone? Had she gotten dehydrated? Did she need a protein bar?

Mined.

Manu had gotten his way. Desperation had forced the hands of the high command. Mining across the arrival vectors of Windworn and Sleepless Beacons would definitely stop the enemy from pursuing into imperial space. But it also meant all straggling Phene military ships were trapped on this side.

"Arthas, give me strength," she prayed.

"Ap?" That soft voice, tentative and terrified.

"Hang on, little sister. We've got this." She wasn't so sure.

"I . . . I have to . . . to go . . ."

The mundane horror of the poor kid pooping her pants cleared Apama's mind wonderfully. That and a pungent scent the membrane's scrubbers couldn't eliminate.

"I'm not laughing at you. Sorry, sorry, I'm really not. Laughing is a stress reaction. I'm laughing because I remember how humiliated I was the first time I did it."

"You . . . did it?"

"Yes. All lancers do. In training they require us to stay out so long that we crap our membranes. So you've passed the test. You're promoted to pilot apprentice."

"R-really?"

"So I vow, on the honor and duty of Arthas. Who are you dedicated to?"

"We don't. I mean, I'm not supposed to say. It's a secret." Then through the stink she immediately added, "The body of me belongs to the basilica, I guess. The riding part of me belongs to emptiness, the place of absence."

Apama registered the words but didn't answer because her comms finished its full reroute and kicked back in. The fleeing military ships were already too far away for her to risk chasing them, and anyway a Chaonian squadron ran in pursuit. An enemy fleet approached, hours away still, headed for Sleepless Beacon where the fast courier drifted with its message on loop, a message the enemy couldn't read or understand.

The girl said in a soft voice, "Are you going to blow us up? I guess that would be fastest."

The resignation in Giolla's voice sickened Apama. She was just a kid, practically a baby. It wasn't her fault she'd been born a Rider. It wasn't Tadukhipa's fault either. They hadn't volunteered for the military. You had to be an adult to do that, to accept the risks, to choose duty, to understand finality.

What were her options? Seedless and Windworn Beacons were blocked by Manu's mining strategy. The fleeing squadron was headed toward Hellion Beacon, its last option besides surrender or death. Not a bad option, with Hellion's reputation as a zone troubled by piracy and illicit smugglers. It had originally been a janus system but was now a terminus because its second beacon had died in the Apsaras Collapse. She'd seen that beacon up close, stained with a glorious neon-glow aura in the shape of spiny starburst, an artifact of the cascading failure. If a ship had access to an Argosy tow chain it could depart Hellion Terminus and take a roundabout way via the Trinity Coalition back into the empire.

Roundabout. An idea niggled at the back of her brain.

"You ready to take a long trip, Teegee?"

"What do you mean?"

"I'll explain if we get to stage one."

"If?"

"Each hour we stay alive is an hour we are still alive."

"Is that some kind of wisdom of the ancients?" the girl asked as sourly as only a terrified, stressed adolescent striving to act cool-headed could sound.

"Negative. It's what lancers say when they're in a battle zone."

"Oh. Like we are now?"

"Like we are now."

The Valiant One Listens to the Crackling of an Unanswered Comms Link

Makinde sat at a sensor console in the command center of the battle-ship *Red Hare,* watching a ship die. The damaged cruiser *Vermilion* hung in space against a backdrop of brilliant stars and a looming gas giant striped with swirling pink and red clouds. Flashes of energy splintered along the cruiser's cracked hull as it hit another mine. Life support still glowed from secure compartments but half the ship had vented from impacts. Lifepods and shuttles released from the dying wreck like seeds scattering.

He'd been so pissed when he'd missed out on the battle of Molossia. Now here he was in Sleepless System as the already battered and exhausted Sixth Fleet took a beating from a lethal combination of weapons fire and mines. They'd expected to drop through into Sleepless and slug it out with dreadnoughts. They hadn't expected a mine-field in the path of any and every ship dropping through. Beacons were sacrosanct because they couldn't be repaired, and also because anyone who hindered the flow of traffic through a beacon hurt themselves as much as they hurt the enemy. Still, it took guts to make such a call. The mines had definitely slammed shut Chaonian forward momentum.

The *Red Hare* had hit two mines and suffered six javelin and two torpedo impacts. The siren had ceased blaring after the first impact but the battleship was big enough that mines couldn't rip it apart without a lot more impacts. *Boom. Boom. Boom.* Battle was exhilarating. Not the taking-a-beating part, but the adrenaline rush of knowing he could die at any moment.

With each inhale he sucked in the lung-searing smoke churning through CIC as ventilators surged, scrubbing the air. On the console he tracked the shimmering heat trails of seventeen Phene torpedoes streaking toward the dead-in-space *Vermilion*. The one advantage the Chaonians had was that the Phene had to fire their volleys horizontal across the beacon arrival zone while the Chaonians could fire outward at will.

From the command dais, Zàofù spoke in his bland monotone. "Target torpedoes. Send the *Rapid* back through with a message to halt all incoming vessels. Send in *Bulsajo* and *Otso* to pick up survivors. *Turul, Henery,* and *Roc* halt forward movement and make ready to circle around the beacon and drop back through into Karnos System. All ships target the hostile fleet beyond the minefield to cover our retreat."

The crane marshal was so old school he used a battleship as his flagship; he hadn't transferred his command over to one of the new Tulpar-class heavy cruisers as Eirene had. She'd commissioned the new ships; to a longtime marshal like Zàofù they were as yet unproven. He was conservative in his choices, but Makinde had to admire the man's phlegmatic calm in the face of disaster. Point-defense cannons on the *Red Hare* reached out to engage the torpedoes, the steady rumbling of their fire shaking the chair Makinde sat in. A moment later the battery joined the fusillade, pairs of huge, long-spooling energy cannons from the previous generation of warfare, equal to the main guns on the Phene dreadnought.

"'Ware! 'Ware the *Bulsajo*," said comms.

Everyone looked at the visual. The view tilted to focus on the *Bulsajo*. The corvette shuddered as it hit a mine.

"Stay in the lane already cleared by the *Vermilion*," muttered the marshal to himself. He dabbed at his eyes with a handkerchief. Everyone was tearing from the smoke. Makinde had sent Dozer off over an hour ago when damage control identified but couldn't reach a stubborn smoldering burn.

He pinged. DOZE?

ALMOST SEALED THE LEAK! BETTER AIR SOON! WHAT CAN
I DO NEXT? CAN I STAY WITH DAMAGE CONTROL? CAN I?
CAN I?

AFFIRMATIVE, YOU BIG GOOF.

A tremor buzzed under his hands. With a sleeve he wiped away a
smear of blood concealing the console's screen. Not his blood. The blood
of the spacer who had been sitting here as they'd dropped through.

"New array of torpedoes incoming." He flagged them over to weapons. A countdown opened on all the consoles. He kept grinning and
then thinking it was terrible to be so wired up with excitement and also
they were really screwed if all that ordnance reached them, even this
brute of a battleship, and then grinning again. "Shit, there's two more
dreadnoughts lighting up."

"All guns respond." Zàofù might have been ordering dinner. "*Bulsajo,* report the status of your beacon drive. Can you drop through or
do you need to abandon ship? Time is short. We must retreat before
that volley reaches us."

"We are clear for beacon drop and we still have helm control," replied the *Bulsajo,* "but our torch drives are compromised. We need a
tow and a push."

"Confirmed. *Roc* will assist. *Turul* and *Henery,* cover her. *Freki,* move
forward to assist the *Otso. Otso,* your report?"

"Eight lifepods still at large. Sending trajectories of four to *Freki.*"

"Confirmed," said the marshal. "Comms, get me a comms link to
the *Vermilion.* Is anyone left on board?"

For ten seconds the entire bridge listened to the crackling of an unanswered comms link: wheezing ventilators, a high-pitched ringing, a
muted popping like fireworks exploding ecstatically inside a confined
space. A shriek that might have been a human voice or just the screech
of torquing metal. Makinde felt his tongue go dry in sympathy. Many
might be trapped, waiting for the air to go or their wounds to kill them.
If the virtual zoomed in they'd see corpses adrift in the vortex of the
dying ship. As the cruiser listed, its trailing curve hit another mine.
The explosion blew a hole in a stern compartment already weakened
by stress.

A shuttle emerged from the belly of the *Vermilion* and shot toward
their position. A message pinged in: Senior Captain the Honorable
Linn Ei signaling that she was last off.

"Marshal, I have confirmed one hundred and eighty-nine evacuated personnel, including thirty-one with me. Confirm four hundred

and thirty-two dead and one hundred and seventeen unaccounted for or unreachable, to my shame."

"We are waiting for you, Captain. You took the hammer and thereby saved the rest of us."

Now they could only wait as the hostile torpedoes narrowed the gap, a slow dance toward collision that made Makinde's hands itch as he watched the console tick down the time. The *Roc* grappled the *Bulsajo* alongside and swung out of sight around the beacon, hugging tight to the curved surface so it wouldn't become an easy target. The conjoined ships were moving fast ahead of the *Turul* and the *Henery*. It didn't take long for them to show up again for a brief visual when, from the arrivals zone, you could see a ship approaching you down the narrowing tunnel made by the beacon's spiral toward what engineers called the *aura*. Spacers called the moment of transition "the blue flash" although it wasn't really blue or a flash but more like a bubble popping out of existence as if it had never been there at all.

The *Roc* came in the lead with the *Bulsajo* loosely tugged behind, reliant on its helm to keep it from colliding. The cruiser released the cable and vanished into the drop. Sixty seconds later the *Bulsajo* hit the flashpoint, but didn't vanish. It sailed right through and kept coming, coasting back into the arrivals zone. Its beacon drive had gone off line, too damaged to tune in to the beacon.

The captain of the *Red Hare* said, "Marshal, if the *Bulsajo* can maneuver, and apply some braking, I can shift position to get in their way. We can clear Hangar 2 so they can put their nose up our ass. The impact will bang us up but we can take it. Then we emergency cable them to us so they seem like part of the same ship. It should fool the beacon."

"Do it." Zàofù left the details to the captains.

The torpedoes streaked steadily closer. Only a handful had been caught by the defensive guns. Phene missiles were lethally smart. The clock ticked steadily. With a jolt the *Bulsajo* punched into the battleship's Hangar 2 but it was just as the captain said: the *Red Hare* could take the damage and keep going. Finally, some good news.

"All retreat."

Otso and *Freki* grabbed the last lifepods and changed course, swinging around the beacon, no longer firing, all power to shields. *Red Hare* held position as the *Vermilion* shuttle sped across that last gap toward them. As the largest ship in the Chaonian fleet, the battleship could hold the rear guard and pick up Captain Ei and the last survivors of the *Vermilion*.

Three hundred klicks. Two hundred klicks. One hundred klicks.

A moving shadow on the console caught Makinde's eye. Debris? A lifepod spun off course? Just as he leaned closer to trace it, the shuttle sheared off course, struck by a missile and sent tumbling. The little vessel hit a mine and came apart in a deadly flash.

"Fuck!" cried Makinde as, around him, the crew shouted in dismay or cursed in anger. "What was that?"

"Fucking lancer," said a chief at weapons. "Bloody hells. It must have slipped through the mines to take a last potshot."

"Dammit, how did I not see it?" Makinde wanted to pound the console but he clenched his hand instead.

"Ensign, this isn't on you. They're hard to spot because of their shape, their shielding, and their low torch residue," said the chief.

"All accounted for," said Zàofù. He looked grim but he wasn't a ranter. He'd seen too much in his life. "Weapons, give me a cone volley. Get that lancer."

The battleship shuddered as javelins were launched.

"Eight minutes to mass torpedo impact," said Makinde.

"Helm, change course to round the beacon." Zàofù did not say "retreat."

Ahead, the other ships hugged the outer curve of the massive coil like winged ants flying around a wagon wheel. As they circled around to reach the other side of the beacon they shifted into a column and, one by one, dropped through the massive spiral. The ships remained visible well into the spiral, right up until they hit the aura. With each ship he held his breath as it dropped . . . *Turul, Henery, Otso, Freki* . . . and did not reappear. They'd made it through.

Behind them, the *Vermilion* drifted, her hulk blotting out stars in shifting patches. So briefly he thought he might have imagined it, a rhomboid shape whirled past like a jaunty farewell, a hand flicked in scorn. Fucking lancer.

They lost visual sight of the cruiser and dropped through, last to fall. The universe vanished. He was a spark of valiant light burning in nothingness.

Then all the alarms were blaring. They had returned to Karnos System.

Makinde's ring buzzed against his finger, startling him. Once the injured spacer had been evacuated from CIC and Makinde had slid in to take her place, he'd gotten so into his duties and the focus of battle that he'd forgotten he wasn't a lowly ensign fighting the good fight, proving himself. He was a fucking Companion to the new queen-marshal. Talk about whiplash.

The message flared just beyond his right eye, a private communication from Sun herself. Damn, life was strange.

YOU ALIVE?

He grinned and pinged back. I AM ALIVE! THE PHENE MINED THE ENTIRE ARRIVALS ZONE LEADING OUT OF THE BEACON. NO SHIP CAN GO IN OR OUT NOW. WE LOST THE VERMILION AND HER CAPTAIN FROM OUR VANGUARD OF EIGHT. THE BIG GUY KEPT HIS COOL. BUT I GUESS HE WOULD.

The clock ticked on. A spacer cycled past with tea and hot biscuits that the galley had somehow kept cooking under fire. A damage-control crew swept in, starting to pick up the scatter of debris from a burst pipe, an electrical fire, and a shattered console. In the strategos chair, Zàofù was calmly speaking to an adjutant who recorded his words onto a tablet.

The ring buzzed again. I EXPECT AN AFTER-ACTION REPORT IN ONE HOUR. DON'T MAKE ME REPEAT MYSELF.

His racing pulse eased as he realized he wasn't going to die, not yet, anyway. What a strange place this was where he now found himself. Normally a high status Core House scion like him would work his way up the line to a ship of his own and, if he proved himself, command of a squadron or, if he showed aptitude for infantry, a Guards division. A solid career, a marriage alliance arranged by his House, duty to the Republic fulfilled. But he'd been struck by an unexpected missile and his trajectory altered as he'd spun into the gravity well of Sun Shān.

"Honored Companion?"

He looked up to see a medic standing nervously in front of him, clearly in awe of Makinde's exalted status. So weird. Then he followed the medic's gaze, which was fixed on his left arm. A bloody gouge cut through the flesh above his elbow, a barb of shrapnel sticking out, plugging the wound.

"What in the hells? I didn't even feel anything."

A Creature Molded of Dread and Wonder

With Hetty beside her, she boarded the captured command ship via a cutter. They landed in the only hangar that hadn't taken crippling damage during the battle. Descending the ramp, she examined bulkheads painted with a monumental scene of gardens lush with flowering trees, a paradise inhabited by brightly garbed youth carrying pots of incense and baskets of flowers, stern soldiers and stoutly earnest magistrates holding banners, spritely dancers and cheerful musicians in procession toward a triple pair of buildings seen in the distance: a basilica, a domed Unity Hall, and a cross-shaped Exchange.

"Is this the royal hangar?" she asked Isis. "With all this decoration it can't be an ordinary hangar."

"It could be. I've fought the Phene my entire adult life, and I still would never claim to understand them. Frankly, I find it wasteful and distracting."

"It's beautiful," said Sun. "Striking. Imperial."

Hetty said, "It tells a story they must wish is true. Perhaps it is. Or maybe it's the tale, the legend, they desire to claim as theirs."

A tall, imposing marine colonel waited at the base of the ramp. His armor was scorched but whole. Blood had dried on the side of his face. On the regular comms channel he pinged over a casualty list onto the queen-marshal's active action network. It took her a moment to remember that this reception was for her, not for her mother.

She found his ID. "Colonel Wallace. Good work by you and your boarding teams. This is the first command ship ever captured."

He gave a crisp nod. "Your Highness, I have unexpected news. It seems when the Rider fled, he left his family behind."

"His family?" Sun glanced at Isis.

"Riders don't have families," said Isis. "Infants are handed at birth over to the Rider Council, raised among their own, and served by the Incorruptibles."

"They identified themselves as the Speaker's family," said the colonel. "Including two children and a spouse."

"I didn't know Riders got married," said Sun. "What might that mean?"

Hetty said, softly, "We do not know what Riders may require when they grow up and take their promised place. It would not be so strange for them to seek the same and ordinary gifts of life that other folk expect will be their part. It seems to me that even a mighty queen might wish for simple pleasures and quiet hearths."

Sun could read nothing in the tranquility of Hetty's expression. Were the words meant to sting, or as a promise? Yet as the marine colonel and his battered squad led her into the astonishing depths of the ship, every wall a procession leading onward, her mind could not settle on simple pleasures or quiet hearths. She kept thinking of how Speaker Baragesi had gotten away. Slipped from her grasp. She'd been *so close*.

"Your Highness?"

Isis's voice brought her sharply back. She'd walked past where the others had halted. They were waiting for her to enter a restricted core area guarded by marines.

She rubbed her eyes, feeling the hateful pressure of fatigue. Her mind cycled through a sequence of needful actions: Eat a meal. Sleep a few hours before too much stim consumption hit with its staggering backlash. The aftermath. The victory. The toll.

"Your Highness, you need to eat and rest," said Isis. "This can wait."

"No, we do this first." Sun shook off the claws of exhaustion and went in at the head of the group.

They cycled through the sequence of interior airlocks. "Once the Speaker escaped, I'm surprised they didn't blow up the ship. That's what they usually do. Are the supposed family definitely civilians?"

Colonel Wallace nodded. "Definitely civilians. The Incorruptibles on board include nonmilitary workers as well as apprentices and even families with children."

"Not the kind of thing Queen-Marshal Eirene would ever have allowed," remarked Isis. "Slows you down and makes you vulnerable."

The last airlock cycled clear. Sun stepped into a reception room fitted with four divans embroidered with floral motifs. Gardens everywhere! So many gardens! Eight chairs meant to accommodate people with four arms. A formal meeting table that seated sixteen. Everything official in the Phene Empire ran in multiples of four, which always felt ill-omened.

The murals on these walls displayed famous locations from the empire: the floating concourse on Axiom Prime, the processional way on Anchor, the plain of triple-headed Cyclops in Auger System. The views reminded her of Kaspar's drawings, his only escape from the enforced solitude of his early life.

Two marines stood guard in the empty reception room. One had a strapping height unusual among Chaonians.

"Solomon!"

"Your Highness."

"So you were on the boarding team. Any observations?"

"It was my first boarding action. I thought they would shoot at us more. A lot of what they did felt like delaying tactics, if you know what I mean." He broke off, glancing toward Colonel Wallace as if concerned he was speaking out of turn.

"Go on," said Sun.

"It would be hard to blow up a ship this size but they could have set charges and done a lot of damage to us along the way. They didn't."

A tickle nagged in her mind. "Isis, get me the telemetry of departures from the command ship. Especially any departures that occurred after the departure of the courier the Speaker was on."

"Yes, Your Highness."

"Anything else, Solomon?"

"I'm sure nothing that won't be in the colonel's report," he said with the judicious temporizing of a person accustomed to dealing with hierarchies. His lips curved up as a memory grabbed him.

"What?" She hadn't known Solomon long, but she knew he had an open, honest character. He was no schemer or backstabber.

"Things that remind you . . ." He shook his head, trailing off.

"Go on."

"That they aren't so different from us."

"Yes?"

"My squad and I entered a wardroom. There was a Phene officer hiding behind a counter in the galley. She said she was a cook but she wore lancer wings. I thought it took a lot of brass to lie like that when we were pointing guns at her."

"Lancer pilots are known for having nerves of adamantine," said Sun. "What happened then?"

"Obviously she knew the ship better than we did. There was a hidden security entrance out of the galley into a smaller wardroom. Frankly, Your Highness, she faked me out, offered us food."

"Food?"

He chuckled. "To distract us while she got the other door open. She locked it behind her but we burned through and used suction to eliminate an acid attack."

Colonel Wallace said, "That entry created our breakthrough into the secured residential core. The guards and stewards surrendered rather than risk a battle that might injure or kill their charges."

"Are all of the prisoners being held in this compartment?"

"No, Your Highness. Most are being held in separate living quarters. We've processed them all."

She tapped a fisted hand against her mouth. "The lancer pilot Ensign Solomon encountered. She escaped into the residential core. Is she among the captured?"

"I don't know," said the colonel.

"Did you get a good look at her face?" Sun asked Solomon. "Would you recognize her?"

He gave a self-amused laugh. "I'm not likely to forget."

"Because she faked you out?"

"I do respect a good move like that. But mostly because she was really striking."

The other marine on guard pulled a face. "Buddy, don't even think about it. Four arms, man. Unless you're into that creepy kink."

"Fuck off," said Solomon without any heat. He wasn't one to lose his temper, but it was clear he found the other marine's comment distasteful.

"Colonel, have the ensign identify her. If she's not among the prisoners then we have to ask where she might have gone."

"We are sweeping the ship for hidden compartments, Your Highness."

"Very good." She moved into a secondary chamber fitted with life-pods and an air seal to a closed launch tube. "The Rider's family chose not to escape even though they had this option?"

"The launch tube is damaged. I don't know why they weren't able to escape with Speaker Baragesi in the courier. Press of the battle, I expect."

"I see."

The far door opened into a spacious room that, unusually for the Phene, had walls that weren't painted. Instead they displayed a streaming image of a mountain landscape. Flighted creatures spun on the wind. Clouds snagged on icy peaks. The landscape was so stunning that Sun halted on the threshold to stare as the others moved into the room.

Belatedly she realized the prisoners had all stood. Kneeling was not the Phene way. She respected their pride.

There was an older man and an older woman. The other adult was a woman with a lovely face and an air of attractiveness despite her four arms. She had a baby tucked against her right hip and held the hand of a boy perhaps twelve years old, although it was hard to guess children's ages because imperial Phene were generally taller than Chaonians. Four stewards wearing the ivory uniforms of the Incorruptibles waited at the walls alongside more Chaonian marines.

In the room, Hetty and Isis paused to wait for her to take the lead. It was an odd feeling to lag behind. She didn't like it, and was annoyed at her own distraction. Isis was right. She needed to eat and rest, however irritating it was to be reminded of these vulnerabilities.

Bracing himself with a cane, the old man paced forward with measured dignity. Strangely enough, he had Phene height but only two arms. He approached Hetty who, like Sun, wore the standard red-and-gold officer's uniform. Pressing his palms together in a standard Yele courtesy, he spoke to Hetty in laborious Common Yele. The words sounded memorized and were difficult to understand.

"Your Highness . . . gracious kindness . . . have mercy upon us . . ." He finished as if expecting the executioner's javelin to pierce his chest.

One of the most splendid things about Hetty was her sense of the absurd. She had too strong a sense of propriety to laugh, or mock, this mistaken identity. But Sun knew every least twitch of Hetty's expression: her lips pinched together as she suppressed a smile, even as the lift of her eyes revealed pity for their plight.

She said, in a kind voice, "I'm not the one you seek. I pray you, Sun. Come forward lest they fear you mean them ill."

A steward hurried forward, flushed with concern, and whispered in the ear of the old man. His hands convulsed as he clutched them together. The old woman spoke frantically to the younger one, and in her turn the younger woman caught in a sob of fear and dropped to her knees, cradling the baby as if to protect it with her own body. It repulsed Sun that they feared her. How could that be honorable? Better to scrub it clean right away. She walked forward, aware all at once of the sweat and grime on a uniform she'd worn for tens of hours.

"I am Sun."

Before Isis could translate, the rest of the family dropped cringingly to their knees. What kind of monster did they think she was?

The old man spoke in a rush of Phenish.

Isis said, "He asks that you take out your anger on him alone for the terrible disgrace of his mistaking another person for you."

"Enough! Tell them my Companion Hestia is also Sun." She waited impatiently as Isis managed to get this message through, then said, "Tell them they will be treated as . . . don't say prisoners. Honored hostages?"

"Guests?" suggested Isis. "I know that word in Phenish."

"That's better." She extended a hand. After a fateful pause, the old man took it. She assisted him in standing, then in turns helped up each of the others. The boy gaped at her as if she were a creature molded of dread and wonder.

"You are under my protection now," said Sun. "We'll arrange transport to more appropriate quarters as soon as we are able."

As Isis translated Sun's words in her rudimentary Phenish, Hetty walked over to Sun and lowered her voice. "As hostages their worth is gold. You have secured a means to bring the Phene to you in hope of making peace to get them back."

"*Peace*." The word sounded discordant to her ears.

She left the suite. In the passageway she turned to Colonel Wallace. "No disrespect must be shown to the prisoners. Send Ensign Solomon back to me once he's finished reviewing the intake records."

Walking between Isis and Hetty, she returned to the hangar. The outer doors stood open and in their place a shimmer marked a transparent barrier to keep air in and vacuum out, a Phene technology Chaonia did not possess. A cohort of field engineers were already on board to analyze the system.

Her shuttle was waiting but she halted to stare at the stars beyond, their presence a message from the past. By dropping through beacons she could reach a solar system long before her descendants would see the light that shone on her when she arrived there. The past travels in the body of the present as a constant companion. It is only the future that humans fall sightless into without knowing what they will find there. But fate isn't just the command of Heaven. It is also a matter of strategy.

She zoomed her vision to get a detailed view of the detritus of the recent battle. A powerless, heatless lancer tumbled through space, no longer pursuing, no longer pursued. A hulked frigate was being evacuated by shuttles hauling survivors to the *Boukephalas*. It trailed scraps of debris amid the ice crystals of a burst water tank.

Her thoughts ticked through coiling strands of information. Windworn and Sleepless mined. Skirmishes still being fought in this system. Many Phene ships fleeing to Hellion Terminus, a dead end for beacon travel while at the same time a potential escape route with strategic importance. Messages pinged in from Nisaba with respect to Chaonia's allies on Karnos Prime, who wished desperately to speak to her. The dead must be honored and the wounded praised.

Exhaustion had wormed its way deep into her bones but victory hummed in her veins. Burned as a soul-cutting light. Yet the stars in their silence and the captured ship in which she stood reminded her that the Speaker for the Rider Council had escaped alongside at least half of the Phene fleet.

She turned to Hetty and Isis. "You two will embark on the *Banshee* for Chaonia. I need something from the palace in Argos. You're the only two I trust to get it."

44

I Am an Honorable Man

Even after a month at the Royal Palace on Chaonia Prime, horizons confuse and amaze Zizou. When he's not on duty, drilling, or sleeping, he has taken to climbing up onto a decorative slab of roof atop a balcony overlooking the Bay of Argos. From here he can watch the sun rise with his back wedged into a wall to brace himself against vertigo.

The island's retaining wall rises ten meters above the sea. Some mornings rough water splashes high enough to spray his face. Other days, like today, waves caress the rocky shallows in quiet measures. The sun hasn't yet risen so it's not quite light enough for him to see ripples and foam, but the taste of salt and the rhythm of the swells also communicates. Growing up on the wheelship of Wrathful Snakes Banner he learned to listen to the ship. Its steady respiration without which every living creature on board would die. The ticks and tocks of all the interlocking pieces that keep a ship operational. The fragrant green wheel with its fields and hydroponic canals and arthropoda vaults. The silence of the maze of Lady Chaos, spinning in weightlessness at the center of the rings. Her knot of destiny can never be unraveled because it lies beyond the power of short-lived humankind to untangle eternity.

Someone walks onto the balcony below. He can't see them, and they won't know he's here if he stays still. Maybe they are also come to watch the sun rise.

A scent of incense drifts on the air, as if the newcomer has just arrived from making an offering. The fragrance reminds him of Persephone Lee. Of how she kissed him in the holy basilica of the Phene. Of how he kissed her, blindfolded so he wouldn't strangle her, making the experience a memory blended of the feel of her body, the texture of her clothing, the press of her lips. The words she said and the slightly hoarse timbre of her molasses voice. *They want you to think you are master of your own fate, because it gives you the illusion of control, and that feeds their purpose.*

So it's a jolt through his whole body when the unseen person on the balcony speaks in a low voice. "I'm glad you came. We should leave now. Immediately."

The voice's husky timbre grips him by the heart. It's *her* voice. Persephone Lee's voice. For a wild instant he tenses, making ready to pitch himself over the roof's curved rim and swing onto the balcony. He can throw an arm across his eyes . . . an arm around her warm flesh . . .

"Honored Manea, that would be unwise," says a stern baritone. "The thirty days of mourning are not over until sunset. There is a protocol to observe. A public offering to make before the evening's formal departure, which has already been scheduled. You would not wish to insult the memory of your dear departed by sneaking out of the palace like a criminal, would you?"

"I would not wish to do anything to insult Eirene's memory. But Uncle Marduk just pinged me to say he can't attend the sunset ceremony. He promised he would personally escort us to Lee House. Doesn't it seem suspicious he suddenly can't come just now?"

"Have you no message from your mother?"

"Didn't they tell you, Kadmos?"

"I've been restricted to the estate with no comms."

"My mother was called out of system right after Eirene . . ." Her voice caught. "After it happened. I've only gotten four messages from her. The phrasing is formal, like a bureaucrat checking in. Doesn't that seem odd to you?"

"As governor of Lee House the Honored Moira has a great many responsibilities. It's not at all odd she might be called away to deal with a serious security breach or an internal matter that threatens the republic. But I had not heard."

"Because you were detained at the estate, without comms. Even my messages to you were refused, until yesterday. Why did they lock you down?"

"I was accused of abetting Aisa's act of violence."

"That's ridiculous. Why would they suspect you?"

"Because I tutored you children."

"I'm not Aisa's daughter!"

"I tutored your cousins as well. Because I chose to retire to the estate after your marriage, that is seen as suspicious. It wasn't until the Honored Marduk offered testimony that I was able to convince the authorities it was coincidence that Aisa and I were at the estate together before the assassination. But I do blame myself. She should never have been trusted."

The fourth consort of Queen-Marshal Eirene sighs on the edge of a sob.

The tutor says, "What is it you fear, dear child?"

"I fear Prince João."

"Has he threatened you, Manea?"

A seabird's mournful cry pierces above the water's sough. Why would Consort Manea fear the Royal? Both are consorts of the deceased queen-marshal. Multiple alliances are a common arrangement among people who use marriage as part of negotiations. Such an alliance is sealed by offspring, or by an exchange of resources, or by handing over one family's child into the keeping of another family. It's one of the ways the banners keep their bloodlines heterogenous. They trade youth between wheelships to start a new life with another banner. It's a noble path. The planet-bound civilizations engage in similar customs. That's how Prince João, a Royal of the Gatoi, came to marry Eirene. They each brought something valuable to the negotiating table. Who benefited most? he wonders now.

Sun is queen-marshal but half foreign in a republic that distrusts foreigners. The Honorable Manea has given birth to a healthy child who is Chaonian through and through.

Manea says, "You know I'm right. It's not safe."

The tutor sighs. "Yes, perhaps it would be for the best if you leave quietly. Do you have a plan in mind?"

"We leave right now. Inanna and I only need to get to Lee House. Mother's people will protect me until she returns." She laughs with the anxious tremor of a person who is genuinely frightened. "The gambit Persephone took at the wedding banquet gave me the idea, if you can believe it."

"Escape by boat. But there are scylla and charybdis."

"Charybdis don't rise until the sun is higher. And Resh taught me how to tune a screamer to confuse the scylla. She wasn't as pissy toward me as the twins were. You know that."

"Ereshkigal had an honorable soul," the tutor agrees. "Very well. I will assist you."

"Meet me at the interior dock in twenty minutes." Their footsteps recede.

Zizou waits a full minute to be sure they're gone, then heads across the roofs. Piquant scents rise from flowering plants in the Memory Garden of the Celestial Empire as he circles the queen-marshal's private quarters. The route is exhilarating, more of a challenge than his usual drill because of the nature of planetary gravity and the slipperiness of damp tiles. As a shortcut it allows him to drop into the second consort's private courtyard in five minutes.

A banner soldier on duty notes his unexpected arrival with an open hand. He clenches a fist in reply and dashes past. Colonel Evans greets him at the door into the Royal's private suite.

"Zizou? What haste?"

"Consort Manea and Princess Inanna with the Lee House tutor are leaving the palace by boat in twelve minutes from the interior dock."

The colonel goes in, leaving him waiting for fifty-eight seconds. Then the door slides open and Prince João strides out, pulling on black gloves. His face wears a glower as merciless as the heart of Lady Chaos.

"Zizou, attend me. Colonel, I've just received word Hestia and Isis are arriving on a highly classified mission. I'll deal with this matter before they get here. Is everyone else in place as per the original plan?"

"Of course, Your Highness."

Zizou falls into step behind the Royal. The prince has no compunction about cutting through the chamberlain quarters. People scramble to get out of his way. Questions thrown at him go unanswered. As a Royal he is not obliged to reply.

There is something going on here Zizou does not understand.

They arrive at the entry porch to the interior docks in eleven minutes and thirty seconds. No palace marines stand guard. That's odd, since there are usually soldiers at every gate between sections, a standard precaution in a republic whose stability and power are built on violence. If Queen-Marshal Eirene had not allowed confidence to lapse into hubris, she might still be alive today.

The portal letting into the interior dock is blinking red with an overlay message stating "closed for maintenance." The Royal strips off the glove of his right hand and presses the bare palm to a square screen. A shimmer of light reads his left eye. Blinking red turns green. The door whisks open. João tugs on his glove as he enters.

The interior is dimly lit. Boats bump against a wharf. Water sloshes against pilings. The space smells of brine, like the big vats in back kitchens of Cafeteria Row on the wheelship where Zizou grew up. A handheld lamp shines at the end of the wharf, its aura glowing golden over the face of an elder. Another figure stands beside the tutor, her face hidden in the shadows.

"Turn your back, Zizou," the Royal says, then walks forward. "Honored Manea, I'm afraid you can't leave just yet."

An intake of breath. "Are you here to kill me?"

"Kill you? No one wants to kill you. You're well loved in the palace and far beyond. Did you not know?"

"Not well loved by you." There's a pause before she speaks in a ragged tone. "You've cut off my comms. What do you want?"

"I want what I've been promised. If you want to live, you should wrap that lovely scarf over your face. Don't look my banner soldier in the eyes."

"He's the one who tried to kill me at the banquet, isn't he?"

"He tried to kill Persephone Lee first. Then you. Interesting, is it not, tutor?" The prince uses a masculine form for the elder.

"Are you addressing me, Your Highness?" says the baritone voice Zizou heard on the balcony. Its tone suggests a canny campaigner who knows he has an escape route.

"I am indeed addressing you. Abdul-Lee Kadmos Rèn Aljiu, isn't it?"
"It is."

"Do not attempt to unmoor the boat. I have no bone to pick with you, but I will not hesitate to have my soldier kill you if you do not obey."

"Would killing me be wise, Your Highness?"

"Have you some sheltering wing that shields you? The queen-marshal left me in charge of the palace during her absence from Chaonia. It's my bailiwick to make security decisions."

"I am an employee of Lee House, not an employee of the palace. Governor Moira Lee will not take kindly to violence done to one of her household."

"Moira Lee is dead. She cannot protect you."

Manea sobs once, then catches herself and says, in a tight whisper, "I knew it."

Water sloshes against pilings. Wind moans through the bars of the sea gate.

Manea's harsh breathing steadies. Louder, harder, she adds, "Did you have my mother killed so you could go after me with impunity, is that it?"

"You mistake the matter. Your mother is irrelevant to my interests."

The words are pebbles in the maze of Lady Chaos, thrown on the path to make feet slip.

"You're lying. If you didn't have her killed, then how did she die?"

"In a shuttle accident, so I have been informed," the Royal remarks blandly. "I will not bother with condolences. She was bigoted, and personally unpleasant to me, but her lack of courtesy is immaterial to the larger strategic issues at hand."

"An accident?" Her wild laugh turns into another sob, quickly stifled. "Who believes it was an accident? I'm not naïve. Even if you think I am."

"Then you understand why I am here." He taps Zizou's shoulder. "You may turn around, Zizou. Search the bags and their persons to make sure they are not carrying weapons. Avoid looking the honored consort in the eye. I know you recall what happened the last time you did that."

"Your Highness."

Zizou scans the wharf's closed storage doors, the eight boats lashed to moorings, the sea gates with their vertical bars. Sunlight undulates across the water. The slap of a wave startles him out of his lull. The constant chaotic movements of planet-side light, air, and substance continually nag in his head.

The tutor is an old man, upright, with an unwavering gaze, age-whitened hair, a beard, and hands held out and open to show he carries no weapon. Zizou pushes away the two duffels with a foot to get them out of reach, then pats down the man. A small multi-tool with fold-out blades and implements. Nothing lethal. He sets the multi-tool onto the wharf's decking and kicks it toward the prince.

The woman's face is wrapped in a white mourning scarf, looped so its fringe drapes over her eyes. Quick thinking on her part. She can see but the swaying ends of the fringe disrupt his gaze. In the palace, people speak of her as dignified in bearing and gentle in disposition, a caring individual temperamentally suited to the role of a selfless consort who strives to soothe and energize their ambitious spouse. In other words, nothing like Prince João.

Of course he'll never be able to study her famously piquant looks, the much-described glamour of her adoring gaze on her beloved spouse, the petals that are her lips. Her resemblance to her cousin Persephone. She wears loose trousers and a hastily belted tunic, very casual garb for the palace, more like a chamberlain's uniform. In fact, possibly it is a borrowed uniform, worn as a way to slip past unsuspecting people in the early-morning work rush. A sling holds a baby against her torso, an infant past its earliest months but not yet of walking age. Her left hand cups its little head. In gesture she is a veritable Khepat, mother and protector of all living.

The baby's face is exposed. Its round cheeks are pleasingly fat. He would have liked to see its eyes—babies always have such bright eyes—but it sleeps. By the evidence of an astringent fragrance lingering beneath the pee-and-milk smell of a baby, he suspects it has been drugged to keep it quiet.

Her, not it. The baby had been announced as a girl child, which seems premature to him, but they hold different customs here. Breath rises and falls on its fragile chest. Lips like buds, a plump nose, and eyes tight shut.

He pats her down and checks the baby—you can hide a stinger in a cloth sling—then neatly rifles through the two duffels. The search produces nothing actionable, only the commonplace detritus of everyday life. Consort Manea's bag contains mostly clothing and gear for the baby while the tutor's produces the expected kit of a person making ready for a long journey at short notice. Suspicious.

He feels the approach of the prince at his back. The Royal uses Zizou's body as a shield between him and the unknown element represented by the tutor.

"I appreciate your patience, Manea. You may embark on the boat and make your way to Lee House."

"Why are you letting me go?"

"Your safe passage was part of the bargain. You may leave as soon as you hand over the child."

She stiffens. "What bargain?"

The tutor says, "What is your intention, Your Highness? It's a baby."

"Babies grow up to become rivals. I'm surprised at you, tutor. Surely you know the history of Chaonia as well as anyone. We use different mechanisms of social control among the Gatoi banners."

"Savages," hisses Manea. She takes a step away from the Royal, both arms wrapped around the sleeping child. "Kadmos, can't you do something? My comms to Lee House and the chamberlains' office are not responding. I'm pinging Uncle Marduk but he's not answering . . ."

The Royal steps up beside Zizou at last. Although his clothes today are dyed dark, the fabric is shot through with glimmering threads that mimic the neural networks every Gatoi is born with. In daylight Zizou had not noticed the presence of the pattern in the fabric. It only betrays itself here where the gates bar most of the sun's rising glow.

"As I said, you may leave once you hand the child over to me."

"Kadmos?" Manea sobs.

The tutor looks at her and then at the prince. He says nothing. He does not act.

"The baby is not who you are here to protect, is it?" says the Royal to the tutor.

Manea drops to her knees as if all the air has been punched out of her. Her body curls over the baby's tiny body.

"Kadmos?" she gasps.

Gravely, the old man says, "I am sorry, Honored Manea. The infant is not under my purview."

"Gracious Heaven, accept my tears," she whispers as at a shot to the heart, the piercing metal of betrayal.

"Oh, of course, how could I not have seen it before?" says the prince. In an excess of emotion, he adjusts his sleeves like a man readying himself to meet a long-sought lover. "Zizou is the proof. You're Nona Lee's agent in Lee House, aren't you? Watching over her clones. Educating them. Observing them."

Head bowed, Manea says flatly, "It wasn't my mother who sent you to help me."

"That depends on how you define who your progenitor is," says Kadmos. His brow wrinkles with the troubled look of a man who wishes to act decently in life, but Zizou can already tell he will not raise a hand.

"That's why Uncle Marduk's not answering," she says to the swaying boardwalk, unable to lift her eyes to unforgiving fate. "That's the bargain you mean, isn't it? I live but Inanna dies."

The Royal remains unmoved by her trembling shoulders and scathing anger.

"What if I rip this scarf from my face? What if your banner soldier murders me? You'll be blamed!"

"And the baby will still die," says the Royal. "But you will be dead too."

Zizou does not like the turn this encounter has taken. The air thickens under a weight of cruelty. It is wrong to slaughter the innocent. To toss babies into the fiery furnace.

Manea says nothing more. Words have withered in her belly.

The Royal is replete with victory, not gloating but sharp with purpose. "Zizou, take the child from her and kill it."

The words hit with the relentless pressure of a jackhammer. The sentence must have fallen through a toxic cloud and, in a spasm, come out opposite to its original meaning. He was raised to obey as his sacred duty. But you do not murder children.

"Zizou? Did you not hear?" The Royal's impatience hangs as a threat.

Manea bows her head. The tutor stands unmoving, awaiting events.

His grandmother and all the elders of Wrathful Snakes Banner taught that the young must be raised to take the place of the old so the banner will live on. But the Rider who captured him told him the wheelships sold a percentage of their own children to the Phene. And it's true the empire employs banner soldiers as weapons, manipulating them with a neurological leash without their consent. It's true that after he went to the Phene, his personal neural network was additionally programmed with an engineered hallucination over which he has no control. It's true the Phene officers fed them on a diet of honor and sacrifice.

They want you to think you are master of your own fate, because it gives you the illusion of control and that feeds their purpose. That's what Persephone Lee said to him. Is he always to be nothing more than a tool, a puppet used by others for their ends?

"No."

He steps away from the Honorable Manea, once the beloved consort of Queen-Marshal Eirene, now a pawn in the ugly game of power.

"I will not. I am an honorable man."

"You disobey a Royal?" The prince looks confounded by this act of defiance.

"I will not murder a baby."

"The baby is going to die regardless."

Zizou thinks maybe he can grab Manea and escape on the boat. If she knows how to steer such a vessel, and he guesses she does. Prince João is strong and smart but he is not a banner *soldier*, trained to the highest level of expertise and furthermore shot through with enhancements to speed, strength, agility.

The thought dies as the portal whisks open. Colonel Evans enters at a jog, accompanied by four banner soldiers. The four banner soldiers surge forward to surround Zizou like points on a compass. He knows them by their battle names, as they know him by his. Four is too many for Zizou, for they are all as accomplished as he is in their different ways: a Marta, a Kōhei, a Wilma, and a Hank. They do not look at him. Why would they? He has turned his back on the covenant by refusing the command of a Royal.

With the arrival of Colonel Evans and her squad, the fight in the Honorable Manea's body dies. She knows what her choices are, so she makes one.

Rising, she inclines her scarf-shielded face toward where Zizou stands. "My thanks, soldier. Please don't harm yourself in a battle you can't win. I won't forget that you alone stood up for my child."

He does not answer because there is nothing to say. It's all very well to crow about honor when your noble speech makes no difference to the outcome. He is ashamed.

Her head lifts with an expression like wrath set in reserve. "Blessed Heaven watches our actions and judges who we are. I choose to live. I accept the responsibility for my selfish choice. But this crime is on your head, João."

She steps down onto the lower dock. Kneeling, she unwinds the sleeping baby from its sling. In silence she plunges the infant underwater. In silence, she holds it beneath the surface.

From here Zizou cannot see if it kicks. If it struggles. The seconds tick past. Ten. Twenty. Forty.

Fifty.

A minute.

Manea is shuddering, weeping, choking. From this angle he can see her arms to the elbows and then only the rippling shadows of the water.

The tutor says, hoarsely, "Enough, Honored Manea. It is enough."

"Fuck you," she says as calmly as if she is ordering her supper. But she rises. She steps up onto the boardwalk holding the limp baby to her breast.

Colonel Evans walks forward expectantly.

There is a long pause. Stillness, drenched by grief and cold rage.

Manea wraps the baby tightly in a blanket and hands her to the colonel as she addresses the Royal. "I pray you, let her be given the same dignity in death as Eirene. She deserves that. She was never a threat to you or your daughter."

The prince's eyebrows lift with an unfathomable expression of emotion. Magnanimously he says, "You are free to go, Manea."

When the tutor reaches for her duffel, she snaps, "Not you. None of you. I can steer the boat on my own."

Grabbing a duffel, she swings it onto a vessel, releases the line, leaps aboard, starts the motor as a sea gate claps open, and pilots the boat out onto the open water.

The sound of the motor recedes.

The prince watches until he can no longer see the boat on the water, then turns to Colonel Evans. "I have underestimated Manea Lee."

"I sense we all have, Your Highness," she replies.

Kadmos coughs like a man restraining himself from a caustic comment.

The prince addresses him. "I have released Manea to Marduk's supervision."

"I take it that Marduk is now governor of Lee House," remarks Kadmos. "Well, Manea was always his favorite. His sons are not as endearing. Nor as strong-minded, as you belatedly comprehend. You've made an enemy today, Your Highness."

"You've discharged your duty and have no further function here. It's time you leave Chaonia and join your exiled employer. Do you understand me?"

Kadmos's gaze slides over to examine Zizou. Speculation cascades along tiny shifts of expression. "Nona Lee would be very interested to examine this individual, Your Highness. To dissect the work done on him. I can see he is delivered to her."

"Can you indeed?" says the prince with a sardonic laugh. "But I'm not inclined to extend a hand to Nona Lee. You may go, tutor. Make haste to depart this system. I recommend you do not return."

Kadmos bows. Without a backward glance or a supportive word he leaves the dock.

When the man is gone, the Royal walks to Zizou. The four banner soldiers take a step back. This close Zizou can see the gleam of a deep network in the Royal's eyes that give him access to a wider range of communications and information than that allowed to ordinary banner soldiers. The Royal's jaw is tight with anger. But he manages a well-modulated tone as he speaks the ritual words.

"Where the heavens above did not exist, and the earth beneath had not come into being, there dwelled the cosmic waters, which are the substance of all. Out of this ocean rose Lady Chaos, who gave birth to the eleven exiles."

The banner soldiers kneel. After a hesitation, Zizou does too. Normally the Royal will extend their hands, palms up and open, and the banner soldier the Royal is addressing will place their palms atop the other's. But Prince João offers no connection. Without the offering of fealty, Zizou has no permission to speak.

Colonel Evans says, "Thus Lady Chaos said to her twelfth child, the last born, the Royal: protect my offspring, and in exchange they will serve you when you call. You have called us, your banner soldiers, into your service according to the ancient covenant."

The prince answers. "I am born beneath the banner of Royal, child of Nanshe, child of Ashur, child of Tanith to the tenth generation. By the binding of the crown of light, I assert my right to demand your service until I release you. But I do not release you. I repudiate you."

The four banner soldiers each take another step away, leaving Zizou alone in his disgrace which they have no part of, because they obeyed.

"I strip from you your battle name. You have lost the right to wear its burnished honor. You may no longer call yourself a banner soldier. It is done. It is done. It is done."

The Royal turns his back. Colonel Evans turns her back. The four banner soldiers turn their backs. He is no longer one of them, living in the moment of impact without future or past. He is no longer Zizou, elegance with precision.

The realization drops as through a beacon, opening a space into a new world in which he is no longer called Zizou but can only be addressed by the name his grandmother gave him. When he left the wheelship he left his birth name behind. Yet if he is no longer a banner soldier, then what is he? Can he even go home? Would they take him back? Or was he truly cut loose, as the Rider said, never to be allowed to return? Maybe he was no longer anything, a wanderer without companions, a name without a purpose. *Kurash.*

45

Because I Am Coming After You Wherever You Are

As the royal cutter *Banshee* made its final approach to Karnos Prime and the newly renamed Command Orbital Station Destined Triumph, Hetty reported to the secure compartment. Isis had slept on a cot in the observation space for the entire voyage from Chaonia Prime. The colonel was armed and ready when Hetty entered, bearing the unlock codes.

On a royal cutter a "secure room" was normally used to secure treasury or high-value tech, and rarely for prisoners. Hetty stepped up beside Isis, comfortable in the presence of a woman she had known for half her life, one who had trained her alongside the mourned and murdered Octavian.

The compartment had a counter next to the far wall, where a silent marine stood guard at all hours over three cells. One was empty. One held the lifepod and a bank of monitoring equipment. In the third waited the young banner soldier who was no longer a banner soldier, whom she could no longer address as Zizou. He wore the patterned leggings and knee-length jacket favored by off-duty palace chamberlains, the only clothing she'd been able to get hold of in the short time she and Isis had been on Chaonia Prime. The prince had been going to send him to the Krinides mines. Hetty had calmly pointed out that Sun alone could request the young man to remove the ring she had given him, so to Sun he must go.

Aware they were near their destination, the disgraced soldier stood at attention, noble in aspect, handsome in feature, and with the build and posture of an individual who can explode from stillness into destruction between one heartbeat and the next.

"You and I have known each other long enough, Honored Hestia," said Isis, "that I can tell you bluntly, I believe this is all a very bad idea."

"I know you have no love for what he is, but he served Sun both loyally and well."

"I can't argue with the assessment, but before the incident with Prince João he was bound by the Gatoi code. And before that by the neural leash the Phene use to restrain the banner soldiers they hire. Now he is a weapon that could go off at any moment. What binds him?"

"His loyalty to Sun. That is enough."

Isis slanted a wry look at Hetty. "*You* would believe loyalty is enough. My duty is to keep killers away from the queen-marshal. As the recent death of Eirene should remind us both. Anyway, my initial comment referred to the Rider. Ah!"

The door into the secure compartment opened. Norioghene Hope entered. Hetty knew the woman distantly. Her Hope House–born father had not been close to that branch line, and Hetty had spent more of her childhood years off-planet than on. The rigid lines of House courtesy made her nervous, since she'd been caught out wrong-footed more than once as an adolescent, asking the wrong questions of the wrong people at the wrong time, or forgetting to ask the right ones. It was no wonder Sun's confidence warmed her. Sun did what she wanted and let the rest go hang.

Norioghene gave Hetty a nod of acknowledgment, then said to Isis, "Has Sun given you any idea of what she intends to do with the Rider? Eirene would never give me the go-ahead to do more than passive scans. Perhaps Sun will be bolder. We can't learn more until we physically take her apart."

Isis raised an eyebrow. "Is that what you will advise, Honored

Norioghene? Kill the Rider and perform an extensive exploratory autopsy?"

"This suspension is of no benefit to anyone. As for the Gatoi, I don't understand why you didn't have him put down. I'd love to examine his neural network."

"His fate is in the hands of Queen-Marshal Sun."

The cells were meant to be soundproof with a one-way view wall but he clearly was aware of their presence. Hetty had stood guard over Octavian's funeral pyre with him, shared food with him. His refusal to obey Prince João's orders at the palace was not the act of an individual gone rogue. Yet honor could make a person dangerous in ways impossible to guess at beforehand.

Norioghene was going on. "I hope Marduk can exert some control over Prince João, because I am not the only one who doesn't like the way he swans around the palace as if it is his to rule. You can't trust a Gatoi."

"Sun won't welcome such words, Honored Norioghene."

"She would do well to listen to those of us who served Eirene. People like you, Colonel."

A ping from Sun buzzed into the ring network, causing Kurash to blink. Hetty read the curt message: COSDT PIER 8. AWAIT MY ARRIVAL.

The proximity alarm rang three times. The cutter shuddered as docking clamps seized hold. The watch bell rang and the 1MC buzzed with the bosun's whistle: the queen-marshal was aboard.

The instant the cutter had dropped into Karnos System, Hetty had sent ahead a packet, so Sun knew the whole. When the hatch opened and the queen-marshal strode in, she walked straight to the cell holding the Gatoi and released the seal.

Norioghene hissed between her teeth, while Isis stepped sideways to get a line for a shot. Sun clasped her hands behind her in a position of confidence. Her mouth was relaxed, her stance easy as he took in her presence.

He touched hand to heart, then lowered it and approached. Isis raised her stinger. Without looking back, Sun waved at the colonel to desist. He halted an arm's length from Sun. He was half a head taller but his height did not overwhelm Sun's presence. She looked him up and down. Hetty bit her lower lip, unaccountably anxious. Even she did not know what Sun would do.

Sun extended her right hand, palm up. He dropped to his knees as if shot. After a hesitation, he rested his hands, palms down, on hers.

"I cannot rescind the act of a Royal, nor would I reject the command of my sire. By his word, you are no longer a banner soldier. You still serve me as my bodyguard."

"Your Highness," he said in a tight voice. "I refused an order. He was right to repudiate me."

"That you objected speaks in your favor. There is no point whatsoever in murdering an infant who will take years to grow up."

"Easy to say now the deed is done and your own hands clean of it," muttered Norioghene. Like all of Eirene's Companions, she had made much of the baby, whether through required performance or actual affection.

Sun gave no sign she'd heard. "I have a mission for you. You will journey as my envoy to the Conclave of the Banners. Bring to the wheelships my offer. Let each banner shed the chains of their arrangement with the Phene Empire. Let them withdraw their soldiers from the Phene military. Let the wheelships join me in a mutual alliance. In exchange I will give them the means to unlock forever the engineered leash the Phene impose on the banner soldiers."

"That is a generous offer, Your Highness," said Norioghene. "Are you sure you want to give up such an advantage now that we possess the Phene leash technology?"

"To coerce people to fight for me? There's no honor in whipping the unwilling into battle. We fight for Chaonia's dignity, her honor, her glory. That is our shared enterprise. Likewise, it would be dishonorable to enslave my own cousins."

Sun gave Norioghene a hooded glance and returned her attention to the young man. She rested her left hand atop his head. "What do I call you?"

His innocent youthfulness was striking compared to his lethal abilities. His shyness appealed to Hetty but she did not mistake it for weakness.

"Our birth names do not leave the wheelships, Your Highness."

"You spent months aboard the *Keoe* under my jurisdiction. I claim the right to call you by the name you gave to Commander Rahaba."

He swallowed, then spoke in a low voice. "Kurash."

"Kurash, the Honorable Hestia will see you immediately to the *Huma*."

"Am I to go with him upon the mission?" Hetty asked. It wasn't that she wanted to leave Sun, but the successful dash to Chaonia Prime to fetch the Rider had left her flushed with a sense of competency and an ambition to tackle more such independent projects.

Sun's beautiful lips pressed and then parted as her thoughts ticked through the hidden message of Hetty's words. Hetty had lived through a dark year after her diplomat father's murder. At one point she hadn't gotten out of bed for seven days. By temperament, she was more an analyzer than a leaper. Even as she braced herself for Sun's decision she admired the swiftness of Sun's decisiveness.

"I need my full complement of Companions beside me. But you are correct that I should assign a notable and Honored Companion as lead envoy to the wheelships, in charge of the mission. I'll send Precious Jīn."

Norioghene shot her an accusatory look.

Sun caught it with the ease of pure confidence, that brilliantly attractive fire, before returning her focus to the young man. "Kurash, there's a packet of instructions waiting for you with Captain Shì. Do you have any questions? Any objections? Let me hear them."

By this gesture she gave him leave to speak as a citizen to their queen-marshal rather than as banner to Royal.

"I will serve as you ask, Your Highness. Your safety and your security, and that of your companions, is mine to defend to the death."

"So will it be."

She caught Hetty's eye. Hetty restrained a disappointed sigh. She nodded, took charge of the young man, and led him toward the docking bay where the *Huma* waited.

"Wake up the Rider," said Sun as she examined the unconscious individual sealed inside the lifepod.

Norioghene Hope did not obey. She remained on the other side of the cell's raised threshold, toying with a percussion-echo baton, used to knock out a banner soldier in full neural flood. For an instant Sun saw Norioghene as a hostile, who might all along have been engaged by Moira Lee or the treacherous seers of Iros to do something about an heir they wanted out of the way.

She'd never give anyone the satisfaction of believing even for a millisecond that she saw herself in any way as vulnerable to attack. But she did cast a glance at Isis.

The colonel took a step toward the older Companion, saying mildly, "Honored Norioghene, if you'd prefer, I can assist the queen-marshal."

Norioghene's eyes flickered at the title, but not, Sun thought, in anger at Eirene's daughter. More as at grief rubbed raw. As a reminder of her changed status:

"I regret my mother was not able to see this campaign through," Sun said, "but her great enterprise will live on to polish her glorious memory."

Norioghene's hand tightened on the rod. "What do you hope to achieve by waking the Rider?"

"You have stood guard over this valuable prisoner for many months. I would offer you the honor of waking her, but if you prefer not to do so, I have the codes."

Sun placed her palm against the control panel. It read her retina, her hand, the aerosol of her breath, and unlocked to allow entry.

"I'll do it," said Norioghene. "I can wake her without removing the restraints."

"Anyone would be physically weak after months suspended in a life-pod."

"We don't understand Rider physiology so it is best to be cautious. But in addition, lifepods have been refined so as to mitigate some of the worst effects of long-term suspension. It isn't the same as being put in a medical coma."

A motor whirred, turning the body to a forty-five-degree angle so the riding face was visible through the transparent segment of the upper shell of the lifepod. Mist puffed into the interior, clouding the inner surface of the clear plate. A timer began counting backward. Sun set herself to wait. People often thought her impatient—she knew that— but they were wrong. She knew how to wait when there was a con-firmed objective and a clear timetable. It was hesitancy and indecision she objected to.

Isis knew her moods, so made no attempt to converse.

Like all her mother's Companions and trusted marshals, Noriogh-ene felt obliged to give her opinion. "It's a bad idea. Every word you say to her will be heard by every Rider in the empire."

"That is indeed my intention."

In silence they waited until the green light blinked to show the next phase was ready. The outer plate rolled back, leaving in place only a paper-thin transparent sheet like a soap bubble. A jet of air whooshed through, stirring the surface. The eyes of the ordinary face blinked several times rapidly, then slowed as the body fully woke. Her eyes shifted side to side but all she could see was an opaque segment of the interior shell. Her features twitched before smoothing into a tight mask as memory returned. The woman had a cruel mouth, twisting with enmity. Her lips shaped words as if curses, and then she stilled as a stronger consciousness took hold.

The lines of the riding face stirred, stretched, and came to eerie life. The eye slits opened. She saw Sun, while Sun stared onto a blank and fathomless void. Beyond that void lay all the Riders in the empire.

"I hope I have your attention," Sun said.

There was a pause as of many voices conferring all at once.

"Queen-Marshal Sun," the Rider's voice whispered, harsh and thin. The gaze shifted to take in Norioghene Hope as if drinking her in.

Sun said, "What may I call you?"

The Rider's lips pressed so tightly together that they became a line. A stark refusal. No matter. This person was not the one she sought.

"I am in Karnos System, as you know. Do I address Speaker Baragesi?"

"He listens among us."

"Speaker Baragesi, I wish to assure you that your family is unharmed, and will remain unharmed in my custody."

The captured Rider murmured, "I told you that claiming families would create vulnerability."

"We all have families," said Sun, "as the Rider Council certainly knows, since they engaged the services of the seers of Iros to attempt to kill me and to assassinate my glorious mother, Eirene."

"The Rider Council had nothing to do with the murder of Eirene."

"Did you not? Then you will certainly be amenable to returning Kiran Seth as surety of your good intentions."

"You have attacked us unprovoked," said the Rider. "What of your intentions?"

"Unprovoked!" Sun swatted at the air as at a bad argument buzzing around her like a fly. "Your ancestors invaded Chaonia and trampled us under your feet. You fought the Yele, more than once. I have taken up my mother's cause to stand as the leader of the Republic of Chaonia and the Yele League to right the wrongs your empire has done to us. Need I list all our conflicts? The assassination of Eirene by a murderer tied to a known agitator and agent who you shelter as an ally was simply the latest act of a belligerent power. But now I have prevailed over you in battle. I have defeated your fleets, taken into my custody your ships, those not destroyed. They belong to me now because you fled when you could not stand against me."

She had to pause to catch her breath as at the end of a strenuous race. Hadn't the attack on Karnos been a marathon conducted over days and months and years? It was a destined triumph no one but Eirene—and Sun—had believed possible.

The Rider sighed with the disdain of hundreds. "You mock us with this unseemly boasting. But out of concern for the peace and health of our imperial subjects we are willing to offer terms to you as representative of Chaonia. We agree to exchange pledges of friendship and to form an alliance of peaceful coexistence."

"That is not an offer. This is an offer." She took a step closer, filling the Rider's angle of view. "Speaker Baragesi, on behalf of the Rider Council you may approach me in person and request that I return to you your family. The Rider Council may sue for peace by acknowledging my place as high admiral over your defeated forces. And you can return to me Kiran Seth, who I have reason to believe resides in your territory under your watch. Meet me on my terms, and anything you persuade me to give you will be yours. But if you intend to fight, then fight rather than run away, because I am coming after you, wherever you are."

She pressed the control panel over Norioghene's startled protest. The shell sealed. Mist swirled into the lifepod in a fresh storm as the Rider pressed her body against the restraints as if to tear them off. The fog inside grew too thick to see through. When the white mist cleared the Rider had sunk back into suspension.

Sun left the chamber with an indignant Norioghene clipping at her heels.

"Why didn't you keep negotiating with them?" Norioghene asked. "It's what Eirene would have done."

"I am sure it is. But there is nothing to negotiate. They lost. They haven't yet understood what that means."

46

The Wily Persephone Is Not a Screamer

I have to see him before he sees me. Obviously. Otherwise I'll be dead.

Hetty pinged me when she entered Karnos System, and I immediately looked up my academy rack-mate Ay Jí Alimerishu, now an ensign assigned to the fast frigate *Huma,* which is part of the *Boukephalas*'s escort group. I get myself on board because the officer of the watch can't say no when one of the queen-marshal's Companions arrives for a social visit with an old friend.

Ay takes me to the officers' mess, where we share tea and pastries the way we used to at our favorite teahouse on breaks at the academy. We bonded over being among those unable to go home for Founders' Week and Celestial Week. I tell her my cunning plan while she rolls her eyes so hard that if they were artificial they would by now be on the floor.

"You've got it bad, and that ain't good," she says. "It's been a year since you saw him, hasn't it? Usually you would have gone through at least two other crushes by now."

"I saw him at the palace just after Sun became queen-marshal."

"I see. The flames got fanned. But I have to ask. Are you absolutely sure you want me to sneak you into the quarters he's been assigned? He could kill you before we got the door open no matter how loud you scream. I mean, if we can even tell one kind of scream from another."

"I am not a screamer. I'm more into quiet ecstasy."

"Am I dead yet?" Ay remarks to the ceiling.

I finish up a coconut bun and lick my fingers. "I've got this."

"Like anyone could ever stop you, not even Solomon. Where is he? And where is your glamorous cee-cee?"

"The big squarehead is on duty. Ti is in attendance on Sun for the review of troops and the launch of Idol Faire."

"Aren't the queen-marshal's Companions meant to be in attendance for that?"

"I snuck out. Ti's covering for me."

"Must be nice." She does that business of wrinkling up her nose as she decides whether to say a thing that might piss someone off. As always with Ay, it's a yes. "You know, Ikenna and Minh got berths on the *Boukephalas*."

"Does that irk you? They have less chance to rise in the ranks there than you have with the most-decorated fast frigate captain in the fleet."

"I won't forget you told me that." She stands with an assist from her leg brace, polished until it gleams. "This way."

A fast frigate is the oldest baseline fleet ship, fast, maneuverable, and with enough weapons power to do damage and enough speed not to have to stick around to get pummeled in return. The Chaonian models have six decks. Officers' quarters take up a portion of Deck 3 and include special billets for temporary passengers like diplomats, high-ranking officers being taken to a new posting, and the occasional high-value detainee.

Ay leads me roundabout by taking me to her cabin, which she shares with another ensign, who is currently on duty. Our route to the quarterdeck takes us past the guest billets just as I get a ping from Hetty: ETA 15

Ay stops short, causing me to bump into her solid frame. Since she was the only person in Stone Barracks almost as short as me, I can see over her shoulder onto a terrifying vision of a glowering Marshal the Honorable Precious Jīn. She's standing in the passageway with a campaign duffel slung over her broad shoulders. The glare she's giving an intimidated lieutenant is exactly the look a person angry at someone else gives the hapless innocent who happens to be in their line of sight. An experienced combat veteran, she catches our movement and turns.

I duck down so she can't see my face. Ay isn't anyone to her, a random ensign of no account.

"Unbelievable, what nerve to send me on this petty gallimimus chase." Eirene's veteran Companion addresses the passageway at large before she goes inside the billet. Ay and the lieutenant exchange a glance. He's seen me, and when Ay waggles her hand as a signal, he trots off, happy to be shed of any further complications.

"In here." Ay opens a secure billet. "Lucky for you I was assigned to Deck."

As soon as we are inside, she latches the door as the lights come on. A secure billet like this one is poured out of a hard ceramic mold so there are no objects that can be removed to make weapons. There's a berth with a thin mattress, a locker, a sink and shower, a toilet behind a screen, an alcove desk with a bench, the whole thing colored a horrifically neutral blue that would drive me to vandalism within three hours.

"Are you sure?" she asks.

I nod because I can't speak. My pulse races like a motherfucker until I wonder if my heart is going to explode out of my ears. Ay frowns, pats my forearm, and says, "About the lights."

"I have a lot of practice with jamming lights."

She laughs. And she leaves.

I have just enough time to jigger the lights before I hear them. In pitch blackness I feel my way to the screen and step behind it. The door opens, admitting a shaft of light from the passageway.

Hetty says, "Will you be well?"

"My thanks, peerless Hestia. I know my duty. I am content."

His voice shears through me like blades cutting open my heart. The door shuts. The lights don't come on. His duffel drops to the floor with a thump. He shifts, and at first I think he's tapping at the control panel, and then an arm has snaked around the screen and a hand grasps me at the elbow.

"Ow," I say.

His intake of breath makes me almost delirious with a feeling I can't describe. Infatuation. Desire. Leaping off a cliff's edge for wanting the sensation of falling.

"Don't turn on the lights," I add breathlessly. My cheeks are flushed and my heart is pounding.

He releases me and whirls, his back thumping against the screen that stands between our bodies. I lean into it, imagining his heat and his flesh a centimeter away from my lips.

"Zizou—"

"I am no longer Zizou," he says harshly. "You should not have come here, dauntless Persephone."

I'd kick myself if I had a clone next to me. "Kurash, I mean."

"Who told you this name?"

"Oh, uh, shouldn't she have . . ." I detest casting blame on others, so I shift gears. "I mean, shouldn't I know?"

"It is mine to tell to those I choose to confide in, not others' to tell on my behalf. Birth names are a sacred trust, not a common road for all to walk."

Whew. His prickliness makes me adore him even more. I press my cheek to the cool ceramic screen to get ahold of myself.

"Please accept my apologies," I say awkwardly in the Gatoi language I have laboriously worked on learning over the last year. "I know not of this custom. I wanted to—uh—to speak to you before you go."

"I know what you imply by 'speaking.' For my part, I have thought of you often, dauntless Persephone. Every day, in fact."

My pulse is a hammer trying to knock me out cold. The formality of his words, and that he replies in Common Yele, is a basin of ice water cast against my face.

"But I have disgraced my calling, and been repudiated by a Royal. What two individuals share in intimate congress must be clean, not tarnished. I am tarnished."

"Do you regret what you did?"

"I do not regret it and would refuse again, even knowing what my refusal cost."

"Then how are you tarnished, if you made the honorable choice not to murder an infant in cold blood?"

His voice drops to a harsh whisper. "Do you know the most shocking thing I learned in my training as a banner soldier? That infants die every day because we bring violence to their homes. They are not our intended targets. But their graves mark our path."

When I think of the speeches we were given at the academy I know I could repeat back to him the justifications and the rationales, but I don't want to. I grew up in wartime footing. By not one iota do I regret Chaonia's war against the Phene. But even I can see this is neither the time nor the place. Even I can see he is something more, or something different, or something changed. My body still yearns to press against his but my honor, and his, has put on the brakes.

"I've presumed," I say. "I apologize. If you want me to leave, I'll leave."

"It would be best," he says hoarsely.

By all the Eighteen Hells, I misjudged my moment badly.

I scrape out words. "May you have a successful mission."

When I slide out from behind the screen he does not move. His lean body is all shadow except for the tracery of light in his hands and along his cheeks, the breath of neural circuitry every Gatoi is born with. And which in every banner soldier is enhanced to make them stronger, faster, tougher. The better to be flung into the furnace of battle and burned to ashes.

I pace out the distance to the door. Just as I set my hand to the latch, he takes two swift steps. His hand grasps mine hard enough I can't shake it. Yet his thumb brushes my palm with a gentle pressure, a promise, a seduction, a farewell. The touch shudders me to my core. My breath hitches, and I'm hot and trembling.

Then he lets go.

I'm too choked to speak. My limbs are rusted metal, frozen in place. Somehow I open the door and slide out into a passageway mercifully empty except for the Honorable Hestia Hope and my buddy Ay. They stand companionably next to each other, wearing identical guilty flushes as if they've been caught gossiping about me.

"Oh dear," says Ay.

Hetty tucks a hand under my elbow. "I feared it might fall out this way."

"You did?" I suck in a syrupy breath, hoping to have enough dignity to not burst into a snot-filled cry.

"The constant orbit of his life was struck. It's torn asunder, cast adrift, lost helm. Like any ship that loses course he must seek fresh coordinates to make his way."

A tear trickles down my cheek. With the casual intimacy of longtime rack-mates, Ay wipes it away with a finger.

"There, there," she soothes, not without sympathy. "I remember the time when you—"

"I know." I wipe my nose ungracefully with the back of a hand.

Without another word Ay escorts us to the quarterdeck. Even as stunned as I am I see how her shipmates stare to see her walking with two of the queen-marshal's Companions, and her a mere citizen ensign, not a Core House scion. Her social standing is about to skyrocket.

We take our leave and are whistled off the *Huma*.

He's not for me and he has the wisdom to know it. Even if it weren't true that he will kill me if he ever sees my face again, who am I now compared to who I was when we first met? As one of the queen-marshal's Companions I can do what I want because I'm a Core House scion and an intimate of Chaonia's ruler, complicit in her decisions. I'll never again have the same freedom from expectation I hoped and planned for when I was pretending to be a citizen cadet aiming for a modest career in the fleet: to serve the republic and honor my dead sister's memory.

Ensign Persephone Li Alargos might have met an off-duty Gatoi soldier as an equal. Hung out. Got cozy. Talked about the future, as if such a thing could exist. The Honorable Persephone Lee lives in elevated circumstances with responsibilities no humble citizen is burdened by. Not that an honorable has it worse, or harder; not at all. But we carry the freight of rulership on its long journey forward through the generations. So we are told from the earliest age: that we are the bearers of Tradition, the shields and spears of the republic, the wiser heads and the gauntleted fists.

Hetty has the gift of silence. My pulse slows and my brain churns back into gear. In the greater scheme of things, my broken heart is a mere pebble on a road that doesn't belong to me. She keeps her hand tucked into my elbow as we make our way down Pier 8 and onto the main concourse where the big event is unfolding.

As we move into the edges of the crowd, for an instant I swear I glimpse my father moving through the press of the assembly. But after I blink the figure shifts to show a profile, and it isn't him. He was never there. I'm seeing things I wish were true: a father who cares for and watches out for me as Sun's father cares for and watches out for her; a soul mate with a bond like the one Sun and Hetty share selflessly and unconditionally; a mother who nurtures her children with what they need as Ti's mother nurtures her and her little brother.

Heaven is hard to depend on. The sages would say we must assess the times and our circumstances and decide how to act. We can't change where we came from. We can only toss it into a locker from which we hope it can't escape and move on, sadder and, if my experience is anything to go by, probably not much wiser.

47

Invasive Seed

A single lancer was not a priority to Chaonia. Apama had avoided the busiest octants of battle by taking a roundabout route toward Karnos Oct, its two small moons, and the system's seventh beacon. After two Anchor days Apama and Teegee no longer noticed the smell. After three Anchor days they depleted the food supply. Teegee complained about having a rash "down there." But no Chaonian ship pursued their flotsam-like path.

The oxygen percentile in the air was starting to drop when Apama was able to cut power and glide into the shadow of the inoperable beacon.

It was huge, as big as a small moon, if a small moon had been brewed out of a light-swallowing substance like polished ceramic and extruded into the shape of a spiral coil. To travel by beacon, ships dropped into the wider spiral mouth, and exited out of the smaller spiral opening into the beacon's linked system.

The surface of living beacons gleamed with a whispery glow pulsing deep in their opaque coils. This beacon was dark. It didn't even have a sickly aura or a toxic glow, as many broken beacons did. It was just plain dead.

But not even dead beacons were left unattended. Since every beacon had a control node attached to its outermost rim, the nodes of the inoperable beacons were crewed by security teams. A boring duty in this backwater. Perfect for her.

She bellied the lancer around the curve of the spiral as if along the blackened bones of a behemoth. The planet had a local name but the Phene called it Gdansk and had expanded two of its orbital habitats into shipyards to take advantage of its mines.

As soon as she came into visual sight of the control node she sent a targeted burst at its comms array, a standard query to confirm it was under Phene control.

The node replied. *Query? Whodat?*

"Teegee, input your emergency cipher."

A hesitation. Then, "Done."

Ten seconds later a security clearance code streamed into the lancer, together with a diagram of the node's rescue airlock. Apama steered cautiously in. The control node looked like a bulbous growth stuck onto the spiral arm, its size impossible to judge compared to the immensity of the beacon, against which the lancer was a mere flea on the gleaming arm of a petrified space kraken.

A light winked within a cleft on the node. She slid into a hangar just large enough to take a shuttle. The hangar shut behind them. Lights came on, and the atmosphere reading spiked to breathable levels. A comforting mural greeted them: a paradise of giant ferns and bold magnolias gave shade to festive picnicking parties.

An officer and a senior specialist with armament bars waited behind the transparent wall of an inner airlock. The officer signaled an all clear with the lower right hand to show the node was still in Phene hands.

Usually deck crew sealed and unsealed pilots in and out of the membrane but there was also an emergency kill switch. She triggered it. The membrane sagged like a balloon losing air.

First she pried the little figurine of Saint Laranthir off the console in case she ever had a chance to return it to Greensleeves. Then she detached the membrane from the interior, clambered out, and clipped herself to a safety bar. After she was secured, she helped the girl out. Teegee's legs were unsteady but she stayed on her feet. The membrane slumped into a sticky heap around their boots. The stench was appalling.

"Lieutenant First Class Apama At Sabao, permission to come aboard," said Apama, with a salute, trying not to breathe through her nose. "To whom am I speaking?"

"Lieutenant Second Class Aristotle Cu Baccay." The tinny voice of the young officer buzzed through the comms. "You have a Rider with you?"

Teegee tugged off the air filter, threw it to the floor like a child having a tantrum, and pulled down her hood. Her tense shoulders relaxed as the face on the back of her head opened its squinched-up eyes and moved its lips in a mimicry of someone having held their breath too long even though Riders didn't have lungs. Not as far as Apama knew.

Both spacers clasped all hands in the sign of respect. "Rider, we are at your service," said the officer. "What is your order?"

"A shower," said Teegee. "I'm so gross."

"You're a trooper," said Apama.

"Ugh. I stink."

"Yeah, well, I stink too. So there."

The girl giggled, exactly as Apama had hoped. She broke off, eyes going into nystagmus.

Apama signed for the others to wait. A brave little scrubber whirred out from an alcove to clean, the mech's vac, brushes, and mop ready to go.

Tadukhipa whispered, "Anchi."

Wasn't that the name of the captured Rider?

Giolla blinked as she turned to Apama, all business now, stink forgotten. "Tee has a message to be delivered via cipher to units undercover on Orbital Station Sabuncuoğlu."

"The main governmental habitat orbiting Karnos Prime?" Apama asked.

"Yes. It's urgent. Classified Council business."

"Isn't Karnos Prime under Chaonian occupation by now?"

The officer said, "Our comms specialist can double-baffle a cipher that won't be traceable back to here. We send private messages to our families that way all the time to get past . . . well, never mind. The panel to your right will give you access."

The girl unlocked the panel and typed, pausing twice to rub tears from her eyes and mucus from her nose. "Done. Can I clean up now?"

The hangar had a decon chamber for anything and anyone entering the control node. Apama had zero qualms about showering with others since that was standard practice in flight school, but with Tadukhipa awake she could not bring herself to undress in front of every Rider in the empire, and she sure as the hells wasn't going to embarrass the girl by pointing that out to her. She asked the girl to go first while she and the lieutenant discussed the situation.

The girl vanished into the decon compartment.

"So far this planet has been outside the battlefield," Cu Baccay said when the door closed behind Teegee. "Obviously the enemy's not going to harm a beacon node. I've been alerted by the Gdansk superintendent that the local authorities intend to surrender the shipyards intact. They'll leave us alone as long as we don't interfere. Do you want the in-orbit garrison to blow up the shipyards?"

"The shipyards are out of my pay grade. I need you to get rid of the lancer so there's no trace we've been here. Sleepless and Windworn are blocked by mines. I need another route back to the empire."

The lieutenant scratched his head. "The only other route back into the empire I know of would be through the Trinity Coalition. You'd have to drop into Hellion Terminus and then arrange for a paid place in a tow chain to get across the gap to Tsurru System. Then you'd have to get a beacon from Tsurru System to Kumbala System. Then you'd have to arrange a second Argosy passage out of Kumbala System to Harahuvati System, which is part of Mishirru Province. Then you'd need beacon passage again, but it's a pretty straight beacon-to-beacon route to the Triple As and you'd get a military escort. But you're talking at least six months' travel time."

"How realistic is that option?"

"Many of our ships fled to Hellion. I have comms with a couple of officers on tenders and tugs who are going to convoy out that way, see if they can escape the Chaonians, six months be damned. They'd be honored to take on the responsibility."

She chewed on her lower lip. "The *Strong Bull* is at Hellion Terminus.

Its knnu drive might still be working. But it's a long way across this system to get to that beacon. Military ships are the first place the enemy will search." She sighed. "I wish I had a long-haul freighter."

"A long-haul freighter?" Cu Baccay shrugged. "Where does that get you?"

The specialist finally spoke. "Oh, I see what you're planning."

"You do?"

Although not as tall as the officer, the specialist had the rangy build of an athlete and the confident look of a person who's won a few competitions. "Sure. You want to take the caravan route through the Hatti region and Hesjan territory around the outer rim of beacon space. To Tranquility Harbor."

The officer objected. "You can't get to Phene space by going through the Hesjan territories and along the Skuda Reach. There's no beacon route out there."

"There *are* beacon routes out there, ma'am," said the specialist. "But they're all broken up now with dead beacons along the line. You can still make the journey. It's just there are gaps to cross along the way. Caravans go that way."

"What's a caravan?" asked the officer, thus making it clear they had grown up in the Triple As.

"A caravan is a civilian fleet made up of freighters. How do you think people out on those broken beacon lines trade and communicate with the rest of us? The caravans have business agreements with regional Argosy fleets who hop them in tow chains across the three gaps along that route. No, wait, there are four gaps if you include the Proxima haul. Anyway, the point is that because of Skuda raiders, Gatoi brigands, and Hesjan corsairs, every caravan overseer requires each freighter captain to hire a licensed security team for the duration of the round trip. That is, in addition to the freighter crew. Extra people."

"I didn't get your name," said Apama, her interest sharpening.

"Senior Specialist Gurak Se Xar." He used male designators. "How do you know that route, ma'am? If you don't mind my asking."

"I grew up on Tranquility Harbor. I used to go to the docks to see the caravans come in. I especially loved the corsairs with their motley crews and wild symbionts."

"You don't say! My grandparents came to Na Iri from Tranquility. I grew up on Na Iri Terce Orbital Habitat Matoas. An invasive seed."

"Invasive seed?"

"That's what the locals call imperial Phene who settle in the Karnos and Hatti territories. Listen, what if we can get you to Na Iri?"

"The Chaonians control that system."

"Things are very confused right now. The Chaonians are still fighting skirmishes across Karnos System and chasing after the ships headed to Hellion. It seems they're also holding a ceremony at Karnos Prime to install new dynasts. The Hatti systems have been a crossroads for trade forever. People around here know how to smuggle."

"What happens in Na Iri?"

"My grandparentss won a concession from the Oreella Syndicate to work as long-haul security for the caravan route from Na Iri to T-Harbor. You're hired."

"That might just work." Apama puffed out a breath, allowing herself to relax for the first time in days. The shortening of T-Harbor's name proved to her satisfaction that Gurak was who he said he was. "It's a small universe. And a fortunate one. In the name of the Founders and on behalf of the Council, we are going to save this girl or die trying."

The Wily Persephone Meets Her Maker

The one-klick-wide shell of the concourse is all curves and air beneath a glittering framework of vacuum-worthy scaffolding. Beneath a transparent dome floats a real-time virtual model of Karnos System with eleven planets, seven beacons, and too many moons to easily count. The exosphere bristles with Chaonian military vessels, magnified so no one can miss they are present.

Spacers and Republican Guard stand on the gleaming deck in disciplined ranks at parade rest. On a makeshift dais a complicated ceremony overseen by Beau Qiáng highlights Sun's benevolent support of the new dynasts of Karnos. The elders look enough alike to be siblings. Sun accepts a crystal sceptre from the headdress-wearing pair as if she is their heir, a polite fiction that gives advantage to everyone involved. Ignoring Isis's disapproving look, she keeps hold of the sceptre with no apparent concern that it might be a weapon meant to blow her up.

A band breaks into a victory hymn. Streamers flutter and sparklers twinkle. On Chaonia we'd be attended by hundreds of wasps recording our every smile and sneeze, but there's no Channel Idol in Karnos System. Not yet, anyway. Hornets hover at intervals. I have no idea how news gets around in Karnos. Maybe this is going out live or maybe it will be edited for later consumption. The locals must be wondering what will become of them as people who a mere ten days ago were subjects of the Phene Empire and are now at the mercy of the upstart

Chaonians. There will be Phene military watching too: besieged ground forces seeking a clue as to whether they'll be allowed to surrender or forced to fight to the death. Phene ships in the outer reaches will keep an eye on the activities of the victorious queen-marshal while they seek a chance to sneak out of the captured system and chart a route home. Space is big, and ships are small. The Chaonian fleet can't mop up every piece of flotsam.

Sun faces the crowd. She speaks to those present and to those at home who will receive this recording in days or weeks.

"This destined triumph we offer to the memory of the glorious Eirene. In honor of her life and her victories I proclaim eight days of festivities under the banner of her beloved Idol Faire. Let all strive to win."

She turns the proceedings over to Beau and makes her way off the dais in the company of the dynasts, helping them down the ramp like any good niece, laughing and joking. The troops erupt in a cheer as Beau introduces Ji-Na, whose swirling ribbon dance and incandescent smile became famous throughout the republic when she lost Idol Faire to Alika two years ago. Rumor has it she followed the fleet because of her love for a hard-bitten soldier who chose duty over passion. Shoot me now.

Still, it's a touching story even if Beau came up with it. Who doesn't love the purity of a romance that spans war and self-denial? I could be Exhibit A.

As the band gets into the groove and Ji-Na spins colors through the air, the troops begin clapping along. There's not a single person on the concourse who has four arms. Why would there be? The Phene were occupiers of what was once an independent confederation. We're about to be occupiers, too, but we and the people of Karnos and the Hatti territories worship at the same temples, revere our ancestors, and speak mutually intelligible forms of Common Yele.

Makinde trots up all bright-eyed and bushy-tailed like an overeager first-year cadet. "Oi! Here you are. Better hustle, or you'll be late."

"Won't you be late too, in that case?" I ask.

"I can't be late because I'm on duty. The Honorable and very handsome Alika sent me since you were ignoring your pings."

"Alika sent you? What? He's our boss now?"

Makinde raises both hands. "Don't put me in the middle just because you two don't get along."

Hetty takes advantage of our conversation to extend a finger toward one of Dozer's tentacles, which is peeking over Makinde's back. The symbiont unwinds toward her, and they make contact. Hetty laughs. The symbiont flushes deep pink.

"Doze likes you," Makinde says to her with his dimpled grin. "But we need to get to the reception."

We stride almost in unison. I have to walk faster because I'm the shortest but that's what makes me so good at endurance races. You may outpace me in the beginning but eventually you'll drop back or drop out while I keep chugging along.

This habitat is the orbital administrative center of Karnos Prime and thus all of the system, so the concourse has multiple function rooms available for visiting dignitaries. On the deck Sun is taking her time moving along the ranks, greeting soldiers and spacers as she likes to do, hearing their stories. Isis and the elite Shields have fanned out across the concourse, on high alert.

We reach the entry to a formal hall just as Norioghene Hope strides out with a dark and stormy expression. She taps her ear, not noticing us, and says, "I'm on my way. Keep everything locked down until I get there. That shouldn't have happened."

Hetty and I exchange a glance but Norioghene is already gone. The inrushing flow of the crowd sweeps us into a fancy official reception. People glide through security nodes into a hall set with tables at the front for the high marshals while local notables and lesser officers make do with chairs and standing room at the back. Sun sent Jade ahead to arrange security for this part of the event, and naturally it looks as if Jade has done a stellar job. Marines are posted at intervals designed to give them immediate access to any potential disturbance.

A swell of sound rises behind us: Sun has arrived. Jade pushes forward to escort Sun to the seat of honor, a piece of gratuitous showmanship that catches Alika's attention and makes the former Idol Faire winner frown. He has his ukulele case tucked under an arm. I'm sure he'll be fine.

All the marshals rise. She waves them down. The Karnos dynasts seat themselves on either side of her. A beautiful woman dressed in pale drapery comes forward with a pitcher. She's either a professional campaspe or someone's marriageable child, as she smiles gracefully and pours a beverage into crystal glasses.

I hurry over. Surely the first lesson of being queen-marshal is not to drink or eat anything that hasn't been prepared in your trusted kitchen or tested for poison. Before I get there Sun lifts the glass to salute the dynasts as they salute her.

"To the liberation of Karnos. The Phene are no longer your masters, nor need they ever be again."

"To the liberation of Karnos," they agree. They look delighted, as the faction raised to power in the wake of the Phene defeat. Or as they would be if they were about to poison the triumphant marshal and cast Chaonia into a succession war.

Sun lifts her glass toward Crane Marshal Zàofù, who looks as alarmed as I am, then toasts toward the nearest wasp. Every Chaonian ship in-system will be watching this banquet interlude as a cutaway from the main event of Idol Faire's newly launched competition. All will wish to see their glorious new queen-marshal in the flush of her magnificent victory. She knows whose eyes are upon her.

With cup held high and in a ringing voice she proclaims, "To the liberation of Karnos. To the illustrious and the brave who achieved it."

She drains her glass. Everyone cheers and claps.

I scramble over to Alika. "Why didn't you stop her from drinking?"

"You ever tried stopping her?" For once we share a look of complete understanding. "I'm uneasy. The marines and the engineers have been doing security sweeps for days, but it's a big, crowded station. Keep your eyes open."

Attractive individuals garbed in mirror-scale gowns or beaded tunics carry trays through the back-of-the-hall crowd offering canapés and drink to the assembled Karnoite notables and lesser Chaonian officers. A clot of boisterous merchants laughs loudly at a joke I didn't hear. Administrators jostle like molecules crowded too close. I study the faces of the locals. Thinking I'd seen my father makes me search for the telltale eyes of a seer of Iros. Their sister organization, the Oculi, are said to have only one cyclops eye, but I've never met one in person to confirm it.

I do note a gold-mantled memoirist wearing a half mask—an adaptive breather—who has one organic eye and one camera eye. The sight of her artificial eye reminds me of Eirene. Murdered by my mother. I pause as a tremor of emotion washes through me that I can't even identify, or maybe I just don't want to admit I'm relieved she's gone. Did my father deliberately instigate the assassination or was Aisa truly acting out of her own self-centered motives? Maybe no one will ever know. I'm honestly surprised Sun didn't replace me, but as always, she charges along the most unexpected road. I'm so grateful to be here. I owe her.

A raspy voice speaks behind me.

"You must be Persephone. Well. Well. Well. You really are the shortest."

If lightning snapped up my spine and exploded out of my head I would not have been more scorched. I don't know that voice and yet I absolutely do because it sounds an awful lot like my own. Sucking in a breath, I spin around.

An older woman stands planted on the deck as if she is the rooted pillar around which the rest of the universe must turn. One of her eyes bears a gruesomely deep scar slashed across the orbital, with a metal-gray prosthetic patched in place of the missing eyeball.

For a sickening pause I stare as into a time-torn mirror at myself as I might look at sixty. If I were a handbreadth taller and stout with prosperous age. If my limbs were braced by flexible pressure wires used by spacers who spend too much time in micro-gravity. If my hair was streaked with silver. If my complexion was still smooth and probably from a distance youthful but up close like old porcelain fractured by the fine lines of radiation-induced aging. If I were missing an eye and sporting a scar where the eye once was.

"I wonder if it was the nutrient bath. That was a bit of an experiment. Or perhaps intrauterine growth restriction, since you were so much smaller than your brother at birth. I wasn't able to monitor Aisa's caloric intake. I'm sure she didn't eat enough to support two. She was always fussy about food as a child. Your grandfather indulged her because she could wheedle him. It was disappointing that a man so competent in other ways could not see what a narcissistic little shit she was. It must be a relief to know she's dead and can't plague you anymore. How Moira put up with her all those years I don't know."

I open my mouth and, when only a faint gasp emerges, close it again. My words have been swallowed into the unfathomable void.

"I received good reports about your quick-wittedness from Moira but now I have to wonder if she was just sweetening a soured patch so as not to make me second-guess leaving her in charge of Lee House. Given how badly she handled Ereshkigal."

My chin twitches. Blinking afflicts my right eye, the eye Nona is missing. Nothing computes. "Resh?" I say like a sad echo.

"Indeed. Ereshkigal was my biggest failure. Stubborn. Oppositional. Disloyal and dishonorable—"

I punch her.

The pressure wires detect my coming blow, and she sways sideways enough that my fist doesn't connect full on but glances off her chin. Staggering, she almost falls.

Immediately I am surrounded by marines. They chivvy me out of the banqueting hall and into an empty lounge before I have caught my breath. Probably I will never catch my breath. I'm panting as if I've just climbed forty-three flights of stairs up to the Eyrie on the sky-tower. My trembling legs can't carry me so I sink onto a bench. The instant my butt hits the seat I pitch forward, elbows braced on thighs, and rest my head on my hands.

Nona Lee is alive.

I mean, I knew. Why create an engineered hallucination to kill someone who isn't alive? But that's not the same as meeting your maker out of the blue in a noisy celebration on a foreign planet celebrating a hard-fought triumph.

Ti sails in like a resplendent ship arrayed in celebratory colors. She hands me a glass, and I set it to my lips and down it in one gulp. A burn stings down my throat and up to my eyes. As I gasp, she hands me a second glass.

"I thought you might need two."

"Fuck," I say, and down the second. The báijiǔ hits in a bracing slug. I blink back tears as I finally catch its hint of sweetness.

The marines standing in a defensive ring around me step back as Sun strides in. She halts a meter from me, careful of my personal space. Someone wearing too much lipstick has pressed a victory kiss to her cheek, leaving the stippled red outline of scrumptiously full lips.

"I hear there was a scuffle," she says.

"Did you know she would be here?" I demand.

"She's been Eirene's agent for years, working this region as our liaison with disaffected factions. How do you think Eirene was able to supply captured banner soldiers to my father's lab? Most of them came through Nona, so we have her to thank for the discovery of Zizou. Kurash, I mean."

Was it less than an hour ago that my heart broke?

"Why didn't you warn me?"

She shakes her head. "You would have known if you'd read the fifty-two-page classified report Hetty put together, as I have."

Ti murmurs, "It was on page eighteen, was it not, Your Thoroughness?"

Sun offers Ti an appreciative nod before returning her stare to me. "I am surprised, though. You strike me as someone who can roll better with the punches."

I clench my hands, feeling the press of rage in my heart. "She insulted my sister."

"Ah. I get that."

The deck vibrates. We all look around. A shudder rumbles through the superstructure. As I jump to my feet Sun turns to address Isis. Before a word leaves her mouth another jolt tunes the bulkheads like a discordant note.

A ping lights up the military network: **EXPLOSIONS ON PIER 5 AND PIER 3.**

49

Fortunately the Wily Persephone Doesn't Have Time
for This Family Tête-à-Tête

Isis shouts to be heard above the klaxon's howl. "Your Highness, don't you dare run *toward* the explosion on a habitat."

"What makes you think—" Sun's comment is cut off by cascading pings and alerts on the military channel. Every habitat lifeboat has released, like hundreds of marbles spilling outward on all vectors. Spinning so close to the habitat, they can't be shot by our ships for risk of hitting the habitat.

As abruptly as if a switch was flipped, the network link goes dead. The klaxon cuts off. Sun tilts her head, listening to voices from the hall. The hum of ventilators reassures me we aren't all about to asphyxiate. She pings her ring network, and we all ping back. Only Solomon and James don't reply. Solomon is still seconded to the *Suvannamacha* and James is off on a mystery mission.

"Your Highness," says Isis, "we are evacuating to an emergency shuttle on Pier 7."

"No, we aren't. I'm securing the *Banshee* on Pier 8."

"The royal cutter will be a target. I advise against it."

"I am going to secure the Rider."

Memory nudges me: Norioghene leaving the reception. "The Honored Norioghene put the cutter on lockdown an hour or more ago."

Sun rounds on me, eyes flaring. "What?"

I explain what I heard.

"You didn't report her comments to me at once?"

"Uh, you were drinking a toast to the victory. I would have had to interrupt right into the middle of the ceremony." I don't add: in front of everyone and all Chaonia.

She raises a hand aggressively toward my face, very like her mother. "How clear do I need to make it that this is why you are my Companion? You act as my eyes and ears, not just as a shield. Your job is to understand my needs and goals so you can anticipate what is urgent and what can be left until later and how you can act in my place if need be. Anything to do with a Rider is urgent. You should have alerted me and gone after her. Do I need to list everything out for you, Persephone?"

My burning-hot face is saved from more of this fusillade by the arrival of the other Companions racing in with stingers in hand. Candace has her battle fans out and places herself at the door. Ti commandeers marines to bring over the battle vac suits she made sure were stored in this secure lounge in case of emergency. She checks us one by one as we seal in.

"Where will you go?" I ask as Ti finishes with me.

"I'll assist Nisaba. She's overseeing an orderly evacuation of the hall."

It's hard to let Ti go but I must. She's not a combat-trained cee-cee like Candace, even if she is in many ways as much at risk as those of us who charge into battle. A mechanical alarm starts to hoot. The fail-safe workarounds have begun to come on line.

"I'm not able to make contact with the royal cutter," says Sun. "Follow me."

Isis looks as if she's seen a boulder rolling down a ramp toward where she is trapped. Who can stop Sun? João is in Chaonia, and Eirene is dead. The colonel falls in at the queen-marshal's side, ready to take any hit meant for Sun onto her own body. As we run, a grim instinct chews at my gut that we missed the starting gun and have fallen too far behind to catch up.

The central toruses of the habitat are encircled by an outer ring broken into segments called piers. A pedestrian corridor connects the concourse to Pier 8. Normally passengers and civilian workers would be using this corridor, but when Chaonia commandeered this orbital habitat it sequestered all piers for military traffic.

Sun waves us to a halt at a checkpoint set up five days ago at the end of the corridor.

"Report," she says to a bloodied lieutenant holding a drained stinger.

"It happened so fast." The young lieutenant speaks in the shocked tone of a person taken by surprise as an abrupt spasm of violent death tore through a boringly peaceful duty shift.

Wasps scout ahead, buzzing along the high curve of the ceiling toward a thick screen of smoke. Is there a fire? Stinger flashes flicker from inside the smoke. All the wasps go dark.

Makinde says, "Send another wave of wasps. I'll send in Dozer behind them. Ou'll hug the wall and be hard to spot because of ou's camoskin."

The little decapod extends a tentacle toward Sun and its tip flares red, blue, green, gray.

She raises an eyebrow before saying, "Go."

A second flight of wasps pours onto the curve of pier and races out of our direct visual sight. We watch through their cameras as they approach the smoke. Makinde clips Dozer's view through to us. As the wasps are shot down in short order, Dozer uses the topography of decorative reliefs to ooze forward into the smoke. The smoke isn't fire; it's a screen. Dozer's cameras use expanded wavelengths to trace bodies, people sprawled on the deck, rivulets of blood. A slapping sound repeats over and over again like a wet rag being swung repeatedly against a wall. Another volley of stinger bursts sweeps the open space. Two smoke-obscured figures drag a third into the airlock. With a whoosh and a hiss, the docking seal to the royal cutter closes. It locks with a red light and a triple warning blat.

Behind us, a phalanx of Republican Guards races up with stinger-proof shields to take their place alongside the Silver Shields. Out on the pier, fans kick up at last. The smoke begins to disperse.

"Advance," says Sun.

A line of Shields goes first, Sun tucked right behind them. The long curve of the pier lies quiet except for the groans of wounded and a bit of scuffling. A weak voice hails us from the checkpoint set up where the royal cutter is docked, but Sun doesn't give in to the impulse to dash toward it. Dozer flows forward. Ou's eyes are our eyes, and then our own eyes survey the docking area. We pick our way through fallen marines and Guards. Whatever injuries I saw at the battle in the industrial park, whatever rough wounds glimpsed on shipboard, are nothing to the carnage of bodies blistered by point-blank stinger blasts and gashed as by a whirl of physical blades. The checkpoint looks like a tornado hit it, portable barrier walls toppled and smashed, a clerk's desk broken against a bulkhead as if it were flung by a giant. I count ten dead marines wearing the shield of the royal cohort—elite forces, not push-overs. A body stirs, an arm feebly rising, a voice croaking with a sound no one can understand, garbled by blood in the lungs.

"Medic!" Sun kneels beside a spacer whose clouded gaze isn't for the queen-marshal but for a vac-suited enemy slumped beside the locked docking seal. It's clear they think the dead hostile isn't dead yet, but how could an individual so torn by injuries still be alive, much less keep fighting? The suit is burned, slashed open, guts gleaming moistly, the vac mask ripped, an eye missing, fluids down the face that can't disguise what we all see. A neural tracery beneath the skin whose silvery light gutters as all biological functions irreversibly cease.

"Banner soldiers." Sun rises to make way for a medic.

"Where did they come from?" I ask as my mind locks into a kind of cold shock, seeing and then setting aside the horrific sight because I can't freeze up now.

A hoarse voice from farther down the pier calls out, "Chaonia, hold your fire." A marine with hands raised limps into view out of the last swirls of smoke.

"Report," says Sun.

It's not clear the soldier has identified her as the queen-marshal. "It happened so fast. First the alarm. Then a lifepod attached to the docking ring where the *Huma* had just departed. The lifepod was broadcasting an emergency signal. Said they were running out of air. But it was an attack. The Gatoi came bursting through . . ."

He topples to his knees, pitches forward onto his face. His back is covered in blood. A medic runs forward. Guards spread out, but the battle has left Pier 8.

Sun turns to a late-arriving colonel wearing a security badge. "Did any other lifepods dock on this pier besides the one that attached where the *Huma* just departed?"

"No, Your Highness. All berths on this pier are filled as per standard procedure."

"Very well. To confirm: have all the seals on Pier 8 been coded to Chaonian military standard?"

"Yes, Your Highness."

"Link an override emergency chute to the *Banshee*'s aft emergency airlock. Hetty, return to central operations—"

Hetty's expression reflects her annoyance.

"—to do what I'd send James to do if he were here. Operations will be scrambling to restore our link to habitat comms. But I want an immediate track of all lifepods released. Was the mass release done to cover this attack or is there more going on?"

Hetty grabs a pair of marines and heads off at a run.

Sun looks Isis in the eye. "We're going in."

"Your Highness, I must object—"

"You may certainly object, but we are going in. They can't have fit more than one arrow into an eight-person lifepod. There's one dead here, so ten hostiles left. Six units, me with the vanguard, a Companion to lead each of the others. Shield-bearers at the front. The cutter has three decks and six companionways. Lock down all lifts. Kill, not capture. Our target is the secure compartment where the Rider is." She pings a schematic to us. Entering through the airlock doesn't look good: fish in a barrel for the enemy to pick off.

She adds, "Alika, you'll attack first through the emergency chute at the *Banshee*'s stern to draw their attention. They may not know I can unlock the seal from this side, so let them think you are our main attack. Once you've engaged I will enter with my unit. Razin, Makinde, after me in that order. Jade, you follow Alika's unit through the chute. Focus on clearing a path and covering my route to the secure chamber. Perse, you'll float to see which opening clears fastest and go in as rearguard to mop up."

I'd love to complain, but this isn't the time, and to be honest, she's not wrong. I may detest Jade but if I were in charge I'd make the same decision. Comms remain dark, filled with a hiss like background radiation tuned to sound waves. Maybe James could figure out what was done to comms, but that's out of my rating. What am I good for, anyway?

We get a hail from the engineers deploying the chute out of an emergency airlock fifty meters away. "We have a connection."

"Let's go."

Alika's unit vanishes into the airlock. Jade makes ready to follow. I collect my unit and drop back equidistant from the two entry points. Sun unlocks the main docking seal and advances behind a phalanx of heat shields. The battle is on. From the emergency chute only silence; from the main airlock a muted storm of constantly echoing pops and burps, almost comical if you didn't know.

The military network stutters into life. Connections flash, go dark, then restore at 23 percent. A survey of exterior cameras shows me military ships detaching from the piers as evacuation proceeds. Tenders sweep up lifepods into their massive holds. I trawl through the chatter but nothing I see or hear waves a red flag. Yet I can't help but wonder why I thought I saw my father. I request authorization to tap into all habitat cameras. I have images of my father stored in my network, and I source a couple of short clips of him walking and hitch them to a classified search engine. My request is immediately put on hold due to overload. If James were here this would go a lot faster.

Razin's unit pushes through the docking seal and out of our sight. Sun and her unit have either cleared the gangway or are all dead, but I think we'd know if she were dead. A second medical unit rushes up and starts treating casualties. A new file of Guards jogs up, led by Candace. They shove past Jade's unit and into the chute ahead of him, obviously on order of Alika.

In their wake arrives Zàofù with a head full of steam and, at his side, Nona Lee. Of course they are old friends. They fought as young ensigns in the desperate days forty years ago when Eirene's three older brothers struggled to hold the republic against constant external attacks and, one by one, died in hopeless battles.

Nona strides over to me with a grin that horribly looks just like mine when I'm about to drop a wicked joke on an unsuspecting classmate.

I'm honestly grateful when Jade waves to get my attention. A ping falls in coordination with the wave: ADVANCE, ASSHOLE. WE HAVE CLEARANCE INTO THE CUTTER.

Makinde still hasn't entered the docking seal, so the chute it is.

"Gotta run," I say to the woman who I am but am not.

"I'll come along. I have a lot of experience with banner soldiers. For one thing, never go straight up against them down a passageway, but I guess that ship already sailed. Do you think Sun is dead yet?"

This is going to be fun.

I gesture *forward* in the commanding way we were taught at the academy. My unit of sixteen races forward. Engineers flag us into the chute. Jade's unit is already in. The rigid surface of the chute sways slightly; in the academy we ran rescue and reconnaissance drills just like this. Shields push out in front of me as we pass through the emergency airlock.

Inside the *Banshee*, the 1MC howls on repeat. CONDITION RED CONDITION RED. HOSTILES ON BOARD. GAS IN VENTILATION SYSTEMS. CONDITION RED CONDITION RED.

Nona shoves past me and points at three individuals. "Split into three groups. You, descend to Deck 1. You, straight on 'til morning. You, ascend to Deck 3. Converge all lifts toward the secure chamber. Your job to is give cover, and to make sure no banner soldiers escape. Blow off their heads, it's the only thing that stops them except percussion echo." She hands out stubby batons to her designated three. "These must make skin contact to work. Go."

She grabs my arm before I can bolt after one of the groups. Her grip is the claw of blood kinship: unshakeable no matter how you try to escape.

"You're coming with me, Persephone. I want to observe how you function. It kills me to have had to release my treasured creations to others without my direct oversight."

The avaricious gleam in her eyes scares me. Fortunately we don't have time for a family tête-à-tête because she is already moving down the central passageway, running as if she isn't worried at all about hostiles who might pop out from a cross passage or closed compartment and blow off her head. She's got a target in mind: the officers' wardroom. Its hatch glares red.

She bypasses the panel's retinal and palm matrix and punches in a string of numbers on a keypad. "They've forgotten all the old analog codes," she remarks.

The panel cranks out a spritely chime that my grandmother, peace be with her, used to hum. The hatch unlocks. Nona undogs it, cracks it open, and shouts through. "Chaonian assault force coming through. Code five aught nine."

"Confirm eight seven six," replies a ragged voice from inside.

We shove through. An ensign wearing a mask dogs it behind us. Without further comment Nona strides through, headed for the galley, as fourteen heads watch her and, belatedly, turn to regard me with desperate eyes.

"Shelter in place until the all clear," I tell them as I trot after her. Two people lie on the ground without masks and they sure look dead. The others are wounded, unconscious, on oxygen, or armed. "Any word on the captain?"

"Commander's dead. Who are you? Who's in charge?"

"Queen-Marshal Sun. I mean, I'm not Sun but—"

"Oh thank goodness," murmur several of the officers. I'm not sure if they're thanking goodness that Sun is on board or thankful that my unprepossessing self isn't the glorious queen-marshal after all. Nona has already moved on. More questions pepper my back as I dodge into the galley in time to follow her down a narrow pantry. It's dim, lights low over refrigerated drawers, dry goods shelves, and racks of liquor.

"This is a dead end," I protest.

"Watch and learn, grasshopper. Though 'grasshopper' is perhaps not the right choice since they only reproduce sexually. Rotifer doesn't have the correct ring to it. Did you know in certain species of ant, the queens produce new queens through parthenogenesis? There's even a variety with separate male and female gene pools." She gropes around in the darkness behind the final wine rack. "Here it is."

"Here what is?"

"The royal cabin. This cutter used to be top of the line. As per fleet tradition, any royal compartment remains restricted access. I'd guess Sun doesn't know about it since Eirene took *Banshee* off her frontline fleet. Ah. Got it."

With a click and a clunk the rack swings inward, a secret door into an empty shell of a space between bulkheads barely lit by a single dim red LCD. Noises reverberate strangely, a metallic hail, a smothered pounding, a whoosh. There's only residual air, but we're in vac suits so atmosphere is immaterial. Nona plucks a bottle of brandy from an otherwise empty shelf.

"By the hells, has this been sitting here all this time?"

Still carrying the bottle, she opens a door into a narrow galley. We hurry down its length and enter a sumptuously decorated dining room that stretches into an attached lounge whose sofas are secured with slip-covers and on into a bedroom with mirrors on the ceiling. Definitely not my kink. All this time she chats like any elder reminiscing about the old days, an unstoppable and soporific force.

"I was assigned as an ensign to this cutter. That was during the Pselkis Campaign. Forty-five years ago, whew. My main duty was to smuggle in his lovers, of which there were many and most of them enlisted. To visit the queen-marshal. Jīnzhā, if you're confused. I also couriered whiskey and brandy. And a rotgut he liked that was brewed in a vat in the Elm Shipyards. There was a catalytic compound absorbed into it he was addicted to. He wasn't a personally pleasant man, I'll tell you that, but he was physically courageous and he would have done well as queen-marshal if he hadn't been knifed through the eye into the brain by a banner soldier during a boarding action. So I know of what I speak about passageway battles and Gatoi."

A constant rhythmic hailstorm serenades us, getting steadily louder. We're closing with the firefight, not that Nona has broken a sweat like I have.

"Get ready. The next door opens directly into the secure compartment. There should still be a guard's counter three feet out from the bulkhead where the door opens. This door does not show up on the other side unless it opens, which Sun must not know about. Funny how age gives you an advantage. Here we go." She punches the panel with a closed fist.

Training kicks in. As the door slides open I automatically bunch up low and burst through. Immediately I slam into the back of a banner soldier who is using the security desk as cover. I'm not sure who is more surprised, but the Gatoi brings a weapon to bear first. Nona clubs the Gatoi over the head with the bottle, which shatters. Brandy spills down their faceplate and obscures their vision for just long enough. As I fling myself sideways, their shot misses because of that split-second blindness. Nice.

I roll out of the way of a vicious hammer of an arm meant to smash my head against the counter. My torso hits the Gatoi's knees hard enough to set them briefly off-balance. Nona shoulders them sideways, out past the cover of the security desk. They're faster even than me and catch themselves and pull back in.

But it's enough time for shots from the door to slam them against the bulkhead, hit at least four times. Not that four hits by armor-piercing slugs is enough to put down a Gatoi. They shoot back toward the hatch, joining the cacophony of yelling and shooting, a hailstorm around me like I'm caught in a lethal pinball machine. Without looking my way the soldier swings their stinger around to point right at me. Nona kicks their arm. The blow isn't hard enough to do damage but it swings their head around so they see her face.

A telltale flash and stiffening. An engineered hallucination triggers a reaction. Just like Zizou.

If I do nothing, he'll kill her and I'll be rid of her in truth, the walking talking proof of what I really am.

I grab his leg but I'm not strong enough to hold back a banner soldier in full flood. He lunges to fix his hands at her throat and slam her against the bulkhead. I head-butt him, and although his hands don't shift his gaze flickers to me.

The neural flash happens a second time, giving me a split-second delay, which if I were better at hand-to-hand combat would be enough, but I'm not. I'm flung onto the deck with a hand pressing through the fabric of the vac suit to compress my jugular vein. With the other he's still choking Nona. Even shot multiple times he can kill both of us at once. My vision starts going black as the tunnel of death races to greet me.

A point-blank shot into his head sends bits of vac suit and fragments of skull and brain splattering into my faceplate. The pressure of the Gatoi's grip releases. Recoiling, I tip backward onto my ass, like I did during our first-year virgin firefight exercise at CeDCA, thus winning me the nickname of "Perse" forever.

Sure enough, just like the first time, there stands Jade Kim all torn up with a shoulder wound and blood splattered down on their leg, looking heroic as fuck with arm outstretched and perfect profile, having saved my backside right before I got tagged with a kill-shot. Only this is real.

"You're welcome, asshole," says Jade, and more insults are surely incoming, except just then there is an explosion, heat, shouts, followed by a horrific harsh stench like grilled meat seasoned with copper and charcoal and sulfur and chemicals.

My vac suit has ripped, and I gag on the stink and choke down bile as I stagger to my feet. My body throbs, but no time for hurt. Beyond the security desk lie bodies, blood, splatter, scorchmarks, a very dead Norioghene Hope with a half-severed arm and her head wedged against a control panel. In the secure chamber the last surviving banner soldier has used the neural circuits of their own body to overload and thus fry the lifepod's controls, which now wink red. The Rider's body lies burned amid a haze of ash and smoke.

Sun stands over the banner soldier who, horribly, remains alive, struggling to get up and keep fighting but whose legs no longer work.

The helmet of their vac suit has cracked and fallen open to reveal a person whose scarred face suggests they are a veteran of many hard-fought battles.

There are only three banner soldiers in the compartment, two with brains blown out. What the passageways back through the ship look like I can't yet imagine, but I'm guessing the casualties are bad. It's impossible to take in this kind of violent death, but isn't that what we're bred and trained for? Take it in and keep going. Sun's expression as she examines the twitching hostile is unfathomable to me. Fury that they stole the Rider from her? Respect for their courage? Regret and indignation for soldiers compelled to fight for unworthy masters?

From down the passageways shouts rise: "Medic incoming! Medic! Medic!"

Sun moves at last, drawing a baton from her belt. She presses the rod against a line of exposed skin and triggers the de-leashing program. The soldier's hand relaxes.

Sun says, "Where the heavens above did not exist, and the earth beneath had not come into being, there dwelled the cosmic waters which are the substance of all. Out of this ocean rose Lady Chaos, who gave birth to the eleven exiles."

No one speaks in the compartment. Even the groaning wounded have fallen silent, or perhaps they have died.

The soldier's whisper stirs the cold air, harsh with oncoming death. "Thus Lady Chaos said to her twelfth child, the last born, the Royal: protect my offspring, and in exchange they will serve you when you call."

Sun nods. "I call you now, according to the ancient covenant. I am born beneath the banner of Royal, child of João, child of Nanshe, child of Ashur to the tenth generation. By the binding of the crown of light I assert my right to demand your service until I release you."

One of the soldier's hands flutters. Sun takes it between her own and bends closer even as we all wince, awaiting some counterattack, an insidious dagger to the throat. But the hoarse voice keeps on, as faint and failing as the fading of smoke. "I am born beneath the banner of Blood Tide. I am bound by . . . the ancient covenant and by the . . . crown of light."

Sun rests a hand on the shaved head of the dying Gatoi. "You know my name. What do I call you?"

The reply is so soft I only hear because of enhancements built into my body. "My battle name is Yuzuru."

"It is an honorable name among the people. Flawlessly executed."

A last breath. The last spark. The letting go of death. To where does a soul rise? Who greets it in that far place?

"You are free," Sun says.

She steps back from the smoking lifepod and drops to a knee. At first I think it is a show of respect and then I realize she is wounded. I lunge forward and catch her by the elbow. Blood is smeared down the front of her vac suit. She leans against me in a show of weakness I never imagined, but the fierce mind churns ever onward.

"The Riders would have known the instant they saw me and Norioghene together. Then getting her to lead them to the right ship with a false message."

"Wait," I say. "Wouldn't that mean . . . there's another Rider still in-system?"

"There has to be, for it to have happened so fast. I'm going to need James . . . no, dammit, Hetty . . ." Her eyes start to roll up before she jerks herself back to consciousness.

Nona paces a circuit around the torched lifepod. "Not sure what I can manage with these remains but I'll try."

"I haven't given permission for illegal experiments." Blood beads on Sun's lips.

My back and shoulders have started to flare with red-hot pain but I don't budge.

A medic appears beside us. "Your Highness, I need to lower you onto the deck."

"Hetty, track the time stamps to see what the farthest distance an in-system Rider could be from Karnos Prime based on the time that passed between when I spoke to the Rider and this attack occurred. Coordinate a search. Any anomalies."

"I thought I saw my father but I'm sure I was mistaken," I confess in an excess of deathbed honesty, because I'm suddenly sure Sun is about to die. My chest squeezes, vised by dread.

"Of course the seers are involved. All Phene military ships still in-system must be captured and searched. Bring in the Third Fleet from Troia. Access all shipyards . . . refurbish ships that can be made ready in under a month. Two months. Get Soaring here. Metis, too, in case Father gets any more bad ideas. And Ti's brother. Go yourself to fetch them, you and Ti."

"Yes," I say, surprised and gratified to be given such an important mission.

"Keep Soaring safe. Keep them all safe. I know how to play this now."

"Out of my way!" Isis's voice pierces the background chop of fans, alarms, and comms all blaring. "Clear a path for the medical team. Move! *Move!*"

"War council may need delay," Sun remarks before her eyes roll up and she collapses onto me. With a surge of terrified energy, I hold her up.

At that very moment my search ping returns. POSITIVE MATCH ON PIER 3, ONE HUNDRED AND SEVENTY-THREE MINUTES AGO. NO CURRENT SIGHTINGS AVAILABLE. SUBJECT NO LONGER ON HABITAT.

50

A Dead-End Bit of Musing

The storefront of the company Responsible Freight Solutions had the stripped-down look of a family business run on a fraying thread. Apama knew the type well. As a child she had run errands for such places in exchange for ration chits.

Despite the company claiming eight long-haul merchant freighters available for hire as a measure of its success, its office didn't even have its own lavatory but rather shared facilities with other establishments stuck in a dead-end lane with businesses like Lucky Pawnbroker and Best Price Traps & Drains.

Past the door of Freight Solutions, a tiny waiting room with a hard bench was overseen by a thuggish-looking clerk at a battered desk. The office itself, where they met with the owner, boasted two consoles with the look of a backwater grandparent's tech, a big wallboard with writing in a script Apama could not read, and a folding table with two folding chairs. One of the consoles displayed a routine administrative screen that displayed the real-time position of Orbital Habitat Matoas circling Na Iri Terce, the splendid glowing coil of the Kaska Beacon vanishing at intervals behind the planet.

The other console was playing a program mandated for universal viewing by the conquerors. Although the sound was turned low, a murmur of music escaped to accompany a woman spinning a dance out of colored ribbons. The performance was skilled but what Apama couldn't understand was how the dancer maintained that unforced smile without it ever faltering. Maybe she really loved what she did.

"All this charming chitchat aside, what's the catch, Effie?" A two-armed and light-complexioned Hatti man with a white beard and bushy white eyebrows sat facing Gurak Se Xar and the specialist's wiry, witty old aunt.

"Haven't I always said you're the catch, Hector?" Aunt Effie toasted him with the cup of coffee he'd offered when they'd come in.

A flash of mischief in his expression gave Apama a glimpse of a roguish younger self. "We did get into some trouble back in the day."

Aunt Effie chuckled. "We surely did."

"But we're both respectable businesspeople now. I know your rates. These are too low for a two-year job running security all the way to T-Harbor and back. What's the catch?" His gaze shifted to take in Apama and the hoodie-wearing Teegee where they stood on either side of Gurak. "I didn't know you had two nieces."

"I only have one niece. That sweet girl." Aunt Effie flicked the fingers of her lower right toward Teegee in a gesture that conveyed the intimacy of family. "But you're right, there is a catch. We're being paid to smuggle out a lancer pilot."

"Whew." His whistle brought a thump at the door.

The young thug stuck in their head. "Dede? Everything okay?"

"It's fine, Renn. Don't let anyone in."

Renn gave Apama a glare, which she answered with a dead-on stare of her own until the thug accepted defeat and withdrew.

Effie said, "It's not a lower rate. It's the danger rate."

Hector stroked his beard. "The Phene government is paying you to smuggle out a single lancer pilot? Isn't there prize money from the Chaonians for turning in high-value military and administrative assets?"

"No respectable imperial Phene will take Chaonian prize money," said Effie.

His eyes quirked like restless caterpillars. "And yet, with our two stubby arms, we Hatti-folk were never imperial Phene, just provincials. Are you asking me to say yes and then turn her in to give you cover so you don't get blamed?"

Apama stiffened. Gurak tapped her upper with the back of a hand. Teegee had not uttered a sound since they'd entered the office. The girl was rigid with nerves, sure the ploy would not protect her. Guilt was written all over her in a way Apama prayed would be taken for adolescence.

Effie had a grin like a floodlight, blotting out the shadows made by Teegee's nerves. "You forget how well I know you, Hector. I know you disguise the other half of your business behind this rundown office. I know you love sticking it to the Office of Declarations and Tariffs who tax every kilo of cargo whether living or dead. Tell me you'll see this smuggling job through, and I know you'll keep your word."

"But why?" he asked. "What's special about this lancer pilot?"

"She's the only survivor of the command ship's lancer squadron.

That means something to us who honor the Exchange. It's a matter of pride and honor."

Would he bite? He gave Apama a once-over, measuring the likelihood she was a lancer pilot while not giving Teegee a second look. In family businesses, teens learned the ropes early. They went out in an unofficial capacity, just as this girl had done in accompanying Baragesi. Her presence was nothing unusual, her hoodie standard teen gear, and she had the correct blend of general features to be plausibly related to Effie. Apama did not. Apama also knew how to deploy the cocky posture of a lancer pilot to keep Hector's eyes off Teegee.

"All right. But only because I owe you one."

"You do owe me one. With this, we're quit."

"I hope not quit, my dear. Never that. But we can start with a new slate."

Effie extended her lower arms. "We are in your hands, my friend."

He grasped her fingers. "Bend up every spirit to a full height. I'll do it just for the challenge."

"I knew you would. And your coffee is as bad as ever."

He chortled as she drained the last of it. "I have a contract to deliver a shipment of Flare to the Skew-Neck Skuda at Flood Terminus. I was waiting for the current situation to settle down before I smuggle illegal drugs through Chaonian military lines. But at some point I'm going to have to test to see if the Chaonians are as short-sighted as the empire was in these matters. I'll send *Overly Devoted* on the next caravan, which is scheduled to leave within an eight-to-twelve-day window and still has open slots, so good timing for you. Leave these three with me and send the rest of your security team over by oh five hundred."

"Done."

Apama took a step forward. "I'd rather return with you, Auntie, and come back with the team."

"You don't know Hatti, do you, lass?" said Hector. "Or you'd not object."

"My apologies," said Apama.

Aunt Effie said, "Nothing is as important to Hatti-folk as an honor debt."

Apama nodded cautiously. "Like a lancer's honor."

"I wouldn't know about that," said Effie. "My point is that Hector owes me an honor debt that this exchange will clear."

She tipped a nod to the old man and went out.

Hector turned up the sound on the festival program. What was it called again? Idol Faire! A band was playing a song she recognized.

"Turbulence," by the handsome aristocrat. Hearing its melody reminded her of the Chaonian marine she'd dueled with on the *Virtuous Heart*. He'd been astute and effective. Had he pulled his shots and missed her on purpose? There was a dead-end bit of musing if there ever was one.

The song ended and the program returned to a roundtable discussion in progress, a convoluted argument about rhyming structures in poetry between several individuals labeled "grammarians." Uncle Hector opened a hidden door and ushered them down a steep ladder into a storeroom.

From there they pulled on stevedore overalls bearing the mark of a local habitat dock-loading consortium, and in this garb accompanied a pallet of goods to a pier. It was a basic sleight of hand. The overalls gave them cover as they walked in plain sight. Renn supervised the pallet, wearing a Responsible Freight Solutions badge. Once the pallet passed a cursory declarations inspection but before it went through Chaonian military security, people out of Apama's sight instigated a loud argument. Renn hustled Apama, Teegee, and Gurak into the tight confines of a container. Apama did not like being helpless but she reasoned that Aunt Effie was putting her nephew at risk too. Anyway, she'd run out of options. As much as it galled, she had to trust Teegee's life to the hands and loyalty of others.

51

The Epitaph of an Uninspired Life

You do not have the right to enter here. Leave now. Get back before I throw you out.

A twisted dream of Hetty's voice turned on her in anger and rejection, pushing her into a crawl space as black as a starless void. Body pinned down, crushed beneath a thousand kilos of sand. Mouth filled with rocks. Seen from within the tomb of silence, the water's surface glittered far above, rippling with the promise of air and light. The diver had no breath left as she fought to rise only to slam into a barrier inscribed with the epitaph of an uninspired life.

Sun, daughter of Eirene. She finished her mother's work competently enough but accomplished nothing of her own. Here she rests among the others whose deeds will be lost in the churning of the Gyre that is time and memory passing in the Archives of the forgotten, the broken shards of the Celestial Empire. These they are, who become merely stairsteps upon which greater souls ascend toward the mountaintop.

No.

Never.

Erupting out of the deep like a spiny charybdis she thrashed her way upward. Her eyes flickered. Opened to a smear of yellow light and a mellow repetitive beep that settled into sync with her pounding heart.

She was awake.

Memory rushed in like waves filling a parched basin. The Rider was dead, stolen from her in a lightning suicide raid. She had won the battle of Karnos, but what did that matter when those who had planned and succeeded in killing the Rider were still at large?

We have to go after them, she said, but no sound emerged from her lips.

A hand touched her shoulder.

"She's awake." Isis.

She had a memory of an object blocking her mouth. A breathing tube! She couldn't speak! No, there was nothing in her mouth, not anymore. She just couldn't form words with her voice. A lethargy of drugs and muddy pain hummed in her bones and dragged on her aching flesh, but her mind was cutting upward out of the drowning waters. She spilled her awareness down through her body. Was it all there? Feet. Legs. Hips. Torso. Hands. Her left arm was pinned. Secured, that was it. She raised her right hand, flexed it open and shut as people around her voiced astonishment.

She signed, wanting them to take the breathing tube out: Mouth. Mouth.

The palace physician in a red cap bent over her. "Your Highness, please be patient—"

The man was summarily moved aside and Isis's stern face swung into view. "Your Highness. Your breathing tube was removed three days ago. The physicians are finishing a round of tests. You've been heavily sedated and sustained multiple serious injuries, so it's going to take some time. You must accept this process, however frustrating it will be."

Sun gave an affirmative sign although it killed her to acquiesce.

Medical personnel moved around the space. Most of Sun's body was hidden beneath a sheet. By the measure of the beeps, her heartbeat had steadied. In the background a voice spoke in medical jargon that she was too muzzy to separate into understandable words.

Hetty materialized at her bedside, pale with exhaustion. This specific frown was known to Sun. It meant Hetty was determined not to shed tears. When she spoke, her words emerged as slowly as if Sun were a fragile invalid who needed to be coddled.

"You were quite badly hurt. Your network's down. You had three surgeries. You're stable now. Ten days have passed. All's well. But you must give them time to work and let them do their job."

She moved back to accommodate a second flurry of medical people swirling around the bed that confined Sun. It wasn't a tomb. She was alive. She would recover because not to recover was unthinkable.

Makinde spoke in the distance. "I told you it would be okay! She'll recover."

"Go tell Alika." That voice was Persephone's. "He'll want to know, and he'd rather hear the news from you than from me."

"Can you blame him? Who doesn't love to see my adorable chubby face?"

"Me, when I am kicking your butt on the next training run and never having to see you at all, until I lap you on the track after klick ten."

"Don't hurt me, gnat." His laugh chased away as he moved out of earshot.

Why were they happy?

No, they were relieved.

The physician reappeared. A look of ecstatic delight lit their face. "Signs look excellent, Your Highness. I hear you're concerned about the intubation. That's done now. The tube is out. You've been breathing on your own for three days but we continue to test your blood gases and it's all fine. There's a minor infection in your throat from the tube but it's responding well to antibiotics. Please be patient."

From the side, Isis remarked, "Think of it as another test and trial at the academy."

Sun knew how to excel at tests and trials. You had to focus on each one and not get distracted. She faded out for a while, then roused again. This time the room came into better focus. The sheet was pulled back. Her chest was encased in a ceramic shell. Her right leg and left arm immobilized. The wall opposite had windows onto another intensive care room, where Alika sat in a wheelchair with a clear medical mask covering half his face. He was looking her way, anxious expression clearing as Makinde spoke to him. Then the medical crowd converged around her bed, cutting off the view. They asked her to cough, measured oxygen flow and potassium levels, tested the sensitivity of her limbs.

Not one told her she was fortunate to be alive. These physicians had served Eirene before her. The eldest had served Eirene's brothers. The gods bestowed fortune or took it away, but that didn't mean people stood helpless before fate.

She would not succumb to the tomb of silence, to the damning epitaph carved onto a mausoleum wall. A monument however mighty was nothing but cold stone. Archives got broken and lost in the gyre of eternity. She had higher aspirations.

At length they sprayed her throat and moved away.

This time she was able to form words. Her voice sounded raspy and raw.

"When can I get up? How soon can I eat? Did you capture Kiran Seth or the missing Rider? What news of Phene movements? What are the reports from Chaonia? The disposition of our fleets? Is Soaring here yet, Perse? I need the *Keoe*."

Isis said calmly, "Your Highness, I'll call in High Secretary Nisaba. She can read you the most recent briefings."

A commotion stirred by the door. Beau shouldered past Persephone only to be halted by Hetty placing her body between him and the bed.

"Let him approach," said Sun. Pieces of her mind still floated dreamily but she was capturing each of those drowsy scraps and murdering them, letting her thoughts expand. Enough of this convalescence.

The historian strode up to the bedside. Sun raised her right hand to indicate he should speak. A gesture was all he needed.

"Your Highness, reports have reached the Fleet and the Guards that your situation is grave."

"Stable," said Isis.

The historian gave her a look. "'Stable' is a mealy-mouthed word meant to deflect bad news. With Idol Faire suspended before it got a chance to start, rumor has taken hold that the queen-marshal is dying. As the official Idol Historian I strongly recommend you allow me to arrange a public visitation. In fact, I have eight hand-picked veterans who fought in the recent battle waiting anxiously in the reception area. They should be rewarded for their courageous actions by being allowed to attend at your bedside. Their testimony afterward, and the visual evidence filmed by wasps, will give proof to Chaonia that you live and are recovering."

Sun ignored the inevitable protestations. "Let them in."

Isis muttered an objection off to the side but Beau had already hustled out.

Sun shifted. "Help me sit."

A familiar medic appeared at her side. "I can raise the bed a limited amount, Your Highness."

"Ensign Minh, what are you doing here?"

"You asked for me specifically."

"Did I?"

"That's why I was added to the team. It's Lieutenant now, Your Highness."

"That's right."

The bed buzzed as it raised. The height wasn't as much as she wanted but Minh's smile had the steel edge of medical personnel who will not be bullied by a patient, not even by her.

"One at a time," said Beau from the door. "No loud voices. Be brief."

First came a burly Republican Guard with a shaved head half covered with wound-seal, one arm in a sling and the other ending in a stump below the elbow. His face was radiant with excitement.

"Your Highness. We thought you were dead."

"Takes more than an arrow of banner soldiers to kill me. Tell me your name, and how you came by those injuries."

He was a citizen soldier from Thesprotis who had taken part in the ground battle on Karnos. After him a pair of older marines knelt with hands pressed to their hearts, but she made them stand and address her because were they not fellow soldiers? They'd both fought in their youth at the Battle of the Esplanade, and at the battle of Karnos had been involved in boarding a Phene cruiser under heavy fire. A damage-control spacer from the *Suvannamacha* who singlehandedly shut down a burn before it hit a vital wiring artery. A comms tech had survived the hulking of the frigate she served on. A Guardsman seated in a wheelchair with both legs in casts who had fought in Ná Bō's division and witnessed Jade Kim take command after the death of the marshal and most of her officers at the planet's famous Citadel.

"Your Highness, I don't mind saying the honorable won our trust by their swift actions. That one has good instincts. We veterans can't say that about every young officer."

"You too have served the republic well with your swift action and courageous strength, Sergeant."

Each time she attempted to lift her left hand to give them a sign, and each time she was surprised all over again to find she could not.

The eighth was a young officer. "Lieutenant Amity Jīn, Your Highness."

Memory spat out a link. "You are the highest-ranking officer to survive the destruction of the *Vermilion*."

"I am, Your Highness." She looked ashamed.

"You will be granted a promotion to the rank of senior lieutenant and command of a corvette."

"Your Highness!"

The officer was eased away as Beau moved up beside the bed and began to speak about the Chaonia capacity to endure hardship and fight with a toughness no foe could match.

The words blurred together. The bright clamor of her thoughts was being dimmed by a wave of fatigue. Thus did ambition give way to decline. This would not be her road. Lieutenant Minh cut into view and ruthlessly guided the still-speaking Beau out of the way. Isis loomed over her with a glower.

"What is making me so tired and my mind so slow?"

"Your grave injuries, Your Highness. And the painkillers."

"Less of the painkillers."

"But Your Highness—"

"Was I unclear?"

"No, Your Highness."

"Where's my comms tiara? When do I get my network back? What of Phene warships? Prisoners?"

"You must rest, Your Highness," said the nearest physician. "Two of your Companions are on duty at all times. You are well protected."

"Isis? My questions?"

"We have secured twenty-eight Phene military vessels and eleven support ships, including one heavy cruiser. I do not have an updated total of prisoners. Oh! My thanks, Honored Hestia. Two thousand, six hundred, and forty-one as of yesterday."

"Only twenty-eight ships? Didn't I get intel that at least one hundred and twelve ships dropped into Hellion Terminus? Didn't I order pursuit?"

"The Phene mined the arrival zone just as they did at Windworn and Sleepless. We have ships caught in Hellion System but no word on what happened to them."

"Can the mines be cleared? Hellion is a dead end, so the Phene can't get reinforcements or resupply."

A new presence moved into the room. People murmured and stepped aside as if to avoid being run over. Even fierce Minh backed away. How odd.

A harsh voice broke in without asking for permission to speak. "Of course they can get reinforcements and resupply. Hellion Terminus is one end of a knnu route to Trinity Coalition."

"Go on," Sun said, thinking it odd how quickly Persephone had gotten old. No, that wasn't Persephone. Through hazy vision she recognized Nona Lee wearing a Chaonian uniform tailored in the fashion of forty years ago. Maybe it was her original uniform.

Nona had learned the habit of independence. It showed in the way she ignored everyone else. "I've heard that the enemy admiral who took command of the situation in Hellion is the capable Yele commander, Manu. He doesn't need those mines to work forever. He just needs time to negotiate with the Argosy mothership that is sitting in Hellion System right now."

"Then they can escape." The thought stung through her like tidings from an ill wind. Yet a connection nagged at her thoughts. "That's how you must have traveled back and forth between Hellion and the Trinity Coalition, because Trinity is where you've lived in exile, isn't it?"

"A canny question for a person as doped up and badly wounded as you are. The Ousoos Argosy runs a regular trade schedule between Hellion and Tsurru System. I have a long-standing agreement with the Trinity as part of my smuggling and spy operation."

"We have to go to Trinity. Kiran Seth . . . the missing Rider . . . escaped."

"Your Highness, you must rest or you will not recover," said the senior physician.

The necessity was galling but the flesh made its demands.

"Trinity is out of Chaonia's reach," said a voice in the distance, receding fast.

Sun wasn't done speaking, not with such a gauntlet thrown down.

"Nothing is out of our reach. We will keep climbing."

He Had Never Thought to Ask What Would Become of Them All in the End

Kurash decided the least worst choice for meal times was to sit at a corner table in the *Huma*'s mess hall. Most importantly, he could trust his back to the bulkheads. Also, people were likely to get waylaid by acquaintances and friends before they made it all the way to the corner to stare at him, the living breathing disgraced banner soldier with gleaming neural enhancers woven through his flesh. He could cover his arms and legs, even wear gloves if it came to that, but they could see who he was in his face.

It wasn't that he wanted to be alone. He'd grown up accustomed to community during the activities where humans are often naturally social: eating and drinking, education and crafts, games and exercise, theater and dance, prayer and singing.

War.

As Lady Chaos taught: What is war if not a shared occupation that requires cooperation to succeed?

The first days on the *Huma* constituted a slow transit from Karnos Prime to the Na Iri Beacon followed by the drop and a slower transit to Na Iri Terce and its Kaska Beacon. During this time the crew respected his space. Maybe it was better to say they had been glued to reports about the queen-marshal's condition. Clips of the recovering Royal speaking to Guards and spacers played on loop, accompanied by a tiresome but authoritative commentary. Of course the crew had a great deal of work, and he was a passenger with no mandated duties. He had once been a weapon. Now he was something he had no name for because the banners had no name for what he had become.

No, that was self-pity talking. He was Queen-Marshal Sun's personal messenger. The ring gave him purpose.

He sipped at a broth swimming with noodles, herbs, and starchy kernels of maize in a glorious concoction of flavors and textures. It reminded him of home, where grandparents' cooking wove together the days of childhood.

Was he meant to ride out the voyage in solitude? He'd seen people hanging about the gym to watch as he cycled through his training routines. His arrow would have joined in; the exercises were meant to be done in a group. But his arrow were all dead, as far as he knew.

"Ah! I've been looking for you."

Marshal the Honorable Precious Jīn seated herself at his table. She had a glass of dark beer but no food.

"As Sun's representative, you are allowed to take your meals in the officers' mess," she added.

"This is not the only mess hall?" he asked.

She chuckled. "This is the enlisted mess hall. There is also a chiefs' mess and an officers' mess and a captain's mess. How long have you been with the fleet that you haven't sorted that out yet?"

Her amusement reminded him of the first rotation of Phene military he had trained under, when he had been fresh off the boat as a brand-new banner soldier in the empire's employ. They'd laughed at the ignorance of the young soldiers in their care. At first he'd thought their laughter was meant kindly. Later he'd wondered if it was scornful. He'd never figured it out.

"I have never served on a Chaonian warship."

She leaned toward him with an inviting smile. "An ambitious young soldier like you with no lineage or academy connections and no experience in the fleet would do well to secure yourself a sponsor. A knowledgeable and well-connected individual who can teach you what you need to know and introduce you around."

By the slight dilation of her eyes and an elevation in her pulse, "teaching him what he needed to know" had taken some predictable turns in her mind. She had an avaricious look, and she was his superior in the Chaonian military order as well as the lead envoy of this mission and thus his commander as well as being his elder, and thus deserving of his respect. What was expected of him? What was required? This wasn't the kind of thing a superior officer would say to a recruit in the banners.

She smiled warmly. Perhaps she read his silence as assent.

"It's the duty of those of us who have the status and skills to smooth the path for the future leaders of the next generation. We've all been where you are now."

He was sure she had never been where he was now.

"Eirene spent two years in the Yele League, essentially as a hostage for her brother's good behavior. She was allowed to attend their most prestigious military academy. Besides that, a famous admiral took an interest in her and took her under her wing, as they say. Eirene couldn't have been much younger than you must be."

The pause offered him a chance to mention his age.

Movement caught his eye. Relief flooded his limbic system with such a surge of adrenaline he had to release a trickle of calming drugs to avoid a flare. The young lieutenant who was Persephone's friend was cutting toward him across the mess hall like a javelin thrown.

"Marshal! I beg your pardon. With respect, I've been tasked to collect the ensign."

"You have?"

"Captain's orders, Marshal."

The lieutenant didn't ask permission, and Kurash didn't wait to get it. On board a ship, captain's orders took precedence over the table conversation of a high-ranking individual who wasn't commanding anything. He spoke the polite words he'd learned were appropriate for taking your leave. People throughout the mess hall watched him return the tray and make his way with the lieutenant to the exit. When the door shut behind them he finally exhaled.

The lieutenant gave him a friendly grin. "Ugh, that must have sucked. I'm Ay, by the way. I don't know if you remember my name."

"I am Kurash."

"We all know who you are, because you have the disadvantage of being the most notorious person on this ship. Persephone said to keep an eye on you. So did the Honorable Hestia. I arrived just in time."

"You did?"

"They have some weird mentoring customs up there at the top of the heap, if you don't mind my saying so."

"Why would I mind?" he asked as they headed forward along a passageway.

She shot him a glance. "Let me just clarify before we go any farther down this road. Marshal the Honorable Precious Jīn is casting bait at you."

"I don't know what that means."

She rubbed a hand over her eyes like a speck of dust had gotten in them. "Whew. The Honorable Hestia wasn't kidding. Okay. If you were from around here you'd have known what was on offer when the marshal sat down to chat you up. Like I said, it's an old custom in which an older honorable takes a young ensign under their wing for seasoning."

"You mean sex."

"Yes, often it's sex, but it's not just sex. It's giving them a hand up by introducing them to all the right people, giving a chance to crew on the best ships, and get experience and training the average honorable will never see."

"Did this happen to you?"

"Me?" She laughed.

A passing spacer glanced their way, gaze flickering as it settled on Kurash, the one who was out of place.

"I'm a citizen soldier so, no, nothing like that happens down in our neck of the woods. That's some warped kind of honorable shit, if you ask me. I mean, I don't care what people get up to as long as they are adults and it's all consensual."

"Are the young ensigns you refer to allowed to say no?"

"That's the question, isn't it? We can debate consent until the titanosauruses come home. I'm sure some consider it a great opportunity. Or even something they've dreamed about. People say Eirene was forged by her two years in Yele. Power dynamics are always complicated. For example, what if you don't really want to but you know it's your best path forward to the big command you hope for? Or what if you think you have to go along because your House won't support you if you don't?"

A vivid memory flashed of the dark water rippling around the Honored Manea's arms up to her elbows. His heart clenched so tightly he stutter-stepped and had to consciously steady his pace. Ay glanced his way, waited in case he had something to say, but his tongue was dry and his throat was hollowed out.

She went on. "I don't blame Perse one bit for getting her ass out of that Core House hothouse the instant she had a chance. I will say this. If the marshal is targeting you because you don't have the background to know where you stand, then that's wrong. If you want to take the path she's offering, we can go back to the mess hall."

"No!"

She laughed in a friendly way, and let the laugh ride as her reply.

Because she was a friend of dauntless Persephone, he decided to take the risk of being open. "As you can see, I don't know what's expected."

"I'm here to be your friend, if you want one." Her look was knowing, reading the heat that rose in his cheeks in response to her words. "I don't do sex, Kurash. I mean your friend like a friend."

"Like a fellow soldier in an arrow? Comrades in arms?"

"That works, if it works for you."

"It works for me."

She punched him on the arm, and he tensed even before her fist connected, and at the contact—the blow was not at all hard—he had to step back and spurt out a dose of calming meds to prevent himself lunging at her. His neural patterns flared on his face.

She flashed a hand up to her eyes. "Whoa. What was that?"

"I am made to be a weapon. My apologies."

"You've nothing to apologize for. I guess you couldn't read that punch as a gesture between friends?"

"Among the banners we request permission before we touch another person with nonlethal intent."

She whistled, the tone cut with a tendril of nervousness. "Got it. No arm punching. No forearm bumps. No stealing food off your plate."

"You aren't fast enough to steal food off my plate."

She laughed as if he'd made a joke but he was just stating the truth.

To cover his discomfort he asked, "What is a forearm bump?"

"I'll explain later. I actually do have a mission I'm hoping you'll accompany me on. The captain has charged me with tracking down and purchasing a stock of barako. It's a drink the Phene like that he got a taste for while on patrol out here. We're in a holding pattern waiting for clearance to drop through the Kaska Beacon. There's enough time for me to make a run to the local habitat. You interested?"

He was.

The corvette had two hangars. The smaller was home to a pair of utility shuttles. Ay seemed to be on amiable terms with everyone she met, all of whom she knew as part of her shipboard duty. She introduced him to the hangar deck crew, the pilots, and a squad of marines who would accompany the flight. Her easygoing manner sanded away some of the suspicion with which the crew regarded him. Not that they became warm or familiar, but as if he were a person they might reach détente with. It helped that he wore a fleet uniform like theirs, although his bore palace rather than rank insignia. The clothes marked him as one of them even if his neural enhancers set him apart as one of the enemy he had once been.

"What's that baton?" a marine asked as they strapped in to shuttle seats.

"Part of the uniform."

As senior envoy on this mission, Precious Jīn had eleven batons in her keeping. He had the one Sun had personally given to him. For that reason he kept the baton on him at all times. It was a reminder of how the Phene had abused and controlled the banner soldiers under their command. A reminder of how the leash had been removed from him via the program embedded into this baton, while a yet deeper level of his neural programming remained unaltered.

Most importantly, the baton served as a reminder that Sun had not cast him away as her father had. Maybe that was because she was not a true Royal, for she had grown up in an alien culture rather than on a wheelship. What her father had taught her about her heritage meant something, but it also meant she did not know the banners as one born and raised there did. She knew the idea of them. She knew her father's memory of them, for he too was separated from the wheelships by many years and the choice he had made to live outside the banners. But she didn't feel bound by those customs.

Banner soldiers who were sent away to fight held to their customs and language by keeping to themselves. The Phene had explicitly forbidden fraternization. Obviously the Phene hadn't trusted the mercenaries they employed. Why else use the leash? When he closed a hand around the baton he felt its eerie tremor resonate through his flesh as a harmonious partial. The final reminder of who he was.

The shuttle got clearance to dock. They unstrapped, unsealed, and disembarked past a higher-than-normal security screen. The habitat was under Chaonian military control, mostly Republican Guards who gave him startled looks as he walked beside Ay. The crew split into three groups with an hour ticking in their networks, each with a list of comestibles to obtain. They'd be running deep into rim space, and with each drop farther out from major beacon routes the familiar local comforts people liked to have on board would get harder if not impossible to find.

When he thought back he wondered if perhaps that was the one thing they didn't tell you after you marched in your funeral shroud onto the ship that would take you away from your home forever. That you would never again taste jellyfish pudding. That you would never again skate the exterior sphere of the labyrinth on frictionless boots as glow-wires lashed streams of color around you and your age cohort. That you would never again ascend the evacuation spire and from that perch be able to watch the wheelship roll onward upon its eternal journey.

Once free of the docking ring the smothering level of security eased. He'd been through five habitats in his brief time as a banner soldier. Mostly his arrow had been confined in holding barracks while waiting for new assignments, but as long as they had no demerits they were allowed liberty each evening, roaming together to see the sights, stopping at a drinking establishment, eating from a food counter as a break from barracks food. In fact he and Ay were now passing a strip of food counters where locals arrived with big meal boxes to buy what looked like an entire family's supper.

"Here, over here." Ay's fingers closed on his sleeve, tugged, then abruptly let go. "Sorry."

"You are used to touching people."

"My friends and family, yeah. I got excited. My aunt was stationed on this habitat for a few months. She said I have to try the local bean pancakes."

She hurried up to a chest-high counter. On the other side a cook poured out streams of batter onto a griddle with the speed and intensity of an old hand. He was startled to see the purveyor was imperial Phene, their four arms working with astonishing coordination.

This individual didn't have the manner and speech of the other imperial Phene he had ever encountered. They spoke in the local patois, a dialect of Common Yele thick enough that Ay struggled to understand it, and wore their hair piled up with decorative flourishes he'd never seen in the Phene military but which the two-armed locals preferred. A child assisted at the cart, wiping the counter, bringing more batter from a cooler, washing the silicone serving sleeves to be reused for the next customers.

He and Ay collected their food and moved to a tall table to eat standing up. The pancakes were crunchy and a little sweet with a taste new to him that sparked an alert in his system for trace levels of something it identified as ptalquiloside. Standing next to Ay as she ate was the best part because eating alone felt wrong. She consumed the pancake with the interest of a person who knows enough about flavor to really think about what they are eating, and she offered factual comments on its texture and seasoning. The new taste was a plant called fernbrake.

The child drifted over to stare as they worked their way through second pancakes, these with yam and nori.

After a few moments the child said, "You have one of those circuit faces."

The adult's gaze flashed up from the behind the counter. "Nanoy! Let the customers eat in peace."

"It's all right," said Kurash to the adult, and then to the child, "I didn't know you saw a lot of banner soldiers out here anymore. They'd have left now that the Republic of Chaonia controls this region."

"They're not soldiers," said the child. "They're grease roaches."

"Nanoy! There is work to do!"

The child hurried off to clear plates from an adjoining table.

"Apologies, officers."

Ay's easy smile smoothed over the moment. "No worry. Cute kid. Any chance you know the direction to"—she blinked to check her network—"Sunrise Market?"

The cook gave directions, clearly relieved to see them go, although Kurash could not know whether it was his presence or their Chaonian military uniforms that made the adult nervous.

They rode a spoke to a different torus and ascended two decks to reach a large commercial hub.

"What is a grease roach?" he asked Ay.

"I dunno. Looks like the market is this way."

She kept walking but he paused. The harmonics in the baton had shifted. Anyone who wasn't wheelship-born wouldn't have noticed but the discordance jangled in his nerves. Ay had almost vanished into the bustle of the hub with its many aisles and lanes by the time he realized what he was hearing.

The baton was reading the presence of leashed banner soldiers.

He hurried after her, deftly slipping and sliding through the crowd at a speed that would have sent any nonenhanced person careening into multiple collisions. He caught her up. His movement brought her around.

"What is it?" She gestured at her own face to say she saw something in his. "Are you okay?"

"I need to check something out, something to do with banner soldiers."

"You think that boy really meant there are banner soldiers here?" She stiffened. "Should I call an alert?"

"Let me scout. Where will you be?"

She squinted, thinking it through, then nodded. "Okay. Check it out. I'll be in that aisle over there. See it? With the beans and roasting carts. I'm slinging you a location ping. Send me one back, and you're good to go. Keep your eye on the time."

He had been fitted with an add-on Chaonian network after he'd boarded the *Keoe*. Compared to his own neural enhancers the system was sludgy and half the time his neuronics interfered with it, but it remained workable as a means to connect with other Chaonians, who as children had chips implanted for immediacy of access. And for surveillance, although none of them seemed to see it that way. Then again, they thought of their government as a republic with a temporary military leader when really their ruler was an autocrat however much they might admire and respect her.

He and Ay parted. The harmonics guided him. The central market hub with its loud and exciting commercial activity gave way to an outer ring of storefronts hosting services like air filter repair, residential plumbing, and cable assembly and wire harness.

The farther he got from the central hub the less cared-for the area looked. Dried stains on the deck no one had cleaned up. Dust in unswept corners. A person dressed in unkempt clothing huddled against an empty storefront, eyes closed, smelling of Flare and urine.

Shocking, really, considering that every meter of a wheelship was considered sacred ground to be cared for and cherished. He found himself at a junction where two lanes branched into the outer shell of the ring. Both lanes were missing some of their light fixtures. Shadows fell like curtains across closed doors onto silent shops. To the left, signs for a "bargain" tailor, a "cut price" undertaker, a "no problem too dire to fix" vac suit repair. The baton drew him into the spinward lane.

A storefront promised Responsible Freight Solutions. He slowed his steps to see if the harmonics stung more against his hand. No, not there.

Lucky Pawnbroker next door was advertised with an image of a pterosaur clutching a gold disc. Seen through a window, jewelry sparkled beneath shelf lighting. Not there.

An empty shop whose door had a smashed-in panel. It was telling they had to lock everything or abandon it as insecure.

A door labeled as a public lavatory.

The last storefront had only writing on its door, in the local script, which he couldn't read. A translation program came up with *Best Price Traps and Drains*.

The baton hummed discordantly. He pushed open the door into a small front room. A counter ran the length of the space. A two-armed person wearing a scarf wrapped around their hair sat behind the counter, bent over a screen. There was no one else in the space, but there was a door behind them with a seal and a lock beaming red. The baton's hum sharpened.

They did not look up as they said in a rote monotone, "If it's an emergency blockage I can't help you unless you have an emergency token to put you at the head of my list. If you want a standard traps or drains cleaning, fill in your designation on the handheld. It's easier to book online. I've got nothing sooner than twenty-two days out. Don't blame me. I'm understaffed and overbooked. Also, we close for siesta in five minutes and I'm prompt about that, no wiggle room."

When he did not answer, the person looked up. Their eyes widened.

"What the fuck? What are you?" They pressed something on their wrist, waited for his reaction. When he gave none, they swore, barely standing their ground and then only because they had nowhere to run. "Shit. I'm not doing anything illegal. No one else will employ them, and it's honest work."

It wasn't possible, was it? Banner soldiers, here?

"Citizen," he said in polite greeting, using the neutral term.

"It's citizen♀," she said, using the female-specific like a counter-strike, as if he should have assumed and thus known.

"Citizen♀," he corrected. "Where are they?"

She tensed. "Why do you want to know?"

"I need to speak to them."

"By what authority?"

The question stymied him until he remembered the ring, the uniform, the frigate. "By the authority of Queen-Marshal Sun, whose envoy I am."

"The Chaonians trusting a Gatoi envoy? Who would do that?"

"Her father is a Royal of the banners," he said, and was instantly annoyed with himself for playing into the woman's prejudices, as if Sun's father's birth wouldn't be just another mark against her. The hum in the baton shifted, the targets moving away.

Enough. He hopped over the counter with an ease she hadn't seen coming.

She side-stepped away. "They work here under a licensed and legal labor permit. I even got a shutdown implant so I can control them if they become violent. But it doesn't work on you." Again she pressed at her wrist.

"You can open that door or I can break it."

She muttered a curse as her trembling hands keyed in a code at the panel. The door groaned and scraped aside. It needed repair. Who let doors get to this state? It was disrespectful as well as dangerous in the case of a habitat-wide environment emergency. He eased through, sensors on alert for atmosphere loss. What assaulted him was a smell of rancid grease.

The space was dimly illuminated by a single thumbnail bulb no brighter than a night-shift passage light. He switched to night vision to see a living quarters, almost a prison, really, except for a back door with a red lock light gleaming. Two cots, each with a thermal blanket neatly folded on top of a smooth sheet. Two of the portable carry-chests allotted to banner soldiers. One was dented, and the other had a series of deep gouges along one side as if it had barely fended off a mech claw. The floor was scrupulously clean. An empty bucket and a folding mop were shoved beneath a small table with a basin, and a battered aluminum pitcher set on the tabletop. A towel hung from a hook. A covered bedpan was tucked under one of the cots.

Most of the space was taken up with a tall metal cabinet. He cracked open one of its hinged doors. The sour fat smell emanated from inside. It was a storage unit where bulky protective gear could hang next to shelving for equipment. The interior was empty, but the smell remained really dire, touched with an eye-watering tincture of ammonia, hints of feces, and a fishy bitterness with a metallic sting.

Her shape appeared in the door, again with the wrist. He whirled into a battle crouch. His neuronics flashed like the warning given by an ancient creature of the Celestial Heaven who flared its wings before it attacked.

"I'm not trying to hurt you! I'll alert station security if you don't answer my questions. It's my right! Are you registered to be here? Otherwise people like you aren't allowed on station."

The back door buzzed.

She brushed past Kurash and unlocked the door panel. It slid aside to reveal two people standing in what looked like a makeshift decontamination chamber. Protective suits hung from hooks, dripping slime. Cleaning equipment and two small mechs sat on the deck behind them.

"Do you know this officer?" she said to the newcomers.

Kurash stared in shock as two individuals cautiously entered the room, one with a pronounced limp. The dim light brightened to reveal their faces. The skintight coveralls they wore were bodysuits that fit beneath protective gear. The baton's harmonics bit into his skin like needles prickling but he could see with his own eyes. Their exposed wrists were tagged with the yellow cuffs of Avalanche Banner. The taller had a terrible scar across half their face, mouth lopsided from the burn, one eye scarred shut, and the ear on that side was hidden beneath a keloid scar, if the ear even existed any longer. The shorter had a badly damaged leg secured in a makeshift brace that looked in need of repair.

"Where is your arrow?" he demanded. "How is it you live here?"

"Who are you to ask?" replied the shorter.

"I am—" But he broke off, because he wasn't. Try again. "I am an envoy of Queen-Marshal Sun."

"The Chaonians?" The shorter barked a laugh, answered by a cough from the taller. "You're not Chaonian. You bear the mark of Wrathful Snakes Banner."

"I was born under that banner."

"You are no Royal. Where is *your* arrow?" The taller's voice was little more than a whisper thrown through lips warped by scarring.

"They have returned to Lady Chaos."

"Ah," said the shorter. "So you survived with disgrace and dishonor."

The accusation burned. The proprieter shaded her eyes against a flare of light in his neuronics, then lowered her hand as he controlled his anger.

"I mean nothing by it," the shorter went on. "We two also survived with disgrace. Our injuries make us useless to the Phene. They left us behind when they evacuated their forces from this system. That is why we are here."

"Like I said," broke in the proprieter in her too-loud voice, "I have a legal permit for them to work. They get paid per job. They pay for the rental of the equipment and their lodging and water and air use. All aboveboard. They are lucky to have work at all. Most people don't want your kind around but I don't mind because no one sees them, because they work in the drains and maintenance tunnels out of people's sight."

Kurash wanted to ask why they had not returned home after being left behind like broken equipment not worth repairing. But he wanted to show respect first of all.

"Is there a name I can call you?" he asked.

They studied him with the resigned suspicion of people who have endured constant scorn.

"My battle name is Sobers." The taller lifted their chin proudly.

"Versatile and adept."

"My battle name is Wüst," said the shorter.

He nodded in respect. "Singular focus."

"Is there a name we can call you?" asked Wüst.

"I was a recruit once but now I live a different life." It galled him to speak his family name as if it were public currency. Yet wasn't that what Sun called him now? "I am Envoy Kurash. As I said, I serve the queen-marshal of the Republic of Chaonia."

"How can that be? Once they have leashed us, the Phene never release us."

"The Phene don't, it's true. But Sun's sire is Prince João of the banner of Royal. He married Queen-Marshal Eirene many cycles ago. He chose to fight the Phene Empire by breaking their hold—their leash—

over the banner soldiers they hold in their employ. That is why I am—"
He broke off. His mission was classified.

He drew the baton out of the loop that held it to his belt. "Why I
have the means to remove the leash. It's a simple process, like breaking
a circuit. I can do it for both of you right now."

They stared at him as if he had started speaking in a language foreign to them.

Again the woman raised her hand and pressed at her wrist. Sobers
and Wüst immediately spasmed, folding forward as they staggered and
fell to their knees.

Before, he had been too focused on the door and his target to notice anything. Now he felt a sensation like a feather brushing along his
bones, a faint tickle that reminded him of when he was Zizou and in
training and how the Phene trainers would compel him harder harder
harder to push himself until he dropped half dead with exhaustion.
Then nursed back to health. Pushed past normal limits again and
again until pain becomes normal.

She hissed in frustration. "Why does it not work on you?"

"What is it you possess?" He knew he ought to speak more politely
because he was a stranger here, but she had attempted four times now
as if pointing a weapon at him. "It's a leash trigger. You're compelling
them."

"I am doing no such thing! They work here of their own free will
and recognizance. Habitat law requires me to have this on-off switch.
They can't hold a work permit without me having this to stop them
from going on a berserk."

"Have they ever acted as if they are not ordinary human beings?"

"We all know what your kind are. What you can do. What savagery you have perpetrated. There's nothing wrong in demanding a
fail-safe."

"What you call savagery is behavior compelled through the very
leash you have just used to put them on their knees."

"Whatever you say," she retorted. "But it is the law here."

"Are there others of you working on this habitat?" he asked.

Wüst and Sobers still knelt, although they were no longer convuls-
ing. "We don't know. Nor would we seek out and confront those from
other banners."

As you have confronted us, Wüst did not add, but Kurash heard it anyway. He saw it in the way they remained kneeling.

"I can free you from the leash," he said. "Don't you want that?"

"What happens to us then? We will lose our labor permit and have nowhere to go. No way to eat. No means to live. We did not lose our lives honorably in battle. So we accept our circumstances."

"To live like this?"

"Have you some other recommendation?" Wüst's mockery had a jagged edge.

He wanted to tell them where he was going, what he was doing, but he couldn't in front of a civilian who might sell the information. Clearly she needed the credit, which was exactly what his teachers had explained was wrong with economic systems that generated such inequality. People came to value money and its access to power more than loyalty and honor.

"I can bring your case to the wheelship conclave. There must be some measure by which you could be allowed to return home."

Wüst lifted their gaze, hands clenched. "We would not bring such dishonor upon our families."

Sobers nodded in agreement. "Ghosts do not return to haunt the banner."

"I'd be grateful if you left my premises," said the woman, gaining courage from her employees' refusal. "I'm doing you a favor. If I call station security, they'll contact your commanding officer to take charge of you."

Marshal the Honorable Precious Jīn would be all too happy to intervene, and not in a way this woman would like.

A ping dropped in from Ay: CONDITION? WE NEED TO BE BACK ON SHIP IN 30. PLEASE RESPOND.

He wanted to fix things for them but he hadn't even realized banner soldiers could survive the war they had been trained to die in. It wasn't just that he had never seen any retired banner soldiers. He'd barely been deployed for half a cycle before he'd been captured, so it wasn't surprising he'd seen so little of the universe. It was that he had never thought to ask what would become of them all in the end.

He should have. He would now. He would find a way to use the authority, however small, that Sun had granted him. There had to be a way, even if he wasn't sure what a future looked like for people like him. Like them.

"I won't forget you are here," he promised, but the words burned bitter on his tongue because he had to walk away and leave them behind.

53

If We Are Fortunate

Apama lay with her eyes open in the dark of the security team's barracks compartment on board the freighter *Overly Devoted*. Every lancer pilot learned to be attuned to the creaks and pops and vibrations of a ship, its cycling frequencies, crew moving about its passageways on their daily routine.

Or gone quiet as the ship was boarded by hostile military.

Smuggling Teegee aboard the merchant ship and dropping into Kaska System with a clean manifest had been the easy part. Everyone on the sixteen-person Se Xar security team knew who Teegee really was. No one on the freighter's crew did.

So far so good. But Kaska System was two beacon drops away from the battlefield, which meant its inspection protocols hadn't been disrupted. The ship had to clear Chaonian Tariff and Security Control before they would be allowed to drop through the next beacon, after which they would join the gathering caravan.

After a beep of warning, the hatch clunked open. Chaonian marines fanned out through the lounge with its couches and table, the two rows of racks back by the showers and the head, and a closed door into a tiny solo cabin which had Team Leader Dunya Se Xar's nameplate on it but in actuality had been set aside as Teegee's refuge.

Apama's bunk was in the first set of racks so they would get to her first. A beam of light lit her face as she pretended to be as surprised as if she'd been woken out of a dead sleep. "Hey! Hey! I can't see," she said in Phenish.

"Up! Up!" shouted one of the marines in Phenish.

She made a point to struggle a bit with her blanket, as if it were caught in her legs, and left it rumpled on the thin mattress as she ducked out of the rack to stand at attention. She was wearing her usual sleeping gear, loose boxers and tank top.

Seeing her shorn-short hair they asked her to turn around so they could look at the back of her head, as if she might be a Rider hiding from them in plain sight.

One rack down Gurak was rousted out. The door to the solo cabin got a few whacks with a baton before it opened. As planned, Dunya and tall, lanky Carmelito stumbled out. They were supposed to be wearing scanty night clothes and the shamefaced expressions of two guilty lovers, and Dunya did indeed have on a short sleeveless shift and a frown, but Carmelito had decided to emerge butt naked and not one bit ashamed of it.

Apama appreciated the professionalism of the startled Chaonians as they went back about their business. They didn't harass or leer. They didn't tear stuff out or throw things on the floor, but they weren't lackadaisical either. They shone lights into every rack to make sure they hadn't missed anyone. Under-rack and side-rack lockers were opened and efficiently searched, no tossing gear onto the deck, no smack talk.

Nor were they chatty, like her marine had been. Not that he'd been her marine. Safe at a distance, that's how she liked her irrational crushes, and weren't all crushes irrational when you came right down to it?

What was Gail up to? Easy to think now of his easygoing cheer with wistful longing, when during the months on board the *Strong Bull* the code of conduct mitigated against a relationship within the chain of command. Who else could she think about to distract herself while hoping and praying the enemy would not find the precious thing hidden right under their noses? She conjured up images of Bartholomew's most adept and pleasing outfits. A diaphanous silver ankle-length jacket came to mind at once, of course, that he'd worn to great acclaim for the Procession of Fans. A traditional lace-drenched houppelande for a basilica ceremony with a sheer shawl of palest green like new leaves, and his long hair braided into a crown decorated with shimmering gilt stars. On the Feast of Anchor Eve, an elaborately wrapped and pleated festival robe paired with a conical hat from which hung strings of beads like a curtain hiding his face.

The security weapons used by the Se Xar team were tagged. Identifications were logged. Four sleep-cycle team members in the barracks; four off duty, about their business elsewhere on the ship. Another four on duty had been logged. The other four members of the security team had been remanded to general caravan use and were currently aboard the Remora-class freighter that conveyed the in-system merchant vessels through beacons. This was the sleight of hand: because she was underage, Teegee wasn't a registered employee but a family adjunct and didn't have to be listed on the official manifest.

The marines did a final tour of the lounge, the head, the showers while Gurak and Dunya watched with arms crossed and Carmelito stood there like a work of art, which he was, and he knew it. Apama was pretty sure the marines were mostly fascinated not by his lithe muscularity but by his arms. They just could not get over the four arms, as if they didn't look inadequate with two.

None of them were her marine, but then again, no marine elite enough to be boarding the *Virtuous Heart* would be doing grunt boarding duty in Kaska System.

After examining the manifest and consulting via their network, the squad leader gave an all clear and they left. Apama closed hands into fists to avoid pressing a palm to her palpitating heart, which would seem all too guilty if the marines returned suddenly, hoping to catch them unawares.

Gurak said, "By all the saints, 'Lito, put that penis away. We've seen enough of it to last us for the rest of the voyage."

The joke cut a little of the tension. Dunya tossed Carmelito a sleep skirt and went to her rack to get dressed. They waited out the rest of the boarding procedure being played out at the cargo ramp and cargo compartments, the airlocks, the bridge. Apama knew how to wait.

Thirty-eight minutes later the ship got its release and an official seal allowing passage through the next drop. Dunya went out.

Apama pulled the mattress off her rack. A concealed switch released the base. She swung it away to reveal a coffin-like smugglers' drawer that ran along the length of the racks. Teegee lay on her side, ordinary eyes shut, riding eyes open.

"Whew," Giolla said with a whistle of relief as she squeezed out with Apama's help. "That wasn't so bad."

Tadukhipa whispered, "I thought it would last longer."

"I'm so sorry, Rider," said Gurak. "It's the best we can do. It's meant for illegal cargo, not for people. The illicit drugs are in the other compartments."

"It's okay," said Giolla, answering for them both, as she often did. Her gaze strayed toward Carmelito, clad only in the loose sleep skirt, torso bare, and she immediately looked away. "We do drills like this starting at five."

Apama exchanged a horrified glance with Gurak. "Five years old?"

Carmelito grimaced. "They confine you in tiny spaces at five years old?"

Gee's color heightened as she glanced shyly toward him. "It's an isolation tank. Sensory deprivation. It's how we start learning to communicate with our Rider, and our Rider with us. When you're little it's really hard to block out all the real-world distraction and hear what they are trying to say so we do exercises like—"

"We're not supposed to talk about training," Tee broke in.

"Oh!" Gee blushed. "Of course we aren't."

Gurak pointedly coughed. He crawled back into his rack because it really was his sleep cycle. Carmelito looked far more embarrassed to have heard this minor disagreement between Tee and Gee than by all his parading. He hastily headed for his rack, leaving Teegee to beckon Apama to follow her into the solo cabin.

Apama shut the door. "Are you really all right?"

For once, Tee spoke first. "I don't mind. I can go somewhere else and I don't feel a strong connection to having a body. It's harder for Gee."

"I just pretend I'm hiding from Chaonian marines who want to take me prisoner," said Gee. Both girls laughed.

"Can't you see what she's seeing?" Apama asked. "My uncle Dasa was able to copy down a message. So he must have been able to see what a Rider was seeing through Zakurru well enough to render the script."

Teegee was standing so Apama could see both her faces in profile. It was eerie to watch the balance and contrast of expressions: Giolla's more mobile face pulling a grimace that seemed more regretful than anything; Tadukhipa's gaze flickering toward Apama and away as her thin mouth flatlined. The girl raised her lower right hand, one finger pointing up as if toward a heavenly ear.

"Council protocol means Council secrecy," Apama said hastily, remembering that every Rider in the empire could listen in to this conversation. "I get it. Apologies."

The girl sank onto the bed next to Apama, shoulders slumped. After a moment, Apama took Teegee's lower left into her own lower right.

"Are we safe now?" Tadukhipa asked.

"No, we're not safe. Chaonia also controls Hatti and Samuha Systems. Once we reach Rosetta System we'll enter cartel-controlled space. Even then, about half of the Hesjan cartels are allied with the republic and the other half are independent corsairs, so we'll still be in danger."

"Every beacon passage will be like this?"

"Yes. You're a lancer pilot now, remember?"

"I'm not a lancer pilot, not really," said Gee.

"No, you're not. But I can call you an honorary lancer pilot. We escaped the *Virtuous Heart* through more difficult circumstances than these. If we are fortunate, the hardest part of this journey will be dealing with boredom. And you having to keep your hoodie on whenever you're outside this compartment so the freighter crew doesn't figure out who you really are."

"If we are fortunate."

Apama wasn't sure which mouth had spoken. Maybe they both had.

54

Like a Parasite Burrowing In

When the marshal began turning up at his personal exercise sessions in the *Huma*'s gymnasium, Kurash asked Ay for help. At the next session Ay and four other members of her duty shift showed up to train with him alongside the august marshal. Soon he had to add a second session per ship day to accommodate the number of crew who wanted to "train like a badass Gatoi."

Of course no one could outjump, outlift, or outlast him, but simply to complete the full basic workout, a routine warmup for banner soldiers, became a badge of honor that allowed crew to swagger about the passageways of the frigate.

Eventually, many days into their journey, the captain took him aside due to yet another spectacular injury suffered by a spacer eager to emulate him.

"I like what's going on with the crew," Captain Shì said. "I could even see a version of this training becoming fleet-wide standard for personal fitness. It's something you could talk to the queen-marshal about, since you have her ear. But you've got to put additional safety measures in place. Harnesses for the bar and rope work. Lower the wall heights. We Chaonians are a tough bunch, but it needs regulation. I don't know how you people are built to sustain those impacts."

The captain smiled winningly at him. He was a good-looking man, no longer young but young enough to bear none of the obvious markers of advancing age. He did that thing Chaonians thoughtlessly did all the time: he tapped Kurash on the forearm without asking, accompanied by another flash of his appealing smile. "If you want any help with that, let me know. I believe the queen-marshal would support new protocols. It's a good way to rise in her esteem, if that prospect interests you."

Later over the meal designated as supper he asked Ay, "Was the captain also offering to mentor me in exchange for sex?"

She laughed. "I doubt it. Scuttlebutt is he's monosexual and not in your court. He does a lot to give young officers a boost up if he thinks they're promising. And he has a reputation for being fair-minded. Also he famously led a brilliant frigate formation against a dreadnought at the battle of Na Iri. The queen-marshal trusts him, which is why she gave him this duty. I might complain about not being posted to the *Boukephalas* like the rest of my rack, but in other ways this is a better opportunity."

"Is everyone in Chaonia looking for a ladder to climb?"

She gave him a long look. "If you don't move, someone will shove you aside to get to the front. I don't know how much you know about our history."

"I have read several Chaonian accounts since I came into Sun's service."

"Yeah, so the lesson we learn from our history is that we can sit passively and be overrun the way we were in our grandparents' day. Or we can push all ahead and not let others take what is ours. The Phene still owe us recompense for the years of occupation in Chaonia, don't you think?"

"It was not my war nor my people."

"Aren't we now your people and thus your war?"

He had no answer.

Being an envoy included meetings that weren't operations objectives for a mission followed by after-action reviews for those who had survived. The political nature of the discussion was something Kurash had no experience of and wasn't sure how to process, so his mind tended to wander while the others droned on.

As a boy he had played throughout the wheelship and thus absorbed its rhythms and contours. As an adolescent he had learned the basic skills necessary for an adult to function as a useful part of the wheelship. But when he had been sent into the maze at the age of seventeen, as all children were, Lady Chaos had drawn her veil of poison over his head. Thus he was declared dead and his body assigned to one of the trade lots destined for the empire. It was an honor to serve the banner on this path. He had gone willingly, not that he had ever conceived of refusing.

Under the Phene he had trained as a soldier. He had endured conditioning and further enhancements to his neural system, so much chronically acute pain day after day that even now, more than a year after his capture, he woke from sleep surprised that flesh and bone could lie quiescent, content, neither aching or flaring. That dreams could be sweetly arousing rather than violent and exhausting. That he could wonder where dauntless Persephone was and if he would ever touch her again. If he should have refused her offer, as he had. If maybe he should have grasped for the hour's bliss she'd offered. What would that have felt like, in the dark where the eyes are not your means of communication but rather the pulse of the heart, the gasp of pleasure, the rapture of skin against skin?

"Kurash? Did you have anything to add?"

He startled, realizing he had almost dozed off seated at a strategos table as the marshal quirked an eyebrow at him.

"Or do you always think with your eyes shut?"

The rest of the diplomatic team chuckled except for the marshal's secretary, a white-haired old man with a prosthetic hand and an air of disdain.

The words of the Rider clung to his back like a parasite burrowing in. If they were weapons the Phene had bought, then had his wheelship truly sold him?

"I understand my role in the mission. You will offer the technology to the conclave in exchange for an alliance. I am proof the technology works."

"You also represent Sun's pledge to take banner soldiers into her employ once the leash is removed. You are Chaonia's surety."

"I am no longer a banner soldier."

"That's not important."

"It will be important to the conclave. I would like to introduce one more subject to the negotiations."

Her eyebrows quirked. "What is that?"

"The matter of banner soldiers who fulfilled their contracts with the Phene but were abandoned by the empire when they had no more use for their services."

"Wouldn't that be like leaving a charged stinger with no fail-safe out on the street for anyone to shoot themselves with?"

There was a bit of scattered laughter.

The secretary glanced toward the marshal before speaking to Kurash. "You filed a situation report about your encounter on Orbital Habitat Matoas."

"I received no answer."

"It's Phene business, not ours," said the marshal. "According to what I understand from the report, those individuals are no longer fit to be soldiers."

"What does Chaonia do with its disabled soldiers?"

The secretary's prosthetic hand twitched.

"Does it throw them onto the streets to beg?" Kurash thought of the elegant Tiana's father, who never spoke ill of the republic but whose prosthetic arm had an industrial, utilitarian look at odds with the honorable secretary's supple, lifelike hand.

"We honor our commitments to those who honor the republic. People receive the medical care they need. Those who cannot return to active duty are offered work that fits their new capacities. Like Xiákè." The marshal turned to her secretary. "Are the speeches and gifts in order? Then we're done until we reach Danu."

She caught Kurash's eye and made a gesture that he should stay behind while the others departed. The secretary paused at the door.

"Go on," said the marshal impatiently.

The door shut. They sat alone in the meeting room where, Ay had told him, the captain would meet with his officers. The ventilation system hummed with a reassuring steadiness. The marshal had a veneer of hard competency, and he got the impression people rarely if ever said no to her or to any of Eirene's Companions. As his grandmother had once said to him, people who get accustomed to wielding power can easily come to believe they are entitled to it instead of being granted authority on loan from the ancestors and from the generations to come.

"Have you given any thought to my offer? You have a great deal of promise, Kurash. Your situation suffers from your ignorance of Chaonian politics and history. You still think like a banner soldier. That's no way to gain influence."

He had thought about this inevitable moment for a while, played its parameters through his head as the arrow, before an action, would be briefed on its mission. What if he said yes; what if he said no; what if he temporized? Arrows did not temporize. They shot straight and true into the heart of the conflict.

"My thanks, Marshal. You do me a great honor, but my answer must be no. Your way is not my way. Your goals are not my goals. I serve Queen-Marshal Sun."

"For as long as she remains queen-marshal."

What could she mean by such words? He said nothing as she went on.

"Not everyone is enamored of her reckless, intemperate style. She almost died in Karnos. And for what? To save a Rider who was no use to her anyway, just for pride's sake. She lacks Eirene's subtlety and ingenuity and will soon wreck herself on the shoals of her inflexible nature. Mark my words."

The blunt speech astonished him. Precious Jīn had been made lead envoy because she was a high-ranking Core House honorable in her own right and a Companion of the deceased Eirene with a notable military career. Reputation burnished her more than any symbol of rank or jewel of ornament. She could say what she wished and yet, to his ears, her remarks sounded treasonous.

Did Precious Jīn know the Honorable Manea's baby was dead? Sun and Prince João had no reason to broadcast the unsavory news. Even Lee House might prefer to keep it quiet, given that they had looked the other way. Kurash had told only Sun.

That being so, Precious and any of Eirene's other Companions who had never really liked Sun might yet pin their hopes on a growing child for whom they could act as advisors and guardians. And if not that child, then another heir, someone more malleable. Someone not Sun. Someone who the fleet would acclaim as long as Eirene's marshals spoke on that individual's behalf.

He tucked his right hand over his left to feel the pressure of Sun's ring. He could not imagine anyone else who would have acted as Sun had acted on the day when the Phene had attacked the industrial park. She had thrown him into a situation where he could easily have betrayed her to the Phene and she'd never have known until it was too late. He would never betray the trust she had shown in him.

What was Sun doing now? The *Huma* was running ahead of the news.

He rose. "Marshal, I must keep my attention on the immediate battle ahead."

"There you go, speaking as a banner soldier. Diplomacy is not a battle. It is a dance between charm and duplicity, so Eirene always said. Offer the other side what will benefit them but benefit you more. A free lesson for you, Kurash." She smiled, a handsome woman accustomed to accolades and success. In the aftermath of the smile her mouth flattened like a warning that her generosity only went so far.

"I hope in the future to understand Chaonia." He gave the gesture appropriate to taking a respectful leave of an elder.

55

What Nightmare Intrusion Disturbs the Peace of the Valiant One?

Makinde stood in the viewing bulb of the *Dufa* as the courier approached a striped gas giant in Hellion System. Standing in the viewing bulb gave him a private bubble, an hour to himself alone before his daunting assignment commenced. Comms chattered in a soothing sonic background.

"All in X-ray one, this is Delta Tango Alpha eight eight tac niner one two, sector Echo Bravo one to Echo Charlie four, over."

"This is X-ray one one two, Alpha Station."

"*Kilo* nine three five, this is *Kilo* actual, interrogative time to resume your station, over."

Out there, invisible against the immensity of space, a Chaonian armada was mustering. The mundane exchanges of ships as they jostled for position at the assembly point pleased him far more than the splendid and overwrought "One Hundred Days" of funeral games for the fallen and associated victory celebrations he'd been subjected to in Karnos System. Not that he begrudged any of the ceremony and honor heaped upon the dead. Not at all. It just had been a lot.

Still, holding the hundred-days festival and commemoration was a smart military move by Sun. The ceremonies had provided much-needed rest and recovery time for spacers and Guards as well as ship repair and rearranging depleted squadrons. Meanwhile, as all eyes were funneled to the spectacular Idol Faire performances, pugilist competitions, and illustrious philosophical debates, the slow and dangerous work of de-mining Hellion Terminus's arrival zone had proceeded piece by piece without fanfare. It had taken crack Chaonian engineers and ordnance ratings over seventy days to clear a way through.

Anyway, Sun had badly needed the recovery time, however poorly she had used it. Even as her physicians protested, she'd planted her medi-couch at the front row of the audience halls. Later, when she could sit upright, she'd wheeled herself into the thick of the debates. Who knew she could relax, banter, and drink with no talk of battle? In a way she hadn't, because she had been keenly involved in monitoring the Idol Faire competition the way she kept track of everything that mattered to her: full bore. There were rumors she'd begun a passionate fling with the winner, Ji-na, which Makinde doubted since the ribbon dancer sat in frequent attendance at the medi-couch of the Handsome Alika. Channel Idol had likely concocted the salacious gossip to make the intense young queen-marshal seem more *relatable*.

The door into the viewing bulb whisked open. Beau Qiáng entered, accompanied by two philosophers. The hells! What nightmare intrusion disturbed his peace? Did merely thinking of Channel Idol magically extrude forth a tendril of its shambling monstrosity? How had these three civilians gotten onboard the military courier?

Dozer gave a beep of interest, flushing pink with excited extroversion, but the historian did not look up toward the ceiling where Doze had affixed ouself.

"Honored Makinde!" Beau hailed him, thus forcing him to nod although he wasn't in the mood to interact. "What a shock to discover that after all our hard work to open a path into Hellion System, the Phene we hoped to fight here have been taken onto the tow-chain of an Argosy Titan! Two hundred Phene ships, including dreadnoughts, as well as uncounted troops! What does Sun mean to do?"

Makinde waggled his eyebrows with fake surprise. "Has Sun not told you? After all, you seem to be everywhere these days, right in her pocket."

"The queen-marshal gives me access because of the value of my work," said Beau with a proud lift of his chin. "The citizens of the republic crave news of our intrepid campaign. I am the only historian properly placed to give it to them."

"Then I can't possibly have anything to add that you aren't already aware of." He grinned as the historian grimaced, looking stymied.

"Is that a Hesjan symbiont?" asked one of the philosophers, Yele by his willingness to crash into a conversation without being invited. The man gave a speaking look to his supercilious companion. "I've never encountered a bionic enhanced escort in the flesh before. They call them 'bees' for short, you know. There is debate as to whether a sheen of personality is an indicator of consciousness or merely a construct. But I suppose—haha!—we can ask the same of most humans. What say you, Honorable Companion? Makinde Bō, I presume. I saw you at the head table with the queen-marshal. She is sharp as a tack, and so well read! I wanted to debate her iconoclastic view of the argument against destiny but I didn't have the chance."

"There's the dead beacon!" cried Beau, perhaps deliberately interrupting the philosopher. He pressed hands against the viewing bulb as if he hoped to melt through into vacuum, an escape Makinde could not help but long for as he considered his chances of getting out of the viewing bulb without further exposure to pontification. Beau's expression of yearning gave way to a doleful speech as the image of the beacon and its neon-colored aura grew larger.

"The harbinger of collapse. The memory of a thriving throughway, a busy and prosperous cultural hub as it was eight hundred years ago, and yet now nothing more than a signpost to failure. A jumping-off point for hazardous enterprises. And yet in another sense it marks a gateway to that wretched hive of crime and iniquity, the Trinity Coalition."

"Are you recording yourself?" Makinde spotted a wasp back by the door.

"Life is a stage," said Beau. "War is a performance. In the end we will be judged not according to our deeds but according to what people say of our deeds long after any of us can affect the discourse."

ZAP THE FUCKER. THE WASP, I MEAN he subvocalized to Dozer. So he'd never have to see that smarmy speech replayed.

BOSS? THE WASP IS NOT HARMING YOU.

"My queendom for a symbiont without a conscience," he muttered.

"I beg your pardon?" Beau asked, turning around.

The philosopher brightened. "That's it exactly! Are morals dependent on consciousness?"

"Why, look! What star awaits!" cried Beau in the manner of a bright bronze bell ringing loudly so as to drown out its rivals. "Is that the Titan which we sail to meet? So huge we can aspire to see it with the naked eye even at this distance?"

The philosophers surged forward, jostling for the best position as might troödons over a bone. By their excited gabble he could tell none had seen a Titan-class vessel in person before, although why should they have when all their lives had been led in beacon-rich zones?

"If you'll excuse me." He got out while they were distracted.

The door shut. Dozer pinged a wordless ?

"They annoyed me. Can't a person get peace and quiet around here?"

His ring network lit with a message from Sun. BOUKEPHALAS IN-SYSTEM. STATUS?

He pinged back. ALMOST THERE

Alika waited in the courier's lounge. He had recently graduated to leg braces but it was the two prosthetic fingers that bothered him most, because he had to train them and they might never be as supple and responsive as the ones he'd lost. He was practicing so intently he didn't look up as Makinde entered. He knew who it had to be. No one else could have walked in without permission.

Makinde had tracked down a photo of Alika at thirteen, an unprepossessing lad brought into the palace to become one of Princess Sun's Companions. All images of the Vata House scion subsequently vanished from Channel Idol for three years. When new images re-emerged, he'd become the cute youth of your crush-laden adolescent dreams. Rumor whispered he had undergone cosmetic surgery, and maybe it was true or maybe he'd just matured in a fortunate direction. Whichever, Makinde respected him for the way he had not complained about a single thing during his painful convalescence from the severe injuries he'd taken on the *Banshee* raid. People thought Alika difficult, and he was, but you didn't win Idol Faire or become Sun's right-hand spear by being a slacker.

"We there?" Alika asked while still playing.

"Almost."

On top of everything else Alika had taken serious damage on the right side of his face. The surgeons had saved his eye, but Alika was more concerned that his pitch hadn't been compromised. All in all, he wasn't quite as perfect as before, and now sported manicured beard stubble to hide the scars along his jaw. Makinde thought he was more attractive with this beaten and battered look. If he'd met him anywhere else he might have tried to get to know and even court such a man. Like his grandmother, he was old-fashioned and wanted a life partner, not a roll in the hay or even a passionate sexual fling. Nothing against sexual flings, but he was no Persephone.

Thoughts had a way of spilling onto his tongue, especially when he was worried about an upcoming test or trial. "Did you see any of those erotic Phene dramas Perse found? She could not stop talking about four arms! Gods, what is wrong with her?"

"A question for the ages," remarked Alika. He strummed a final set of chords and set the guitar into its case. He rose carefully. The door into the galley opened and his cee-cee Candace entered. She nodded at Makinde before giving Alika's uniform an elaborate once-over. She'd also been wounded, but by good fortune her injuries had mostly affected parts of her body already artificial from injuries she'd received in the famous industrial park skirmish over a year ago, so her recovery was less complicated.

Of course Makinde had skated through the brutal fight on the *Banshee* without a scratch, because he'd been last to board, even after Persephone. It was embarrassing and also a drag. How was a person meant to win honor and renown if he never had a chance to actually scrap? He'd far rather slug it out than play diplomat.

The wardroom door chimed to announce the arrival of the *Dufa*'s captain.

"After you," said Makinde, letting Alika set the pace. The captain escorted them to the courier's number-two shuttle, a little armored larva of a boat that carried twenty, although there were only the three of them and five crew on board for this mission.

As they reached the rendezvous point Makinde expanded the visuals into a big virtual 3-D map filling much of the cabin space. In the wake of the battle of Karnos, over two hundred Phene ships had fled to Hellion Terminus. Lacking the resources of Windworn and Sleepless Systems, the retreating defenders had only been able to lay a slapdash array of mines. Once the Chaonians had broken through, they'd expected another battle. Instead, they'd found an Ousoos Argosy Titan with most of the Phene ships attached to its tow-chain as it made ready to depart. Sun had sent him and Alika as envoys in advance of the main Chaonian fleet.

He went back through the interim report, anything to keep his mind off whether he would fuck up his prepared speech. Twenty-nine severely damaged Phene ships had been abandoned, now crammed together in parked orbit around a gas giant. One of these, amazingly, was a dreadnought, so that at least was a prize. Chaonian engineers were already going over the abandoned ships with a fine-toothed comb. Even so, he doubted Chaonians could operate them. The Phene were smart about how they locked use of their most advanced equipment, like ships and computers, by requiring operators to impress four palm prints from the same individual all at once. Four arms were certainly a creepy human genengineering choice to make, but Makinde respected the Phene for making the best use of them in as many ways as possible. Like that one clip Perse had replayed at least five times . . . never mind. Stop thinking. It would be hideously embarrassing to walk into a meeting of this importance with an erection.

Reacting to Makinde's emotional flare, Dozer beeped interrogatively from where he was stretched along two seatbacks. Candace reached from the row behind and with one of her furled battle fans gave Doze a playful tap. The two began fencing, Candace switching hands at intervals. Alika kept his eyes closed. He looked a little gray, but all the physicians said that he, like Sun, was lucky to be alive.

If not as bogglingly gargantuan as the Alabaster Argosy Titan, the Ousoos Argosy Titan was still massive. It was one thing to see a Titan and its tow chain at a distance and another to actually go on board. Nerves made Makinde loquacious.

"Hey, Alika, do you have a thing for Ji-na? I mean, I don't believe the gossip about her and Sun—"

"Shut up, Baby Mak."

"Ouch. Hit a nerve? Or are you just missing James?"

Alika sighed. "Are you twelve?"

That hurt, especially when Candace stifled a laugh. Her hand strayed to touch a butterfly-embroidered ribbon she'd used to tie back her long hair.

The problem with being a Companion was how easy he found it to get sucked back into first-year antics at the royal academy, as if he were still mobbing with a cohort of recklessly immature honorables who had never lived in a dormitory before. Not that the other Companions behaved that way, but that he didn't have a handle on how to jockey for position among his peers, especially as the youngest. Maybe he should reflect more on his tour on the *Sunbird* and how duty-minded veterans conducted themselves.

As they approached, the Titan opened a maw into a hangar so large that multiple ships were docked along its length, much like a Remora freighter. Makinde set his network to measure the size of the hangar and estimate how many ships were docked inside, but the link went gray, blocked by the Argosy.

He tested the ring with a ping to Sun.

After a lag, Sun's reply dropped in: RECEIVED.

The ring network was Gatoi technology. A gift from her father that was precious because it could not be hacked and could connect when other networks went off line or out of range. They were about to test its capacity now. Just as he was testing Dozer's capacities. The symbiont flowed off the seats and flattened around his torso beneath his uniform jacket like a thick layer of armor, warm against his skin.

"Doze," he said softly, "record everything. We'll analyze later."

ALREADY ENGAGED! ANY OTHER ORDERS?

"Keep your tentacles quiet." He glanced down as the two tentacles wiggled their sensor stalks up out of his collar and shaded to the color of the uniform's buttons.

Grappling lines towed the ship to a dock. The shuttle crew remained on board.

No welcoming party greeted them on the other side of the airlock, only a small, closed compartment built for a scan. A technician could be seen behind a transparent wall. This individual was tall like Princess Soaring. They wore their dyed orange hair in four braids and an orange tunic to match. Their gaze flicked over the arrivals as if they were cargo being cleared of contaminants. Not even a register of interest in or recognition of their humanity. Whew.

When the scan blinked green, a door opened and they went through. Alika eyed the long ramp of a corridor ahead, then started walking. The gravity was definitely lighter than Chaonia Prime, which was a blessing because the lower grav made Alika's ascent easier. After about half a klick they reached a checkpoint where red-clad security people required them to divest of anything the checkpoint deemed a weapon. Candace had to relinquish a basket of fruit conveyed all the way from the Garden of Precious Memory at Dodona Temple on Molossia Prime. Dozer either raised no objections or blended into Makinde's body heat.

They were ushered into a foyer. Beyond sprawled a spacious terrace-like compartment whose outer wall offered a view onto space. The lights were dimmed to a reddish glow that would not interfere with stargazing. On a dais, a seven-person band softly played a jassy melody. Attendants carried trays laden with bowls and glasses. Chattering individuals sat at a curved bar and at tables angled for the best view. The terrace quieted as the newcomers entered. He had to refrain from laughing because the setup reminded him of a famous bar fight scene from *Old Honcho and Baby Bee*. Dozer subvocalized the anticipatory theme that in the show always presaged a skirmish. Sayre Guī Alsura would have loved this.

Alika halted to allow the attention to settle on him. Dozer's tentacle sensor-stalks twitched as ou scoped the scene for later analysis.

An elderly woman sat cross-legged on a cushion at the top of a low plinth, like a living god. Her body looked frail but her voice boomed.

"Don't tarry! Come forward so I can see you."

Makinde pinged to Sun: AUDIO WORKING?

Alika's injuries made his approach stately and courteous. Makinde held position at his right, while Candace walked a pace behind to his left, carrying the embroidered silk that was the only part of the courtesy gift she'd been allowed to bring through.

They halted before the plinth. The woman looked them over with mouth puckered as if she found their presence sour. "I am Adele Karsh, ancient of the Trinity sisters. Which of you is Sun?"

Alika inclined a bow with the respect due to an elder. "I am Captain the Honorable Alika Vata. This is my fellow Companion, Lieutenant the Honorable Makinde Bō, and Lieutenant Candace Jiāng Alyǎnshī. We carry with us the greetings of Sun. We invite you to return to the *Boukephalas* with us to meet with her in amity and goodwill."

"Me, to approach her? I think not. The Trinity Coalition has controlled this vital passage for six hundred years of unbroken authority. We are not upstarts to be called before a youth who parades about with delusions of importance because of a pair of lucky military victories."

ALL GOOD. Sun's reply dropped in.

"However," Adele Karsh went on, "I am willing to offer to the Republic of Chaonia the same friendship pact the Trinity Coalition has long maintained with the Phene Empire."

"What might that be, Gracious Elder?" Alika asked with the stalwart courtesy hammered into every young Core House scion, although Makinde could tell by the pitch of his eyebrows that he was offended by the woman's dismissive tone.

"Why, nothing greater nor lesser. Chaonian-flagged merchant ships may avail themselves of the services of the Ousoos Argosy. We ply the three knnu routes from Tsurru to Hellion, Meli to Nalanda or Sankore, and Kumbala to Harahuvati. The Argosy does not give discounts. That would be unfair business practice, favoring one client over another. But the Argosy does offer bulk rates for conveying ships in a tow chain. In return, we take a services and insurance tariff. That's beyond the fee charged for transportation, just to be clear. The tariff is necessary to secure full protection."

"Surely you understand that to Queen-Marshal Sun, your arrangement to transport Phene military looks like aiding and abetting our enemy." Alika had his game face on, and he knew how to stand and how to stare. He looked awesome, the perfect Chaonian honorable and officer.

"You Chaonians may think whatever you wish. I'm not involved in your war. I'm here to do business, so pay up or get out."

"But you *are* involved."

She snorted. "How so? Pray, do enlighten me, pretty boy."

By not a flicker did Alika betray if the attempt at a condescending insult had hit its mark. He tipped his head toward Makinde.

Makinde swallowed twice, licked his lips, cleared his throat, and launched into his speech. "Gracious Elder and Wise Karsh—"

Her scornful cackle disrupted his memorized words. "What demand are you going to make that I will certainly refuse? Are you even old enough to be a soldier?"

His lips parted with a retort, and then he sucked it back. The effort steadied him. He met her glare with an unintimidated gaze of his own. "Gracious Elder and Wise Karsh, the queen-marshal seeks redress for an injustice. A fugitive who murdered one of her household has fled to this system."

"What does a random fugitive have to do with the Trinity?"

"It may be he has purchased passage on this very Titan. Or he was allowed to embark with the Phene vessels you have locked into your tow chain when you might be more prudently advised to allow Chaonia to take the Phene ships as prizes in war."

"I hope you aren't thinking of firing on a Titan," she said sardonically. "That would be, shall we say, imprudent and ineffectual. We made the deal to convey the Phene ships before you arrived. Anyway, I fail to see why I should care about this personal matter of a random fugitive, hatchling. You're eating into my timetable. Cut to the chase."

"Sun requests your cooperation. She wishes only to pursue the criminal into coalition space. Once she has retrieved the individual in question, she will retire back to the territories she controls."

The old woman had a bark of a laugh. "Don't be ridiculous. Why would we countenance a military advance into our sovereign territory?"

Alika signed to Makinde that he was taking over. "What about the Phene?"

"The Phene? I already told you. This is a salvage operation, a transit passage, if you will, for which the Trinity is being amply paid."

Alika gestured with the authority of a skilled performer letting his audience know he has his next melody in hand. "Likewise, what Sun requests is no military advance, Gracious Elder. It is a retrieval, nothing more. We ask merely the same courtesy you have shown to the Phene. Do we not all pay tribute to justice, according to the venerable sages of the Celestial Empire, who said—"

"Yes, yes, I know what they said. If the queen-marshal lost a criminal she was pursuing, it is no concern of mine. In the Trinity Coalition we do not discriminate among adversaries. We allow independent operators to use our services the same as any others, as long as they pay our fees and the tariff. Our task has always been to facilitate mutual aid in pursuit of profit, not to involve ourselves in political disputes."

She snapped a finger. An attendant hustled over, bearing a tray laden with glasses and plates of finger food, and set it on the plinth. Something in the light and the view of the tray blurred faintly, as if there was a force field around the pillar. After it cleared, the old woman plucked a fluted glass filled with a tar-colored liquid. Holding it in her right hand, she eyed Alika as if he were one of the snacks on the tray. Or maybe she was just letting them know she did not intend to extend the most basic hospitality to her visitors: no deal, no drinks.

"We of the Trinity have had a long and prosperous arrangement with the Phene Empire. We are businesspeople, not politicians. As I said, we are willing to extend the same terms to the new rulers of Karnos System, for as long as they can hold on to their gains. You may take this message back to your queen-marshal. My vessel and its tow chain will be departing Hellion Terminus for Tsurru in twenty-two hours. The Weinstein bubble is already powering up, so my schedule is fixed. If the queen-marshal wishes to seal a trade agreement with me, I will be available to meet with her for the next twelve hours. Although, since her flagship has only just entered Hellion System, I suppose she won't be able to reach me within that time frame. You are dismissed."

56

Pah. Pah.

Sun sat on the viewing side of a one-way glass wall. The room on the other side had the look of a relaxed schoolroom and daytime lounge. It was part of a larger laboratory dedicated solely to the study of Kaspar Yáo Altjeker.

Twelve hours after the departure of the Ousoos Titan and with Sun's agents infiltrated into its tow chain, the *Keoe* had arrived in Hellion System through the Karnos Beacon. Sun had transferred over to be greeted by Soaring, Persephone, and Tiana. Now she watched as a door opened and the boy entered the lounge alone. He wore loose trousers, a long-sleeve shirt, and a knit cap pulled tightly over his head that covered his ears and brushed the tops of his eyebrows.

His body and facial features were beginning to mature with puberty but he still looked like a boy, and it was with a child's restlessness that he perched on the edge of a chair. He glanced toward a second door in the lounge but it hadn't opened.

Behind Sun, the door into the viewing room opened, bringing with it a fragrance of sandalwood. Tiana took a seat beside her. Normally poised and calm, the cee-cee sat with a rigid back and hands clasped tightly together.

"It's been so hard not to be able to greet him," she said.

"We can't risk that his Rider might hear your voice or register your presence."

"I know, and I accept the necessity. But think about him. Finally freed from the prison of being tentbound in Tjeker and able for a year to run about the *Keoe* as he wishes. Only to be forced back into confinement in the lab and one greenhouse because we brought the *Keoe* to you. Poor Kas. What a terrible burden."

Sun noted the cee-cee's clenched jaw. "No new title for me? Was the effort too much? Did you give up?"

The challenge brought a flash to artfully painted eyes. Tiana was a superb cee-cee, so smoothly attentive to the needs of others it might seem to the unobservant that she had no needs of her own. But no one graduated first in class at Vogue Academy who wasn't ambitious and relentless.

"Not at all, Your Attentiveness. I was merely playing fair, given you had first a family tragedy, then a battle to fight, and afterward a grievous injury to heal."

"Your consideration is noted. You can take off the gloves at any time."

"So be it. You shall have your challenge, Your Competitiveness."

Sun smiled, about to retort, but instead leaned forward as the Honorable Hanifa Nazir entered the room beyond. The researcher was accompanied by the boy's tutor, Ioane, who was one of the Solomon cousins and thus a nephew of *Keoe*'s Commander Rahaba.

The tutor sat opposite the boy, a table between them, and smiled encouragingly. "Are you ready, Kas?"

The boy's lower arms were crossed defensively, and his uppers set with hands flat on the table as if he was thinking about shoving himself to his feet and bolting. After a moment, he slumped forward. "Okay."

"It's all right to not like this."

"I don't like when it wakes up. I can feel it crawling inside my head."

Tiana gave Sun an accusing look but said nothing.

Sun said to her, "You can't make a problem go away by ignoring it. I have received a steady stream of reports as they test the Rider's capabilities in prudent and contained experiments. There's no threat to your brother. No indication it can possess his body or take him over and move him about like a puppet."

"Yes, I've read the reports too, Your Thoroughness. I also grew up with him. I've seen the Rider try to take control of Kas."

"Yes. Surely it helps Kaspar to know how to react and respond when that happens. To give him tools to protect himself."

"That is a theory everyone subscribes to. So be it."

The Honorable Hanifa brought over a clear headband wired for various levels of observation and gave a signal meant for the people on the other side of the one-way wall. In the room with Sun and Tiana sat two technicians wearing headsets. One was a de-leashed banner soldier who had been retrained as a technician.

The boy looked at Ioane with a suspicious frown. "This isn't the usual schedule."

"I know. But it is today's schedule. You'll get a special surprise afterward."

"I'm not five, to need a bribe," he muttered.

Tiana snorted, probably amused by his tone.

"That's fair. Our schedule changed, so that's why we are doing this now." Ioane gave Kas a sympathetic smile. Sun had heard everyone who worked in the lab treated the boy with affection because he was a friendly boy who was eager to please but not a pushover. Whatever his core personality, he had been raised by decent, good-hearted parents who loved him for who he was and not for who he might be. A quality conspicuously lacking in Sun's own upbringing. So be it, as Tiana would say.

The boy groaned under his breath. As if ripping off a wound plaster, he tugged off his knit cap and liner. He had no hair, not even tufts. At first glance the back of his head looked smooth, but then its contours revealed the lines of a half-hidden face sunk deep in what was slumber or unconsciousness, no one was quite sure.

Hanifa settled the band sideways over Kas's head to leave both front and back face clear. After she'd attached a series of electrodes, she retreated behind a screen.

Ioane rested a hand on Kas's right upper. Gave an encouraging nod.

The boy shut his eyes. He sat tense in every muscle, braced for an attack.

After a stretch of silence, the flat sketch of a face on the back of his head shifted infinitesimally. The closed eyes wiggled. The mouth parted into two thin lips and a faint sound came out. *Pah. Pah.* A string of whispery sounds followed, with a rhythm like words although in no language Sun had ever heard. The eyes opened, slits shifting back and forth as would a person caught between enemies, trying to gauge who was going to strike first. All the face could see was a wall, currently blank.

"What does it wake up from?" Sun mused. "When the cap seals it away, is it still aware of itself? Has it lived most of its existence as if in a sensory deprivation prison?"

Tiana turned those spectacular eyes on Sun, mouth twisting into a grimace. "Are you criticizing my parents for protecting Kas?"

Sun quirked an eyebrow. Tiana rarely revealed anger so openly. "Not at all. Under the circumstances, knowing the Phene would have taken any steps to kidnap him if they could find him, most parents would have done the same. Unless they believed it was for the best to hand their child over to the Council. Since they didn't, they did what they could. That doesn't change the situation for the Rider, does it?"

"The creature's a parasite. I don't feel any sympathy for it. Do you?"

"In a way the Rider has been in a prison for its entire existence."

"I wish Kas had been born as a normal boy. I'd gouge out that parasite if I could."

Ioane gave a hand sign for Kas to start.

Kas said, "Are you there?"

"Pah. Pah."

Was it playing a game with them? Rejecting their overtures? Rendered mentally deficient because of the long years of mental and psychological darkness it had endured? What was a Rider anyway? How did it develop? Like any child, did it need learning and seasoning? Or was it already a personality with knowledge and skills siphoned off from whatever Council-joined thoughts Riders might share?

Sun had only interacted with the captured adult Rider three times, all briefly, but the difference between that Rider and this one was shocking.

"Queen-Marshal Sun has asked us to show you slides," said the tutor. "Would you like that?"

"Nuh. Nah. Peh. Bah."

Was it babbling like an infant who didn't yet speak a language? Was it mocking them with nonsense? Sun shifted uncomfortably in her seat. Riders felt like abominations to her. Yet they were also miraculous. And she felt sympathy for the Rider's plight, even as she prolonged it. What had her mother said so long ago when they'd discussed why to avoid actions that were legally condemned as war crimes? Sun had said, because they were wrong. Eirene had answered, *But I'd do it, if I thought it would work.*

It was a stark and honest assessment by a woman who had stopped at nothing to gain power for Chaonia. Maybe Sun wasn't so different from her mother as she had often told herself she was. In some ways it was a sobering thought when she had worked so hard to define herself as her own person, and yet she could not help but compare herself to the most successful individual she had ever known, Chaonia's beloved Eirene.

The wall tuned to an image of the floating concourse aloft above Axiom Prime.

"Can you share the image you are seeing with K?" said the tutor.

"Oo. Oo."

Kas closed his eyes, face squeezing in concentration. "The floating concourse."

The image changed to a view of the Processional Way on Anchor Prime.

"The Processional Way."

The plain of triple-headed Cyclops in Auger System, which Kas dutifully repeated. According to the reports Sun had read, this was a standard sequence.

An image of a Phene dreadnought.

The boy opened his eyes. "Nothing. Just like a gray screen."

"Can you work with us?" said the tutor in a kind voice. "Once we master this sequence we can move on to another batch of images."

A full minute ticked past.

Kas grabbed for the knit cap. "It's refusing, just to be a jerk."

From beyond the screen Hanifa said, "Patience, Kas. It may be Qíshì doesn't have enough context to share it with you."

"What does 'not enough context' mean?" the boy asked sullenly.

"They might not know what it is. We don't know how the process works on the other side, do we? Let's continue with familiar images and get back on track."

Sun said, "Did the Rider give themself the name Qíshì?"

"We came up with the name," said Tech One, the former banner soldier. "We have to call them something. Whatever a riding consciousness is, this individual has sapience even if we don't understand what they are."

Beside Sun, Tiana shifted restlessly, rubbing a shoulder.

A lush photo of a bamboo forest filled the wall for thirty seconds before being replaced by a view of the famous horned lighthouse on Sogdia Limit.

"Bamboo forest. Lighthouse with horns." Kas sounded bored.

A new image appeared on the wall, a column of loading cranes like the skeletons of big dinosaurs lined up within a vast tubular scaffolding. The habitat was so large that merchant vessels were moored inside it, as along docks. Where the habitat curved out of the field of view, the docklands gave way to industrial wasteland. There was nothing green anywhere, odd on a habitat. Grim and unwelcoming.

"Brachiosaurus Landing, that's what I call this one," said Kas jokingly. Then he blinked several times and his mouth dropped open in surprise. "Wait? What? Tranquility Harbor? Is this place called Tranquility Harbor?"

Ioane leaned forward with excitement. The two technicians looked at each other with raised eyebrows.

"Is this a new image for the Rider?" Sun asked.

"Knowing the name is what's new," said Tech One. "Which means a new connection has happened between Kas and Qíshì."

Tiana rose. "My apologies. I don't have the heart to watch any more of this."

Sun signed permission for her to leave.

After Tiana was gone, Sun rested her chin on her hands. As images appeared and vanished on the wall, the Rider stared as if starving. Devouring a long-denied feast. Desperation made any creature vulnerable and dangerous.

Kas's Rider was a danger to her, she knew that. Not because it—they—Qíshì—might betray her movements to the Rider Council, although that possibility had to be guarded against. But because Qíshì had never been given a reason to be loyal to Chaonia. How could she persuade the Rider? Was there anything Qíshì wanted?

She tapped her comms. "Isis."

"Your Highness." The colonel's response flashed immediately into her network. "Princess Metis has secure quarters on the *Keoe* and seems to have weathered the voyage well enough. She keeps asking for sun, and no one is sure if she means the light of a star, or you."

"I'll come over to greet her. I want you and Eleuterio to supervise the preparation of a chamber suitable for Metis within the lab complex. Put the room adjacent to Kaspar's suite. I want to introduce her to the Rider."

"Your Highness, is that wise?"

"I don't know if it's wise. It's a hunch."

"If the Rider Council sees Princess Metis, won't they know where Kaspar is? Kiran Seth may have revealed her existence to the Phene."

"Even if he did, he would have told them Metis is imprisoned in Lee House, because that's where he thinks she is. It's no risk to this expedition."

"The risk is that the Rider Council will know you have a Rider."

"I disagree. The risk is that this Rider might already hate its host and its jailers. I do not fault Kaspar's parents, but in protecting their son they may have driven the Rider into the arms of the Council beyond our ability to persuade it of our goodwill. Metis has a kind and harmless soul. She could be the means to befriend this entity."

"Do you think Riders are human?"

Sun cocked her head, considering the question. "In the days of the Celestial Empire, it is said different people in different lands claimed others were not as human as they were themselves. If a mind exists in the human brain, how is it not human?"

"They're parasites."

"You aren't the first to say so. But if a host takes no obvious harm from their presence, then can they truly be described as parasites? What if they are symbionts? Or a mutation that arose at random from the genengineering work the Phene did on themselves? Surely we can as easily posit that the Rider is as much a part of Kaspar's mind and body as is Kaspar himself. Even if the boy wishes it were not, there is no way to disentangle the two. It may seem a Rider is a mind apart from a body but, in every case, each Rider is unified with a body. The issue isn't the Rider. The issue is the Council's hoarding of resources, the way it coerces any person born with the mutation to serve it whether it wishes to or not."

"A compassionate view, Your Highness."

"Riders are not monsters."

"Your Highness." Isis's bland reply was all the disagreement she was willing to offer.

"Just because they scare us doesn't make them monsters. Even all of that is beside the point. The Riders are an advantage beyond compare. That's what matters."

In the room beyond, Kas still had his eyes closed. His features twitched as he concentrated. Sun thought he was becoming interested despite himself as the parade of images continued and, one by one, he with his face turned away from the wall could describe what his Riding face was seeing.

You're Not Supposed to Know This

Like many in-system freighters, *Overly Devoted* had a starscape lounge with a view window. The compartment provided a place for off-duty crew to relax, game, sing, recite, and meditate during the long stretches of in-system travel by torch drive.

At the moment, everyone was at duty stations, leaving Apama and Teegee alone in the lounge. They stood side by side at the window, marveling at the view of the waiting Titan. Arriving through the beacon at Nusrat Quince, the freighter had detached from the Remora-class ship that hauled them through the beacon from Rosetta System and had proceeded in a loose caravan with thirty-six independent freighters and three hired corsairs to Nusrat's heliopause. The little fleet had stayed on high alert because this was territory where raiders and brigands might show up, but the outward journey had been mercifully uneventful. Now here they were, about to join the tow chain of an Argosy Titan for the first of four knnu hops on their roundabout journey to T-Harbor.

"That's really just a mini-Titan," said Apama.

"*Mini?*" Teegee kept turning her head to give each of her faces time to look.

"The motherships are a lot bigger. They can tow a thousand ships, like in the ancient poem. So yeah, compared to that, sure. But a mini-Titan is about four times bigger than the biggest dreadnought. That's why we had to have ten dreadnoughts fitted with knnu drives to make the raid on Molossia, because they could only each haul about sixty to eighty ships. Even that was a risk because dreadnoughts aren't built for knnu drives. But it worked. I mean, except for the battle part." She rubbed her eyes, wondering if she would ever see any of her compatriots again. They might have fought and died in the battle of Karnos and she'd never have known.

Teegee used the zoom panel to get a closer look at the Titan's tow chain. Ships were being grappled in and fixed into place at one-klick intervals along the rigid scaffolding that trailed behind the huge ship. There were five "chains," and the incoming freighters were directed to specific positions to keep their weight and number balanced. It was an intriguing sight, like a monstrous jellyfish collecting little fish along its tentacles. Beyond the Titan's massive bulk, Nusrat's star shone, so distant she could look directly at it.

"Why don't they just hook up the Remora we came in with all the freighters already docked inside?" Gee asked. "Wouldn't that be more efficient?"

"But less profitable, because each system the caravan goes through wants a cut. So the freight lines deal with a different entity at each stage. They hire a local corsair escort. This Argosy will convey us to Orfeo System, where we'll pay a Remora to haul us through a beacon to . . . I can't pronounce that . . . and from there to Segovia System, where there's another gap and we'll pick up another Argosy. But locals wanting their piece of the pie isn't the only reason. A knnu drive creates what's called the Weinstein bubble. The bubble has to stay stable, so you'd need a Remora on each chain to keep the mass in balance. There's just not enough traffic out here to support that many ships. Nobody's going to haul rocks to an asteroid belt, right?"

"We don't learn much about things outside the empire," remarked Gee in the tone of a teenager who has only recently realized how much the adults are keeping from them.

A warning chime alerted Apama that someone was keying the entry code into the panel outside. "Hood up."

The girl tugged up the hood to cover Tee's face. Aunt Effie might trust Hector for old times' sake, but the bounty for a captured Rider was staggeringly high. Dunya had mentioned the girl had terrible burn scars on the back of her head from a recent accident and needed a change of scene to work through the trauma. So far the ruse was working: the freighter's crew treated her kindly and didn't remark on her shyness.

The door slid open and the freighter's junior crew member came in. She was barely older than Teegee but had the confident sheen of a kid who grew up working in the family business from a young age.

"Hey, Chenoa," said Gee with a blush.

Despite only having two arms, Chenoa was a pretty young woman who had a flirtatious grin that she had tried without success on Apama, although Apama had put money down against Gurak that the flirting was going to work on 'Lito. "Hey, yourself. This is your first knnu passage, right, Gee?"

"Uh. Yeah."

Chenoa waved them back from the window as she pressed a few buttons and released a bar. "Time to seal this window. I get all the fun jobs."

"We don't get to look out when we're inside the bubble?" Gee asked.

"There's nothing to see out there except oblivion. You know what I heard?" Chenoa leaned closer, confidentially. Gee's blush deepened. Oh dear. "People who stare into knnu space go insane. Except Navigators."

"R-really?"

Chenoa glanced at Apama, who couldn't decide whether to laugh or scold. "Well, it's a rumor. No one knows, because every freighter seals off its windows. It's bad luck to leave them open. None of us ever come in here during knnu passage."

"Is that bad luck too?" Apama asked.

"No. Family custom in our case, I guess. Every ship has its weird habits. When we have passengers, they use it if they want. I mean, your team could." A blank wall rolled across the view window, and the compartment abruptly felt smaller and yet more secure. "You have to admit it's kind of creepy, if you think about what is lying on the other side of the bulkhead that you could see if you accidentally opened the seal. I mean, if you get cut from the tow chain, you'll be lost in space forever."

Apama snorted. "Technically you'll just be very far away from anywhere else with only a torch drive but . . . never mind."

"Yeah, see, you'd be dead either way. Might be better to go insane." Chenoa waggled her shapely eyebrows, which were dyed a neon gold. Her hair was sculpted in a garish tricolor mo-wave, and her jumpsuit fit too tightly, but her choice of presentation wasn't any of Apama's business. "Gotta run. See you around, haha, as if we can go anywhere once we're locked into the chain."

Chenoa went out. As soon as the door shut, Teegee pulled back her hood.

"Do you think it's true about insanity and oblivion?" Tee whispered.

Gee said, "Were you allowed to look onto space when you went with the Styraconyx Fleet?"

"No. I would have, though, just to know I'd stared oblivion in the face and oblivion had stared back."

Teegee grinned. "You would, wouldn't you? I would, too! We could sneak a look, couldn't we?"

"Oh no, never ever, not if opening the seal goes against shipboard superstition. But I'll ask Dunya to request permission from the captain for the security team to use the lounge while in transit."

In other words, by the second day of a projected forty-two-day knnu transit, Teegee was spending most of her off-duty hours in the lounge.

She and Apama were currently alone there. The girl sprawled along the topography of pillows she'd slung on the floor, hoodie peeled down. Both her faces were watching a racy theatrical drama from a hundred years ago in which everyone talked at an old-fashioned clip with strangely measured phrases and a lot more skin showing than in any of today's more buttoned-up popular dramas.

Apama had her tablet on her lap, open to an unclassified Phene military map, which she was comparing to the manifest the security team had been given by the freighter's captain. The silence was broken only by dialogue from the drama. The sound cut off abruptly, and the girl sat up.

A furtiveness in her expression caught Apama's attention. "What is it?"

Gee chewed on her lower lip. Tee's eyes shifted back and forth as if she were double-checking to make sure no one else was in the compartment. But weren't other Riders always with a Rider? She scooted toward Apama as if to take hold of her arm but halted. Shrugged her shoulders self-consciously.

"Have you had sex?"

Apama blinked. Yet how was the question surprising? Teegee was sixteen.

"Yes, I have. Although it is a personal question to ask someone."

"Do you . . . do you masturbate?"

Apama felt her cheeks grow warm, as ridiculous as it was for her to get embarrassed about such an ordinary human act.

"I'm sorry," said Teegee, and shifted back.

"No. No. It's fine. It's just . . . it's not the question I was expecting, or even any question about . . ." Saints, now she felt awful, because she remembered being this age. Surely it was worse for a young Rider raised in the constantly supervised confines of the creche. "Don't they talk to you about sexuality?"

Gee snorted. "I bet you would enjoy it if a physician gave a lecture about sexual positions and behavior, and then asked everyone to fill in a survey about how often they touch themselves. Because if your Rider is awake then everyone will participate with you if you're, you know . . ." She waved her lower arms as she blushed.

Apama closed her tablet. "Yeah. I can see how that would be off-putting."

The girl scooted closer again. "How did you find out? About sex?"

"You mean besides from boring school lectures and annoying parent lectures?"

"Yeah."

It took a lot to drive a teen to ask this question of someone not in their age cohort. Apama had to model sharing and trust. Anything else would be unkind to this child whose life had been regimented to a degree Apama couldn't fathom. Yet anything she said would mean telling all the Riders who chose to listen in. But surely since Teegee had made herself vulnerable, the decision had to be for her.

Maybe that was why her mom liked Dasa and gave *him* respect. Why, when she had worked for the Council, Mom had shown all the Riders who had sex with her that same respect, had looked them in the eye, even though looking exposed her.

Teegee grasped Apama's wrist. In a whisper, Tee said, "They can't hear me."

"What?"

Gee murmured, "You're not supposed to know this. We didn't even believe it was true until we found out yesterday for sure."

"That what is true?"

She turned her head so Apama looked at the Rider's sketch of a face. Tee's visage was similar in some ways to Zakurru, Baragesi, and the others, but after so many days in proximity, Apama knew she would recognize the dissimilarities that made Tee an individual, not a collective. Something sweeter, shyer, reluctant, and brave.

"The bubble is like a blanket of silence thrown over me. I've never been alone before. I mean, I'm never alone because I'm always with Gee. And there are ways to close doors to all the radiance so it doesn't crowd me. That takes years of practice. But it's just me here, right now."

The *radiance*? She let that go for another time. "You're saying Riders can't communicate with a Rider who is inside a Weinstein bubble?"

Teegee said nothing. Silence is assent.

"But Zakurru went on the Styraconyx campaign . . ." She pressed her uppers against her cheeks, thinking it over. "That doesn't mean he was necessarily communicating with other Riders while the fleet was under knnu drive. It just means he could communicate as soon as we transitioned out of the bubble at the heliopause of Molossia System. That would be plenty of time to coordinate with the Tanarctus Fleet coming from Karnos."

Teegee's fingers tightened on Apama's hand. "Do you see why I'm asking now?"

Apama whistled. "Wow. *Wow*. Okay, listen. I completely get why you're asking now. I'll make you a deal. For every question you ask, I get to ask one of you."

Both girls' eyes flickered. If they'd been separate people in separate bodies, they'd have exchanged glances like people do who speak without words, knowing each other that well. How unlike Dasa and Zakurru they were, not servant and master. Even Gil and Baragesi acted more like associates who shared a body but with Baragesi the benevolent boss.

Gee said, "Deal."

Tee said, "Deal."

"Okay. No getting offended at questions. None of us have to answer if we don't want to or if the answer would violate ethics or security protocol. You go first."

"How old were you when you did it the first time?"

"Seventeen."

"Was it . . . nice?"

Apama chuckled. "Sure. It felt good physically. But she wasn't my big crush or anything. I was mostly focused on getting to flight school. That's two. My turn. Do you ever get any privacy? I mean, in your life in the creche."

"We all share a barracks room. But there aren't that many of us. Six in my age cohort. And we are the largest of the four youth cohorts right now."

"How are the age cohorts divided? If you're allowed to say." In a year living with her sire she'd not been allowed to learn anything about the creches.

"Newborn through six. Seven to twelve. Thirteen to seventeen or eighteen, depending on when you graduate to roamer, which starts at about eighteen and ends when you become a full member of the Council. Are you glad you found out who your sire is?"

"No."

The girl flinched as if she'd been rebuked.

"I mean, yes, because it meant meeting you, Teegee."

"You don't have to say that."

"I mean it." She grasped Teegee's right hands with her lefts. "I really do mean it about meeting you. It's only . . ." Could he really not hear? The idea that Teegee was playing a deep game wouldn't wash. "I don't like Zakurru much and I don't think Dasa likes me. Are you ever curious about your birth family? Do they tell you anything?"

Teegee gave a big sigh and shook out of Apama's hands. "No. The records are sealed. I checked. Also it's rude to ask. It's unfair to people who couldn't keep us, or who wouldn't have wanted to keep us."

"The Council changed all that. Surely you could ask now."

"The rules changed for the adults. Not for the creche. Can we get back to sex? We may never have another chance like this in our lives. I thought maybe . . ."

Oh saints. Here it came.

"Carmelito's not that old. His body is really hot."

"Yes, we have indeed all been invited to admire his body in the showers and at shift change. I mean, nudity is commonplace in military barracks. That's not the issue."

"Is it wrong I think he's attractive?"

"Of course it isn't. He's kind of a dick, and he has a dick, as we've all noticed. But don't forget that like Gurak and the others he's putting his life on the line to save you. Loyalty and courage is also an attractive quality."

"He is kind of old. I asked him once and he's almost twenty-one."

Arthas give her strength. This was like trying to choose your target at the same time you were spinning out of range of a hundred missiles headed your way. "I don't have anything against age differences once people are adults, but you are still underage and that makes 'Lito a little old for you."

"You said you were seventeen when you first did it. I turned seventeen in Anchor years a few days ago."

"You didn't tell us!"

"People make a big deal of age when one minute you can be underage and the next minute an adult. I communicate across impossible distances. The empire rests on Rider shoulders. I barely escaped a battle. And had to send a message to a special forces unit that probably resulted in the death of a Rider. Of Anchi. I know her! Knew her. But I'm too young to be responsible for my sexuality?"

Apama pressed the heel of a hand to her forehead. "Don't you have any way to block people out or, I don't know, close the curtains for an hour?"

"First you have to learn to see into the radiance. After you learn how to see, it fills your head all the time. Eventually most of us can learn how to politely look away, but it's harder and never opaque because it is so complicated."

"I'll bet."

"I mean, my unusually precocious skill is politely looking away."

"Is it? Huh. It makes sense. You have a lot of discipline and control."

The girls blushed. "Thank you. We can't say more. Except there are some who can never look away. I feel bad for them."

Apama thought about her mom's experience. "Don't they tell you about the workers who, uh, service Riders?"

"You have to be on your first official roamer tour before it's allowed. The service workers are supposed to be secret. How do you know about them?"

Whew. Did she want to go there, or not? Sometimes you had to make the leap.

"My mom was one. That's how I was conceived."

A tense silence dropped. Was the girl embarrassed for her? Scornful? Shocked? Teegee traced a pattern like a writing script on her knee, then looked up.

"What's it like? Having a mom?"

"Oh, honey."

Gee slumped. Tee's eyes narrowed to slits, not quite shuttered.

"Listen, listen." Apama grasped hands so all connected, linking them as family. "I have a great mom and she's great and she cares about me and looks out for me and annoys me and I can tell her anything I want her to know except once I became an adult and left home I wouldn't be telling her about who I had sex with even if she butts her head into my business and asks sometimes. But the point is, I'm fortunate. Not everyone is fortunate with their blood relatives. You're not alone in that. Also, you have me now, like finding . . ."

"A sister?"

"Yeah. Your big sister. Which is why I can boss you around. And hear your secrets. If you want to tell them to me."

"Is it weird I want to try sex right now because none of them"—she waved an upper toward the ceiling—"can possibly know?"

"It isn't weird at all. It's totally normal." It was so unfair to these children, but she couldn't say that. And she just could not bring herself to put a roadblock in the way of what might be Teegee's only chance to explore what it meant to be a sexual being without hundreds of Riders peeping over her shoulder.

"Do you think 'Lito would even want to?"

"What do you mean?"

"Am I pretty enough? And don't say I am, because either I am or you're lying to make me feel better."

Apama smiled wryly. "Intimacy makes you vulnerable to rejection. It takes courage."

"There's also Chenoa." Gee tugged on an ear, a self-conscious gesture she'd not made before. "I kind of like both Chenoa and 'Lito."

"The problem with Chenoa is she's freighter crew and they don't know and can't know. Sex is close. We can't risk her finding out what you are. If she did, even if you swore her to silence she'd probably tell her crew, because her crew is her family."

"I understand. She sure is hot though . . . don't you think?"

It was exactly the kind of question a young person unsure of their budding sexuality would ask. Is my taste normal? Am I okay? "She is definitely hot even if she does only have two arms. That limits your options."

"Oh. Oh! I see. I suppose it would."

Carmelito had the sort of personality that craved attention but he was loyal to the clan and a responsible worker, never skiving off his shifts or taking shortcuts on his chores to save time. He was vain enough to want to be known as someone who gave as much pleasure as he received. Would he break a young woman's heart or could he treat Teegee without condescension? Would he feel obliged to agree even if he didn't really want to? Teegee wasn't wrong about the slippery slide of age, of attraction. She wasn't wrong about the weight of empire on her shoulders.

Apama released her hands. Of course the words that popped out of her mouth were the very ones her own mother had once said to a sulking, reluctant daughter who certainly didn't want or need a tedious sermon about things she already knew from her wise and worldly adolescent friends. "Okay, Teegee. Here comes the annoying but necessary lecture about respect for and recognition of any problematic aspects of the situation as well as the importance of mutual consent."

Teegee leaned toward her with twinned smiles both nervous and eager. "Okay."

58

A Speech in a Briefing Room on a Captured Phene Dreadnought

The high command awaited Sun in a briefing room on the captured Phene dreadnought. The ship's name translated as *Formidable Bull* or *Strong Bull* depending on who you asked. A vivid depiction of this horned mythological creature from the Celestial Empire adorned the bulkhead behind the head seat at the table. As Sun entered, she walked toward the image. A painted individual was grappling with the beast's horns while a second vaulted over its back and a third was poised behind its hind legs to catch the vaulter. What danger, beauty, and skill! In the ancient Celestial Empire lived bold and honorable people who dared to grab fate by the horns. What might kill you also gave you wings if you confronted it. No one could win who cowered on the sidelines when the formidable bull charged onto the court.

She stood poised on a cusp. She could consolidate Chaonia's hold on the Karnos and Hatti territories, confirm the treaties that cowed the Yele League and the Hesjan cartels, and return to the palace on Argos to rule the stable queendom as would a steward for its future.

Or she could grapple and leap.

In Chaonia the high command met at an oval strategos table, a nod to the republic's principle of equality of citizens. The empire chose a more hierarchical format for its meetings, reflecting its contentious history of factional disputes. She reached the head chair and gestured for those in attendance to sit, preferring to stand as she considered her audience.

Her Companions, except James and Razin, currently seconded to other missions.

All the marshals who had fought in the recent battle, with the exception of Crane Marshal Qìngzhī Bō, left in charge of the Karnos System garrison fleet. Officers like Angharad Black who she had promoted to fill marshalships emptied by death or by the departure of veterans she had retired from the front lines and assigned to support duties. Other notable ship and division commanders.

Of Eirene's Companions, only Zàofù Samtarras and Grace Nazir were present now that Norioghene Hope and Nà Bō were dead and Precious Jīn sent off to meet with the banners. Tomyris Vata had been assigned full oversight of Kanesh and the Hatti territories with their crucial resource and transport concerns, and Sun had neutralized Marduk Lee by making him governor of Lee House and regent of Chaonia in her absence.

The path may be clear to those scouting from atop the promontory that overlooks the horizon of what can become. But clarity of vision is not enough. The skill to fight is not enough. Longing for a greater battle is not enough. No one in Chaonia succeeds alone. Like the athletes painted onto the bulkhead behind her, the behemoth can only be surmounted by a team working together, in concert and with a full measure of will. They must want it, not begrudge it, not be forced to it.

Her audience waited. Her Companions knew what she was going to say. Others suspected. Of the rest, they would soon understand. The ones who launch into the most magnificent storm will be gilded with the most brilliant sheen of honor. Anyway, what is war if not a gamble? What is destiny, if the hazard does not match the reward?

Wasps hovered to record it all.

"We stand today on a dreadnought whose guns and lancers have taken countless Chaonian lives. This fight was begun by the empire generations ago when they invaded Chaonian space. When they pressed their boots on our backs. It has been the work of many years and every citizen to reach this day. All the territories who owe allegiance to the dynasts of Karnos System are liberated. This is the message I send to the empire: You are done here. You will not come back."

She paused to give the words time to soak in.

Zàofù had the right to speak without being called on. He rose and of course she gave way to his seniority and worthy reputation. "This is the culmination of Eirene's great strategy, honed and wielded over twenty years. You have done well, Sun. It is time to garrison Karnos and return to Chaonia to enjoy the fruits of our triumph."

Spoken like the old man he was. But she could not say that aloud!

"Is this a triumph, Marshal?" She gestured a signal.

A light came on behind her, a virtual column in the form of a casualty list. Names fell past images of hulked ships trailing wakes of vented wreckage. The list of known dead was long and, as death must be, always shocking. Marshal the Honorable Nà Bō. Lance Corporal Sukja Rèn Alcotai. Captain the Honorable Linn Ei of the *Vermilion*. The final known visual of the shattered *Vermilion*, of whom 158 out of a crew of 737 had survived.

"We defeated the Phene in Karnos. We are still analyzing the damage we did to them. By all accounts we hurt them badly. But did we hurt them badly enough? Do you want to give the empire time to rebuild and rearm? They gave us time, after our fleets were battered at Molossia. Had they pressed their advantage we would have struggled to defeat them, although I never doubt our fleets will defeat any enemy who attempts to stand against us. Shouldn't their delay be a warning? To the Phene, the Karnos region is merely conquered territory, not the imperial Phene heartland. Have any of you forgotten they are more populous, richer, armed with resources and wealth we can only dream of? We can't afford to relax. We must press on while they are destabilized and on the run."

"Press on where?" Grace Nazir demanded, secure in his status as one of Eirene's legendary spears. "The Phene have mined both Sleepless and Windworn Beacons. The lesson of the *Vermilion* is we will be wasting ourselves by throwing our ships against an impenetrable wall."

"That is correct." Zàofù broke in as if he had been about to say the same thing and wanted to make sure everyone knew it. "Even if we are able to break past the mines and accept the catastrophic losses it would entail, there is no way to pursue. According to our best maps of imperial Phene territory, both those beacon routes lead through a series of beacons to Anchor System. We would be forced into a funnel, a corridor of deadly firepower down one beacon after the next, concentrated through dreadnoughts and heavy cruisers. Even if we defeat them at Windworn and Sleepless, they'll mine each system as they leave it behind. There's no path to victory."

Sun gestured agreement. "That's right. There's no path to victory through meeting them head on, on their terms and on their ground. But do we mean to accept this temporary stalemate? Are we really going to let them block the trade that is the lifeblood of Karnos? Won't our allies decide we are worse than the Phene if we destroy their prosperity? Blocking beacons is an act of war! We can all agree about that."

Heads nodded around the table, mostly among the younger officers but a few of the veterans as well.

"That isn't all. Our treasury needs replenishing. The empire has taken enough from us. It is time for us to take from them what they stole generations ago: our treasury, our people, our hopes for a peaceful future! And what about my mother? Do we mean to allow the Phene to get away with her murder?"

Grace Nazir jumped up. "Eirene's murder was not a political act by a foreign power. It was the act of a woman who held a personal grudge."

There was the opening Sun had hoped for, a gap in the line.

"Was it also a personal grudge that a seer of Iros tried to murder me on Kanesh's Esplanade? That Command Orbital Station Destined Triumph was attacked by Phene mercenaries during our peaceful celebrations? Chaonia's most valuable prisoner of war murdered in front of our eyes? What an insult to us!"

Sun scanned their faces, seeking resistance, doubt, ambivalence, and the ardent brightness of those who were already with her. With a grimace of frustration Grace sat, giving way.

Good.

"We will never be at peace as long as the Phene can attack us. We will never be at peace as long as the Yele League can send one envoy to sweet-talk us while my mother's own spouse Baron Voy deserts Chaonia to bargain with the Rider Council on behalf of the League. We will never be at peace as long as we pretend a bigger, stronger enemy whose fleets can communicate across any vast distance of space instantaneously won't strike back. An enemy, need I remind you, willing to murder one of their own Riders to make sure none ever fall into our hands."

"The truth of your words does not change the reality," said Zàofù. "The Phene have blocked the only routes into the empire. Even were we strong enough, we can't get there from here."

"Can't we?"

She nodded at Persephone, standing unobtrusively at the back. Above the table, a three-dimensional map of the local belt of stars spun into focus.

"The heart of Lady Chaos is a knot. But there are times when what we perceive as a knot is easily unraveled. We need only remove the linchpin that secures us to the wheel of rote decision making. We are only confined to obvious solutions if we refuse to seek out different ones."

Zàofù shook his head. "You said yourself we don't have the Phene ability to communicate instantaneously. That limits our options. I don't make the rules that govern the universe. I merely abide by what can't be changed."

"That is what I would say if I were you, Marshal. But I am Sun. I don't see what can't be changed. I see a chance to make new rules. Do you know why I brought so many Chaonian ships to Hellion Terminus?"

"Because we had hoped to capture Phene vessels and troops. But their admiral arranged for transit passage with the Ousoos Argosy."

Around the room, people nodded in resigned frustration. Sun waited for the restless discontent to ripple through the gathering and for stillness to settle. Once their attention returned to her, she continued.

"What if I told you the heart of Lady Chaos is a complex interweaving of beacon routes, knnu routes, and the gaps created by the collapse of the Apsaras Convergence eight hundred years ago? For example, let us consider Karnos System, a seven-beacon hydra system. In the collapse it lost only one of its beacons. Thus it remains a crucial crossroads system with multiple strategic routes."

She guided them through the map.

"One beacon leads to Aspera System and thence to Troia and onward to our beloved Republic of Chaonia. As we have discussed, two routes lead through Sleepless and Windworn respectively into the heartland of the empire. Two routes lead via Na Iri and Tarsa respectively into the Hatti territories. These routes link inward to Kanesh and outward into Hesjan-controlled regions and the Skuda reaches. Finally, Karnos's sixth working beacon has dropped us here, into Hellion System, which was once a janus system and is now a terminus. But Hellion is not a dead end. It is a back door. This back door leads through the Trinity Coalition and connects to the Yele League in one direction and to the empire via Mishirru in another."

She looked toward Zàofù, expecting the objection to come from him, but his thoughtful expression surprised her. He was chewing things over in his head, too canny not to start making the connections.

It was Grace Nazir who sighed with the exasperation of a veteran forced to hear the reckless ideas of an ignorant newcomer. He was known as more of a blunt-force instrument than a sophisticated strategist. "The nature of the Trinity Coalition makes it unsuitable for campaigns, if that's what you're suggesting. It's all very well that the three Trinity systems are linked by beacons to each other. But to get to any one of them you have to make a knnu passage. It takes too long, it's slow, clumsy, and would be ruinously expensive for a military force. Beyond all that, any attack run through Trinity can only happen with the agreement and support of the Ousoos Argosy, which is under the command of the Karsh and her sister rulers."

"The Karsh is already cooperating with the Phene."

"For payment!" objected Grace. "That's a commercial transaction."

"The Karsh claims it is a commercial transaction as a smokescreen, but by every strategic and political measure it is an alliance by Trinity with the empire. They are aiding and abetting our enemy because it profits them to do so, and because they think we can't stop them."

Heads nodded all around. This, at least, everyone could agree on.

She went on. "I sent all of you a clip recorded on the Titan. You have seen the defiance and contempt with which my own honorable Companions were treated by the Karsh not thirty hours ago. She made it clear Trinity is nothing more than a criminal enterprise with no respect for justice or universal law. If we don't close this back door, the Phene will pay whatever it takes to the Trinity to let them use this route to attack us. And we won't be able to match their price."

Grace tugged at his lower lip as his brow creased.

"It's not just our control of Karnos at risk. With the cooperation of the Trinity, the Phene can transit fleets through Trinity into the League. With the seers of Iros egging them on and Baron Voy negotiating for a new understanding between the League and the Council, they will be able to sway the League to their side. We all know it's a short and easy three-beacons hop from Yele System to Chaonia. Imagine the Phene and the Yele raising common cause against our home worlds."

In an excess of drama, Beau had recommended little flashes of light at this point in the speech, centered around Chaonia, Molossia, and Thesprotis Systems, as if planets were exploding. Persephone and Makinde had objected and been overruled. Sun watched the officers wince as each flash went off. In that moment, each was seeing their own household or favorite neighborhood noodle shop die.

"Even that threat is not all. Because while we may have placed a few strategic mines at Windworn and Sleepless Beacons merely as self-defense, we can't be sure the enemy won't attack through those beacons anyway. We will have no way of knowing when they destroy their own minefields and decide to punch through into Karnos in concert with an attack via Trinity, because they can coordinate it all with their Riders. Because they can take the losses and keep more coming. In a war of attrition we will win every battle and ultimately lose the war."

Zàofù had started tapping his fingers onto the table's surface, recording numbers into his personal network. He wasn't ignoring her. Far from it; he was calculating, eyes narrowed. Grace crossed his arms but didn't speak.

Sun said, "And that's still not even all the options open to them."

Her sip of water was timed to get everyone on the edge of their seats.

"Because there is *also* a long-shot route that the Honorable Persephone Lee has identified. It is a long-distance trade route that runs from Karnos System along the outer rim of beacon space via four or five short-haul knnu gaps and some short beacon connections all the way to a system known as Tranquility Harbor. Yes, it's an unlikely scenario. It's a very long journey that could take as much as two years for transit time, not to mention the expense, the knnu gaps to be negotiated, and the ever-present risk of raids by unaffiliated cartels and

Skuda brigands. But what does the empire have, if not time, wealth, numbers, and Riders to connect them all? A Phene fleet can sail at any time from their own Tranquility Harbor and, in combination with fleets running through the Trinity Coalition, can attack our home systems from multiple directions. Which is exactly why my mother took control of the Hatti region to begin with. To protect Chaonia."

As Sun spoke, Persephone used a pointer to trace the routes and stars, the main paths and the vulnerable back doors.

"Our fleets are the best, but on how many fronts can we realistically fight with our smaller numbers? We remain surrounded. Beset from all sides."

Now her mouth genuinely was parched. As the map faded from view, she took a long swallow of the iced lychee tea Eleuterio had set beside the glass of water. Following her lead, officers sipped at their own tea. She set down her cup.

"In the wake of all this information, let us consider the name Kiran Seth. He is a seer of Iros who is the husband of Eirene's murderer as well as a man who was given access to much of Lee House's security apparatus. Some of you know him. What you don't know is that he personally murdered my bodyguard Octavian on the day of my blessed mother's wedding banquet."

A murmur rushed through the room like a gust of wind through trees.

"He fled Argos on the same day one of Chaonia Prime's industrial parks was hit by Phene special forces. A raid based on information he gave to the Phene. That raid might as well have been a fist up our asses."

Crudeness was Eirene's style so everyone twitched to hear such words from Sun. While they were off-balance, she tossed her grenade.

"Kiran Seth fled to the Phene Empire. For all we know, he's already sold them the secrets of our security apparatus in exchange for asylum. He was seen on Command Orbital Station Destined Triumph not an hour before the banner soldiers attacked the *Banshee*." She nodded toward Alika, still wearing his leg braces. Her own injuries had been infuriatingly debilitating for too many weeks, but the less said of that the better.

"How can we know he was in command of that mission?" asked Grace.

"We had removed all Phene military from the station. Someone had to be present in person to use the compulsion we call the leash to command the banner soldiers. It took many hours of investigation but we traced his movements. We now have a recording of him departing the station on one of the lifepods released at the moment of the attack to confuse our sensors and ships. That lifepod was eventually picked up by what appears to be a long-haul freighter, which dropped through into Hellion System. And that's not the end of his journey."

She waved a hand to bring a new image into focus, one enlarged from Dozer's scope during the meeting with the Karsh. Persephone's algorithm had identified Kiran although he had donned a different style of hair and clothing. "Here he is, on the terrace of the Ousoos Titan when the Karsh insulted my envoys. It's simply not true that the Karsh does not involve herself in political disputes. Why else aid a known fugitive who she claims she has never heard of? Why else aid a criminal who has harmed Chaonian interests multiple times?"

She snapped a finger and the image vanished.

"Consider where we stand now. The Rider Council has only recently undergone some manner of internal upheaval. The imperial fleets have lost two major battles in a row. We've inflicted significant damage and casualties, disrupting years of expertise and experience the Phene cannot quickly reproduce."

Again she studied her audience. All, even Grace Nazir, leaned toward her, awaiting her next words.

"This is what I propose. We attack and take over the Trinity Coalition. By holding Trinity at the same time as we hold Karnos, we cut off the Yele League from the empire and secure both our Yele allies and our own home worlds."

She waited for an objection. This time the silence lasted a full thirty seconds before a grizzled old ship captain glanced first at Grace and then at Zàofù and said, in a low voice, "It's not possible. It can't be done."

"Of course it can be done. Crane Marshal the Honorable Nona Lee has secured the cooperation of her smuggling associates, people she has worked with for thirty years. She's already in transit on board a merchant vessel that's part of the Ousoos tow chain that just left for Tsurru System. Alongside hundreds of Phene military ships, I note. Captain the Honorable Razin Nazir is with her, in command of a group of elite Guards. Nona is well placed by means of her long knowledge of Trinity to locate and uncover the Karsh's physical vulnerabilities. The military attack against local security forces and the retreating Phene is up to us."

"But our ships are stuck here, because we don't have a Titan or a Navigator," said Grace in the tone of a person who has just played his winning move.

Eirene might have gloated for a moment. She could be petty like that. But Sun saw no point when the battle was won.

"We have both. My sister Soaring has arrived in-system with the *Keoe*. As an Argosy Navigator, she can oversee the sixty-day journey it will take to make the knnu passage to Tsurru. The *Keoe* can't tow a thousand ships as a mothership Titan can, but she can tow two hundred and forty vessels. With the way prepared by those I have sent ahead, we will be ready and Trinity will be taken by surprise.

"By the peculiar grace of destiny, we are in the best position possible. We can hide behind our shields. Or we can strike. This opportunity will never come again."

59

The Damning Evidence

The marshals and officers filed out in a buzz of furious commentary.

"Marshal, please remain," she added as Zàofù reached the door, last to leave as if reluctant to let go. To her Companions she said, "Go on. Isis has assignments."

As they left, Tiana entered with a tray of tea, poured it with her usual flair, and offered a cup to the old marshal, who was clearly taken by the cee-cee's skill, grace, and beauty. Sun nodded at her.

"Your Loquaciousness, will there be anything else?" Tiana smiled in the way she had of acknowledging power without submitting to it. It was a rare gift, one Sun respected.

"That's all." After the door shut behind the cee-cee, Sun said, "I've received word that James has boarded. He has something to show us."

As if on cue from Channel Idol, the door opened and James entered with his flatcap perfectly straight on his curls, which meant he was feeling smug. Not that James didn't usually feel smug, but then again, he was good at what he did.

He halted at a respectful distance with a slight bow. "Honored Father."

"James. I was wondering where you had got to, since Sun did not fill me in. You have been separated from the command for quite a long time." Zàofù's side-eye toward Sun was masterful, even annoying, but she let it go.

"James, did you retrieve and deliver the person I requested?" Sun asked.

"Sayre? I did! A strange choice for a cee-cee, but honestly, she's great. You can't put anything over on her. I swear she almost boxed my ears once."

Zàofù looked alarmed. "What individual dared attempt to box your ears?"

"The Honorable Makinde's new cee-cee," said Sun. "I requested her personally."

"She told me about this awesome prank she and a shipmate pulled on Baby Mak."

"I can't wait to hear about it. *Later.* Display the evidence."

"Hold on, hold on, I do not have the hang of Phene networking. It's all physical, like they don't trust the cloud. Not that they're wrong about that, on security terms."

While he talked, he set a cube on the table in order to project a portable strategos field. He fiddled with its tunings for five minutes as his father sipped at his tea and Sun waited with the perfect composure of knowing she was about to see her accusations confirmed with concrete evidence.

"Here we go."

A visual popped up to display a four-dimensional virtual web of connections. As James brought specific linkages and dates into focus, Sun addressed Zàofù.

"I and my people have labored for over a year to discover who placed Hestia Hope's cee-cee Navah into my household. Navah was directly responsible for the deaths of Perseus Lee and Duke Guī Alargos when she tried to assassinate me on Molossia. I also hold her responsible for the death of my bodyguard Octavian."

"Sergeant Major Octavian Yíng Alhesperus died in the battle of Molossia. Do you dispute that? I note you claimed otherwise in your speech."

She cocked her head to the left. "Did my mother really never tell you the truth? Octavian was shot with a late bloomer by Kiran Seth de Lee as I and my Companions were leaving the wedding banquet."

"Heaven's breath! That explains—" He broke off, wiping his brow with a handkerchief.

"Yes, it explains how Aisa Lee got the late bloomer she used to murder my mother. But before all that happened, my mother ordered me to bury the evidence of Kiran's complicity. That's why no one suspected Aisa would be a threat."

"I see."

Sun thought he would say more but he didn't. Was he troubled? Skeptical?

"That's water under the bridge now she's dead." Sun gestured toward James's tower of evidence. "Naturally I wondered who was behind these murders and why they wanted *me* dead. It would have been easy—too easy—to blame Moira Lee."

He frowned. "Moira's hostility to you was public knowledge."

"Less to me and more to my father," she said with a sharp smile triggered by the memory of Moira insulting her father on Command Orbital Station Yǎnshī. Sun knew how to bide her time, and so she had. Moira would never insult her father again. "That's neither here nor there. Lee House is loyal to Chaonia. Nothing implicates Moira. I remain convinced she was unaware of Kiran's actions and unable to perceive Aisa's complicity. She wanted me discredited but she didn't need me dead. She certainly did not want Eirene dead."

"I'm listening, Your Highness," he said with more respect than he had heretofore shown to her. Had he liked Moira? Or was he simply reassured that Sun could see truth past her own dislikes?

"Some months ago I sent two of my Companions to Yele Prime to dig into the seers."

"You should not have flouted Eirene's authority. Didn't she exile those two?"

Sun saw no need to argue the injustice of a matter now resolved. "They found evidence that Hetty's cee-cee Navah was hired by the order of the Oculi."

"The sister order of the seers of Iros?"

"That's right. Navah was not *of* the Oculi but she worked *for* them. In fact, she came originally from Pelasgia Terce."

He blinked several times like a fussy old man, but then a flare of enlightenment widened his eyes. He turned to James. "Is this true?"

James manipulated the visual to expand a set of lineages and residential coordinates. Zàofù leaned forward to examine the numbers and diagrams closely. All the energy sagged out of him and he sat back.

Sun waited him out.

Finally he said, "Are you saying this Navah is linked to Prince Jiàn?"

"She was the daughter of a chamberlain in his service. She concealed her origins and hid their tracks. The seers wanted me dead as part of a deal with Jiàn to put him forward as queen-marshal in the event of Eirene's death."

"Why would they believe that would work? Jiàn may be Nézhā's son, but he has little support inside Chaonia. He didn't grow up at court so no one knows him. He hasn't proven himself in battle. Eirene made sure of that. To be blunt, Eirene was more favored of heaven than her brothers ever were. You are of her womb. Jiàn is not."

"That's my point. To become queen-marshal, Jiàn is entirely reliant on Yele support. He would be beholden to the seers, the Oculi, and any factions who gave him the resources to make his play. They would control him. Chaonia would become a vassal state in all but name to the League. The League Congress has already voted once on the question of whether to void the treaty with Chaonia. We had enough votes this time, but the seers and their allies will try again, just as they'll never stop trying to kill me in order to get what they want. According to his own public statements, Baron Voy has been negotiating with the Rider Council. He and they are probably parceling out who will get which systems in our territory. Do you want a puppet of the Yele League to rule Chaonia?"

"Of course not."

"That is why we need Trinity. As long as the empire can communicate with factions among the League, as long as Kiran Seth can escape without consequence, we'll be fighting this undertow."

James indicated the damning evidence in its swirling colors built in unassailable virtual architecture.

She waited for the silence to grow taut before she dropped what Alika would call the final cadence. "Marshal, even with Trinity in our hands, the Yele won't stop as long as Jiàn gives them hope they can create a fifth column."

She clasped her hands behind her back in parade rest as a signal she personally could do nothing more and awaited Zàofù's decision.

He rose like a man whose joints hurt. At the door he paused to look back, a man whose courageous deeds in war and absolute loyalty to Chaonia had lofted him to the position of Eirene's most trusted marshal.

She added, as if she'd just thought of it, "By the way, I have it in mind to raise Anas's rank to kite marshal and give him command of the Second Fleet. Meanwhile I'm sending you back to Chaonia with the worst wounded, the ones who'll have to be mustered out. Once there, you'll be given full authority to rearrange the disposition of the fleets and task forces left behind in Chaonia and Karnos. Leave a sufficient home guard and garrison detachments. Bring the rest to me as reinforcements. To Trinity. That's where I'll be by then. You're the only marshal I trust to carry out the task."

He met Sun's clear, hot gaze. His own was clouded but steady, his tone calm with the weight of his years. "Your confidence honors me, Your Highness. I will see to it that Jiàn can no longer trouble the republic."

60

Interlude at the Tail End of a Tow Chain

Captain the Honorable Amity Jīn gives her reflection a final look before she leaves her cabin. On the days she expects a fleet-wide message to arrive from the *Keoe* she puts on her service dress uniform as if she were going to physically meet with Queen-Marshal Sun. The peculiar circumstances of a knnu transit demand a high standard of morale and discipline. She's not one to boast of her ribbons and medallions but small details matter when the crunch comes. Most of the spacers on the frigate *Bennu* fought at Karnos. They know she's one of twelve battle-field promotions to captain of her own ship. She has a lot to live up to.

She studies the scar on her jaw and tests the new joint in her elbow, which functions better every day although it's still stiff. An alarm chimes. Time to go.

She heads forward toward the bridge. The name is an artifact of the Celestial Empire, what her scholar aunt calls "a shard of the past which we hold in our hands without truly understanding what it meant to our ancestors."

As she passes the door into the officers' wardroom, it slides aside. Ensign Semisi Fairweather Alsuva trots out, carrying a tray of freshly baked buns. When she gives him an inquiring eyebrow he says, "For the tactical training." She ducks in to grab a sealed bulb of freshly brewed tea. Along a bulkhead, the panels for the wardroom lifepods shine a steady green. Ventilation hums. All stable, all ahead.

"Anything else, Captain?" From the galley, Petty Officer Thea James Alhonolulu gestures toward a cooling rack of ginger buns, sweet fried sesame buns, and compsognathus-tail buns. The smell is divine.

"I'll be back later," Amity promises.

A marine undogs the hatch onto the bridge and swings it aside. As she enters, the officer on watch calls out, "Captain on the bridge."

Vanna vacates the captain's chair, but she waves him back. "I'm here for the drop."

She passes the forward hatch and into the narrow service passages that thread the heavily armored fore of the ship. Part of a beacon drive has to be in the ship's bow, because it is not a propulsive drive but more of a message a beacon registers before it translates the ship in a seeming instant through its coil and across vast distances into the coil of its linked beacon. The *Bennu*'s engineers have taken advantage of the enforced downtime to perform a complete maintenance cycle of the beacon drive components. She avoids their current work areas in the bow because calibration and cleaning is a tricky process, easy to contaminate or throw off tune.

One of the armored fore compartments was rigged before departure for the grapple that connects each ship to its place in the tow chain. The *Keoe* has five chains. Four are placed equidistant around the outer circumference of the ship's circular stern and the fifth in the center, which the *Bennu*'s crew jokingly calls the navel string. Ships attach like beads along these parallel, rigid tubes that extend behind the ship inside a one-hundred-klicks-long elliptical Weinstein bubble. As the last ship in the central chain, *Bennu* is the last to receive the daily check-in.

By the usual standards of a knnu passage this is quite a short trip, a mere fifty-five to sixty days if they remain on schedule. So far fifty days have passed without incident. Nevertheless, it is a long time to go without radio or network contact with another ship, habitat, military station, or planet. The structure of a bubble and the drive itself produce radiation across the electromagnetic spectrum that saturates sensors with so much noise on every waveband that comms between ships are basically hopeless. In addition, ironically, the military ships' modern comms don't interface with the Argosy's antiquated network. Because of the speed with which Sun launched her fleet from Hellion Terminus there wasn't time for fleet engineers to work up a solution, so for now each ship flies as if alone except for the *Keoe*'s clunky physical system.

The uncanny silence sets everyone on edge. She can smell the heightened nerves as a chemical metabolizing in sweat and filtering through the ventilation system. It's as if the closer they get to Trinity the more tense the crew becomes. Isn't that true of battle no matter how a fleet or an army approaches the front line?

She reaches the workaround compartment and ducks inside.

"Captain, according to schedule we should have incoming in five minutes," says Spacer Guyson Ueda Alargos, on duty with Ensign the Honorable Trajan Hope by the pneumatic tube that ports into the tow chain.

They're both in vac suits, as required. She dons one of the emergency spares. A physical switch flips over, marking the arrival of an object. A bell rings. Ueda turns a crank. There's a clunk and a thunk. The spacer unscrews a cap and fishes out a cylindrical container while the ensign records its receipt in a logbook.

Amity opens the container. She gives a glance at the "all stations normal" entry in the scroll tucked inside, and hands it to Trajan Hope, who will record the *Bennu*'s current operating conditions on the scroll and send the container back. It's a terrible way to maintain contact with the Titan, but on the other hand, a catastrophic failure on any towed ship can't be dealt with while in knnu transit anyway. At least Titan command would know where to look first when they reemerge into normal space.

She'll never complain about beacon travel again. That one weird drop as into the void, and you're through. None of this waiting, helpless, unable to do anything but cycle through a daily routine. How the ancestors survived their thousand-year voyage intact psychologically she cannot fathom. Maybe they didn't. As Aunt Evelyn once remarked, someone hacked and smashed the Archives on multiple Titans, leaving the survivors with disconnected shards that are all the knowledge that remains of the lost Celestial Empire.

It's the data storage capsule she came for. She records her presence in the logbook, sheds the vac suit, and takes the thumb-sized device with her.

Back on the bridge she commandeers a tactical alcove and plugs in the capsule to clear it with her captain's code. The content is marked green for all hands.

She unplugs and makes her way off the bridge as Vanna says, "Captain off the bridge."

After descending three decks she heads aft.

Every Day Eight of the shipboard week the queen-marshal, on the *Keoe*, sends a special recording. Amity has made it her tradition to premiere any all-hands recording on the mess deck. Partway there the passageway is blocked by yellow barricade tape. Up ahead a spacer is working on an open electrical relay panel. A second spacer stands the regulation three meters away, holding a rope attached to the engineer at the panel.

The spacer holding the rope looks her way. "Passageway is secure."

"Very good."

She backtracks to a perpendicular corridor and cuts over to a parallel passageway that leads to a different hatch onto the mess deck. It's not a scheduled meal time but nevertheless people congregate here when off duty, chatting with friends or playing through their battle scenarios yet again. A couple of amateur musicians work their way through acoustic renditions of recent songs popularized on Idol Faire by the Handsome Alika. "Wherever you stand be the soul of that place."

His Idol Faire days are over. It's Marshal the Honorable Alika Vata now. He's the commander of the task group *Bennu* is assigned to.

Her entrance doesn't disturb the flow of relaxed chatter. It's longstanding tradition that a captain does not come to the mess deck to give people work to do. She veers over to Thea, who is seated at a table with another culinary chief.

"Didn't I just see you?" she asks with a smile.

"I got off duty and came down here to remind Isabel that her cooking isn't as fancy as mine."

"Slander," says the other chief. "And I have the awards to prove it."

"Also I figured there'd be a recording from the queen-marshal. Is that it?"

"It is."

Amity heads to a master control panel. More people are filing in expectantly. Everyone can access the recording via shipboard comms, but humans like to congregate when there's good news to enjoy. The part of the job that brings people together appeals to her far more than the gut-churning adrenaline shock of battle. She's not sure she's a good spacer. She's just the highest-ranking officer who survived the *Vermilion.* Nothing heroic in that. She's ashamed, and if she ever gets her hands on a lancer pilot she'll do something, but she's not sure what.

After seeing death up close in the minefield in Windworn System she can't help but think all the paeans ever sung to the bravery of frontline combatants can't capture even an iota of what it means to stay behind to stop a circuit from exploding, knowing you'll die in the attempt but hoping others will live; what it means to be stuck on the wrong side of a sealed airlock as the air runs out in your breached compartment and you can't move to reach the controls; what it means to order a wounded lieutenant onto a lifepod while you stay with the broken ship and its dead to the bitter end.

Increasingly she's thinking that after her tour is over she'll apply for a post in one of the ministries. Rites and Culture, maybe. A well-managed bureaucracy can bring stability to a careening situation.

She plugs the capsule into the panel and presses play.

Usually an all-hands program is a tightly filmed inspirational speech, Sun addressing the troops as if they are gathered around her in an intimate audience chamber, accompanied by a tactical scenario for the ships to run. Sun is big on training. Amity is sure that, by now, she could navigate the three Trinity systems blindfolded and pinpoint which planets, moons, orbital habitats, and on-ground fortified cities are most crucial. The key, Sun says, is adaptability and speed. Act fast but don't get tied into a single course of action.

Not this recording.

Cheers greet an opening montage that begins with a two-minute pan of the smiling Ji-na. Her ribbons curl and wind around her like the skein of history, ever moving, never tangling, a pattern hard to read because it seems to move so fast and yet in retrospect it all makes sense that it had to unfold exactly that way.

The performer's twirling image fades out to general groans and some chatter as to whether the rumors are true that the queen-marshal took the beautiful winner to her berth. Who wouldn't, given the chance? Really!

The screen is taken over by a stern image of the Idol Historian, as he styles himself. His montages and scripted sidebars are always a highlight of the weekly recordings. Under his clever direction, a history of the Trinity Coalition unfolds.

No fleet has ever successfully attacked the Trinity Coalition. The recording drops into a briefing between the queen-marshal and her high command, which must have taken place at Hellion Terminus before the fleets departed. Using a 3-D visual, the Honorable Persephone Lee explains how the Coalition became central to the political alignments in the post–Apsaras Collapse. Beacon routes used to run all through the region, but in this region, called the Middle Gap, most connections failed when the thirteen beacons of the Apsaras home world underwent some manner of cataclysmic breakdown. It's likely some star systems got cut off so completely that one day they were receiving ships on the regular and the next they were fated never again to have contact with the rest of humanity.

The three star systems now known as the Trinity Coalition became an island because they remained linked to each other in a Tinker-Evers-Chance convergence. This fortunate chance was enriched by a coincidental geometry. While physically distant from each other, each one of those star systems happened to be physically close to one major trade node, close enough that an Argosy could cross the gap in fifty to seventy days via knnu drive. Thus, Meli System is unusually close to Nalanda System and Sankore Systems, which each lead via three working beacons directly to Yele Prime. Kumbala System lies a short gap from Harahuvati System, itself three beacon drops from Destiny, the heart of the old queendom of Mishirru and now the seat of a provincial government under the empire. Tsurru was a mere six light-years from Hellion Terminus, which is why the latter had become a haven for smugglers seeking to circumvent the empire's heavy imposts.

Chance is strange. If the beacons linking Meli, Kumbala, and Tsurru to each other had failed in the great collapse, there would be no Tinker-Evers-Chance "island" on which its triumvirate of rulers had constructed their authoritarian government. There would be no short-haul Argosy routes that allow ventures and trade to travel from the Phene Empire into the Yele League without having to go through Chaonia.

Channel Idol calls the Trinity Coalition a pirate den filled with crime and iniquity. Queen-Marshal Sun says the triumvirate is holding Chaonia hostage by refusing to offer a treaty of friendship and cooperation. In her lecture Persephone Lee points out that Trinity is key to securing communication and transport across half of the vast span of inhabited worlds.

A virtual map of the known human worlds and functional beacon routes wraps around the figure of Sun. Seated at the strategos table, she addresses her audience: those in the room with her and those in the greater assembly at which all citizens of Chaonia have a place.

"The empire began this quarrel in the days of our great-grandparents. It is up to us to end it. Risk is merely a stepping-stone to reward. What can Chaonia not accomplish when its citizens strive together for the common good? With what conspicuous valor and unrelenting determination have Chaonia's fleets withstood the assaults of the empire's dreadnoughts? We remember Sergeant Ah-Nee Jiāng Almatajap of the Twelfth Division during the assault on the Citadel on Karnos Prime, who although wounded in the neck by shrapnel continued to calmly identify targets for her sniper cohort. We remember Lieutenant—now Senior Lieutenant—the Honorable Amity Jīn who with a shattered arm and without thought to her own safety pulled eleven spacers from a fire-ravaged compartment on the *Vermilion*."

Amity flushes with both pride and shame as the crew gives a spontaneous cheer, which they politely cut off as the queen-marshal goes on. It would be rude to drown out her praise of courageous service members. "We remember the crew of—"

The ship shudders. Comms crash. Her personal network, linked to the ship's internal network, starts blinking: it's gone off line.

"Captain to bridge," she says, clicking through. No answer.

Every good spacer learns to feel their ship. It's instinct, an awareness. Inside a bubble, attached to a tow chain, ships seem to be at rest.

They're moving, and that's not good.

An alarm starts blaring. Emergency lights tick on alongside the regular lights. Gravity is still working. People stare at each other, stand up, sit down, a welter of confusion, then look toward her because the captain always knows what to do, right?

She taps her command code into the galley's master control panel to break through the flood of chatter. "This is *Bennu* actual. Status?"

The lag feels as if it lasts a year. Thea James hustles up with a vac suit.

A crackle of static clears and Vanna says, "We're moving. We don't know what happened. Nothing on the whiskers."

The whiskers are extended tactile sensors like wires attached to the ship and sticking out half a klick along ten vectors. It's Argosy tech cobbled onto the military ships, their only contact with the outside because of the sensor whiteout.

"I'm coming forward. Atmosphere tight all compartments. Crew all repair lockers."

She seals on the vac suit even though life support hasn't been compromised, but if anything is drilled into spacers, it is that fire and breach will kill you faster than you can get on your vac suit. The announcement to set damage control stations broadcasts around her. Spacers begin moving to their assigned stations. Their faces are creased with trepidation but their bodies follow the drill.

The chief accompanies her as they hustle forward. "You have any ideas?"

"I do not. We were assured these tow chains don't break. And I don't see how any ship in normal space can attack a bubble that's traveling too fast for it to perceive. So that leaves equipment failure or—"

She breaks off as comms blink on. Immediately she is poured into the bridge's monitoring screen as helm and engineering flag velocity and trajectory. This is not good. This is very, very bad. Has something happened to the Titan? But if the *Keoe* or the knnu drive failed, the bubble would destabilize and collapse. Sensors are still saturated, which means they're still inside a working bubble.

A proximity alarm flares. The forward whisker turns red with warning messages: *Incoming. Incoming.* Something physical is sliding toward them with force. Pressure hits the starboard forward whisker. What in the hells?

The instinct that saved her on the *Vermilion* seizes her. She grabs a no-grav bar as she broadcasts on the captain's universal channel, "All hands, all hands, brace for impact. Starboard side."

She can still feel in her flesh the jolt of mines exploding against *Vermilion*'s hull, as visceral a physical memory as the cooling of her beloved grandfather's skin after his death when she had rested her cheek against his arm. She braces.

Expectation isn't enough. Nothing is enough. The slam hurls her to the ground, her grip wrenched from the grab bar. It's like running into a gigantic wall that punches back.

Regular lights go out. Contact with the bridge vanishes as if physical fiber lines have been severed. Alarms clack on and off and on again.

Life support chugs onward like the stolidly built system it is, emergency lights indicating passageways and doors. More whiskers flare. She reads the arc of their information as debris peeling back along the *Bennu's* hull in smaller impacts more like hard slaps than gut punches. She routes a message to engineering in the stern.

"Damage report? Atmosphere?"

"Showing extensive containment breach across multiple forward compartments, Captain." The disembodied voice has the contained tension of a person who has just realized they are watching a disaster unfold. "Our telemetry for the forward beacon drive is no longer showing up on the feed."

"At all?"

A gulp of emotion, quickly controlled. "The whole front end may be gone."

Amity feels her eyes blinking as if to stave off the visual battering of a howling, fiery chemical outflow against her visor. She's on the *Vermilion* in her vac suit peppered by particulate matter being sucked outward, the explosion came so fast, no one thought the Phene would mine the entry vector out of the beacon . . .

No, she's on the *Bennu*. She's captain. This is her call. Get a grip.

She pings the CIC pod at the center of the ship. "Report."

"All compartments forward of frame three six are not reporting at all. Catastrophic breach. We think we've been hit by another ship."

She slams through an all hands via the 1MC. "All hands, this is the captain. The ship has been struck by an unknown object. There is a catastrophic breach across the front of the vessel. Seal all compartments. All personnel suit up and tether. Every compartment and division report your status to CIC. All personnel report in. Submit muster reports to the bridge. Investigators report status of all compartments forward of frame four zero. I'm taking charge of damage control and rescue."

The pressure of a touch on her arm. Startled, she looks around. Thea is still with her. "Captain, with respect, may I accompany you to CIC?"

Amity is no longer a lieutenant to charge into the breach, to oversee rescue crews from the front line of destruction, to throw her own body into the fray. There are personnel whose job it is to do the dirty, dangerous work. They are well trained. Training means survival. They know what to do. She has to command.

"Okay, okay," she mutters to herself. She pings her XO: Take charge of damage and rescue forward. Hayma's affirmative pings back in two seconds.

Amity and Thea unreel flexible tethers and hook to the bar system built throughout the ship. With Thea beside her as a steadying influence she heads aft, their tethers sliding along above them. It reminds her of a holiday her family took in the alpine badlands on Thesprotis Terce, the thrill of the eight-day rope-line trek along cliff faces and across scissor canyons. Now that she thinks about it, she realizes this popular holiday choice for teens is a good introduction for emergency shipboard routines.

Damage-control personnel with sturdy mechs trot past. A file of marines in full battlesuit follow at their heels. All hatches have to be passed with multiple fail-safes. Everyone is vac-suited and tethered. Have they been attacked or is this a horrible mechanical failure?

People don't look up as she enters CIC to the officer on watch's "Captain in Combat." Everyone's attention is fixed on their console. On the ship-wide screen the recording from earlier is still playing. The Idol Historian has segued into narrating a triumphant montage of great moments from the battle for Karnos. Angharad Black's *Rakhsh* and its fierce escorts pound the Incorruptibles fleet. Sun with the *Boukephalas* streaks away in a bold pursuit of the Speaker. "Our visionary queen, marshal of our fate—"

"Turn that off," Amity snaps.

Thea says, "I'll bring provisions," and cycles out.

From the evidence of internal monitors it looks exactly as if something huge smashed at an angle into the stem of the *Bennu*, shearing away the beacon drive and an unknown number of forward compartments, including the grapple-station where less than an hour ago she stood alongside Ueda Alargos and Trajan Hope. The starboard hull has taken substantial impacts but its armor has held with minimal breaches and only one fire, already contained; two dead, nine injured.

Every ship has a counter for personnel to check in. As of seven minutes post initial impact, fifty-two spacers have not logged their presence and must be considered in distress without access to comms. Or dead.

All the exterior cameras aft of the breach are working, but they show nothing except the smeary oscillation from the saturating effects of the knnu drive. Only Titans have the means to pierce the forward curve of a bubble with a single hook of a sensor that can catch on what Argosies call an anchor, a weighted signal that tells them they are reaching a known system. Navigators use some kind of neural enhancement combined with secret skills and interdicted maps to navigate a crossing. Trade secrets aren't shared with outsiders. So it's fortunate the new queen-marshal has a half sister who is a Navigator. Perhaps it isn't luck. Maybe that was Eirene's plan all along.

She crosses to the auxiliary helm and brings up the "order of march" that displays the disposition of Sun's fleet along the *Keoe*'s tow chain. A bubble remains stable along its entire elliptical inner layer as long as there is no significant movement of mass inside; thus the rigid chains. So they don't dare use their torch drive to halt their momentum for fear of creating more widespread havoc.

She says to Helm, "What will happen when we hit the trailing edge of the bubble?"

Helm looks up with a strained expression. Stress wipes the spacer's name right out of her head. "Either our motion destabilizes a portion of the bubble and we drop past into normal space. Or it doesn't destabilize, and we hit."

Amity winces, then realizes that everyone in CIC is looking at her and has seen her wince. Tension spikes in the compartment even beyond what was there before. One spacer rubs their eyes. Another coughs. "Fuck," someone mutters, leaning over numbers on display on their console. The ID operator whispers, too loudly, to their supervisor: "I heard no ship can survive collision with the inner layer of a bubble. We'll disintegrate."

"Will it be too fast for me to chug down my secret stash of báijiǔ?" retorts ID Sup with a spacer's grim humor.

Amity struggles to put on a calm expression. "Helm, what's your estimate for when we will reach—"

The impact arrives more as sound than as movement, a resonant thrum that swells into a roar. The ship tumbles as if caught in a slow-motion churn of breaking waves so powerful and with an amplitude so high that the huge vessel literally rolls aft over stem and also portwise. Everyone is flung against their tether as gravity flips out, turning off to counter damage. A bulb of tea spins through the air as the corvette shakes and vibrates as if rolled along a monstrously endless break.

and then

quiet

stillness but for the gentle roll

tethered humans soft in freefall

Comms have fallen silent. Life support blinks at orange. They still have atmosphere and emergency power.

She plugs into the fiber line. "Engineering. Report."

No one answers. Has her ship lost both stem and stern?

"Joe? Are you there?"

A buzz against her palm. A tinny baritone. "Engineering. Shaken, not stirred."

All her air gusts out and it takes her a moment to find words. "Good to hear your voice. Damage assessment?"

"We're running a full check."

"Get this roll corrected."

"On it." In the background from the central engine control compartment she hears a loud *pop* and a shout and several people swearing, succeeded by the half-hysterical laughter of people relieved they aren't dead. Engineering clicks out.

"Captain?" says the ID Op. "Did you see this?"

Exterior cameras have flickered on. They are back in normal space. Of the Titan, the tow chain, and the Weinstein bubble and its wake there is no sign. She doesn't expect to be able to see them, not if the *Bennu* tumbled out of the bubble. In even a few minutes they would have fallen light-hours behind.

An image comes into focus on one of the elevated viewscreens. A camera array on the spine forward whisker broadcasts a stark view of the stem of the ship. It's gone, sheared off as if a ragged knife sliced partway through the forward compartments, followed by a giant's hand torquing and twisting with malignant strength until a fragment was ripped free. There's not even debris, not even bodies adrift along the hull as she would have expected. She flips through camera angles and begins shaking with relief: the stern of the ship is intact. These warships are tough.

"Captain, we've got a distress signal."

The signal is the standard SOS followed by the voice of what sounds like a brand-new graduate fresh out of the royal academy. "Mayday. Mayday. Mayday. This is Ensign the Honorable Felix Hope of the *Seker*. We have suffered catastrophic damage and have lost all thrust. Requesting immediate assistance. I say again, we need immediate assistance. Does anyone copy?"

Sweat slides to her lips, and she licks away the moisture. Her eyes are wet. Her elbow throbs. Her vac suit seals flicker for a terrifying moment before stabilizing to green. She can do this. These are tasks every spacer runs through a hundred times as standard drills.

"*Seker*, this is *Bennu* actual. Report your situation."

As they wait for a reply she says, "Where is it? I don't see anything in visual range."

Damage reports pour in. She fills in time by collating them with her ship's blueprint. Except for the catastrophic loss of the stem of the ship, they have weathered the blow far better than she had feared. Not counting crew in the missing stem, they've taken seven deaths but minimal casualties—mostly contusions, breaks, and concussions.

"Captain." ID Op raises a hand. "I have located six ships."

"I have another six! No, eight!" cries ID Sup excitedly, although it's nothing to be excited about. Has the entire tow chain fallen apart?

"Five more," says ID Op.

Her hands have gone cold but she can't panic. "Open comms to all vessels."

She studies the order of march. Sun split the Eighth and Second Fleets between the five tow chains according to their place in the coming assault. As part of Task Group Copper, the *Bennu* upon arrival in Tsurru System will head for the Kumbala Beacon. The task group's mission is to take speedy control of Kumbala System before its ruling Magava can muster an effective defense.

The reply from the *Seker* arrives. "*Bennu,* I am the hells glad to hear from someone. Preliminary observations suggest the tow chain forward of our position was cut through, possibly by shrapnel. The ship sustained numerous impacts from small-scale debris before we made impact with a big object."

"The big object was probably us," interposes Helm.

Amity gestures for silence. The message is still playing.

"Our torch drives have taken severe damage and the replacement parts were lost in a compartment breach. We have multiple breaches. Mass casualties." His voice quavers, but he coughs and manages to go on. "Engineers working on life support but all our oxygen recyclers have taken damage. We have eighty-two crew alive. Sixty-eight working lifepods. I am the highest-ranking officer. Sending preliminary velocity and coordinates. *Seker* out."

She knows how to play these tiles. "Well done, Ensign Hope. We are assessing our own situation and making contact with other vessels. As soon as we have a confirmed heading and ship count we will analyze possible rescue maneuvers. Over."

OS Navigation chimes in. "Captain, their coordinates check out. If their torch drives are out it doesn't look good for them. They're moving away from us in the opposite direction faster than we can catch them if they can't slow themselves down."

She chews on her lower lip, catches herself, and stops. "Shrapnel? What in the hells. Whatever happened kicked it backward hard and fast."

Navigation flags the *Seker*'s probable path. "Because of its angle of exit and the force of the impact, it is now moving more or less back toward Hellion Terminus."

"Do you know where we are?"

"I do. I've completed a full sweep of our stellar neighborhood." A diagram pops up. "Hellion System lies four point five light-years away, here. And here is Tsurru, at point three one light-years. We are headed at a slower velocity on this trajectory."

"So if we do nothing we'll miss Tsurru and continue coasting in interstellar space." She opens comms to Engineering. "Joe, take a look at this telemetry. How soon can you get engines back on line?"

"We are running a full safety check. One hour and thirty minutes."

"We need to get a course correction and calibrated acceleration before we are kicked so far out of range we have no hope of reaching Tsurru."

"Understood. One hour is the best I can do."

"I'll give you forty-five minutes."

The hatch opens and the XO staggers in, vac suit covered in ash and blood from whatever Hayma was dealing with up front.

"Hayma, you'll stay in CIC secure second until further notice. I want a full accounting from life support, supplies, and lifepods."

"What are you thinking?" Hayma asks.

"We change trajectory as soon as the engines are clear to go. Even at full torch speed it will take us fifteen or more years to reach Tsurru."

Fifteen years.

Every person in CIC falls silent and stares at each other as the ugly truth sinks in. But in her head, Amity can still hear, and will always hear, the klaxon on the *Vermilion* as it died with no hope of ever reaching safe harbor.

"We can manage it if we rotate personnel in and out of lifepods to reduce oxygen and supply load. We'll operate with a skeleton crew."

Sensor One says, "We have identified another two heat signatures that may be debris clusters or hulked vessels not responding to transponder pings."

Comms perks up. "Captain, I have multiple incomings."

"Route me a conference call in my office." She gives a nod to Hayma. "Do a physical circuit of the ship."

Bennu's crew gets back to work. The XO heads out. An updated casualty list starts scrolling on Amity's network, but she can't let it distract her from the hard choices she'll have to make.

She surveys the captain's office with its strategos table, tea set and hot water, chart drawers, and a door into her private cabin. She is too hyped up to sit, so she paces around the small oval table as her crew in CIC arrange a 3-D display as a virtual grid above the table, each ship labeled and placed in proportional distance with reference to its comms lag time.

This is going to be a tricky conference.

She hasn't heard back from Ensign Hope yet and marks the *Seker*'s spot with a placeholder. Blank placeholders mark the possible hulks. In total, twenty-six or twenty-seven vessels seem to have been separated from the bubble, depending on whether you count the hulks as one ship or two. Almost 10 percent of Sun's assault fleet. She collates the positions of the ships against where they were on the order of march.

Senior Captain the Honorable Abiye Bō of the light cruiser *Raijū* takes charge. The *Raijū* is amazingly still linked via rigid tubing to five ships; they were the last in their chain and somehow emerged out of the bubble intact.

Someone more clever than her is plotting a four-dimensional graph of the Event, as they all start calling it. Based on the ships that fell out of the bubble, only two of the outer chains were affected, although that's bad enough. It seems possible that debris from collisions severed the tail end of the central chain just forward of the *Seker*. It will take months for a radio signal to reach Tsurru, if there are any survivors from the main fleet to receive it or anyone in Trinity willing or able to respond.

She asks, "Catastrophic failure? An attack?"

"Gather all the data you can," says Senior Captain Bō. "Everyone must do a thorough sweep of their ships for possible weaknesses and especially sabotage."

The ships fall into two loosely proximate groups, one including ships within striking distance of the *Raijū* and the second around a squadron from the Second Fleet whose senior-most commander turns out to be an academy cohort buddy of Abiye Bō. Sensors are constructing data from the two dark bodies but Amity is already sure it is a ship cut in half and probably dead with all hands. It's within range of the cruiser.

Captain Bō says, "We need to make for Tsurru. We'll make better time if we advance in two loose groups and angle our routes to meet up in a year or two. Ēnlái?"

After a lag, the other commander's reply drops in. "I'm collecting my stragglers and evacuating personnel, equipment, and supplies from the three ships we have to abandon. We'll set course as soon as that is completed."

"Very good, my friend. Captain Jīn, you must change your trajectory in order to meet up with me. You're holding together pretty well now but I don't like the look of these readings from your front end, what's left of it."

"Understood. I am awaiting return message from the *Seker*." She pings over the last coordinates. "I'm going to need to mount a rescue mission. Their torch drives need repair with parts they no longer have. Their life support is compromised."

His lips pinch as his weary eyes read the screen. "They're too far away and headed in an opposite direction without means to decelerate."

"What are you saying, sir?"

"I'm saying they are out of luck. As fortune wills it, none of us can catch them with any chance of returning."

"But—"

"'Where are the hapless shipmen? Disappeared, gone down, where witness none, save Night, hath been.' That's an order, Captain." He gives a last, pitying look and signs off, his final words like a tolling bell.

For five minutes she just sits there, stunned and sickened. They don't even know if the *Keoe* and the rest survived the Event. These ships flung upon the empty shoals of Night might be all that is left of Sun's audacious armada.

The door chimes. Thea enters bearing hot tea and a bowl of curry noodle soup with sweet potato. "Eat, or I'm not leaving."

Amity shakes herself out of her stupor. The captain has a job to do, and she means to do it. After she eats she calls down to Engineering and loops in her XO.

"Joe, Hayma, can we rig a shuttle to go uncrewed on autopilot after the *Seker*, carrying the replacement parts they need? If we fix its helm to their transponder I think it should chase them until it catches up, even if it takes two or three years."

"We lost three shuttles when Hangar 1 was breached," says Hayma. "Dispatching such a mission would leave us with only one functional shuttle."

"Yes, it's a risk, but we should rendezvous in about forty days with the *Raijū*. This is the only chance for the *Seker*."

"The chances it will work are vanishingly low," says Hayma, as she must.

"It is a long shot," agrees Joe, "but it burns me to walk away without trying anything to help those poor souls."

"Then we're agreed," says Amity. "I'll come down to Hangar 2 and supervise."

As she makes her way through the ship, she sees the crew at work with resolve and determination. The grim jokes haven't started, not yet, but they will. They're doing what they have to do. So must she.

When the reply comes in, she takes it.

"This is Ensign Felix Hope on the *Seker*. *Bennu,* if you read me, I am sending a list of critical replacement parts that we need." His voice sticks. She can hear how he takes a breath to steady himself. The murmur of voices in the background. Someone says reassuring words. Brave words. "I'll be sending a list of the dead. I have asked the survivors to record messages to home. Those will come in the next transmission. Please respond. Are you there, Captain?"

She rubs away the sting of tears. She knows how to leave because of the cruel calculus of survival.

"This message is for *Seker* actual and the crew of the *Seker*. This *Bennu* actual. My name is Amity Jīn. I'm here, Felix, I hope you don't mind if I call you Felix." She speaks into silence, words that will not be heard for hours and all too soon not for days and then weeks and then months. "There will be always be someone on this line, for as long as it takes."

61

Not That It Takes Much to Set All the Wily Persephone's Flares Alight

Even though the *Keoe* is a baby Titan, with a minimum crew requirement of only 8,448 spacers and a maximum passenger capacity of only 18,523 souls, or fewer if cabin holds are converted into massive lab complexes, it's by far the biggest ship I've ever been on, massively larger than the *Boukephalas*.

In a ship this big, a fixed system of ventilation will create dead zones, permanent eddies, and other problems that across generations of knnu travel can wreak havoc on a contained population. Cause mildew to grow in a backwater greenhouse, for example. So at certain times of ship day and week the ventilation patterns shift, vents opening or closing. Except for dedicated maintenance shafts and major corridors, all other passageways on the ship *also* open and close at intervals. Maybe it's a useful way to make sure locked routines don't atrophy minds. You can't get there from here the way you did yesterday or last ship year. Definitely I'm that restless individual who likes the challenge.

I leave my suite and head out for my daily "predawn" run on what the crew calls the ring road, a permanent artery that carves a big oval around the equatorial axis of the hull. It's a through route for equipment, large-scale group movement and training, and for people who want to bike, skate, or run with no sharp corners and on a dedicated exercise lane. Since I like sharp corners and messy traffic patterns, I've mapped routes of varying lengths that cut through the interior of the ship and loop back to the ring road.

I set out at an easy pace on my favorite ten-klick loop.

First I pass an exercise arena where I fall into time to the beats and cadences of drilling Guards. Then the closed doors of a barracks on sleep cycle. A laundry. A row of repair shops and snack bars. A sports garden where a few late-shift crew are playing table tennis. A teahouse that is playing the most recent program put together by the Honorable Beau, who I privately call by the art name Bombastically Pleased with Himself. Although he's not wrong about telling people the story you want them to see in you.

Living quarters. Offices. The sealed doors of a lab complex and, next to it, a gymnasium where banner soldiers are doing calisthenics. I halt to stare through a transparent wall. They are sleek and fit, powerful and confident. Like Zizou—no, *Kurash*—they were sent off to be soldiers with no training for any future beyond war.

Freed from the controlling leash of the empire, what are they training for? Who are they if they are no longer mercenaries fighting for the Phene? Sun has talked about incorporating them within specialized cohorts of marines, but her marshals argued against it and there isn't a Chaonian who would trust them enough to fight alongside them. I like to think I'm open-minded but I'd have a hard time feeling comfortable with a Gatoi at my exposed back. In a way the ones Prince João saved are voyagers in a liminal zone whose destination remains undetermined.

Where is Kurash this very moment? Is he thinking of me? I swear I can still feel the press of his fingers on mine before he let me go.

A lean, mean, very attractive woman with sinuous neural tattoos has been running a routine on a set of bars. She flips with graceful strength to the mat and turns to look at me through the clear wall that separates us. Is her stare challenge or curiosity? She could crush me to a pulp if she chose, and who wouldn't want to go that way, really, choked to death by powerful thighs?

I move on.

A sharp right takes me into the central core of the Titan. A catwalk vaults over the vast Garden of the Celestial Home. The garden's winding paths are a favored place for people to walk amid the greenery, but I like the view from above, the way the smell of vegetation and running water lofts on a whisper of a breeze. At the center of the garden floats a huge sphere suspended in space, although in actuality it is fixed by clear tubes to the bulkhead. This is the Heart Temple of the Divine and Pacific Lotus Queen. The heart of every Titan is found in the labyrinth path enclosed within the sphere. I'm told it's a shipboard tradition for crew to walk the maze for clarity.

Not me. I like the ability to see what lies before and behind me, so I keep running. No distractions.

When I reach the far end of the catwalk I veer onto a freight corridor and head outward, back toward the ring road. A company of marines pounds past, running in unison, voices raised in a call-and-response whose words I can't understand. Squarehead Solomon jogs past at the rear of the company, and I remember he got a bug up his ass and has started making his unit learn basic Phene. What a weirdo. His head flickers my way but he doesn't greet me, nor would I expect him to. I reach the ring road and I've just turned aft toward the aft-port galley when I spot a familiar face standing sentinel outside a strategos-equipped conference room.

Jade's cee-cee has only been with us since Hellion Terminus. Mèimei is certainly her work name, not her given name, but I don't know her given name. As a graduate of Vogue Academy she has the polished smile down pat.

"Honored Persephone. Peace be upon you."

"And upon you, peace. What's all this then? A locked door?"

She looks startled by my vehemence. "The Honored Jade is engaged in private study and has asked not to be disturbed."

"Has the Honored Jade, indeed?" I set palm to red-blinking panel and it admits me as it would admit any Companion or Sun.

What I'm hoping to find on the other side I'm not quite sure, although whatever it is should hopefully involve Jade being gruesomely embarrassed at being caught in the act. What I find is a darkened conference room with its strategos system displaying a virtual 3-D render of Tsurru System.

Jade stands within the halo of the star, manipulating fleets like a sorcerer trailing light from clever fingers. Their gaze lifts to meet mine.

"I asked not to be disturbed, but naturally it would be you."

"Haven't we gone over these scenarios one hundred times already?" I ask as I study the layout of the system's seven planets and three beacons. The planets are all beauties, one dusty marble in the goldilocks zone and the others swirling with tumultuously attractive atmospheres that would kill you in a hot second. "I haven't gotten any new information."

"The key to skill is drill," Jade answers tendentiously.

"You're such a swot."

"The difference between us, asshole, is that I prepare while you rely on luck and your mystifyingly loyal friends to keep your head above water."

"I can't help that you don't have the skill of cultivating friends."

Jade's snide tone always brings out the worst in me. "Anyway, I know the plan. Take control of the Trinity Coalition through speed, surprise, and superior firepower. To which end, Alika is now a fancy marshal, unlike you and me. He and Makinde will bomb through straight to the Kumbala Beacon to drop through before anyone in Kumbala System realizes they're coming. The grand Kite Marshal Anas Samtarras and the Second Fleet will charge into Meli System, with Hetty along to do any fix-up needed because that's the route leading to the Yele League and Hetty has the mad Yele skills from her scholar dad, and with James along to crack open the infamous Trinity treasury which is rumored to be held at the Matrone's Hive."

"Are you telling me this just to interrupt me? Or are you trying to annoy me into paying attention to you?"

"I'm not done. I am assigned to the auxiliary corvette fleet that will provide adaptability to Marshal Angharad Black as she secures Tsurru System, isolates the mothership Titan for seizure and occupation, and captures or destroys any Phene ships that might still be in-system or provide additional support to the ground assault on the Karsh's head-quarters. Which is being led by Sun, right here."

I cup my hands around the dusty planet with its smoky green seas and a beacon whose dull black surface marks it as dead.

Jade stands a mere two steps from me. Too close. Too far. Darkness reminds me of other dark rooms lit only by virtual sparks and the heat of clandestine sex. A smile quirks those perfect lips as if my thoughts are as brightly visible as the hazy glamour of the sun in whose heart Jade stands.

"And I am assigned to the assault on the Karsh's citadel, as you also know," says Jade. "Were you not paying attention? Or did you have something else in mind?"

To pretend I didn't hear, I expand the dead beacon and admire its smooth spiral coil. Jade takes a step closer, like a solar flare licking outward. The reflections of stars shiver along the bulkhead as an all-too-human shadow passes across them.

"I wonder where this linked to, back in the day," I say without look-ing up.

"Surely that goes to Hellion Terminus."

"Why would it go there? The two stars are next-door neighbors in astronomical terms. Why waste a beacon when that beacon could drop you into a system one hundred light-years away instead of four? For all we know, it linked directly to She Who Bore Them All."

Jade laughs curtly. "Every beacon-obsessed engineer thinks every dead beacon must be the drop that leads directly to the Apsaras home world. We'll never find it, any more than we will ever return to the long-lost Celestial Empire, if it even ever existed. Anyway, all the beacons in the Apsaras home star system died and left it stranded. Even the Argosies can't find it."

"How would you know what the Argosies can or can't find?"

"Wouldn't you like to know how I would know?"

Jade has crept up the way they always do, insinuating the lithe readiness of that body into my personal space just close enough to set all my flares alight. Not that it takes much to set all my flares alight.

"Sun said Soaring was off-limits for us Companions," I point out imperiously, "in case you've been trying to seduce Argosy secrets from her."

Jade sighs on a breath like cinnamon and cloves. "You know, Perse," says the person who gave me that one-syllable nickname instead of something respectable.

"Yes, I do know her."

"Surely you can do better than that tired retort." The silky voice takes on its most exasperatingly coaxing tone.

"I could." When I turn my head to look up at them we are close enough that I could lean forward and kiss those slightly parted and exceedingly inviting rosebud lips. I've been here way too many times before, in a dark room with a locked door.

But.

The only thing hotter than a smug but annoyed Jade Kim is a forbidden secret map of the beacon routes from before the collapse. My thoughts have already strayed in that direction because I know where one is, here on the *Keoe*, dangling just out of reach. So frustrating.

Something in my manner exudes distraction.

Jade frowns and takes a step back. "What's gotten into you?"

I lift my chin. "I'm not the easy mark I used to be."

Jade says nothing, as if my words don't compute.

The virtual map spins. There's got to be a way to get to that old beacon map without pissing off my cee-cee or Sun. Jade is looking genuinely concerned now, no doubt afraid they have lost their touch. But in truth, I realize with some surprise, it's not them, it's me. *I'm over you. Mostly.* I give a dismissive parade wave and leave them to it. The door huffs shut behind me.

I say to Mèimei, "You are correct, the Honorable Jade is studying. Apologies for the disturbance."

It takes only two minutes to jog to the aft-port galley where Nanea kin Kavan crews as a baker. It's 0500 on the twenty-four-hour ship clock of the *Keoe* and the early shift is prepping for ship-wide breakfast.

I pause just inside the door, not calling attention to myself. Watching Ti with her mother burns sweet and bitter in my heart. Working side by side they roll out ropes of dough and braid them with the ease of long practice. The two chat so comfortably that for a moment I think I will drown in the regret of what I never had.

Captain Vontae Yáo Alaksu strides in, wearing the uniform of ship security. My father never put his arm around me to give me an affectionate squeeze, only the ceremonial yearly blessing of a hand placed atop my head when we sang an ancestral hymn in the Temple of She Who Preserves and Delivers Voyagers. *We reap what our ancestors sowed. What we sow our descendants will reap.*

"I thought you'd be on duty, Sweetpea?" I hear her father say to her. *Sweetpea.* How adorable. It suits her.

Ti pauses to check the time stamp in her virtual network. "Not yet. Twenty-nine more minutes. I'm not giving up a single one."

Ouch. I guess I am just a job to her.

But that's unfair. I'm feeling pissy, like I always do after any close encounter of the Jade kind.

Her dad slips a rolled-up tablet from his sleeve pocket and opens it on the counter, away from dustings of flour. "Kas has a new drawing for you."

Ti flips the end of her scarf out of the way. "Is that a new flower?"

"So I hear. He could tell you its taxonomy and history. I was more interested in the mechs they're adapting to clear out a stubborn growth of mildew that got into the secondary greenhouse compartment. It looks to me as if it only cropped up after we entered knnu space. Kas is sure it has to have been contaminated at some point on the journey from Chaonian space to Hellion Terminus. Maybe the Guards division we took on board in Karnos brought it in on their boots."

"That sounds like the Guards, never cleaning their boots," remarks Nanea drily without looking up from the countertop.

"Burn me!" He snags a hot bun off a cooling tray and takes a bite.

Nanea gives him the casual smile of a person who loves and is loved. Ugh.

Resh is long turned to dust adrift in interstellar space. Perseus was taken from me even before that, although he didn't die until later. I have long been an interloper listening in on warm-hearted calls home from other cadets, watching pure romances bloom between classmates, and avoiding Channel Idol's smarmy but popular ongoing real-life series *Love Amid the Spears and Shields,* except for a tear-jerker episode about devoted childhood sweethearts sent to opposite fronts who never saw each other again. That was satisfying.

Ti is still studying the drawing. She's always willing to take time to appreciate the work others have done. With a sigh, she says, "Wish I could hug him. How ironic he can't be allowed to see me."

"The queen-marshal learned that lesson the hard way. Just can't take the chance the Riders will figure out where he is and who he's with."

"I know, Dad. But all those years they never found him means he can protect himself. And that decision is selective. The queen-marshal has her cousin visiting him and thinks it's fine because supposedly the Phene don't know Princess Metis is with us now. But how do the Phene know where I am? Or who I am?"

"This war won't last forever, Sweetpea."

She sighs. "I guess I'm just envious. I wish it could be me."

I never had an affectionate childhood nickname. The first person who ever gave me a nickname was Jade Kim, and it was meant as an insult, which is why I adopted it as a badge of honor.

Vontae adds, "Nan, can I have another bun?"

"Have I ever been able to stop you?"

They all laugh as at a familiar, loving joke.

I could insist Ti start duty early. Make up some excuse. But until we boarded the *Keoe* for the knnu passage she hadn't seen her family in a year, and I'm not that cruel, although I might be that selfish.

That's when she looks my way, because she knew all along I was here. She beckons, inviting me in. Her parents are gracious. If they resent sharing her with me they give no indication.

"Perhaps you will come to dinner again, Honored Persephone?" Nanea says. "I can make samosas and tagine again. Or something different, if you'd like."

"My thanks, I am honored to accept," I say, as I think about where the map might be stashed in their quarters. It's not clear they know what they have. It's not clear they don't know. As difficult as it is to imagine, maybe I should just come right out and ask.

"Did you have a question?" Ti says, adept at reading my moods.

That's when I feel the tuning of the ship change. It's subtle but my ear is good and my bones concur.

My ring vibrates with a message from Sun. PERSEPHONE. JADE. FLAG OFFICE NOW.

Ti's eyebrow goes up. She blinks through to the ring network, but she's gotten no message, which means it is a military emergency.

I say, "Stay here. On call."

I hustle out. Once in the passageway I break into a run for a final eight-hundred-meter sprint that brings me out of breath and sweating to the hatch into the secure compartment Sun has taken over as her flag suite. It's adjacent to the captain's suite. Commander Rahaba does not run her Titan like an Argosy, but I have a feeling that on an Argosy ship this compartment would be the living quarters of the top administrative functionary who worked in tandem with the ship's captain.

The marines on duty let me through. What was once a lounge has been turned into a strategos meeting. Six people are present: Me. Sun. Isis. Commander Rahaba. Marshal the Honorable Grace Nazir, who will be in command of the Ninth and Twelfth Guards for the ground assault on Tsurru Prime. Marshal the Honorable Angharad Black, looking relaxed and legendary while sipping at a flask that probably contains whiskey, which means things are about to get interesting.

Sun leans with both hands braced atop the strategos table. Its virtual projection displays the fleet in its final approach to the heliopause of Tsurru System, which has a pop-out showing the dense blot that marks the anchor.

Sun waves me over. "We have commenced transition to normal space."

"Wasn't that supposed to start in twenty-one hours?"

Commander Rahaba is seated at the opposite narrow end of the oval table. On shipboard she does not need the braces she wore planetside, although she still uses a cane. She says, "The energy dynamics from the incident two days ago have hastened our arrival, according to the Navigator's readings."

The Navigator in question is Soaring, but she isn't here, which means she is on the bridge tuning the final approach, or however you want to describe a technology kept so secret it might as well be magic, like in the ancient tales. The door opens and Jade hustles in, beads of sweat on their forehead and breathing like they sprinted the whole way, which they certainly did. I flash a *victory* gesture. Jade pretends not to see.

The commander says, "Is this everyone, Your Highness?"

Sun nods at Jade. "Yes. After going over what's known of the incident, I'm leaning toward sabotage by the Karsh as the most likely explanation."

"Sabotage!" I expostulate.

"Commander Rahaba and Princess Soaring can find no indication of internal failure. However, we can't determine anything until we reach Tsurru. In preparation, I'm rearranging our order of action and preparing to shuffle around a few ships. Persephone, you and Solomon will assemble a task group of onboard shuttles, cutters, and corvettes with a company of marines and a cohort of engineers."

"You're taking us off Marshal Angharad's task group?"

"I'm giving you your own command. I need one of my Companions to oversee the operation to locate and secure the twenty-eight nonresponsive ships. Be prepared for any eventuality, including resistance from the Coalition's local security fleet. I'll be back in touch in twelve hours to game through options and possible courses of action and reaction for the upcoming attack. Any questions?"

A packet drops into my network listing the personnel and ships now under *my command*. I can't fuck this up. "No questions."

"Dismissed," says Sun. "You'll launch the instant we clear."

A timer starts ticking on my network. Fuck. We have eighteen hours to put this entire operation together, and that's considering we have no idea what we're going to be up against, since no one knows what happened to the tow chain except that ships stopped responding to the pneumatic message system. Based on physical measurements emanating from the chain, it's likely they are no longer attached.

Solomon and I set up a staging area off a corvette hangar. We rope in our old CeDCA rack-mates. I put Minh in charge of an emergency rescue medical cohort on a corvette equipped with four rescue shuttles. Ikenna tracks personnel, ships, supplies. As I wait for personnel and supplies to arrive, I match unresponsive ships with their place on the tow chain.

"Look at this," I say to Solomon. "Chains 2 and 3 are the affected ones, but two ships from Chain 5 also aren't responding. That's an odd pattern. Do you really think it's sabotage and not equipment failure, or an attack?"

"How can anything in normal space cut through a bubble?"

"I don't know, but if anyone knows, the Argosies would know, don't you know?"

"I wouldn't presume to know."

I slap him on the arm for the principle of the thing.

He whistles softly. "You want to ask Princess Soaring?"

"She likes my crass jokes, but I'm not sure she's going to confide Argosy secrets to me on that basis."

"No, I mean, here she is."

I've been hunched over a console, face-deep in logistics. As I sit up, her shadow falls across me. She's a quiet one, not a partier. Mostly she keeps to Navigator territory, a special deck off-limits to anyone not of their guild. When she's not on duty she's close to Sun. The way they interact, you would never know they hadn't known each other all their lives.

"Princess!" I say intelligently, hopping to my feet. It's not her height that intimidates me, although she is taller than Solomon. It's that she has the glamour of a person who dresses well, never loses their temper, and trusts themselves enough to like who they are. In other words, she's got what Tiana has, without the exceptional beauty but with the added punch of high status and the privilege of being received with dignity and honor anywhere she goes.

She acknowledges me with a gesture but her gaze has fastened on the mockup I've made. "Drive failure and tow chain collapse have been known to happen, but sabotage remains the most likely scenario."

"I guess it fits with the Trinity Coalition's brand of criminality." I scratch my head. "We still don't know how the Phene got possession of ten knnu drives for their attack on Molossia. Do you think they got them from the Ousoos Argosy?"

She smiles wryly. "Even if they wanted to flout that Argosy interdiction—we don't loan knnu drives to non-Argosy groups—they don't have ten knnu drives to lend. But that's not why I'm here. There is a thing I wish to tell you in person. Look here." She uses a virtual stylus to trace the elliptical shape of the bubble. "A stable bubble can't be punctured or crossed. Once we emerge from knnu space, you should look first along our wake."

"You're saying we're looking for wrecks and debris."

She shrugs elegantly in agreement.

"Does that mean ships can't get kicked out of the bubble?"

"It is theoretically possible. A bubble might destabilize in places due to localized movement. In such cases a ship might cross into normal space. The force/mass coefficient did alter when the incident took place. But if they did fall out of the bubble, then they are far behind us now."

"Like archaeopteryx chicks who lost their mother on a vast and treacherous ocean, only worse because they've also lost the means to cross the water?"

Her smile has the sweetness of crystalized ginger: first the sugar and then the kick that makes your mouth burn but in a good way. "Something like that, although when I was in fifth form I was assigned to a fowl hatchery. Archaeopteryx chicks are cute little fluffballs and will peck out your eyes if they have the chance. As I know from personal experience."

She has dazzlingly violet eyes that I suddenly realize look totally artificial beneath the numinous glow of the rhombus embedded in her forehead.

Reading the abrupt horror in my expression, she chuckles.

"Oh the hells, you're having me on," I say.

She gives a polite bow of acknowledgment, an Argosy gesture, not Chaonian. "You are any easy mark, Honored Persephone."

"Please, call me Perse."

She glances at Solomon, who has his I'm-trying-not-to-bust-out-laughing face on. "My thanks for the courtesy but I cannot, Honored Persephone. It would be rude."

"Asshole also works."

She covers her mouth with her hand, eyes crinkling up with the kind of embarrassed smile I love to winkle out of people to get them to like me as they decide I'm no threat. But we don't have time for my bad jokes.

She takes a breath and lowers the hand. "This is no time for levity, is it? What I want to show you is the pattern of flow currents present within the hauling radius in the hours before the incident."

"Oh, I see," I answer, hoping to impress her with my sagacity. "That will help us plot a likely distribution of debris so we can get to wreckage faster."

"That is correct." She hands me a memory capsule. "How you Chaonians do not secure separate and unconnected physical components for high-value information will never fail to puzzle me. Anyone could hack your personal network at any time."

As a scion of Lee House I know all about that. "We have fail-safes."

She frowns. "So you believe."

What I do have is one of Ti's portable tablets, which she gave me to share a set of drawings Kas had done that she thought I'd like, as well as a set of erotica shows I lifted from a Phene ship in Karnos System and keep secured off my own network because I'm a scion of Lee House and know better. I slip the tablet out of my sleeve. "Will this do?"

She examines the tablet. A pulsing rhythm chases around in the depths of her rhombus, and she nods. "That is acceptable."

After transferring the data and giving me a tutorial in how to read it, she takes her leave. As chief Navigator on the *Keoe* she guides the transition. All over the Titan, people batten down the hatches and prepare for battle stations, taking their last naps and eating their last meals. We are headed into what will be a war zone as soon as we reach it. No one knows if the retreating Phene fleet will attack the moment we arrive. No one knows what the Trinity will have ready to meet us.

After our conference with Sun, Solomon and I embark on the corvette *Hræsvelgr*. We buckle into pressure couches when the chime rings and Rahaba's deep voice booms out over comms.

"This is Commander Rahaba. Countdown to transition. Secure all personnel and loose ropes."

"Loose ropes?" I ask Solomon.

"Argosy cant."

"In eight. In five. In three. In two. In one."

The tuning fork I carry in my sleeve pocket vibrates. My body feels as if it is being pulled through a fine mesh of intangible particles that ring in my bones at A-432. We hit a patch like a bumpy road for thirty-two seconds and then it's as if we never left normal space. Outside cameras, comms, and arrays snap back to life.

"Release," says Captain the Honorable Freya Lee, a Lee House cousin so distant I have never met her much less heard of her before today.

The *Hræsvelgr* kicks out of the hangar, torch drives on standby as momentum carries my little task force of twelve ships away from the cliff-side of the huge *Keoe*. My first real unit command. I'd feel sick but there isn't time. I unstrap from the secure couch and scramble to the corvette's strategos dais, hooking in like a boss.

The first thing I see as we come clear of the *Keoe* is its tow chains, ships strung like beads receding over eighty klicks into the past. This is the most complicated part of the assault. Ships are releasing from the chains, some more smoothly than others, as they form up into their designated fleets and streak away. The royal cutter speeds from the *Keoe* to the waiting *Boukephalas* and its escort. Sun is on her way to do something rash and brilliant, her signature style. On top of all that, she's got to be pissed about losing her ships to dirty sabotage instead of clean battle.

A distant burst of energy marks the beginning of the attack. Second Fleet under the command of Anas Samtarras has fired the first shot as it races toward Tsurru Quince and the Meli Beacon. The *Keoe*, under the wing of Alika's task group, vanishes from visual sight. All that's left here on the heliopause are twelve little ships and their dauntless if inexperienced commander looking for the proverbial needles in the incomprehensibly vast haystack that is space.

Me.

Get a grip, asshole.

The Grand Sanctuary of the Vestal Trinity

Sun rode the *Boukephalas* down from the heavens to the Grand Sanctuary of the Vestal Trinity. She and her strike team weren't in the battle cruiser, of course, since Tulpar-class vessels weren't built to land on a planet. They led a vanguard of heavily armored drop-ships accompanied by cutters, screaming down onto Tsurru Prime.

The circular site was visible from the mesosphere, with its four concentric rings of walls like a vast and colorful target offered to the sky. According to Nona Lee, the outer wall created a perimeter around the entire complex. The first ring housed warehouses, drone barracks, and tithing offices. The second wall enclosed administrative and residential compounds. The third wall, a mere four klicks in diameter, set off a restricted area with gardens beneath layers of clear roofing. The fourth wall was a single klick in diameter, the "eye" that housed the seat of the Karsh.

An opening salvo had bombed the roadways and railways leading to the Sanctuary. Sun was attacking in coordination with a landing of the Ninth and Twelfth Guards under the command of Grace Nazir who, after his initial skepticism, had grown positively enthusiastic at a chance to really stomp some Trinity butt. He was a man straightforward in his military thinking.

Sun had kept the plan simple: slow down the enemy's movement capabilities, keep their defense forces busy, and strike directly at the Trinity's heart.

The Karsh had brought this battle on herself. Sun had offered the woman an alliance, but she had kicked it back in Sun's face. Such disrespect could not be tolerated. It made Chaonia look weak, and it just plain pissed Sun off.

She checked her network. In orbit, the *Boukephalas* and its escort group were establishing local dominance around Tsurru Prime. Alika's task group with the *Keoe* and her escort had twenty-one hours remaining before it reached Kumbala Beacon. The Second Fleet was already engaged in battle as Anas's flagship *Kanthaka* drove toward Meli Beacon, a mere nine hours out now. Their operations were streaming a live analysis of hotspots in the battle, a crippled Chaonian frigate sluggishly retreating, a hulked Trinity corsair being evacuated. Trinity's scrappy defense force wasn't going to go down easy, but they would go down.

None of the Phene ships who had fled Hellion Terminus seemed to be in Tsurru System, which meant they had already dropped into either Meli or Kumbala. Thus not her immediate concern.

The engines changed pitch as the turbulence of descent increased, rattling everyone on board. Twelve minutes to landing. She was entirely in the moment. Totally focused. Totally alive. There was nothing else like this.

She opened comms to Razin, who was with Nona Lee's advance infiltration force. STATUS?

No reply, and no location mark, which was unusual but likely meant they had entered a shielded area in the same way Persephone's and

James's rings hadn't worked in the underground lab beneath the industrial park by CeDCA.

A ping vibrated into her ring from Persephone, as if responding to her thought.

> MULTIPLE DEBRIS CLUSTERS CONFIRMED. SPLITTING OUR
> FORCES TO INVESTIGATE.

Sun tapped back an affirmative. No need to say more. Either Persephone could handle the job, or she couldn't, in which case Solomon would take over, and Sun had nothing but good reports about his ability to keep his head under pressure.

Ten minutes to landing.

She used voice for Jade. "Over. The Guards are on target to hit dirt five minutes before you do. Are you ready?"

"I am." Jade always sounded ready, and at first she'd thought it was part of a competitive performance play to get attention and praise. But their successful actions at the assault on the Citadel on Karnos Prime had convinced her Jade was genuinely gifted at ground operations and at staying levelheaded amid fire. A secondary command on this crucial operation offered a perfect testing ground for that theory. "I have an open comm to Razin but have received nothing since the coordinates she pinged in one hour ago."

In a firefight, an hour might as well be a year. For all she knew, Nona's advance party had been overrun and the plan dead on arrival, in which case she would be sending Jade into an ambush. Zàofù would doubtless tell her to call off Jade's cohort, set a static line, and try a more conservative approach.

She said, "I have no current status from your rendezvous party, so be prepared to go straight into flack. Probable that we will lose communication."

"Understood."

The copilot's voice broke over comms. "Brace for landing."

The drop-ship flipped in that stomach-lurching way they had, head over ears in a final slowdown. They hit with a jolt hard enough to rattle everyone's teeth. The engines cycled to a new hum. Hail-like thumps peppered the hull. Local fire.

Sun and her elite marines unstrapped. They had armor suits built for mobility and speed, able to withstand light fire. A noise clunked. Two ramps slammed down. Attack cutters screamed past overhead, laying down covering fire to clear a path.

"Go. Go. Go."

Sun hammered down the ramp with Isis beside her and the company behind. Telemetry fed into her network, building a real-time map. The two Guards divisions had landed at the outer wall, blocking the roads from external threats and beginning a push both outward and inward.

Sun had landed in the "eye."

The central Sanctuary was a triangular-shaped pavilion at the center of a circular plaza paved with stone and decorated with fountains. Tsurru Prime had Destiny-standard gravity but a marginal atmosphere prone to acid rains. Therefore, the toxic spray drifting off the fountains made it difficult to approach the seat of the Karsh without that august ruler's permission, since the ancient one controlled all the entrances into the Sanctuary. The ruler could demand any who came before her first disrobe from their seal-suits and unhook their breathers. Power gives you the means to place others at a disadvantage in relationship to you.

A firefight broke out on the far side of the plaza as the other half of Sun's unit headed in, drawing some of the fire off her advance. She raced for the pavilion entrance as local military in tricolor uniforms scrambled to lay down a hailstorm. Impacts staggered her, sent her to one knee as her shield cracked. Coming up from behind, Isis shoved her sideways into the cover of a blocky fountain. Impact sites on Sun's bodysuit shone with a fading blue, the armor radiating the force up and down to disperse it. A seam was cracking at her left elbow joint. Her thigh ached, the old injury waking up. The shield was damaged beyond repair so she shook it off her arm.

"Your Highness," Isis began in that tone.

"I don't want to hear it."

She flung the shield to her left to draw fire and dashed out to her right. This time she broke from fountain to fountain, using the thick spray to obscure her movements. It helped that she had the knack of picking out targets at a run. Octavian had trained her well. From this distance all she needed was to knock them off-balance, disorient them. Give her squad time to get across the plaza to the entrance.

She reached the monumental triple arch first. Beyond lay the pavilion, the heart of the Karsh's Sanctuary and the visual representation of her power. A more cautious soul would take cover behind one of the big columns to take their bearings, but that would give the defenders time to place a bead on her, so she charged past into the central pavilion. Behind her, marines collided with tricolors, going hand-to-hand.

Amulet ribbons painted with symbols hung from a high-beamed scaffolding. Their ten-meter lengths writhed in the air as a wind swung through. They were clearly positioned to dazzle and disorient the people who entered the Sanctuary intimidated by the Karsh's inhospitable power and then forced to shuffle forward with labored breathing and skin stinging from the touch of icy toxins. But the banner-like ribbons gave Sun an advantage since their fluttering lengths provided visual cover as she used their swaying and swirling to dart forward from one to the next. Isis caught up to her. Where had Isis been? Was that blood on her visor? No matter; she was mobile and had a shield. More marines appeared, spreading throughout the pavilion as they picked off the last of the tricolors. The scattershot noise from the other side of the pavilion meant people were still fighting.

A transparent dome about half the height of the pavilion's roof stood at the center like a bulging cornea. Beneath the dome rose the three "thrones" representing the Trinity's rulers. They were not chairs but plinths suitable for displaying statuary, and each wide enough on their flat tops to accommodate a cushion.

Sun had attacked the Grand Sanctuary on the principle that it was crucial to make a statement by taking charge of symbols of authority. She who holds the Sanctuary holds one-third of the heart and power of the Trinity.

So she didn't fully expect that Adele Karsh would be waiting for her. Speaker Baragesi had fled Chaonia's fleets in Karnos. Why would a ruler of a far smaller polity not run also, hoping to fight another day? That the Karsh would be arrogant enough to meet her head on was a chance Sun chose to take.

And her instincts again proved correct. For there the old woman sat, atop the tallest of the plinths. Her body was as small and frail-looking as Alika had reported. Looks can be deceiving, as Makinde had pointed out in his separate report. A weapon rested on the Karsh's lap. Her grasp on it was as relaxed as any sharpshooter who treats the gun as if it is one of their own limbs.

Sun pushed past the last amulet ribbon. The heavy fabric slithered along her body as if trying to cling to her form, a sensation not displeasing but more like an invitation whispered from whatever gods inhabited this place. *This too can be yours.*

Sun halted at the edge of the little dome. She gestured toward Isis and the trailing marines to stay behind the ever-shifting screen of the swaying ribbons. Shields up. Guard her back.

"You must be Sun," said the old woman with a searing expression of disdain on her face. "Do you know who I am and what I represent, that you bully your way into the chosen Sanctuary of the Vestal Trinity without invitation?"

"I expected you to run."

"I am too old to run. Nor do I ever intend to abandon my seat. But since you have forced your way into my hearing, I suppose I must be willing to open negotiations."

Sun cocked her head to the left, considering the statement. She understood stubbornness, but she had had enough.

"The time to open negotiations was at Hellion Terminus. Now you can surrender. In another hour we will control the planet. In another day, this system. In three days, all of the Trinity Coalition will belong to Chaonia."

"A presumptuous timetable. No one has ever conquered Trinity."

Sun began to pace a circuit of the dome's circumference, studying its transparent material and a smooth flooring that supported the bases of the plinths. Drops of blood spattered. From her arm? Her thigh? Wounds that didn't fell you could be tended later. She kept walking.

"What I don't understand, Eminent Karsh, is why you refused to negotiate at Hellion Terminus. You could have had a profitable alliance with Chaonia. Yet you rejected it."

The Karsh did not shift her position to follow Sun's path as the queen-marshal worked her way around the dome's curve and behind her back.

Sun went on. "Did you believe that by yourself the Trinity Coalition could defeat Chaonia? Were you given assurances the Phene Empire would lend its retreating ships to your defense? Perhaps the Yele League, or some breakaway faction within the Yele League like a representative of the seers of Iros, made promises to you. Promises you unwisely believed. Or perhaps you simply did not believe I could follow you here with my own Titan and my own Navigator."

The old woman's tone was scornful. "There is a reason, brash youth, that we in the Coalition rule by threes. The ancient one brings wisdom to the table of governance. The Matrone offers stability and sustenance. The Magava provides the fresh ideas and vigor of youth. Because youth is not meant to rule alone. You will crash and burn because there is no one with the courage to check you. I will not bow before you, who ought to show proper regard for your elders."

Sun came back around into view of the distinguished visage. Adele Karsh had the hard expression of a woman who has presided over many unsavory decisions. Her short silver hair was brushed upward into a crown-like appearance. She wore no adornment except for a handsome white brocade jacket embroidered with gold thread in horned moons and trefoil knots. While the Magava and Matrone of the Trinity had limits to the term they could serve, a Karsh, once installed, could sit on the cushion of power until she died. Her role in the Trinity was precisely that she had lived a long time and thus brought the lessons of experience and institutional memory to the deliberations of the triumvirate. Rumor had it that Adele Karsh was 140 years old and had prolonged her life by drinking the blood of youthful sacrifices. Sun doubted the story. Not that people wouldn't happily sacrifice the lives of others to benefit their own selfish desires, had they the chance, but no one need die for a transfusion to happen. Not unless the person receiving the donation desired the cruelty of a mortal flourish, the final prick of a blood sacrifice.

Even Nona Lee's illegal clones weren't immortality, although that did not answer the question of why Nona Lee had created them.

Stay focused.

She said, "Here I am, Eminent Karsh, come to pay my respects. Be assured I will demand full restitution for the lives you have cost me. Did you sabotage the tow chain?"

"Self-defense is not a crime. You chose to invade us. Chaonia was offered the same terms as any other trading partner."

"I am not 'any other.'"

Sun took several steps back to examine the dome, plinths, and old woman through various filters in her network. All read with the same outputs. She would never have known were it not for Dozer.

She silently pinged Jade a ?

No reply. Was that a faint tremor of a firefight felt through her boots?

Keep her talking.

"The terms are unconditional surrender," said Sun, tipping her head to meet the Karsh's glare. "I am willing to show deference to you and the other two members of the triumvirate if you explain what you know about how the Phene illegally acquired knnu drives and Navigators to guide them. And if you reveal how you managed to sever the tow chains."

The old woman chuckled. "An absurd request."

"An Argosy pledges safe passage. The Ousoos Argosy has betrayed the Argosies' most treasured traditions and ideals."

"Your history is sadly lacking. Why do you think the Apsaras Convergence developed in the first place? Why do you think they conceived the urgent idea to build the beacon routes? It was to combat the rise of war among the Argosies, a slow-burning series of slow-motion conflicts that threatened the web of contact between star systems. But technology is a tool, not a morality. The peace that beacons bought by sidelining the Argosies has come with a greater price than the Apsaras engineers ever imagined. The beacons brought us people such as you, Queen-Marshal Sun. Aggressors who speak of honor when what they mean is that they have the power to do as they wish."

"You rule the Trinity as a haven for lawless marauders and criminal enterprises. Are you scolding me?"

"I am content with what I have. Can you say the same?"

"Why should any soul be content? Are there not always more secrets, greater enlightenment, yet to discover?"

"If there are, you will get no answers from me."

Adele Karsh broke off, chin rising, eyes widening at a sound or sight Sun could not hear or see. Certainly the commotion was not present on the plaza nor amid the rustling amulet ribbons that seethed in a rising wind, revealing and concealing the figures of Sun's soldiers ready and waiting for an action that was, in this case, happening elsewhere. Sun had been the distraction, the only one prominent enough to grab the Karsh's full attention. No one else could have fooled the ancient one into thinking the attack was coming through the plaza.

Raising the weapon, the old woman fired. Her body convulsed at an impact. A second. A third. She slumped forward, folded double, head to knees, and slid limply off the cushion. Where her head moved past the edge of the plinth it vanished as though excised.

Sun raised a hand to signal *Wait* to her unit.

An unseen force dragged the body off the plinth and into nothingness. A strange swirling energy like smoke topped the plinth. For twenty-five seconds—a seeming eternity—it spun around and around and around in a vortex. Then an out-of-focus shape stepped into the vortex. Energy like insects coalesced around the shape, filling it in, patching in and out of colors and textures until there stood Jade Kim atop the pillar like a deity, softly shining. Behind Sun, one of the soldiers whistled softly. Several cheered.

Jade's lips moved. Words emerged, out of sync. "Can you read me?"

"Is the facility secured?" Sun asked.

"Not yet. We are going room by room. There is substantial resistance. They have traps, gas, and blast doors."

"Did you make contact with Razin?"

"Verbal contact only, for ten seconds before a blast door shut. The Honorable Nona Lee's party is besieged in the northwest quadrant of the complex."

"Any idea why they would have ended up there when you entered from the southeast? And the target was the Karsh's seat in the central chamber?"

"Unknown."

"Very well. Secure the central chamber and assign a unit to remain at this plinth for communications to the surface. I'm coming in." Jade pinged in a rough diagram of what was so far known of the underground complex. Sun turned to Isis. "You will remain here to keep this area secured and to relay comms."

Isis took her duties as bodyguard with the utmost seriousness, but she also understood tactical needs. "Yes, Your Highness."

Sun said, "Second squad, with me."

She pinged the drop-ships to have a full company meet her at the entrance coordinates to the underground complex. All gates out of the central plaza had been secured by Guards. A Wolverine met her on the other side. She and her squad piled in. The vehicle sped on a service road past fields, sleepy canals, and decorative gazebos perched on tiny islands surrounded by placid ponds. She used the time to check in with each of the unit commanders of the Guards, under heavy fire as they secured the warehouse district building by building or moved outward along the roads and railways.

A full company of Shields met her at the gate at the second ring. The tricolors there were dead or prisoners. They sped around the exterior of the second wall. Smoke rose from buildings. A rattle of stinger fire announced a skirmish close by. At the point of entry, a squad of marines waited to escort her.

"Our comms don't work inside, so we're using runners," said the sergeant in charge, a woman Sun had worked with before.

"Very good, Cleo. Lead on."

The underground complex was clouded with smoke, ventilation whining as tendrils were pulled toward overworked exhaust shafts. They raced through connected corridors without running into any fighting, then turned a corner not into the central chamber as she had expected but into Jade Kim. The Companion had thrown up shields at an intersection of two passageways to create a protected throughway. Stinger fire and the occasional impact slug slammed into the shield barricade from the passageways on either side while marines popped off shots in response.

"What's this?" she asked.

"We found Nona Lee under fire in a chamber farther in. We cut this route through but she won't evacuate."

"Why not?"

"She wouldn't tell me. I guess I'm not important enough."

"I see. That way?"

"I'll come with you!"

"No. I've brought my own squad. You need to clean out these passageways and take control of this entire level. Do you need a plan of attack?"

Jade bristled, as Sun had known they would. "I'll get it done."

"See that you do." She ran on with her squad.

One hundred meters past the barricade brought her to a hole cut through a maintenance shaft to provide entry into a chamber beyond.

"Air filters secure, they have tried numerous gas attacks," said the corporal who was on guard at the hole, not recognizing Sun.

Inside a large, square chamber she found Nona Lee's ragtag squad of auxiliaries. Nona had refused a marine or Guards unit for her infiltration, preferring to work with local people trained to her specifications who knew the territory. Sun didn't immediately see Nona, but Razin had been pulled to one side with two other unconscious casualties.

"What happened?" she asked after checking to make sure Razin was unconscious, not dead.

"She was incapacitated by the first round of gas, but is stable," said one of Nona's people. No name tag, but outfitted with a medic's kit, gloves stained with blood.

"And those two?"

"Gut wound, not stable. Concussion and crushed hand, stable."

Sun's platoon spread out to reinforce the two other entry points. One was a sealed blast door and the other a hatch to a lower level that had been exploded open and was clearly a vector for all kinds of unpleasant attempts to make the chamber uninhabitable. A number of shattered shields littered the deck around the opening, and a pair of marines were welding pieces of a console together to create a barrier. An immediate drop of flash-bangs down through the hatch by her marines gave them breathing room, if you could call it breathing, given the stinking haze that obscured the chamber. What was burning?

At first she did not see Nona Lee amid the banks of consoles and shelving. No, there she was in the back, pulling physical folders from a shelf and dumping papers into one of several metal bins and cans where other papers and folders burned to create that sulky, smoky fire.

Sun trotted over. "What is this?"

"Records," said Nona Lee without looking around. "The consoles contain all classified coalition records of the Trinity's official enterprises. The physical records pertain to all offline and out-of-the-cloud activities. The stuff that even a criminal coalition doesn't want anyone to know about. It's how the Karsh keeps the people of Libertalia under her thumb."

"Libertalia?"

"A place. Where people pay to conduct their business off-network without legal oversight or the interference of Trinity enforcers."

"Ah, I see." She did not say "like your clone lab" but she didn't need to.

Nona added, "The Karsh has informers everywhere. Thus these records. I've been waiting years to do this. That old bitch murdered one of my progeny and there wasn't a thing I could do about it without risking the others, as well as all the work I was doing for Eirene."

"A grim toll. Yet you remained loyal to Chaonia."

Nona halted in mid-reach for a final clump of folders on a shelf. She turned around. The resemblance between her and Persephone was clear, even with age, the patched eye, and whatever specific hardships Nona had endured in her sixty-plus years. But there is far more to character than genetics. The woman's stance and the cut of her shoulders gave her the look of a lethal barrier her enemies would not easily overcome. Her leg braces suggested a frailty that had been compensated for to create a new method of strength. The aesthetic of how she carried herself offered a window onto a person who had chosen to illegally clone herself in the teeth of what would be universal condemnation and a prison sentence if anyone found out.

Nona said, "Do you intend to stop me from destroying these records?"

"I'm not a blackmailer," said Sun. "Nor do I believe you will betray Chaonia. But you've endangered many squads of marines by making this detour rather than sticking with the stated goal."

"Is it a detour? You have to smoke out this entire nest of scorpions regardless. I've left the consoles intact so your people can get to work on them. Have at it. It's all yours. Do you have a ship waiting?"

"Why?"

Nona tossed the sheaf of folders into the flames. "Right before we entered the complex I received a distress signal." She gave a one-shouldered shrug to indicate they both knew what she was talking about and thus needn't speak its name out loud.

"I see," said Sun. "So naturally you wish to go there immediately now that you have dealt with covering your tracks by destroying the incriminating evidence."

Nona's expression suggested Sun ought to know better. "I meant it when I said it was a *distress* signal."

"How well do you know Kiran Seth de Lee?" Sun asked with abruptly inflamed curiosity.

Not by an eyeblink did Nona reveal any emotion beyond her already obvious impatience. "I warned them against him."

"That's not the story Moira told Persephone. She said you encouraged the liaison between him and Aisa. Which makes me wonder if he was complicit in your . . . experiments."

Nona's mouth flickered with distaste. "Even as a girl Moira had a way of phrasing things to give shine to herself. As it happens—"

An explosion shook a quake through the floor. Shouts broke out below. The marines guarding the hatch to the lower deck began shooting downward. One fell back, wounded, to be replaced by a second.

A marine shouted, "Is that hatch cover you were fixing up done yet or did you stop for a cup of tea?"

Sun jogged back to the hole in the wall and into the corridor. The pops and echoes of weapons fire intensified as she ran back to the barricade at the intersection. Jade and the rest of the unit was still hunkered down.

"Was that explosion you?"

"No. I don't know what it was, and we don't have comms, so . . ."

A whistle warned them of an incoming messenger. A runner staggered into view along the passage that led back to the entrance, wearing the colors of the Twelfth Guards. The soldier dove down beside her.

"Your Highness. The entrance has been bombed by tricolors. It's blocked by debris. We can't get out or receive new reinforcements until our forces clear the wreckage. It'll take hours."

"I see." Sun turned this new information through her head. "Jade, with me."

Jade easily matched her on the sprint back to the records chamber, and had the good sense to remain silent.

In the records room, unflappable Nona Lee was running her finger down the last shelf that held paper folders as if she had all the time in the world to make sure her laboratory remained incognito.

"Marshal," Sun said. "We're trapped. Give Jade the coordinates to your lab."

"Why?"

Because I gave the command! Sun tamped down her anger. Yelling at an elder would not solve the situation, even if Nona Lee only thought about her own personal situation in the midst of an emergency. "Because we have no time to waste. We still have access to the plinth. Jade will transfer the coordinates to Isis, who is in the Sanctuary above us. She can send a corvette to investigate the lab."

"They won't be able to get in."

"Give Jade the name of whoever will be able to get in, from whatever organization you have arranged in-system. *We don't have time.*" She raised a hand. Everything was clear, sharp, pristine in its focus. In these intense moments she could feel events bending to her will. "Squad two, with me. Squad five to follow. This nest of scorpions isn't going to clear itself."

She pitched two flash-bangs down the hatch. They burst on the deck below in a series of hollow thumps and firecracker snaps. In the lull that followed, Sun dropped through feet-first into the thick of a stunned and surprised enemy as, behind, her squad scrambled to keep up.

The Wily Persephone Does Not Aspire to Be a Fucking Glory Carnotaur

I open a window to conform to my order of march: eight corvettes, four cutters, and utility shuttles for close-in work. Ikenna monitors my personal comms. He loops me in with the commanders of each vessel. For the time being we sit idle as we approach possible targets.

The ops sup console is crewed by an older lieutenant whose name I have forgotten but who wears a CeDCA pin on her right shoulder epaulettes. In fact, her shoulders are as wide as Solomon's although she's a head shorter. She must have played rugby at the academy. I'd bet my life on it.

She's using the record of currents Princess Soaring gave me to trace from the *Keoe*'s arrival coordinates backward along the rippling energy of the wake's trail.

"Got something," she says. Bìyù Yáo Alcyrene, that's it. Gave me the white-eye when I came on board, intimidated by the presence of one of the queen-marshal's exalted Companions. Obviously she doesn't know my history, but as Ti would remind me, even if she did, I'm Core House to people like her. "I have identified four packets of debris at possible flow points."

She pings over velocities and vectors. Three of the debris packets are moving in more or less parallel motion, already ten thousand klicks away and receding toward the heliopause. They get labeled Packets 1, 2, and 3. Packet 4 is spinning off at an angle that will take it through Tsurru's outer asteroid belt unless we reach it first. Comms sends out standard pings to see if we get any answers. Sensors sweep for heat and energy readings. I wonder what happened to the rest of the missing ships. This debris doesn't remotely amount to the mass of twenty-eight vessels.

Captain Lee catches my eye. "Honorable, we're seeing a shift in hostile forces from an orbital habitat at Tsurru Nonce. A squad of corsairs and gunships headed this way."

"What's their earliest ETA?"

"Sixteen hours."

"Hold position. Sensors?"

Yáo Alcyrene says, "I'm reading residual heat and energy from Packets 1, 2, and 3 consistent with debris. Combing through the heat signatures now. I'm getting fireflies but not much else."

"Could it be survivors?"

"Undetermined."

"Comms?"

"No apparent distress signal from Packets 1, 2, or 3. But I've got wiggle on Packet 2's frequency."

"Wiggle?"

"At this distance onboard comms inside a ship's fiber system would be difficult to confirm. More likely it is the slow collapse of an energetic shipboard system. A drive tone. You know?"

I do know. I pull my tuning fork from my sleeve and unhook headphones from the console I'm seated at. "Separate it out and send it over."

An alarm rings as we approach the dispersing wake. The hull rumbles. It's like getting hit by a wave, rock and roar, and then we stabilize.

Ikenna starts bouncing in his seat. "I've got Packet 4. Marginal energy readings consistent with the lowest level of emergency power. Discrete but multiple faint heat signatures that might be lifepods or suited survivors sheltering in a hulk. Hold on. Comms, did you get that?"

"I absolutely did!" says the ensign at comms, looking like she's just been given the best gift of her life, and maybe she has. Another CeDCA grad, I note.

She amplifies a message, its basic SOS repeating, followed by the crackle of a voice. "This is *Bulsajo* actual. We have lost main power. We have casualties and survivors on board. Please respond. Out."

The relief is so profound I have to wipe my suddenly damp forehead and swallow before I can speak coherently enough to patch in. "*Bulsajo,* this is the Honorable Persephone Lee on the *Hræsvelgr,* in charge of the rescue and recovery operation. You have arrived in Tsurru System. Send a full sitrep. We are on our way and will arrive at your coordinates in . . ." The captain drops through a number.

I didn't specialize in tactics at CeDCA since I had been aiming at beacon engineering, but I've been training in Sun's circle for over a year, which means the basics have been pounded into me. I place the corvettes in a defensive formation with the cutters in the lead. Off we go. The hostiles are still moving, possibly after us and possibly to intercept the *Rakhsh* or the *Boukephalas*, but if I were them I'd want to scrap with us, not with battle cruisers.

Even with all this, visions of fireflies are still dancing in my head. With the headphones sealing my ears I tap my tuning fork against the railing of the strategos dais and press it against my arm while I test the faint background wiggle off Packet 2.

Beacon drives are weird things. Sometimes I think the universe is a voice both too loud and too soft for human ears to perceive. From my personal research based on not enough test subjects, every ship when it drops through a beacon vibrates at the same tuning as a scylla's song. Beacon drives are always vibrating. Singing, if you will. The vibration of the drive in concert with the frequency of living, breathing humans on board the vessel is what triggers a beacon as the ship glides through its coils.

The vibration of my tuning fork tells me there's a beacon drive somewhere in Packets 1, 2, and 3, which would mean the stem of at least one ship drifts within that debris. It's not my gut or my heart; it's my diaphragm that tickles my instincts and tells me to take a deep breath.

All this time Solomon has been seated at a side console, scanning readouts, but he's attuned to my moods and comes over.

"Let me listen," he says as he plugs in with a separate headset and shuts his eyes to concentrate. After three minutes and forty-eight seconds, he opens his eyes.

"Repetitive taps," he says.

"Can't be taps. There's no sound transmission."

"That's not what I mean." He thinks it over. "Interruptions. Like someone opening and closing a door."

"Ikenna, can you separate this out and amplify it?"

It takes ten minutes. The entire bridge listens to what sounds eerily like a repeated SOS if you had an off-line but functional beacon drive, no functioning radio comms, and a clever engineer or tech who was alive at one point to set it up. Or maybe it's just an artifact of the system. A broken fragment of a ship adrift in the solar wind at the edge of a star system.

We've got hostiles incoming. The *Bulsajo* needing rescue. This whisper could as easily be background radiation. But I don't think it is. I'm not very religious, but I trust my big sister and the objects and skills I inherited from her.

"*Bulsajo*, what is your weapons status?"

Their captain replies. "No way to charge main cannons, fire control is basically shot, but I've got all my missiles. I can be very angry if you tell me where to shoot."

It's my call.

"Lieutenant Solomon and I will proceed with the *Hræsvelgr* and the two cutters to Packet 2." I identify the senior-most of the remaining captains; another CeDCA graduate, twenty years in. "Captain Jí Alargos, you will proceed with the rest of the task group to the *Bulsajo*. Put it under tow if you can. Otherwise evacuate the survivors and rendezvous with the fleet. Captain Lee, send hornets to Packets 1 and 3. I want a complete sweep for life signs. Send mimic wasps with them to try to draw off a gunship or two. Corvettes, be aggressive, but if the hostiles bypass us, don't pursue."

Not one person tries to talk me out of my rash plan. I suppose they might secretly hope I get blown to bits, but I think those are admiring looks they cast in my direction as I make my way off the bridge. Captain Lee pings me to recommend two damage-control ratings and four shuttle pilots from her crew for a boarding mission. Proximity to the queen-marshal is a heady brew, and I don't mind savoring it. If this isn't just a wild gallimimus chase I'm leading because I've placed too much stock in Resh's tuning fork.

We speed toward Packet 2, teasing out more and more complex information as we close the gap. Nothing can hide our torch drives, but we have to hope we'll be ignored by the hostiles in favor of pursuing the flashy corvettes and the prize represented by the stricken *Bulsajo*. We get utility shuttles ready. I put Solomon and his team on the *Orange* while I take the *Gold*. Minh accompanies Solomon while Ikenna accompanies me.

Comms gets busy. A battle lights up around Tsurru Prime. The first drop-ships land and disgorge troops on the perimeter of its major city, Triparadeisos. If the delayed chatter is anything to go by, Jade Kim is in the thick of it, leading two full companies in a high-prestige operation in support of Sun's very visible and showy attack on the Grand Sanctuary. Fucker.

Pay attention, asshole.

The other fleets are still in transit to the Kumbala and Meli Beacons when I receive confirmation from Captain Jí Alargos that they have made physical contact with the *Bulsajo*. Twenty-one minutes later we glide up to a bizarre debris artifact that is almost impossible to recognize as part of a ship. A bounce-back confirms it is the fast frigate *Bennu*. Or what remains of the *Bennu*.

The shuttles release. The *Orange* approaches on the other side, out of my visual sight. Solomon pings me on comms so everyone can hear. "We have identified a signal flag set to confirm an entry point. Going in."

The *Gold* slides under the raggedy torn hulk. Breached compartments have spilled their guts and yawn like gaping mouths, cold and empty. We're also getting thumped by objects, including twice by corpses adrift in the debris field.

I say, "Identify human remains and bring them in."

Ikenna says, "Got a visual SOS."

Someone has seen us coming and is standing in an airlock in a vac suit with an emergency lamp blinking the oldest naval code. Unlike some, I do not aspire to be a fucking glory carnotaur leading elite units as part of the main event on Tsurru Prime, but maybe I can save a few stalwart survivors.

"Get me a tether," I say.

"How about me?" Normally Ikenna wears glasses, but we're all vac-suited with our visors up so it's spooky goggles. He gives me the owl stare he used in maths class when he'd finished the entire test early and I was only halfway through.

"Of course, you. Why did you even ask?"

We match velocity and shoot over tethers. It's an easy slide to the twisted hull. Magboots keep us fixed to a surface and we all have secondary lines. Fifth squad follows, while I lead the way to an open airlock to find a vac-suited person waiting for us.

"Report in, Spacer." I cycle through frequencies until I get a match to the channel they are using.

"Guyson Ueda Alargos. I didn't think anyone was coming." The poor soul sounds like they're hyperventilating.

"Casualties? Survivors? What happened to the rest of the ship?"

A traumatized face stares back at me, bewildered by my questions.

"Can I get past and clip into your ship's wiring?" Ikenna asks.

"Oh. Yeah." Ueda is blocking the gap into the interior. The airlock is only partly opened, like it's been forced. "But we lost power when we got cut off from the rest of the ship."

"Where is the rest of the ship?"

"We don't know."

"We'll debrief later. Have you located all survivors inside the hulk?"

"I think so. Yes. There's one compartment we couldn't get open. We felt tapping from inside but . . ."

He stops speaking. He's clearly been days in this condition.

I use my best speaking-to-anxious-first-years voice. "We have two squads coming onto the ship. Once we have confirmed location of all survivors, we will evacuate you onto the shuttles. Can you lead us inside? Just breathe. Slow breaths. We need *your* help."

The glaze of shock starts to clear. "Okay. Okay," he says to himself, as if he's been saying this word over and over the last tens of hours as his mantra of survival. "You can plug in here, but there's a better node in the beacon drive housing. But . . . But . . . We stacked corpses in there. I don't know."

"Okay," I say, to prod him.

"Okay. Okay. This way. Watch your vac suits. There are razor edges where you don't expect them. We lost one person . . . But that was days ago. Okay. It's okay."

Ikenna gives me a look with a tip of the head that I recognize from the academy anytime our rack of five had to deal with a cadet who was falling apart under pressure.

I give the *Eyes open* sign and wave him on ahead of me. Fifth squad has lined up behind, two remaining on hull sentry duty.

I use the ring network to ping Solomon. ENTRY?

WE ARE IN.

CONDITIONS? I reply.

FUCKED UP. I'M BEING TOLD THE ENTIRE FRONT BEACON
    DRIVE HOUSING AND ASSOCIATED COMPARTMENTS
    WAS SEVERED FROM THE REST OF THE SHIP IN A
    CATASTROPHIC IMPACT. I CAN'T BELIEVE ANYONE
    SURVIVED.

We arrange a path for mapping and a time for an eventual meetup. Sensors on board *Hræsvelgr* and *Otso* are scanning the debris and sending me updates. Eleven corpses have been fished out of the flotsam.

As we work our way in through passageways and torqued hatches with barely enough space to squeeze through, Ueda starts talking at a rapid clip.

"The captain had come up to get the message. She likes to come up when the weekly speech by the queen-marshal comes in so she can take it down to the mess and premiere there, not that it doesn't screen everywhere on the ship, but it is a courtesy, I guess you see what I mean, she was okay, really new and young, she survived the death of the *Vermilion* . . ."

"Hold on," I say. "Is the captain among the casualties?"

"We don't know. She'd gone aft. Me and the ensign got the reply message sent off and we closed up and then all of a sudden the impact and I . . . and the compartment breached and . . . the tether . . . okay."

"You lost the ensign?" I ask carefully.

"No, no, Trajan survived, they're still with us, but they broke bones and we had to put them in a stasis pod, it just didn't stop, we were rolling endlessly, people went mad, tore off their suits just to make it stop . . ."

"Hey!" I grasp his arm as his pitch rises and he starts to hyperventilate. "It's okay. You're in normal space. In Tsurru System. We're here. Take a breath. Out. In. Out . . . In . . . Do you need to be transferred to the shuttle?"

"No no no no no, I have to make sure you find where everyone is. Okay."

"Okay. Breathe. That's better." He's not calm, but his eyes aren't so white and his pulse has slowed, so as we proceed I give him a little more information. "The leading theory is that the Trinity sabotaged two of the chains. The queen-marshal is safe, but some ships have gone missing, including the *Bennu*."

We reach a short stretch of normal-looking passageway with four closed doors and one sealed hatch with a green light that signals atmosphere beyond.

"What's in there?" I indicate the hatch.

"An intact launch tube and two missiles."

Spoken like a Chaonian. We don't stop fighting until the last breath has left our bodies and, if we can rig a booby trap as we go down, not even then.

The next hatch takes us into the command and control room for the beacon drive, which looks scrambled from being shaken and jolted but is otherwise intact. Vac suits turn as we enter. In this space the survivors have set up a medical bay, rest zone, and refueling station for liquid meals and air rations. Eleven lifepods are secured to bulkheads with the worst injured suspended inside. Ikenna pushes over to a node and plugs in his module, pulling in a pair of *Bennu*'s tech specialists.

"Lieutenant Yacouba Pfau Alnanjing." A grizzled old CeDCA veteran floats up to me holding a manual clipboard. "Thanks to all the holy ones that you found us."

"Report."

"We estimate that these remains represent eleven percent of the ship. The rest was sheared off. There may have been survivors who made it into the other part of the ship, if any part survived. Here's the manifest with our best estimate of the number of spacers and marines who were likely to have been in the forward compartments at the time of the event. It includes confirmed deceased."

"Where are the rest of the survivors?"

"We established three safe zones in separate compartments."

"Mark your people for an orderly evacuation. We've got another squad coming in from the other side. I'm going to do a sweep."

Comms from the *Hræsvelgr* crackle. "We have two incoming hostiles. Corsairs."

"Accelerate evacuation. Lieutenant, there's a mechanism in every ship to release the beacon drive core. Is that still working?"

"We haven't checked, Captain. We were too preoccupied."

"Not an accusation. You're doing well."

I head out to meet Solomon by the green-glowing hatch.

He says, "A corvette and two cutters can hold off two corsairs as long as we can maneuver. Let's get this ship evacuated."

At that moment we both receive a ping from Isis on the ring network.

URGENT. SOLOMON, STAY WITH THE RECOVERY OPERATION.
    PERSEPHONE, PROCEED ON YOUR FASTEST SHIP
    IMMEDIATELY TO LIBERTALIA AND THESE COORDINATES.
    SUN'S DIRECT ORDERS.

"Libertalia?" I say. "What kind of name is that?"

He gives me a look. "Didn't you read the briefing?"

Reflexively I make a rude gesture in his direction, but I say, "Go on."

"A habitat cluster governed under a nominally free charter, which means the Trinity let criminals and privateers operate out of there without oversight in exchange for plausible deniability of their actions."

Plausible deniability. I have a bad feeling about this.

I say, "Two cutters against two corsairs isn't good odds."

"Yes, but the *Bennu* has two missiles and a working launch tube. I have an idea. So you're good to go, as if either of us have a choice. Sun's orders."

He's correct, as usual. I ping Ikenna to accompany me and leave Minh with Solomon. Once back on the *Hræsvelgr* I ping Isis a private query on the ring.

She replies as immediately as distance allows. "Investigate a distress signal."

"Where am I going?"

"Nona Lee's base of operations. She's unable to go herself. She says you're the only one who can get in past the fail-safe lock."

Oh fuck. As much as I'd like to, I can't argue with that.

64

Blown by What Fortune They Could Not Yet Know

The fighting hadn't reached the top floor of the citadel known as the Matrone's Hive. Hetty entered its suite expecting to find the Matrone tendering her surrender or braced to battle to the death. Instead, the office and parlor were empty. A sweep by Guards revealed no dead bodies, no trapdoors or hidden closets, no aircar landing pad on the tower's triple-domed roof, and no one trying to escape down the lift shaft.

James came clattering up the stairs with his hand-picked squad of hack-and-slashers. He whooped as he scanned the spacious office with the Matrone's official desk surrounded by a bank of lesser consoles for trusted drones. Hetty stood behind him, resting a hand on his shoulder, as he started pulling up screens from the desk.

"The first thing people like this do is grab the money and run," he said. "It's good we got up here so fast. If I can close all the escape routes, we can get our hands on Trinity's treasury."

"A mighty sum, if rumor's true."

"It is."

"We're also meant to capture the Matrone. I'm not so sure we haven't missed that mark."

He'd stopped listening, hunching forward over the desk as his fingers wove and tapped with the peculiar grace that belonged to James alone. His job was to break through the Hive's privacy locks that screened physical vaults as well as the vast system of credit housed in coalition servers.

She explored the suite. The bedchamber was a utilitarian space intended for people who have to pull long shifts and need a place to nap and shower. It wasn't a place to sleep overnight, much less lie for an hour and contemplate the nature of the universe or the particular heat of Sun's body spooned around hers.

The adjoining parlor had divans set in conversational arrays and a long table inlaid with images of bees. Floor-to-ceiling windows looked over the city of Melissa, the capital of Meli Prime. Doors let onto a curved balcony. Outdoors by the balcony railing a pedestal table bore a moisture ring from an object recently removed. Hetty set a hand on the latch.

"Honored Companion, I recommend against it," said Captain the Honorable Justice Bō, her designated attaché for the Trinity mission. "There may still be snipers."

"Do you think so? I'd guess they all have fled."

"It's true coalition troops fight for money, not for duty or honor. Nothing to keep them in the city now we've taken over."

Hetty opened the doors and stepped out into the chilly air.

From the citadel tower the city looked like a patchwork blanket unrolled across a river plain. Storm clouds loomed to the north. Booms of artillery fire shivered the air. The city's comptroller had surrendered yesterday, together with most of the coalition management offices. The head of the system's feared security bureau was dead, shot by an unknown assailant and left in the street for the Chaonians to find. The Eighth Division was currently demolishing a line of police entrenchments seventeen klicks to the east.

From the height, it was clear there was no civic planning involved in the city's layout. The first settlers had built residential compounds, then expanded on top of the older foundations. Marketplaces had burst open like flowers shedding seeds into a tangle of stalls and shops. Everything in Trinity focused on the mercantile. The only green lay in the famous Mother Gardens adjacent to the citadel.

Bears and Wolverines trundled through the streets on patrol. A few locals had ventured out in search of supplies or to check on kin or shops. Their figures were like scraps of paper thrown to the wind, blown by what fortune they could not yet know.

She had been to Melissa before. The memory stung not because it wasn't sweet and tender but because it was.

She turned to Captain Bō. "Now James is here, I'll leave this work to him."

"I'll attend you, Honored Companion."

"No need. Prepare to breach the basement vaults."

"Do you think we'll find the Matrone and her staff barricaded in there?"

"She's somewhere in the city. That we know."

"Sensors haven't picked up an emergency escape tunnel. The marshal had us ring the city before the assault began, so she can't have gotten out on the ground or by air." The captain cleared his throat and, after Hetty nodded, went on. "Honored Companion, I can sense you are looking for solitude. I mean no disrespect, but allow me to assign a squad to shadow you. I don't want to have to answer to the queen-marshal."

Hetty smiled wryly and signed acquiescence. It would be irresponsible of her to get other people into trouble just because she had the sentimental urge to make a pilgrimage into her past.

She took the spiral staircase down ten floors, wondering all the while if the citadel tower was a refurbished Argosy tow-ship in whose shell the Matrone had built her ruling tower. The back of the Hive included living quarters and an extensive kitchen for feeding the indentured servants, colloquially called drones, who lived in the Matrone's household.

The battle had been swift and decisive, but for Hetty's purpose all the paths through the exercise yards, garages, warehouses, and Hive workshops were blocked by wreckage and fallen masonry. There was no way through the citadel to the garden.

Not this way.

The main Hive was a massive administrative complex with hundreds of rooms staffed by outside employees as well as indentured ones. From an office coat check she grabbed an abandoned winter coat. What had happened to its wearer? Were they dead? A prisoner? Had they run home to a flat in the city and hoped to blend back into civilian life as the occupiers established a new regime?

She and Sun had talked many hours about the decision to attack the Trinity Coalition. *What do you mean to do about the coalition's political and economic situation*, Hetty had asked, *if Trinity should fall?* Sun had said, *Trinity* will *fall, and it will rise as before, only now it will be beholden to me.*

Tugging on the coat, she left the Hive by its main entrance. The monumental entrance staircase was intended to intimidate envoys, supplicants, debtors, and small-time criminals brought before the legal apparatus wielded by the Matrone. Those who couldn't pay the large fines imposed would be bound for a term of service into Trinity's massive indentured labor force.

Wearing a local coat over her uniform gave Hetty a disguise. She had always had the skill of effacing herself. Her fathers had loved her, no question, but they were a dyad so attuned to each other that at times they forgot she was part of the family. What she called the years of exile, when Papa had been assigned as Eirene's official diplomatic envoy to Congress Moon in Yele System, had perfected her ability to glide through the corridors of her academy and the back halls of power as softly as a Taraxucum seed dispersed on the wind. It helped that Father was Yele born, not of Chaonian stock, which gave her a more gracile and taller frame than most Chaonians. Meli System's short knnu route took it to either of two Yele League systems, so over the generations the city of Melissa had absorbed a number of Yele immigrants, often fleeing one step ahead of the law. Because of this, Hetty's height allowed her to walk abroad without drawing a second glance from locals, as long as she hid her uniform beneath a coat.

The squad had split into units of three and shadowed her from a distance, so as to grant her some privacy while still protecting her. Her stinger was holstered out of sight under the coat. Her military clearance and discreet escort allowed her to pass patrols without them stopping her, even if they did give her curious glances. Twice she heard her name whispered as a soldier recognized her.

Going the long way around hadn't been part of her plan, but she was glad of the detour. Instead of entering the garden from the citadel side, via its service entrance, she entered through the same gate she and her fathers had used seven years ago.

They had approached the entrance arch along the wide promenade amid many other visitors. The garden was open to the public, for a fee, three days out of every local month. Her fathers walked arm in arm as they always strolled when on an outing. She followed a few steps behind like the icy tail of a blazing comet. Father would glance back anxiously at intervals to make sure she was still there. Papa knew exactly where she was without looking because he had an expansive sense of people and their fields of mood and presence, a form of echolocation that made him an excellent diplomat.

Once through the entrance the crowd had veered onto the path that led to the famous rose garden. Father took a step as if to follow the crowd but Papa gently tugged him in a different direction. They made their way down an innocuous side path past a heritage garden depicting a quaint reconstruction of a supposedly authentic village from the Celestial Empire. Papa already knew what his daughter wanted to see, even though she had only mentioned it once after he had announced she could accompany him on a diplomatic trip to Meli Prime. The Trinity Coalition wasn't a travel destination, because to reach it travelers had to take a knnu hop. Also, of course, visiting a criminal enterprise run by a ruthless triumvirate wasn't anyone's idea of a relaxing holiday, except for those with unsavory tastes or felonious aspirations. But the chance to go had felt like an adventure. It meant getting to spend more time with her fathers than their schedules on Congress Moon permitted.

She'd been fifteen and desperately lonely, in furious correspondence with Sun via courier, slow missives that took weeks to get to the palace and back to her, with her heart poured into her words. It was Sun who had mentioned the Hive Garden and its rarest specimen, the ice rose, because the species had been part of the princess's botany study.

The diplomatic visit had not encompassed winter on Meli. Even though Papa had known an ice rose doesn't bloom in warm weather, he'd taken her to see its plantings anyway. He'd understood the heart must also wait to flower.

Today the Hive Garden wasn't open, but who was to stop her from walking in? The escort fanned out. She knew the route without having to check a map. Such patterns burned permanently into her brain, an inheritance from Father. She paced past the heritage garden and was surprised to discover humbly clad gardeners harvesting winter greens. They wore the striped sleeves of drones, an economic class legal in the Trinity Coalition although banned elsewhere. Father had written at indignant length about the plight of workers caught in such a barbaric system.

Seeing Hetty, the gardeners shot to their feet and bent in subservient bows. No citizen of Chaonia need grovel like this. That was the pride and honor of the republic: every citizen had the right to speak their mind before the queen-marshal.

"Please carry on your work, pay me no mind," she said in her flawless Yele. No roughhewn Common Yele for her but the precise rhythm and tone of the literary and scholarly establishment so prized in the League and so lacking in Chaonia's crudely antique dialect.

Three of the Guards lingered behind to keep an eye on the gardeners. Perhaps it was a little odd that a day after their city had surrendered they were out working. Yet what was strange about needing to eat?

She passed an orchard of persimmon and cold-hardy mandarin oranges. A fence surrounded the winter garden with its beds of yellow aconite and starry glory and its trimmed shrubs of bright red winterberry, jasmine, and camellia.

The center bed held the garden's prize collection of ice roses. It was being tended by another gardener in a stripe-sleeved coat. This older woman knelt on a pad as she packed down loose soil around a tiny rosebush. She glanced up when Hetty halted two meters away. Her gaze caught on the Guards standing back by the fence and returned to cut straight to Hetty's heart.

"You thought they would be in bloom." The voice had a smoky timbre and an alto's range, low and soothing.

"Do they not bloom in winter?"

"Yes, they do." The gardener smiled. "But only when it snows or sleets. That is why they aren't called winter roses but ice roses."

"It's true I'd hoped to see them in full flower."

The gardener cast her eyes toward the clouds pressing across the river plain like the advance of an invasion fleet. "Can you not feel the change in the air? The storm is upon us although its bitterest consequences have not yet begun to fall."

Hetty licked her lips. It was indeed colder than it had been an hour ago. The wind had gained a biting edge, the vanguard sweeping in.

"You are not so accustomed to winter, I think," said the gardener. "We who know our home's seasons can see the ice bearing down upon us. Your eyes are on the roses, for to you this storm brings beauty as well as triumph."

"I did not think to meet a sophist here."

"Ah, but all experienced gardeners are sophists in their way."

That the woman was an experienced gardener was evident in the rich array of well-kept plants. There were sixteen rosebushes, all with mist-pale buds furled tight. The promise of a bloom seemed so close it was painful, yet with the coming storm came also encroaching dusk.

Even on the trip here with her fathers they'd been told never to walk out after dark, only to take an armored car. It was a strange caution heard by a girl who at eleven had regularly explored with Sun, Percy, and James through the night markets of Argos with only their cee-cees in discreet attendance. A bizarre warning after living for two years on Congress Moon where Yele adolescents routinely studied for their exams in chattering packs at tea carts and sweet shops before they trooped to poetry slams and philosophical debates and café concerts that lasted until midnight.

Even were Melissa not already known as a city unsafe at night, no one wise walked the streets of a newly occupied city after dark unless they were a soldier on patrol. As if in reminder of this brutal fact she heard the whine of an aircar passing overhead. Both she and the gardener looked up. A Peregrine-class striker dropped at reckless speed toward the citadel's walls. It was headed for a landing, which meant a high-ranking officer, maybe even a marshal, had come to oversee the decanting of the citadel's treasury. Since the only marshal in-system was James's older brother, Anas, fireworks would soon start.

Probably she ought to go and rescue James.

"Yet here," remarked the gardener, sitting back on her haunches as she studied Hetty with a new sharpness, "why stand upon ceremony with a polite stranger who talks of sophists and phrases her speech in a careful rhythm? There is a saying here on Meli that honey after dark is best explored in a house where dancing is allowed."

"What house is that? A ballroom, do you mean?"

The gardener's eyebrows raised archly. "Have you not the same phrase where you come from? I meant one of our many pleasure houses. Meli is famous for them. I know of a few that may tempt you, if you'd like me to show you. They open at dusk."

Hetty stiffened. She recognized the distinctive eyebrow lift. She'd seen this same woman seven years ago. On that day the woman had been wearing an elegant suit, not a gardener's dirt-stained tunic. Papa had been introduced to her while Father and Hetty stood amid the crowd, for they were merely family, not important political people who must duel diplomatically with a canny and vicious opponent. Her dark eyes on Papa had been as brutal as a honed blade.

She was the Matrone, hiding herself in plain sight as a drone.

Hetty schooled her expression to bland conformity as she pinged James.

MATRONE IN THE HIVE GARDEN ICE ROSE PLOT DISGUISED
   AS A GARDENER. THOUGHTS?

James could be erratic when deep in his beloved systems, but in this case his response was instant: WHERE ARE YOU.

Hetty pinged: STANDING TWO METERS FROM THE MATRONE

KEEP HER TALKING

"Have I said something to offend you?" the woman asked.

"Don't such establishments lack worker rights? What pleasure is there in unwilling love?"

"If people fall irresponsibly into debt then they must make restitution where they are best suited to do so."

"That's a philosophy I cannot praise. Debt is a form of violence when misused."

"And invasion by a foreign fleet is not a form of violence?"

"Sun offered an alliance to the Karsh. The offer was thrown back into her face. The Phene remain a threat, so we will act to shield Chaonia against our foes."

"You are a person of some importance, I perceive. The snow will not begin to fall before the sun sets. Let me grant your wish, Honored One."

"What is my wish?"

"A rose that smells as sweet. Look." The woman shifted to indicate the tiny bush, not half a meter tall and with but a single bud waiting to bloom. With her trowel she cut into the soil.

"I mean no harm! Won't that disturb the plant?"

"Is the garden not already disturbed? Is the citadel not already fallen? The tides of power wax and wane. But here, Honored One, do not distress yourself. This particular plant normally resides elsewhere and is in a pot."

Now Hetty realized the soil was loose because it had already been disturbed. For some inexplicable reason the gardener had just dug a hole and placed in it the potted plant, which she was now clearing back out. Wind raked through the garden, clattering amid branches. The thunder of artillery rumbled in the air. A shout brought the gardener's head up with anticipation.

The clap of footsteps. An exchange of speech.

A man entered the garden with a commanding stride and a pair of adjutants hurrying to keep up. Hetty knew him at once: tall for a Chaonian, with the same curly hair as James. His features aligned with an arrogance that young Hetty had thought alluring. She had had a little crush on Ensign the Honorable Anas Samtarras when she was twelve and he had just graduated top of his class at the royal military academy. Everyone said he was destined for great things, and here he came, the youngest kite marshal in the history of the republic and commander of the victorious Second Fleet that had defeated Meli's security forces and defense fleet.

"Hestia, here you are." His haughty gaze fixed on the gardener.

The woman sat back on her heels and looked him up and down as if she had all the time in the world. "You look like the sort who might be interested in an evening's visit to one of our most luxurious pleasure houses. Exotic House, perhaps, so full of surprises."

He shot her in the head.

65

Blood That Someone Else Would Have to Clean

Hetty jolted back as the woman collapsed onto the ground. She hadn't even seen Anas draw his stinger.

He took two steps forward and shot the woman again, point blank to the brain stem. The flesh heaved. Blood spattered onto his boots and uniform.

Blood that someone else would have to clean, Hetty thought at random, mind skittering.

It wasn't death that shocked her. She'd pulled broken corpses from damaged compartments. Had applied rescue breathing to a spacer who'd asphyxiated from smoke inhalation but not saved them. Had prayed beside Papa's corpse, holding his cold hand for hours before the pyre.

It was the speed. The detachment in his expression.

Anas turned to his adjutants. "Get the body collected. We'll need a confirmed match before we can announce the Matrone's death."

The wind was picking up with a sharpness that hurt her exposed face.

A ping from James slid in. DID ANAS GET THERE YET?

She replied with a wordless affirmative, all she could manage.

"Always best to avoid the mess of a trial." Anas took several steps away before pausing to look back. "Are you coming? Did you hear the news?"

She shook her head.

"What? Aren't you on military comms? James didn't alert you?" His right hand twitched. "I'll have to slap some sense into that useless slug."

"Pray don't, Anas," she said. "I like James as he is."

"You're the only one." His glare was meant to burn. She'd addressed him with familiarity although he was older and outranked her on the military scale.

But she was one of the queen-marshal's Companions. She inclined her head with a rigid smile, her throat still choked from the shock. Let him scratch at that!

He shrugged and headed back the way he'd come. It was obvious he had arrived to deal with the Matrone in person. James must have alerted him. For some reason her feet would not move, not until a trickle of blood oozed toward her as if it sought living flesh to call home. She stumbled a step back, then caught her breath and bent to retrieve the potted rosebush. The Matrone's outflung hand was slack, marked by calluses. The woman had dug in gardens before.

"Honored Companion, the disposal squad is on its way." An adjutant looked after the retreating marshal. "We can handle this from here."

"Of course you can. My thanks. Snow's coming soon."

She followed Anas. He was not the sort to slow down to allow someone to catch up, so she did not try. Her squad closed in around her as they walked back to the citadel. No one offered to carry the pot and she did not want to relinquish it. The bud was exquisite, its petals as white as snow. The weight and solidity anchored her.

The tower lift had been restored. She put on a burst of speed and slipped in before its doors closed. She and Anas were alone as the lift rose. Bits of dirt from the pot shed onto the floor with little plinks.

His brows shot up. "What in the hells is that? Some kind of weapon?"

"It is the past, and also what's to come."

He snorted. "Whenever I'm like to forget you were half raised in the Yele League, you say something that reminds me. Not that there's anything wrong with the Yele that a little roughing up can't cure."

There was no answer to that, so she did not attempt one.

His eyes flickered as he read something on his network. "I'll have my final report sent over to you within the hour, as is due you as one of

Sun's Companions. We did have to deal with an unexpected number of Yele ships that were allied with the Phene fleet. They were negotiating for a place on a tow chain into League space but didn't get away in time. One odd thing though."

The lift halted so smoothly that for a moment she thought she would float right up off the floor, but that was likely a reaction to the lighter gravity on Meli Prime. The doors opened onto the top floor.

James burst into view from the direction of the office. "Hetty! The hells! You scared me! I thought you'd be murdered."

"Really, James," said Anas as he strode past his brother and under the arch that led into the parlor.

James gripped Hetty's arm so tightly she winced. "Please don't leave me. I begged to be sent to Sun as one of her Companions in order to get *out* of the hell of being hung on iron trees." The bush jostled against his sleeve and he looked down. "What is this? Oh! How beautiful!"

She nodded. "I know just where to put it. Come with me."

She walked into the parlor and stopped short. An elderly man in uniform stood at the head of the dining table, which was set for a meal. He had the same curly hair as his sons.

"My greetings, Honored Marshal. You've come far. And I must say, so unexpectedly."

"Honored Hestia. Indeed I have, as I will relate." Crane Marshal Zàofù watched Hetty proceed across the parlor to the balcony doors. "Is that a rosebush? Has it been scanned for explosives?"

Hetty indicated the latch with a tilt of her chin. James opened the door, and she went out to the lonely pedestal. The damp ring on the table matched the diameter of the little pot. The Matrone had taken this of all her possessions and tried to save it. The act had cost her life.

In the garden, the corpse would be placed in a body bag and taken to a forensics unit. Anas wasn't wrong. This way was easier for Chaonia. The last traces of her blood would soak into the soil. Perhaps more roses would bloom because of her death. Why had the Matrone sought to save the plant? A strange fate to walk into.

She closed the door behind her, washed her hands, and took her place at the table. The meal was set for five with the empty seat belonging by tradition to the queen-marshal, here in spirit if not in physical presence.

"Take that stupid cap off, punk," said Anas.

"Your tone," scolded their father, but he gestured to show James that the cap did indeed need to come off.

James gave Hetty a long-suffering look as he dragged the cap from his head and scrunched it up on his lap.

Sun had sent Eleuterio with Hetty and James. The factotum glided in to deftly command the flow of platter-bearing adjutants. After the crane marshal made a toast, they ate. Once the main courses were finished and sweets brought, Zàofù broke the silence.

"You've done well. It seems all three systems of the coalition are under Chaonian control. I hadn't thought it possible."

"Anything is possible with Sun," said Hetty.

The comment occasioned an uncomfortable pause, broken by the crane marshal with a clearing of his throat. "How did your first full fleet command go, Anas?"

"We had some fierce fighting, first in Tsurru System to reach the Meli Beacon. Here in Meli System we had to skirmish with a task force of Yele ships. The Yele are among the best when they're on their game. It would have been a harder fight but fortune favored us when the admiral's ship was stricken by an internal accident that poisoned the air. They lost quite a few people, including their commander. Manu, his name is. Don't you know him, Father?"

"Is there more than one Admiral Manu? The man who went over to the Phene when the League wouldn't give him the command he thought he deserved? His death is excellent news for Sun. But I confess to puzzlement. I had thought all the Phene ships would retreat through Kumbala back into Phene territory."

"That's the interesting part," said Anas. "From interrogation of prisoners it appears Manu split the retreating fleet. He kept all the auxiliary Yele ships and crews with him while sending the Phene on to Kumbala."

Zàofù rubbed at his chin as he considered this strategy. "To what end would he split an already beleaguered fleet and himself return to Yele? As an exile, Manu could not expect the League to welcome him back, not after they had voted to hold to their treaty with Chaonia."

"Ah, well, that's the thing, isn't it? He reckoned he had enough force to proceed through Yele without confrontation and make a lightning attack on Chaonia Prime. A brilliant scheme that would have taken advantage of Sun's tendency to push her vanguard and leave her rear unprotected." Anas tipped his glass reflectively, the amber-colored liquor sliding up one side and back down. "Had time and fate been right, Manu might have accomplished great things. As it was, the Yele force went to pieces when they lost him. Bad chain of command, if you ask me."

"Good fortune for us. What of Trinity Coalition forces?"

"Meli System has a disciplined home guard but not enough ships to hold out against us, even with our reduced numbers. Still, it's a good thing you brought timely reinforcements."

"In truth, I had not realized the reinforcements were coming here to Trinity," said Zàofù with his habitual frown. "According to Sun's instructions I brought two fleets to make a show of force through the Yele League. At Yele System the two fleets split, the Sixth with me continuing to Nalanda System and the Ninth under Amoy's command to Sankore System. My understanding was the maneuver was meant to cow the League, to make sure they don't try anything while so many of our ships remain outside republic space. I thought after reaching Nalanda we were to turn around and make our way back through Yele to Chaonia and on to Karnos. Imagine my surprise when in Nalanda I was met by a Titan running under the flag of the Alabaster Argosy. They took us onto their tow chain and conveyed us here. The Ninth Fleet is meant to arrive from Sankore with a different Argosy within twenty to forty hours, so my Navigator informed me."

"If anywhere in Trinity thinks to hold out, this will end that hope," said Anas.

Zàofù nodded. "I was among those skeptical of Eirene's alliance with the Argosy all those years ago. And of Sun's more recent embrace of her half sibling. But the association has given us an unexpected advantage."

Hetty smiled, feeling smug. "Sun sees the branching paths that others miss. Both strategy and tactics."

"She's so good," James broke in.

"You'd say so," remarked Anas.

"Tell me how she isn't," retorted James.

"Yes, of course, she's brilliant." Anas returned his attention to the venerable elder with a meaningful lift of his noble brow. "And your other assignment, Honored Father?"

The crane marshal gave Eleuterio a pointed look. The factotum swept the attendants from the room and closed the doors.

"Jiàn is dead. So that's done."

"Well done or ill done?" Anas caught Hetty's expression and gave a scolding shake of his head. "It's no comment upon Sun. She's proven herself in battle."

James said, "The seers of Iros had their hooks in Jiàn. Chaonia is well rid of any chance they might place a puppet on the throne."

"James is correct," said his father. "The evidence did not exonerate Jiàn. As well, I do not care to take the chance that unscrupulous folk would take advantage of our absence to make trouble at the palace. While Marduk Lee is attending to his duties as regent in a systematic fashion, and things continue at home in the well-ordered way established by Eirene, nevertheless the question of succession raises its head. With Trinity under our control, perhaps Sun can finally be persuaded she needs to marry and get an heir of her own womb. Or someone else's."

James's eyes flickered as he carefully did not look at Hetty, but she had no reason to believe the other two saw her as anything except one of Sun's Companions. Nevertheless, she took a sip of wine to give herself something to do.

Zàofù added, "Frankly, Eirene would have done better to marry Sun to Manea, if elevating Lee House was her goal. But theirs was a love match, and who among us can stand in the way of true love? And certainly not against Eirene when her mind was set. Regardless, I had several comprehensive discussions with Prince João on the matter."

Hetty glanced at James, who fanned himself with his cap as at a lucky escape.

Anas said, "Oh, to be a fly on that wall."

"No need to be a fly, in that quaint expression, since I can tell you the whole."

Anas waved an airy hand. "A brisk summary will suffice, since I am not among the palace chamberlains to need to busy myself with Sun's personal affairs."

"Marriage and an orderly succession is never a ruler's *personal* affair, Anas." Zàofù indicated the others with a gesture. "I hope you two, Hestia and James, can bring your influence to bear upon Sun in this regard."

"Of course," said James. "She always listens to me."

Anas snorted.

"The prince her father entrusted me with a letter which I will deliver to her. No doubt complaining of Marduk Lee's regency." He flicked fingers as if shooing away the fly on the wall. "There's always someone in the palace squabbling over precedence or which office has authority over which benefice. I am content that Marduk is a good administrator. He was a good choice by Sun. As for the other, we may hope Sun will listen to her father. He certainly has influence over her. But enough of court. What other news from the campaign here?"

Hetty sent a message to Eleuterio that he could resume service. As he brought in an aperitif she said, "Do tell them, James, of your discoveries."

James brightened. "It's early hours yet. Early days, really. But we have made headway in excavating the Coalition's treasury. I expect to gain access to everything: the vaults, the bullion, the credit servers, the indenture lists, the tax rolls, and the entire apparatus of protection payments and criminal enterprises who pay for the privilege of operating here without oversight."

"What will be done with all this?" Zàofù asked. "The republic's treasury needs an infusion after Eirene spent it down to almost nothing."

"Sun already told me her plans," said James, recovering his usual smirk. "It will be distributed as pay, as prize money, to pay for repairs and rebuilding of ships, habitats, and cities that took damage, and to refurbish the shipyards in Molossia and Troia. Also to commission new ships and pay for more training camps."

Anas said, "The coalition has an extensive and compliant workforce. Those drones can be leveraged as well."

They fell into discussion, the father and eldest son in general agreement while the younger son tossed in occasional grenades. James had irritating quirks, and he was a little immature for a twenty-two-year-old, but because she had watched him grow up she had a fair idea that what made him tick was how inadequate a quirky boy had been made to feel standing beneath the prestige of his esteemed father and beside the success of his admired elder brother.

Night had fallen. When she turned to look outside, snow had begun shimmering down. From inside, the balcony was too dark for her to see the rosebush.

All their comms brightened with identical pings: a courier had dropped in from Kumbala System bearing a message from the queen-marshal. The curt order called for the high command to gather at the Magava's Grove on Kumbala Prime.

"I thought she was still on Tsurru Prime," said Anas. "The assault on the Karsh's Sanctuary met with some setbacks, so I heard. But I must suppose she finished them off and couldn't wait to move on."

"If there's one thing I can say about Sun, it's that she can't wait to move on to the next thing," said James. "I liked the quiet life."

"You did not," said his brother. "You were always causing trouble."

"The trouble I caused didn't alter the destiny of multiple star systems."

"Why would she go to Kumbala and not come here to Meli?" asked Zàofù, ignoring this byplay.

Anas rubbed his smooth, handsome jawline. "Mmm. She put that hatchling Alika in command of the Kumbala invasion group. I don't mean to say he isn't a fighter, I can't fault him for his courage, but he jumps the gun and gets himself and his troops into trouble. Don't you think, James? You're always complaining about him."

James gave his brother a wicked smile. "I received a private message from the queen-marshal asking for a report on my activities. Father, if I may be excused."

"Of course, son! Go on. You're doing invaluable work." Zàofù beamed. He could be dull, and overbearing, and a blowhard, but he genuinely loved his sons. It was the thing Hetty liked about him.

James tugged on his cap and left the table.

She checked her network with a blink. Checked again. Nothing but the message sent to all the commanders.

Was she to receive no private message? Had Sun nothing for her to do? Had she been sent to Meli as a sop to her pride, so she couldn't say she'd not been given a mission like the other Companions?

No, that wasn't fair. Sun was scrupulous about her promises. After the battle at the industrial park she'd listened to Hetty's complaint about how being left behind made Hetty seem weak and unworthy to the others. Or perhaps James hadn't received a private message. Maybe he'd said so in order to make an excuse to go rather than be forced to linger at the table.

Fortunately, his departure catalyzed the other two. Anas took his leave to return to his command. Zàofù's adjutants had arranged for quarters in undamaged diplomatic lodgings near the citadel. At last she sat alone at the table as Eleuterio's assistants unobtrusively cleared it around her. The Samtarras men could be a lot to endure for a long dinner. She missed her dads and their quiet discussions of phoneme inventories or the technology of bureaucracy.

As Eleuterio took out the last of the dinner settings, James crept almost comically back in, looking around like an anxious thief.

"Are they gone?"

"They are, dear James. You can relax. It's fine."

"I liked it how it was before all this. It keeps speeding up, and I'm not sure we should be headed on this course. But Sun will be Sun." He sighed.

"You're tired. It will seem brighter come the dawn."

"I guess." He flung himself on the couch. Within one breath and the next he fell asleep. She took off his shoes, fetched a blanket from the bed-chamber, and laid it over him. In the office people were working, faces transformed by the flow of information into shifting sculptures of light.

She'd been thinking about the rosebush but was almost afraid to go look for fear of the disappointment. Yet no one who hesitated could keep up with Sun.

She turned the latch and stepped out onto a thin blanket of snow fresh enough to sink effortlessly beneath her feet. It was dark and her eyes hadn't adjusted. A snowflake tickled her nose. She turned her face upward and caught the delicious feathers of cold on her tongue. When she reached the railing she clutched it with chilled fingers, a smile pulled from her. The city gleamed softly, lit at intervals by streetlamps that hadn't been shot out. A Bear on patrol with an accompanying squad of Guards trundled past with a growling hum. Her gaze dropped to the plant.

The bud had opened, petals unfolded. The snow's kiss transformed the white flower to a translucent bloom as if it had become in truth a rose grown from the most delicate ice. A rare treasure whose beauty had but a brief span under the heavens.

Zàofù's words about Sun needing an heir came back to her.

Sun wasn't hers, nor would Hetty ever demand exclusivity. A queen-marshal must lead, fight, and administer, and must marry to seal alliances and provide a successor. What she and Sun shared lay outside duty and responsibility and was therefore not constrained or confined by the architecture of public political life. It was a rare treasure. It was what she cherished most. That was all that mattered.

A ciphered message chimed into her network bearing not the sixteen-pointed sunburst of the queen-marshal but the eight-pointed sunburst sacred to She Who Rises as the Sun in transit to the eight-spoked wheel that represented the truehearted and unwavering Charioteer.

DEAREST ONE, COME AS QUICKLY AS YOU CAN.

The Shock of Seeing Her Own Lifeless Face Makes the Wily Persephone Want to Smash Something

People lie all the time. They lie to enemies and rivals, to strangers and friends. They lie to their loved ones. They lie to posterity, hoping not to be caught. And the most harmful lies are the ones we tell to ourselves.

Approaching Libertalia, the *Hræsvelgr* swings wide around a chilled-out ice giant. The planet is attractive to the human eye, as any glimpse of a reminder of home will be if home were a place you missed and loved. This planet even has a few debris rings to give it an ornament of elegant glamour like the whisper of a future crown.

I sit in the *Hræsvelgr*'s CIC wondering why I haven't received any messages from my destination. Isn't there meant to be a contact person?

We slide into view of a satellite that I think is the moon our destination, until the cameras enlarge and enhance it so we can get a closer look.

Our destination isn't a moon after all. It's a beacon, a monstrously large spiral artifact with a dull ceramic surface.

A rush of astonished murmuring races through CIC as we all stare. What emotions the others feel I can't know. But I am stupefied and staggered, because according to every beacon map I have ever seen, Tsurru System has three beacons, one to Meli, one to Kumbala, and the dead one anchored to Tsurru Prime. This beacon makes an incontrovertible four, which means there must also be at least a fifth since beacons always appear in star systems in prime numbers. I desperately want to search the system, but I have to stay focused on my mission.

Why have I been sent here, of all places?

Unlike the broken beacon in Hellion Terminus, this beacon has no undulating aura with potentially toxic qualities. It's just a big dead object, intact but nonfunctional.

However, a dead beacon is a built structure. The inert surface creates a lot of solid ground in a stable orbit. As we close in and our camera views get higher resolution and more detail, they reveal the surface of the beacon is pitted by growths. At first look the growths remind me of cocoons attached to a coiled branch, if the branch were as massive as a moon and the pupating organisms destined to become freakishly vast monsters. Many of the cocoon-like habitats connect to each other by sealed freight-ways. These transport networks string the habitats into tens-of-klicks-long conurbations lit by sparkling lights or sheltering behind the shields of solar arrays. Others sit alone, antisocial. Vulnerable.

Libertalia is a dead beacon.

No one builds on the surface of a beacon. The surface of a living beacon will kill you if you come into direct physical contact with it, which is why beacons have shielded control nodes for their engineer, comms, and security crews. Broken beacons with toxic auras have to be avoided, and even their nodes are off-limits. But because no one understands the causes of the collapse, dead beacons are treated as if they might come on line at any moment. Therefore their nodes house a bare-bones crew just in case, and as a mark of respect and an expression of sanctity for the neutrality of the beacons on which we all rely.

I guess an authoritarian criminal enterprise like Trinity isn't too concerned about sanctity, and since they run things here, there's no one to stop them doing what they want.

The corvette parks itself at a cautious one hundred klicks out. My boarding group approaches the coordinates on the *Gold*.

The target looks like a cluster of eight warehouse-sized mushroom domes secured to the beacon by short, thick stalks. The pilot circles once as sensors scan for weapons, but nothing raises any alarms, which strikes me as odd. Given how large the cluster is, it also seems strange there is only a single docking ring with two berthings and no ship or utility boat in sight.

We ease in. Dock. Seal. Scan. There's air beyond but no signs of life. The microgravity makes me feel queasy as my balance struggles to make sense of the environment. In off-planet training during the academy I learned I could tough out the dislocation and nausea and it would ease quickly, not like some who vomited for the entire two-week training run. Lucky me. My high tolerance for microgravity conditions, which many Chaonians don't have, is one reason I qualified as a beacon apprentice.

The squad of marines takes point. Ikenna and I follow through a double airlock. The marines wave us into a vast domed space that planet-side I'd call a great echoing ruin. It's about the size of CeDCA's rugby pitch and seats. Dim lights shine in the scaffolding above, just enough to turn the jumble of equipment on the deck into a hells-scape of threatening shapes. There's a breathable atmosphere, and a weak gravitational pull toward the beacon's center of mass. The kind of microgravity that a planet-born person like Nona Lee could have been working in for years to cause her to need the body scaffolding she wore when I met her in Karnos System.

The elevated walkways, hooks, platforms, and lifts rigged from the dome look like the kind used in loading and unloading freighters. Forklifts, mini cranes, and dunnage are scattered in lanes between intermodal containers.

"Do you register that sound?" Ikenna asks via comms.

I raise a hand to halt the advance of the marines. The noise is a faint *plink plink*, like a slow drip from a broken faucet into a metal basin. I'm not a musician, but I'm good at sounds. There's something off about this that raises my suspicions.

I unseal my vac helmet and tip it back. The air has a metallic odor, the temperature hovering at the freezing point of water. Ikenna looks toward me while the marines keep their eyes on the shadows and the light.

The silence weighs like a message. No sound. The plink is being routed through the comms system for us to hear, which means we are dealing with a hacker or someone with access to the Chaonian military network.

Hand signs can't be overheard on an audio comms channel.

Comms compromised. Spread out. I will flush out the intruder.

There's just enough light we can all sign, and it's possible the lurker is counting on it. As the marines move forward to new positions, I tip my helmet back on and say through comms, "Show yourself. I know you're there."

No answer. No movement or heat beyond our own. Our sweep turns up nothing except stacks of bedding crumpled on its floor in one of the containers, as if people slept here like vagabonds, refugees, or illegal transports.

Two passages lead out of the dome, each sealed with an airlock. The first airlock I attempt opens into a passage-tunnel of about twenty meters that has been blown up through the middle, leaving ragged edges and a gap too wide to leap. Because the domes are set up on thick, vertical stalks, we have no way to quickly bridge that gap. I ping an image to Captain Lee so she can task an onboard engineer to build a temporary airtight bridge if necessary, standard combat procedure.

The other passage has a sealed panel, blinking with a shiny gold ✦. Kadmos's star, from the Lee House school channel.

"Fuck," I mouth under my breath.

Ikenna comes up beside me and asks, in sign, if I need him to break into the panel.

I sign a negative, keep that hand held aloft in *Hold*. We don't know what lies beyond the hatch except that if this is really Nona Lee's lab then it means

it means

it means I came from here.

I don't want to go in there. But one thing I learned after Resh died is you have to jump in to the deep end, because no matter how clear the waters look from above no one can know what they'll find under the surface until they dive down.

I pull back my helmet and look straight into the pinhole camera. I peel off my glove and press my right hand to the panel. This is why I was sent. After an agonizing eleven seconds, the hatch rolls aside.

Because my left hand is still raised, the marines don't move. My distraction saves their lives. The intact passageway beyond the hatch is crisscrossed with a shifting net of crackling energy. My network flashes a warning: the voltage will kill on contact. Ikenna hisses in surprise.

At the other end of the tunnel, twenty meters away, stands Kadmos. Tall, gray-haired, distinguished, serious, he wears his formal tutor robes as if he has just come from a Lee House classroom. No vac suit. No sign he is concerned about atmosphere loss.

"What are you doing here?" I blurt out.

"I need your help, Honored Persephone. I can't get into the laboratory, but you can."

If my heart congealed into a block of ice, I would not feel more frozen. A terrible realization lumbers into my thoughts. *He knows.*

Was he working for Nona Lee the entire time? The hells, of course he was. It could have been Kadmos who blackmailed Solomon at CeDCA on behalf of his true boss, Nona. She was just keeping an eye on one of her creations. If true, then the surveillance never had anything to do with Lee House, which means Aunt Moira told me the truth and so did my father. I can't get my head around it.

Ikenna whispers, "Who is that?"

The one adult in Lee House I trusted.

Kadmos says, "Offer a drop of blood to the threshold sensor, the mark of a palm on the floor. When it clears, pass through. The security lasers will form again behind you. The others must wait until you and I have cleared this entryway and powered down the security program."

"How did you get through?" I demand.

"I hold a key that allows me to pass this far. However, the hatch at this end is secured from inside. No one is answering my hails. We don't have much time. The lab is wired to blow up." He pauses to check his network. "In ninety-seven minutes."

"That's an awfully convenient time-dependent deadline. And a long lag time for lab blower-uppers if they've already gotten away."

"I suspect the perpetrator was hoping the owner of the lab would return in the interim without suspecting there is a problem."

"Ah. And get blown up with it." Thinking of what Nona Lee said about Resh, I feel a surge of sympathy for the theoretical bomb-setter. Which begs the question, who wants to blow up Nona Lee and her illegal lab?

He sighs because I'm still stuck on my side and he on his. "If you do not desire to assist me, Honored Persephone, then I suggest you clear the area."

"What will happen to you?"

He smiles in the wry way I'm familiar with from my many years of schooling in Lee House, a man who took teaching seriously but did not strut and preen about himself. "The security fail-safes have allowed me in this far, and have trapped me here since I now can't get out or get in. So here I will stay. But I would prefer you live, since you have that option."

That's torn it. He betrayed me and the others all along. Yet he is also the man I admired, who made us laugh, taught us things that weren't in the prescribed curriculum, and was endlessly patient as he checked up on our studies and our quiet lives as the most privileged of already privileged children in Lee House. I can't leave him to die if there's any chance I can save him.

I advance to the threshold, where the outline of a golden handprint shines against the ceramic-alloy decking. I kneel and place my hand in the print. The proportions are the same but my hand is slightly smaller. Was it the nutrient bath?

Heaven help me.

A pinprick point stabs my palm. I jerk up. Ikenna steps forward.

"Halt," I say. "Stay back."

Blood swells, beads, and a drop falls onto the print. I inhale. Exhale. Inhale. The print flares with a light so bright it causes an autonomic response as my secondary eyelid shutters to protect me from the glare.

The print fades. The light in the tunnel shifts as the network of beams vanishes to be replaced by glowing squares like stepping-stones amid the matte-black flooring.

"Hey, are you sure about this?" Ikenna's gaze on me ticks like a time bomb that will soon go off. He is sharp enough to put puzzle pieces together even when he doesn't have all of them at hand. I'm the one who won't start until I count the pieces to make sure they're all there.

"No way out but through," I say with a wink and a smile, as a proper legend would do.

I walk into the tunnel, one stepping tile at a time, waiting for a snap, a hiss, a burning pain through my flesh, but the way stays clear as the security net rebuilds behind me. The killing beams separate me from my rack-mate and the marines. Maybe a person always has to leave a place that seems safe in order to find out who they are, or maybe I'm the anomaly.

Thirteen steps seem like an eternity but they bring me to Kadmos's side, a place I always feel comfortable because he is the one adult in my life who wasn't always telling me what I ought to be doing to fit their goals for me. Or so I once believed.

"What's next?" I ask.

He indicates another panel. "The key allows me to record my presence on this panel, which is why I'm not dead. But I can't open the door."

He's been here before. I feel sick. But naturally there is no time for any heart-wrenching conversation. A reckless vexation overtakes me. Since my palm is still oozing blood, I press it merrily onto the panel while staring at the camera pinhole, figuring some combination of blood, retina, and palm print will identify me. If I truly honestly am an illegal clone of the notorious civilian-massacring state-sanctioned terrorist and apex bitch Nona Lee, the hatch will open.

The red light atop the panel turns green.

The hatch opens.

A gush of reeking, noxious air spills over us. I reflexively suck in a breath that coats my mouth with the taste of rot, as if smears of liquidized tissue are adrift in the ventilation system. I clap down my vac helmet and trigger my air filter. The space beyond is pitch black, seething with a weird movement I can't identify.

I flip through channels until I find one that hooks into Kadmos's array. "Are there lights?"

His helmet headlamp snaps on. Its beam spears into the darkness across a rippling surface of what looks like water.

I ping Ikenna on military comms. "See if you can find access to main power for the complex. Get it running. Also, see if you can cut off the power to the lasers." I ping a status report to Captain Lee on the corvette and to the pilot on the shuttle.

Kadmos and I stand on a walkway situated one meter above the floor of the dome. This elevated path hugs the curve of the dome, a ring road wide enough to take cargo traffic. Tiered bleachers rise at intervals, like viewing stands looking across the central floor of the dome, which is where the liquid has collected. It can't be more than a few centimeters deep, because even with no lights our headlamps reveal markings. This dome is a sports complex, a big recreational field with what looks like a running track and, inside the track's loop, a pitch for rugby, cùjú, cricket, and other ball-oriented team sports. How odd. Or maybe not odd at all.

Where is the drip coming from? Who is broadcasting it?

The air checks out as breathable, if foul smelling. A quick analysis of the liquid confirms it is water.

I flip my helmet back up, bracing myself for the stench.

"Kadmos," I say softly, "where might we find the source of a drip? Especially one that could have flooded the field."

"As I recall, there is a wash-and-water station at the changing rooms, which are adjacent to the entry to the residential dome."

"Residential dome?"

"This is a habitat, not just a lab."

He and I have been using our old Lee House school link, which works on both our networks because of proximity. As we hustle along the boardwalk I check to make sure I'm on "receive only" for the military comms. "How many of me were there?"

"You mean of the cloning experiment?"

"Yeah. That."

"There were several preliminary batches that failed. The successful batch numbered eight."

I've gorged on too much resentment and too many lies. "You were tutoring her clones and reporting back to her on our progress. You were the unidentified male voice who called Solomon at the academy to check in on me. You were always working for her, weren't you?"

"I was, Honored Persephone."

It's like someone shoving a scalding-hot stake into my ear and pulling it out and shoving it back just before I get used to the cessation of pain. Step back. Focus. Concentrate.

"Is this place really wired to blow up in ninety-three minutes?"

"Now eighty-seven. Yes."

"How can you know?"

He pings me a frequency and a privacy code that dumps me into a comms network for the lab. I should ping it directly to Ikenna but I have to trawl it first for incriminating evidence.

There is indeed a countdown to destruct ticking away, with a flag that states that the entire complex will be vented and sterilized. I assume the beacon is impervious to whatever will happen if we can't find the charges. Obviously it's a system Nona Lee set in place long ago in case she needed to hide her dirty work.

My network spots a gleam of body heat, a living person who is not moving. Although the lights are still off, no other sign of human life pops up in my sensors as I sweep the dome.

"I'm going to run ahead," I say to Kadmos. "Keep scanning for threats. See if you can figure where the charges might be laid."

"I see you have learned some command skills while in Sun's retinue."

"Swim or die." I take off, my feet pounding into the darkness as my headlamp scans the path ahead.

The wash-and-water station is a rectangular shelter with a roof and no walls. It is level with the playing field and thus its floor glistens with a sheen of water. On a step-up in the back runs a row of bleacher chairs. A person is lashed to a seat, slumped against the cords. At first glance I take him for an adolescent boy who looks an awful lot like me five years ago, had I been taller and male. As I run up, the head raises and the eyes blink, focus, sharpen. He gives me a look as if I am the hired entertainer who came so rudely late to his party that the guests have already departed.

He has a gag in his mouth and wears damp athletic shorts, a sweaty singlet, and sodden cleats. Even woozy, dehydrated, and disheveled he strikes me as better-looking than I have ever been. Fortunately it turns out he's more of a jerk too. As soon as I get the gag out of his mouth he coughs with a dry hack and speaks in a raspy tone.

"That took long enough! Who are you? Where are you from? Did Aganippe send you? Why haven't you gotten the lights on? Did you catch him yet?"

"Slow down. I need more information and fewer demands."

He gives a disgusted sigh, coughs raggedly, and strains against the cords. "Why haven't you cut me free yet? Aganippe would have been here hours ago, unlike you, so he must have found her. And Despy's dead . . ."

The youth's voice falters. He chokes down dry heaves that sound like exhausted sobs. I consider the metal cords that bind his torso, arms, and legs to the seats, then recall the beacon medallion I purchased on Yele Prime. Its edged hook neatly slices through the cords. Freed, he sags forward with eyes shut, gasping as circulation stings through his body. Kadmos hurries up, panting from the exertion of his jog.

"Honored Dimitar! What happened? Where is Despoina?"

The kid is not too exhausted to rudely scold his elder. "You were told not to come here again unless Mother specifically requested you."

Indignation consumes the last of his fading energy. His eyes roll up in his head, and he faints.

"Well, fuck me, and I don't mean that literally. He calls her *Mother*?"

The overhead lights pop on in a fabulous glare like the excitement building before a big match.

A ping drops in from Ikenna. POWER ON. TUNNEL STILL BLOCKED. AM TRACING CONTACT SIGNATURES LOOKING FOR EXPLOSIVE CHARGES IN THE COMPLEX.

I spot a faucet, which is indeed dripping, although other water mains must have broken to cause the extent of this flooding. Cups sit stacked on a counter. I fill one up and gleefully splash its contents over the youth's face. He sputters awake and comes up fighting, which I easily sidestep because he's bleary and weak. But he manages a punch at Kadmos that catches the tutor off guard and sends him stumbling backward.

"Hey! Leave him alone!" I grab the boy's shoulder and kick the back of a knee so he topples. Solomon taught me the best arm lock. "Settle down! Kadmos and I are here to rescue you. And to stop this complex from blowing up. So I'm going to release you and step back. Then you're going to stand up, and we'll work together to save the lab. Get it?"

"Let go of me, shrimp!"

"Oh my stars, what a burn. How will I ever recover from the shame, because no one has ever before thought of that insult for me due to my short stature and wiggly personality."

I let go and step back.

He staggers to his feet and turns to loom over me, ignoring Kadmos, which strikes me as foolish since Kadmos has a stinger. "You must be number six. I've heard about you."

"Nothing good, I hope. I wasn't aware we had numbers. What number are you?"

His smile is cocky and self-assured, as if the heavens have anointed him multiple times because it gives them such pleasure to do so. "I'm number eight. Of course."

"Ah, the favored one. I'll call you Eight."

The sullen adolescent emerges in his expression. "I'm Dimitar."

I give him my best "don't fuck with me" look. "I have a lot of questions but two urgent ones. First, do you know where the charges are and how to turn them off?"

"What charges? I got knocked out by gas and woke up tied to the seat."

"This complex is set to blow in seventy-three minutes. Second question. Are the people who attacked still here?"

He starts blinking, by which I gauge he is trying to contact someone, anyone, within the lab complex.

"We need a plan," I say, "but I need more information. What happened? Just the bare bones."

"It was an ordinary day. We got a message from Mother nine days ago that she had arrived in-system via the Karsh's Titan and we should go on high alert."

"So she didn't come here?"

"She had an unspecified task to complete."

That tracks. "Go on."

"Then he came."

"Who is he?"

"The seer."

"The *seer*?" The merciless hand of fate tightens on my throat.

"Kiran Seth. No reason for you to know him . . . Wait, were you one of the pair given to him?"

I catch myself on a seat before I topple.

Not given by Nona to Aunt Moira. Not to my mother. Given to *him*.

Has my father been Nona Lee's coconspirator all along?

My mind goes blank and my skin goes cold. Of course he has.

In his calmest tone, Kadmos says, "Honored Dimitar, time is of the essence. If we can't find the charges then we must evacuate all remaining personnel."

Set it aside. We have to move. I pitch my voice to the tone I used as a child to boss Percy around. "Dimitar! Ping me the map of this complex. Now!"

Shaken, he fumbles around. "Uh, uh, I know it's on the network somewhere."

Thirty-three agonizing seconds later a map drops into my network. I shunt a copy to Ikenna, his eyes only, and order him to make sure his group and the shuttle get clear if we can't return that way. I don't send the map to Captain Lee.

"Is there a list of personnel?"

"I don't know anything about that. Despy is admin."

"Where can I find her?"

He sobs.

As we speak I'm scanning the blueprint of eight mushroom domes linked by passages. The warehouse where we entered. The sports dome. A residential dome. A service dome. A greenhouse dome. Two domes designated as work space and laboratory. The eighth dome is blacked out.

"What's up with this one?"

"I don't know. It's off-limits."

"Off-limits to who?"

"To me."

There's a sulky tone! I am too wise to mention it. "Will it open for me?"

"I don't know."

"Where did Kiran Seth go?"

"Oh." His gaze flashes up. I stare into a mirror of my own eyes. "That's where he went."

Fuck.

"Can you turn off the tunnel security between the warehouse and here?"

"No. Despy won't give me clearance because she says I'm too immature—"

"Never mind. Is there another exit?"

"There's an emergency shuttle in the residential section."

"Can my shuttle land there?"

"I don't know."

In fairness he *is* just a child, sullen, scared, and shaken. "Kadmos, you clear the residential section. Find the shuttle and any survivors. See if the military shuttle can come in there. Dimitar, can you enter these two work and lab spaces?"

"Yeah?"

"Sweep them for anyone alive. Place an all alert onto your complex-wide comms system. Everyone to meet at the shuttle in the residential dome within fifty minutes."

I take off before they can ask me where I am going. The map is easy to read so I sprint to the tunnel that connects the sports dome to the greenhouse dome. The hatches open seamlessly for me. I race through the humid air of a garden laid out with hydroponics tanks, soil troughs, and airy vines snaking across scaffolding. A sprinkler system spits water like the last gasping breaths of a dying beast. Water puddles everywhere. I splash along a wide path toward a hatch designated on the map as the only entry point to the blacked-out dome.

Debris lies on the path ahead, smeared with color. No. It is a corpse, the first human I've seen besides Dimitar. I kneel to examine a person dressed in ordinary linen workday clothes made bloody by fatal wounds. Sprawled down a side path I spot a second body, who my sensors tell me is dead.

The dome is silent except for the tick of sprinklers trying to spurt out the last of their water, the burble of a drain, and the *chunk chunk chunk* of a laboring ventilator.

A fight that happened hours ago converged on the far hatch as a last-ditch stand. Death should never be easy to witness, but I don't have time to fight feelings of pity and disgust as I pick my way through a group of corpses. Fourteen, because I count them. The dead ought to be counted. They aren't garbed as soldiers but all have weapons fallen by their sides. All wear the same commonplace garments. There's no sign of the enemy who cut them down. By the scatter of the attack and the ruthless efficiency of the trail it left I am beginning to have an idea I don't like.

The final hatch stands before me, closed and dark. I grip my stinger, take a breath, and release the control panel.

The hatch opens. Air gusts out into a zone of lower pressure. I dodge through and seal it behind me so as not to vent the garden dome. The passageway has dim walkway lights that guide me across. The far hatch is stuck open with half a meter of clearance, enough for me to squeeze through. The dome beyond has a trace atmosphere and no lights, as if it is not on the same circuit as the rest of the complex.

It is a lab. I swing my headlamp back and forth as I advance into the silent wreckage. My gut churns with a flood of emotions I have no name for, only that they hurt. This is where I was conceived, if my genesis can be called conception.

Someone has moved through on a smash and grab, wires hanging from the wall where a console has been torn out, a scorched lab bench, broken chairs, a dead person in a lab coat.

And another body.

It's me.

I jolt back, heart bursting out of my chest. *Breathe,* Solomon would tell me.

The body wears a classy teal suit of tunic and trousers with an ugly, bloody gash across the chest. She's maybe twenty years older than I am. Comfortably heavyset. Her hair, falling out of a bun, is black like mine with gray strands that stand out under the stark light. She wears pink lipstick and purple eyeliner. My gaze sticks on her face. My dead face, as if reality has ripped asunder and shown me a glimpse of my death. Of Resh's death.

Tears burn in my eyes as I'm flung into the past, to Resh's funeral, not that there was an actual body.

No. Concentrate. Time is running out.

A flash of red catches my eye like someone winking at me from hiding. I flick off the headlamp and wait.

It flashes again to my left. I walk away from my dead face to a lab bench where, right out in the open, a rectangle with spiny tendrils is attached to the floor.

James disarmed an object just like this one: a Phene bomb.

The hells.

Past another crumpled body and more melted, mangled consoles I see a second bomb. Once I see them, I can't unsee them, placed every ten meters on the deck. But why did they place the timer on such a long run?

My school network from Lee House tickles in my head like the whisper of a ghost. The past has come knocking. A message drops into my network, and I know who it is from.

My father materializes as a hazy visual half obscured by the dark. He's bloodied and disheveled in a way I have never seen before in a man who knew exactly how he wanted to look even though he could not see himself in a mirror. My daughter's heart grips with fear for him, scared that he might be injured. Then I remember why we are both here.

He wears not seer's robes but a vac suit. In his left hand he grips a baton. Behind him I see people moving in flashes of light. The flickering patterns on their faces reveal them as banner soldiers, under his command. They are destroying the lab, just as the Phene destroyed the lab in the industrial park. Was Nona doing experiments on banner soldiers here? But if so, why does Father care? He's not here to eliminate banner soldiers.

The recording stutters and starts, coarsened by a background whine. "If you are hearing this, then you are my daughter Persephone. This complex is rigged to blow and there is nothing anyone can do to stop it. You may think I am merely a tool of the seers, but this action I take to preserve and protect you, Persephone. I suppose by now you distrust me too much to believe me. You display a stubborn allegiance to Sun. She is not worthy of you. Even so, I will not take you to task. As the father who raised you, I command you to save yourself. There is nothing here for you. This isn't who you are. This is merely a starting point. Once this facility is destroyed there will no longer be a forensics trail to link you here. You don't belong to her."

The message fizzes out. After a loop of silence it shudders back to life and starts playing again. Curse him! I mute the loop because I can't think when I hear his voice.

Military comms chimes, a signal from Captain Lee. "Honored Persephone?"

I can call in the *Hræsvelgr* ordnance squad. We have an hour. But then they'd have to enter this place. If any of them put two and two together, then not even Sun can protect me and Manea, or even that obnoxious youth.

"On my way," I answer. "We need to evacuate."

I bring back the private message's sound. What is that background whine like a small craft drive? Ah. That's how they departed.

I release targeted bursts of water from my suit supply. The water gets sucked to a hole cut into the decking in the base of the dome. Their escape route. When I shine a light into the gap, it pierces ten meters through airless space to the surface of the beacon.

Wading through death makes me reckless. The shock of seeing my own lifeless face makes me want to smash something into smithereens. The ghost's whisper pokes at my network, trying to get back in to drill through my heart using my father's rational voice, always so objective and measuring, the man who didn't want you to make excuses for your failures and who would give you an approving nod if you hit the target so you kept trying to hit the target just to get that nod. Resh adored him, and she hated him, because even though she couldn't have known what she and I and Manea are and how we came into the family, something deep in her knew how badly wrong we all were together. That we were a lie.

Resh made her choice.

I stare down at the opaque surface of the dead beacon. And I decide. Fuck it. For once in my hells-cursed life, I am going to touch one of the mysteries we live with.

I jump. The beacon exerts enough microgravity that I float faster than is comfortable but slowly enough to be safe. I land deftly, bent-kneed, and straighten. I am standing on the surface of a beacon. The gods do not annihilate me with their fearsome eye for my blasphemy.

The mushroom complex sprouts above and behind me. When I pace out from under the dome, the heavens greet me. The blue-green gas giant catching light. The furnace of the system's sun. The wild sweetness of the myriad stars like sparkling flowers strewn across a vast, dark meadow.

Some of these stars we live beneath. Some we will never know except as strangers out of the past. The ancient sages said there must be intelligent life in the universe, but time and distance are so unfathomably vast that we could span millions and yet never touch another sapient existence.

I crouch and set a gloved hand upon the beacon's surface. It is hard. It registers cold. No heat. No breath. No life, although I could not tell anyone why a part of me is sure a beacon can live. Why I wonder if maybe the beacons are trying to talk to us when we drop through, or maybe all we hear are the waves of eternity soughing against the shore of our short lives.

"Perse?" Ikenna is so worried he's forgotten to use my title on the public channel. "Uh, I mean, Honored Persephone? Can you report in? Where are you? There's a corsair incoming. It's claiming to be a friendly and has the Chaonian military codes to prove it, but we need to get you out of there in case it's a ruse."

Too late. Lights blink in the distance. A hover-ski skims close to the surface of the beacon, headed for me. It's built like a smaller version of a Phene battle chariot with an ovoid chassis, a curved railing for support, and a crossbar for control.

As it glides in to settle next to me, I am unsurprised to see my progenitor.

Nona Lee latches into the Lee House school link with a spindle as her icon. Her voice is as harsh as ever. "Hop on. There isn't much time. The corsair will cover our escape."

"Aren't you going to try to save the lab?"

"Aren't you?" she counters.

I flush, the heat of my blood its own betrayal.

She smiles, the pull of her lips warped ominously by the curve of her vac suit's faceplate. "Well. Well. Well. I wasn't sure you had it in you."

"Had what in me?"

"It's for the best. Too many people now know this complex exists, even if they don't know what for. I have a hidden backup lab in place for just this eventuality."

"He killed your people. Your . . . Despoina, was that her name? Don't you want revenge? Or justice?"

Her expression flickers with a cold calculation that terrifies me far more than Eirene's brutal charm or Sun's impetuous assurance. "You don't know me or my aims or what I want. Now come along."

I don't budge. "Come along to what?"

"After our successful if rather bloody takeover of the Grand Sanctuary, Sun has seen fit to leave me as the new Karsh of the Trinity Coalition."

"You!"

"Me! Surely you're not surprised that was the deal I made?" She clucks disapprovingly. "Anyway, Soaring is assigned for now as Magava so she can coordinate knnu passages. Hestia Hope chose an accounting drone as acting Matrone."

"Drone?"

"Indentured workforce. People who fell into debt. Farming indentured labor is one of the sources of the coalition's wealth. We shall see how long this new Matrone lasts, although she must know enough about the Hive to have engendered Hestia Hope's confidence. That young woman does not strike me as a fool. Now, as I said, come along. The charges Kiran set are meant to destroy this lab specifically, but I've long since wired the entire compound to blow should it come to this."

She and my father, in league all this time. It's too much to process as the clock ticks.

"I have my own way off. I'm not going with you. I don't belong to you."

She laughs. "Take your chances, then, Little Six. I'll be waiting when you've had enough of Sun's voracious appetite for glory."

The hover-ski lights up. I step back as it races away, headed for the residential dome. I check the map and ping Ikenna on military comms.

"Pick me up at these coordinates."

The one thing I can do when my thoughts tumble through a riot of confusion is to run. So I run along the surface of the beacon two klicks out, away from the doomed complex. It's halfway to flying, and a tiny voice in my head wonders if I should just launch myself into space and drift into eternity. But I ignore it.

The shuttle swings by for an easy grab. After I'm hauled up and sealed through the airlock, I make my way forward to the cockpit.

"Did another vessel depart the complex?" I ask the pilot after I strap in.

"Yes, ten minutes ago. Your orders?"

"There she goes!" Ikenna exclaims.

The complex blooms, shattering into a debris cloud that flickers with

444 · KATE ELLIOTT

spurts of flame doused as the air vanishes. We endure a shock wave and, when the worst is past, circle back around to view the pulverized remains. Whatever was once there will be difficult to reconstruct by salvagers and investigators.

I don't know what to feel. Shock? Grief? Anger? Relief? When I close my eyes my dead older face lies slack on the ground before me, with her vibrant pink lipstick and her purple-shaded eyes.

"Honored Persephone? Your orders on the corsair and the other vessel? Shall we follow?"

"No. We return to Sun."

She Had Loved Him

Because assembly was at 0714, Kurash arrived at Hangar 1 at 0644 per arrow standard: always reach your target first.

Ay was on duty. She hustled up, almost grabbed his sleeve with excitement, and withdrew her hand before she touched him. "Come and see!"

The hangar crew had gathered at an open hatch onto what everyone called the "goldfish bowl," an observation bubble that could be retracted and sealed for battle. They made way for him to move into the bowl-like space. Hand-and footholds allowed viewers to move around to viewing perches from which a person could see approaching ships or an astronomical marvel, for example the dusty blue-and-yellow-green planet whose facing hemisphere shone like a greeting. His gaze stuck on the searing circle of light that was the system's star.

Ay elbowed him. "Don't stare at the sun. You'll go blind. Didn't you learn that as a child?"

"No. We didn't have a star. We are not born beneath a sun. We are born at the heart of Lady Chaos."

Everyone around him fell silent.

He added, "We are voyagers. That is how humans reached these worlds. We honor our forebears by not straying from the path they forged through the furious heaven."

"Is that where you come from?" asked a specialist, pointing to an object growing in size as they approached it.

A wheelship rested against the immensity of space, the visual enhanced and expanded by the optics of the observation bubble. At the age of eleven every banner child who survived the first census was taken via elevator to the end of the evacuation spire. From this distance they could see the wheelship in its entirety: the huge outer torus, a smaller inner torus, and a yet smaller docking ring, all connected by spokes to a sphere at the hub, the weightless maze around which life and destiny spin.

That trip to the tip of the spire was the only time he had seen with his own eyes the Wrathful Snakes wheelship where he had grown up. When he had been marked to become a banner soldier and left his home on his journey of honor, he had departed inside a cargo ship. Not even a screen for a final visual. Their old lives were severed. The chosen ones had attended their own funerals. Like the ancestors, they left a place to which they would never return.

So it hit hard to see what had once been home.

It was not his birth wheelship, of course. But the shape and its purpose welcomed him. He understood its structure and its endlessly rising horizon. He understood the layers of its cosmological atmosphere, consumption and recycling, a slow wheel that turns endlessly around the heart of Lady Chaos, which is all that was, that is, that will be, the ever-shifting maze of She Who Bore Them All, progenitor of the eleven banners and of life's mystery and death's inevitable embrace.

Was this why all the Chaonians exclaimed so when they viewed any habitable planet from space? To him a planet was an intriguing astronomical object that had no emotional connection beyond that, no matter how lovely its patterns might look.

The wheelship was parked in a halo orbit at the L1 point of Danu System's ninth planet. As a warship from a potentially hostile entity, the frigate was denied permission to dock.

The diplomatic party embarked on a utility shuttle. He sat next to Marshal the Honorable Precious Jīn for the two-hour approach. She was a tactile person, and held a physical tablet, which she tapped through as she reviewed sets of schematics that seemed to represent Chaonian knowledge of the structure and layout of a wheelship.

"Is this the ship Prince João was raised on?" she asked him.

"It is a Royal wheelship."

"Is there more than one Royal wheelship?" She really loved leaning into his physical space. In any other circumstance he would have gotten up and moved to a different seat, but Sun had given him a job to do, so he would do his job.

"There are three."

"Yes, I see it noted here. Royal wheelships are smaller than banner wheelships. The hells! Given the size of this, that must be something." She angled a look at him as if to gauge his temper after their last conversation.

He kept his gaze on the back of the seat in front of him.

She gave a tiny huff of displeasure before going on. "Let me see. Royal wheelships serve as neutral ground for all banners to meet. The conclave I will speak to is made up of Royals? Is that correct?"

"No, Marshal. A conclave is made up of representatives, one from each of the eleven banners. Each banner sends an elder for a term of office as one of a sitting conclave. The conclave votes on matters pertaining to the health of the clans."

"So the Royal wheelships are more of a staging ground for cooperative enterprises among the banners. Cooperative ventures like raids, perhaps?"

"Ventures are not only violent operations," he said. "Such raids are less common these days, except in the outer reaches of the beacon system."

"Yes, where there are no planetary fleets to fend them off. It says here the Royal wheelships also serve as trade emporia between Gatoi and outsiders."

"Marshal, among the banners we do not use the word 'Gatoi.' To use the term here will offend people."

Her smile was not so much warm as it was satisfied to have pried this splinter out of him. Her right shoulder shifted several centimeters closer to his left arm. He held still, feeling his jaw tighten.

"I will remember not to use the word." In fact, he realized, it was the first time she had used it in conversation with him. "How fortunate you are here to advise me. How clever of Sun to send you as her unofficial representative for this diplomatic mission. Your people will respond more kindly to a familiar face, I am sure."

He wasn't so sure. And he felt very isolated. He had requested Ay as one of the diplomatic party but his request had been refused, so he was trapped on board with the marshal's personal entourage, all of whom had not a whit of interest in him except as Sun's pet "savage."

He touched the baton he carried. Its surface slid inert against his palm because its neuronics and his were in tune. Nothing about the humble one-meter baton revealed the gift coiled within its circuits. The means to halt the Phene from doing to all the many other banner soldiers what had been done to him. Had he not had the leash removed, Prince João would have compelled him to kill a baby.

Sun wanted no one coerced to fight for her. She asked for something harder and higher.

"Secure grapples. Lock in." They docked.

A strange rushing roaring filled his ears like pressure venting. A shiver of light-headedness raced through his head and ran in a wave down his arms until his hands tingled as if his neuronics were glitching. He felt a rush of weakness, of doubt. He gave himself a spurt of calming psychotronics. The sensations subsided. It was just nerves, the same as he'd had the first time he'd gone into a battle.

Was this going to be a battle?

The marshal readied her retinue at the airlock, a marine colonel beside her, Kurash next to her secretary. The group was filled out by another seven individuals according to the protocol that any entering group should number eleven souls.

The airlock opened. His first breath of the cool air punched him back in time: a boy seated on a bench beside his beloved grandmother with her scent of lemongrass and ginger from the tisanes she drank every day. The aroma of the mulch in the wheel's endlessly rising forest and gardens. The fragrance of plumeria. A sour touch of aloe. The flutter of wind socks as the powerful ventilation system that breathed air through the vast cavity of the torus kicked into a high cycle.

He was Kurash again, the boy with feet dangling from the bench, kicking; he was always restless. Clambering. Running. It was so hard to sit still.

A voice broke into his thoughts just as the baton attached to his uniform's belt altered its hum to recognize the presence of another neural system.

"Marshal the Honorable Precious Jīn. You are come as envoy from Queen-Marshal Sun of the Republic of Chaonia. We recognize your presence on the wheelship of the banner of Royal."

A person wearing the colors of Royal faced them, hands clasped behind their back in a stance meant to convey peaceful welcome. They had taken the role of Gatekeeper. Their long, graying hair was pulled back into the topknot adults used for formal occasions. The Royal also wore shoes, which meant this area was considered a contamination zone unfit for children.

The marshal recited a set of memorized statements acknowledging the formal welcome and asking for permission to board on behalf of Chaonia's ruler. The Gatekeeper gave rote replies. Their group cleared the airlock and entered a compartment where adults acting as Sentinels told them to deposit their weapons.

The hum of the baton remained steady. No one on a wheelship bore a programmed leash within their neuronics and thus triggered no discordance in the baton's harmonics. The marines handed over their stingers, and they were all cleared to go on. No one looked at him, not even the Gatekeeper. He was just another Chaonian uniform.

They entered the trading post where outsiders bargained with a wheelship's trade representatives. Goods from both outside and inside were on display in stalls. Kurash stared. It was such an ordinary market space but utterly out of his experience, since no banner child ever walked in the emporium. Everyone wore shoes; he was wearing boots too because he was the same as any other outsider who could not be allowed into the spaces where people lived. Even when he'd departed as a banner soldier he had not passed through a contamination zone. The newly deceased were marched through a sealed quay onto a cargo ship.

Yet he smelled spicy chapuline tacos cooking down one of the aisles, just the way his grandmother spiced them. Acorn bread fresh from an oven. A clamor of voices speaking Common Yele in variant timbres and rhythms as outsiders bargained with locals on the market floor.

"Are you coming?" Secretary Xiákè paused to wait for him. "I can't help but notice how their gazes skip right over you."

"I see." He did not want to have this discussion, but now that the man had raised it, he could not help but notice he had become a null object that did not exist to the bannerfolk. Outsiders moving through the emporium stared at him because he was an anomaly. *The* anomaly. Everyone else fit their category: banner or not-banner. A sense of dislocation assailed him, as it had when the prince had stripped him of his battle name. Who was he, if he was not what his people had made him? If his people could not see who he was now?

He was Sun's envoy. He had to focus on the mission. With a sense of relief he entered a chamber where two adults waited behind a table. The marshal sat opposite the elder, who had taken the role of Interface. The marshal presented her diplomatic papers. The elder studied and then returned them. Tea was served ceremonially by the other adult, who wore the robe of an Etiquette.

The Interface said, "You may bring two individuals with you to the conclave. The others will wait at the emporium, where they may shop or entertain themselves until you return."

"A divide-and-conquer strategy to dispose of us?" the marshal said as if in jest, although there was a tough tone beneath her words.

"If we wanted you dead, Marshal, you would be dead already. João, child of Nanshe, child of Ashur, child of Tanith to the tenth generation, is a child of the banner of Royal. We do not forget that he went out to fulfill the conclave's determination that an alliance with Eirene of Chaonia would be to the benefit of the wheelships. We will hear from the representative of João's child because it is her right to be heard by us, as she has requested, although she is not herself born into the banners. I will leave my Etiquette to entertain and guide your people in whatever way you deem appropriate. Now, if you will choose your companions."

The marshal beckoned Kurash and Xiákè over. "I am ready to proceed."

"You may bring two individuals," said the elder.

"I have designated two individuals."

"There is only one person with you."

The marshal looked at Kurash with a questioning quirk of an eyebrow. "Can you explain this?"

He kept his voice pitched low as if it might be forbidden for his voice to be heard within the wheelship. "Those chosen to be banner soldiers are declared dead. They may consider me to be a ghost."

"You must come with me for the demonstration."

"I will attend you as long as they do not stop me."

"I'm game," she said with a chuckle, finding it all a bit of a lark. "Colonel, you'll attend me as well."

The Interface led them through a hatch and into a secondary spoke, a domed walkway that connected the docking ring to the hub. A slight curve in the spoke made the hub invisible from here.

The marshal said, "We are not going outward to the giant wheel? I had looked forward to walking its famous endless rising horizon."

"Outsiders are not allowed on the wheel. This way. Clip into the walkway. The gravity will lesson as we approach the hub."

"No tramway or train?"

"If any of your group need accommodations I will gladly have an Etiquette fetch a wheeled chair."

"We can all walk. I'm just surprised there's no tram."

"Such a conveyance wastes resources better used for more crucial operations."

"More crucial than diplomacy?"

"Marshal, wheelships are designed to honor the journey of the ancestors, who traveled for many generations without engaging with outsiders. Diplomacy is a tool but for us it is not a necessity."

A deputy checked the two Chaonians to make sure they were correctly clipped into the walkway. Kurash knew the drill already but he might as well have been a ghost, a presence avoided and never acknowledged. He carefully took a place in the file behind the secretary and in front of the colonel because he could not bear if one of the bannerfolk came too close, even "accidentally" bumped him, as if he were a piece of furniture; it would be the crowning insult.

In other circumstances he would have enjoyed the walk and its steady sense of lightening, called "the ascent toward Lady Chaos." The spoke was as plain as the pedestrian tunnels under the Wheelhouse in Argos, although cleaner and with less echoing noise, only the flutter of light footfalls as they sprang forward. The passage dead-ended in a transparent bulkhead overlooking the spherical zero-gravity maze of Lady Chaos with its shifting paths and deadly puzzles.

The marshal grinned. "Is that where we are going? It looks like a three-dimensional version of the labyrinth in the Heart Temple of the Divine and Pacific Lotus Queen. An intriguing puzzle to get lost in."

"This way," said the Interface, indicating a humble doorway.

They unclipped from the walkway and, with a lightness like an up-lifted soul approaching the divine, mounted a stairway up to a chamber grafted atop the spoke. Its dome was also transparent, offering a splen-did view of the slowly spinning hub, the gleam of the distant planet, and the stately roll of the ever-turning wheel.

This chamber had two levels: the deck on which visitors stood in their shoes, and a raised floor with mats where the conclave elders sat on cushions. All wore formal white jackets wrapped with a sash, strip-ping away much of their individuality. They sat here as representatives for communities, not on their own behalf. Eleven banners hung from stands, each symbol behind the elder who represented that banner. Violent Storms with its charging bull. Blood Tide's oliphant with five trunks. Arsenal's battleship turret. The five-headed naga of Deluge. Avalanche's yellow bands. Thunderbolt's lightning. Venom's fangs. Magnificent Dragon. Ravenous Wolves. Riot.

He had skipped over Wrathful Snakes because he knew it would hurt to see the intertwined caduceus of his own tattoos. Wheelships carried a larger population than even Titan-class vessels. Young chil-dren stayed within a local district but adolescents were encouraged to roam. What if the Wrathful Snakes elder was someone whose face he had glimpsed as a child? It was possible.

It was.

It was a plump, round-faced woman with a short cap of age-whitened, curly hair and the wire-framed glasses she'd only begun to wear after she stopped working in hull repair.

It was his grandmother.

The formal white jacket looked odd on her, disguising the grand-mother he knew, because it was nothing like the garishly bright yarn shells and vests she knitted for herself and her extended kith. She was knitting now, a woman who needed something to do with her hands while she listened to a family discussion, a neighborhood dispute, a child's excited story. She had a wide circle of enthusiastic acquaintances and five grandchildren. Even so, fair-minded as she famously was, everyone knew he was her favorite, the one she coddled a little more than the others because he had the sweetest temperament. She had loved him.

Yet now she did not look at him. She listened to the marshal's presentation.

Queen-Marshal Sun brings before the conclave the collected results of tens of thousands of hours of laboratory work. This work has revealed the presence of a leash, a neurological means the Phene imprint onto an already existing neuronic network. Through this leash they literally control the actions of the soldiers they hire from the banners, as strings control marionettes. Through this leash they force the banner soldiers in their employ to fight far beyond normal limits and even unto death. It is the queen-marshal and her father Prince João's greatest wish to end this unethical practice. Sun is sure the conclave, once it hears the appalling truth, will accept her offer, her gift, of a technology that will free banner soldiers from this deadly and unethical compulsion.

When the marshal finished her statement the elders looked at each other with skeptical mouths and crinkling eyes. Outsiders might think they were communicating telepathically but the elders of a conclave were fitted with a special comms link so they could talk to one another on a completely private and unassailable network. It was a version of this network that Prince João had gifted his daughter many years ago. Kurash's ring, on his left forefinger, was hidden beneath a pair of formal dress gloves.

In conclave, elders took the title of their banner.

Blood Tide spoke. "What is it that the new dictator of Chaonia seeks in exchange?"

"Why, the queen-marshal of the Republic of Chaonia seeks only to end this injustice. There are no strings attached."

Arsenal snorted. "Of course there are strings attached. This so-called gift is intended to destabilize the banners."

"How do you figure that?" Precious asked with a flash of annoyance. She was a soldier, not a diplomat. An odd choice, when all was said and done, to lead this mission. More persuasive envoys could have been found, surely.

Wrathful Snakes answered. The familiar rough-hewn voice of his grandmother, who still had not acknowledged his presence even by looking his way.

"We on the wheelships must live in balance with our available resources. There is no other way to survive. We trade surplus to the Phene."

Surplus?

"Surplus?" The marshal could not hide her distaste. "What can you mean? Humans are not excess agricultural products to be exported to orbital habitats and mining stations that need food. Are banner soldiers not your own children?"

The knitting needles clacked in an unbroken rhythm. "We may regret the necessity of their departure, but if we do not cull our population then we will suffer. This we know from our histories. When a population exceeds its resources, death will come one way or another. We have chosen this path to keep our environment healthy."

"Are you saying you don't want this freely offered technology that will benefit your own people?"

"You do not understand us, Marshal. But Prince João does. This is a poisoned chalice."

"How do you mean?"

"All of us born to the banners are born with the neural pattern in our bodies. It enhances our survival by allowing us advantages of strength, reflexes, endurance. But we do not program compulsion into our own people. What happens to the ones we sell to the Phene is the business of the Phene. What do we need this technology for? By offering it to us, Queen-Marshal Sun is implying we will work with Chaonia to reduce or eliminate the empire's deployment of banner soldiers. We are not tools to be used in Chaonia's war of aggression. I call a vote."

"With no further discussion?" objected Thunderbolt. "No discussion of whether we ought to allow the Phene to abuse our own people in this cruel and unethical way?"

"No further discussion?" the marshal echoed, looking stunned by the cavalier way the conclave was treating the mission and the offer.

Kurash too was stunned. His hands seemed not to belong to him. His legs had turned into immoveable stone. Lightheadedness washed through him, and he had to give himself a spurt of calm, too much, followed by a sting of alertness. Everything collided against the dull pain oozing outward from his aching heart.

"We need no discussion," said Arsenal with a glare toward Thunderbolt; old rivals, he thought. Prince João's chief aide Colonel Evans was Thunderbolt Banner. No love lost between these banners.

The marshal was still struggling to comprehend the speed at which she was being rejected. "You mean to just throw away the lives of your own citizens without even the courtesy of a ceremony to honor the dead?"

His grandmother answered in a tone grown harsh with impatience. "We have already honored the dead. Those chosen to serve as banner soldiers die before they leave the wheelships. We hold their funerals, at which they take part before they leave. We mourn them, as we mourn all our honorable dead. Then we continue on our journey. That is the cycle of life, is it not, Marshal?"

He could not bear it any longer. He took a step forward and spoke before the marshal could attempt to command him not to. "What of banner soldiers who survive their time with the Phene? What responsibility do the banners have toward those who served honorably and faithfully but were abandoned by the empire?"

"That's a good question," said the marshal, pouncing on his words. "Do you have an answer for this person, who is an honorable son of the banners?"

Grandmother addressed the marshal. "No honorable child of the banners would dishonor the banner by rejecting their destiny according to the will of Lady Chaos. As for wandering ghosts, they are not welcome here."

She would never look at him. He understood that now. She had buried her grandson Kurash with genuine tears and watched as the banner soldier Zizou marched away to die, carrying the socks she had knitted for him. But the body standing here—his body, his breath, his soul—was no longer part of her world.

They voted eight to three to reject Chaonia's offer out of hand. Thunderbolt, Venom, and Riot the dissenters. Agitation in the ranks. But in the long history of the banners, there had never been a time when the wheels had turned through the heavens united, not since the dark day they had scattered from the rage of Lady Chaos, the primordial one, She Who Bore Them All and who with a lash of her tails sent them fleeing the wreckage of her nest, cast adrift on the glistening ocean of stars.

Precious Jīn lost her temper, or maybe she succumbed to her pride. "Reject Chaonia's offer if you will. But this is not the last you have heard from us." She turned her back on the elders and beckoned to her attendants.

His grandmother's gaze flickered his way, and she shut her eyes hard as if to blot him out. He did not want to move. He wanted to show that he belonged still to the family he loved and had been required to leave. He had never questioned his fate.

"Kurash!" snapped the marshal.

His grandmother's eyes flared with shock as she heard his intimate name on the lips of a foreigner, spoken in public for any ear to gather into itself, shared as if the name she had herself given him was a mere commonplace. She looked down at the knitting, a pattern growing into a recognizable pair of socks. Her silence and her disgust exploded in his heart like a killing blow, the percussion echo of shame. Now they all knew he had been stripped of his battle name.

He fled after the others.

He caught up where the marshal was clipping herself into the walkway as the Interface waited some paces away.

Kurash said, "You mustn't give up so easily. You can bargain harder. Stay in the fight. That's expected. If you ask for another meeting and sweeten it with some trade goods, they will hear you again. It's what Sun wants. She has a reason for everything she does. She's thinking two or three moves ahead."

She rounded on him. "Three moves ahead! What rubbish! She's reckless and self-obsessed, just as Eirene said. This is a waste of time. We can't trust the Gatoi because we've never been able to trust the Gatoi, not that petty schemer João and not these arrogant savages who think they can treat me, a marshal of Chaonia, with such bald contempt! It was a fool's errand to begin with. We are done here. Come along."

She headed wheel-ward along the spoke. He followed, head down, reeling from his grandmother's rejection, from the marshal's temper. It was all he could do to set one foot after the next while ahead of him Precious outpaced the dour Interface quite rudely and kept going as if the Royal were a mere speck of dust too unimportant to be acknowledged. Kurash fell into step with Colonel Jin, who stayed behind the Royal to keep an eye on this potential hostile.

The marshal had drawn her secretary ahead with her. She bent her head toward his to speak in a confiding murmur. Kurash amplified his hearing.

"Eirene would never have begun with such a clumsy overture. But it serves us well. In truth, this mission has worked out better than I had hoped. Sun's reputation is high because of the Karnos victory but with each setback it will erode. Then we will be positioned to replace her."

Replace her?

His despair and self-pity burned off in an instant. Adrenaline flashed through him, wiring him taut, ready to leap. The colonel glanced at him, aware as any soldier must be of a change of tension.

But he was no longer in an arrow, to be flung against a target. He was no longer Zizou, elegance with precision. He was no longer the old Kurash, the boy who had tagged after his beloved grandmother and obeyed her every wish. He had to find out who this new Kurash was, the one who had been lashed by the tail of Lady Chaos onto a new trajectory, cast into an unknown map with but one known star.

Protect Sun.

If a Wily Persephone Is Dragged in a Lounge and There Are No Rack-Mates Around to Hear It, Does It Really Count as an Own?

All traffic from Tsurru System into Kumbala System is stuck in a holding pattern at the Kumbala Beacon because so many military ships are lined up and waiting to drop through. On board the *Hræsvelgr*, the crew engages in predictable grousing as we wait our turn in the queue, but I don't mind at all.

"Look, look," I say excitedly to Ikenna. We are sipping tea in the officers' lounge where I am glued to an expanded live visual of the beacon coil as the massive *Keoe* maneuvers to position itself to drop through without scraping the interior curves of the coil. Several shuttles speed away from the ship while they can still leave. The coil begins to pulse as it tunes into the beacon cone at the stem of the mini-Titan. "This confirms my new theory that beacon coils were designed at a size to prevent mothership Titans from being able to utilize them."

"Your new theory? From this minute?" Ikenna groans. "One ship's transit is not confirmation of the intent of the Apsaras Convergence."

"Nobody appreciates my brilliance."

"So you constantly remind us."

There are only two other officers in the lounge. One is a junior lieutenant napping on a couch. The other is a baby honorable fresh out of the royal academy who is fetching a tray of tea for the bridge. The ensign gives a side-eye toward the sight of a vaunted Companion bantering with a mere citizen officer and CeDCA graduate. I give the ensign a smile and a nod, and they blush and hustle out with the tray.

As the door slides shut, Ikenna rolls his eyes. "Stop scaring them, Perse. You're just being mean."

"I don't have a mean bone in my body."

"You and Jade Kim in a dark closet says otherwise."

"Shut your face."

"It's not as fun to tease you if the others aren't here. If a Perse is dragged in a lounge and there are no rack-mates around to hear it, does it really count as an own?"

"You're worse than Squarehead."

"Has Solomon checked in yet? Or Minh for that matter? Ay's off on that wild gallimimus mission with your last bad crush, so that sucks."

I ignore Ikenna in favor of pinging first Solomon and then Ti via the ring network. STATUS? I'M IN THE BEACON QUEUE AWAITING DROP.

Tiana replies instantly. DO YOU NEED ME THERE?

NO NEED. MEET UP ON THE OTHER SIDE.

When Solomon doesn't reply I say, "The rescue task force must have dropped through before the *Keoe* arrived."

My ring lights with an incoming message. I'm startled to hear James.

"Hey! Are you still in Tsurru System? Where are you?"

"In the queue at Kumbala Beacon. I thought you were in Meli System."

"I was. Check your ship's monitor."

I spot the battleship as it moves toward the queue. "Are you on the *Red Hare*?"

"I am. Transit time to Kumbala Prime is shorter to come via Tsurru System than to take the direct drop from Meli into Kumbala. Come over! Hetty's here too. We're moving our task force into place to be next in line to drop through as soon as the *Keoe*'s escort group clears."

"Queue jumper!"

"That would be my father. Your corvette is in position ninety-two for transit and I see twelve cruisers from Second Fleet coming up. I guarantee Anas will kick the likes of your corvette down the queue even more. Your choice."

I jump to my feet. "Ikenna, grab your duffel. We're switching ships."

"Don't we need permission from . . . Hells. I just can't get used to you being an honorable, much less a Companion."

An hour later we are boarding the *Red Hare* through the dignitaries' hangar. The ship's XO awaits me. He's a middle-aged Samtarras scion, cousin of the venerable crane marshal.

"Honored Persephone. We've made a cabin available alongside the Honorable James . . ." The man trails off, eyes widening, as Tiana enters the hangar from an inside door.

She's resplendent in yellow, hair tightly braided and pinned up with jeweled butterfly ornaments that catch the light. "Commander, if I may. The Honorable James has sent me to escort the Honorable Persephone and Lieutenant Ikenna Sì Alluòyì."

Dazzled, he gives way. Ti includes every officer and spacer on the receiving deck with her most gracious smile before she sweeps us off the hangar and into a passageway. It's a short walk to one of the flag suites.

"When did you get here?" I ask. "And why?"

"There was nothing for me to do on the *Keoe*. So when Hetty . . . when the Honorable Hestia and the Honorable James arrived in-system I transferred at their request."

When did Ti start addressing Hetty so informally?

"You aren't required to act as their cee-cee," I say, not at all grumpily.

"Colonel Isis has been acting bodyguard to Sun for over a year. James has no one except household staff. Not that he's the type to complain. And if I may remind you, Honored Persephone . . ."

"Burn her," mutters Ikenna.

"The Honorable Hestia gave up the ring she would normally have granted to a formal licensed cee-cee so Solomon can have one. As the only cee-cee currently in-system it seemed fair for me to agree. Anyway, I was so bored that my parents were starting to get on my nerves. And the other thing—the thing I can't do—was bugging me so much I figured better to transfer over and get back to work."

"I get it." We exchange a glance without needing to say Kaspar's name.

In the entry foyer to the flag suite a marine stands guard next to a calligraphy scroll with a poem about the loyal virtue of heavenly ships. There's no time to admire the masterful stroke-work before we enter the parlor. James is hunched over a strategos table while Hetty reclines on a couch, reading. She rises with a smile so big that suddenly my face hurts and I realize I haven't seen her in months, because for the knnu passage she and James traveled in a ship attached to the tow chain while I was on the *Keoe*.

Before I know it, I'm giving her a hug and I hardly know how to describe the warm feeling inside me that I had grown accustomed to lacking. The serotonin of friendly human contact. The simple pleasure I once felt in company with my sister and brother when I was little.

"It's been so long since last we stood together," says Hetty, releasing me.

I walk up behind James, snatch the cap from his head, and slap him with it.

He doesn't look up. "I knew you were there."

I try it on my own head. "Perfect fit. What do you think, Ti? Is it the right style for me?"

James sticks out a hand and waggles his fingers. "Give it back, asshole."

Because I don't have a mean bone in my body, I hand it over.

"Missed you," he says grudgingly as he smooths out the fabric on the tabletop. "Kind of. Not really."

Hetty smiles. "Sit, sit, we'll have a toast and supper too."

Ikenna looks around desperately at the sumptuous furnishings, a beautiful calligraphy scroll signed by the crane marshal himself, a sculpture sealed inside a sphere depicting an escher-looped waterfall.

The presence of a strategos table signals this as a suite reserved for people of the highest military status. Not to mention Crane Marshal Zàofù's illustrious son, who hasn't greeted Ikenna, because why would he think he had to?

Ikenna edges after Ti as she walks to the door into the galley. "Uh, Tiana, perhaps I can assist you in some way."

"Has the Honored Persephone not introduced you, Lieutenant? Your work on deciphering source codes in Phene military computer hierarchies might be of interest to the Honorable James."

James jolts up to his feet with an excited grin. "You did that? I looked over your algorithms. They're very good. I didn't know you and the Honorable Persephone knew each other or I'd have asked to meet you."

Ikenna gives me a speaking look.

"I forgot you wouldn't have met," I temporize. "Ikenna was one of my and Solomon's rack-mates at CeDCA."

"Like Ay," says Hetty with a gracious nod.

Ikenna brightens at the mention of Ay. I gesture for him to go to the strategos table with James, then wash my hands and sit on a cushion opposite Hetty in a screened-off dining area. Ti serves us chilled ume-shu. Hetty tells me about the Matrone's Hive and I tell her about the *Bennu*. While we talk I use the tabletop as a screen to keep an eye on the *Keoe*'s slow progress into the beacon coil. It's honestly exciting to see how tight the fit is; how close the hull passes to the inner coils. If I were standing on its hull, I swear I could reach out and touch the beacon as the big ship passed through.

Ikenna begs off supper and flees to the officers' mess. So it is just Hetty, James, and me for an intimate repast, whose delicacy and flavor provides a welcome change after the standard fare on the corvette.

Our conversation is random and easy. James and I enjoy picking apart the Pompous Historian's newest Exclusive, a slickly edited thriller about the attack on the Grand Sanctuary. It's a rattlingly invigorating hour using animated reconstructions and actual hornet and body cam footage that will play to great acclaim back in the republic once it reaches there in three or four months. Hetty finds Sun's act of leaping alone into the waiting enemy less amusing than James and I do, even knowing her squad jumped right in after her and that she got through with what she, in her riveting post-battle speech, refers to as "only minor wounds." I wouldn't call a scapula fracture, two rib fractures, a hip puncture, multiple contusions, three broken fingers, and a concussion "minor wounds," but I'm just an endurance runner, so what would I know?

We are joined for a fruit-and-sweets aperitif by the crane marshal himself, stern, not a jokester at all, which requires us to speak only of worthy things in worthy tones. He is accompanied by the formidable Marshal the Honorable Angharad Black. Normally a war hero like her would totally intimidate me. Unfortunately I've had enough to drink that I'm unusually loquacious upon the subject of my new obsession.

"It makes perfect sense if you think about it," I say with no rackmate to stop me from embarrassing myself, not that any of them would.

"What makes perfect sense, Honored Persephone?" asks Angharad, who has the sort of genial hard-ass temperament I aspire to. I can't help but notice how her gaze now and again touches on Ti with appreciation while at the same time she pays attention to my thesis.

"It makes sense the Apsaras engineers wanted to develop a faster means to travel between star systems. But what if they also wanted to undercut the power of the Argosies while they did it? For generations the Argosies controlled who and what and how people, ships, and populations could move between star systems in the local belt. They controlled exploration and expansion. Of course, it's possible the size of the beacons simply reflects an engineering limitation. Because we don't know where to find the Apsaras home world and any records we would discover there, we can't know. But what if it wasn't an engineering limitation? What if the Apsaras engineered the beacons so the mothership Titans can't use them?"

Angharad nods sagely. "To kill their fucking monopoly. An intriguing theory."

"Unprovable," says the crane marshal with his most serious face.

James says, "Yes, but it's as good an explanation as any, Father."

"How then do you explain that mini-Titans like the *Keoe* are fitted with both knnu drives and beacon cones?" objects Zàofù.

I wave a hand. "I haven't done exhaustive research into this, not yet, but from what I can tell, it seems the class of ships we call mini-Titans were developed after the beacon system was built. As if the Argosies designed a smaller Titan that would fit through a beacon. It's not as if the Apsaras could change the beacons once the system was in place. Think of it from the point of view of the Argosies. The crucial difference between the *Keoe* and the mothership Titans is the difference between towing two hundred and eighty ships and one thousand ships. The energy load is similar either way, and anyway the original Titans were built to haul as many ships as possible because of the need to move vulnerable populations out of the Celestial Empire. My point is, all else being equal, larger ships always make more sense for an Argosy. The Phene dreadnoughts could handle the energy load of a knnu drive but could only tow sixty or seventy ships each, according to our estimates from the Molossia attack."

"Even if true, what does this matter to us now?" Angharad asks.

"Well, for one thing, where did the Phene get those knnu drives? Argosies keep everything about knnu technology secret. It's in their organizing charter. No Argosy can just hand out knnu drives or Navigator services."

"That is a hells-good question we've not yet answered," says Angharad.

Zàofù sighs. "We've not been able to trace the origin of the knnu drives or how the Phene were able to get hold of ten, which is an astounding number to randomly find lying around."

"Not the work of criminal salvagers on the hunt for a bigger piss pot," agrees Angharad. "A concerted operation by professionals who knew what they were doing and why they were doing it. Still, at Molossia we kicked them in the face hard enough to hurt."

She smiles her sophisticated war hero smile at Ti, who has just at that moment halted beside her to fill up her glass. Ti is not coy, nor does she play games. She knows who she is. She meets the honorable's gaze for a fraction longer than one might expect. A message? An offer? A promise?

My pulse spikes. I pick up my glass but it's already empty.

Comms give a warning chime. "Set beacon stations. Transition in five minutes."

We close up our glasses like petals furling and anchor ourselves with straps.

"Take all weigh off the ship."

The gravity cuts.

The transition bell rings.

The ship rolls and we fall through.

The seers of Iros like my father say we fall through beacons no matter which direction we enter, that there is neither up nor down. A pulse of movement cycles on and on just out of my range of sight like the heartbeat of a vast invisible beast. Ships slide through an impenetrable opacity toward pinpricks of distant stars. A whisper like Father's voice threads through my unspooling thoughts.

This isn't who you are. This is merely a starting point.

As in a dream I see a shrouded figure seated by a young woman. Her face is shadowed and her garments too dark to see. Only her hands are bathed in light as she reaches for a radiant crown shaped like a halo adorned with glittering spikes.

We drop into Kumbala System.

Comms crackles above a klaxon's blare. "Incoming debris. All hands brace for shock."

"Captain, status?" The marshal politely projects the reply so we all hear.

"We are cleared to move through the debris field. It is from the battle five days ago. Looks as if the Larissan Centaur Division took apart the main column of enemy ships that fled this way. I hear the Phene were trying to make it to an Ousoos Argosy mothership waiting out by the heliopause. Marshal the Honorable Alika Vata captured the *Bountiful* after a heavy engagement."

Hetty, James, Tiana, and I all react with minute gestures as our ring network delivers incoming from Sun. **ASSEMBLE AT KUMBALA PRIME**

Zàofù says to the captain, "We accompany *Keoe* to Kumbala Prime. ETA fifty-three hours."

He rises, and we all scramble to our feet to pay our respects.

"Do you need me for anything, Father?" James asks in a tone that sounds suspiciously like hope.

The marshal turns at the door to look back. "You, James? Your duty is to serve Sun. Anas will be along soon if there are any remaining maneuvers or task forces to finish off."

James looks away as his shoulders sag.

The marshal departs. Angharad takes her leave as well. Although we are Companions, without Sun among us we must seem like junior scrubs to a veteran of her stature. The liquor has filled my head to the brim with unspoken words that tremble on my tongue. I almost blurt out to the others about Nona's lab but I mustn't. No one can know.

"Not even Hetty," I say before I realize I'm speaking out loud.

Ti sighs. "You're not as badly inebriated as one would think given your small mass compared to the large amount you imbibed."

"Is this Vogue Academy diction?"

"Let me put you to bed."

I give Hetty a sloppy kiss on the cheek, which makes her laugh, but when I attempt to grab James's cap so I can slap him with it he dodges faster than I can react.

"Shit. I *am* drunk if you can fake me out." I rub my face. "Where do I sleep?"

Ti leads me to a three-room cabin attached to the flag suite. It sports a tiny bedchamber, a tiny office, and a tiny parlor fitted with a sleeping alcove for my cee-cee's rack, which is screened off by a curtain. While I shower she sorts out my gear and sets my pajamas on the bed.

"Go help James and Hetty," I offer magnanimously, but mostly because I feel cringingly awkward around her for some reason I can't explain. "They need the help more than I do."

She laughs.

"They do! They didn't spend five years at CeDCA like I did. I'm fine until morning. No need to check back in. I'm fine."

Fortunately she leaves before I twist myself into knots. Then I have nothing to do because I am sorry she left. I lie on my back on the bed with a virtual screen expanded above me, studying our transit of the debris field. Phene hulks fade past. Trawlers sift for corpses within the flotsam and jetsam. I spot a pair of dark-running lifepods and use comms to flag a cutter that's searching. A pair of Larissan Centaur-class frigates jauntily skim past as if gloating over their kills but maybe they too are searching for survivors.

The hull designation of a big vessel looms into view. It takes my network seven seconds to translate the Phenish letters on its side. *Legbiter,* destroyer class. The derelict slides on into the oblivion of its death. Following in its wake come a pair of Scarab-class haulers. Are there military-grade shipyards in this system? How can I find out when James and his crew haven't yet fully cracked the Trinity's network?

I think of Tsurru's fourth beacon and how I haven't found official confirmation of a fifth. Does Kumbala System also have more than the three beacons?

I fall asleep in the middle of searching a map of the system.

Much later I wake up. At first I don't know why. Then I hear a feather-light whisper. My door is open, and the lights are off in the parlor beyond. I slide from the bed and tiptoe to the door, staying to one side so my movement won't be noticed.

Someone laughs low and smoky with an edge so suggestive my spine tingles and I ache with remembered anticipation. It's been way too long since my last bad crush and what did I get out of that anyway? Heartbreak from a single kiss.

The parlor is dim with only a muted track of path lighting along the floor. Nevertheless it's enough for me to recognize Ti's silhouette. She's leaning at the door into the passageway, where a tall person stands backlit by the night-shift lighting.

The person in the passage speaks with the intimacy of postcoital pillow talk. "I would far rather see the radiant glance of your face than the famed fighting ships of the Larissans in their glittering ranks."

"I'm honored, but I won't hold you to that when the next battle comes and you are awaiting reinforcements."

The lazy laugh falls again. I can hear in it every stroke and kiss and orgasm gathered up like treasure. "What gift is worthy of such splendor, Tiana?"

"I'm no longer in the Campaspe Guild, to accept gifts. I do this for myself, Captain."

"Please. Call me Angharad."

I slink back to bed, unseen, and pull my blanket over my head. Not my business. Not my business.

Of course I can't sleep. The door closes. There's an interlude of quiet rustling as Ti goes to bed. I count my blinks but eventually give up and, with a sigh, tune back into military comms. Fortunate me. History never sleeps. The Pompous Historian has uploaded a preliminary public report on the battle for Kumbala System.

In the dark cave beneath my blanket, I watch the action unfold, the Phene bombardment to cover their retreat, the swift and effective attack of the Larissans while Alika's fleet charges onward to the edge of the system to capture the Magava's mothership Titan, the *Bountiful*. If there was a battle on the surface of Kumbala Prime, Beau's chosen not to include it.

In the background, steadily receding, the Tsurru Beacon pulses as ship after ship drops through on our tail like the steady drip of that most crucial question: Why is Sun having her entire fleet assemble here in Kumbala? The Trinity Coalition has three beacon-linked systems. Its three Argosy routes face Yele, Karnos, and the Jewel Road to Destiny in old Mishirru. Shouldn't we be headed home via Karnos or the Yele League? Instead we are falling endlessly through, and I understand to the very core of me that there is no return possible to the world we lived in a year ago.

If the Gods Allowed

The Magava's Grove on Kumbala Prime was a complex of buildings and temples woven amid a thousand hectares of woodland. This sacred forest had long ago been planted with trees native to the Celestial Empire. For eight days Sun presided over the funeral rites for the fallen, pyres burning, prayers chanted, offerings made. She was always in the thick of it, speaking tributes to the dead, visiting wards of wounded, eating with enlisted in their mess halls, announcing the forgiveness of debts incurred by spacers and soldiers, and rewarding generous bonuses fleet-wide to be paid out of the Trinity's captured treasury.

On the final night the queen-marshal took her place in the seat of honor at the evening banquet. In a large open-air pavilion heated with a hypocaust system against the bitter cold, she hosted the marshals and highest-ranking officers in the now-united Eighth, Second, Sixth, and Ninth Fleets. Musicians, dancers, acrobats, and renowned pugilists provided a stream of entertainment as course after course was brought to already heavily laden tables. Liquor flowed freely. Laughter abounded. Crane Marshal Zàofù was seen to smile twice, once at a caustic joke made by his son Anas at the expense of a Yele colonel who had been laid flat by a petite pugilist the man had drunkenly propositioned, and the second time during the performance of the acclaimed ribbon dancer, Ji-na, as she directed the flow of her ribbons to trace a triumphant battle through the air.

At oh hundred by the shipboard clock, zero hour, dead of night, the banquet ended with a speech from Sun at her most exuberant, broadcast throughout the fleet. She praised the command, the spacers and soldiers, the ships, and the famous Chaonian discipline and toughness, only briefly referencing the wounds she had herself taken: her left hand was still in a splint, a medical brace wrapped her ribs, and a contusion had yellowed along the left side of her face.

"What we do, we do for the common good of our beloved Chaonia. When we act together, the impossible is achievable."

With huzzahs, the gathering broke up and people departed, singing. The bright lights of the pavilion were switched off at midnight according to the holy tradition of the Grove, which Sun followed according to her practice of showing respect for local temples. Dozer slithered away to the doors that led to the kitchen, where the cee-cees had gathered in the shadows to chat to one another as they wound down from the night's revelry. Guards stood farther out in a loose ring, not visible but always present.

Sun and her Companions remained seated at the high table scattered with half-finished platters and empty bottles. Eleuterio hung silk lanterns in the shape of the Chaonian sunburst. Under this auspicious illumination Sun called for another round of wine.

James started to yawn and tried unsuccessfully to stifle it when Persephone prodded him on the arm with her usual gadfly teasing. "Now what?" he asked. "I guess we won."

"We aren't done." Sun didn't look tired at all. "We are still spears in flight."

The glow from the lanterns fell on her face. With darkness surrounding her as the emptiness of space surrounds a brilliant star that alone has the power to radiate light, she had never appeared so like a legendary figure as she did now. She wasn't smiling, precisely, but she exuded an energy that must attract all eyes to it because of the extraordinary intensity of her expression.

"I hope we're not done!" Makinde slapped a hand emphatically on the table. "I haven't even had a chance to get into a real fight yet. I always have to sit and wait. Do I have the worst luck, or what?"

With her braced, broken-in-five-places leg stretched out straight before her, Razin gave him a masterful side-eye and, with a bandaged hand, raised a glass ironically to him, after which she slugged down its contents.

"We make our own luck," said Jade disparagingly.

At these words Persephone stirred, as if with words bursting on her tongue, but instead chose to say nothing. For once Jade wasn't paying attention to her because their gaze was on Sun, who began.

"Karnos has fallen. The Speaker of the Rider Council fled in ignominy in the face of our attack. The defeated imperial admirals blocked their own beacons with mines, like cowards. Their best strategist is dead by a random accident."

She paused as if she'd caught the edge of a whisper. Maybe she heard the murmur of old gods who dwelt within the forest, or maybe it was just the winter wind.

"Those who scoffed at my plan to punish Trinity for the Karsh's insult now walk as conquerors in these spear-won systems and are enriched by their shares from the Hive's treasury. Even they now recognize this as strategically crucial territory that bridges routes to all the great powers. Our victory gives Chaonia an advantage even if our numbers and resources remain dwarfed by the empire's wealth and population."

Hetty nodded as she always did, never failing in her support.

Sun nodded in answer. "It is time to alter the balance of power."

Jade lifted a glass in a toast. "Fate is not just the command of heaven. It is also a matter of strategy."

"Shoot me now, suck-up," muttered Persephone, but no one paid any mind to her grousing.

"Why stop here?" Sun asked in a confiding tone. She held Hetty's gaze longest, ever clear, then got to her feet as if one evening spent in a chair at peace was as much as she could endure. "Karnos and the Hatti territories were independent before the empire conquered them and turned them into provinces. What of venerable Mishirru? Does the ancient glory of our first queendom not deserve liberation from the imperial Phene yoke placed on it a hundred years ago?"

"Will you ever be satisfied?" James asked. "What outcome will content you?"

"Why should any outcome satisfy me? Why should I seek contentment?"

He rubbed his eyes, then took off his cap and set it on the table.

Alika leaned forward. His ukulele was nowhere in sight; since becoming a marshal he no longer carried it with him everywhere. At some point he had left the Handsome Alika behind, perhaps for good. "The *Bountiful* is ours. I left Princess Soaring on board to get acquainted with its network and to make it clear the Ousoos Argosy is under Chaonian authority."

With a smile, Hetty said, "Is this the night that launched a thousand ships?"

"It's a completely ridiculous idea to invade Mishirru," said Persephone, "but—"

"I can't wait for this genius insight," James interrupted with his cheekiest grin.

Persephone grabbed his cap off the table and slapped him with it before she arranged it at a jaunty angle on his head and left it there. Then she went on.

"Think about it. I don't know what strategic benefit liberating Mishirru gives us. That's your job, Sun. I do know the old Archives, or what remains of them, can be found in the Gyre. And the Gyre is in Mishirru. Even then, so it is said, that's only possible to reach the Gyre if an aspiring pilgrim is given the blessing of the Great Mother Queen and her holy sisters. I mean, I know the Archives are so old they probably only contain outdated information, but it's said people who go there bring offerings of new information in the hope of being admitted to the stacks. If we can gain admittance to the Archives, we might be able to get hold of up-to-date maps of how the beacon routes run throughout the empire. An accurate map of how best and fastest to get around via beacon inside the empire is information we don't have. I don't think the Phene are going to leave classified maps lying around. I'm still putting together my best guess of how the routes work from Sleepless and Windworn into the three capital systems. We might even find maps of the pre-collapse routes at the Archives. Wouldn't that be fascinating?" Her eyes went glassy with excitement.

Sun lifted her gaze to the darkness beyond the frail aura of lantern light, the night that awaits all living things at the end. "The Archives contain all that is known of the Celestial Empire. Records from the world that was, before the fall. The most ancient lore of the final battle and the many heroic deeds of those who made humanity's survival possible. The personal accounts of the last emperor, my namesake. Maybe even the location of the Celestial Empire itself in the distant heavens."

No one replied. What was there to say? Humanity had left behind a dying world, so they had been taught. Although the Argosy fleets had fled humanity's home world three or four thousand years ago, every child grew up with the memory of the Celestial Empire woven into their lives. Its fragments and ruins were the foundation on which all else was built. Mishirru, Yele, the empire, Chaonia, the Hesjan and the Skuda Reach and Gatoi, the Apsaras who had overreached with their engineering, and remote systems like Belt of Jewels, Jade Skirt, Sacred Mountain, the Ring of Ravenna, isolated Fortuna, and the mysterious Asmu: the star systems and confederations of the local belt encompassed humanity's home now. Yet in some unfathomable way, they remained eternal refugees from a place to which they could never return, a stubborn wound that will never fully heal. Or maybe the dream of the Celestial Empire was nothing more than a snatch of song heard across an impassable barrier. Had the legend been constructed like any ark, built to protect those huddled inside so their descendants can survive the assaults of time and chance?

"How can we know anything for certain, if we don't for certain know anything at all?" mused Sun. Then she smiled her most captivating smile, the one that aimed its dart into the heavens like a missile on fire. "But I have a solution to all these questions. If the sun arises at dawn, then we have more work to do."

In darkness, Sun led her Companions along a path through the Magava's Grove, dedicated to the third and youngest aspect of the Trinity. The Karsh's Sanctuary of sunset and death; the Matrone's Hive of the zenith propagators; the Grove of dawn with its promise of a new day.

A cold wind rustled the branches of the trees. The Grove stretched away on all sides through tumbles of rocks and along stream-cut slopes. The slender trees faded into shadowy fugitives lost amid the night. Stars shone brightly overhead as scattered clouds sped westward. In the heavens, the fleets had gathered like a host of divine spirits arrayed for war.

They crossed under a series of slender wooden gates painted red and gold, although it was difficult to see color in the predawn gloom. Zàofù and the senior marshals had objected to Sun walking into a secluded wood with no escort. But the Grove was an ancient and sacred place, and Sun would not disturb its traditions.

Anyway, if she could not protect herself, then what was she? If her Companions could not defend her, then she had chosen poorly. Everything that had happened since her mother's death proved she had chosen well.

Let the Phene come at her with their fleets and their assassins. She had prevailed against them. If the gods allowed, she would prevail again.

She walked at the front of their group carrying the ice rose Hetty had brought her. The translucent flower gleamed beneath a remnant snow that dusted its open petals. There was just enough ambient light to discern the path. They made their silent way down its winding curve. Even James and Persephone spoke not one word as the sheltering trees gave way to a windswept promontory overlooking a sea.

The path fanned out to become a semicircular plaza whose edge was enclosed by a simple railing. A long pier-like structure extended as a skywalk into the gulf of air. Waves slapped rocks far below. The air tasted of salt and of something more, the scent of a world that was not Chaonia Prime. Was this not the fragrance of triumph?

The promontory faced east, where a glow gained strength along the horizon. On the plaza, two acolytes of the Grove awaited them, shockingly barefoot and clad in light tunics that left their limbs exposed. With gestures the acolytes indicated where they should stand, Sun at the point with her offering and her Companions spread out behind: James, Hestia, Alika, Persephone, Razin, Makinde, and Jade.

Half the sky lay bare. The wind died. The waters stilled.

A third acolyte stood in the shadows at the end of the skywalk. He began to sing. Softly at first, the curling melody wrapped back around itself as it slowly built in volume and intensity as if through purity of devotion a prayer could raise a star out of the abyss of blanketing night.

The words flowed aloft on an elegant melody, lifted by the beauty of a human voice. The other acolytes joined in. The language's cadences had been born long before people set foot on this world. The song had traveled as far as humanity itself across the ocean of stars.

Light splintered as the rim of the star pierced the horizon. The ascending disk spun a shining path that reached across the waters to those who waited on the shore.

The song lifted toward the heavens:

Let destiny be born to embrace her fortune and her fate.
She Who Rises as the Sun will dawn in glory and yet sink into darkness in
    the end.
Live in the day that is breaking.
Let the soul breathe her perfume into the universe.
Let the heart radiate with splendor.
Arise. Arise.

70

Interlude: an *Old Honcho and Baby Bee* Adventure

The august Titan named *Bountiful* sails on her majestic way through the ever-spanning night mantled by stars. Her tow chain attends her in immaculate order lest they be flung into the empty void to drift helpless through the millennia of time and distance.

In space, sound does not carry. Inside the womb of the mothership, however, a klaxon frantically wails the all hands.

Its hoot pierces even the recesses of the flag suite lounge where an overworked cee-cee might hope for peace and quiet as she tries to catch up on the most mundane of her duties. It is not to be. There is always a new emergency. Old Honcho sighs, weary to her ancient bones as she sets aside a torn uniform sleeve that needs mending.

Never in her long life had she dreamed of wanting to become a Companion's companion. What a crock of spoiled eggs. Her one youthful glimpse of the exalted sphere of a palace detail revealed itself as a life with too much flattering and too little free time. But even a skeptical and sarcastic veteran can't say no to the queen-marshal's personal request.

Meanwhile, Baby Bee is flattened and splay-legged against the ceiling, pretending to be in power-down cycle.

"Get your tentacle out of that conduit before it shocks you."

Dozer stealthily withdraws the tip of a tentacle from a node while gleaming the pink of innocence.

"Don't try to fool me, little one. That fleet sailed four thousand years ago."

The klaxon's blare clicks off and is replaced by dire tidings announced in a clipped tone over the 1MC. The queen-marshal is missing and no one can find her. Sabotage has happened, just as the Young Master has been hinting for days. Boarding parties are loose and causing havoc. Fuck.

Someone has to get to the bottom of these ongoing attacks, especially since they are trapped for the time being on board a Titan with a population as numerous as a city. Since no one else seems able to, Old Honcho will get the job done.

Baby Bee detaches six of its legs and, dangling in preparation for a drop, beeps interrogatively.

"Yes, you can accompany me. If you promise to not get into anything you don't have clearance to access." She doesn't have a direct link to the symbiont as the Young Master does, but over the half a year she's been in his service, she and the symbiont have worked out a complex system of color, movement, and sound that allows them to communicate basic concepts quickly so text messages and a slower direct camera stream need only be used on occasion.

The galley door swings open. Tiana emerges wearing a figure-hugging flight suit that will no doubt distract a younger enemy. She carries several satchels.

"Here, Sayre," she says, handing one over. "I made supplies for you, me, and Candace. The rest are on their own."

"My thanks."

"Do you know where you're going to start?"

"I do."

"Can I come with you?"

Old Honcho chuckles. "No dice, my young lovely."

"You'll regret that decision." Tiana has a smile so gracious it is a weapon.

"My thanks for the rations. As long as they're not poisoned."

The other cee-cee tips a two-finger salute to her, then leaves the lounge. A heady fragrance of sandalwood and ylang-ylang drifts in her wake like a threat.

Baby Bee lets go of the ceiling and rolls tight so as to hit the deck spinning. Old Honcho checks in the satchel to see a day's worth of neatly wrapped bento boxes. So thoughtful. Or suspicious. Tiana can go either way, or all ways, really. It is a Vogue Academy skillset this old honcho utterly lacks. But Baby Bee crawls up her leg and attaches to her back, and she is content to be who she is if it means this little sweetheart trusts her.

She slips on her boots at the door and grabs an emergency air filter. Eleuterio waits in the entry foyer, armed. All of Sun's entourage take the same training as the queen-marshal and her Companions. You never know when your baggage train might get hit, or your queen-marshal disappear, kidnapped or assassinated by onboard hostiles eager to take over and probably in league with shadow factions.

She opens the outer hatch a crack and lets Baby Bee probe. Ou blinks a warning. She closes the hatch. Comms are blocked, which means no network access. After forty-five seconds she tries again.

"Good fortune, Sayre. Dozer, you too, little buddy." Eleuterio hoists his stinger in case they are about to get raided.

Baby Bee waves two legs before slipping into the passageway. She signs a reply to the factotum as she follows. Ou is racing away at speed down a corridor as wide as a street. They've been eight weeks on board the *Bountiful,* and yet still the huge mothership Titan's proportions disorient her. But she knows where they have to go. Baby Bee carries a full schematic in case her memory needs prodding.

Ahead, the passageway dead-ends in a three-way junction. The main hatch on the facing bulkhead is closed, blocking access to the next compartment. The popping of stinger fire echoes from both directions.

Baby Bee overrides the security panel of a ventilation grille and unscrews it, easy when you have multiple appendages. They get inside the crawlspace with the grille back in place just in time. Keep calm and carry on. A squad comes running in retreat; a green-band-wearing individual stumbles and falls, scooped up and dragged onward by comrades. There is a pause as shouts chase after them, followed by the sizzle of stinger fire. Baby Bee silently secures the grille's bolts.

In a ship the size of a small city, the maintenance tunnels are the arteries, lymphatic system, and nerves woven through the vessel. She climbs down to an oversight walk that parallels the deck's sewage and waste lines. The smell makes her eyes water but she isn't going to use up her air filter just to cut stink.

With Baby Bee rolling ahead and her on a zip cart, they fly sternward toward the tow chain housings and their transit docks. The main battle for control of the ship will push toward the Navigator's bridge at the bow, directly behind the knnu hook. If hostiles can break into the bridge and capture Soaring Shān, they'll have a crucial advantage when, or if, negotiations start.

But Soaring isn't the only royal prize. She is just the obvious one. You don't survive to become an old honcho if you overlook the dark-dinohippus candidate.

In the first five klicks of the ten they have to cover from the midship flag suite to the rear, Baby Bee alerts her five times to movement in the throughway. Three times they keep going since the clamor is in a different artery, once they hide behind a powered-down sweeper mech as an orange-banded squad runs past, and once they ambush a blue-clad trio of hostiles and leave their bodies shoved into a storage locker alongside sewage rakes and a suction hose. Seven minutes after the fifth encounter, main power goes out and emergency kicks in with its red glow. They keep going.

The ship she wants is attached on the chain named Loyalty. She waits in a lightless side passage a quarter of a klick from Loyalty's transit dock as Baby Bee oozes ahead. The little symbiont can extrude a comms filament at need. With the network down, she connects this filament to her feed, allowing her to see via ou's infrared. A squad guards the entrance to the Loyalty transit dock, stationed amid a scattering of downed bodies. There has apparently been a fight here not long ago.

Providentially she recognizes the silhouette of the person in charge. She sends a burst message down the filament to Baby Bee, then extends her stinger to become a cane and taps forward down the dim passageway so the sound travels before her.

"Who's there?" a voice calls from the darkness.

"Dozer? Sayre?" Young Master waves the others back. "What are you doing here?"

She slings the satchel off her back. "My job, Young Master. I've brought provisions."

"Oh, excellent! It's been hours since we ate."

"What happened here?" She indicates the bodies lying on the deck.

"The first thing Persephone did with her units was to start grabbing tow chain transit docks, so I thought I'd better nip that in the bud. Her devious mind is always up to something."

"Is she dead?"

"Too bad, but no. Solomon brought a unit in and saved her ass. Say what you will about Alika or Jade or Razin, but Solomon is one tough cricket—"

He is smiling cheerfully right up until she slaps his shoulder with a poison pin while shooting three of the now-relaxed soldiers. Don't they teach these young sprouts never to let down their guard? Baby Bee takes out the other eight; ou's legs are all armed. They drop with groans and curses cut short.

The Young Master falls to his knees, grimacing. "How could you—? I thought—"

"You thought we were on the same side? Rash of you, Young Master."

She dumps the satchel beside the bodies, figuring it might implicate Tiana. She and Baby Bee hurry through the triple airlock sequence and into the big tube itself. A mini-Titan like the *Keoe* has to make do with two-meter-in-diameter rigid chains down which physical comms can be sent via a pneumatic system to the two hundred or so ships it tows. But motherships can create a more robust bubble. Knowing the journey would last generations, they built the tow chains as hollow tubes so it was possible for small numbers of people to move up and down the tow chain for emergencies, maintenance, and security. Therefore these chains have tracks for two-person pods, some to carry cargo and others fitted with a seat. Here on the Loyalty transit dock, one passenger pod slot is missing, as she expected.

Because the queen-marshal's advance fleet bridged the gap from Hellion Terminus to Tsurru System being towed by the *Keoe,* few knew in advance about the more complex mothership tow chains. No reason for any Chaonian to understand Argosy technology. But an old honcho might have scrambled about a few odd adventures in her scrappy youth, including a stint as the lowest-ranking and thus anonymous enlisted personnel in then–Princess Eirene's retinue when she was sent on an ambassadorial mission by her older brother to the Alabaster Argosy. Young Sayre had been too clever for her own good, always making the wrong kind of trouble, and she'd never forgotten what she observed and learned.

It is easy enough to release a passenger pod ahead as a decoy and follow in a cargo pod with Baby Bee beside ouself with excitement, crawling all over the inside of the pod and fiddling with anything that sticks out from the bulkhead or has the shape of a control panel.

"Don't poke a leg in that fixture. No. No!"

What was she thinking? *No* never worked with any of her four children or nineteen grandchildren except timid, compliant Asteria, who was doubtless destined to a soothingly boring career in the backwater machinery of the bureaucracy.

"I'll tell you a story."

Baby Bee turns both tentacles in her direction.

"I'm not saying anything more until you come over to me." She attaches herself to the bulkhead as the pod eases out from the hangar. Once free of the Titan's gravitational field she feels the annoying nausea and disorientation of weightlessness. Acceleration offers a bit of relief as the pod gently picks up speed. She pats her leg.

Baby Bee flows over and snuggles up against her, pulsing with excitement. Pod lights blink to indicate they are approaching the first stop on the tow chain. She checks the schematic stored in ou's capacious memory. The first ship is *Boukephalas*. With a tap of her fingers she sends both pods onward. According to the schematic her target vessel is anchored in position 88 of 132 ships on Loyalty Chain. Too much mass shifting position too quickly will destabilize even a mothership's bubble, so this is no high-speed transit system. It will take over an hour to get there.

"According to legend it took a century or more for all the great Argosies to depart the dying corpse of the Celestial Empire. During that time, some Argosies fled together while others ran alone, never to be heard from again, for space is vast and within its tangled dimensions we are not even as significant as grains of sand."

As the pod speeds onward she tries not to think about how vulnerable they are in a fragile tube. She wonders if any of the ships gone missing on the passage to Trinity survived, and she's dead certain a single cargo pod won't. She shakes off the thought. Go down that road and your gibbering mind will dissolve into nothing. It's better to tell a story.

"But what about the Argosies who wanted to travel together to the same place, you may ask. To the people traveling inside a Weinstein bubble, it's as if they are cut off from the rest of the universe except for the hook of the knnu drive. It pierces the bubble by means I don't understand and therefore is in contact with ordinary space. How could two or more Argosies stay together and not lose track of each other?"

Baby Bee stirs excitedly.

"My little friend, I don't know the answer to that question. But since they managed it in the ancient days, it must have had something to do with the hooks being able to communicate or transmit information to adjacent Argosies. Be that as it may, in time the first Argosy discovered Landfall System with its marginally habitable planet. It placed an anchor at the heliopause of the system to guide its Argosy siblings to its side. It's said the great motherships of the ancient Argosies were larger even than this grand Titan. I know. Hard to imagine. It's said each mothership housed one hundred million souls inside their womb, and towed five thousand ships behind them. That doesn't seem feasible to me, but what do I know?"

Baby Bee streams a short message through the filament. THERE ARE ONE THOUSAND FIFTY THREE SHIPS [1053] ATTACHED VIA EIGHT [8] TOW CHAINS TO THIS VESSEL ACCORDING TO THE FINAL SCHEMATIC DOWNLOADED BEFORE DEPARTURE FROM KUMBALA SYSTEM

"That is correct, Baby Bee."

The symbiont pulses with delight.

"But let me continue, because I have a point, and it's about you."

ME! ME!

She smiles, then grows serious. "In the generations following the first landfall, more Argosies did indeed arrive. Most people were eager to get off the ships and make a new life planet-side. In those days, the idea of living on a planet had the gleam of legend. Was the Celestial Empire not a holy planet now lost to us? These populations spread quickly along a string of stars that were close together by galactic standards, stretching from Landfall to heaven-sent Destiny. This territory was eventually named Mishirru because it was the border between the long night of the voyage from the Celestial Empire and the new day as humanity found a safe home. Mishirru was but the first step into a crowded stellar region rich with star systems blessed with habitable planets, what we call the local belt.

"But here is the warning I need to give you. Because far back in the early days there was a conflict among those who established the venerable queendom of Mishirru, she who is the first and the last and attended by Fire and Splendor. We don't have the particulars. Some say it was the avatars of the gods who went to war in their new heaven. Others claim the Argosy leaders fought each other. Some say the last Argosy to arrive had replaced its entire population with clones bred and programmed to exterminate. Some say the motherships' artificial intelligences went rogue and tried to kill all humans."

The symbiont grays out a little, hearing such horrible tidings about artificial intelligences. She scritches ou's bulbous dome, and the skin mellows to a pale and hopeful yellow.

"These are all stories of dubious provenance. The histories are unreliable. What we do know is that someone or something broke into the Archives, the precious treasury of knowledge brought across that thousand-year trek. The Archives were fractured. Erased in the way torrential rains wash topsoil from vulnerable slopes and leave only bare rock. Imagine being given one hundred pieces of a thousand-piece jigsaw puzzle and being told to reconstruct the full image. Of course the attack on the Archives was a terrible crime, although some said it was an inevitable accident of time and distance. People say we can never know the truth of the Celestial Empire, nor should we pretend we can. That's a question outside of my pay grade.

"Humanity spread outward from venerable Mishirru. Some wished to explore. Some to live apart. Some to seek resources or territory they could claim for their own. Some who sought change left Mishirru's hierocracy to create new forms of political organization. A thousand years after landfall, a collective that named itself the Apsaras Convergence built the beacon routes and by this means destroyed the dominance of the Argosies forever."

She paused with a sigh. Baby Bee tapped her on the thigh.

"Yes, anyway, the point is that you, Dozer, must keep your head down and your arms pulled in tight as long as we are in Mishirru. It's said the priests confiscate symbionts and turn them into scrap. Do you understand? No games."

Baby Bee turns a bright, anxious orange.

"Good, because I mean it."

Their cargo pad passes ship after ship, military vessels crammed with spacers, Republican Guards, allied forces, and Phene prisoners. This journey is a gamble of such audacity it is hard to know whether to laugh or to cry. She admires Sun's boldness. Yet is this gamble any greater than that of the original Argosies themselves? Before she left Chaonia, Sun laid an offering at the altar of her namesake She Who Rises as the Sun, so it seems fitting she honors the legendary divinities of the past by emulating their fortitude and fearlessness.

At length Old Honcho identifies the upcoming eighty-eighth ship, the *Keoe* itself, placed this far back in the tow chain by Sun's order. If another attack happens, and more ships get cut loose, then it is hoped the *Keoe* can escape from the Weinstein bubble and gather the lost into its smaller tow chain. That way they wouldn't be lost as the other ships had been, a defeat that gnaws at Sun although she rarely speaks of it.

Sayre halts the cargo pod a quarter klick from the docking mechanism. With her air filter in place, she eases out to a maintenance walkway running along the inner wall of the tube. Resting her hand on its curving bulkhead, she imagines the voyagers of old being granted permission to make a trek on foot from a ship at the back of the tow chain all the way to the great Mother at the front, a pilgrimage to the holiest of temples.

Then she thinks of the emptiness that lies beyond. No, enough of that.

She pulls herself forward using handholds. After a few meters Baby Bee gets bored at her slow speed. Ou winds two legs around her torso and uses four to pull ouself and her faster than any human pace.

At an emergency airlock, she overrides the lock with codes available to Sun's Companions and their cee-cees. Weightlessness flips her over gravity, with down being the wrong way. She thumps hard onto a deck on her back. The two spacers on duty at the airlock are so surprised to see her that she easily tags them before they can react.

She flashes her cee-cee credentials. "My crew or dead? Your choice."

They choose to join her crew, although under these circumstances they might jump allegiance in a heartbeat if something better comes along. She has to be fast.

"Hold the cargo pod here."

Keeping an eye on the cargo pod will keep them busy, especially since it means they believe she is returning soon.

She knows the *Keoe* pretty well after the journey from Chaonia to Hellion Terminus to Tsurru System. Using Baby Bee as her scout, she makes her way to the laboratory complex in the center of the ship. The passageways are silent. The repercussions from the current battle on board the *Bountiful* will take a while to filter down its tow chains. She wonders how civil disobedience and attempts at rebellion survived back in the ancient days when the Argosy leaders could simply cut off a ship from concourse with the rest of the fleet. A person might spend their entire life wandering the restricted compartments of a minor cargo hauler while knowing a fabled mothership lay out of their reach forever, even though it was so very close at hand. Old honchos didn't much like despots sitting atop the heap of power. Better to be a republic where all strove together under the leadership of a capable queen-marshal to gain freedom, wealth, and security for every citizen.

She reaches the laboratory. The problem with the people attacking on the *Bountiful* is that they have forgotten that Sun's royal cousin Metis is on the *Keoe*. Soaring is a foreigner and always will be. Metis has a mental disability, it's true, but she understands more than people think she does, and most importantly she is Chaonian through and through. Sound of body if not fully of mind.

The one who controls the queen-marshal's throne, even if they are not the queen-marshal, is the one who controls the republic.

Inside she confronts a startled group of lab coats going about their business unaware of the tumult beyond and puzzled by her appearance.

"Princess Metis? No, she's not here."

Because an old honcho doesn't take people's word for it, she checks through the living quarters for herself. The young princess is indeed not in her suite, but Sayre notices an open door into the interdicted level of the laboratory. She's never been allowed in that part of the complex. Curiosity killed the compsognathus. But that doesn't mean she's not here to win.

"Go check," she says to Baby Bee.

Ou chirps with excitement and vanishes down a ladder, filament stretching to keep her connected to ou's camera. The lower level has an oddly residential air but with more security measures. What is this place? Who opened the door?

The view oozes along the ceiling of a spacious sitting room, empty except for a single individual wearing factotum garb. The individual is leaning over a table with hands holding open some kind of half-disintegrated folded map bearing an elaborate geometric design. Their face isn't visible from this angle but the figure sure looks like the Honored Persephone. Why would the Companion be skulking around here, pretending to be a noncombatant, instead of engaging in the fight?

Old Honcho is about to ask Baby Bee to cross the ceiling to get a better view of the map when a joyful, high-pitched laugh surprises her and attracts the symbiont's endless interest in human beings and their doings. It slithers fast toward another open door. A tentacle hooks around a corner to spy into a parlor-like setting where a boy of perhaps fourteen sits at a table. He wears a knit cap even though the ambient room temperature is warm according to readouts. He has a good-natured, open expression, and is laughing excitedly as he leans against the woman seated next to him. She has an arm around his shoulders. It takes a moment for Sayre to realize the boy has four arms.

The woman is Tiana.

Why does Sun keep a Phene child hidden on her ship? One even an official palace cee-cee like Sayre with classified access wasn't told about? What can possibly be so precious about a mere child? Did Eirene keep a secret Phene lover with whom she had a child? It's too unlikely, and Chaonians would never ever accept a four-armed queen-marshal. Never. It would spit in the face of the republic's entire history.

What is Tiana's connection to the boy? As the two speak it is clear theirs is a relationship of long standing and genuine affection. There's something familiar about his face but she can't pin a tail to that deinonychus.

She sets aside the situation. Whatever this boy represents, Tiana has beaten her to the goal. Has someone gotten to Metis before her? According to the Young Master, Persephone secured this tow chain as her first move.

She recalls Baby Bee and in haste returns to front room where the lab coats have gone back to work. Using the full force of her palace authority, she demands they give up the princess's location.

The lab coats aren't happy about her intrusion, but she'd made sure to acquaint herself with Metis on the journey from Chaonia. She'd had an uncle with similar behavior patterns who'd spent decades of his life withering away in an alcove of the community room in the family compound. Young Sayre had thought him a piteous figure until she'd discovered he was skilled at backgammon, with its stark lines and regularized actions. He never talked, but he'd play if you set a board in front of him.

The lab coats trust her, therefore, and she gets the information she needs.

The waiting cargo pod turns out to be needed after all. She kill-tags the two spacers who've faithfully kept watch—a sad betrayal but necessary to cover her tracks—and heads on toward the end of the line. This time she goes directly to the main transfer point of the troop carrier *Surabhī*, bearing a battalion of Republican Guards fresh from home, part of the reinforcements brought in by Crane Marshal Zàofù. Marines wearing palace badges wave her forward with smirks, like the joke is on her. And it is, because the airlock disgorges her onto a big hangar directly into the teeth of a noisy, violent firefight.

Debris lies scattered across the hangar, visible as humps and twisted ridges in the dim red glow of emergency power. Streamers like ten-meter-long ribbons spin disorienting patterns across the debris field in a steady blast of wind from various directions, creating a constant visual shift as lines of sight get blocked and then reopened in seconds. It is wildly disorienting. Several squads are trying to push forward to reach the big doors into the main part of the ship but they keep getting slammed back by a fierce defense. Numbers dwindle. Bodies collapse as they get splashed with killing shots.

She spots a balcony overlook where a beam of light illuminates a young woman staring down at the carnage with an expression of puzzled interest. Metis, at last.

"Can you get up to her?"

Ou skitters away, blending into the bulkhead.

A hand taps her shoulder, planting a sting. "You're dead, comrade."

"Dammit! Colonel Isis, I thought you were on the *Bountiful*."

"That was your first mistake. I can't believe I walked right up to you like that. You're usually cannier."

The old honcho smiles. "I usually am, aren't I?"

Isis gives her a sharp look and is about to reply when a whistle blows. Everyone stops moving. A few groans and laughs echo in the space as people shuffle up to their feet. Main lights snap on. A figure outfitted in a Republican Guard uniform climbs atop a crate and pulls off a combat helmet.

Sun raises a hand for attention. "Establish your base of fire before you go in. That's why you aren't making headway. Back to positions. We'll run it again."

Turning, she sees them. She jumps down and runs over. Sweat trickles down her face. Smudges like patches of dried oil speckle her nose and jawline.

"Is the exercise complete already? Is there a winner?"

Sayre pulls off the kill tag on her shoulder before she answers. "The exercise was still underway when I departed the *Bountiful*, Your Highness. Dozer is claiming custody of Princess Metis on my behalf."

"You can't win if you're dead, and you're dead because I killed you," says Isis.

"Irrefutable, Colonel. But the Honorable Makinde is also dead, so perhaps that makes Dozer the winner. According to cartel protocol, a symbiont has protected status as a courtesy sapient."

Sun laughs as she looks toward the balcony. Dozer has attached ouself to the railing and, by swaying six legs and two tentacles, entrances the smiling Metis. "I was wondering if anyone would come after my cousin. I didn't want her startled by the events, so I brought her with me. Very good, Sayre. I should have known your experience would give you an edge. Anything to report? Criticisms? Observations?"

Sayre thinks about Tiana and the boy. If it was indeed Persephone disguised as a factotum, then it's possible Persephone deliberately forfeited her chance at victory in order to sneak Tiana onto the interdicted level. That would be an act of generosity unusual to see in the competitive realm of the honorables.

"Sayre?"

"Nothing, Your Highness. As far as I can tell, most people kept the focus of the exercise on the *Bountiful*. As for my choices, I wanted to think about what other modes of control might be open to me since I don't have a division at my command."

"Very good." Sun's nod of approval carries an uncanny power, like being bathed in the divine favor of a celestial deity.

Old honchos knew better than to be swayed by shallow charisma and weighty authority. But Sun has a rare quality Sayre cannot explain. Her superb physical and intellectual training combine with a dexterity of mind and the conviction of her principles to give her confidence and resilience. Yet even with all this, there is something more, a gift of vision that allows Sun to see beyond the playing board that confines the moves of everyone else. Why else did she leap to conquer the Trinity Coalition when any other would have settled for the Karnos victory rather than trying to bridge what they saw as an unbridgeable gap? How else are they now on their way to venerable Mishirru?

A marine wearing the badge of the Silver Shields trots into the hangar from the transit dock. "Your Highness!"

"Sergeant."

He hands over a scroll. "Your Highness, Princess Soaring sends her best wishes and says she has suspended the exercise. The passage has gone more swiftly than her initial estimate. The Argosy will reach Harahuvati System in thirty ship hours."

Sun unrolls the scroll and, eyebrows raised, reads it silently. When she releases one side, it snaps closed against her other hand. "Send an all hands throughout the fleet. Make ready. We will meet the Belt of Jewels Road and advance to liberate the people of venerable Mishirru from the hated yoke of the Phene Empire. We must be prepared for any eventuality that awaits us."

71

The Wily Persephone Doesn't Dare Lick Them

I'm not used to being in the spotlight. When I was a girl, that honor belonged to my older sister, the eight-times-worthy hero Ereshkigal. She was gold and jade, the most promising young officer in the fleet, daring, disciplined, and dutiful. Of course Resh eventually sacrificed herself to save the Second Fleet, so maybe death is the lesson a person should absorb about what standing in the spotlight gets you.

I am standing at the top of the royal corvette's ramp. The glare of Destiny's G-class sun makes me blink as my eyes adjust. My formal palace dress uniform has no climate controls built in. Sweat prickles along my skin. My neck feels damp beneath the press of my hair. In the ten seconds I've been exposed to the low humidity, my lips have dried out, but under the circumstances I don't dare lick them.

Not in the face of this intimidating welcome reception.

The corvette was instructed to land at the dignitaries' airfield on a windswept plateau. From the top of the ramp I look over a plaza filled with rank upon rank of silent figures sheathed in ankle-length golden capes. They have ignored the eight marines who descended first and await me with boots on the ground as my honor guard. I am, so the waiting multitude believes, the most important to emerge, the queen-marshal's noble envoy to the Imperishable, the Caretaker, the Great Mother Queen, she whose names cannot be numbered, and her sisters Fire and Splendor.

Behind the last rank, the plaza splits into three processional ways. To my left a road departs at a forty-five-degree angle to the east-southeast. To my right, a second road departs at the opposite forty-five-degree angle west-southwest. These roads take separate paths that ultimately descend via an escarpment into the holy city of Everlasting.

The third way lies directly in front of me: a canal straight south toward the original Theatron. The sacred temple dedicated to the Great Mother Queen was founded about three thousand years ago when Argosies forging outward from Landfall discovered this hospitable world. Those who set foot on Destiny's verdant lands and walked the shores of its turquoise waters and sucked in painless lungfuls of its air said it must be destiny that their travels had brought them to a fate-saturated ground where humanity could at long last start anew.

It's a nice story. While some part of it might even be true, it is unclear from this distance of time how we can possibly tell. No one alive then had ever seen, much less set foot on, the home world of the Celestial Empire, because they had been voyaging for a thousand years. So no one really knew for sure if this planet had all the grace and beauty of humanity's long-lost birthplace as it had once been.

People create narratives to serve a purpose. That's what the Pompous Historian says as he crafts dispatches to be sent home. It's in our interest that the citizens who support Sun's noble endeavor can follow the campaign and praise the valor of the fleet and the righteous pursuit of their queen-marshal. The Honorable Beau may be a bore when he starts in on his interminable lecturing about the strategic uses of history and the tactical weapon of public opinion, but he's not wrong to bring Channel Idol along for the ride. There's a lot any one of us can learn from his approach.

Tiana emerges from the interior and halts beside me. A sigh ripples through the ranks, perhaps because Ti looks dazzling with her hair braided and wrapped into a pillar atop her head and her body draped in glittering yellow robes slashed through with deeper hues of orange-brown and rust red. While she does not observe the rites of the Great Mother Queen, she is a graduate of Vogue Academy as well as a devotee of the Campaspe Guild, and thus a person who shows respect by looking her very best.

I'm just fortunate I have a formal palace dress uniform, or I would be the saddest drab envoy in the history of the universe.

"Ready?" she murmurs.

The marines await us at the base of the ramp with ramrod posture and the serious faces of people who aren't afraid to get into a scrap. I do not glance toward them. The biggest part of my act is not to reveal that one of the marines is Sun, gliding into Mishirru in disguise. She claims it is to scope out a feel for the political situation, but I think she enjoys the challenge.

I raise a hand to acknowledge the waiting crowd as I start down the ramp, Tiana at my back. Dozer is wrapped through her towering hair, because ou is a clever little symbiont whose camera can record everything we see and hear and gather information beyond those frequencies as well. There are no Channel Idol wasps here.

The instant my right boot hits the dirt of Destiny the formation erupts with unison stamps. The scene swirls as every soul turns in place. Their capes flow outward. They begin to sing. Voices blend and glide in a soaring welcome. I am shaken to the depths of my soul by the way the melody pierces my flesh as if it were lost to me and is now returning home.

As my network scrambles to find a translation for the language, the singers become dancers who stamp feet and clap hands to create a rhythm. The ranks separate to leave a path for me and my escort, as if the waters of a flowing golden sea part to allow me to pass through.

Yet I hesitate because the territory seems so strange: a welcome made of music and movement rather than speeches. A boot nudges mine. Octavian's sergeant major cap pulled down to obscure her face, Sun edges up behind me.

Why she assigned me to be envoy to Mishirru I cannot know. Alika would fit in better with this scene. Yet here I am.

I walk into the gap, Ti beside me, marines at my back. Fabric ripples and shines as the dancers spin. My boots slap the pavement in time to the beat as I walk toward the canal with its calm waters and lotus blooms.

A pier attaches to the stub end of the wide canal. A barge waits, its railings braided with garlands of flowers. I board at the head of our group, which includes Isis, Candace, and Sayre in their military uniforms bearing gifts for the temple. Attractive attendants usher me to a noble divan that is, to my relief, shaded by an awning. I am invited to sit, so I do. Tiana is invited to sit beside me. She gives me a lifted eyebrow, and I dip my chin to indicate the cushions. I don't mind if she is mistaken as my consort. Safety in numbers. She's better at this. Wordlessly but with many gracious hand gestures the attendants offer food and drink. The eight marines spread out to the stern and the sides. Sun stands next to Solomon at the prow. His size helps disguise her air of command. Sailors cast off and begin to pole us forward.

The Theatron lies one klick away, according to my network's measuring instruments. The canal is one and twenty hundred meters wide. On either side wait companies of three or six or eighteen or sixty or more, standing in tableaux like statues awaiting the kiss of life. The barge moves slowly. As we approach, each group comes to life in turn with a song sung just for us, or an explosion of dance or acrobatics, of juggling or instrumental music, of martial arts or deftly wielded fans or flowing streams of ribbons to remind me of Ji-na, who has turned down every opportunity to return home to Chaonia. It is like a parade if, rather than the parade marching past us, we are the ones moving along stages of the route as if from one grandiosely blooming flower to the next. We could have walked the distance in a quarter of the time it takes to be conveyed in this lazy processional. Yet the effect is utterly charming as I sip sweet wine and nibble candied ginger and salted nuts. As each group of performers finish, I salute them with a lift of my cup and they bow in answer. I could get used to this.

Standing motionless at the prow, Sun keeps her eyes on the prize that lies ahead: the Theatron's entry arches. A chorus of children welcomes us with a stately hymn as the barge bumps the arrival pier. We disembark onto a forecourt.

An elderly woman walks forward from the central arch. Her braided wisdom hair and wide-set facial structure look familiar. I'm sure I have seen her before, but how could that be possible?

"I am the caretaker, an honored priestess of the Divine Worship of the Great Mother Queen and her sisters Fire and Splendor, under whose sheltering arms all Mishirru takes refuge and receives sustenance. You are well come here."

She greets me with striking informality by taking each of my hands in hers and giving me a greeting kiss to each cheek. She is shorter even than I am, and it is a bit odd to look down at those keen dark eyes. They examine me as if all of my flaws and strengths have been laid bare by the scalpel of her gaze.

She says, as portentously as if she has been following my earlier discursive thoughts on the history of this world, "Thus was the Queendom of Mishirru founded. It stands as a frontier between the long voyage endured by our ancestors and the promise offered by the star systems of Landfall, Arafel, Cataract, Scepter, and Alabaster, each of which had a marginally habitable planet that was, in turn, discovered and settled before Destiny herself. So are you come, Honored Persephone, to the promised haven. Let your sojourn here be bountiful beyond your expectations. Let this become a refuge to you in time of need. Let your crown of endurance give holy Mishirru new centuries of stability. Let your descendants thrive with the breath of the Queen, the Fire, and the Splendor awakened in their hearts."

As uncomfortable as this little speech makes me, I have memorized the proper diplomatic phrases. We come in peace to honor the venerable ancestors. We support holy Mishirru's autonomy, which has for too long been denied by the occupation of the Phene Empire's syndicates and fleets. As representative and envoy for the queen-marshal of the Republic of Chaonia, I ask for but one boon, that these gifts be worthy of presentation to the holy temple sacred to the Great Mother Queen of Mishirru, she whose names cannot be numbered, who carried in her womb a thousand million souls out of the wreckage and into the promised land.

Tiana is more adept than I am at the universal sign language which, like the fleet-standard ideograms, offers a basic means of shared communication when two or more languages are being spoken. As I speak, she signs, even though the elder spoke to me in the same Common Yele I reply in. But her signing allows the children and others around us to understand my message.

"Please accompany me," says the caretaker graciously.

We pass beneath the arches and find ourselves standing at the lip of a vast amphitheater. Its semicircular stone seating is built into the steep slope of a high hill. The seats create a viewing platform that overlooks Everlasting. The holy city spreads out from the base of the escarpment and extends along the banks of a wide river.

The caretaker descends down a central ramp. We follow, Sun in front as if my point guard, so it is Sun who, of us Chaonians, sets first foot upon the round circle called the orchestra, where any performance takes place. The circle of ground is flat, nothing but pavement—no statue, no altar, no throne. When I think of the splendid parade of music and dance that greeted us along the canal I realize we have already experienced a taste of the spiritual heart of holy Mishirru.

A railing rings the outer edge of the orchestra circle to mark its perimeter but also, I suspect, so no overexcited performer accidentally stumbles over the edge of the cliff and falls a hundred meters to an unpleasant and messy death. Beyond the railing, a rectangular platform enclosed by a second railing thrusts out from the promontory like a foreshortened pier. Above us fly a dozen splendid rippling kites the colors of fire: red, orange, and gold.

The caretaker leads us around the edge of the orchestra rather than crossing its mosaic pavement, which depicts the Celestial Emperor resplendent in a gold cape. Grasping her golden trident, the emperor holds off a wall like a seething storm of ashes and smoke as refugees stream onto waiting ships. Of course it wouldn't have happened like that. Argosy ships are too big to land on a planet, much less be able to take off again. But a story speaks to the heart, not to the facts. It happened so long ago, and at such a great distance, we cannot possibly ever know the truth as the people of those days experienced it.

The elder opens a gate in the railing that lets us onto the rectangle. Sun goes immediately to the edge as if she means to leap off the cliff and, like the kites, soar aloft. I give Isis a startled glance because we have all seen footage of Sun jumping alone down through a hole in the floor to battle the Grand Sanctuary's stubborn defenders on the level below. At this point I wouldn't put anything past her.

She merely braces herself against the stiff wind and stares over the city in the manner of a particularly alert sentry. Octavian would have preceded her in just this way, no reason for a hidebound old queendom to guess anything unusual is going on.

The rest of us crowd onto the platform. Below lies a terrace carved into the cliff face where people have gathered amid flower-bedecked pillars. Elegant servers bring around trays with drinks and finger food. It has the look of a lovely party. Is this the cunning prelude to an ambush?

As the platform begins its stately descent, the folk below look upward in unison, lift their arms, and break into song.

"I am honored by this elaborate welcome. You have brought out so many performers."

She smiles. "Oh no, Honored One. These are elected representatives who serve in our Congregation. That is what we call our advisory council and assembly. Everyone in the holy queendom knows this welcoming song from childhood."

"Ah, as we sing hymns in Chaonia from the earliest age."

She inclines her head, although I can't tell if she is agreeing or just being agreeable. "We have gathered our cardinal and ordinary congregants to meet with you, as you requested. You may judge for yourself the political currents here in Mishirru by speaking to those whose work has been to govern and administer beneath the yoke imposed on us by the Phene Empire. I am sure you will find their comments enlightening. Is that not why you have come? To assay our political sentiments and sample the timbre of our hospitality?"

Her gaze flicks to each of the marines. Does it rest a fraction of a second longest on Sun before returning to me? "Although you come armed."

"An honor guard is how we show respect in Chaonia. I assure you our greatest wish is to grasp hands in friendship on amenable terms."

Tiana taught me the phrase. The elder presses crossed palms to her chest in answer. I think she approves.

I add, "I have hoped to personally present these gifts as a show of courtesy and respect to the Great Mother Queen."

"So you have," says the elder. "If you please, let me introduce you to those who have come so far to greet Chaonia's envoy. You may know the cardinals by the red elaborations on their capes of office and the ordinaries by the green."

I am already floundering in terms I don't understand, and I'm not sure how to ask without seeming unprepared. The caretaker has a keen eye for my confusion.

"Think of yourself as a cardinal and the Honored Tiana as an ordinary. One makes decisions and the other has the authority to carry them out."

"So by that analogy, Queen-Marshal Sun is the cardinal and I, her envoy, am her ordinary. Is that what you're saying?"

"You grasp the analogy," says the elder.

I think my heart will burst from pride at getting the answer right.

The platform halts. She opens a gate. As I step onto the terrace, a server offers me a glass of amber-colored liquid. With glass in my hand I suffer myself to be led forward into the assembled people. The congregants do not number more than two hundred and, as if by long training or a great deal of drill, they have formed themselves into neat clusters that create curved receiving lines so I may meet a few, take a sip of the bracing sweet-spicy liquor, and then meet more. I will never remember all the names I am bombarded with, sounds that fall oddly on my ears, but Ti will collate them all and give me a list tied to faces later. My job is to draw attention as my polite marine escort casually spreads out.

Their unthreatening manner allows Sun to walk through the ranks of the locals and listen to what they are saying. They speak a descendent of Common Yele riddled with two thousand years of intermittent separation from Yele. The elder spent many years as a trade envoy moving throughout the beacon network, so she translates where I struggle to understand. My inability to easily comprehend the vernacular here is part of our plan, since it highlights my foreignness.

Sun, on the other hand, spent two hours every day on the *Bountiful* studying the language so she can eavesdrop on what the people of Mishirru say to each other when they think outsiders cannot understand.

I let my attention slip off Sun as I press forward in my role as envoy. Mishirru is a very touch-oriented culture. Hands press mine in warm greeting, accompanied by a kiss to bless each cheek. Once we are talking, words may be punctuated by a light tap to the arm. It's comforting for a tactile person like me. Maybe too comforting. Maybe it lulls me.

An older ordinary says, "How lovely to see new faces here."

"We are delighted to be here on this graceful and beautiful world."

A cardinal wearing a badge depicting a bow and arrow says, "As I am sure your sensors have told you, the Phene military garrison withdrew from Destiny System when it became clear your fleet had arrived in force in Harahuvati System. We have you to thank for their departure."

"You consider their departure a blessing?"

A young cardinal breaks in with eager intensity. "We have never been on good terms with the Phene. You know our history with them, I am sure."

I look at the caretaker for help with translation. We didn't learn this part of Mishirru's history at the academy, or if we did I wasn't listening that day, so I temporize. "I am sure my understanding of the events would be improved by hearing your account of the matter."

Around me, the cardinals and ordinaries applaud in appreciation of my diplomatic wit. I could get used to this.

"You are all too kind," I add.

A new person is brought forward and introduced to me by a name that sounds to my ears like "the swimmer through the waters of history." Without any obvious direction, the assembly shifts positions as the individual steps up onto a riser, as onto a stage. I'm asked if I need a chair to sit, and I politely decline.

After an introductory prelude that seems to be a prayer of thanks for the gift of voice, they begin a recitation. The melodic timbre of their words makes the gist easier for me to understand, together with the help of a real-time translation program. The recitation has a childish singsong feel, not annoying but soothing. The gathered folk respond in unison with expected refrains.

The holy queendom of Mishirru in its compassion and wisdom sheltered the voyagers as they built new lives on the newly discovered planets and in the newly discovered systems after their long journey, their thousand-year-long journey, from the ruins of the Celestial Empire. But always amid the gentle fields, weeds arise, the malcontents. These were the folk who wished to break the holy laws that kept the peace. These were the restless ones, those who chafed at the tasks given to them meant to benefit all, those who dug into dark corners best left untouched, those who dared to alter the holy order of the human body by changing its appearance in the most interdicted of ways. Their malign experiments were drawn from the very root of the reckless explorations that had brought about the ruin of the Celestial Empire. Always agitators and discontents find each other. When the tinkerers went too far, they were taken apart from each other, they were separated, as it is said, "divide that which harms from that which it will harm." But in secrecy these factions joined hands. They stole ships, and fled the holy queendom in the dead of night. Away they fled, stealing from the common good that which they wished to cultivate for their own selfish purposes. By their appearance we shall know them, and thus they were called Phene.

For generations the Phene agitators kept to themselves as they spread across the local belt, far from the holy queendom. When the Apsaras Convergence built the beacon system, even then the Phene were hesitant to return to the land they had scorned and robbed. In time, trade was reestablished. Only after the collapse of the beacons did the cruel empire rise, and as empires will, its hunger could not be appeased. So it happened that 143 Destiny years ago, the Phene returned with their Riders and their ships. They forced the Great Mother Queen to travel to Anchor, where they imprisoned her under the guise of "honoring" her and never let her return to Destiny. Thus they yoked the holy queendom under the whip of their harsh rule and crushed the holy order of our land beneath their merciless heel.

Whew. It's quite a story, especially told in a deft blend of melody and rhyme.

At the moment of harsh whips and merciless heels, I look around. Ti remains beside me, intent as she records the accomplished rendition. Isis, Candace, and Sayre guard the gifts meant for the Great Mother Queen, should I be allowed to enter her august presence and make my case for Chaonia's friendship. But what if we miscalculated through ignorance? According to this tale, there is no longer a queen in Mishirru. Who can Sun negotiate with?

I belatedly think to count my marines.

Only then, far too late, do I realize Sun is missing.

The Repast I Have Laid Out for You

Sun recognized the long recitation from her language study. It was a poem taught to children and had been useful in the early stages of her learning. Unfortunately all the locals on the terrace had turned their attention to the performance, which meant no one, not even in the back ranks, was whispering their real opinions to each other as she eased past. She'd taken her fill of the view of the city, the river, the distant fields and forest said to be exactly like the lost Celestial Empire. The planet Destiny had been named in honor of the fated haven said to await those who survived the anguish of loss, the ordeal of passage, and the adversity of the last tormented decades aboard the overcrowded motherships before they had reached Landfall.

To her eye, the servers had the posture of soldiers rather than attendants. It's what she would do to keep an eye on a visiting dignitary whose alliance she wanted but whose motives she doubted. She walked to the back of the terrace. Behind, via twelve arches, lay a grand chamber hewn out of the rock. Shafts of light struck like spears across its mosaic floor, glinting on bits of glass embedded as the eyes of peacocks and kestrels and in the wings of proud ibis. Servers with trays crossed back and forth on paths laid across this magnificent floor as if it were a garden in truth, not an image made of many smaller pieces welded together into a grand tapestry.

At the back of the hall, a pair of arches led deeper into the rock. From the lit archway the scent of cooking drifted with a wholesome perfume. Her mouth watered as she smelled fresh bread and baking coconut. A clatter of busy voices accompanied the clatter of a busy kitchen.

By the unlit archway stood an individual draped in a gold cape, watching her. A gloved hand raised like an invitation. The figure stepped backward into the darkness.

Challenge accepted.

She crossed the hall and entered the dark passageway. Footfalls faded into the gloom ahead of her, a disappearing shadow chased with glints as the cape rippled.

Did they intend to lure the marines away one by one and then . . . and then what? Kill them and hand them over the Phene as testament to their loyalty to imperial rule? No. She'd never have come to Mishirru if the queendom had a recent history of devoted subservience to empire.

As she walked onward the light faded until the archway became a pinprick of light. She could no longer hear voices from the terrace. When the light grew too dim for her to see, she doffed Octavian's cap and blinked her infrared lenses into place. They were uncomfortable so she didn't like to use them, but needs must. The figure in the cape had vanished but a promise of heat lay ahead.

The passageway ended without fanfare. She stepped into a domed chamber whose high ceiling sparkled with stars linked by traceries she at first thought were beacon routes and then realized were meant to represent constellations. Only they were no constellations she had ever seen, and the stars did not stand in the sky as they did on Chaonia Prime. She set her network to map the arrangement and let her gaze drop.

She stood on the edge of a circular chamber whose far walls she could not see. But there were people waiting here, as still as statues, strangely shaped, and wearing elaborate headdresses.

No, they *were* statues. They were women with the heads of lions, a mythical creature out of the iconography of the Celestial Empire meant to represent powerful goddesses not confined to a single form. Each wore a star's spiky halo as her crown of power. There were so many that faces and bodies faded into the darkness in the way that the past fades from memory.

Closer to the entrance, the lion-headed statues became human-headed statues of stately queens, each face unique in age and expression, and all crowned by the haloed star. The closest rank formed a semicircle of stern rulers clustered around a modest table, on which sat a lit lamp. Two platters of food and two goblets waited on the table, obscured by the shadows. Two wicker chairs faced each other.

A woman stood behind the far chair. She was in the prime of mature beauty, shining in a figure-hugging dress that shimmered as if woven out of gold. It was the same style of garment the statues wore, although theirs were carved. Clearly aware of Sun's presence, she said nothing, but she sat.

Sun approached, amused by this lure. The woman's intensely attractive eyes took her in with the rich intelligence and sly smile of a person who knows something you do not.

Reaching the table, Sun gestured to the empty chair. With a dip of her chin the woman invited her to sit. She kept her hands on the table as if to assure Sun she held no weapon, as if there couldn't be a thousand stingers aimed out of the darkness.

Her hostess spoke in a musical alto. "I am Splendor, the youngest facet of the Imperishable. Thus I am sister to the Great Mother Queen, the heavenly ruler of the world, she who was stolen from us almost one hundred and fifty years ago. So are we all become orphans of the storm that afflicted us. You are Sun, daughter of Eirene, queen-marshal of the Republic of Chaonia, called by some Victor of Molossia, Champion of Karnos, and Liberator of Trinity. What is it you seek here in Mishirru?"

Sun wasn't going to bother to ask how they had known. It wasn't so difficult, even if it was annoying that her attempt at subterfuge had been so easily pierced.

"I seek an end to war with the Phene Empire."

The woman smiled as at an answer she expected. "How do you mean to accomplish this feat?"

To be treated as if she were predictable was definitely irritating. "By keeping my strategic vision to myself."

The Splendor laughed, oh so musical and charming. The domed chamber had some mechanism by which the laugh's echoes spilled back at them like a waterfall of delight. Laughter was an answer, of a kind.

"Part of my aim must be clear to you," Sun added, not without a measure of impatience for this sort of grating political theater. "Mishirru made no effort to block my fleet from entering her territories."

"If you come in good faith, your good faith will be rewarded."

"I'm listening."

"As a show of good faith on my part I will tell you that when the empire took over, they immediately placed Mishirru's best ships and spacers under the control of Phene syndicates. Our fleets were sent to garrison other systems and guard frontiers other than our own. For example, our elite Pitati Fleet is stationed at Picket, facing the disagreeable Asmu, who prefer not to speak to the rest of humankind but who sometimes steal our children. So it would be disingenuous of me to allow you to believe we of Mishirru gave way before you in the hope of gaining your favor."

"You're saying Mishirru does not have the military means in-system to fight Chaonia."

"The Phene garrison this system, not us. *Their* fleet withdrew when the news reached here of the arrival of a mothership Titan in Harahuvati System towing your substantial military presence. The stance of our holy establishment remains neutral, as it always has. Again I ask, what is it you seek?"

"I seek information I can find only here."

A nod, inviting her to continue.

Start small. "Where did the Phene get ten knnu drives?"

"I see. To that end, what is your plan?"

"I am told I may find answers at a place called the Gyre."

"The Gyre has long been banned from human travel except through the auspices of a small and knowledgeable group of unbanned guides who must agree to lead you into its interdicted core. Are you willing to undertake this perilous journey?"

"How is it perilous? Is the Gyre not the resting place of many of the original celestial fleet? Would it not also be the case that the most complete Archives remaining in existence might be found there?"

"What would you want with such a fabled object as a complete Archives?"

"Who does not wish for knowledge? To understand the past? To assay possibilities for the future? To discover secrets lost or hidden?"

"Some knowledge is best left hidden." The rings on the Splendor's hands winked in lamplight like glimpses of concealed truth.

"Perhaps. But I have military reasons as well. For example, Chaonian military intelligence does not possess a complete map of the empire's beacon routes. Can you give me that?"

"We are Phene subjects, not their allies."

"Your Pitati Fleet would have had to cross the empire to reach its far frontier facing the Asmu."

"With Phene officers at the helm."

"They don't share their Riders either, a strategically sound decision. But these are surmountable obstacles. That I am here now is because I do not shy away from chasing my vision."

"Vision is a harsh taskmaster, a treacherous bedmate, and an uncertainly trustworthy partner. You might prefer to live a long and prosperous life and on your peaceful deathbed pass your legacy on to a grateful and numerous progeny. Why struggle with the impossible?"

"Only deeds proffer immortality."

"Yet the Celestial Emperor died in her time."

"We sing the pain, the courage, the heart, the storm-wrought wreckage through which the Celestial Emperor and Her Loyal Charioteer led the plague-struck people. Legend makes fame, and fame outlasts the lives of mortal creatures."

"Thus we sing. Even so, bright-mantled Sun, deeds may be lost.

Archives may be shattered and their shards tossed into the furnace of oblivion."

Sun shoved her chair back, making ready to stand. "I did not come here to be mocked."

"Nor do I mock you. Stay, brave queen. Will you not eat of the repast I have laid out for you, in honor of your coming?"

So intent had she been upon the duel of words that Sun had neglected to recall the feast, its platters in shadow, the goblets half filled. Hospitality was a gift not to be shunned. It went against the most ancient custom of humanity, and anyway it was bad diplomacy.

"My thanks."

The Splendor used a rod to shift the lamp's louvered shades, causing its mellow golden glow to fall upon the platters and illuminate their fare. Sun stiffened, rocked back by surprise. The "food" was made of precious stone and gleaming gems hewn with the greatest skill to resemble a beautifully designed meal. The goblets held not liquid but crystal cunningly carved to seem like sparkling wine.

"Is this meant as a jest? How am I to eat stone and jewels?"

"Are these not treasures valued like to glory? Many seek them as if they are more precious than any other part of life. Yet glory will not feed your hunger. You reject the humble offering of bread because it does not suit your majestic vision. Nevertheless you must eat as any of us must eat. We are all dust in the end."

"I take it I am meant to learn a lesson. Is humiliation the price I must pay for an alliance with Mishirru?"

The Splendor's smile was as gracious as a gentle wind cooling a hot day. "How you receive the lesson is the choice you make, brightmantled Sun."

Keep your temper in check.

Sun struggled with a surge of temper regardless. But she knew better than to give in and lose the battle. Instead, she picked among the platters, admiring the workmanship as a way to let her anger dissipate. The main platter was arrayed with amethyst ube, a remarkable nest of pale gypsum sculpted into a mound of rice, and sinuously molded strips of silver in the shape of noodles interwoven with carnelian carrots and serpentine greens. A granite bowl held the model of a fig cut in half to display a meaty red-pink interior. She caught it up in her fingers. The stone was as warm as memory, a crystal cracked in half to reveal the treasure others might overlook because of its modest exterior.

"Let that be a gift to you," said the Splendor. "All that we have here in Mishirru lies within your power to take."

"Does it?"

"You know it does, else you would not have come."

"What do you want in return?"

"Only this, that the Phene depart. We have been waiting for the promised liberation. Let it be you, if you will it."

"Me?" Despite herself, Sun closed her fingers around the carved halves of the fig and tucked it into her sleeve pocket as a private gift for Hetty.

"When their ships sailed into gentle Mishirru, the Phene took away with them our Great Mother Queen. They took her to Anchor to stand as surety, as hostage, for our good behavior. Of course she is long since dead, there in the iron city, severed from her heart, her dust, her children, and no successor allowed to take her place on the soil of Destiny. The line of the Fire has devolved into appointed commanders trained at Phene behest and assigned to the admiralty of the Pitati Fleet, where they serve well out of the way on the imperial frontier. I alone, the line of Splendor, keep the hearth warm for that which we await."

"What is it you await?"

"The queen who can restore what was taken from us."

"You speak slightingly of my vision but look to me to restore your holy line?"

"Am I wrong about you?"

Sun relaxed. "Of course you are not wrong, holy one. If I am enthroned as Mishirru's Great Mother Queen, according to your custom, then any assault by the Phene upon any system within Mishirru's boundary of refuge is an assault on me."

"That is correct. Mishirru's fate would be bound with your destiny unto eternity."

The fierce and splendid longing swelled in her heart. It rose within her like the splintering dawn on Kumbala Prime as the bright star pierced the horizon and cast its spear-like rays across the waiting ocean. Night must be succeeded by day. Arise.

But she said nothing. In truth, and to her own surprise, this offer was nothing she had strategized for. Instinct had brought her to make the leap from Trinity to Mishirru, sure she would find answers to questions she had asked all her life that she didn't even fully understand. Who are you? Why does this restlessness in your spirit feel as much like regret as desire? Is regret just another name for that which we are not willing to risk and thus can never attain?

The woman went on. "We have endured many long years under the weight of Phene rule. But we have been patient. Long ago the Gyre spoke of an unconquerable sun that would rise to obliterate our night of bondage."

"The Gyre speaks?"

"Many gnomic messages arise out of the background chatter that is the sonic landscape of the Gyre. The Great Mother Queen may travel where she wishes within the boundaries of her queendom, may she not? Although I grant you, there is some risk in traveling to the Gyre, which is why it is banned. In the past those who made the journey often did not survive it with their minds intact. As well, the passage takes at least six months there and back again. But should we become your subjects, we will, as is our tradition, sustain and heal and strengthen your fleets while you embark on this journey. We will keep them safe and treat them as our own family."

Perhaps it was a cunning trap to dispose of her and destroy her fleet.

But the lion-headed goddesses had their own way of speaking. Their gaze was a pressure of time and tide, of spirit and will. She could walk among them without fear, and they would welcome her.

You had to leap when an opening presented itself.

It was a better deal than even she had dared to hope. She'd known Mishirru had a contentious history with the Phene, that they hated the empire's rule. In this same way, many in Karnos had been happy to see the Phene and their fractious syndicates and interfering Riders be forced to leave. Millions of people tied into indentured servitude in the Trinity Coalition had no reason to fight to the death for rulers who used and abused them for their own power and greed, so the resistance to the Chaonian invasion had not enflamed the entire population of the coalition but only those who benefited from Trinity's authoritarian rule. Thus also she had sent Kurash to determine the disposition of the banners toward her, information she did not yet possess, as well as adding a second mission he should soon be receiving.

Fate is a matter of strategy.

"I do fancy some of that bread I smelled earlier," Sun remarked.

The Splendor clapped her hands as a summons. A gold cape shimmered out of the darkness to become a smiling woman bearing a tray of bread fresh out of the oven and beside it a bowl of salt.

Sun savored the bread's delicious fragrance as her mind spun through the weight of the hidden past and the unknowable future. Her father would scold her for her rashness. Isis would demand a taster be brought. Alika would offer to taste it for her. James would make a sarcastic remark to divert her attention. Persephone would try to steal the bread before Sun noticed it was gone, so she'd have no chance to eat it.

Razin would silently pull the tray out of her reach to let her think over her decision before she took the final step. Makinde would accidentally rip off a hank for himself before he realized it was meant for her. Jade would point out the pitfalls and advantages and measure them against each other to determine the winning try. Hetty alone out of all of them would simply let her be what she was meant to be.

The lion-headed goddesses and the halo-crowned queens watched.

She pulled off a hank of the warm bread and separated it into three segments, one as a symbolic meal to share with the distant Fire, one for Splendor, who accepted the piece with a smile, and one for herself, bread and salt shared between them.

Mishirru was hers. As long as she survived the trip to the Gyre.

73

You've Got That Look on Your Face

When the news arrived via courier, the *Huma* had just dropped into Olynthus System after the long return from Danu System. Kurash was in the training arena with the frigate's third and fourth squad of marines. As part of Sun's household he was technically in command of tactical sessions but Esen, the company sergeant, had twenty years of combat experience and the blunt egalitarian manner of citizen soldiers, so Kurash worked in collaboration with them to design and implement scenarios.

He was seated in an overlook watching a simulated boarding action in the arena below. Many of the marines had noticeably improved their reaction times and speed, while a few were stubbornly stuck where they started. He wasn't sure if the latter were working less hard or simply had been in top condition and training to begin with and so didn't have much space to improve. Like the Phene special forces, Chaonian marines were strong and fast and tough, but in the end they still weren't banner soldiers. For one thing, they were valued, not used up and disposed of. They had families waiting, and a chance for a life after this was all over, whatever *this* was.

The door opened and Ay swung in to sit beside him. She'd just gotten off duty and had brought snacks, something she liked to do for her friends because she came from a lineage of professional cooks. Since it made her happy to feed people, he could never say no even if he wasn't hungry.

"What? They won't let you play anymore?" she asked as she set the box on her thighs and opened it.

"They have a difficult time with my enhancements."

She laughed. "With anyone else, I'd think that was boasting about sexual prowess."

Kurash cast her a mystified look. "Why would someone boast about a sharing meant to be intimate and private?"

She sighed the way she did when he said something that reminded her that he wasn't Chaonian. "Turnip cake? Haw flake? I forgot to bring rice crackers. You like those."

Comms crackled. "This is your captain. All hands assemble on Hangar 2 in twenty minutes. Come as you are."

The sergeant blew a whistle. The exercise slammed to a halt. People dispersed rapidly. Kurash checked in with the sergeant before making his way to his cabin. Ay trotted alongside and came into his cabin with him, seated cross-legged on his rack as he stepped into the shower stall and stripped out of his soggy, sweat-drenched workout suit.

"He said come as you are," Ay pointed out. She set the food box on his little desk where, he knew, she would "forget" it. Then he would have to eat it because she would ask him later if he had and be disappointed if he hadn't.

"I will come as I am about to be," he said.

She laughed. "It's not like you're not fast. Okay. The news has got to be something to do with what happened to the fleet in Trinity, don't you think? We haven't received a single dispatch from the queen-marshal in six months."

"Seven and a half," he corrected as he wiped down his body with a towel.

"Holy hells. Imagine going off-network for that long. Makes you wish we had a few Riders, eh?"

He remembered the eerie way the Rider's eyes flickered as a signal might toggle on and off in the depths of an unfathomable network. "Have you ever come face-to-face with a Rider?"

"Wouldn't it be face-to-face-to-face? How does that work?"

"Having spoken to a Rider, it is difficult for me to imagine any of them can ever be trusted to bow before anyone but their own power."

He pulled on a uniform he'd gotten from Supply, work gear lacking insignia that allowed him to not stand out more than he already did. Everyone on the *Huma* knew him. He didn't need to advertise his status, not as Core House nobles seemed determined to always do, as if they feared they would lose their elevated rank if it were not continually flagged into the order of daily life. Probably that's how it did work in hierarchical systems. Yet who was he to judge? His own grandmother had sold him.

"You okay?" Ay asked as he emerged from the stall. "You've got that look on your face."

He gave her a reassuring smile as he latched on boots. "What look is that?"

She sighed as her gaze flicked toward the deck.

"You can say it."

"A look you didn't have before the wheelship. It's not my business but, if there ever comes a time, I am a good listener."

Her tone unwrapped the outermost edge of tightness that had ground unceasingly in his chest over the long ship weeks as the *Huma* crossed from Danu System back into Acre System with its beacon. When he lifted his eyes to meet hers, she smiled gently and said nothing more, although she got to her feet.

"Come on, or we'll be late because of your excessive attention to decorum," she added in the bossy manner of every older sibling and cousin everywhere in the universe.

They made it to assembly with four minutes to spare. In transit, the hangar was a big echoing space, its shuttles and gunship tucked into garages in the deck below. People took a place in rows and columns in the order they arrived rather than separating into units. The diplomatic group under Precious Jin's command had taken over the front row but Kurash simply stood to attention next to Ay. He liked being one among many; that was the way of the wheelships, and even if he was no longer of the wheelships he could not shake the habit and the wish. He received a number of nods as people filled in around them where they stood toward the back of the formation. The last hustled in with thirty seconds to spare. No one on the *Huma* was late, not without a steel-clad excuse.

At exactly twenty minutes from the original announcement the captain strode into the hangar. Crew had shifted a big stepladder in front of a bulkhead. He climbed up, holding an amplifier.

"I bring today a republic-wide announcement received one hour ago via courier. Queen-Marshal Sun sends her greetings to the citizens of the republic. The Chaonian Fleets and Guards have triumphed over the collective resistance of the Trinity Coalition. With our courageous and undaunted efforts we have laid to rest its criminal enterprises and inhumane practices. Trinity space lies under the benevolent hand of a republic governor, in the name of the citizens of Chaonia."

Cheers and applause broke out. Kurash puzzled over this remarkable announcement. His first, and only, duty station as a banner auxiliary for the empire had been Hellion Terminus, his arrow assigned to board suspicious ships that might be carrying foreign agents or contraband. Hellion's proximity to one of the Trinity worlds made it a magnet for such activity while Trinity's Argosy looked the other way.

He leaned closer to Ay and said, "I thought it was impossible to attack Trinity."

"At Karnos isn't that what the queen-marshal said? The impossible is not just achievable but necessary."

The captain signaled for quiet. "Channel Idol has forwarded several reports on the Trinity Campaign. I'll play the summary."

The lights went down, and everyone quieted. A three-dimensional deck-to-ceiling visual took form against the bulkhead. The palace's official Idol Historian appeared to introduce the tapestry of events. The Karsh's insult. The bold decision to cross the void using the *Keoe*. The shocking sabotage of the tow chain. The toll of missing ships. The fleet battles in Meli and Kumbala Systems. Sun's attack on the Karsh's Sanctuary. A sunrise from the Magava's Grove.

With a glittering ocean of possibility stretching away to the horizon behind her, the queen-marshal addressed her fleets and armies. The camera began with her entire body in the frame; she never mentioned the injuries she'd taken but they were apparent from the leg brace, wound seal, and shoulder cast. As she spoke, praising the toughness and courage of the troops, the steadfast effort of the citizens at home, and the sacrifice of the dead and the lost, the view slowly pulled in tighter and tighter until she was head and shoulders above them all.

She announced that the treasury of Trinity had proved to be so vast that it would provide funds for the beleaguered shipyards and training camps and to expand agricultural zones and transportation networks. The top-level management of the Coalition had been captured, those who weren't dead, and remanded to work in the Krinides mines where the rare metals that powered the torch drives were excavated. But there was more beyond even this. Payday, of course. Cheers roused, dying down as her image raised a hand to request their attention.

Prize money for those who fought at Karnos as well as an additional pot for those who had braved the Trinity campaign. She named a figure that meant nothing to Kurash.

Shouts and cheers thundered through the echoing hangar. People jumped up and down, they embraced, they slapped each other on the shoulder. After three minutes of uproar, the lights came up, and the captain called for quiet.

A wit called out, "How soon do we get back to the front? I don't want to lose out on any more prize money."

"You're not losing out on any today, because it hasn't been disbursed yet," said the captain with his genial smile. "When it is, a bursar will be assigned to assist crew in routing their prize money. I know all of you have parents and clans who will benefit from the queen-marshal's open-handedness. And there's more. The *Huma* has received specific orders from the queen-marshal herself."

The hush deepened. For a ship, especially a modest frigate, to receive the queen-marshal's personal notice was a signal honor.

"To that end, we will be docking for four weeks at the shipyards here to get adjustments to our torch drives and some weapons enhancements before we proceed to our next assignment. Meanwhile, every ship of the line has received a preliminary credit for immediate short-term use. Light duty will commence for two weeks. You will receive a staggered schedule for liberty on the orbital habitat."

He paused. Not a single soul in the crew made a peep.

"I remind you all of the *Huma*'s pristine reputation. Don't let it be sullied. You are guests on Orbital Habitat Mecyberna. Treat its citizens with the same respect you would treat your honored grandparents. There's always a bit of Hesjan influence in these outer systems, so I will repeat for any of you who didn't hear me the first time you joined this crew: the state-regulated gambling clubs, sex parlors, virtual games, and local markets are within legal limits. Any of you picked up by local security for fighting, public drunkenness, or solicitation of any black market venues including and especially exploitative sex bars will be put in the brig and flagged for transfer. Other ship captains may turn a blind eye to that kind of thing, but I don't. We are the best frigate in the fleet. I don't intend for that distinction to change. Congratulations, citizens and honorables. You are dismissed."

The silence exploded into a storm of voices and movement.

Ay almost slugged him on the arm and pulled it with a laugh. "Hey! You have to come on the town with us! We'll do the rounds. Whoa!" Her eyes popped open as information registered in her private network.

"What is prize money?"

Her surprised blink made him self-conscious. "You didn't get prize money? How do people get paid in the banners beyond their monthly guarantee?"

"The wheelships do not utilize a credit system. Such a mechanism is for trade with outsiders."

"How did the Phene pay you?"

"They did not pay us. We belonged to them."

She whistled. "You are blowing my mind. That's some criminal-level shit. Indenture and slavery were outlawed in the republic hundreds of years ago."

The subject shamed him but for once she didn't notice and kept talking.

"As part of Sun's household you must have an account to draw on for expenses. I don't know how things work in the palace. Maybe you don't even show up on the books. Tell you what, I'll front you credit. We can work it out later. You have to come drinking with us. The best chun comes from this system. And my aunt will kill me if I don't try some of the local truffle risotto. With treatment, the soil on Olynthus Quart turned out to be compatible with eighteen species of truffle. Think about it!" Before he could ask her to explain what a truffle was, she spotted a friend and trotted away, waving to get their attention. "D'Elle! Hey! First round of chun is on me!"

He remained in his place as the hangar emptied. Precious Jīn and her entourage walked past, headed for the exit. Seeing him, she veered over.

"Kurash! Here you are. I feel you've been avoiding me since the wheelship."

"Honored Marshal."

"I'm leaving the *Huma* and returning to the palace."

His chin came up sharply. "Sun told us to return to Karnos."

"Sun's not in Karnos, is she? Who even knows where she is? Or if she's even alive, considering her proclivities as that unctuous little potted summary of the Trinity campaign portrayed so raptly. I will make my report on the failed diplomatic mission to the Gatoi to Marduk at the palace. Are you coming with me?"

Was this an invitation and, if so, to what exactly? Just then his network pinged with a message from the captain. **Meeting immediately.**

"My apologies, Marshal." He was unaccountably relieved to be shed of her.

74

Untethered by Any Harness

Sun's new mission for him was direct, dictated across a gap of time and distance.

Thirteen days later he looked down from orbit onto a planet labeled Pelasgia Terce. The world had a restless look he could not make sense of as he scanned its image in the lounge of the royal courier *Muninn*. He was the sole passenger. The crew remained polite but left him to eat alone. He missed the *Huma*'s camaraderie.

Enough self-pity. He turned his attention back to the image. The planet had a few scattered static areas labeled as islands, but mostly the surface was liquid.

The alert pinged on the lounge door, the captain asking permission to enter. Kurash was pretty sure that normally a ship's captain entered an open lounge as they wished, but within the hierarchy of a tyrannical dictatorship any member of the queen-marshal's personal household was elevated to an exaggerated importance by dint of proximity to the throne.

"Enter."

The door whooshed open. Captain the Honorable Utu Lee glanced nervously around the lounge as if expecting another banner soldier to leap out and murder him. He was no older than Kurash, which seemed young to be in command of a royal courier. "Lieutenant, we will be docking in one hour. A shuttle awaits you at the habitat. I think I mentioned already we aren't atmosphere capable."

"You did mention that."

"Ah. Yes." The captain studied the planet's image as if trying to think of something to say. He cleared his throat and essayed a laugh. "Ha! All that water and not a drop to drink. I guess the ancients tried to build up the shallows, but except for the two island chains they couldn't get anything to stick, so this place has always been a backwater."

His pause and drawn-out look meant he expected a reply, but Kurash felt he had missed something important. As the silence dragged on, the captain added, "Get it?"

"What is it I am meant to obtain?"

"I suppose you Gatoi don't know about river systems because you grow up on spaceships. Never mind. My father says . . ." He broke off. Coughed. Scratched his head. "Anyway, we are almost there."

"My thanks," said Kurash, making a note to ask Ay about river systems and what it might have to do with what the captain had said. Did it relate to the term "backwater"?

The planet's orbital habitat was a basic ring-and-spike configuration. They docked twenty-three minutes after their scheduled arrival time. The rumpled stationmaster met them on the pier with stiff-backed deference.

"Captain Lee. And how is Regent the Honorable Marduk? I was honored by his attention when he visited five months ago with Crane Marshal Zàofù."

"I don't suppose you get many visitors here," said Captain Lee as he scanned the run-down docking area and a wheezing mech that was polishing the deck.

"Indeed, I did not expect to see anyone from the palace again quite so soon." The stationmaster's voice had the exhausted timbre of a person who hasn't recovered from his last argument.

Kurash broke in. "I need to go to the surface, to the settlement Potemkin."

The stationmaster's eyebrows shot roofward as Kurash displayed the jade pendant Sun had given him. "Apologies, Honorable. Our supply shuttle already went down with the palace committee."

"A palace committee?" Kurash looked at the captain, who scratched his head.

"I hadn't heard about any palace committee coming here," said the captain, "not that my father tells me anything."

"Yes, well." The stationmaster had the anxious mannerisms of a person eager to move trouble off his dock without getting punished for it. "They descended about twelve station hours ago. They arrived to inspect the ponds for the palace kitchens. Apparently there were some contamination issues with the last batch of salt."

The coincidence struck Kurash as odd. Regardless, he had a limited time frame to get back to the *Huma* in Olynthus System, three beacon drops away. "The habitat must have another shuttle."

"We do have a work shuttle available but it's rough. No fancy acceleration couches and no dinner service."

Captain Lee laughed, by which Kurash determined that the second part of the statement had been a jest.

"That will be acceptable, Stationmaster. How soon may I depart?"

The stationmaster gave him a measuring look. "You must be part of Prince João's retinue, eh?"

"I serve Queen-Marshal Sun."

"Of course! Of course! No offense intended. This way, please." He started walking and, when only Kurash followed, turned back with a startled look. "Just you, Honorable?"

"Just me."

Once they were out of earshot the stationmaster sighed and remarked, "That lad doesn't take after his father, does he?"

"Does he not?"

"Marduk Lee has a distinguished military career, besides being one of our late, lamented Eirene's Companions. A good choice for regent, if you don't mind my saying so."

"Why would I mind?"

"Haha. A cunning jest. You know how it is. I don't see people from the palace often but I do see them coming through because of, well, you know. I'm sure that's why you're here. What a maiasaurus nest it all is, busy busy busy. But everything is shipshape and under control, hatches secure, I assure you."

"Of course." Kurash had learned to keep people talking when he wasn't sure what they were talking about. Usually comprehension came into focus after enough words were spilled.

The stationmaster was happy to go on and clearly relieved to be away from the captain, who was evidently one of Marduk Lee's unfavored sons. Kurash had to blink away a vivid image of stern-visaged Manea with her arms in the dark water. He released a spurt of inhibiter to smear out the flashback.

"I'm not sure why the new queen-marshal has to be away from Chaonia for so long, but these are cheering victories, are they not? Everyone always said those Trinity criminals couldn't be touched, but I guess Sun showed them! Opened up their treasury, too! I received word we are to get an upgrade to our docking system as well as a replacement shuttle. Maybe that is just because Prince João is one of those who prefers Pelasgia salt . . . maybe you are too . . ."

Kurash waited out the pause, evidently meant for him to make some manner of shared confidence. When he did not, the man went on.

"But I like to think Sun is taking care of us now she has the means to do so. We all knew the royal treasury was empty even if no one talked about it. Still, Eirene saved us from far worse. The sacrifices she imposed on us were worth it, weren't they?"

"Do committees from the palace kitchens inspect often?" Kurash asked.

"Erratically. Sometimes it simply depends on if there's been a power struggle inside the chamberlain's office. The kitchen fights are the worst, I'm told. Pelasgia salt is a prestige item. I guarantee this planet would have been abandoned as an official settlement a thousand years ago if not for the unique properties of this salt. Here we go. Do you have a time frame, so I can add it to my schedule?"

"I'll keep you posted."

"Ah, yes, I see. Of course. Of course." He winked to imply he understood that something classified was underway.

Kurash reflected on this complicated subject as the shuttle descended into the atmosphere. The pilots spent the entire reentry arguing over the respective standings of the republic-wide premier rugby league. The cargo specialist sat as far from Kurash as humanly possible and kept her eyes fixed on a flexible tablet folded out from her sleeve. There was no one else on the shuttle.

On the final approach he got a good visual of the islands. According to a report Sun had appended to his orders, a semicircle of uninhabited "fore islands" acted as a wind and tsunami break against the prevailing weather system. The main atoll was made up of an outer ring of islands that were salt flats, which surrounded an inner island linked to the salt flats by cargo bridges. From above, the arrangement looked as pretty as a matched-jewel setting worn by a hand-fasting couple at their wheel-ship community feast. Dauntless Persephone might wear such a choker and necklace drapery . . . but he flinched as his mind's eye pictured her. An ugly sensation writhed in his chest, garbling his thoughts. His hands tightened.

She wasn't here. The engineered hallucination would only trigger if he looked her in her real face. In her real eyes. Therefore, he could never see how she would dazzle.

The engines changed tone. The shuttle got permission to land and, with a bump, came to earth. Gravity made its presence known, strangely comfortable compared to the heavier clutch of Chaonia Prime. One reason the early colonists had tried so hard with Pelasgia Terce, so the history claimed, was that its gravity was said to be closest of any known planet to that of the ancient home world of the Celestial Empire. But Kurash had learned the hard lesson that what people said might disguise the truth rather than illuminate it.

After the shuttle's ramp gasped open, he set foot on a salt-dusted and wind-swept island. There was another shuttle powered down. The doors into a low building opened and a person hurried out. Kurash walked to meet them, leaning into a powerful wind.

The chamberlain had a frown meant to intimidate. "Who are you? I wasn't informed of any new arrivals."

Kurash displayed the jade pendant and handed over a handwritten paper note marked with the personal seal of the queen-marshal, a form of private communication meant to deter eavesdropping and hacking.

"The hells!" After reading the note, their color changed. "I see."

Kurash plucked the paper out of his hand. He had a survival lighter built into his left knuckles. The chamberlain jumped back as a flame bloomed, caught the paper, and burned it into ashes that spun away on the wind.

"I am Lieutenant Kurash. How may I address you, Honorable?"

"I don't recognize you from the palace spatharioi. Are you one of Prince João's people?"

"I serve the queen-marshal."

"My apologies. Of course you do. That's why she entrusted you with this task. Well. Yes. I am Chamberlain the Honorable Toa Lee. The regent left me in charge after . . ." The man glanced around the empty runway as if to make sure no one was trying to spy, although Kurash was pretty sure the wind's bluster covered their words.

In the distance, whitecapped waves carved lines across the lagoon. The six cargo bridges looked different from down here, functional scaffolding instead of beautiful jewelry. The outer islands barely rose above the water, dark lines separating sea and sky. What was it called again? The horizon.

"This way, Lieutenant."

As they walked toward a cluster of buildings adjacent to the airstrip, the honorable rattled on. "It's not really an atoll. It's modeled on atolls with the addition of the barrier islands. Even so, once or twice a year we get a storm system from the north that wreaks havoc. That's why I was surprised to see the palace committee. This isn't a good time of year to visit. On top of that there's a storm winding its way toward us, though it might blow past. But I don't have the authority to turn away one of Eirene's Companions, even if the blessed Eirene is no longer with us."

One of Eirene's Companions?

Sun's instructions had said nothing about her mother's inner circle, only that this settlement was under high security, with limited access.

They reached a secure building guarded by a pair of bored marines who snapped to attention when they saw Kurash's face. The jade pendant made another appearance to convince the marines he was legitimate. He could tell they wanted to ask questions but were too disciplined to do so without permission.

The chamberlain released a progressive set of locks. The interior room was set up as a clearinghouse with a counter and a desk, currently empty, and behind these a vault sealed with a hatch. "This place is desperately understaffed but the hardship conditions make it difficult to keep folks here unless they're assigned or grew up here and don't want to leave. Which is too bad because there's a lichen that grows here that has unusual medicinal properties . . . oh dear, I won't bore you with my rant on this subject. All people want to talk about is the prestige salt. In here."

Behind the unlocked hatch, a ramp led down one level.

"Nothing can be buried deep here without excavation hitting the water. But that's what they say in the palace too, eh? This is where we store the harvested salt before it is shipped out. No one can enter here without my authorization. Back here."

"Back here" was a refrigerated vault with shelves and drawers labeled as foodstuffs and medicinals stored in bulk for Potemkin's temporary-duty population.

The chamberlain indicated a deep-set drawer. "Set your jade pendant on the panel. The regent set the seal to release only on the queen-marshal's authorization."

A buzz, a light, a click. Kurash stepped back as the chamberlain rolled out the drawer. Inside lay a corpse.

The man was young but not a youth. Cold air breathed across his pallid lips and curled around his twisted, broken legs. He bore a faint resemblance to Sun around the chin and in the angle of the nose, but if Kurash hadn't known he was looking at Sun's cousin he might not have remarked on the similarities. He pulled a pin out of the pendant and pricked the chilled flesh, then held it up as a mechanism inside the pin sought a match.

"A sad end to a dutiful life," remarked the chamberlain. "Too bad about the accident. But it could have happened to anyone."

"How so?" Kurash asked, careful to not reveal the extent of his ignorance. Sun's message had tasked him with confirming that her cousin was dead, but hadn't mentioned how he'd died.

"I don't mean to speak ill of the dead. Folk around here do get careless on a pleasant day when they're crossing one of the bridges and don't wear their safety harness because it's a hassle to get on and off. A gust of one hundred klicks or more can come up out of nowhere. We were fortunate we were able to fish him out of the lagoon, but he'd drowned by then. Poor lad. I suppose the queen-marshal wishes to lay him in state at the palace, not that he was ever there since he was five years old. I remember him when his father was queen-marshal. A friendly little fellow, he was. Used to run about the courtyards waving a sword and shouting that he was stabbing Gatoi—"

He stiffened and his face flamed red as blood rushed to the surface. Kurash could smell his embarrassment and fear.

"I understand," he said in an even tone. "I need to convey the body without it being obvious it is a body. Perhaps it could be wrapped and then concealed within a transport box of salt secured for the queen-marshal's kitchen?"

"Yes, yes, yes, certainly, yes." The man could not stop bobbing nervously as his cheeks stayed flushed. "I can have the body ready in four hours. You can wait here, or if you would prefer there is a decent bakery in the village. I can ping you when the, uh, package is ready."

"Where did the palace committee go?"

"Oh! Ah! They went to pond five, which is next in line to be harvested. They intended to check for impurities. I hadn't realized the last batch was a complete ruin, but of course that would have been before I got here."

"I thought all of Eirene's Companions left with the fleet, besides the regent, of course."

"So did I, but evidently Precious Jīn was sent about some other diplomatic errand to a nearby system. An old friend of hers from the kitchen staff prevailed upon her to add this stopover to her mission."

Precious Jīn. A spike of adrenaline flared. The chamberlain yelped, startled by its brightening, and Kurash tamped down the surge.

"Do they know about—?" He indicated the body.

"Oh, no, no, no. Strict secrecy. Cousin Marduk put me on this detail himself, you see."

"Marduk Lee was one of Eirene's Companions alongside Precious Jīn. He might have shared the news of the death with her."

"That I couldn't tell you, but Precious sailed with the fleet to Karnos a year ago now, isn't it? I got the impression from a passing comment she made that she hasn't been back to Chaonia since Eirene's death."

"Did she ask about the prince?"

"In a courteous way. I told her the official story, the one the crane marshal put about."

"Which is?"

"That the prince went on a pilgrimage to the temple at Dodona to pray for his aunt since he was not able to attend her funeral."

"If Marduk Lee and the crane marshal know he's dead, why didn't they take him away to the palace for a customary funeral?"

The man rubbed his chin, cleared his throat, and sighed. "I suppose, Honorable, that the crane marshal wanted proof to show to Queen-Marshal Sun, should it come to that. Since you are here, so it has."

"Pond five, did you say?"

"Yes. In truth, I'm glad you're here. I don't mind saying to one of Sun's household that I found the marshal's arrival a little odd. If you want to see them, the fastest way to get there is through town and then to tower five. The route is marked. Everything is marked so no one can get lost when a storm blows in too fast to get to shelter. Repairing the routes is an endless task."

"I see. Thank you." He considered the swiftly shifting parameters of his mission. "I was also tasked with checking in on Prince Jiàn's household and making sure they've been settled with sufficient funds. Is there a palace or estate nearby?"

"Oh, no, no, he lived in the town alongside everyone else. He didn't even have servants or anything, nothing beyond three factotums, a cook, and a cleaning staff. Or so I'm told. I never met him. Marduk sent me here afterward to keep an eye on things. No one among the permanent inhabitants has a bad word to say against Prince Jiàn. Anyway, besides these landing-zone buildings and the safety shelters at the salt ponds, everything is in town. It's not too bad for a temporary assignment. There's the bakery, as I mentioned, a night market twice a week in the community hall, a Yele-style salon for performances, and even a little sports league, although I grant you the competition isn't much." He trailed off, rolled shut the drawer and, after he locked it, added, "I'm talking too much. My apologies."

"Honored Chamberlain, it is my pleasure to hear of the ordinary goings-on of the people who live here. I believe my orders will allow you to be relieved of your duty after I have left with the cargo."

The man sagged, shoulders slumping with relief. "Thank goodness, I surely hope so. Not that it has been bad, of course not, anything in service of the palace and my good cousin Marduk, but . . . I do miss Argos. I know the gourmands say this salt tastes special and can't be replicated elsewhere, but it doesn't taste any different to me."

Kurash thought about how Ay would polish off the conversation. "Let me leave you to your work, Honored Chamberlain. I will go into the town to discharge my duty."

The chamberlain took him back topside and pointed the way, although in fact the roads and paths were indeed all marked by sturdy safety railings and stubby light poles set every meter. What storms demanded such precautions? He looked at the sky and its shredded clouds. The wind was constant and strong but not debilitating.

The chamberlain pointed northwest. "You see that line of darkness? That's a stammer-cloud ridge. It could pass us offshore or pick up and hit us directly in an hour. Let me show you how to clip in. Everyone wears a harness."

The harness was similar to the harness used by the Phene when they broke in new banner soldiers through a grueling test course that usually resulted in 90 percent casualties and a few deaths. The officers broke them so they could put them back together the way they wanted them to be.

The thought made him hesitate, he who never hesitated. Putting on the harness was like putting back on the leash and thus putting himself back into the hands of people who wanted to break him. He didn't want to be broken again. He wasn't sure he had the strength, not after his grandmother had turned her back on him.

Angry at this weakness, this betrayal of the core of himself who had sworn an oath at his wheelship funeral that he would serve until biological death, he roughly tugged the harness on, over his unmarked uniform. After clipping into a safety rail he headed off at a run for the town, which lay five klicks away through fields of dense ground cover and stubborn lichen.

The island looked flat from the landing strip but was rumpled like a disturbed blanket. By this means the builders had created a more sheltered zone for the island's ten thousand inhabitants. He felt the wind lessen as he entered the town through an open gate.

The main street looked like a showpiece, with brightly painted storefronts and a spotless deck. No, not a deck, a street. Nevertheless the pavement looked as clean as if it had been sprayed down this morning. The town's high wall and additional layers of shifting, wing-like structures directed the force of the wind away from the ground, although there was still a constant breeze. The numerous drains would allow runoff from heavy rains to pour away from the buildings.

There wasn't much traffic on the main streets. About half of the businesses were shut and locked. Maybe it was meal time or work time, almost high noon, so his timer told him, the star rising toward zenith, bright but cold. In the sixteen minutes it had taken him to run the five klicks, the temperature had dropped by five degrees. What did that mean?

No sooner had the thought registered than a shrill alarm began to blare with a *hoot hoot hoooooot*. He hurried through the streets, raising a hand to those he passed in the way Ay did on the ship. This disguise together with his unmarked uniform and the moaning klaxon allowed him to pass townspeople without incident. There were other people around wearing military garb. Soldiers and spacers walked everywhere in the republic, because that was the measure of Chaonia, wasn't it? Every citizen served their entire life, in whatever way they were capable. Anyway, by the evidence of the klaxon, they had their own trouble coming and didn't care about a random passerby.

The central market district gave way to a ring of parks, schools, and training facilities. Past these lay the residential district, domiciles built low to the ground with generators spinning on their roofs.

The compound in question stood at the outermost rim, against the town wall. A protected porch gave shelter as he rang the entry bell. He could have just walked in, but instinct made him wary of using the aggression of royal power.

A door hissed open. A woman wearing a sour expression and a palace factotum's hummingbird badge looked him up and down and said, "What do you want? We already had visitors today, and they didn't have any news."

"I have news."

Her eyes widened. "Let me see your identification."

He displayed the pendant.

She gasped, pressed a hand to her heart, and lost blood in her face, going ashy. Once she had recovered her ability to move, she showed him into an audience room fitted out for entertaining. She abandoned him amid its couches and game tables without a word, fleeing farther into the compound. He waited in the center of the gracious chamber.

A portrait of a couple dominated the space: the prince's honored parents, Queen-Marshal Nézhā standing beside his consort, the Hesjan honcho who had betrayed her husband to her treacherous allies among the cartels. She had fled, leaving behind the five-year-old Jiàn, who Eirene had tucked away into this exile. At least she hadn't murdered the boy.

He blinked away a sudden rippling of dark water that flooded his vision, and doused his racing heart with a spurt of psychotropic drug.

The door opened.

Four individuals entered, one of them the woman who had answered the door. Each carried an implement that looked innocuous but could be used as a weapon: a cooking knife, a gardener's spade, a mechanic's crowbar, and a metal-tined rake. The four spread out, moving like trained soldiers to encircle him, but he wasn't concerned.

A fifth person entered the space. They were attractively garbed in a light, flowing gown, and carried a baby on their hip. The little child had bright brown eyes beneath a tight cap of curly hair, and a familial resemblance to the handsome couple in the portrait.

The adult's hair was wrapped up to create a tiara-like ornament atop the head. Fastened around this headdress was a symbiont like a meter-long, hundred-legged ribbon.

His neurons flared in preparation. Everyone took a step back.

The person said, "Ou isn't armed. Identify yourself."

Symbionts were always armed, so the statement was a lie.

"I am Lieutenant Kurash, a member of Queen-Marshal Sun's household. There is no record of a small child being present in this household. Are you a Hesjan honcho?"

"I am the child's mother. I am Hesjan born. But I am simply a member of the cleaning staff. All my provisional work papers are in order."

He caught the gaze of each of the attendants in turn, making sure they knew he knew exactly where they stood in relation to where he stood, before again addressing the woman. "This species of symbiont is assigned as a class-four military-grade weapon, and is generally reserved for high-level cartel honchos, especially family members intended for cross-cartel alliances."

Her expression crumpled briefly with a grimace, and then she controlled it with a hard inhale. "The marshal was here only hours ago, looking for Jiàn. She was sure he'd be here. She hadn't heard anything about a pilgrimage to Dodona. Do you have news? He's been gone for months. He's never been allowed off-planet since Eirene dropped him here as a boy."

She did not say *Is he dead?* but he heard the question in her tone, and saw expectation in the defensive way she hugged the child. Hesjan-descent children were linked to a symbiont at one thousand days, so this child was not yet that old. Which suggested Prince Jiàn had contracted a secret alliance only recently. What kind of encouragement would bring about such a decision, with all it implied about his wish to create a successor for himself?

"Prince Jiàn is dead."

She sobbed once, her whole body shaken, then fell silent as the child looked concernedly up at her. The attendants staggered as though they'd been struck.

"Where is his body?" she whispered. "May I not even pay my final respects?"

"I am here to deliver a message. Go home and never come back."

"But the marshal said it was all arranged, now that Sun had left the republic we could . . ." She closed her mouth. She had said too much in the way of people unmoored by shock.

"The marshal can't protect you or your child. You can wait here until Prince João arrives, as he inevitably will."

"That wouldn't be so bad, would it? He's so kind and gracious."

"Have you met him?"

"Yes, he came to visit, oh, almost three years ago. Before Eirene died, at any rate. Jiàn said the prince has visited before and always brings appropriate gifts."

"Did he see the child?"

"No, I was pregnant, and not yet showing."

"And at the time you did not mention the pregnancy to the prince?"

"Jiàn said not to. He said to say I was a member of the staff, so that's what I pretended. I don't know why he insisted on keeping our marriage secret. He had sent word of it to Eirene, and she had not objected. Why would Prince João care? And what could he do about it anyway?"

Had no one prepared her for the job of being an illegal and secret consort to an exiled, disinherited prince whose survival hung by the thread of his aunt's love for her brother and her sense of fair play?

Unless people had seen it for themselves, people did not understand how fast and inexorably a banner soldier attacked. He sparked his neuronics and *moved*. Two attendants were down before the others had time to make a shout of surprise. In six more seconds he had tossed the four implements onto the deck and stood, not even out of breath, facing her. The symbiont was already in motion with a writhing fall from her shoulder to the deck that twisted into a slithering explosion toward him. He leaped over ou before ou could shift direction, and ripped the child from the consort's arms. With a spin, he placed the child between him and the drone just as ou arched up to spit killing toxins.

"Disarm!" she cried, as he'd guessed she would. She burst into frantic tears.

No one came, because there was no one who could protect her, and she was only just realizing that. She was no Manea, girded of stronger scaffolding than anyone had suspected. She hadn't an inkling of how many knives waited beneath the sparkling glamour of the palace and its dreams of power.

The child wailed. He set it on the deck and stepped back, keeping a cautious eye on the symbiont's twitching legs.

"If you want the child to live, you will go home to your cartel and never set foot in Chaonian space again. That is the only warning I can give you."

"If you aren't from Prince João, then who sent you?"

"I belong to Sun's household. This is her act of mercy, not mine."

Yet that too was a lie, wasn't it? Perhaps Sun suspected there was a child involved and knew better than to demand from Kurash a form of submission to her authority that he would refuse. Because this was the measure of her. She asked for all you had, but she would not coerce it from those who didn't want to give it of their own free will.

He left the compound. The klaxon had fallen silent, having done its duty. Now it was up to people to do what they knew had to be done.

The north gate out of the town remained open. The air was even colder than it had been an hour ago. As he jogged up the ramp out of the town's protected vale his internal sensors indicated the wind was now nearing gale force by the Beaufort scale. The ridge of clouds had grown in size or had moved closer or both. Planet-bound proportions remained difficult for him to parse.

Pitching his body against the wind, he pumped his way to tower five. A stream of foot traffic passed him heading back toward town, everyone clipped onto the railing. People in grime-smeared and salt-dusted harvesting gear shouted at him as they passed. He ignored them, and no one came after him. At length, legs and arms flushed and throbbing from the effort, he reached tower five.

The bridge stretched from shore to shore, thrumming softly as the wind sang through its scaffolding. The conveyor belt and the lift had been halted. Crates of salt sat chained to the base, awaiting transport after the blow. A party of miners descended from the sheltered walkway, not noticing him where he concealed himself by one of the tower's massive legs. He hadn't seen Precious Jīn but when he telescoped his vision along the length of the bridge he spotted three more parties making their way back.

He raced up the stairs tucked inside the tower. Once he reached the top, he saw that the walkway wasn't completely enclosed by a wire cage. It had no roof, so he climbed up and out and slung himself over the side to the conveyor belt. The bridge was already swaying slightly, and the wind was determined to pluck him from his precarious path. Using the cargo belt's sturdy cross rungs as a horizontal ladder, he crawled out underneath the bridge's walkway, hanging above the lagoon. Waves lashed on shallow rocks. Now and again a thread of spray brushed his face, the water surprisingly warm.

The first party clattered past on the walkway above without seeing him; all miners with the resigned look of people who have dealt with these conditions before.

A second party consisted of two arguing administrators, one of whom kept dabbing at a bloody nose with a red-smeared handkerchief clutched tightly in bruised fingers.

". . . rude! There was nothing wrong with that batch!"

"Shouldn't we help them? They're struggling."

"Let them struggle! I've never been so insulted in my life!"

The third party moved with erratic, staggering footsteps, fighting the wind. This wind was indeed something to fight and to fear. But wind was also a weapon of Lady Chaos. He had survived worse trials in her maze. He had survived worse in training with the Phene. He would pay later for the energy he was expending now, but wasn't there always a cost? At least in his case, right now, he would pay for his own exertions from his own flesh, unlike Manea or the unnamed honcho who, if wise, would take the child and run as fast and as far as possible.

Precious Jīn's commanding voice lifted as if to challenge the gale. "Move along, Xiákè! We need to get off this structure before the full force of the storm hits."

"I'm sure I've sprained my knee."

"Can you two not support him better? I'll report those administrators for just leaving us behind. I'd never have come over to this hellsbitten salt pond if we didn't need to keep up the pretense that we aren't here because of Jiàn—"

He swarmed up the wire cage and dropped down behind. She swung around, her combat instincts still sharp. The other three hadn't noticed as they battled onward toward tower five, their palace robes flapping wildly around them.

"Kurash?"

For an instant and an eternity she stared as the wind howled at his back and battered into her face. Her surprise was complete. He lunged. She grabbed her stinger and shot point-blank, but the sway of the bridge threw off her aim. A hot pain burned across his thigh, causing him to stumble. He rolled as she shot again, this time branding his shoulder. His boots hit her knees. She went down, but caught herself as she brought the stinger back to bear on his face.

He kicked her in the side of the head and as a follow-through slammed a hand down on her wrist, breaking it. The stinger fell. She dropped hard, stunned.

Any moment now her companions would look back, wondering why she wasn't ordering them to move faster. He hoisted her body on his shoulder. A stab of agony pierced his shoulder with the movement but he'd been trained to ignore pain. With a boost of adrenaline he flung her up. She caught on the wire wall's rim, arms dangling out and legs in. He crawled up, thigh burning with each pump of his leg. Blood flowed from the wound, but the rain washed it away. Grabbing her legs, he heaved her lower limbs up and over as he clung to the wire. With a shove, he pushed her off the bridge.

She plunged fifteen meters into the shallows, smashed onto the rocks facedown, head slumped below water. A shimmer of blood rose to the surface. The whitened rims of curling waves brightened with pink highlights.

The others kept walking, didn't even look back. They hadn't heard over the roar of the wind. Soon enough they would realize what they had lost.

He clambered down the outside of the wire wall, locking his fingers around humming wire, pressure down to the bones as the wind tore at him. The gusts were staggeringly powerful, and once he almost lost his grip when his wounded shoulder buckled under the strain, a fresh injury tearing in already damaged flesh. Only by timing his movement with a gust was he able to swing back beneath to the cargo belt. He hooked the harness onto a safety rail intended for maintenance workers and edged his way to an emergency platform. Here he wedged himself into a tiny ledge of safety as the clouds roared in. His right shoulder throbbed brutally; something was fractured. The muscle in his left thigh burned as if a hot drill was grinding into his flesh. He coaxed down the pain with a surge of drugs, letting the neuronics start their slow if unpleasant healing protocols.

Rain lashed the bridge in a frenzy. Below, the surge tossed the body amid the rocks like flotsam. He had to wait under cover until he could get away unnoticed and never be explicitly linked to the death of a respected and high-ranking Companion, even if Precious Jīn was a traitor. As for his own actions, he had simply followed Sun's lead. Whatever people might suspect, the accusation must be difficult to prove. He did not know for sure what Sun would do if the death was definitively linked to him, and even if it was, who could act to punish him if she refused to? She didn't yet know about Precious's betrayal, but there was no reason for her to treat the marshal differently from her cousin Jiàn. Splinters lodged in the flesh had to be removed.

The acute agony of injury numbed to a persistent ache as the first dose of drugs took hold. His body needed treatment, but like all banner soldiers he had been molded to keep going long past the pain. He would just lie here a little longer.

The storm pounded the atoll with shrieks. A strange, delighted sound like laughter haunted his ears. What caused that noise? The front of rain moved past. The drowning torrent slackened, although the wind still tore. Shapes moved in the lagoon. Creatures rose out of the waves, inexplicable to his eyes, something like the winged mušḫuššu his own Wrathful Snakes banner was named after and yet unlike anything he had ever seen beneath Lady Chaos's creation, nothing that humans had brought with them from the Celestial Empire of ancient memory.

Untethered by any harness, they danced on the boundary between wind and wave like children at play, joyous and filled with energy. What drove the humans into shelter brought them freedom.

75

Interlude in Port Shivakiar

Petal wakes up before the time clock rings to roust them. She grabs her day robe and slips out of her bunk, grateful she was assigned to a bottom tier, and tiptoes down the length of the sleeping compartment. All is quiet.

Past the privacy curtain she enters a spacious compartment with divans, two twelve-chair dining tables, two pīng pāng qiú tables, two gaming alcoves, a mirrored dressing and cosmetic area, and a full lavatory with showers and separate toilets, enough that people don't have to wait ten in line for an hour before shift starts.

In the pleasure house on Meli, the drones had no lounge of their own to relax in, much less any free time. They were either working, cleaning, or sleeping, and meals were supervised, their portions measured.

Here, at Port Shivakiar in Aila System, they have an entire lounge where they can sit on a cushion on the floor or on a plush divan, play a game or watch Channel Idol. She'd never heard of Channel Idol before the Chaonians came but she enjoys its bright and easy programs. Besides the poetry recitations and history lectures there are musical contests, dance-alongs, and dramas. She likes *Journey to Landfall* best, even if she can't figure out why the mothership commissioner's pampered daughter looks exactly like the struggling young janitor on a half-forgotten and isolated tail ship in its tow chain.

Channel Idol is always on. Right now the Idol Historian is narrating the recent coronation of Queen-Marshal Sun, which confused Petal until she found a sidebar program that explained that, in the Republic of Chaonia, Sun is the highest ranking marshal, called queen-marshal, while, in Mishirru, she is being crowned as Great Mother Queen, which is a different title and tradition. Anyway, the ceremony is beautiful to watch, and that's what matters.

As the local sun rises over Destiny's famous Imperishable Temple, Sun receives a crown shaped as the spiky halo of a star's bright aura. Singers and masked dancers accompany the ceremony in a solemn ritual, the proceedings interrupted at intervals by the historian's authoritative explanations. The haloed crown makes the young queen look like a figure out of legend. She has a very serious expression and a look in her intense dark eyes that pierces the farthest horizon.

Petal sighs. Before the Chaonians came she never thought much about a different life. A whispering voice nags her now. What if she could become someone else? But how would she get to a different place than the one she grew up in? Her mother worked in Meli's famous Exotic House, and her child was required to do the same because the debt hadn't been paid. Where the debt came from Petal has never figured out, and her mother never said before she died but she often cried at night and sometimes had nightmares, although she told her daughter it was nothing, just a wandering ghost who couldn't hurt anyone but her.

The curtain swishes aside as other early risers appear. The triplets Calix, Calla, and Calypso sweep in and go straight for the counter where bean broth, salep, tea, hibiscus juice, and water are set out at all hours. No house clerk monitors what they drink so as to add it to their indenture account.

Flor brings her a cup of salep and sits down. "I heard a rumor. We're going to be given shore leave."

"What is shore leave? Do we have to pay for it?"

"I don't know. But Joya heard Kole tell Lily that he'd heard an officer say there is to be a party in a fancy villa on the planet. Our unit has been picked to go. I guess it's so fancy we won't take the space elevator but they'll fly us down in a military corvette. It won't be so bad, right?"

Petal doesn't know why Flor asks her for reassurance but she always does. "If it's no worse than this, then it won't be so bad."

Flor toys with her own cup of salep, turning it around and around. "That one high officer . . . What do they call them?"

"A marshal."

"You're so good with language! I can't understand their way of speaking Yele. Anyway, I think he likes you. He keeps asking for you, doesn't he?"

Petal shudders.

"Was he . . . cruel?"

"No, nothing like that. He's fast, so that's good, and then he likes to talk and have me listen. It's just my mama warned me never to get my hopes up. She thought a man loved her. He brought her dresses and jewelry and took her to fancy parties and fancy villas."

Flor nods to encourage Petal to go on.

"She dug out her implant because . . . because she had stars in her eyes. As soon as he found out she was pregnant he complained to the boss. She never saw him again. And she had to pay a big fine for having me."

"But she loved you." Flor sighs, and they lean into each other. They both lost loving mothers, although in starkly different circumstances.

"Whoever he was, he just wanted to parade her around because no one had ever seen anyone like her before. He didn't really want *her*. So what do I care about the attention of a high officer? I'm just grateful I can drink salep every day without having a debit put on my tab. I mean, I think they aren't charging us for it."

Flor gazes at the coronation, propping her chin on her hands. She has a delicate, thin-nosed face and unusual white-gold hair that is natural, not dyed. It's a feature as rare as Flor's blue eyes. Exotic House boasted that its stock was brought in from the farthest reaches of the great beacon network, including uncommon gems like Petal's mother and Flor herself, sole survivor of a pirate attack on a merchant ship.

Flor cocks her head, studying the image. "I was glad when we heard Queen Sun killed the Trinity, all three of those bitches," she remarks in her gentle voice. "What do you think we'll get for breakfast today?"

The locked outer door chimes. Everyone in the lounge stiffens. It's too early. Ever since their unit was removed from Exotic House on Meli and transported to a secure compound inside Port Shivakiar to serve the Second Fleet, their days have been tightly structured.

They all stand as the door opens, because that's what the boss at Exotic House requires them to do. Flor starts to cry silently. Petal grips her friend's hand. Calla puts an arm around each sibling, hugging them tight. The others who weren't up yet crowd in from the barracks. At the pleasure house you would receive a demerit and a fine if you weren't waiting and ready.

The supply officer they have been instructed to call "Chief" enters, accompanied by two people. One wears a uniform Petal does not recognize, but it reminds her of Queen Sun's military uniform because it has sunbursts on the shoulder the same way Exotic House drones wear a badge in the shape of the flower called "bird of paradise" to mark the pleasure unit they belong to.

The other person is a tall woman with a scarf knotted around her head. She wears an ankle-length gown with a sash, its fabric densely embroidered with goblets, clamshells, and red umbrellas.

The woman says to the chief, "Turn that off, if you please."

"But Citizen, it is the queen-marshal's coronation as ruler of Mishirru."

"It is, and we've all seen it five or ten times since it took place three months ago, have we not? I, for one, have memorized the entire ceremonial sequence and could sing and dance it for you right here. Does anyone wish to join me?"

Her gracious smile and playful tone surprises a laugh out of many, including Flor, but Petal keeps her mouth shut. Channel Idol snaps off for the first time since they were disembarked onto the big space-wheel habitat. The silence has an odd, anticipatory texture. But it isn't truly silent. A habitat hums and whirs and breathes, not like a living thing but like a machine that can never sleep because it is conceived of and built to be a tool for people to use, a purpose it did not ask for but is fated to carry out. That's what her mother once said: She Who Weaves can't be escaped once she has knitted her damning kiss into your bones.

"I am Tiana Yáo Alaksu. I am accompanied today by a palace clerk and factotum, the Honorable Eleuterio Andas. I am also accompanied by Chief Vernon Sakai Aldodona, whom you know. Please, my comrades, feel free to sit."

She gestures toward chairs and cushions. No one sits.

In a low voice, the clerk says, "There are thirty-six individuals in this unit, according to the records."

The woman goes on, careful to speak slowly and in short sentences. She is easier to understand than many of the Chaonians.

"I stand before you as a citizen of the Republic of Chaonia. I stand before you also as a representative of the Campaspe Guild. Has anyone spoken to you about your rights? The Republic of Chaonia is a signatory to—they have signed—the Campaspe Guild's universal statement of rights for sex and recreation workers."

Again she waits. No one speaks. Is it a trick question? Is she waiting to trip someone up? She's wealthy looking enough to be a high-status campaspe, the kind who has attracted a rich patron.

The chief looks puzzled. "I didn't know people outside the republic fell under the guild's umbrella, Citizen."

"It's a common misconception," she says with a patient smile. "That's why we are doing these inspections throughout the fleet while we have the time. To make sure all people who became attached to the fleet after the Trinity victory are aware of their rights."

"But they were debtors. They were part of the treasury the queen-marshal took possession of."

"Is indenture how we deal with debt in Chaonia?"

"Of course not! All Chaonians proudly serve the republic and in return the republic cares for them."

"Are humans merely objects, to be treated as property?"

The chief shifts nervously, cheeks flushing with emotion as he dips his chin. He has run the unit for six months now with strict regulation, the power to whom all must defer except the officers. So it shocks Petal to see him defer to this woman who has just said she is a campaspe, however elegantly dressed. In Meli, the pleasure house drones were among the lowest-status workers, meant to be discarded when they were no longer profitable. The worst fate was to be expelled from a house onto the uncaring streets. It was traditional to make expulsions in winter.

As if she can feel the anxiety of the drones, the woman raises her right hand in the gesture, palm outward, which means "fear not."

"You are allowed to leave this service at any time. You should all have been given the right to refuse this duty on the day your pleasure house was brought onto this ship as a unit. If you wish to return to a hometown or a family, you may file an immediate request with the Honorable Eleuterio."

No one speaks, although a few people glance at each other.

"I understand some of you and perhaps most of you may have no way to return to your families. Perhaps you have no families to return to and have remained with the unit because you have nowhere else to go. The Campaspe Guild is an auxiliary guild but it is not an official part of the fleet. You may request to remain with the fleet as an apprentice spacer. If you pass the basic tests, you can be trained in a new specialty. In order to do this, you must apply to become a provisional citizen of the Republic of Chaonia. You can start that process by filing an immediate request with Eleuterio."

The triplets whisper excitedly to each other. The woman's gaze shifts toward the noise. Her interest sharpens as she studies their faces and forms. They are impossible to tell apart. That is why they are in Exotic House although in every other way they look commonplace, unlike individuals like Flor, the Skuda-born Joya, and Kole with his shimmering tattoos that light up like fireworks when he has an orgasm, which makes him very popular with a certain kind of customer.

The woman goes on. "You have the right to work, if that's your wish. You have the right to refuse this work and the right to refuse a customer. If any of you have been told you must accept every customer who asks for your service, then know you need not. There should be a panic button in your workrooms. This safety feature is required under the auspices of the Campaspe Guild. If any of you have been mistreated, you may file an immediate complaint with Eleuterio. You should also be receiving a base rate of pay. You don't have to be a guild member to ask for that, but you may need to set up a credit instrument to receive pay. Again, Eleuterio is here to help you with that."

Again she pauses. More people whisper to each other, a growing undercurrent of excitement.

"I am aware some among you may not believe me. You may fear my statements are meant to expose troublemakers, that I hope to find people to punish. Sex work is an intimate and personal job. It should be your choice to engage in it and yours to leave when and as you wish. You are not to be coerced. Not to be moved wholesale from indenture in the Trinity Coalition into service in the Chaonian fleet where you don't even have freedom of movement."

"But we are treated better here," says Petal, angry that this well-dressed, well-fed woman can't understand the most basic aspect of survival. "It's not so bad."

When the campaspe looks at Petal her smile softens but the shine in her eyes remains hard. "I am glad to hear you are treated better here than you were treated in the coalition. That is not the same as having access to the full rights due to you. Would you take up a different line of work if you could? I'm sorry. May I know your name?"

"I have no other skill," says Petal with a shrug. "I might as well stay here."

"You're good with languages!" Flor opens her big blue eyes toward the woman. "Petal can speak ten languages, at least."

"Can you?"

"Not really." She elbows Flor, hoping her friend will shut up. It's not safe to draw attention to yourself. "I can't really speak anything but Trinish. I can get along in Common Yele and High Yele. I can make myself understood in Larissan Yele and now Chaonian Yele. I know a little Phenish and some Mishirruvian."

The woman's laugh is amused or surprised or maybe mocking. "Is there more?"

"I know some Jewelsprach, from Flor. I know a little Ravennan and a few hundred words of Skuda. And . . ." She hesitates, but why not? The entire situation makes her angry. "And Vaeonic Guoyu."

"What is Vaeonic?"

"My mother's born tongue."

"I've never heard of it."

"No reason you should. She came from Asmu."

"Asmu? Isn't that a fable place? A tiny enclave of mysterious magical hidden folk who live beyond the last beacon in the Phene Empire?"

"It is a real place."

"Have you been there?"

"I was born here. On Meli, I mean."

"I see." The woman didn't believe her and was too polite to say so. "Language skills are very useful. Can you read and write also?"

"My mother only knew Vaeonic small script. She never learned Yele characters or Trinity script. The boss didn't allow us children to learn. And we didn't have time."

"You sound like an intelligent person who would do well on an aptitude test and could qualify for training."

"Can I go with her?" Flor asks, grabbing Petal's hand. "I'm Flor."

The woman takes in Flor's exotic looks. "Are you born on Meli also, Flor?"

"Oh, no, no. I was born on Belt of Jewels. That's how Petal knows Jewelsprach. I taught it to her so we could have a secret language we can speak to each other when we want to gossip or complain without the boss hearing us and charging us a fine."

"Flor!" Petal hisses, elbowing her again.

"Would you go back to Belt of Jewels, if you could?" the campaspe asks.

"Of course I would. I have family who must be wondering what happened to us, to me and my mom and her cousin, I mean. They're dead. Our merchant ship got attacked by pirates and they captured me and sold me. Are you saying there's a way for me to go home?"

"Flor! Shhh." How can she be so dazzled by the woman's gracious manner and intrusive questions pretending to be kind? That's how they get you.

The woman indicates one of the tables and the clerk sits. "Please, give your information to Eleuterio. If you'll start, Flor, we can see what we can do for you. Are there other questions?"

Flor is so naïve that she releases Petal's hand and stumbles over to the table as if in a daze. Nothing good will come of this. She'll hope, and then she'll cry.

Everyone starts to talk at once. People begin lining up behind Flor. The woman goes over to the triplets. Something about them has caught her interest.

The door opens. No one notices at first because the order of the morning has been turned upside down and inside out. But Petal notices as a curly-haired man strides in with his retinue behind him. He always looks annoyed but right now he looks extremely annoyed.

It is the marshal. He never visits this early, so that means someone sent him a message. The campaspe is in big trouble now.

The marshal pulls up short as the woman turns around to face him. He speaks in his curt, commanding voice. "I received a report that an unknown party had come on board and was interfering with shipboard routine. Who are you?"

She does not appear troubled by his aggressive question. "Marshal Anas, may peace be with you this fine morning."

"And upon you, peace," he says automatically, then grimaces, looking even more annoyed, which is a lot considering he is a man steeped in arrogance. He's never struck Petal or yelled at her or even insulted her in any way, but being near him always makes her flinch. "Chief, what is going on?"

"She's a representative of the Campaspe Guild, Marshal."

He snorts angrily. "So *that's* why I heard that several Trinity units brought here have gone on strike."

"They have not gone on strike," says the woman as if the marshal does not intimidate her. "They are asserting their rights, according to the law of the republic and the charter of the Campaspe Guild."

"Get out before I whip you." He raises a stinger, angry in a way Petal has never seen him before except that one time when he was complaining about someone who disobeyed his direct order.

The woman's calm expression does not falter. "Are you sure you wish to threaten me, Marshal?"

"Are you trying to intimidate me? Are you even a citizen or just some jumped-up provisional sex worker—"

The door opens for a third time, which, Petal knows from every Channel Idol drama, means the final hammer blow is about to hit the nail.

A tall, elegant woman enters. "Tiana? Did you call me . . . *Anas!*" She breaks off as if too surprised to finish.

"Honored Hestia," he says through gritted teeth. "What brings you here?"

"I come here on behalf of Sun, of course. While she is on her expedition to the distant Gyre, I have remained to make a survey of the fleet's chain of supply and all the personnel and ships and arms."

"Who is this cheaply perfumed campaspe? You seem to know her."

"Perhaps the two of you have not yet met," says the noblewoman with an arched brow. "Though I confess I'm sure you've shared a room."

"How can that be? Ridiculous."

The campaspe gestures toward herself with a flowing movement like the opening of a dance. "I am Companion's-companion to the Honored Persephone, who is currently traveling with the queen-marshal."

"Oh, I see. I didn't recognize you without paint and ornament." His lips twist.

"Indeed," says the campaspe. "I have found many see only what they expect on the surface, but no matter. I am sure you would not wish any irregularities in the Second Fleet's supply chain to come to the attention of Sun. The Honored Hestia and I are just doing our duty as part of Sun's household to make sure every aspect of the Fleets and the Guards meets with the high standard our military has long lived up to. Of course the situation with Trinity brought unexpected wrinkles. Hard to know how to deal with all of its *assets*."

"How dare you speak to me with such disrespect!"

"Anas," says the noblewoman. She has a quiet demeanor but a spine like steel shivers into view, and he huffs and he puffs and he backs down.

"This is ridiculous," he mutters. Then, like lightning, his gaze strikes Petal. She is starting to know him well enough to see a decision spark in his thoughts. His glance toward the campaspe. A chance to land a blow. "Petal! Get your things. You're coming with me. You'll be in my household now. The clerk can make the appropriate transfer."

She is trained to obedience, having experienced the lethal consequences of her mother's final attempt to escape. "Yes, Marshal."

She hurries into the barracks to her bunk. It has a small locker where she has tucked her cloth bag with her receiving gown, a change of work clothes, a cleaner's apron, her mother's four-tined comb and beaded hair pin, and the ear cuffs she stole off her mother's corpse before the body was sent to the Matrone's gardens for recycling. Everything else that belonged to her mother was taken by the boss for salvage or sale. She takes off the day robe, folds it up, and pulls on her receiving gown, which fortunately isn't sheer even if one seam is slit halfway up the thigh.

Footsteps pad up behind her. The campaspe has followed her into the barracks.

"Petal, if I may call you that. Do you want to go with him?" She has such a lovely voice. Everything she says sounds sincere.

"You are a very elegant and highborn person."

"I am not, I assure you, but go on."

"I don't have a family or a clan to go back to. I grew up in the pleasure house. I had my first client at thirteen. I was fortunate because my mother wouldn't take a bigger payout for them to auction my services off before my menstruation started."

She pauses, waiting for a shocked face.

The campaspe nods. No surprise. No false protestations. Clear eyes.

"He is a high officer," Petal says.

"Among the highest," agrees the campaspe.

"Can you offer me better?"

The campaspe has the look of an apsara, a celestial messenger of divine origin whose strength lies not in her beauty but in her courage, her intelligence, and her ability to reach out to her multitudinous sisters. "He knows I can't. He himself skirted the law to bring indentured workers from Trinity into the Second Fleet for his own convenience, not just you campaspes but other workers as well. I can only offer you the rights you have, and the chance to become a provisional citizen. It isn't much, but it would be yours alone."

"Didn't you just say you are a companion to a high-status person?" Her smile is a crooked wisp. "So I did."

"If I join the marshal's household, I will be no different from you."

"In some ways, yes. But I have a contract which gives me legally created rights. Households are bound by obligation, which is a different relationship, in some ways more secure and in others less safe."

Petal shrugs.

The campaspe nods. "If you ever need my help, contact me through the Chaonian network. It is your right as a member of a Core House household to be fitted with network access. I'll check in later to make sure you are well."

"Of course you will," mutters Petal. She hurries out, suddenly afraid the marshal has left without her, that she's missed her chance.

But she has underestimated how angry he is, tapping a booted foot as he waits by the hatch. Why wouldn't he be angry? A lower-class person has thwarted him and insulted him in public.

Even so, she can't help but veer over to where Flor is sitting opposite the clerk.

"Are you going, Petal?" Flor trembles as she grasps Petal's arm.

"You could come with me. I'm sure his household has room for one more."

Tears spill down Flor's cheeks as she jumps up and embraces Petal, her voice a hoarse croak. "I want to go home. The clerk says I can go home."

"It's all right, Flor. You have a family waiting for you."

Despair chokes her, but she swallows it down down down because she isn't selfish. She kisses Flor on each cheek, hugs her tightly one last time, and releases her to step away.

The campaspe stands at the curtain, watching her with a gaze Petal cannot make sense of. Pity? Compassion? Hope?

"Petal! Come along. I'm in a hurry."

"Yes, Marshal."

Hope is for fools.

76

The Gyre

Sun rarely slept long hours, but she slept particularly poorly on the *Corpse-Eater*. Once they'd arrived in Cataract System she'd had to transfer off the *Boukephalas* onto a local Crow-class ship. Mishirru's religious establishment controlled all travel to and from the Gyre.

When she woke after another restless cycle in a cramped stateroom, she first, as was her habit, checked her strategos network to see what needed her immediate attention. But of course she had no access here. It was like walking in the dark with a muffling shroud pulled over your entire body, and she didn't like it. Instead she rewatched the message her father had sent for her with Zàofù. She had seen it ten or twelve times, maybe more, but nothing soothed her in the same way: the excessive care he took to frame himself in his outdoor courtyard at night with lit lanterns behind him. A long indigo jacket embroidered as the heavens with the sunburst ascendant, shining over all. His habitual manner of alternating dry lecture filled with unasked-for advice with illuminating observations on current palace factionalism. The random bursts of praise that warmed her soul.

"Look over the list of eligible marriage candidates that I've attached. They're all of highest Core House lineage, prominent and respectable, but without ties to Marduk, who already has too much power, mark my words. Still, he was the best choice in the moment. Your instincts are excellent, as always, my unconquerable Sun."

Once the message played all the way through she could breathe more evenly, but she was still awake. She dressed and made her way forward to the ship's shrine. Every spaceship and habitat in the holy queendom of blessed Mishirru was adorned with a shrine just as every village, town, and city had a theatron dedicated to the Imperishable. A shrine might contain three small lion-headed statues of seated queens, or a brass sistrum, or a replica of the halo crown. There was a jar of fragrant ointment so devotees could dab their foreheads before they sang an invocation. The Great Mother Queen and her sisters watched over all their children as arbiters of plenty and of lack, of mercy and of judgment, of life and of death.

On the *Corpse-Eater*, the shrine was tucked into an alcove cut into the bulkhead that separated the habitable compartments of the ship from its forward drive. Sun had no need to worship at a shrine that was now in an intangible way dedicated to her. Humans weren't gods, whatever the people of Mishirru believed. Nevertheless, humans sought to touch the numinous threads that knit together the universe, an imperishable soul that lies both within and beyond the sluggish solidity of a mortal body.

When she leaned against the bulkhead, a slow *thrum thrum thrum* vibrated through her bones, exactly timed to the beat of her heart. It whispered a dispatch from a hundred generations past, when Crow-class ships like this one flew as couriers between Mishirru's star systems. A little Crow's streamlined knnu drive ate up most of the ship's space. The only cargo it could hold was small luxury items or supplies not produced on the isolated habitats it served. Crows weren't large or powerful enough to haul a tow chain or to transport soldiers and weapons in sufficient numbers to carry out an effective attack. Once the beacon system spread across the local belt and couriers could speed along those routes, the Crows became obsolete everywhere beacons reached.

The Gyre could not be reached by beacon.

Generations of spacers had stood at this shrine and listened to these engines pulse. When she rubbed a finger across the mural of Mishirru's eight star systems, painted in a semicircle around the alcove, she traced faint lines where long-haul crew had scratched their names into the wall below the planet, moon, or habitat of their birth. The names could no longer be teased from beneath the layers of paint and the weight of years. They had lived, and now were forgotten.

The resonance changed, pitch dropping. Almost there.

She went to the empty galley, its lights dimmed, the cook not up yet. Cold buns had been left on the counter for the sleep-shift duty crew. As she took a bite she heard a bark of familiar laughter. She stuck her head into the softly lit wardroom. Isis and Sayre sat relaxing with a pot of warmed rice wine. Wing perched on Isis's shoulder, wings furled and eyes closed.

"Couldn't sleep, Your Highness?" asked Sayre, who, after the competition on the *Bountiful,* had taken on a great-aunt tone with Sun.

"I don't have time to sleep."

Isis laughed again. "You'll learn not to ask that question, Sayre. Will you join us, Your Highness? We were trading stories of a few old nemeses we had in common during the Kanesh Campaign."

Sun sat and accepted a small lacquered cup. "Phene?"

"Quite the opposite. Chaonian officers of the old school, the ones Eirene rooted out as she rebuilt our Fleets and Guards. Long gone now. May they rest in peace with all our proud citizens who fought beside them through those long and weary nights."

"To the heroic dead." Sun raised a toast. The rice wine had an elegant taste and a light finish, the kind of spirits a person could sip all night on campaign without impairing their judgment. Or for day after day after day as the Crow flew. No faster way to get here.

Isis said, "Now I understand why you brought the group you did."

Sayre tilted the wry gaze of an old hard-ass at Isis. "I'm thankful every day we don't have to endure what this tiny living space would be like if Jade was on board in constant proximity to Persephone."

Isis shot a glance toward Sun.

"That's why I left Jade in charge of training the new Guards divisions as they integrate into the main force. Alika to blockade Sena's beacon. Second Fleet to get repairs. And Zàofù to get the Eighth and Ninth Fleets back to fighting strength with new recruits. Place people where they can get their job done and not squabble."

Sayre sighed. "The Young Master was very sorry to be left behind on this stretch. I do miss Dozer."

"He and Razin get to take an offering to Landfall," said Isis. "I'd have gone in a heartbeat. They'll dine off that pilgrimage for the rest of their lives. The first footprint. The restored lander. The first permanent structure. The old city under its dome. I shudder to think of what this stretch of Mishirru was like before the beacon system was built. The little orbital habitats we've been resupplying are like prisons."

"I'd guess they are prisons," said Sayre. "Or hermitages."

Any mention of the seers flushed Sun with fresh energy, like a raptor catching sight again of the prey that has eluded it so far. "Do the seers of Iros have hermitages in Mishirru? I thought only the local religion was allowed here."

Sayre's head tilt conveyed puzzlement. "The seers? I was thinking of the episode in *Old Honcho and Baby Bee* where they end up on the desert planet of Skete searching for an anchorite who is the lost heir to a cartel. They get in a big fight in a separatist hermitage where all the hermits are really Skuda mercenaries in hiding."

"I don't remember that one," said Isis.

"How could you forget! When Old Honcho feeds bananas to the hungry barmaids and tosses the peels one by one onto the stairs as the mercenaries keep trying to run up the steps to attack her but slip . . . ?"

"Oh! Yes. Yes! Of course! The artistry and comic timing of their falls!"

They both laughed. Wing startled awake and squawked, then settled as Isis stroked the teacup pteradon's feathered head.

Sun thought back through her childhood: drill, temple protocol, history and philosophy, more drill, the ancient classics of literature and music, military science and an introduction to the healing arts, yet more drill, a pilot's license, and drill. "I never watched the show."

Sayre clucked her tongue. "I didn't realize a palace education was so lacking in refined entertainment."

Lights snapped on in the galley, followed by the clicks, clacks, thumps, and bumps of the cook coming on duty.

Enough of this leisure. Things were about to start happening. She stood. "It's not clear I'll be allowed to disembark once we reach the Archives but I'm going to be ready. I'll need all hands on deck when we arrive."

"We didn't get an alert from the captain that we were arriving," said Sayre.

"The engines changed pitch."

Sun went back into the galley. Ship's protocol on the *Corpse-Eater* was to ignore others unless you specifically needed to speak to them. So although the cook offered Sun a curt bow in acknowledgment of her exalted status, Sun didn't follow up with small talk as she waited for the first brew. Grabbing three cups, she went to the map room. Persephone was already there, manipulating beads along a wire scaffolding, a physical structure the old ship used in lieu of a virtual 3-D map.

"Did you also hear the engines change pitch?" Persephone asked without looking up.

"What happened to the map?" Sun asked. "We've spent weeks refining it."

"Yes, but it was still wrong. We just don't have good enough intelligence on routes and systems inside imperial Phene space. I'm going back to basics."

Persephone had pulled apart the physical map they'd been building, their best estimate of the empire's beacon routes, which they had constructed together based on Chaonian military intelligence and as much merchant and trade route information they'd been able to gather. She had replaced it with something much simpler: a central hub with ten long, skinny limbs.

"Is this supposed to be a diagram of Dozer's nervous system as it radiates outward from ou's core?" Sun asked, not sure whether to be bemused or amused.

"No. It's meant to be the original Apsaras beacon map."

"The original? Oh, I see. Each of the ten—"

"Eleven. This little stub of a line here is only one beacon jump. I'm theorizing it is the first beacon route. A single hop, there and back again. Proof of concept, if you will. But lost to us after the collapse along with the Apsaras home world."

"A reasonable assumption. I can see the engineers would have needed to start somewhere with the simplest configuration. Are you positing that none of the original eleven lines connected with any of the other lines at any point along the network?"

"Yes," said Persephone. "Only with She Who Bore Them All. Like on Yele Prime, you always have to go to the center before you can head out to a different periphery. Maybe the engineers weren't sure at first whether they could put more than two beacons in any system except the central system."

"Maybe they didn't want to give up control of beacon traffic."

"Maybe, but they did give up control eventually when they started adding additional beacons to systems and linking all the routes up to each other. No one knows why the collapse happened. I wonder if the network simply got too big and unwieldy."

"Do you have proof of that assertion?"

"It's plausible but not provable."

"Sabotage is also plausible but not provable. An act of war or rebellion. An accident. Equipment failure. Deterioration. Hard to know without finding She Who Bore Them All, where presumably there's evidence to be found."

"And we can hope there would also be evidence there of how to fix the broken beacons. Whatever the engineers' reasons for linking up the original routes to each other, it's because of that interconnection that we have our current network. I'm pretty sure that what we think of as the main routes today aren't the original main routes." She indicated the map. "I think these eleven lines might be the original main routes."

Sun paced around the table. "How did you come up with this particular configuration?"

Persephone crossed her arms, a sure sign she was hiding something.

Sun added, "Do each of those beads—star systems, I mean—have coordinates? Can you place this onto a map of the local belt?"

"It's just a model." Her gaze flicked away from the table and from Sun.

Ah. Either she didn't want to admit she had no idea and was spinning her wheels for obsession's sake, or she knew something she didn't want to share.

"But look here at where this ship is now," Persephone went on with a seamless change of subject, deftly handled and totally in character.

The table had many moveable parts in addition to the adjustable wire scaffolding. She shifted the map model up over her head, all except the segment that represented Mishirru. The queendom's core systems made a line, represented here by beads on the wire: Landfall, Arafel, Cataract, Oasis, Scepter, Alabaster, Destiny.

"The queendom eventually established control over systems outside the core eight. Like Harahuvati. It's part of the beacon route that links up to the super-distant terminus known as Belt of Jewels. But if I'm right, Belt of Jewels didn't used to be connected to Destiny at all, not originally. Sena System is another example. It is marked as the 'official' boundary between Mishirru space and Phene space. Was Sena on one of the original routes and, if so, which one? Or was it a later addition, one of the added links? I think we can track back and make a guess at finding She Who Bore Them All if we could overlay an accurate map of the original beacon routes on an accurate map of the current beacon system."

"In other words," said Sun, "besides this historical map being a guess, we still lack the map we need of the empire's current beacon routes."

Persephone slid all the star systems back into the sculpture's holding ring. She expanded the area known as Cataract, a red dwarf with two beacons, one of which was anchored to a marginally habitable planet. "I've been talking to some of the crew."

Sun was 99.9 percent certain that Persephone was having sex with one of the crew, but that wasn't any of her business unless it impeded readiness, so she said nothing as her Companion went on.

"They say the region got its name because of an unusual prolif-eration of brown dwarfs in its local group. In the early days, before the beacons, these provided stepping-stones, a 'cataract' of shallows along a river, as it were, that allowed knnu fleets to more easily leap the large distance between Cataract System and Oasis's K-class star. They 'skipped' from one brown dwarf to the next. Now only Crow-class sup-ply ships use this route, because traffic can skip over the cataract by dropping through the Cataract-Oasis Beacon."

"All right, that's interesting," agreed Sun, because it was. "Where are you headed with this?"

"We've stopped at Tomb, Spring, Pool, and Temple." Persephone slid four brown beads representing dwarf stars along the flexible wire, each accompanied by a micro-bead representing an orbital habitat. She pushed a fifth to align with the others. "Oracle is the last dwarf. But there's nothing on any map I've seen to mark where the Gyre is in rela-tion to Oracle. I'm not even sure *what* the Gyre is. Don't you find that strange?"

The door opened as she spoke. James staggered in, rubbing his eyes and yawning. "What I find strange is how uncommunicative the ship's crew is. Does your fuckboi even talk or do you like it better silent?"

Persephone smiled smugly.

James rolled on, not expecting an answer. "It's just so annoying that our network can't interface with the ship's computer system. I can't decide whether the system is just too archaic. Or if it's deliberate ob-struction." He took a long swallow of tea. "I like the tea, though. It's harsh and bitter, like my sleep on this loud boat."

The steady *thrum thrum thrum* ceased.

They all froze in place, waiting as if on a dance floor for the beat to drop.

"What in the hells?" James tapped his ears as the silence prolonged.

Comms gave a loud buzz, followed by a prerecorded message. "Dock-ing in two."

"Two what?" James asked.

"They like being mysterious," said Persephone. "Unlike you, James."

He flashed her a challenging grin. "I'm not mysterious. I'm inge-nious."

"Strange!"

"Marvelous!"

"This is happening faster than I expected," said Sun. "Get your things and be ready to disembark."

"Do you think we'll be allowed to disembark?" Persephone's hand lingered on the beads, spinning them. "I need one of these structures for my very own. I'd take this one, if I could. James, can you help me steal it?"

"Sure, and get tossed into one of those locked-down habitats we passed, never again to bask in the light of a proper G-class star? I don't think so."

Sun left them to it. Of her Companions, James and Persephone complained the most and talked the loudest, but they worked well together because they both used good-humored teasing to negotiate their differences. Not that Persephone couldn't be mean. She was positively cruel to Jade and adept at massaging the story so people thought it was Jade being cruel to her. Jade had never done anything wrong except hustle and excel, and Sun would never fault someone for having ambition. That would be like faulting herself.

She passed six crew members headed toward the stern, where the docking gear and airlocks were. They crossed forearms over their chests and bobbed a truncated bow but did not speak. She had a ready kit packed so was at docking control when the ship bumped five times like a spear pushing through layers of stiff canvas. With a clunk, the *Corpse-Eater* came to a stop.

The captain intercepted her in the compartment for docking control, which overlooked a small hangar with an airlock big enough to take a forklift. The hangar had been crammed with pallets when they'd left Cataract System. At each of the habitats a specified number had been offloaded by personnel from those habitats. No one on the ship had set foot off the ship once they were underway because all the orbital habitats on this route were off-limits, outsiders banned, even ship's crew.

The airlock lights flicked from red to yellow to green. The doors opened. An incoming breeze rustled ribbon-like tags attached to the pallets. A forklift hummed through the door. Tinted windows shielded the features of whoever was inside the cab, or perhaps the vehicle was remote-controlled. One by one it hoisted the pallets. When the last pallet was gone the hangar sat empty. Were they going to receive passengers or cargo? They hadn't at the other habitats. They had only delivered and departed.

Sun took a step toward the hatch that led from the control room onto the hangar deck. The captain raised a hand in warning. For an instant Sun considered ignoring the gesture. Who could stop her, queen-marshal of the Republic of Chaonia, Champion of Karnos, Liberator of Trinity, Imperishable of Mishirru? Not anyone on this crew. Instinct stayed her feet. Mishirru might have crowned her, but she needed to pay attention to what this ancient land was telling her. She did not leap. Not yet.

An individual emerged from the airlock and halted three steps into the hangar. His spectacles caught glints from the overhead lights, the old-fashioned wire-frames an artifact of the elder days. He wore dark slacks and a silver-gray shirt woven of a shimmering fabric. In one hand he held a palm branch, still fresh. On the other perched a teacup dragon no larger than Isis's Wing, its tail curled around his wrist.

The captain coughed in surprise. "That is the prince of the un-banned himself. Usually one of the archivist clerks seals the manifest."

"Why is he called the prince of the unbanned?"

"Many have come from the outside and requested a change of status."

"A change of status?"

"All outsiders are banned. Few manage to get the ban lifted. His story is famous among us. But you would have to ask the Archives to know the whole."

As if he heard, the man below said, "We have had word a visitor seeks an audience with the Gyre. Let Sun come forward if she wishes to be seen."

The captain whistled under their breath, then undogged the hatch.

Behind Sun, in their ready gear, Isis, James, Persephone, and Sayre each gave her a look typical of each individual: loyal caution, enthusi-astic curiosity, a joking mask over a dead-serious core, and age-worn amusement. They knew what she intended, and that none could stop her. Their caution and concern did not anger her, but she didn't have time for it. She descended steep steps onto the hangar deck. A breeze still blew, bringing with it a hot, dry odor like that of heat on rocks.

"I am Sun. Is there a name I may call you?"

"I am the prince of the unbanned. The community here is larger than you might know but closed to outsiders."

"I ask for leave to enter and pose my questions to the Archives."

"You may walk with me, if you dare."

Sun laughed curtly. "If I dare?"

"Those who walk the Gyre do not always like the answers they re-ceive. Do you think you will find what you want to know?"

"I'm about to find out." Part of her was impatient to get on with it after the long journey, but another part enjoyed each little obstacle to be surmounted. Rituals funneled actions down narrowing paths. As her options shrank, her choices grew sharper and brighter.

He turned and, without looking back, walked into darkness. She followed, entering a night-drenched space like a cavern. Her guide had vanished, but the pale gleam of his footprints marked the path ahead, fading behind her as if to conceal her route back. Noises reverberated: the forklift driving away down an unseen passageway and a scattershot echo of distant voices. She could not get a direction for where the forklift or the people might be because of the way the sound bounced.

The quality of the air changed as the ceiling and walls sloped down to confine her. A last glowing footprint vanished to leave her at the outer rim of the habitat's shell. A dull globe of reddish light appeared beneath her feet on the other side of the transparent surface she was standing on. The globe drifted forward to dimly illuminate a walkway, a transparent tube, that extended like a sealed pier into the airless emptiness of space.

She entered the tube and walked about a klick to where it ended in a dome with a transparent membrane. As the globe's light dimmed to a spectral gleam, a staggering view unfolded, a vast vortex of dust turning in a slow gyre around the sullen glow of a brown dwarf.

Is this all there is, a view onto a hopeful star that never burned hot enough to become a true sun? There had to be more than this.

The dome disguised a telescoping property, because she could see with her naked eye that more than dust circled the brown dwarf. A moving carousel of tiny objects looked like specks from this distance, until a distortion in the membrane sprang them into close-up view.

They were ships. So many ships.

Massive Titans larger even than the *Bountiful* were trailed by smaller ships of designs she had never before seen. Were these the legacy fleets that had departed the Celestial Empire four thousand years ago? Placed here as archivists place objects in storage? A mothballed fleet, too valuable to destroy but of no particular use in the modern world. Not unless your admirals wanted ten knnu drives and had the authority to take them. Was this the answer the Alabaster Argosy sought?

She said, "Did the Phene take knnu drives from these ships?"

Beneath her, the globe expanded and brightened like a miniature star going nova. It filled the dome, its light embracing her, consuming her. Within this glowing sphere shadows began to move and twist. They coalesced into a vision that might have been a reconstruction or an actual time-lapsed recording of events.

A Phene task force arrives in-system. No diplomatic vessel parks itself at the habitat. When does an empire ever ask for permission to do what it wishes? The ships get busy with a salvage mission. They pick targets and rip knnu drives out of twelve ships. Then they depart.

The globe began to spin, shrinking smaller, tighter, elongating to form the shape of a human whose skin glowed with an antique gold sheen. Their eyes shone the same sullen red-orange shade as the brown dwarf, as if substellar objects could have consciousness and an avatar.

"You are allowed three questions. That is one."

"You speak for the Archives."

"I am the Oracle who speaks for the Archives. You are allowed three questions. You have two questions remaining."

Sun had hoped for a searchable archive, a place she could bring James and Persephone and set them to work. But anyone who read the classics knew an oracle was fenced about by prohibitions, so she had come prepared with a prioritized list.

Will I find Kiran Seth and bring him to justice? Was anyone else involved in my mother's murder, and if so, are they dead or do I have work yet to do? Will the banners join me or reject me? Is Precious Jīn going to prove my ally or my enemy? Will my father ever stop nagging me? What is Hetty doing right now?

What is my destiny? Why should I stop when I could ignite and burn more brightly than any before me?

But these were not questions for a repository of the past. Oracles spoke of the future as a riddle to be interpreted, or misinterpreted, according to the temperament of the person receiving the prophetic prediction. A good strategist engaged in the same line of work, with or without the hand of the gods upon their brow. She had to be strategic.

"Where can I obtain a complete and accurate sequence of maps of both the current beacon system and of the pre–Apsaras collapse beacon system. Ones that span all inhabited and human-marked worlds of the local belt?"

The Oracle bowed its head gravely, forearms crossed against its chest. Within the sweep of its crystalline robe, a grainy visual played.

Tiny vessels dart amid a habitat shaped like the stacks James made when he built information profiles in the strategos system. As the silvery vessels flit in and out, pieces of the stacks shed like scales falling from a dying leviathan to be vacuumed up by the ships.

"The Apsaras Convergence never cooperated with this Archive by sharing any of their knowledge. Their messengers plundered what they desired from our stacks. If you wish to know the secrets of the Apsaras Convergence, then you must go to their womb system, which they named after the glistening one, the primordial creator, She Who Bore Them All."

The Oracle paused, and Sun knew the hesitation was a lure, an enemy opening up a gap in their line in the hope the other side would charge in and be trapped. The question on the tip of her tongue was easily turned into a statement.

"So it seems you have no pre-collapse beacon data, but you have not mentioned whether you have accurate and complete current maps of the beacon routes."

The Oracle's eyes burned, swirling like the gyre in the slow contraction of a once-mighty energetic force collapsing into obsolescence. The shifting depths of the crystal robes darkened as if information could thicken liquid into solid. A thumb-sized capsule dropped to the deck with a plink.

The Oracle said, "Those who bring shards to the Archives gain our favor. This information was offered to us by the prince of the unbanned in exchange for a place here. Now a copy is yours, although you could have found this elsewhere. It is not rare, merely difficult to prise loose from the hands that grip the power it represents."

Sun picked up a Phene memory device, stamped with the triangle badge of the Immortals' military branch. She smiled with satisfaction. If this proved to be as promised, the information contained here made the trip worth it.

"You have one question remaining," said the Oracle.

Sun knew people thought her impulsive, that she rashly threw herself into dangerous situations because she had an unstable temperament or a reckless streak. Maybe a little of the latter. That might be fair. But she never undertook a risk without measuring what would happen if she stepped back from the brink, if she did not leap down a level in order to break the defenders' hold on the Sanctuary, if she sat back and allowed the Speaker of the Rider Council to escape when she might have a chance to capture him, if she did not drive the Phene from Molossia before they had a chance to deploy the full brilliance of their daring plan.

And she was never afraid to let her heart be the one to dictate her next move. She did not fear the sheer raging strength of emotion that surged behind the cold spear of ambition. Her utmost desire. Her unfulfilled longing. She spoke slowly and clearly so as not to be misunderstood.

"Where is the Celestial Empire of blessed memory?"

The Oracle's shape began to spin, slowly at first, then whirling until it twisted out of a human shape to become a pillar of fire. Images burned inside the flames.

A white-clad goddess sits with prayer beads and a zither-like instrument in her hands, She Who Bears the Wisdom of Ultimate Truth, and yet behind her a mighty river shrinks and dries up and all those it nourished with its life-giving waters must depart as refugees for other lands.

At guard in a desert, a human-headed lion built of stone slowly crumbles.

On a double-hulled vessel sailing on a storm-tossed ocean, a woman uses her hand to measure the angular height of a bright star as she navigates a course toward an unseen land.

Two women seated high upon elephants lead an army against a great host.

A dirigible explodes.

Women whirl in a dance of swords, singing and stamping at the broken gates as they defy the invaders.

An orderly line of exhausted people files onto a cargo shuttle as, in the distance, smoke rises in dense, boiling clouds above a shattered city.

Dust and ashes, the debris left by the passage of ages.

Amid the flames, the Oracle raised two hands, four hands, six hands, eight.

"We are here. We are all that is left of those sent outward from the Celestial Empire in the last days. These fragments. Our ruins. The Argosies fought over us and dismantled us into pieces so no one Argosy might take an advantage over the others. The destruction only ceased when the queens arose and enforced their rule over the feuding Navigators. Much later the Apsaras came with promises of amity and shared sacrifice. They said they would return the navigational charts they stole, but we never saw them again. Now outsiders are banned from our stacks. Only those willing to devote their lives to reconstruction may be admitted to the inner halls. Are you such a one? Do you seek to reweave what was lost from the shards and broken threads?"

An image chased into view amid the golden fire, a fearless rider with spear in hand chasing a foe fleeing in a horse-drawn chariot, their features as familiar as if Sun had seen them adrift in her dreams. Or maybe it was her own features, or a shard of herself being wound into the Archives so it could never leave.

The pillar of fire twisted and re-formed into a glowing human shape, that of an imperious woman weighted down by chains on her wrists and a crown of slag on her head. An expression of longing bled like ichor from a wounded heart.

"Shall I keep you here? Shall I keep you here? Shall I keep you here?"

"You shall not keep me here, Oracle."

"Yet you burn so brightly and your presence would warm us who grow cold as we fall apart shard by shard by shard."

A hiss chased through the air, gaining in volume. The dome was losing atmosphere as if the Oracle was purposefully draining it of air to suffocate her. Sun set a hand on her upper left sleeve where an emergency filter with one hour of air could be detached and hooked across her face.

"My destiny lies elsewhere."

Yet the gyre turned, drawing her into it. The dust occluded the orange-red luminosity of the distant stellar object, more than a planet, less than a star. The abandoned ships were its prayer beads and its prayer. The habitat was dark behind her, the dome a fragile shelter, the oscillating hiss the whispers of the past that can never be fully comprehended. Even the monstrous indifference of space is not eternal. It too will end. Everything will end.

How galling.

The Oracle's voice had the harsh temptation of desire. "Perhaps that which is broken might be repaired. Perhaps worlds long sundered from the rest of humankind may be gathered back and She Who Bore Them All restored to her central place in the network. A person who commands all the worlds can do greater work yet. Perhaps the fractured Archives can be reconstructed. The Celestial Empire reclaimed. You could. You could. You could."

Sun tightened her fingers over the capsule. "Many things are possible. But right now, I have in my hand what I need for the next step I intend to take. And with it in my grasp, who can stand against me?"

"Only you, Sun. You are the conqueror. You are the destroyer. You are the uniter. You the divider. Only you."

77

Her First Glimpse of Home

Apama sat in the passageway, back propped against the closed door of the starscape lounge. In knnu space the freighter breathed, and it ticked, but she missed the hum of a torch drive vibrating in her bones. It was strange to feel at rest while at the same time being part of an anomaly that was moving incredibly fast.

A chime rang, followed by ship's comms: "We are entering the final four-hour approach to transition. All hands to stations."

Two freighter crew members—cousins Arnu and Kuru—came

hustling along the passageway. After so long on the ship, she'd gotten used to their only having two arms.

"Hard to believe we're almost there, eh?" said Arnu with his usual smile.

"Good thing too, eh?" said Apama. "I'm starting to speak Yele the way you lot do instead of the pompously correct League-style the way they taught us in flight school."

They chortled. After a year on board a single ship you knew who you liked and who to avoid. None of the Hatti crew had ever once called her a shell, at least not in her hearing. She'd come to appreciate their kindness. Or, possibly, they just weren't aware of the slur.

"You on guard duty?" asked Kuru. "Those kids, eh?"

"We were all young once," said Apama.

The three shared a knowing chuckle, Kuru being the eldest at thirty.

"Is there a problem with Chenoa being in there during knnu travel?"

"You mean the family tradition." Kuru nodded. "Yeah, no, she asked the captain's permission. For compassion's sake, you know? A good cause." He chuckled.

"Hope Teegee gets over her skittishness, poor mite," added Arnu. "You can fix physical scars but the psychological ones are hard to heal."

"They sure are," Apama agreed, tamping down the nervousness that flooded when anyone on the crew mentioned Teegee's "ailment."

Kuru elbowed his cousin in the ribs, and Arnu cleared his throat self-consciously, prelude to a question.

"Go on," said Apama as her nerves iced to alertness.

"We didn't want to bring it up because it's none of our business, and no offense, and no need to say."

"But?"

"But we were wondering if maybe there was something more to your story. Our captain let slip you're a lancer pilot, which is pretty amazing. But is that by itself enough to hire you on so you can get back to Phene space? Are you from a Triple A syndicate family? An admiral's eldest child, maybe?"

"What! You have a betting pool riding on my true identity, eh?" Their guilty expressions betrayed them. She laughed because, after all this, she, Gurak, and the Se Xar team had managed it. They'd deflected all suspicion off Teegee. "All right. We're almost there, so I'll confess. I'm the offspring of a Rider, although not a Rider myself."

Struck speechless, they stared at her with wide eyes, then laughed uproariously and slapped her on the shoulder. "You had us! You had us!"

They went on their way, chuckling as they argued over what kind of drama her fake story would make: comedy or tragedy? She checked the time. How much longer did she have to wait? Her mom had once called her too much of a romanticist, but Apama had been a pragmatist even as a teen. If romance wouldn't get her into flight school, then what use was it? Lacking syndicate connections or the ability to pay for private tutoring, she'd had to rely on all the extra time she could earn in the local Wing and Ding Scouts unit that encouraged scrapheap teens to see if they were a good fit for pilot or medic training. There were plenty of backwater habitats, moons, and planets where no one wanted to live that needed medical personnel and pilots. Recruiting from the desperate was how syndicates supplied hard-to-fill posts.

Instead she had hit every mark up the ladder to the exalted lancer academy. When she thought of how an invisible hand had been opening doors for her without her knowledge, she no longer felt anger or disappointment. She just wanted to get back to Anchor to make sure her mom was all right.

The slap of footsteps broke into her thoughts.

Gurak strode up. "Do you know where 'Lito is?"

She indicated the closed door.

His brows lifted, then dipped. "I thought she was with Chenoa?"

"They enthusiastically decided to try a threesome for their final act. That's all I ever need to know beyond being stuck here on door duty in case Chenoa's supervisor comes looking, which now strikes me as pointless because everyone knows everything anyway. Except . . . you know. So here I sit like an Incorruptible."

He shook his head. "Chenoa is a risk we shouldn't have allowed."

"That worked when you were seventeen, am I right?"

"We weren't all sex-obsessed adolescents."

"Look at it this way. In a few hours Teegee won't be our problem anymore."

"You say that, but she loves you like a sister, and you love her right back, you can't hide it. She trusts the rest of our team, too. Her big, rowdy cousins. Family ties don't just get cut."

She winced, not sure how to reply. The door opened. Chenoa hustled out, face as flushed as if she'd been halfway to her destination when she had to change course.

She took in the two loiterers. "Oh! Uh."

"It's all right," said Apama. "No one saw anything."

The young woman smiled with flustered gratitude and self-consciously checked her hair and face in a hand mirror. Did she carry one with her everywhere? Not unlike Bartholomew but without his acumen. The 'Litos and Chenoas of the universe didn't move through ruling circles where performance was a political weapon.

"Thanks, eh?" Chenoa hurried off down the passageway while fumbling at her half-fastened clothes. Apama did not turn to look into the darkened lounge where 'Lito was laughing and Teegee was giggling so sweetly Apama thought her heart might break. How would the girl cope with the end of her adventure? Maybe they hadn't done her any favors. Yet having heard that giggle, Apama couldn't regret it. The door swept shut, cutting off the lounge.

Gurak said, "Are we going to get in trouble for this?"

"Who will know, if we don't tell them? They can't read minds."

He gave her a diffident look. "You know, if we weren't on the job and you being an officer and me enlisted, I'd have . . . asked you out."

"You're a good man, Gurak."

"Ouch. That let me down politely."

After her months on Anchor she'd gotten better at this kind of awkward talk, even devised pat answers. "Lancer pilots partner with their lancers. I spend half my time with eyes closed running through battle simulations. I'm not that much fun."

His jaw had set, and she guessed him to be embarrassed. "Maybe. I appreciate the trust you showed in the Se Xar clan. It's an honor to serve the Council."

"Just make sure 'Lito keeps his mouth shut. He means well, but he's going to get drunk someday and spill."

"No one will believe him."

The door opened and Carmelito swanned out, wearing only a sleep skirt. "Who needs belief? They need only look and admire."

"Get your fucking clothes on," snapped Gurak. "By all the saints, 'Lito. Who do you think is going to board this ship the instant we transition into T-Harbor?"

"Maybe I can get a date? They say special *forces* are called that for a reason."

"Get out!" Gurak good-naturedly slapped the back of his head.

Carmelito grinned as he trotted away.

Apama called into the room as the door closed. "You have five minutes."

"You okay?" Gurak asked, watching her restless shifting.

She was fretting about her mom. The long voyage had included eleven beacon drops and four knnu passages. But although Teegee had been in communication with the Rider Council whenever they were in a beacon system, her sire had never passed on any greetings from her mother or mentioned her at all, even though Apama had asked. He was a bully. A manipulator. She hated him. But she could never let Zakurru know. She had to smile and pretend.

"I'm glad I didn't live back in olden days, before the beacons. Back then a person like me would have never have had the chance to leave the habitat where she was born."

Gurak shrugged with self-mockery. "I never had that wanderlust. I'd've been content on a Titan going about my business year after year. I like routine. But you're a lancer pilot, so routine isn't the life for you."

"I won't forget what you and the team have done for her. The risks you took."

"We are all destined for death, ma'am."

"Shut up with the 'ma'am.' I'm not anyone's officer out here."

He gave a salute, she answered with a rude gesture, and they parted companionably as he headed back to the barracks.

She tapped the panel comms. "Can I come in?"

"Affirmative. Lock the door behind you."

The starscape lounge was dim, and a bit musky in scent although the fans had been turned to high. A fully dressed but hoodie-down Teegee was collecting cushions strewn over the floor.

Apama helped her tidy up. "Seems like Chenoa never guessed."

"I don't think so. It would be a lot to expect, wouldn't it? She sewed me a silk balaclava and said it would be more comfortable for the sensitive burned part of my skull and the back of my neck while leaving my face bare. Isn't that sweet?"

"I'm sorry this has to come to an end for you."

The girl stared at the neat pile of cushions she'd made. Her two faces were expressions chasing in counterpoint: a smile against a frown, an anxious wink against a steady stare.

Tadukhipa spoke first. "I don't regret this at all but I'm ready to be back. The bubble is hard for me. I miss the radiance. This world is so dark. I'm sorry, Gee. It's not fair to you to be stuck with me all your life."

"Yeah, but I am," said Giolla in a tone that might have been affection or might have been angry resignation.

Apama took all four of their hands. "I need to know you two are okay with each other, and with what is coming next."

"What is coming next?" they asked in tandem.

The chime rang again. Lights dimmed to red. The hull shook with a grinding noise, a rough entry through the heliopause. Both women grabbed for one of the low-grav bars. Their feet left the deck. Apama floated, enjoying the ride until her feet thumped back to the deck as the mini-Titan and its tow chain reentered ordinary space. Tadukhipa gasped. Her lipless mouth opened as if she were taking a breath, as if she hadn't been able to breathe for days.

"I'm here," she whispered. "I hear you."

Giolla wiped a tear from an eye but she smiled, too. Sad. Happy. Complicated.

The seal over the window blinked green. They released the lock and together peeled it back. Apama got her first glimpse of home in years.

Knnu anchors could be laid anywhere in the outer heliosphere of a star system, usually at a convenient transfer point near an outer planet with a beacon in orbit. In Harbor System the anchor had been sited close to Tranquility Harbor, a massive linked complex of orbiting ship-yards, wharves, industrial parks, and a cylinder habitat whose fields supplied food.

T-Harbor sat in the L-4 point of a gas giant well away from the system's big red star. A beacon was anchored to the planet, called the Sea That Has Become Known for its endlessly swirling atmosphere, but wasn't visible from the window. Tranquility Harbor had been given its name because this beacon linked to the Tranquility System, the fourth-most-populous system in the empire with an astounding two Destiny-class planets, the only known system with such a bounty. Whether via Argosy or beacon, to reach Tranquility, and more distant systems like Sogdia Limit, you had to pass through T-Harbor. Strategic importance made T-Harbor a vital crossroads, even though the system lacked habitable planets or moons. It was a gateway opening in three crucial directions.

"Magnify Docklands," said Apama.

A big ring habitat came into focus, its ragged edges indicating where explosions had torn away compartments and buildings and wharfs. A constant stream of salvage traffic was still going on after thirty years as the damaged area was dismantled and removed to reinforce and rebuild elsewhere. Uneven layers of restored habitat marked the Dregs, where she had grown up like so many others, scrambling to survive. Some never left Docklands. Some never wanted to leave but were forced to go. Some left and never returned.

"What is that ring habitat?" Giolla asked. "It looks like a wreck."

"It's home." Telemetry from the freighter's sensors caught up to the window. An up-to-the-minute view of the local area within ten thousand klicks streamed into focus. "Holy Arthas!"

Gee wrinkled her brows as she tried to figure out what Apama was referring to, then turned her head so Tee could see too. "What is it?"

"There's a dreadnought and five cruisers waiting for you, Teegee. That's quite a parade. Oh look! A command ship, too. You've gotten fancy in your old age."

"Oh. Gosh." She wrung her hands. "You'll stay with me, right?"

"Oh, honey." She hadn't realized it would hurt so much. "You know the Incorruptibles will take you back to the creche. I'll do my best to stay in contact. That's all I can promise."

The girl flung herself at Apama, crushing her body into hers as she began to cry.

"We made it," said Apama through her own tears. "We got you home. You better say goodbye to the others before the Incorruptibles get here."

The leave-taking was a saints-blessed necessity because it made the hours pass as they waited for the tow chain to release them and an official shuttle to arrive. The freighter's crew looked shocked when the airlock opened and a squad of Incorruptibles entered with weapons ready. They were too intimidated to ask questions as an admiral walked down the line of Gurak and the Se Xar security team and thanked them one by one for their dedicated service to the Council and the empire. Even Carmelito was too overwhelmed to posture. There would be a substantial credit recorded in the name of the company and clan, and an offer of Batillipes Syndicate backing. How had Batillipes shouldered its way into this notable moment, Apama wondered. They hadn't been so influential before, had they?

The answer came after their shuttle journey to the command ship *Stalwart Truth*. This squad of Incorruptibles had come from the creche on Anchor where most of the children were raised. Giolla chattered excitedly with the soldiers, all of whom she knew. Tadukhipa also was glad to see them in her less effusive way. But the squad stayed formal. They didn't joke with the girls as the Se Xar security team had, family style. Gee's excitement tempered as she realized the casual atmosphere she'd gotten used to on the freighter had evaporated.

Not one Incorruptible spoke to Apama. She had a seat in the back, a row to herself, like a prisoner. Once they reached the command ship, she walked at the back of the column as they made their way to the residential core. Its entry bristled with more Incorruptible guards as well as ecstatic creche stewards. The true welcoming committee waited in the lounge, as she'd suspected it would.

She spotted Zakurru immediately the way a lancer pilot must identify hostiles amid a range of possible threats. Besides the Incorruptibles admiral there was a Tanarctus admiral and a Batillipes admiral. A lot of big guns. It took her that long to register there was another person in the room who waited quietly at the back with her usual indomitable patience. She was dressed simply, not as for a performance, but the costly fabric and exquisite tailoring and cosmetic styling emphasized her beauty, as if Rana were a trophy to be displayed.

"Mom!" Apama took impulsive steps toward her, only to have her mother signal a halt with a shift of a hand. Shaking as she fought down dread, Apama faced her sire.

"Zakurru. My thanks. I did not think you would come yourself to collect us."

"Tadukhipa has shown great courage as well as a maturity beyond her years. And you, Apama, have displayed a true lancer pilot's ability to spin survival out of a dead end. You will receive a commendation."

"And a return to the *Strong Bull*?"

"The *Strong Bull* was captured by the Chaonians, I am sorry to say."

"Captured?" The words hit like a punch to her sternum.

"Its torch drive was badly damaged. Our ships in retreat did not have time to blow it up before they had to depart Hellion Terminus. So, yes, the Chaonians captured it. What happened after that we don't know. But that was a year ago."

In her mind she could see the battle at Karnos as if it were yesterday. In other ways the memory had faded as if the battle's fireflies had sparked and died a lifetime ago. Her entire sense of time had been utterly disconnected from the ordinary round of life that had gone on without her. "What is our current force condition? What has happened in the last year? You could have passed on news via Teegee."

"Tee? Gee?"

The dislocation of his question, his prim disapproval, was like hitting a wall. Bam. That path shut. "Through Tadukhipa."

His supercilious expression reminded her of how much she loathed him. Dasa hadn't looked at her once. "Yes, we could have, Apama. But what if you had been captured? We could not take the chance of your captors having access to Rider-sent information they would not themselves receive for many months, could we now?"

She should have known better. The journey had made her sloppy, no matter how many times she had run simulations through her head. "Of course not."

"Never mind it, you've done well for the most part," he said with condescending magnanimity. "We will return to Anchor."

"And then?" she asked. "I don't even know what happened after the battle. Did Baragesi get away?"

"He did, I am pleased to say. Although wounded. He recovered and is currently in Anchor dealing with a bit of troublesome syndicate uproar as we assemble a large enough force to put an end to this Chaonian stunt once and for all. Sun has overreached, and we have her trapped in a perfect position. Once we put the proper hammer together, we will crush her and her pretensions. I'll assign you an adjutant to brief you on current force conditions. You have received a promotion to captain."

She glanced at her mom, who gave a shake of the head in warning.

"Thank you, Zakurru. Will I get an assignment to the front lines?"

"You remain more valuable to the Council in other ways." He gestured toward the Tanarctus and Batillipes admirals, who eyed her as if she were the last piece of scrumptious flan on the dessert platter. "I feel sure you have been out socializing with some of the lively young people of Tanarctus and Batillipes Syndicates."

"Sure." The admirals' calculating expressions pressed like a weight on her flesh. "Angursa not along for the ride?"

"Angursa? Ah, that's right. A year ago Paulo was pushing his fourth child on you, wasn't he?"

His tone implied Angursa had fallen out of favor. They'd been in trouble before, hadn't they? "I liked Bartholomew. Never a dull moment with him, and he dresses so well and knows every intricate step of every festival procession."

"You shall wish to avoid his overtures in the future. We shall discuss these details later. There is to be a celebratory feast in an hour. You will get properly dressed. Your mother is waiting to greet you."

Another might have hesitated, or asked for permission only to have it denied, but she wasn't a lancer pilot for nothing. "Tadukhipa. Giolla. Come over and meet my mother. I've told you so much about her."

Teegee was so accustomed to Apama's big-sister routine that she forgot to seek permission from Zakurru. She simply trotted over as everyone stared in shock at this breach of protocol. Zakurru's eyes slit long, and his mouth went flat. Apama grabbed Teegee's wrist and dragged her to the far wall before her mom could gesture another prudent warning. Fuck warnings. She'd earned this, by the grace of Saint Arthas.

"Mom, I specially wanted you to meet because I hope you'll have a chance to see Tadukhipa and Giolla again." She pitched her voice low so the rest couldn't hear.

"She told us so much about you, we're so glad to meet you," said Gee in a rush with a big, goofy, nervous grin, and Tee whispered shyly, "Can you call us Teegee? In private, I mean? In case it's not allowed."

Rana's gaze shot to Apama's face. She had the gift of searching fast and hard for truth and she got it, grasping Teegee's lowers as if they were already family.

"Rana!" cried Apama's sire at this violation of creche formality.

The stewards stiffened, gazes flashing from Zakurru to Teegee to Rana and back to Zakurru.

"Of course, Teegee," said Rana with her most welcoming smile, as if she hadn't noticed the sudden chill in the room. "I hope we will have an opportunity to become better acquainted. Although I'm sorry you had to put up with Apama for so long. She's incredibly difficult, don't you agree?"

Apama snorted.

Teegee looked alarmed, and then puzzled, and then both sets of her eyes widened and she said, "You are joking. Like, making a joke. Like Apama does."

"Yes, it's my sad but effective way of coping. I am so glad you are safe, my dear. My door is always open, if you can reach it." She released the girl's hands as a steward finally hustled over to shepherd the young Rider back into the grasp of the creche. The steward gave Rana a tiny dip of the chin, almost like a silent message of solidarity.

Grabbing one of Apama's lowers tightly with one of her own, Rana murmured, "Thank the saints, my dear girl. I thought I'd lost you." Tears shimmered in her eyes.

"Didn't he tell you where we were?"

Rana's smile altered to one softer and oh so disturbing. She spoke past Apama, and Apama didn't need to turn to know that someone was coming up behind her. "Ah, Zakurru. I have Apama's new uniform laid out and ready, although I'm concerned it might be a little loose. Were they not feeding you properly, my dear girl?"

"Mom! They were fine, and the food was fine," she said loudly. "The Hatti crew on the freighter are good people. They never suspected the truth. The Se Xar security team risked their lives to save us. Not to mention the lancer pilots who sacrificed themselves to aid our escape."

The figure of Laranthir was in her duffle, in case she could return it to Greensleeves. Had she and Fry-baby survived?

Zakurru placed himself between her and her mother. She wasn't sure if it were Zakurru or Dasa who took hold of Rana's wrist. Maybe it was both, for Dasa's gaze darted toward Teegee as the girl was led out a door by the stewards. He stared at her back as he sometimes stared at a ruined page of calligraphy before he angrily ripped up the rice paper and started anew. How much trouble had she gotten her mother in?

Zakurru said, "I have bad news for you, Apama. We received word recently that Admiral Manu was confirmed dead in fighting in the Trinity Coalition."

Manu was dead? Horribly, her first sensation was relief. Then shame for thinking ill of the dead, followed by a disorienting seesaw of puzzlement. "The Trinity Coalition? Why would there be fighting in the Trinity Coalition?"

"Is that all you have to say about the death of an honorable man and steadfast ally? I am disappointed. A steward will show you to your stateroom and help you make yourself presentable for the feast. You have an hour to get ready."

"I can help her," said her mom. "I'll like to. I haven't seen her for a year."

"Rana, you'll attend me. We already discussed this, did we not?"

Her mom's gaze dipped toward the floor, slid toward Apama and then away, and finally returned to meet Zakurru with a calm smile. "Of course we discussed it. Naturally I have been overwhelmed by seeing my daughter again after so long, and not knowing what had become of her."

Had he let her mom dangle cruelly in the wind for over a year?

Now was not the time. She dropped a kiss on her mother's cheek before anyone could stop her and, without looking back, left the room accompanied by a young lieutenant and an elderly steward.

How could she ever have thought Riders were all the same? But how could anyone know what individual Riders were like when the Council spent their lives as strangers to those they ruled? Separation was a choice, not a requirement.

"Captain, this way." The steward showed her to a stateroom with its own partitioned-off lavatory and shower. A pressed uniform with captain's bars and lancer insignia hung ready. "Do you need any help dressing?"

"Could you get me some barako? There wasn't any available on the voyage, and I've been craving it."

"Of course, Captain." The steward withdrew.

Apama turned to the lieutenant, who was young to be so well connected that she was allowed into the inner circle of Council advisors and adjutants without being an Incorruptible. "And you are?"

"Lieutenant Angelika Ru Ruan de Batillipes. The admiral is my uncle."

The influence of the Batillipes Syndicate had indeed risen substantially in the last year. Apama had to get her hands on the controls so she could be ready to fly. "I have a feeling we may be spending a lot of time together. We'll be adjutants together."

The young woman grinned with what Apama hoped was excitement. "Everyone's been talking about how you saved Rider Tadukhipa. I guess if anyone could manage it, it would be a lancer pilot."

"Most of the credit goes to the Se Xar clan, who risked their lives and livelihood to get us here. Please, in private call me Apama. I suppose your work colleagues call you RuRu."

The lieutenant laughed. "Of course they do. My family and friends call me Jelly."

"Angelika. Jelly. I like it, but there must be a story behind that nickname."

"The way I'd stuff myself with coconut pandan as a girl. To be honest, I still do."

The lieutenant was relaxing. Apama knew exactly how stressful it was to get dumped into the hothouse politics of Council and Exchange when you were a flunky rather than a mover and shaker.

She stepped behind the partition and began to strip off her clothing. "I'm glad they assigned you to me to get me up to speed."

"What do you want to know?"

"To start with I'd like to get my lines of sight clear, see what I missed and the basics of how things stand." Apama kept her tone jovial. "Are Windworn and Sleepless still mined? Did we lose Hellion Terminus? What happened to the *Strong Bull*? Did we counterattack at Karnos or is it still in Chaonian hands? What is our current war footing? What happened in Trinity?"

"Wow. Okay. I'll give you a rundown while you change. To start with, the Chaonians murdered the Trinity rulers and imposed their own authority there. Then they advanced into Mishirru."

"*Mishirru?* What happened to our garrison and fleet there?"

"They were withdrawn in advance of the Chaonian arrival. No point in fighting a battle when instead we can keep the queen-marshal and her fleets pinned up in Mishirru. They're cut off both in communications and travel time from home except by Argosy, and that takes forever. Scuttlebutt is the Council has long nurtured a secret plan to kill the republic from within, by creating a succession crisis. Sun is months away from Chaonia even once she decides to return. I don't have details, but from something Rider Zakurru let drop while we were waiting for your ship to dock, it sounds like the operation is well underway."

78

This Is How the Wily Persephone Finds Herself at Port Khayzuran Trying to Break up a Fight in a Bar

The queendom of Mishirru does love a party.

And Sun knows how to throw a party at which she is both the centerpiece and yet also only one among many whirling objects. It started with a grand parade welcoming her back to Destiny after the journey to the Gyre. She stood—no sitting for her!—atop a barge that rocked way too much as she and her seven loyal Companions sailed along the river that runs down the spine of the city Everlasting, pride of Destiny. One arm raised, she greeted the cheering troops and singing locals who massed the shoreline for klick upon klick upon klick. I was the person throwing up over the stern of the barge. What a way to find out I had developed an acute case of labyrinthitis.

So even though I don't like resting for long periods of time because I need to keep moving, it was a relief when Sun called for a twenty-eight-day celebratory arts competition. Modeled on Idol Faire, the contest includes local luminaries like the illusionist Seven Masks as well as Chaonian favorites, like Ji-na, who have accompanied the fleet from the beginning of the campaign. The official description touted by the Idol Historian is that in order to thank the population of Mishirru for so generously hosting the Chaonian military for over two! hundred! days! of rest, recreation, and training, the contest is to be held in various venues across Mishirru's fourteen star systems. Of course Sun has another object besides her love of the arts. There are two beacon paths that connect Mishirru to the heartland of the empire, one via Aila System and one via Sena System. All the huge gatherings and the mass movements of local crowds from one system festival to the next help disguise the transfer of troops and ships piece by piece to these two frontier systems.

This is how I find myself at Port Khayzuran trying to break up a fight in a bar.

In the language of Mishirru they call a drinking establishment with a stage a "garden of joy," which sounds like a very different activity to me. But at the moment in this garden of joy a bunch of rowdy, drunk spacers are facing off against a bunch of rowdy, drunk Guards with the usual insults about which branch of service is faster, stronger, better, and more crucial to Chaonia's mighty victories.

Makinde and I are standing between, arms extended, palms out, trying to keep the two seething masses apart. That's when I notice something even worse out of the corner of my eye. Over by the stage, uninvolved in the standoff, Candace flips open one of her battle fans with a look on her face that is bad news.

"Oh shit," I say intelligently. "Mak, keep this lot apart."

I race down the narrowing gap between the shouting hordes, dodge between tables, and reach Candace in time to grab her elbow before she strikes. Her target is a drunken colonel. He wears Yele insignia, a member of our allied forces.

"Candace! Stop!" I yell before she slices off his nose.

There's an instant where I think she is going to spin and cut off *my* nose, but with a flick of her wrist she snaps shut the blade-edged fan. Her expression is rigid, teeth gritted, eyes wild. "He grabbed Ji-na's ass without permission!"

"The hells he did!" I punch him in the face, and he reels back a solid step before easily righting himself.

"She's a performer! That's part of the job!" the colonel protests.

"Maybe in Yele, but not in Chaonia!" Candace shakes the closed fan at him. I don't think he knows what it is, but he finally registers her insignia and turns his eyes to my insignia. Not that we Companions are flashy, mind you. Core Houses don't flaunt their status in public. The citizens don't like it, for one thing, and it's considered a sign of insecurity among the House-born. But the message is there, loud and clear.

He takes three big steps back as he realizes what I am. My status is a bigger punch to the face than my weak-ass jab.

With the jolly roar of veterans who have been out of battle for too many months, the two sides leap forward and collide. The space erupts into a full-on melee. What happened to Baby Mak?

I'm too short to see over the surge and stumble of the slugfest. I run over to the stairs that lead up onto the stage. Ji-na has retreated to stand with her back against the railing. She's clutching her sticks, ribbons unspooled messily at her feet. Her flowing lace skirt is torn. I wish I'd punched that jerk harder but I don't have time to say anything to her as I race up the stairs to the stage.

A hapless troupe of jugglers are being thoroughly ignored as they gamely continue their deft routine. Their mouths move in rehearsed patter, but I can't hear a word. An ocean of riotous movement swirls along the main floor. Locals stare down from the balcony tiers, watching the eruption. I can't tell if they are offended or entertained. Maybe they think it is part of the contest. Where is Makinde? Has he survived two major battles only to be trampled to death in a boozed-up brawl?

On Chaonia I could just shout through Channel Idol because every personal net and every hovering wasp is part of the overarching web of communication or, as my family would call it, oversight and surveillance. But this is Mishirru so we don't have that kind of coverage. We are dependent on local physical networks like sound systems. I grab a mic stand and yell words into its bulbous depths, but it's turned off so it's mere shouting into a whirlwind.

In fact there's a whirlwind cutting a path across the tumultuous floor, only it is not whirling, it is Sun with Isis and a squad of marines opening a path, Hetty at her side, and Solomon bringing up the rear with another squad of marines. Sun hops up on the stage, grabs the mic out of my hand, looks at it, finds the on/off switch, and triggers a burst of feedback so horrible that everyone in the auditorium ducks and flinches, covering their ears.

She looks over the crowd. There is something in her that expands to fill these moments. What are we tiny humans but gnats soon to die unnoticed beneath an indifferent star? It is Sun who holds in herself a gravity that bends the light and mass of our existence to her.

"Stand tall, good citizens! It is only a harsh noise. Are you so eager for battle that you cannot restrain yourselves for one night? Who doubts your courage? Not I! But perhaps I doubt your discipline! Come. Sing with me, so we can remind ourselves of who we are."

The jugglers include a ukulele player, since ukuleles became fashionable among Idol Faire groups after Alika's win. Sun isn't an accomplished instrumentalist but she can creditably strum basic chords for an accompaniment. Her singing voice isn't memorable but it is tuneful and on pitch. She takes the ukulele and launches into Alika's signature song, whose refrain every Chaonian knows: "Wherever you stand, be the soul of that place."

The locals stand out of respect, and with each subsequent chorus more and more join in, even if they are only humming the melody. The brawl has evaporated and in its place several thousand humans link arms in solidarity as they sing.

A hand grabs my elbow and pulls me around. "Hey! Don't call me Mak. It's Makinde."

I press a palm to his baby-face cheek because I know it annoys him and also because I'm genuinely relieved. "Oh, thank goodness. I thought you'd been trampled to death."

His expression changes, mouth gaping as he stares at something going on behind me. I turn to look. At the base of the stage stairs, Candace has enfolded Ji-na in an embrace. They kiss the way lovers do after a narrow escape.

"Wait. What? I thought Ji-na was with . . . had a thing for . . . Alika."

I withdraw my hand in genuine dismay. "You thought Ji-na was following the fleet because she has a crush on Alika? Whew. My young friend. You are too innocent. Or too something."

"You really are an asshole, did you know that?"

"I had no idea!"

"Unbelievable." He adds, "Has it been those two all along?"

"I wasn't with Sun before the ill-fated wedding banquet, but I believe 'it' budded its first tender yearnings the Idol Faire prior, yes, the one that our handsome Alika won. It was the first year Candace was his cee-cee."

Because I'm looking at the stairs I am looking toward the back wall of the auditorium. To my surprise, I see Ti over by one of the fire exits, which is shaped as a gaudy arch carved to resemble a vulva. Really? A vulva? No, no, it's just me translating. It's a stylized calla lily.

Ti signals *Come*. She's wearing what I call one of her I-am-just-an-ordinary-person outfits, a russet brown work tunic over a skin suit in case of a breach.

"Hold down the fort," I say to Makinde. There are fifteen more verses to go, one for each of the republic's star systems.

As I cross the stage toward the stairs, Solomon asks in sign if I want him to attend but I sign a negative in return. I've known this moment is coming ever since we boarded Port Khayzuran. Ti hands me a light coat to pull on over my uniform. We walk side by side down an exit passageway toward the habitat's main concourse.

"This is about the triplets?" I ask.

"Yes. They were among those who wanted out of the indenture contract. Their situation was complicated because they have no point of origin."

"No point of origin? They appeared as if from the foam of the sea?"

"More or less."

"Did the genetic results come in?"

"They did. It rules out cosmetic surgery. They really are identical triplets."

I nod because I'm wise like that. "So it's possible they are clones from Nona's lab or there were other cloning labs operating in Trinity in violation of universal law."

"It's possible. If they were identical triplets, then why no point of origin? No planet, no moon, no habitat, no ship. Their indenture listing doesn't show up until they first appear in the accounts, aged thirteen. There's no transaction event. No payout to an intermediary as with people who appear in the accounts as a result of being captured for ransom by pirates. They abruptly appear in Exotic House's list of drones."

We merge with the foot traffic on the concourse. Port Khayzuran is a set of connected habitats, including a shipyard, an industrial park, an extensive docking platform, defensive armaments, and the main habitat with a permanent population of one million as well as temporary residents and travelers passing through. In normal times Sena System is one of two major entry points where people can say they have left the empire and entered Mishirru. There is not a trace of Phene iconography in the public spaces; either there never was, or the locals tore it all down when Sun arrived.

I'm shaking, clinging to Ti's elbow like we are sisters or partners or lovers.

"Are you all right?" she asks.

"Brawl. Excitement. Scared. What if they came from Nona's lab? What does that mean for me?"

We cross an open concourse with a transparent ceiling. The view is disorienting, because the ceiling's up is really down onto the planet of Sena Prime. It's a bland world with marginal surface water, nothing to write home about, although people live there for all the reasons people prefer to live on planets. After three thousand years of carbon splitting, electrolysis, and massive planting programs, the air is breathable, and that's a big advantage compared to the risk of being exposed to airless vacuum. The entire Second Fleet is now in-system together with the Eighth Fleet, but tiny ships are impossible to see against the immensity of space.

What we can see are the docks where Sun has put strict controls on civilian traffic. The Jorsha Beacon winks in the far distance, poised on the night cusp of the planet. One of two routes into the empire from Mishirru.

For now, Sun is allowing trade ships to go on to Jorsha after inspection for fugitives, military targets, and interdicted materials. It's in her interest to allow passage, because that way she can be sure the other side hasn't been mined. So far for every ship we allow through, they send one over, like a game of Red Rover. There have been no ambuscades, no tricks, just desperate merchants and delayed travelers and once a cohort of librarians headed for the Gyre and once a party of devoted pilgrims on their very long way to Entering the Waters Temple on Congress Moon, all wearing beacon badges like the one I purchased on Yele Prime.

Did the Phene decide against mining Jorsha because of its trade importance? What if they months ago decided to remove the mines at Windworn and Sleepless as a matter of imperial policy that spread to all their systems in a Rider instant? The Rider Council knows where Sun is. But news of events in Karnos will take months to get to us roundabout via Trinity Coalition.

Ti guides me into a transport pod linked to the string of habitats. We skim a surprisingly long fifty-seven klicks to Port Chaucer, a habitat for temporaries awaiting transit permits and cargo inspections.

"The campaspe unit was moved here with the Second Fleet," Ti explains. "I've arranged to meet the triplets in a public place to assess their situation."

We disembark onto a port ring where people are standing in lines, waiting to get permission to go somewhere. After a short tube ride, we enter a market concourse. Here it is the deck, not the dome, that is transparent. The planet floats below my feet as if I am walking like a god above a vulnerable world. Given the way no one seems to be giving the view a second glance, I am the only one who finds this strange.

In Chaonia, a busy marketplace and public gathering zone would be saturated with Channel Idol 3-D pillars and virtual screens playing at all hours with updates as well as streams of the ongoing Idol Faire performances. There is no embedded public network. Instead, there is a round stage in the center available for live performances. No troupe is performing now, but children are dancing around the stage's oval in groups whose size ebbs and flows as individuals leave and others arrive.

Ti's gaze drifts that way. "That's one of the dances in Mishirru's version of the Landfall story. But see those three children there? That's a new dance. It represents Sun freeing Mishirru from the empire's heavy hands. It's very clever how they use gesture to represent the four arms of imperial Phene."

Dance is more Ti's thing than mine. Normally I'd be interested in how the queendom eschews the virtual in favor of the physical and communal, but right now I'm checking out the packed marketplace. It is crowded and noisy, people in constant motion. Scents and sound sweep over me: the smell of baked 'ulu, the laughter of carefree youth, elders seated at tables playing senet while loiterers give advice.

Ti tugs on my wrist. "I see them. Wait here while I make contact. I'll wave you over."

I find an empty bench and sit, pretending to watch the jubilant antics on the stage while keeping Ti's progress in my line of sight. I don't spot the triplets until she reaches a juice stand. There they are, turning to greet her with wary expressions. I telescope in to study their faces. They've made no effort to disguise their similarity. Height: same. Weight and facial contours: same. Only hair length differs, and even that appears gradated for visual value: short, medium, long. They watch each other as much as they watch Ti. There is something unsettlingly familiar about them even though I am sure I have never seen them before. Did one of the corpses at Nona's lab look like an older version?

Someone sits beside me. Where did my training go? I didn't even notice a body approach. I paste a smile on my face as I shift to check the new arrival, and find myself looking at Princess Metis.

Princess Metis? Why would Sun allow her notoriously environment-sensitive cousin onto an uncontrolled, chaotic concourse? Where are her handlers? I'm so startled that another individual sits on my other side before I realize I'm surrounded.

When I turn, I am looking at Princess Metis. Oh shit.

It's that moment when a hard shove on your back sends you tumbling down the slippery slope of awakening and it is too late by the time your eyes open.

"He wants to see you," says Metis One.

"We are to bring you," says Metis Two.

They speak Common Yele with the refined lilt of the League.

I ping Sun on my ring, subvocalizing a message.

EMERGENCY. KIRAN IS HERE.

GO TO HIM. Sun's reply is immediate. TRACKING YOU.

HE HAS CLONES OF—

Metis One twists my wrist back so hard it breaks my line of thought as I croak in pain. At that moment I realize how much bigger they are, robust, strong, and with the expressions of people who don't see any humanity in me or at least nothing they care about protecting. They are just following orders.

She says, "Take off the ring or our cousins will kill your companion." Cousins?

Oh the hells. The triplets *are* from Nona's lab. And they have Tiana.

"You have three seconds," says Metis Two. "One. Two . . ."

My heart goes cold. My fingers fumble clumsily as I wrestle off the ring. I am just about to ask how they know about the ring when a needle-prick stabs into my arm. A hot sting flows under my skin. My hand spasms, and the ring falls. My lips go numb. I struggle to my feet, swaying. I must warn Ti, call or gesture . . .

Arms embrace me.

"Come along, little cousin," says one Metis in a voice pitched strangely loud as the other Metis scoops up the ring, thank goodness. "You drank too much, didn't you? We better take you home and put you to bed."

The noise of the marketplace smears into static. The planet staggers past beneath my nerveless legs. I am paralyzed, boots bumping on the ground like a puppet's. Saliva smears on my lips as I try to get a word out. What happened to Ti? Oh gods, what if she is dead? Walls converge around us. A hatch opens. A bright light recedes in front of me, growing smaller and smaller until its dot snaps out and takes the universe with it.

79

We Are Already Wandering Ghosts

This time Kurash arrived at Best Price Traps & Drains with a habitat administrator in tow and backup consisting of Ay, Esen's squad, and the captain's blessing for the operation. The entire crew of the *Huma* knew what was going down, and they were waiting expectantly on the ship to see what happened.

A bell chimed as he and Ay walked in. The proprietor glanced his way. "We close in fifteen minutes—" She broke off. Her expression tightened. "*You!* Get out!"

The administrator entered with a nervous look around before setting a tablet on the counter. "I have a writ of cooperation. Are you the proprietor listed here?"

She stared at the tablet, at the administrator, at Kurash, at Ay in her fleet uniform, at the door where Esen had taken an intimidating stance. "What is this?"

Kurash said, "I am here to speak to your employees."

"They're not back yet. A big job—"

"I'll wait. While we are waiting, give me the leash trigger you wear."

She sputtered. "I was granted a permit for this tool by the habitat council."

The administrator tapped the screen impatiently. "Read the writ. The council has revoked your permit."

"What? You do the bidding of the Chaonians now? Roll over and lick their balls?"

"The Chaonians restored our old council system instead of installing their own syndicate governor like the empire did. This isn't a request. I have the authority to revoke your business license if you don't cooperate."

The proprietor slipped a strap off her wrist and slammed it angrily onto the counter. The administrator picked it up as if it were a wrathful snake and offered it to Kurash. He took it.

He did not want to threaten the proprietor, precisely, but she had to understand that it was over. He had learned from his encounter on the wheelship. He had learned from the mission to Pelasgia Terce. No leash controlled him except honor and loyalty. He had the authority to do what he deemed was right, as long as it did not harm Sun or violate his principles.

The proprietor lasted thirty-eight seconds before she gave way and unlocked the panel to the back. The door still scraped, needing repair. The tiny room still stank of rancid grease, the smell so strong that both the administrator and Ay covered their noses and mouths. Only he went inside, hands open and empty except for the strap.

Sobers and Wüst had been sitting on their cots. They stood to confront the threat he posed. They wore the faded and worn duty coveralls all banner soldiers received on entering Phene service. Maybe these were their original set. Seeing him rather than the proprietor, they looked at each other.

He showed them the strap. "This is the leash trigger. Its use has been revoked. I can give it to you and go on my way, but there will be others who have such devices, so giving it to you does not free you."

"What do you want?" asked Wüst. "We already told you our situation."

"And I told you I would not forget you. I now have the means to offer you a new situation. Let me remove the leash from your neuronics."

"And then what?" Wüst gripped hands into fists. Sobers swallowed and licked scarred lips as if making ready for a last-stand battle.

"Then I would offer you a choice. You can be granted provisional citizenship in the Republic of Chaonia according to the normal legal process."

"Which involves?"

"Twenty years as a provisional citizen without breaking any laws and while engaging in some manner of betterment to the republic. Specifically, I can offer you a placement on the planet Pelasgia Terce working in salt production and its associated support services or in lichen farming. The work is hard. The islands are sparsely inhabited and desperate for more people. You would be treated as every other inhabitant."

"Not free to leave."

"Provisional citizenship does impose some restrictions, it's true. Are you free to leave this place?"

Sobers's head dipped, chin down. No.

Wüst said, "They'll just have a leash trigger there."

He drew the baton from its loop on his uniform belt. "This device cuts the leash. The leash trigger does not work on me. You saw that with your own eyes when I was here before."

"Let's say you're telling the truth about the leash. If the other choice is that we stay here, where we aren't allowed to stay except with an employer armed with a leash trigger, then you are not offering a choice if the council revokes our employer's permit for a leash trigger."

He indicated the strap, which neither had touched. "That is yours to use as you see fit. If you choose to stay here, you may abide by the habitat's rules and give the leash trigger back to the proprietor. The third choice is that you join the household of Queen-Marshal Sun. As a member of her household I have the authority to expand my retinue. You would accompany me."

Sobers snorted, but Wüst lay a hand upon the other's arm to quell the scorn. "And where are you going, Lieutenant?"

"I go where Sun needs me. For the moment, I have use of a frigate and the permission of its captain to bring you aboard."

"To bring us aboard with no leash?" Wüst's scoffing laugh was high-pitched and eerie. Sobers's was more of a ragged cough.

"Did I not already say my leash was removed? I walk in Chaonia without a leash. The captain did ask me what would happen if you went rogue. I said I did not believe you would, because you no longer fight for the Phene and have no reason to attack Chaonians. I also pointed out that you both are permanently injured. I can kill you, should it come to that, and I would if I were forced to it. If that is the surety you need to see that I am serious."

They considered his words in silence.

He went on. "You would have the duties of ordinary crew. You would work alongside the Chaonian spacers. You would be allowed to train in a specialty that could serve you later in civilian life. In addition, you would assist me in creating a fleet-wide personal fitness program to present to the queen-marshal, to replace the current training standards. You will find the crew of the *Huma* to be interested in you. They know me, so they won't fear you unless you give them reason to fear."

"If you remove the leash, we must give up our battle names."

"Yes, that is the price."

"Who are we, if we are not banner soldiers?"

"We are already wandering ghosts who can never return home. Any of us could have stepped out an airlock, but we did not."

He met Sobers's gaze first, then Wüst's. They did not flinch from the examination. They had accepted what it meant that they had chosen to stay biologically alive.

"I make this offer to the person within you who chose not to take that step. I don't want to leave you here. Anyone deserves better than being treated as shamefully as you are being treated here. You deserve to be treated with respect. Not just you. Not just me. There are others of us out there, I am sure of it."

"Many humans are treated with disrespect through no fault of theirs. But perhaps you mean other disgraced banner soldiers."

"We were not treated with honor by the Phene. We were treated as weapons to be used and then discarded once they were broken. The wheelships did not tell us the whole truth of the bargain they made. We do not deserve dishonor for believing what we were taught as children. For fighting when we were told it was the will of Lady Chaos that we die in order to serve."

He waited. After a moment, Sobers picked up the strap and stared at it, then handed it to Wüst. They both looked at the baton, which Kurash held not as a weapon but in the same manner symbols of the banners were displayed so people could identify with whom they belonged.

"This is not the path I expected to walk when I left home. I never thought to depart from the traditions of the wheelships and our grandparents. But I am content this also is a worthy voyage. Humans survived because they ventured into unknown territory, not because they resigned themselves to the fate created for them by others. I am not resigned. I try to be an honorable person. Will you join me?"

80

No One Ever Called the Wily Persephone Sweet

When I was little I contracted an illness, as children do. One night, in the throes of chills and sweats and bizarre patterned hallucinations, I woke to find my father seated at my sickbed. He had a bowl on his lap, and he was dabbing a cloth into the water and gently wiping my brow to cool me down just as every normal loving parent would do for their beloved small child.

Then I woke for real, on the Lee Estate in a medical bed with a retired military nurse in attendance. He told me stories about the fighting at Kanesh so hair-raising that later I wasn't sure if I'd dreamed those lurid tales or if he'd figured me out enough to know six-year-old me could only be distracted from my misery by tales so gruesome he made me promise never to tell anyone what he'd told me.

That is how I first met Kadmos.

When I woozily emerge into consciousness, I taste bile dried inside my mouth. My legs are sticky and prickly because I've peed myself. My eyes are stuck shut. My first thought is that at least Kadmos will be there to help me clean up. My second thought is that he is dead. No, he's not dead. He was working for Nona Lee all along. Even then, that long-ago day, he was working for her. Did he care for me at all or were Resh, Manea, and I just part of the job?

"What job?" a familiar voice asks.

A cloth dabs gently at my goo-encrusted eyes. I successfully pry open my lids and blink as my vision hazily returns. My father is seated next to me with a bowl of water in his lap and a damp cloth in one hand.

"It's not you," I say. "I'm hallucinating."

"Yes, like when you were six and caught the beacon sickness."

My body seizes up. Coughing racks me. I double over, hands clutched to my chest as I struggle to breathe. *Breathe.*

The coughs subside but adrenaline courses through my flesh. I am completely awake now, surging with frantic energy. I sit up.

"Beacon sickness?"

He hands me a glass of water. "Yes, it's one of the reasons Nona cloned herself."

"I thought she cloned herself because she is a self-centered asshole."

"That too," he says so casually I can tell he doesn't hear the jest in my tone, and I'm not really kidding, am I? "That branch of the Lee House lineage was susceptible to beacon sickness to the degree that an increasing number stopped traveling outside Chaonia System. As you can imagine, this restriction put a damper on their ability to make careers in the military and thus become prominent and respected at court."

"No wonder they like prisons."

"Lee House proved a natural fit to run the Ministry of Security, Corrections, and Punishment. Your aunt Moira never left Chaonia System, did you know that? I am sure she confessed to you that she was Eirene's favored Companion in their youth."

"She told me those were the most exciting days of her life. Maybe so, compared to the daily grind of supervising spies, torture, and extrajudicial killings as governor of Lee House." I take a sip of water, not sure if I'm dehydrated. Go slow. This is a lot to take in, if it is even true and not just a mind game to throw me for a loop.

"Becoming governor of Lee House was in her best interest, as it gave her an excuse to stay in-system. She might even have had the forbidden affair with Queen-Marshal Nézhā in order to be disgraced. If Eirene knew about the Lee House susceptibility to beacon sickness, then it explains why she trusted Moira."

I take a cautious sip. "Eirene knew Nona before the massacre and exile. Except she was ten or fifteen years younger than Nona. So if Eirene knew Manea was Nona's clone, wouldn't that be kind of creepy? Watching a child grow up into an adult you already know?"

He says nothing.

I go on. "It seems like a risk to raise the three of us so close together."

"You three girls were all given enough external differences—height, weight, hair color, and so on—that people only ever remarked on the strong family resemblance."

The water hits my stomach with turbulence. Too much, too soon. I breathe through the nausea as my mind churns, avoiding the titanosaurus in the room: Why is he being so nice to me? What purpose does this serve?

"Now that I think about it," I say, "Mother never left Chaonia system that I remember."

"Indeed she did not."

"You two didn't meet on Yele?"

"We did not, although she often told it that way later. Aisa is a fearful woman."

"Was," I correct.

He smiles fleetingly. "That's right. So much effort expended by the empire against Eirene, yet Aisa managed what no one else could. Narcissism is a powerful tool in the hands of the right wielder. She has gained the notoriety she felt she'd been denied, has she not? No one will ever forget her name."

His comments appall me. His calm demeanor. His analytical detachment. My own horrible, hateful relief that I don't have to interact with my mother ever again.

"But enough of Aisa, thank goodness. Nona is made of sterner stuff than her sisters, which is doubtless how she has outlasted them. She declared early on that she would rather die than be trapped. Like every other royal academy graduate, she shipped out at eighteen. She never displayed any sign she had caught beacon sickness from the passage."

"She had a child who died."

"Yes. She once told me it was a shock to her when her child caught the beacon sickness and died within seventy-two hours. As I said, that's why she cloned herself. Once she created a successful vat, she produced eight of you. Her legacy, if you will."

"Why only eight? Why not sixteen? Why not sixty-four?"

"Do not be facetious, Persephone. It does not suit you."

At moments like this, it is clear my father does not know me well. It's also obvious I don't know him at all well either, but I am determined to take advantage of his loquaciousness. "All the clones were deliberately taken on beacon passages to see if they had inherited Nona's resistance? Even knowing it might kill them?"

"Yes, that was part of the experiment. Most had no reaction. You and one other became ill, and you both recovered with no evident lingering effects."

I don't mention the visions I see inside the beacon passage. For the first time, I am sorry Nona's lab is gone. Except she said she had a backup somewhere in the Trinity systems. I have to keep my father talking.

"So Marduk doesn't have the propensity in his branch?"

"It's never shown up that I know of, not that they'd tell. Once the beacon sickness starts afflicting more than a statistically random percentage of the members of a descendent branch, it has been shown to metastasize into the next generations, and so that lineage becomes system bound."

"Or Argosy bound."

"Ah. Mm. That's true. The Argosies avoid beacon sickness by avoiding beacons. Regardless, Lee House censors all references to beacon sickness. It's rare enough that knowledge of it can be contained."

"Yes, I can see how people being scared of beacon travel might have put a damper on Eirene's martial ambitions, not to mention Sun's." I chance a sip of water to ease my throat. I have to ask before he decides he's said enough. "What about Metis? If Moira never left Chaonia System, then how did Metis get sick?"

"Ah." He places the bowl on a table. A flash of regret creases his mouth. "That was Aisa's doing. She lost her first child to beacon sickness and could not bear to see Moira happy with a child of her own. I should have understood what she meant to do, but I did not intervene until it was too late."

"It isn't as if you were stopping Resh and me from being sent through beacons to see what would happen. So really no different from Metis, is it?"

He takes the glass from my hand and sets it out of my reach. "Metis was a remarkably sweet little girl."

"Unlike me?"

"No one ever called you sweet," he says, not as a criticism but merely as a statement of fact.

"Wait, what about Percy?"

"Perseus is not genetically related to Nona, Moira, or Aisa."

It's like being punched in the face all over again.

Percy. My brother.

After two years with Sun I've learned how to absorb blows fast and keep moving. He's still my brother. He'll always be my brother.

"Is that why Mother never loved him?"

"Aisa never loved anyone except herself. Surely you understand that by now."

The ship has been humming and ticking around us. The texture of the sound changes as the beacon drive is engaged. I feel it in my bones. Of course I can. It all makes sense now. I lick dry lips. It's time to address the titanosaurus in the room.

"Why are you telling me all this now? What do you want from me?"

"Can I not merely wish to spend time with my daughter?"

"By kidnapping me?"

"The restrictions placed upon me at Lee House often got in the way of our relationship. But we may start afresh with new allies."

"The Metis clones are our new allies?"

"Considering how much you enjoyed playing connect-the-dots games as a child, I'm surprised to hear you ask me such a question."

"Give me a minute. This is a lot of new information to process. I assume you are still planning to try to assassinate Sun. So that would suggest you hope to put a Metis clone on the throne in place of the original Metis. Or is the person I saw in Lee House the original Metis? Maybe she's a clone, too?"

"She is the original Metis. The clones are younger. Nona and I hatched the idea when Metis came down with the beacon sickness and didn't recover."

"What a kind uncle you have been to her."

"I have done my best," he says as my sarcasm flies right over his head. "There is no need for her to be harmed. She can be placed in comfortable confinement."

"So you're saying the Metis clones I met didn't get beacon sickness?"

"All eight Metis clones caught the beacon sickness. Four died."

Which leaves four, two of whom I've met. He probably thinks Princess Metis is still on Chaonia Prime, and I can think of no way to probe for this information without giving away her whereabouts.

"I don't see what this has to do with me. Or where we are going now. Surely not back to Chaonia, which, I may remind you, is under the regency of Marduk and Prince João. Neither of them will be sympathetic to your goals."

"We are going to the empire."

"There's nothing for me in the empire."

"I can give you a throne. Don't you want a throne, Persephone?"

"A throne? Why would I want a throne?"

"When you and Perseus were little you used to parade around wearing a tiara while insisting that Perseus act as your loyal Companion. One time Eirene came unexpectedly to Lee House to visit Moira and she almost saw you in the tiara, which would have been a capital offense."

"For a little child playing pretend?"

"Any Core House is suspect, given Chaonia's violent history of assassination and factional disputes."

I can't argue with that. "What does that have to do with giving me a throne?"

"You will marry Metis and become queen-marshal."

"Wouldn't Metis become queen-marshal?"

"Yes, but you and I would rule through her."

The cunning nature of the plan grows more clear. "What an interesting proposition! May I ask a few clarifying questions?"

"I'd be disappointed if you did not."

"You plan to replace Princess Metis with one of the clones and put the real princess out to pasture in a locked, secret room. What happens to the other clones?"

"Placed in lifepod suspension, should they be needed later."

At least he isn't going to just murder the extras. But isn't that the entire point of clones? To have extras in case your beloved sister Ereshkigal dies in battle? She had all the personal qualities appropriate to a queen-marshal: courage, strength, aptitude, command, charisma, and the ability to connect with people. Did she suspect? Is that why she wanted to die rather than be a pawn in his schemes?

I will never speak to him about her. He doesn't deserve to share my grief.

"Those triplets. Are they from Nona's lab?"

"Yes. They were part of the taxes the Trinity demands from Nona in exchange for leaving her laboratory alone."

"Tiana said they were handed over to the pleasure house at thirteen. The criminality of cloning aside, that also violates established norms of law and decency. Grown folks preying on children."

"The Trinity makes its own laws."

"*Made* its own laws. Maybe you missed the finale, but the coalition is part of Chaonian territory now."

"For the short term. Sun has had more success than anyone could have predicted. Not impossible but certainly improbable. Her luck will run out."

Does he really think I am going to go along with all this? Does it tempt me? I have to be honest. It does not tempt me at all to be a puppet ruled by my father. But if I say no, I don't know what he will do, and that question might be the worst one of all. Am I disposable? Does he care about me at all? The one who wasn't sweet as a child.

Anyway, Sun gave me a mission to complete, so I will do my job.

"When do I get my ring back?"

"Why would you need your ring back?"

Check, as a chess player would say.

"How did you know the only way to remove the ring is to kill me, or for me to take it off voluntarily?"

"I was on Tjeker with the banner soldier."

"Of course you were." I touch my throat, all bruises gone although a tiny nodule scar remains beneath the skin.

"You displayed incredible cunning in the basilica to take the Gatoi out of the battle. At no small risk to yourself. I was impressed."

My face heats, warmed by his praise, but my mouth is dry and the glass of water stands just out of reach. "If I say no, will you kill me the way the Oculi agent killed Perseus, who was your son even if he wasn't genetically related to Lee House?"

"The agent was meant to kill Sun."

"That doesn't answer my question."

He stands. "Nona Lee and I made a deal a long time ago."

"There's a plan with a long view! One of her clones to grow up and marry a grown-up Metis clone. What happens if you lack a Nona clone? Does Nona still trust you? Or did you dissolve the compact when you sabotaged the lab?"

"No plan survives contact with the enemy. The essential fault of the Nona clones is their lack of compliance and deference."

"Manea is nothing if not compliant and deferential."

"You badly misunderstand her if you think so."

"So that leaves me as the chosen one?"

"I would have said so, before."

"Before what?"

"Before you chose Sun."

I've overplayed my hand. "I haven't chosen Sun."

"Of course you have, Persephone. As a child you made it clear you refused to give your loyalty to those you did not respect, but that when you did give your loyalty, you gave it completely. Your loyalty to Sun serves me well because Sun values loyalty. You have correctly ascertained that I no longer see my ties to Nona as necessary. Not when I have the backing of the Rider Council."

Keep him talking. "So you still hope to kill Sun. Then, with Phene backing, place the marshal's tiara on Metis's head, no one knowing the truth?"

"Sun will kill herself through her reckless audacity and excessive self-confidence. She can't possibly succeed if she throws herself against the empire."

"She already has."

He shakes his head with a scornful look for my lack of acuity.

"Piecemeal. She defeated an ill-judged attack at Molossia. She lucked out by facing a divided and arguing syndicate command at Karnos as well as a new Speaker who was too busy trying to placate all factions instead of installing a clear chain of command beneath a single competent admiral. Who the Council had willing and waiting, if they had only chosen to use Manu rather than throwing him away by not listening to his advice until it was too late. The Trinity had come to believe themselves untouchable and were not prepared for a coordinated military attack. And Mishirru? They opened the gates for Sun because it serves their goals, not because they care about her. Those are not triumphs. They are random accidents of fate."

He is the one with hubris, but I'm not about to tell him that.

He checks the back of his hand, then walks to the door.

A bell chimes. An automated voice speaks in Common Yele. "Set beacon stations. Transition in twenty minutes."

Fuck. We really are going into the empire.

I blurt out, "What about Tiana? Where is Tiana?"

"Tiana? Ah." He makes a soft *huh* of satisfaction. "You betray yourself."

Does he have Ti? Did he kill her? I lunge up from the bed, stumbling as my bare feet touch the deck. My legs give out and I collapse onto my ass. The sedative hasn't worn off, as he knows.

"I am the one who maneuvered Navah into position to be chosen as the Honored Hestia's cee-cee. Easy enough, with my Yele connections. What if I told you that I chose Tiana to be your cee-cee because she too is an agent of the Oculi?"

My voice catches in my throat. I want to scream but nothing will come out. I grab the table and drag myself up, grunting with the effort. He presses a code into the locked panel as I grasp the glass of water. He will escape. In desperation, in fury, I throw the glass at him just as the door slides open.

I miss his head by a handbreadth. The glass sails into the passageway, where a pair of four-armed soldiers in white uniforms are passing.

Phene.

The young man walking behind them flinches, ducking aside as the glass breaks on the bulkhead. His shaved head turns, and I look onto another face, a thin, eerie sketch of a face.

The door closes. The hiss of its seal hits me like a kick to the gut. I drag myself to the panel and hammer at it frantically before my legs give way again. I bump my head as I go down. Slumped on the deck, I lie unmoving for a full five minutes, too stunned to move.

A Rider.

Is Ti really an agent of the Oculi?

The ship gives the shudder I recognize as the turbulence created by a vessel undocking from another vessel. Minutes tick past as the torch drive accelerates. It takes me that long to drag myself to a crash couch, whose bizarre array of straps reminds me that the person normally seated here would have four arms.

A bell chimes. Transition in ten minutes.

Before I can strap in, an impact shudders the entire ship, flinging me back onto the deck. My chin takes a hit, and I bite my tongue, tasting blood. Fuck fuck fuck. I can hear the blare of combat alarms but the comms in this chamber stay silent. We are under attack. Where my ring is I do not know, but surely my father is using the ring as a decoy to manipulate Sun.

It takes forever for me to get back up on the couch, and then the straps won't cooperate because we are shuddering and juddering. *Boom boom boom* goes the symphony of battle as the ship takes hit after hit, shields up as it races for the beacon.

Between one breath and the next the impacts cease. We are too close to chance a shot hitting the coil. My trembling hand finally clips one strap into place.

Gravity cuts. I lift off the couch, drifting half out of the strap. My inner ears rebel, and I retch but there's nothing left in me to throw up.

Get a grip, asshole.

I hook a foot around a railing, jerk myself to a halt by locking an elbow around the strap, and grab another loose end with my free hand. With a frantic stab, I clip myself down.

The ship rolls, and we drop through.

I fell in love with the beacon network the first time I dropped through, when I was six years old. For a bright instant I felt myself linked with everything and everywhere, an insignificant node drawn along a shining network. I thought it was just my child's imagination, even though later the experience never went away. After that trip I got really sick, but I never associated the two things and no one ever told me.

This time I see it with new eyes. Faint traceries like gleaming arteries shimmer in the void to create an unfathomably vast network. Ships like droplets of water slide along this web with its complex weave and randomly ruptured threads.

What if the ships I dream I see are the real ships on the move throughout the network, here where time has no meaning? A passage is brief but I cling to the one I am inside, trying to draw out my awareness longer.

Trying to see the ships. Who is moving where right now? Trying to see the routes. Do they match the military map Sun received from the Oracle?

A cold exhalation touches me, the minds of the Gap pressing like ice on my mouth. The divine apsaras whose existence fathoms this insubstantial web that weaves in and out of the physical universe. *Let us in.*

I part my lips and I let them in. *I'm here.*

There aren't really minds or voices. There's just me, letting myself open into what isn't a childish dream but something stranger and far more mysterious, the deepest machinery of a network built on something other than machines.

I see the ship I'm on falling away from the dark gate which must be the door into Sena at the same time we are rising toward a dark gate which must be the door into Jorsha. Or maybe it is rising out of Sena and falling into Jorsha.

We drop through.

The universe reappears, alarms blaring, the panel blinking as comms lights up across the ship. Damage control must be swamped. I hear nothing because my audio remains blocked.

For a long time it doesn't matter when no one comes for me and no one even checks on me, because I am too busy. I unroll the tablet in my sleeve and start recording as much of what I think I saw as accurately as I can. Is this merely a long-haul side effect present in some of those who survive the beacon sickness? What if I did not survive it? Perhaps the disease accomplished what it was meant to do. Perhaps I am become a divine messenger, an apsara who flies along the scaffolding between worlds. I don't feel any different, and my clothing still stinks of dried pee, but my hands are shaking with the sheer force of surging adrenaline as my heart burns with jubilation.

Nothing has changed. Everything has changed.

How Could It Be Enough

Sun set foot on Port Chaucer with a company of marines, a division of Guards, and a firestorm in her heart.

"Search every millimeter of this station. Detain all inhabitants until further notice. Total lockdown." As the Guards dispersed to carry out her orders, a local administrator dressed in cardinal red hurried up.

She spoke before he could greet her. "Have you no visual records of the concourse?"

"We do not, Your Highness."

"How do you know what's going on if you don't have cameras?"

The man gave a nervous bow, sleeves fluttering. "Cameras can be tampered with, Your Highness. More to the point, we do not record people's lives. If there are problems, we assign public health officials who may call in mediators, examiners, and investigators as needed, an effective system—"

"My Companion and her attendant were kidnapped!"

He bowed again, face flushed. What a coward! She stepped forward, raising a hand. A slap to the face might shake loose better information!

Isis angled her body half a step between Sun and the shaking man. "Your Highness, this is not Chaonia. They are cooperating fully with our operations."

"Cooperation is not good enough! I want results. Persephone and Tiana are gone. Their ring signals have vanished, which means—" She broke off, the words incinerated to ash in her mouth by a spike of red-hot fury.

Kiran Seth had been on Tjeker. He likely had witnessed Zizou being forced to remove the ring. So he knew.

She slammed her attention back to the administrator, and with an effort lowered her clenched hand. "Are all the docks under lockdown?"

The man took a hasty step back, hands twitching as he answered in a local dialect thick enough that she struggled to understand. Seeing her confusion he stumbled over his tongue as he tried to translate, but his Yele skills were rough and he cringed to a halt. Would she have to pummel some sense into the dithering fool?

Again Isis interposed her body. "Your Highness, remember Octavian."

Keep your temper in check.

"You are dismissed." Sun was cursed sure she couldn't hold on to her fractured temper a moment longer.

The cardinal hurried off gratefully. She watched his progress, how he called over waiting ordinaries and began to dispense orders. On the concourse the Guards were shutting down businesses and foot traffic. Within an hour the entire habitat of one hundred thousand souls would have come to a standstill. Were Persephone and Tiana still on the station? She doubted it, but she couldn't take the chance that Kiran Seth was lying low until the furor died down.

The rings were meant as a taunt, the gesture a slap to her face.

How had Kiran grabbed Persephone so easily? Had Perse been that careless? Had the trip to the Gyre unmoored Sun herself? *Had she lost her edge?*

"Your Highness," Isis continued, "I would feel better if you were off this concourse, given what happened on the habitat in Karnos. A shuttle from the *Boukephalas* will be docking in twenty-four minutes."

"Very well. We'll repair to the *Boukephalas.*"

They began walking at a brisk clip, not quite a run. Makinde had remained beside her the entire time in his capacity as bodyguard and Companion. The situation had jangled his nerves enough that he had barely spoken, gaze darting in every direction as he assessed threat.

"Makinde! You were there at the concert hall."

"In the middle of the brawl? I was!" He had a shiner to prove it, eye purpling as the bruise set in.

"Do you have any idea why Persephone and Tiana left the concert hall?"

She appreciated that he thought it over before answering. "I don't. Perse was with me at first. Then by the stage, Candace got involved in an altercation over Ji-na, the ribbon dancer."

"I know who Ji-na is."

He coughed under his breath as his gaze dropped to the floor. His embarrassment distracted her.

"I'm not involved with Ji-na," she added irritably.

"I figured that out," he muttered. "Anyway, Perse slugged some Yele officer. Then she saw Tiana over by a back exit. They went off together in a rush."

"All right." To Nisaba she said, "I want two divisions of ships ready to go after the rings in case signal is restored. Hetty and James to command, respectively."

"You think they were taken separately, not together?" Isis asked.

"Why take them at all? Their corpses might be sealed into a lead-lined box here on Port Chaucer."

How dare Kiran Seth get the jump on her? How dare he toy with her like this?

As Sun set foot on the shuttle, both rings abruptly popped back onto the network, in separate locations, accelerating on opposite trajectories toward the outer system. Perse's last two messages hung on her virtual screen.

EMERGENCY. KIRAN IS HERE.
HE HAS CLONES OF—

No message from Tiana. What did that mean?

The rings provided a secure private comms system for Sun and her inner circle. Certain forms of shielding could block the connection but distance was no barrier even if time might be. What no one but her knew was that she could eavesdrop through any of the rings without their bearers knowing. She opened a channel to Persephone's ring, waiting through the lag. All she heard was a crackling hum that an analysis identified as the background noise of a ship's torch drive. The same with Tiana's ring. Multiple possibilities unfolded: They were dead. They were unconscious or asleep. The rings were no longer on them, which begged the question: How had Kiran managed to get them to take them off?

"James. Hetty." She spoke into the ring. Hetty and James had been engaged at separate celebratory events in Sena System, Sun sending her Companions as surrogates for the places she could not reach in person.

"I am in transit to the *Alkonost*," said James. "I'll take the asshole. Hetty, you want to go after Tiana?"

AFFIRMATIVE, Hetty replied.

"It might just be their rings, not them," James warned Sun.

"I know, so why are you telling me?"

"Oi! No need to snap my head off because you're in a temper. I'm just saying as a reminder. Not saying we shouldn't go."

They would go and she would wait, but she could not bear waiting. "On second thought, I'll go with you, James. Perse is the key to this."

Makinde said, forlornly, "What about me?"

"You." She eyed him grimly, and he grinned back, utterly unable to be intimidated, which she liked about him, however irritating he might otherwise be.

"Pack up. Be ready to depart."

"Are you sending me back to Alika? He promised that next time I would get to lead a boarding party myself."

"I'm sending you to Zàofù in Aila System."

Makinde sighed.

She added, "This is it, Makinde. This is the hour, this is the day."

"Oh. *Oh!*"

"Isis, with me. Nisaba, return to the *Boukephalas*. Prepare couriers, as we discussed. Wait for word from me."

Isis cast her a look of concern but not surprise. She had been present throughout the strategy sessions as the marshals and commanders cycled through scenarios: Try this. Try that. What if we went here? What if we went there? No, what if we really went *there*, even though everyone says it is impossible.

Nisaba said, "Yes, Your Highness. The couriers will be ready."

By the time the *Alkonost* caught up to a Mishirru corsair in the outer reaches of Sena System, fifteen hours had passed and Sun was too wound up to sit.

"Your Highness, let me board first," said Isis.

Sun had already pushed herself out of the airlock, tether stretching behind her as she crossed the gap to the hull. The ship's two main airlocks and its hangar hatch were welded shut by apparent weapons fire, but this wasn't damage done by the frigate. An emergency airlock was the only remaining entry point.

"We'll go in through the hull," Sun said over comms. "They left that airlock untouched for a reason."

A squad of marines led by Solomon took position. Sun did not interfere. She'd received training in every aspect of fleet and ground warfare, but that didn't mean she had the expertise of units whose specialty it was. As Octavian always said, trust your skilled people to do their jobs or don't bring them along.

All she knew for sure was that Persephone's ring was inside the ship. The vessel's guns had fired on them as they approached, but in the mechanical manner of an automated program. Once they'd taken out the torch drive all power had collapsed in the ship in a cascading failure that included emergency life-support protocols. So either Persephone was dead or something else was going on.

A ping from Hetty dropped into her ring. WE HAVE TIANA'S RING. SEND IN HORNETS FOR THE PICKUP. DO NOT GO YOURSELF. REPEAT, DO NOT GO YOURSELF. SHIP WAS BOOBY TRAPPED.

WHAT ABOUT TIANA?

NO SIGN OF HER, LIVING OR DEAD. NO HUMANS ON THE SHIP AT ALL THAT WE FOUND. IT WAS ON AUTOMATIC PILOT HEADED FOR INTERSTELLAR SPACE.

The rings were a trap. Curse Kiran Seth to all the hells.

"Your Highness?" Isis floated up beside her. Although the colonel wore a ring, she chose the comms system. "Might I convince you to put some distance between yourself and the vessel in case it is wired to blow up?"

Sun pinged Hetty. DID THE SHIP BLOW UP?

No answer.

Fuck.

She ordered the marines to reel themselves back to the *Alkonost* and gave James clearance to guide a pair of hornets through a breach cut into the hull. Once they were all back on the frigate she raced to the bridge and clipped herself into its strategos dais. The hornets were moving swiftly via different routes toward the ring's signal. She tapped a foot, gripped the rail. Why was everything going so slowly? Each passing minute ramped her one more rung up the ladder of anger. *Keep your temper in check.*

HETTY

No answer. The frigate was moving away fast, putting distance between itself and the drifting corsair. Shields up.

HETTY

No answer, but the signal wouldn't have reached Hetty yet, would it? If only she had a Rider's mind, able to leap instantaneously instead of being stuck in the mire. So slow. So slow.

"Just around the corner from the ring signal," said James. "Which is odd, given the usual specs for a corsair, because we're headed into the engine compartment, where you wouldn't put a living prisoner—"

A burst of light smeared the camera of the leading hornet. It went dead, or perhaps it would be better to say the corsair blew up and took all the hornets with it. Half the bridge crew exclaimed aloud. The other half were already firing at debris tumbling in their direction.

James doubled over as if he'd been punched in the gut.

"Perse isn't on board," said Sun.

"Oh the hells," he gasped. "Are you sure?"

"I am cursed sure Kiran Seth is fucking with us." She so rarely used crude language that everyone looked at her in shock. "He will regret that. But not as much as he is going to regret killing Octavian and Percy and Duke. Do you have the signal?"

James panted, getting his shock under control. "Yeah. Yeah. Got a location in the debris. Sending out a squad of hornets to retrieve."

A ring's signal could not be duplicated or imitated. A few forms of shielding could block it, but nothing short of disintegration could cut off its connection to what her father called the command ring, and an exploding ship wasn't enough to destroy a ring. The technology had been developed on the wheelships so they could track far-flung and dangerously vulnerable raiding groups and foraging parties through thick and thin. The banners took care that all their living people were accounted for. She'd grown up on tales of death-defying rescues and loyal treks to track down a last missing crew member. Care for life was so precious on the wheelships that it wasn't until Kurash that she had realized the banner soldiers sent to the Phene were considered dead.

Persephone was not dead. Could not be dead. Wasn't allowed to be dead.

James's annoying voice broke through, shattering her thoughts. "Sun! Oi, the hells, get up to the bridge and look at this. They're rushing the beacon."

By the time she reached the bridge she could only watch a replay: four beacon-capable Yele-model merchant corvettes had broken holding position in the queue and raced for the Jorsha Beacon. Two had been pounded into submission by Chaonian firepower and, having lost their drives, blown themselves up, thus creating enough havoc that the other two ships had managed to reach what everyone called the beacon shadow: no one fired *at* or into a beacon.

"That's him," she said.

Kiran Seth had used Persephone's ring to distract Sun and get the ship he was on through the beacon into Phene territory. He had escaped. But it was more than that.

He has clones of—

Persephone had sent the message to Sun on the private link, not the link that went out to the entire ring network of Companions and ceecees. He has clones of whom? She would bet her life that Nona had not cloned Riders, if Riders could even be cloned. So something or someone else he thought he could use.

Maybe he had destroyed the lab to destroy the evidence that Persephone and Manea were clones, but to what end? What use was Persephone to him now? Lee House was closed to him. Marduk would never allow him back. Without a Core House's backing, he was just another distrusted foreigner at court.

Nona had to have known who else was cloned in the lab. The veteran had told Sun nothing when they'd met. Had never told Eirene about the existence of other clones, not as far as Sun knew. Nona was a loyal daughter of Chaonia, so Eirene always said. Nona had worked on Eirene's behalf for half her life in exile although she could have done anything else, made a new life for herself, painted herself chameleon-like with fresh colors. But she hadn't. Did Nona have aspirations beyond her place, or was something else going on? Some factor Sun wasn't aware of? Something Nona had kept hidden even from Lee

House? Because there was one other unanswered question: Why did Nona clone herself?

An ensign brought tea but Sun wasn't thirsty. She counted down the comms lag, waiting for an answer from Hetty.

Waiting for an answer.

Waiting for an answer.

Her hands hot. Her eyes cold. A storm brewing.

Hetty's comms pinged in: YES THE SHIP BLEW UP. LET ME KNOW YOU ARE ALL RIGHT.

Sun had to steady herself through a rush of dizziness. Shook her head to clear it, and replied.

> YES. THE SHIP HERE ALSO BLEW UP. THANKS FOR THE
> WARNING. WE RETRIEVED PERSEPHONE'S RING. ON OUR
> WAY.

I am coming after you wherever you are.

She'd known this moment would come. People urged her to turn back, to act with prudence, to say it was enough, but how could it be enough? Could any weapon be content to be held in stasis as a mere symbol?

Did spears not wish to fly?

She sent comms to Nisaba: Send the couriers to Aila System, where the Sixth Fleet was assembling, trickling in under cover of the Mishirru-wide festival events.

She put in a call to Angharad Black, Anas Samtarras, Grace Nazir, Jade Kim, and the other command officers in Sena System: Meet me on the *Boukephalas* to go over for the hundredth time the scenario everyone says is impossible.

It can't be done, Zàofù had said at one of those sessions. *The empire has five times, ten times, our numbers. Maybe through subterfuge you can eke out a partial victory.*

Did you have some trickery in mind? she had asked, aware how many were listening. *We disgrace ourselves if we cannot win openly. No victory is proof unless it is unassailable. The war will never end until we prove once and for all that our fleets are superior. Only then must the Phene concede that we have won and they have lost.*

That was the lesson she'd learned from her eight-times-worthy mother: the impossible is not just achievable but necessary.

Frustration still burned like acid in her belly but she was moving now. There would be no need to make long speeches for a military that had already proven itself capable, diligent, effective, and disposed to fight. All or nothing.

82

The Wily Persephone Decides to Launch a Competitive Group on Idol Faire

My father and I sit side by side on the intercontinental train. Normally I would sit casually, legs tucked up under me, back slumped over my tablet as I grind my arduous way through the academic exercises I'm not all that good at, but I would never be so sloppy as to slump in front of the meticulous man who raised me. As always, he is impeccably dressed in his seer's robes, the tailored layers of off-white bound with a cream-colored sash for contrast. He sits with his back to the long windows, as patient as if we have just finished a heartfelt personal discussion. We travel through an endless expanse of coniferous forest that fades in and out of view as the train passes through patches of fog like the lost opportunities in my childhood when I hoped to connect to the man I admired and loved who never quite seemed to admire and love me.

The trees vanish altogether into the mist and my father in his pale robes dissolves into the foggy backdrop until all that is left of him is the sheen of his seer's eyes like silvery discs turning turning turning as we hum along the tracks . . .

I wake up as the pitch of the torch drive changes timbre. My mouth feels stuffed with cotton and my eyes itch but my stomach isn't queasy. The compartment hasn't changed. The bulkhead is painted with a floral array of vines and flowers, the overall effect strangely soothing.

The furniture remains the same: the bed I sleep on, a molded bench to sit on, and a table with rounded corners, its legs fixed to the deck. A tray of food and drink has been placed on the table while I slept, accompanied by my laundered dress uniform draped over the back of the bench. How polite! I feel like a prisoner of war, and I guess I am, since I am apparently on a Phene ship in Phene territory.

The tiny washroom accommodates my needs while offering no sharp implements. I strip off the loose cotton tunic and trousers I was provided with when an unseen attendant opened up the washroom for my use. I shower, then dress. I'm grateful my tuning fork and Resh's memorial tablet are safe on the *Boukephalas*, because the Phene have thoroughly inspected my uniform and it would kill me to lose these two precious reminders of my beloved sister.

The flexible tablet is still attached to my jacket sleeve but it no longer connects to my implant, which is odd. My ceremonial Companion's baton, which is actually a disguised stinger, is missing. No boots. They must have found the folding knife hidden in a heel. No ring, not that I expected to see it. The subsonic emergency comms embedded in the belt buckle has been tampered with and disabled. My ribbons and medals have been left in place, and the beacon badge remains slipped into a pocket, which means no one figured out it conceals a blade.

All in all, I've fared better than I had hoped, since they seem not to have scanned my body. Maybe my father convinced them not to. He wouldn't want them to guess I'm a clone. But it means I have one other weapon left to me besides the blade in the beacon badge.

I drink water to cleanse my mouth. Afterward I sit down to the meal. If they are going to kill me I don't see why they would bother with poison when they could simply gas this compartment and be done.

The dishes are new to me. I guess at some of the flavors: a peanut tofu stew over heaps of red rice, a tangy sour tamarind broth with peppers so hot my nose starts running, sautéed noodles and vegetables, and long rolls made of paper-thin pastry skin rolled up around a filling that tastes like spicy turnip.

I decide to launch a competitive group on Idol Faire, something with jugglers and saucy comic patter. We will call ourselves Spicy Turnip.

The door lock chimes as it flips from red to green. I jump to my feet. The door opens. My father walks in, accompanied by two white-clad Phene soldiers who escort a bald man. The man is not much older than I am. He is heavyset in the way of a desk jockey rather than in the manner of a stocky, powerful, active-duty Chaonian marine. He is intimidatingly tall, which makes his four arms look both strange and utterly right. I pat at my mouth with a cloth napkin, hoping I have no peanut sauce smeared on my lips.

My father speaks first. "Persephone, I hope you have made good use of this time to consider your options. The Eminent Manishtusu has asked to meet you."

The man turns. He has another face, a janus face, on the back of his head. I have never been so close to a Rider. Never spoken to or met one. Seeing a Rider down the length of a basilica does not count. No matter how many times a person sees an image or illustration of a Rider, it cannot compare to standing two meters away from that eerie face. Pinpricks crawl up my back. My palms sweat. I lick my lips nervously.

The Rider's eyes are like pen strokes that open and close. The mouth is a line and yet it possesses expression and voice. The face is alert, intelligent, serious without looking grouchy. Is that a smile it flashes at me? *It,* or he? Or she? Or something else? Is a Rider the same gender as its body? Do Riders have gender? Where do they exist?

Manishtusu speaks words in garbled Yele that I belatedly realize are his attempt to say "Peace be upon you."

"Uh, and upon you peace." I'm stunned to realize he has charmed me with this simple act of courtesy. I thought Riders were all scary, arrogant monsters.

His riding face looks at my father with a sympathetic glance of entreaty.

"Sorry, I don't speak Phenish," I hastily add in Common Yele before switching languages. "Any chance you speak Mishirruvian? I have a few words."

Manishtusu gestures a negative with his upper right hand. When you are imperial Phene, you don't need to learn the languages others speak because they are required to learn yours. He again smiles as if he wants to connect, to show me he is as human as I am. Is he? That creepy Rider face, and yet I smile back guardedly. I am waiting for the other grand piano to drop.

"This is very lovely and I am honored," I say, the words meant for my father although I do not look away from the Rider. "But why are you here and why am I meeting a Rider?"

The Rider speaks again, and this time I understand two words. *Nona Lee.*

My bubble of good feeling bursts. So much for my father protecting me.

"A demonstration," says my father. He signals to a specific spot on the bulkhead. Of course he knows where the surveillance cameras are located. This is why it's important never to masturbate while in custody.

The opaque bulkhead is not really a bulkhead. It is a barrier that peels away to reveal a transparent wall that looks into another compartment the same size as this one. Father grips my arm and turns me to face the wall. The other room looks like a standard secure detention compartment. It contains four lifepods, three glowing green and one open and empty. Five people stand in the center of the room, backs to me. Four are Phene military while the fifth is a two-armed person dressed in generic military coveralls.

Oh the hells I know where this is going. When I start to pull away from my father, his grasp tightens and he pulls me back. I am a prisoner, not an honored future queen-marshal's consort. If Baron Voy is anything to go by, in diplomatic marriages a consort is often merely a hostage to political necessity.

In the other room, a Phene soldier shifts the two-armed person around to face me. My breath sucks in sharply, a millisecond before their gaze strikes my face. The flash of their neuronics is so bright that I am the only person in both rooms who doesn't throw up a hand or hands in surprise, because I'm braced for it. But even I am not braced for the impact as the anonymous banner soldier slams themselves into the wall, pounding it with their body as they try to reach me. *Slam. Slam. Slam.* Their nose starts to bleed. I think I see the septum break as they again slam against the wall, trying to shatter it and get through. Their eyes are blank windows, their muscles rigid with pumping adrenaline, a killing machine seeking its target.

"That's enough!" I cry, but my father doesn't move.

I haven't trained with Sun and fought with Sun for nothing, as much as I may make light of my military skills. I sweep my father's feet out from under him while twisting my arm out of his hand, spin, throw him to the deck as I turn my back to the wall and drop to hands and knees to show I am harmless, nothing to be afraid of. The two Phene soldiers are on me in a heartbeat, pounding me flat onto the deck. My chin hits the floor in a burst of pain but I'm ready for it. I suck in a hard breath, breathe out slow, accepting the pain, letting it flow through me.

The Rider speaks words in Phenish. After a pause, the soldiers let go.

Coughing, I rise to hands and knees, working my jaw to make sure it isn't broken. When I decide it is merely bruised, I cautiously peek around to the wall. As expected, the banner soldier has collapsed because the visual connection broke. That big of a surge drains a neural network.

Father is seated on the deck, rubbing his head.

"I told you it was enough," I say as I stand. "Let the banner soldier kill me if you wish, but don't torture the poor soul. There's nothing they can do to stop it. They'd batter themselves into flinders before they stopped. It seems cruel. Anyway, why do the Phene care about Nona Lee after all these years?"

"There is no statute of limitations for justice," says one of the Phene soldiers in respectable Yele.

"Whoa!" I jump back, surprised.

The Rider grins, and the Rider's other face, its normal face, also grins, as if both faces are amused at my antics. Are they two different personalities? Or the same?

Does my father know that Sun left Nona in charge of the Trinity Coalition? Had word gone out on civilian channels before he left Kumbala? He had to have been hidden on a random ship on our tow chain. I don't know and I'm not about to ask.

I say, innocently, to the Rider, "I can understand why you would like to bring Nona Lee to trial for that long-ago event. But she's dead. Didn't you know that?"

"She is not dead," says Father. "And justice is patient. The Rider simply wanted to see if engineered hallucination truly works, as their scientists said it would."

"They didn't believe your personal testimony? That you saw it happen? Don't they trust you, Father?"

He looks me dead in the eye with the sheeny gaze that seers have, searching for the lie. "Do you know where Nona Lee is?"

"Out of your reach." I know better than to lie. "Anyway, I am not Nona Lee. I am your daughter. Aren't I?"

"You haven't changed, Persephone." He turns to the others. "As you have seen, the engineered hallucination works. And can be applied more widely."

Sun.

Oh shit.

How long does it take to engineer a hallucination? What do their scientists need to make it happen? Is an image enough? And if an image isn't enough, then how or who or what did the Phene use to engineer Zizou and the others? Did the Phene capture one of my sibling clones to experiment on?

I never would have thought to ask Nona such a question, and the Phene won't confide in me. The wall seals, shutting me away from the banner soldier who would kill me if they could just get their hands around my throat.

"Please sit," says the Phene soldier. The "please" is a courtesy, not a choice.

I sit at the table. A chair is brought from outside, placed backward opposite me, and the Rider sits to face me. My father stands by the door, watching me. The Rider asks questions in Phenish, and the soldier translates.

What is your name? What is your rank? Why are you in Mishirru? What is your relationship to Queen-Marshal Sun? What are Sun's plans? How many ships are in her fleet? How many Guards are in her army? What are her plans? What are her plans? What are her plans?

The interrogation goes on for an hour or perhaps two as my father scans my face for any lies I may tell. But I know how to play this game. I grew up twisting words so they weren't true and they weren't false and most importantly they didn't tell my parents anything I didn't want them to know, because it was the best way to stay out of trouble. The only way. It is oddly bizarre to realize I am better protected by having the rights of a prisoner of war than I was as a child of Lee House, ruled by petty bureaucratic tyrants, shadowy powermongers, and narcissistic bullies.

The weirdest part is the steady gaze of the Rider. Sometimes the Rider pauses and their riding eyes turn to slits as in a holding pattern, even though they aren't gone and don't leave. Are other Riders listening? If they are, what do they make of me? Who am I to them? A pale shadow of the war criminal they hate? Or an honorable soldier who may give them the key to defeat their aggressive enemy?

I say, "How did you learn to speak Yele so well, Colonel?"

"It's captain."

"Captain, surely you have been in Argos. You used the word for 'please' that is local to the folks there. I've never heard people use it outside the metropolis. Wasn't there a high-ranking Phene official who lived in Argos for a few years in exile when his faction got in trouble? Eirene gave him and his family sanctuary for a while. I guess he got swept back into the bosom of empire. I have a vague memory of seeing a Channel Idol program, gosh so long ago, that followed their amusing encounters around the city. Shopping at the market and having to ask what popcorn cicadas were. Navigating the Wheelhouse and getting lost between the Blue Line and the Green Line. Guests at the temple and not knowing how many times to bow. A white-water rafting trip where somebody's child fell in the water and couldn't swim . . ."

The captain's eyes flare. I've hit a memory they can't disguise because it was a real thing that happened that must have scared everyone who was there on that day.

I snap my fingers. "Bartholomew, that was the boy's name, wasn't it? He was the son of the official. Mondragon? Mendel? Mandalor? *Manalon,* that's it. The boy and little Sun were buddies, weren't they?"

"That is enough, Persephone." My father's tone makes me flinch. "Lest you wonder, the banner soldier is on guard outside in the unlikely event you figure out a way to open the door."

The captain looks at the Rider, who stands and says, in memorized Yele, "A pleasure of meeting, it has been, Honored Persephone."

I rise because however creepy the Rider is, after an hour he's just another face and not the unfriendliest one in the room. That would belong to my father. "My thanks. I hope we meet again, Eminent Manishtusu."

I put on a brave expression but I hide my face as the door opens and I don't breathe until the door shuts and I'm not dead. Then I go to the wall, running my fingers along it to see if there is a seam, any way to control it from this side, but I can't discover the least crack or gap. When I press my ear against the wall I hear nothing except the ship, which is all right, because ships always speak in a language of their own and they are far more honest than human beings.

There is one question I did not ask. Not *where are we going?* because either he already told me or they'll never tell me until we get there.

What happened to Tiana?

Is she an agent of the Oculi? The thought sinks me to the deck, head pressed against my hands. My father could be telling an untruth to goad me. Being a seer of Iros does not preclude prevarication on his own behalf, does it? Life is a vale of lies.

My father, the Rider, the captain: none of them return. I entertain myself by running through the usual martial and military drills, over and over and over. Solomon would be impressed. My implant provides a source of study materials, although its dedicated components lack a basic Phenish language program.

Most importantly, I have my images of the antique beacon route map from the photographs I sneakily took on the *Keoe* when I snuck Ti in to see her brother. I have the diagrams I saved from the model James and I constructed during the long return journey from the Gyre. The modern beacon route map Sun got there allowed her to run scenarios.

Time passes, as time does. Trays of food arrive and are taken away. I sleep, and I wake, and everything I do, I do knowing the cameras are watching.

The ship's language shifts with a familiar resonance. The beacon drive has been engaged. A bell chimes. A voice speaks and even though I do not understand Phenish I know it is saying some version of "Set beacon stations. Transition in twenty minutes."

I fasten myself onto the bench. Once secured, I roll out the blank tablet from my sleeve and activate it by resting an open hand on it, skin to surface.

Ten minutes. Does time have meaning inside a beacon? Are linked beacons part of the same structure, contiguous in a way we who exist in our part of the physical universe cannot measure?

All weigh off the ship. My body rises against the straps.

We fall through.

I have a moment. I have an eternity.

The usual droplets slide between gates but the usual trickle is become a flood. Hundreds of ships are on the move, tightly streaming too close together and too fast as they drop through. My fingers tap out patterns on my tablet even though I don't feel its surface because nothing exists except my astonished excitement.

We drop back into the universe.

The tablet displays an undifferentiated scatter of points where I have attempted to mark the position of each dark gate in a general relationship to the others. Maybe I am fooling myself. Maybe I am only telling the story I want to be true.

Hundreds of ships are on the move from Sena System along a beacon route that leads straight to Karnos. Hundreds of ships are on the move from Aila System headed toward Anchor.

In our final weeks in Mishirru, we Companions sat for hour after hour around Sun's strategos table. We drank possibilities and options and wild chances as if they tasted better than wine, and to Sun surely they did. But even if little Chaonia under the command of Eirene was able to leverage its disciplined fleets to gain control of the Hatti region, where the Phene were disliked outsiders in the systems under their governance, that doesn't mean our junkyard hatchling of a republic has the means to beat the behemoth in open war on an open field where their numbers swamp ours.

The door panel flips from red to green. Hastily I swipe my hand over the tablet, erasing the marks. A silent attendant brings a tray of food and a change of clothing so they can again launder my uniform. I'm charmed by their politeness and attention to detail.

As for the map I tried to make, it doesn't matter that the tablet is now blank. I know what I saw inside the beacon. I know what it means.

Outnumbered and outgunned, Sun has launched an audacious attack at the heart of the empire.

Blood in the Water

From Apama's old room the view through floor-to-ceiling windows still faced east across Fair Water. The flash of the rising sun refracted through the glass of Anchor Prime's grand basilica was the only alarm she needed. She rolled out of bed and, bleary-eyed, surveyed her chamber. It had not changed in the twenty months she'd been gone. Staff had kept it clean but not an object had been moved as far as she could recall, and she was in the habit of keeping her spaces tidy.

She padded over to the door that let onto the parlor. It was locked. Too early for breakfast. On the voyage from T-Harbor to Anchor, she had not been allowed to speak to her mother except when they were seated at the same table for formal dinners with syndicate leaders and regional admirals, and then they were always seated apart.

She changed into workout gear folded into a drawer exactly as she'd left it. It smelled freshly laundered, not musty. The route down a level to the gymnasium hadn't changed, and why should it have? She kept looking around as if expecting the world to have come apart and re-formed into a new shape but it was exactly as it had been before. The long journey had disoriented her. She hadn't been in the cockpit of a lancer for so long that she was eager to get a couple of runs in. It stunned her to discover the flight simulator was gone. A piece of her torn out. Zakurru had known she wasn't dead. So why had the specific equipment she'd requested been taken away?

A surge of fury blasted through her like a rough ride through hostile fire. She froze it out and wrapped it up and put it away because it wasn't doing her any good. With lancer discipline she paced herself through a hard workout until the sweat poured and her heart pounded and her muscles burned. Back in her room she showered and changed into a dress uniform.

When the second bell rang, the door that led from her room into the parlor did not unlock. She tried it once. Twice. Three times. Had to stop herself from hammering on the barrier, as if anger solved this kind of problem, because it never ever did.

Wait.

A cream-colored envelope sat on her desk, her full name printed in precise blocky letters. It hadn't been there before she left for her work-out. Inside she found a handwritten message in midnight blue ink on a pale yellow notecard.

The Eminent Tadukhipa and her sister Giolla respectfully request the honor of Apama At Sabao's presence at afternoon tea to be held in the Breakwater Room at 1500. Formal dress required.

The Breakwater Room? She'd never heard of it, not that she knew much about the substantial four-level bunker, as big as a town, that housed Riders and the apparatus of their ruling council. But she smiled. Teegee was up to something.

Her old routine wasn't going to cut it. Zakurru obviously didn't in-tend to give her a new portfolio of duties, not today, anyway. Where might she eat breakfast, in that case? She sent a message to Bar-tholomew: *Back in town. You here? I'll be at Coffee House Savaran from 1000 to 1100 if you want to catch up. Or suggest another time and spot.*

Then she sent a message to RuRu. *Is there a place where attachés and adjutants eat breakfast? Can I join you? Or just let me know so I can eat?*

Always make connections.

RuRu replied within three minutes with a location on Level 1, the public-facing administrative spaces that surrounded Unity Hall. The lieutenant waved from a table inside a cafeteria serving a stream of administrators, officials, and military as they got ready for whatever work they did for Unity Hall. The cooks and servers were young Incorruptibles who looked barely older than Teegee.

Apama grabbed congee, sliced mangos, a warm coconut roll, and two cups of coffee. She took a seat beside RuRu at a two-person café table and pushed a cup over to the other woman. "Figured there can't be too much coffee in the morning."

"Thanks. I'd have waited to eat if I'd known you were coming." The lieutenant indicated her empty plate. "This is where they shake out potential kitchen staff for the Rider levels, so the food is good."

"I've never been here before. I never even knew this place existed."

"Where did you eat? I used to see you all the time at the Exchange, so I know you know your way around there and on the terraces. Do you have a flat in town?" RuRu grimaced. "Never mind. Not my business."

"It's all right." Apama didn't answer the query, choosing prudence. "I'm off today. Thought I would try to catch up with old friends since I just got back."

RuRu waggled her eyebrows. "Anyone *iiiiinteresting*?"

"I was hoping to get together with Bartholomew Kr Manalon de Angursa. We spent a lot of time together . . . What?"

She'd come to know RuRu on the journey back because they'd been thrown together a lot. Not tight friends but work friends. The way she chewed on her lower lip meant she was uncomfortable.

"I don't run with that glamorous set. I'm not a Triple A heritage seed."

They shared a grin.

"But you know, Apama, like I said before, Paulo Kr Manalon got on the outs again. He keeps saying we need better coordination between the syndicate fleets. Batillipes and Tanarctus among others have repeatedly accused him of making a power play to consolidate fleet actions under Angursa's control. That would be tyranny. They mustered a majority and voted Angursa off the war council."

"That's the step before suspension of a syndicate, isn't it?"

"Or disbanding the syndicate. Yeah. So serious stuff. People are angry about the Chaonian victories. They need someone to blame."

"Who do you blame?"

"Blame lies above my pay grade. All I'm saying is, be careful of who you are seen with."

"Thanks for the heads up."

RuRu checked the time. "I'm on duty in ten."

"Hey, quick question. Do you know anything about a Breakwater Room? Here in the complex?"

"Sounds like something that would be on the lowest level of the ridge, doesn't it? A place you would watch the water break on the rocks during a storm. I don't have clearance for Levels 2, 3, or 4. That's Rider and Incorruptible territory. Gotta run."

Apama applied herself to the food, which was good if not as sublime as the meals she'd become accustomed to in Zakurru's suite. Although the cafeteria was crowded, and it was commonplace for individuals to share tables with strangers, no one sat next to her even as people were seeking spots and yet avoiding the empty chair opposite her. It was like having a target on your back. She finished and got out.

She had two hours to kill and no desire to pretend to work if her sire was going to be so petty and cruel as to take away her mother *and* her flight simulator. So she went shopping at the expensive market at the base of the terraces. She bought a silk scarf for Teegee and a set of dress gloves for her mother, and, after some consideration, a bottle of lambent orange ink for Dasa and a tiny blue glass vase for Zakurru. She added an outdoorsy basket of specialty snack foods from various imperial systems for Gil; for Baragesi, a bracelet of polished wood beads appropriate for a niece to give to her uncle. RuRu had confirmed that Gil's family had been captured by the Chaonians but that was all she knew, and Apama hadn't yet seen the Speaker to ask.

Midmorning on a work day, Coffee House Savaran was almost empty. When the proprietor brought her a second cup of coffee, they said, "I don't see many lancer pilots here these days. Seems you're all out at the front lines."

"I'm on family leave," she said. "Shipping out again soon."

"Good fortune with that, Captain. Everything's on edge, in't it? Syndicates quarreling when they should be cooperating. The Chaonians looting Mishirru. They say the queen-marshal enslaved half the population of the Trinity Coalition."

"I don't know much about the Trinity Coalition. Don't they operate with a lot of indentured workers? Still, it's pretty impressive that anyone invaded Trinity successfully. From a military standpoint, I mean. We never tried."

"We didn't need to," said the proprietor with a hint of disapproval. "We aren't war-addicted barbarians, are we?"

She had ten minutes to go, and it was time to change the subject. "Is that ube and coconut cake? Fantastic! I'll have a slice."

A server brought the cake, an ordinary young person with messy dark hair wearing a black apron over nondescript slacks and shirt. The black fabric was unrelievedly somber except for a red enamel badge in the shape of an umbrella. She glanced up to thank them and did a double take. Without the glamour, Bar was almost unrecognizable.

He blinked three times in warning. "More coffee?"

"One more cup, thank you. I was so hoping to meet a friend here but I guess they can't make it."

"Does seem like people are on the move, what with the syndicates arguing over who is responsible for the last few years of setbacks, and the Exchange looking for a scapegoat to blame the troubles on. Like being caught in a lancer's gunsights and not knowing how soon you're going to be blasted out of the sky."

"Makes sense people might feel they don't want to draw attention to themselves. I hope folks have a fallback position. Good military strategy."

He raised a hand to flick an unseen piece of dust off his shoulder, and on the way back down tapped the umbrella badge.

She nodded and said, "My thanks for the cake. It's my favorite."

The corners of his lips lifted. *I know,* he mouthed.

He poured her coffee and left.

She took the time to savor the cake, then went to the Exchange. At this hour meetings and committees were in session, and she had no mandate to involve herself, not as she had used to. However she still had library privileges, so she reserved a kiosk and skimmed through the last twenty-two local months of news. One way to gauge syndicate influence was how often they were mentioned in the talk and analysis of the day. The Angursa cliff got steep right around the time the Chaonian fleet reached Mishirru. The social pages that had highlighted Bartholomew's fashionable presence at processions or parties or festivals stopped mentioning him at all, a clear indicator his syndicate had fallen out of favor. The syndicate system had its strengths but they could also become sharks attuned to blood in the water. No one wanted to get caught as the chum. It was one of the things Apama most appreciated about the lancer ethos. You backed up the other pilots even if you didn't like them, because if you didn't, you would all lose.

The more she read, the more a feeling of dread ate into her chest. When people got consumed in casting blame they forgot they had a ship to pilot. She did a search on guild pins. She vaguely recalled a Red Umbrella Procession from childhood on T-Harbor, vague because she'd never been allowed to attend. Her friends had once snuck out to see what all the fuss was about and ever after called it the box and tool parade, and thus in her memory she associated it with a celebration of machinists and mechanics. It turned out the red umbrella represented the Campaspe Guild, an inter-beacon sex workers' guild with annexes all over the known systems, often in under-served and out-of-the-way industrial zones and backwater moons and planets. *Box and tool.* Of course. She chuckled and checked the time: 1415.

She walked briskly back down the Processional Way under the light of the cold, bright star. At the security entrance to lower levels beneath Unity Hall, she produced the note and with a lancer pilot's confidence said, "I'm expected. I'll need someone who can escort me through."

"What's in that bag, ma'am?"

"Family gifts."

Security searched the bag impassively, allowed her through, and had her wait.

After five minutes an Incorruptible steward arrived and perused the note. "Ah. I see. You're only clear for Levels 2 and 3, and not for the central core. This way, ma'am."

They descended via stairs to Level 3 and then through another security post to reach a secure stairwell down to Level 4. The steward asked no questions and made no small talk so she remained silent. Just another mission.

They emerged into a passageway painted with star systems, each carefully depicting its local resources and famous sights. A hum vibrated through her feet like some kind of motor, but she didn't ask. They passed a long bank of windows onto a vast interior greenhouse modeled after a Titan's sunless agricultural gardens.

"Folks could ride out a siege down here," she remarked.

The steward looked at her for a measuring pause and she couldn't tell whether the stare was meant as a warning to keep away or as silent approval for figuring out a truth she wasn't meant to know. Then the moment passed, and the steward gestured toward a branching passage that led east. "This way."

They approached a blue-green shimmer that grew larger and with it a steady ebb and flow rush of water. The outer passageway on Level 4 was set flush against the exterior of the ridge and about two meters below sea level, so the water surged up and down and up and down the thick transparent wall. Fish nibbled along the foam-laced surface. A pod of the eel-like creatures called sirens twisted out of sight as they headed farther out into the endorheic sea's sun-splashed waters.

"Wow!" said Apama, for once losing her cool.

"I knew you'd like it!" Teegee waved enthusiastically at her from an archway. The girls wore a trim, ankle-length frock the shade of twilight and adorned with glowing beads like stars. It was cleverly tailored to suggest there was no back but rather two differently cut fronts. "My thanks, Castor. I can manage from here."

The steward inclined his head and moved away to take up a station nearby.

Teegee hooked a lower hand into the crook of Apama's lower elbow and led her through the archway. A walkway like a clear tunnel sloped down so they were entirely beneath the water. It opened into a startlingly gracious chamber set cunningly both along and beneath the rocky shoreline that lapped up against the seaward base of the ridge. Waves flowed overhead, breaking into bright spray, spinning into eddies, now and again sucking clean away so sunlight glinted into the space. A dozen tables were arrayed to catch the best views. Divans had been placed facing outward next to the clear walls so people could watch the ever-changing play of water. There were only three other groups eating here, two Rider pairs each engaged in some manner of tête-à-tête and a foursome made up of an elder Rider who she recognized as the former Speaker, grouchy old Kubaba. Her three non-Rider companions wore syndicate formal tunics appropriate for ceremonies and banquets. Was that Uncle Paulo? The table was the farthest away, and his back was to her, so she couldn't be sure.

All the furniture stood so far apart that each table or divan arrangement was essentially a private room. Painted folding screens were available to create additional privacy. Teegee guided her toward one such screen set close to an undersea pinnacle. A swift-flashing school of silvery baitfish grazed amid swaying kelp as spiky sunfish idled just below the surface. Behind the screen a table had been set for coffee with cups and saucers and a tiered ceramic tray artfully arranged with fresh savory and sweet baked and fried delicacies.

There sat her mother, wearing a mischievous smile that matched the jolly pink dress tunic she wore, embroidered with fanciful hot-air balloons and shark-mawed blimps. Her loose trousers were hemmed with tiny fabric puffballs as if she were a seed cloud ready to burst and fly away on the wind.

"Mom!"

She rose to embrace Apama. "Teegee is a clever girl."

Teegee was bouncing on her toes. "Who can say no to me? Sit. Sit!"

Apama sat.

"Did I surprise you?"

"You did!"

The girl clapped her hands. "I thought nothing could surprise you, Ice."

"Ice?" asked Rana.

"My call sign."

"You never told me!"

"Mom! Teegee teased it out of me and now she won't let me forget it."

Teegee looked thoughtful. "Because I thought pilots only get insulting names, like those two we met, Greensleeves and Fry-baby."

"How is Greensleeves insulting?" Rana waved away a steward who had approached in order to serve them.

Apama considered. "I don't know, but if I had to guess it might for example refer to something like her throwing up on her flight suit during gyro training after she'd eaten an avocado salad."

Teegee giggled.

"Let's pretend I didn't ask," said Rana as she took charge of the coffee pot.

The girl brushed Apama's upper right hand. "I checked, by the way. Neither is on the list of known dead, so maybe they were taken prisoner. I felt bad they stayed behind. But I guess that isn't worse than what happened to the ones who didn't stay behind. The ones who cut a path for us to escape."

Rana poured coffee into the girl's cup. "Lancer pilots understand the risk. Otherwise they would choose a different path."

Apama caught her eye. "Mom."

"Yes, I know." Rana poured for Apama and for herself, then sat. "I say we don't waste this lovely view and these delicious treats on morbid subjects. Now here, if I know you, Apama, and I do know you, you'll have binangkal and one of these jackfruit-and-banana spring rolls. What do you prefer, Teegee? The onion and the bean paste hopia, perhaps?"

"How did you know?"

"I have so little to do at formal dinners that I amuse myself by observing what people eat. It comes in handy as a parlor trick when I serve them what they want before they ask for it."

Apama said, "It would come in even handier if you were an assassin like in that old comedy drama *The Last Fork of the Poison War*. Then you'd know which food your target was most likely to choose, and you could poison it with a deadly toxin and they would die dramatically as they empty their stomach."

"Exactly. Only then it would be the last *hork* of the poison war, wouldn't it?"

"Oh, no, Mom, stop," Apama groaned.

"You started it." Rana's deadpan expression made Teegee giggle again.

"You two are so funny." A wistful expression chased across her faces.

Rana set two hopia on the girl's plate and transferred a coconut cream tart to her own. "How you are settling in, Teegee? You must feel a different person than the one who set out with Baragesi and Gil quite a long time ago."

"I do. I informed the creche administrator I would take a week of free time to make new plans. I'm thinking about what changes I'm going to ask for in my schedule and training." She lifted an upper and set a finger to her lips. Apama paused with a sesame dough ball poised in front of her open mouth. The table was configured so a Rider could both eat and talk with her tablemates. Tadukhipa's eyes had pulled into long watchful slits as her mouth sketched a lopsided wave. Giolla whispered, "She's working to tune out the radiance. So the others can't hear us."

"It is always worthwhile to speak prudently and cautiously," observed Rana as she cut the tart into quarters.

Apama popped the binangkal into her mouth. A crackling crust and a meltingly soft interior. She was suddenly aware she'd skipped lunch. She was suddenly aware the sounds of conversation drifting from the other diners had ceased.

An angry voice. "Where is she—?"

Rana's eyes widened with alarm.

Teegee sat straight up, both faces taut with expectation and a sketch of an anticipatory smile.

A body jostled the screen. Apama stood as Zakurru appeared. He was not dressed for the room, as if he'd come from a more casual administrative meeting.

"What is this, Apama?" he demanded. Then his gaze fixed on her mother. "Rana! How are you come to be here? I gave no permission for such a gathering."

Teegee did not rise. Sometimes staying seated was the power move. Tadukhipa said in an astoundingly calm voice, "I need no permission to invite friends to partake of afternoon coffee in my company. My status as a Rider is the same as yours."

"You are not of age."

"I am no longer a child in the creche. If you have a complaint or wish to file a grievance, you may take it to the Rider Council. It is my right to be addressed with respect. It is my right to avail myself of the perquisites of my status."

Heavy footsteps warned of a new arrival to the skirmish. Kubaba rounded the screen. Her ordinary gaze flashed to meet Giolla's and away at once.

"Why is my afternoon being disturbed by this disgraceful interruption? Have you a reservation, Zakurru? Surely you can't have just barged in like an unwanted and ill-mannered Chaonian?"

The girl rose to align herself with Kubaba. Rana moved with the light-footed grace she had, brushing Apama's lower forearm. Apama tilted her chin toward the girl; she did not want to abandon her. Rana shook her head and tugged on her elbow. Teegee caught the movement. Her lower right hand fluttered in the sign for *Later*.

Apama and her mother slipped out from behind the screen and retreated toward the entrance.

Rana murmured, "That was a setup. She's asserting her adulthood."

"Kubaba isn't in power," Apama muttered. "It's dangerous. Is Baragesi nearby?"

"I believe he is in-system but I don't know for sure. There are a lot of fleet movements right now. A lot of uncertainty."

"With the Chaonians in Mishirru, sure. I'd feel uncertain if I were the high command."

"I don't see how they could even consider attacking us. They'd have to fight us at home, where we are strongest."

She squeezed her mother's arm. "Give me a minute. I see someone I know."

She walked to the table Kubaba had vacated, where her three companions waited with impassive expressions. One was, indeed, Paulo Kr Manalon.

"How are you, Uncle Paulo?" Apama said. "I am so pleased to see you again."

He rose, flushed as he looked toward the screen that hid the three Riders. Total silence from that direction, but on the other hand Riders did not need to speak aloud in order to argue. Maybe Tadukhipa was forcing the issue before an empire-wide jury of her peers.

"Apama, I am honored by your notice. Let me introduce you. I know you have already met Bahala Rn Maki, who is syndicate president. This is our cousin Reynaldo Kr Manalon." Reynaldo was a striking man of older years who wore a red umbrella badge alongside the laurel-wreath badge of Angursa, which meant he had an association with the Campaspe Guild that he wished to advertise. How interesting.

"Welcome home, Captain," said Bahala, all seriousness.

"You are quite the savior of the hour, are you not?" said Reynaldo with a flirtatious wink.

"My duty is no different from any other. We are all destined for death."

They answered in kind, then politely walked over to the wall to look onto the sea, giving her and Paulo privacy. She thought over how she wanted to phrase a bland inquiry without speaking any lies.

"I messaged Bar but he wasn't able to meet me as we used to do."

Paulo's bluff confidence had withered since she'd seen him last. His eyes were bloodshot as if he couldn't sleep, and he'd lost weight. He cleared his throat nervously. "You know I hoped for an alliance. I think you liked Bartholomew well enough."

"I do like your son," she said with a smile meant to be heartening. "Who could not? If only I dressed so fashionably and with such panache. And knew all the songs and dance patterns in every festival procession besides. He was an honorary member of a number of procession associations, a great honor . . ." She faltered. Paulo's grim expression shot through her with foreboding.

"Rider Kubaba was kind enough to bring my compatriots and I here today to give us early warning. The Angursa Syndicate has received a vote of no confidence. We are to be disbanded immediately."

"Disbanded? Doesn't suspension come first? So the syndicate can fix whatever problems the Exchange and the Council have flagged?"

"This is political. People are fools." His tone was bleak. "They don't want to hear the truth, so they would rather cut out the truth-teller."

"What is the truth?"

"I didn't like Admiral Manu, but his suggestions were all proven right. We need a single commander to face the Chaonians. Baragesi is a good Speaker and a courageous leader, but he has minimal fleet experience. We need one proven admiral with a good strategic mind to impose a clear chain of command. The ascendent syndicates see my words as the complaints of an embittered loser who wants to bring them down to my disgraced level."

"If I may ask, what got you exiled before?"

"I admit to you, out of respect for the many hours you have endured my company as I tried to broker a marriage between you and my beloved son, that syndicate politics inside Angursa forced me to leave the empire for five years. Eirene welcomed me because she thought she might find me useful. I got along well with her. I appreciated that she's not one to mince words. In the end, it didn't hurt that I could return to the empire with a bit of inside knowledge to share with the Council."

"You must have known the new queen-marshal as a child, then."

"Sun and Bartholomew played together as best of friends."

"How were you able to return home?"

"New Angursa leaders reinstated my branch of the family with the help of Kubaba, when she became Speaker."

"Ah, I see, about ten years ago. Is that why Kubaba is warning you? Because she helped you before? I don't see why syndicates are creating this level of disruption when our military ought to focus on Sun's unprecedented campaign of expansion."

"Angursa's fleet will be disbanded and all our ships reassigned to new fleets so no capacity will be lost."

"Yes, but unit cohesion, surely."

"The other syndicates are greedy. They all want to march at the front of the procession."

"Who did you recommend as high admiral, if I may ask?"

"Well." He cleared his throat self-consciously. "Me."

She couldn't help herself. She laughed. "That was bold."

"Zakurru blames me for Admiral Manu's death and for the defeat at Karnos. He claims I broke the defense and retreated too soon. But I was tasked with protecting Speaker Baragesi."

"Are you the one who mined the beacon at Windworn?"

"I did give the order. The forces at Sleepless followed suit."

"From everything I've read, those mines are what stopped the Chaonians."

"That's not how the other syndicates see it. They call it dishonorable rather than pragmatic. The loss of trade through Karnos has hit a lot of syndicates hard."

A resonant bell tone shook through the air, so loud that Apama jumped. All went silent for twelve long seconds. Only the waters moved as the swells rolled in and broke through the rocks, bubbles and foam churning deep into the crevices, boiling along the walls. A pod of sirens spun into view and vanished. The school of baitfish flashed away, lost to sight. Only a solitary sunfish remained with a flick of its tail to hold it in the sun's light against the drag of the backwash.

Zakurru hurried out from behind the screen, followed by Tadukhipa steadying Kubaba with a hand on her arm. The girl shot a look at Apama, lifting her chin.

"Pardon me," said Apama to Paulo. She hurried over, realizing he had never hinted whether he knew Bar had secretly spoken to her at the coffee house.

An Incorruptible took charge of Kubaba. They made their way toward the door.

"Come with me," said Teegee. She moved fast, Apama trotting beside her through the archway and deeper into the core of the ridge until they reached a pair of lifts secured by Incorruptible guards.

"I'll need to see your clearance, Captain," one said to Apama.

"She is my attaché," said Tadukhipa.

"Of course, Eminence."

Teegee preceded Apama into the lift. The doors closed and the elevator began to descend.

"Where are we going? To the war room?"

"There's an emergency war council." She shook her head. "Keep your head down and no one will notice."

"I am unbelievably grateful to you for bringing me to see my mother, but do you really want to tangle with him?"

"I'm a Rider too." She tapped her ear to remind Apama that any Rider might be listening in. Then she added, "I want your military expertise. You explain things in a way my tutors won't. I know I'm still young and have a lot to learn, but your mother is right. I haven't come home the same as I was when I left."

"It's called growing up. What's the news?"

The lift halted. Its doors opened directly into the bowl-shaped chamber carved deep into the bedrock beneath Grand Unity Hall. Admirals and officers and high-ranking administrators were rushing in from the other entrance and taking seats, a hubbub of voices racing at high pitch, excited, angry, disbelieving, protesting, a wash of sound like a storm battering itself against rocks. Above, in the dome, the virtual map of the empire shone too brightly, hurting her eyes. Sparks kept popping into existence within Jorsha and Alternity Systems, the two border systems whose beacons linked into Mishirru territory. How could there be so many ships in those two frontier systems? Was the map malfunctioning?

Tadukhipa was torn away from her in the flood. Apama grabbed a place at the upper ring of tables. She did not see Paulo or indeed any Angursa representatives. But she did see her sire taking his place in the lower circle. How had he known she'd be with Teegee? Who had alerted him? A loyal steward? RuRu? Ugh. She hated not being able to trust people, but she had mentioned the Breakwater Room to the lieutenant.

The space fell silent as Speaker Baragesi appeared, descending toward the lowest circle. He looked older than he ought; the burden of leadership and the loss of his family had aged him prematurely. Gil had deep shadows like grief under his eyes, and lines that had not been there before, and a frown scored so deep it looked permanent.

When they reached the Riders' circle Baragesi raised his speaking baton. He gave no welcome although for an instant she thought his searching gaze paused on her, noting her presence, before it swept on like a lighthouse's beam seeking ships about to wreck themselves on a perilous shore.

"Our brother Manishtusu sends word from Jorsha. Our sibling Arakamani sends word from Alternity, where she took refuge after she received word that Sun's fleets had arrived in Destiny. The Chaonians have attacked in force and at speed through the Sena and Aila Beacons. They have invaded the heart of the empire."

Silence met this declaration.

Attacked? How? Why? Impossible.

"What do you say, admirals?"

The words opened the door to a tempest of discussion, a whirlwind of competing views, no one in agreement.

Split the fleets into multiple strike forces and come at Sun's fleets through every beacon imaginable, swarming her.

No, no, there must be one decisive battle to finish off her arrogant aggression once and for all.

But where should it take place? Haymarket? Rake? What if she wasn't headed for Anchor but for Auger or Axiom? Or both?

Withdraw the defense forces at Sleepless and Windworn to shore up the defenses at Anchor, Auger, and Axiom.

An outcry: that might allow whatever garrison fleets had been left in Karnos System to invade and increase Sun's numbers. No, it couldn't, because both systems were mined and the Chaonians couldn't break through without extensive damage.

Anyway, how could the Chaonians coordinate a sortie with the fleet in Karnos when they didn't have Riders? It was impossible. All syndicate fleets must be recalled!

But what if Sun was counting on the high command withdrawing fleets from the outer systems and thus decided to push through and attack the outer systems first? What if she meant to go all the way to Tranquility Harbor and meet up with a fleet coming around via the long caravan route, as Tadukhipa had?

This suggestion, from the only officer in the hall wearing an Angursa badge, met with scornful laughter and then catcalls: How had the colonel gotten in here? Hadn't Angursa's representatives been required to resign from the war council?

The colonel flushed with bright anger, then pulled the Angursa badge off her uniform and slapped it onto the tabletop. "You're all fools, just as Paulo said," she declared in ringing tones. She left as the assembly shouted at her back.

"Enough! Enough!" Baragesi raised his speaker's baton.

The Speaker struggled to restore order to the seething groups. Every syndicate was so sure of its righteousness, and all of them were angry at Angursa's parting insult. Or perhaps, Apama thought, they were just furious that the upstart Chaonians had dared to disturb the tranquil peace and orderly rule of the empire, which had served its comrades and subjects so well for so long. How dare Chaonia! How dare Sun! Even the Riders were arguing among themselves, splintered into factions.

In the end Baragesi had to have a sergeant at arms ring the assembly bell four times. Everyone quieted. From the Council floor, Teegee looked up at the highest tier and caught Apama's eye, but what message she meant to send, Apama wasn't sure.

"So be it," Baragesi said. "As Speaker, I have the right to declare my intention and demand it be carried out. Sun has cast a reckless throw. Our forces will gather in Anchor System. We will meet the Chaonian fleets here on our home ground, in numbers they cannot possibly match. They cannot defeat us."

No One in Her Fleet Said *If*

"All weigh off the ship."

Smoke drifted in the bridge and tasted acrid on her tongue, but all the fires on board the *Boukephalas* were out. For now.

"All hands brace," said the captain over comms. Someone coughed. Another person made a comment, lost in the crackle of comms as multiple ships pinged in their positions. One by one they lined up behind the big Tulpar-class cruiser. When they'd entered Refuge System, the heavy cruiser *Stymphalia* had followed the *Boukephalas*. The skirmish in Refuge System had damaged *Stymphalia*'s bow and with it her beacon drive, although the ship could still fight. She was the eleventh ship they had to leave behind as Sun's attack charged from Sena into Jorsha into Agate into Old Spiral and then into Refuge. Even so, she knew Zàofù would be taking the brunt of it as he moved from Aila System along a different route toward Anchor. Badly outnumbered, he was relying on her bold move to succeed in time to relieve him from the pounding he was about to take. Was already taking. She couldn't know because she didn't have Riders of her own. Kaspar didn't count, and anyway she had left the boy in Destiny with the *Keoe* awaiting further orders. Soaring could retreat to Trinity if needed.

All this flashed through her mind in an instant. In a totality.

They dropped through the beacon, falling out of Refuge System—

What lies between beacons?

It isn't nothingness, is it? It is a road.

—and into Haymarket System. The captain helmed the cruiser hard left. They used the beacon's vast spiral as cover, firing out at the local system defense force, which dared not shoot at them. In tight order, closer together than Eirene would ever have allowed, Sun's best ships appeared one after the next, scant minutes apart, a dangerous maneuver that was her only way of taking the Phene by surprise since they knew she was coming.

Explosions shook the *Boukephalas*'s powerful shields. Damage reports streamed in. That was Captain Tan's job, not hers. Telemetry and reports from the other ships also streamed in, headed to James and his team. These details she also ignored except to stay alert for gaps and vulnerabilities. Hers was to direct the battle, to drive the wedge. To see and exploit any opening that appeared.

Haymarket was an intact cerberus system, a valuable crossroads. Refuge Beacon led back through Refuge System toward Jorsha and thus Mishirru. Sandbank Beacon led to Sandbank System and on to Sleepless and thus to Karnos. The third beacon led to Cut Stone System, a single drop from Anchor. A short stab of the spear, if one chose to take it.

With pounding force and perfect discipline and unflinching courage, the vanguard hammered the enemy defense force, leaving space for the Second Fleet under Anas to arrive and head at speed for Cut Stone Beacon. It was the frontal attack the Phene expected. The Sixth and Ninth Fleets under Zàofù were attacking from Aila into Anchor via one route while the other two fleets swung around this way. Phene ships stationed elsewhere in Haymarket System began retreating toward Cut Stone Beacon, hoping to cut off the powerful Second Fleet. A portion of the Eighth Fleet, under the command of Angharad Black, was following the Second to Cut Stone, but Angharad had her own special flanking maneuver to attempt once through the beacon.

By now 238 ships had dropped through into Haymarket. It was the rearguard Sun was waiting for, the rest of her elite task force. With the bulk of the battle moving at speed toward Cut Stone Beacon, she set course for Sandbank Beacon. She had one chance to break through the biggest roadblock, and she meant to take it.

IN-SYSTEM. The ping came from Hetty on the *Khepri*, the Scarab-class ship to which the *Strong Bull* was attached.

Thirty minutes passed as fifteen more ships dropped into Haymarket System.

Alika on the *Sphinx* pinged in, last in the line.

IN-SYSTEM. ALL ACCOUNTED FOR.

A packet from the *Sphinx* dropped into the *Boukephalas*'s network for James, containing the final sensor readings and ship reports from Refuge System. Their attack had demolished Refuge's defense fleet, which was modest and therefore not much of a victory, more a sideswipe as they blasted past. A minimal garrison squadron had been left in Refuge, including the powerful *Stymphalia*. Everything depended on the main strike.

"Proceed to Sandbank Beacon at speed."

After scattered fighting, the local forces were unable to stand against them, and they were hulked or they fled toward the heliopause. By the time the main Phene force who had engaged with the Second Fleet realized Sun's group wasn't also headed to Cut Stone Beacon, it was too late for the Phene to cut them off.

With at least twenty-two hours of travel time before they reached Sandbank Beacon, Captain Tan called for modified battle stations to allow exhausted crew to eat and sleep. A marine came through the bridge handing out stim bulbs and protein bars.

Sun left the bridge. She went first to the mess deck. Two gurneys rolled past: a living marine with a bloody stump of a crushed leg and a dead Samtarras House ensign with a moon-shaped face who appeared untouched, as perfect as porcelain.

"What did you trip over?" she said to the marine.

The man grinned up at her through the ragged edges of his pain. "Some cursed spacer, Your Highness. Those squids keep getting in the way of us boots, right?"

"That's right, but we'll have plenty of action for you later. What's your name?"

"Joram Har Alargos, Your Highness."

"Argos, eh? Where do you get your sweet water noodles?"

"Only at Copper Street Market. My granny won't settle for anywhere else."

"Not from Abundant Waters District?"

"Nah, they don't know how to make it proper up north."

Sun laughed, the sound causing folk to look their way. "We'll have to argue this further. I'll schedule you to take tea with me when you're settled and secure."

"Your Highness! It would be my honor!" For a moment, his pain was forgotten.

She sent a quick message to Nisaba to arrange it. A medic trotted up and, after a brief examination, attached a black tag to the Samtarras ensign.

Sun recognized the medic. "Minh! Any idea what killed her?"

The medic had been so intent she'd not paid attention to who was next to her. "Your Highness! This is one of the casualties we took on from the *Alkonost*."

The corvette had been badly damaged in the frontal attack into

Haymarket. They'd had to abandon ship, and the *Boukephalas* had taken on its crew.

Minh was going on. "Asphyxiation is one possibility. Maybe gas from a broken line. I've seen a couple of cases from that early-model corvette."

"You think there's a structural issue with that specific model that needs to be addressed?"

"It might be."

"File a report when you're done here. Flag to my secretary. She'll have it looked into."

"Of course!"

"And you'd better get Joram into the queue. He'll need all his strength to lose his argument over sweet water noodles with me."

"I don't even know what those are except that Perse used to talk about how great they are," said Minh. "We didn't have that where I grew up."

"Joram'll fill you in."

Sun moved on. She set a delayed ping for Makinde with the ensign's name, wondering if he and the dead woman had been in the same cohort at the royal academy. It wouldn't send until she and Makinde were in the same star system, which they very much weren't right now.

The soundscape of the mess deck had an eerie pulse, awash in groans, medical chatter, the scrape of gurney wheels alongside the clap of footfalls, the steady hiss of the *Boukephalas*'s ventilation system, and the occasional blat of an announcement over comms. The kitchen was in full gear, a strange parallel universe where people were lining up to get a full meal before they took their mandated sleep. The fragrance of roasted 'ulu, mashed 'ulu, and spicy 'ulu fries washed up against the harsh aroma of bodies torn and bleeding and the stink of sweat and pain. A spacer hurried up to her bearing a tray of hot buns.

"Your Highness?"

Past the open cafeteria line she could see into the kitchen. All work had come to a standstill as the cooks and staff anxiously and expectantly looked her way. She wasn't hungry but she knew she needed to eat, and anyway she would never insult an offer like this by ignoring it.

"My thanks." She took a bun, tore it in half to reveal its purple filling, and ate it with dispatch, then gave an acknowledging gesture toward the kitchen. A wave of excitement passed through the staff. She moved on to a spacer missing both hands, the stumps sealed with medical foam.

"Both of them?" Sun asked. "You didn't want to save one?"

"The hatch closed on my wrists while I was still trying to finish my joke," said the spacer, clearly spiked on a dose of painkillers. "Very rude, if you ask me."

"The hatch or the joke?"

"Both!"

They laughed companionably. Sun caught Minh's eye and signaled to her to come over. "This is Lieutenant Lê Altadmor. She's got an excellent multi-tool prosthetic. She doesn't have time now but later she'll come by and show you all of its options."

She moved on, getting names, making jokes, listening to those made loquacious by pain, speaking softly to those who weren't up for a laugh or a chat. None better than a Chaonian spacer. None better than a Chaonian marine. None better than Chaonian Guards. Who can stand against us when we are united in purpose? We have reached this far because of your bravery, your strength, and your superb battle discipline.

Isis appeared. "Your Highness, I am here to escort you back to your suite so you can take a mandated rest period."

A private message from Hetty pinged in. YOU MUST SLEEP. THERE IS NOTHING YOU CAN DO AT THE MOMENT THAT SOMEONE ELSE ISN'T ALREADY TAKING CARE OF.

"Are you and Hetty colluding?" Sun asked, half amused and half annoyed.

"No, Your Highness. We are both wise to your ways."

The buzz of her last stim bulb was wearing off. As hard as it was to sit down, they were correct. She had to be fresh for what lay ahead.

Back in the flag suite she took off her boots, handed her uniform jacket to Eleuterio, drank a supplement-laced booster, and lay down on her bed. It spread so empty without Hetty in it. Her lips formed an endearment, and then she was asleep.

Awake.

She sat up, flushed, heart pounding. But there was no alarm, just a steady murmur of voices in a comforting backdrop. The door was open into the lounge because someone knew her well enough to know that quiet background noise would keep her asleep longer. Silence hypercharged her brain. Solitude brought her mind to spin faster and faster, ceaseless as it whirled.

James was speaking softly, as he could. An answer in a stentorian baritone. A *shhhsh*. Isis appeared at the door, checking before she closed it. Sun signed to her to leave it open. She checked her network. She'd slept ten hours.

"Did you drug me?" she asked, only half joking.

Isis raised an eyebrow. "Your Highness, you were that tired. I'll tell Eleuterio to bring rice porridge and tea."

As she showered Sun leafed through layers of virtual reports. The Second Fleet would reach Cut Stone Beacon in an hour. Anas had sent his interim report. He was charged up and ready to go, pleased at being given a major assignment although he was sailing into heavy weather. His goal was to fight well, always that, and to meet up with his father, who would already be taking the worst of it, absolutely. Four hours to Sandbank Beacon.

If there had been any Phene Riders in-system when they'd arrived, she hoped they'd fled before they realized she was headed for Sandbank. Or they might think the move was a tactical decision to take control of the system and its resources. It would be the prudent thing to do for an invading force regardless. She'd never heard that Riders could read minds, so they had no way to be sure what she would do next.

She dressed in a fresh uniform and went into the lounge.

James sat slumped over the strategos table, head resting on a hand. He waggled the other hand in greeting. Exhaustion carved shadows under his eyes. "My report is waiting for you. I'm going to sleep now."

She nodded, and he left for his cabin.

Isis poured tea and vanished into the galley. The sharp scent of oolong cut right up into Sun's head. She sat down opposite Beau.

"Do you want to see what I've got so far?" he asked.

"Sure." Sun applied herself to the rice porridge. The cook had added a side platter with a savory pancake.

Beau cleared his throat in the self-conscious way he had, thinking about how he wanted to say what he wanted to say as well as how what he said might be received. It would have been more aggravating if she hadn't been aware that she operated in much the same way. It was why she found him useful.

"Our goal is to open the mined route into Karnos System. Then the fleets waiting there can follow you to Anchor in time to reinforce our other fleets."

She savored another spoonful of rice porridge. The war council had gone over this plan a hundred times.

"However." He raised a finger in the manner of a teacher raising a crucial point. "Arriving in Karnos *also* allows you, Your Highness, to communicate at speed with the citizens at home for the first time in over a year."

"Almost two Chaonian years by now."

His jaw tensed at her correction. "I will be sure to replace my working figure with the precisely correct figure when the time comes."

He did not say *if.* No one in her fleet said *if.*

"I intend to have a complete Idol Report ready on the breakthrough courier both as transmission and as packets for distribution down the line. It will be ready for instantaneous play on Channel Idol throughout the republic. The full program will include breakdowns for announcements, for school assemblies, for pillars, and for commuters. I have assembled lengthier versions for academies and universities."

"It can all go forward once Nisaba gives it her seal."

"Of course, Your Highness." He only used her title when he was refraining from a burst of criticism. Nisaba had once told Sun that Beau resented having to clear all his programs through her office, and would Sun speak to him about that, please? To which Sun had replied that Nisaba needed to do her job and leave Sun to do hers, which did not include handling Beau's vanity.

"Go on. I'm curious to see what you've put together and how you've added onto the files you sent home from Trinity."

"Ah! Yes. I'm quite pleased with the result so far." He loved the sophistication of the flag suite's strategos table and used it whenever he was allowed, preferring it to the virtual table in the communications department where Fleet Idol worked. His gestures were as emphatic and enthusiastic as a conductor commanding an orchestra of effects, images, and words.

It took forty-six minutes to run through a tribute to Eirene, the battles of Molossia and Karnos and their aftermath, the Karsh's insult to the republic and Sun's answer, Mishirru's welcome to the Chaonians who liberated them from the Phene yoke with a focus on the grand festival played out across the ancient queendom's venerable star systems. An oblique sidebar referenced the trip to the Gyre and the curious array of brown dwarfs. Makinde and Razin's visit to Landfall featured prominently, including a dazzling slo-mo of the moment when their Chaonian boots touched the ground of the planet whose existence had saved humankind from extinction.

"Hold on," said Sun. "Go back to the Trinity sequence. I did not single-handedly clear the Grand Sanctuary by myself."

"I'm going for the dramatic. For the legendary."

"That's ridiculous." She set down her cup hard, its smack causing the historian to give a start. "Marines and Guards died there, some of them protecting me. I will not have them neglected. Redo that entire section. Less focus on me and more on collective action. The citizens of Chaonia are my partners in this venture. Not my tools. Furthermore, this venture doesn't need false frills and furbelows. The extra paint demeans our achievements by making them look exaggerated. Don't indulge yourself."

He looked down at the table, cheeks reddened.

She signaled to Eleuterio. "One steamed bun, that's all I ask. Sweet. Beau? Do you want anything from the galley?"

"I'm fine."

"Go on."

Beau made a fuss of clearing his throat. Maybe his self-importance made him good at what he did. She couldn't quite tell, and she would never have kept him on if he wasn't a superb synthesizer. He had the gift of creating narratives that allowed viewers to understand the sequence and importance of events as well as feel an emotional punch.

"Given the time frame, Your Highness," he said with exaggerated formality, "it has been necessary for me to create a future template."

"A future template?"

"I have speculated on events according to your campaign strategy. Therefore some of the pieces you see will be a *simulation* of how we hope things will go."

"Very well." She checked her network. "I need to do a ship walk-through before we drop into Sandbank, so go on."

Beau had cast himself in the program as a Knowledgeable Sage addressing the patient citizens of the republic. A diagram atop a simplified map traced the fleet's path from Chaonia through Karnos and Trinity to Mishirru. From Destiny the queen-marshal had had two options. She could return to Chaonia via Trinity, enduring two long knnu passages while leaving an open and vulnerable territory behind her. Or she could go forward, into the empire.

It is this latter path that Queen-Marshal Sun has chosen, intones narrator Beau.

An animation of the operation so far and its hoped-for future unfolds.

The combined fleet in Mishirru divided into two parts. Commanding the Sixth and Ninth Fleets, Crane Marshal Zàofù stalwartly drove forward from Aila into Phene territory. He will proceed via Hunger, Rake, and Gardens Systems to Anchor, fighting all the way, and all without any means to communicate with Sun except vulnerable couriers that will take days to reach her via beacons if they aren't blown up.

At the same time, the Eighth Fleet under Sun and the Second Fleet under Kite Marshal Anas attacked from Sena via Jorsha, Agate, Old Spiral, and Refuge into Haymarket System. Once in Haymarket, the Second Fleet speeds onward to attack Anchor through Cut Stone, taking part of the Eighth Fleet with it.

But Sun splits off and, at the point of a cruiser-heavy vanguard, streaks fast and hard through Sandbank directly to Sleepless System and the mined beacon that leads from Sleepless to Karnos.

It would have been both foolhardy and suicidal to ask the fleets gathered in Karnos to attack through the extensively mined beacon. The death of the *Vermilion* proved that.

But what if the mines were cleared? If the mines were cleared, then all those Chaonian and allied ships massed in Karnos, most of the rest of the Sun's expeditionary fleet, have a straight shot to Anchor via Haymarket and Cut Stone.

However, to clear the mines she has to take control of the star system, which the Karnos-based fleet can't do from the opposite side of the beacon. Yet even if she wipes out the defensive fleet, how can mines be cleared quickly, especially ones invisible to most sensors? It would take too long to sweep them up one by one with multiple Turtle-class shield ships, as the Chaonians had done at the more lightly-mined Hellion Terminus. Defusing mines manually or automatically is another possibility, but obviously the Phene will not cooperate with such a project.

Sun had seen the *Strong Bull* in Hellion Terminus and in that instant had determined to bring the dreadnought with her. Chaonians could not pilot a Phene ship, as they lacked four hands. The big dreadnought's beacon drive was broken. It could not move between systems, but it didn't need to. It could be attached to a Scarab-class ship. Had Sun already had in mind an attack on the heart of the empire, or was it instinct, knowing even a crippled dreadnought might prove useful later?

The local defense fleets along the Sena to Sleepless route have so far been no match for Chaonian discipline and their exceptional ability to attack in formations and at speeds others would not have risked. The Sixth, Ninth, and Second Fleets will bear the brunt of the initial offensive attack as they close in on Anchor against a mighty enemy roused to defend itself from the junkyard hatchling that dares to sting it in its own territory. There is surely a Rider stationed in Sleepless System who will warn the Rider Council that Sun has broken through. She has to rely on the hammer of her bold attack as her ships race through Sandbank System and drop at full speed into Sleepless with the dangerous turning maneuver her ships have mastered, the one that allows them to drop through an entire task force before they have to move out of the shelter provided by the beacon.

Entering Sleepless, the *Boukephalas* and its sister ships press the Phene hard back, away from the Karnos Beacon to buy the time she needs.

The *Khepri* approaches Karnos Beacon with the dreadnought

attached. When the *Strong Bull* is released from the Scarab-class ship, thrusters that have been attached to the hull begin firing.

Beau had animated a mockup of the operation: the huge ship, pilotless, bearing down on the area known to be mined. Explosions shimmering as flashes of light. The dreadnought shuddering, taking hit after hit after hit after hit as it plows through, leaving a debris field behind on its death journey, for it will not return from this level of damage. In the distance, the battle with the local force rages on as the Phene realize too late what the plan had been all along. A flanking maneuver.

Last of all, the royal courier *Glory* streaks through the disarmed minefield into the beacon coil that will drop it into Karnos System. Between one breath and next, it drops out of sight.

An Autonomic Response

After the *Huma* received a classified packet of orders Sun had sent in the wake of the victory at Trinity, the frigate joined the Third, Fifth, Seventh, Tenth, and Eleventh Fleets gathered in Karnos System. The Third and the Seventh took up station by Sleepless Beacon, the smaller Fifth, Tenth, and Eleventh by Windworn Beacon. For the first seventy days, the fleets drilled relentlessly in large-scale battle scenarios as well as the maneuver that allowed almost twice as many ships as normal to speed through a beacon per hour.

After seventy days, each combined fleet divided into five task groups who rotated position at five-day intervals. One group waited in tight column at the beacon, ready to drop at a moment's notice. The second formed up behind the first group as they transitioned out of being the third group, which cycled through a readiness, maintenance, and supply inspection. The fourth group, farther out from the others, continued the drills. The fifth took liberty on one of Karnos Deci's three orbital habitats and what the Chaonians called its "party moon."

The five-day lineup at the beacon was the hardest. Waiting on edge for day after day while not being able to act proved exhausting as well as debilitating to morale. Captain Shì was back in command of a frigate squadron. When his squadron was in position in the first group, he had come to rely on Kurash and his little band of ghost soldiers to keep crews on point. He rotated Kurash and a select platoon of marines onto other ships to introduce the new fitness regimen, layered in with team competitions between groups on each ship and between the ships in his squadron as well. Nothing new, in itself. Eirene had made sure her expanding military was superbly trained. But the ghost regimen, being new, fell into the ranks with fresh appeal. It made people feel tougher and cooler to strut alongside former banner soldiers. The fitness regimen wasn't just about personal fitness. The way the exercises were set up fine-tuned people's ability to work together. An arrow of banner soldiers was only eleven individuals, but their ability to coordinate and act together gave their numbers an outsize effect. Exactly like a well-trained squadron, the captain had observed.

On day 117, Kurash was on the frigate *Montu* leading a squad of marines through Ropes and Ladders Level One. He was hand-over-hand climbing the center rope strung in the training arena as marines watched from below. His ring buzzed, and a message from Sun appeared.

IN-SYSTEM. TRANSFER IMMEDIATELY TO ME ON THE GLORY.

She was here, as she'd said she would be.

From seven meters up he let go of the rope. The watchers gasped. His neural network flared. Body straight and bent forward, legs together. Relaxed. He'd done this a thousand times in training. Half the training with the Phene was learning how to absorb damage in a fashion that left him able to fight, because all that mattered for a banner soldier was that they be able to continue fighting. Dropping, he had the strength and adrenaline to absorb the shock with a double-footed landing, but while still in the air he decided on a forward shoulder roll to take him back up to his feet. It was a better example for the marines. He didn't want anyone trying to imitate him and injure themselves.

"The session is over," he said to the lieutenant in charge of the squad. "We are about to go to battle stations. The queen-marshal has arrived."

"We are? She has?" The lieutenant blinked, checking the network, and gave a shake of the head because no comms had dropped. Sun had to send a message to Crane Marshal Qìngzhī Bō and thence the order would be broadcast fleet-wide.

Which meant that Sun's first message on arriving in-system had been directly to him, the disgraced banner soldier she had chosen to trust.

"Lieutenant Kurash, are you all right? You . . . sparked."

"An autonomic response." It was, but somehow, it wasn't. Sun trusted him still. She had sent him on a mission and he had completed it.

He should have replied to her already!

> IN-SYSTEM ON BOARD THE MONTU. I CAN TRANSFER FROM
> HERE OR RETURN TO THE HUMA AND TRANSFER WITH
> THE PACKAGE AND MY STAFF.

> COME NOW.

"Lieutenant, I'll need shuttle transport to the courier *Glory*."

"*Glory*? Isn't that one of the royal couriers? Did our fleet truly travel all the way from Mishirru and break through the minefield?"

1MC crackled to life. "This is the captain speaking. All hands to battle stations. We have received the orders we've been waiting for. All hands to battle stations."

Two hours later a utility shuttle docked with the *Glory*. By this time the *Huma* and its frigate squadron had already left Karnos and dropped through into Sleepless. Kurash and the two pilots had watched in awe as the column moved in tight order, beads on an invisible string falling one by one through the coil. The pilots discussed where they were meant to go after delivering him, since a courier had no hangar. Just as they latched on they got orders to rendezvous with Crane Marshal Qīngzhī Bō's flagship *Tianma*, in the second group, which would convey them into Sleepless System, after which they could return to the *Montu*.

"Depends on how much fighting is going on, doesn't it?" remarked one of the pilots. They looked at Kurash.

"I don't have any more current information than you do," he said, which was true because Sun had not replied to him since her initial order. Her silence did not worry him, exactly. Her presence in Karnos System was her chance to speak in real time with the garrison force and to arrange any further announcements or orders for farther down the line, to send a message to Marduk Lee or to Prince João that would reach them within eight to ten days rather than the hundred-plus days her message from Trinity had taken to arrive at the palace.

He thanked the pilots and disembarked. Sun greeted him at the airlock as he boarded with the duffel he'd taken over to the *Montu*. Looking him up and down, she spoke briskly, in a hurry to get on with other business.

"Kurash, here you are. Captain Shì sent over the salt before his squadron departed." She indicated a sealed crate that measured two meters by one meter by one meter, a standard shipping container for luxury goods being sent onward in small quantities. "And I am assuming these individuals are what you refer to as 'staff.'"

The captain had sent over the five rescued banner soldiers who had chosen to remain with him.

"It was explained to me that as a member of your household I had access to your household treasury for expenses, and might retain a staff for my personal needs."

"Who explained that to you?" she asked, looking amused. "Precious Jin?"

A spurt of adrenaline—rain, wind, death—raced along his neural network. He damped it down at once but she'd seen it chase across his face and drawn her own conclusions.

"No, not her. It was Ay . . . I mean, Lieutenant Ay Jí Alimerishu."

Sun blinked, gaze going distant. He could practically see the whirring of her brain as she cast for connections. "Ah, Persephone's rackmate from CeDCA. You'll come with me. I want a debriefing."

The soldiers looked at him. The soldier he'd met as Wüst had renamed himself Traps; he had that brand of sardonic humor. Traps raised an eyebrow. His ruined hand had been replaced by a standard military prosthetic and the shattered arm rebroken and rebuilt, still healing, which meant that some of the marines were a match for his sparring skills. That wouldn't last.

"Lieutenant?" Traps asked, as spokesman for the others.

"This is Queen-Marshal Sun. She is your commanding officer. You may trust her."

They all dropped to one knee.

"Up, up," said Sun impatiently. "We don't do that here."

The door into the passageway opened and Colonel Isis strode in, pulling up as she looked over the new arrivals. He hadn't seen her in so long that seeing her now was like viewing her for the first time. A powerfully built woman with an air of mastery and confidence, the wisdom to know what situation she was looking at, when to strike, and when to wait.

The banner soldiers all stared at her and at Wing, who chirped upon seeing Kurash and was allowed to flap over, land on his shoulder, and bump his cheek before flying back. The newest of the soldiers was very young; she'd been on her first assignment at the battle of Karnos when her left leg had been blown off below the knee in an explosion that had killed the rest of her arrow and so she was left behind by the Phene commander in charge when his unit had evacuated.

She leaned toward Traps and whispered, "I bet her battle name is Serena. Harder, better, faster, stronger, smarter."

Traps nudged her and said, "They don't take battle names, Sunshine."

"Oh."

Isis finished her examination of the five soldiers before turning to Sun. "By all the hells, I thought you were joking."

"When do I ever joke about things like this?" Sun replied.

"You think I don't remember some of the mischief you got up to with Hetty, James, and that Phene lad who was in exile at court for a few years . . . what was his name?"

"Bartholomew. We were twelve."

Isis was the kind of thoroughly experienced soldier who could say whatever she wanted. "You'd benefit from a little more playfulness in your life, Sun."

"I'll let you know when I have time. Get Kurash's squad settled."

"Before you go, make sure you ping Nisaba immediately. She just told me that the briefing packet delivered by Marshal Qīngzhī includes a message from Senior Captain the Honorable Abiye Bō of the light cruiser *Raijū*."

"That's one of the ships we lost to sabotage on the Argosy passage."

"That's right. There are survivors."

"Survivors!" Sun's hands clenched, her expression shifting to anger and then a flash of powerful relief, not so much excitement as vindication, he thought. "If anyone can survive that kind of treachery, it is Chaonians. Nisaba, what's this about the *Raijū*?" Her attention shifted inward as she listened to her high secretary's reply.

"Where did you find these soldiers?" Isis directed the question to Kurash.

"Tossed away into the rubbish," he answered bitterly. "Fourteen in total so far, but the others—"

"Not now, Kurash," said Sun, breaking in. "Isis will take charge of the rest of you and show you where to strap in until we reach the *Boukephalas*. We'll sort out arrangements later. For now, treat Isis's orders as if they were mine."

They all looked at him for permission. He signed the go-ahead in the hand talk that arrows shared.

Sun's mouth flattened. In a closed compartment even crippled banner soldiers could take her out but she walked right up to them as if daring them to try it.

"Soldiers! Kurash may be your unit commander, but I am queen-marshal. My direct orders never need confirmation from anyone. If you have any issue with that, then you'll leave this fleet."

Without waiting for an answer she went out. Kurash grabbed his duffel and followed. A courier was a compact ship with tiny living quarters, cramped operating compartments, and vastly outsized engines, built for speed and survival, not for comfort or fighting.

"Your Highness!" A citizen Kurash did not know hustled after them from where he'd been standing by the airlock hatch. Since Sun did not react with alarm, Kurash kept walking.

"Your Highness!"

Sun halted. "What is it, Beau? All of your duties have been discharged and the packets sent. It all looks good. The citizens will love it. Is there something else?"

"Your Highness." The stentorian voice lowered to a stern whisper. "Are you sure you want to bring Gatoi on board? Into the fleet? Won't it look bad, as if . . ."

"As if what? My father is a Royal of the Gatoi, which Chaonians haven't forgotten."

"As if you are reverting to your barbaric heritage."

"My barbaric heritage?"

Kurash swung around to see her megaton stare boring into a tall man dressed as if he hoped people would notice him.

"If I ever hear you use that phrase again, you'll be sent packing. Do you understand me?"

Indignation tightened his face. "Your Highness," he said with rigid politesse, "I understand the nature of public opinion. I do not speak lightly. Bad enough you have brought Gatoi on board and seem determined to entertain them as part of your household when you should be served by stalwart citizen soldiers alone. What's worse, from my perspective, is these are all Gatoi who have fought against Chaonia. They're not noble and beautiful savages. They're scarred. Damaged. Unsightly."

"Unsightly?" Sun rocked forward onto her toes, seeming to swell intimidatingly as anger tightened her face. "The same could be said of many of Chaonia's honorable veterans, could it not? If one were so unwise as to say it."

He hemmed and hawed, then said, "I just meant they aren't the sort of attractive faces you could be surrounding yourself with—"

His gaze had drifted past her—no one really took their eyes off Sun if she was talking to them—and he noticed Kurash for the first time.

The words choked off as if he'd been struck in the throat. He gaped, goggle-eyed, flushing as blood rushed to his cheeks in an autonomic response.

A response to what?

Kurash felt it impolite to stare. On the wheelships, people did not intrude with their gazes when they could avoid it. Sun had the matter in hand. He turned away.

"But that . . . that is . . . the one . . . I saw . . ." The man floundered into the trench of silence.

"I don't want to hear this line of argument again from you!"

Sun turned her back on the man, as she would never do to someone whose martial skill she respected, and led Kurash to the captain's cabin. He set his duffel on the neatly made-up rack she was sleeping in because there was no room for anything else except a private head, a fold-down desk/bench combo, and barely enough room to turn around. She sat at the desk. He stood with his back to the closed door.

She blinked as she checked her network. "Secure yourself with the strap. I've completed all my business here and we are joining the queue to drop through into Sleepless."

Her attention again shifted inward. He guessed by the complex sweep of emotion playing across her face that she was listening to the actual message from the lost ships. Once back in Karnos System, the crew of the *Huma* had heard rumors about a disaster during the Trinity Campaign, but they'd never gotten the full story. He waited.

After some minutes she murmured, "Wow."

For a full minute she sat completely still, absorbing whatever she'd heard. Then she shook herself and turned her gaze on him. "Your report, Lieutenant. Chronological. Be brief but thorough."

He had rehearsed this alone in his cabin more than once. Twenty times, maybe. By now he had the sequence of events memorized and was able to recount each stage of the journey and what people had said and what he had heard without at any point breaking from the account to justify his actions.

Comms chimed. "Set beacon stations. Transition in twenty minutes."

Mostly she listened as he described how he had discovered the first two abandoned banner soldiers and then the long journey to the wheel-ship of Royal. She broke in only to ask an occasional question for clarification.

"Transition in ten minutes."

Now the fateful council meeting, as he struggled to recount its events and repeat the words spoken without betraying the grief that ate at him. She watched him with a gaze so focused and brilliant it seemed it could absorb whatever he threw at it. If anything, the interaction fell across her as an outcome she had anticipated, but he did not want to break the flow of his report in order to ask if she had assumed all along her overtures would be rejected. If she had preferred that outcome. If she had set up Precious Jin to take the fall.

"Then we returned to Olynthus System. That's where we were when the message from you arrived. I went to Pelasgia Terce and retrieved the salt you asked for. I interviewed Prince Jiàn's household. In the course of this I discovered that Precious Jin had flown separately to the planet. She intended to meet with Prince Jiàn. And I heard her say—"

Comms broke in. "Take all weigh off the ship."

The gravity cut. The transition bell rang. The little ship rolled, and they both shifted to absorb the movement. They fell through.

creatures like winged snakes rise out of wind-torn waves pounding on jagged rocks

"So you killed her," said Sun, although he did not recall telling her.

"Yes, Your Highness."

She considered his words with a thoughtful frown.

"If I have acted outside my authority I accept full responsibility," he said. "As for the ghost soldiers, they are innocent of any actions against you or Chaonia, Your Highness, and I recommend—"

She raised a hand for silence, listening to ship's comms, her gaze fixed on her personal virtual screen, the one no one could see but her.

One minute, two minutes, four minutes ticked past. Five minutes. Six.

She came back to herself and relaxed enough that he knew they were in no immediate peril. Yet.

"With regard to Precious Jīn, you did what needed to be done in your capacity as my bodyguard. What do you mean by ghost soldiers?"

"We are dead to our banners. We no longer have the right to carry our battle names. I was taken aback when Traps started calling himself and the others 'ghosts,' but the name stuck. In the banners, you belong to a grandmother, to a lineage, to a wheelship. You belong. I thought that if taking on the role of 'ghost' would create belonging, then let us call ourselves ghosts and give ourselves new names."

"Isn't Kurash your original wheelship name?"

He could now see the irony of how it had all unfolded. "I needed something to call myself before I fully understood the situation. The others had to decide what they wanted to do when I came to them. Thereby they had time to decide what came next."

"What made you search for abandoned banner soldiers? It never occurred to me there could be any liminal space between a banner soldier and a corpse."

"I suppose the Phene syndicates who bought them didn't want to outright kill the injured and disabled ones but didn't consider them worth spending any more resources on, so they simply disposed of them. I found the first two by accident on Orbital Habitat Matoas. After that, I knew to look. On our return voyage to Karnos, Captain Shì gave me leeway to check orbital habitats and moons. That meant our travel time took a little longer, but because of your new orders he knew we would not be called on to act immediately, so he felt he could spare the weeks."

"Just these five, then?"

"No, I found fourteen. I offered them the option of staying leashed where they were, in truly appalling conditions, each one. Or of having the leash removed and settling on Pelasgia Terce."

"Pelasgia Terce!"

"The planet needs more hands to work. Or they could join me."

"I see. Did any choose to stay leashed?"

"No. But one spaced himself rather than choose. May his ghost find the peace he deserves. Of the rest, eight chose to build new lives on Pelasgia Terce. I was able to use your authority to commandeer passage for them and secure provisional citizenship."

"Were you, indeed?" She tapped fingers on the desk.

He waited. Was she angry? Suspicious? Or just answering some other message?

Finally she looked up. "I hold Captain Shì in the greatest admiration. I spoke with him before you got here. He praised your discipline, your ability to work productively with others, and your initiative. Everything you have said to me here affirms his praise."

"The captain has been supportive. He is a good commander. Much credit also goes to Ay, who counseled me on Chaonian customs."

She rose. "Can I assume you are willing to take up your duty as my personal bodyguard? Not as banner to Royal, but as lieutenant to queen-marshal."

"Your Highness! It is my honor to serve you. But . . ."

"But?" Her eyebrow quirked in a question. She clearly did not expect anyone to answer her with "but."

He didn't know how to ask.

After all, she guessed what he meant to say. "You are concerned about the engineered hallucination. For the moment it's not an immediate concern because—"

Anger hit like a storm, creased her expression. A pent-up fury. Coiled lightning that would obliterate anything in its path.

"—Kiran Seth captured Persephone. He knew enough to leave her ring behind, so I have no means to track her. Presumably she is somewhere in the empire."

"A prisoner?" Lethargy gripped his limbs, towing him toward the deck.

She said, sharply, "Soldier, sit down!"

He sat, head spinning. What feeling shuddered through his mind and flesh as if all energy were being drained like blood flowing from a spigot that could not be turned off? Not dauntless Persephone. He had thought . . . dreamed . . . imagined they would meet again now that he could consider himself a person of honor.

Sun rested a hand on his head. "She's either dead, or we will get her back. Meanwhile, I need to know I can count on you for the battle ahead. Can I, Kurash?"

Words rose on his lips. *I am bound by the ancient covenant and the crown of light.* But he wasn't that person anymore. He had lost his battle name and become a ghost.

Yet ghosts could still fight. Ghosts could still live.

"Your Highness, my honor and my life belong to you."

You Have Really Fucked Things up Now, Asshole

Central Defense Cadet Academy trained me well. Imprisoned as I am in a sealed compartment with inert furniture and no network connection, I stick to a strict routine that follows Sun's training protocol. Physical training, military science, operations and management, philosophy and the arts, fleet history and strategy, and field exercises, adapted to fit my circumstances. Because they are stored in my implant, I even read *Analects: On Family and Honor* and *Introduction to Tactical Ethics*, two textbooks I studiously avoided in the academy.

Vacuum-sealed packets of food and bulbs of juice or coffee arrive at precise six-hour intervals through a slot too small for even me to squeeze through. The slot leads not into the passageway, barred by an ordinary security hatch, but into the adjoining compartment, where presumably the banner soldier innocently stands guard with no memory of slamming their body repeatedly against the bulkhead for a chance to throttle me.

The callous demonstration of engineered hallucination enrages me all over again. I feel a remote sort of pity for the banner soldier involved, who would kill me if they ever got their hands on me, but really it is about Kurash. According to the local time stamp on my implant, it has been two Chaonian Prime years since I last saw him. I don't fully recall his face or his frame, more the way his presence made me feel electrically ablaze.

Is he still alive? Does it matter if he is? Of course it matters to him. But for all my cunning plans and my attempt on the *Huma* to re-create the initial breath-stopping thrill of being near him, our situation has not changed. At this point there is no evidence the engineering that forces him to try to kill me *can* be changed.

Thinking of him distracts me for a few minutes from the titanosaurus in the room: *Where is Tiana?*

Was she left behind in Sena System because she was never of importance? Or was she brought with us and is even now elsewhere on the ship obedient to *his* command? My brain has circled over and over again, slicing through *his* words. *What if I told you that I chose Tiana to be your cee-cee because she too is an agent of the Oculi?*

What if I told you a lie that I want you to believe is truth because it will upset you? Because it will turn you against a person you trust. Because turning you against a person you trust will make you more likely to cast your line to my vessel as the last port in this storm. At Port Panic, Tiana believed in me when Sun did not. I refuse to let my father poison me against her.

We have dropped through seven beacons and have not slowed to take on a utility shuttle or courier. Nor have we docked. I haven't felt the telltale shudder of an attached ship being released, not since it happened in Sena System. It's been many days in Prime time, as we say in the republic when we refer to measuring the length of day and year according to the palace in Argos. In that time he has not returned to speak to me, nor has the Rider. I'm surprised Father didn't pop me in a lifepod, but perhaps he prefers to allow me to stew. Maybe he thinks he can break me through boredom. He has another think coming.

Each time we drop through a beacon I am able to add to my map, because even in the glimpse I'm given I can count how many beacons exist in the system we enter. Some are living and open, some are dead and shut, and some are warped with a twisted aura as if they are alive but diseased. Does that mean a ship could go through them? Who would want to try, not knowing the outcome?

I want Tiana to be alive. If he had killed her, surely he would have used the fact to taunt me. Or maybe he is holding that knife in reserve. I wouldn't put anything past him. I wish he'd liked me better growing up. But I suppose it is better he did not. Imagine how hard this would be if someone you genuinely loved and admired and trusted betrayed you so thoroughly.

A bell chimes. Twenty minutes to transition. Ten. Five. All weigh off the ship. We roll and drop in, falling toward the most resplendent star system I could ever hope to see. Eight living beacons shine; three dead ones gleam with the matte black of obsidian. Eleven total.

Before the collapse, the Apsaras homeworld had eleven beacons, one for each of the original janus lines. At some point the engineers connected those original, separate lines to each other to make the network efficient, starting with three-beacon cerberus systems and five-beacon scylla systems. They gave seven beacons to a few systems, like Karnos, Destiny, Auger, and Axiom, thus making them crucial intersections for trade and communications. But only Yele System and Anchor System have eleven beacons.

By no possible route I know of can we have traveled through a mere seven beacon drops to Yele. We have arrived in Anchor.

Wow.

I'm too stunned by the vision of eleven beacons to make sense of the flood of droplets spilling through the network, except so much traffic is flowing toward Anchor.

Then we fall through and I stare at the blank white walls of my compartment.

A klaxon blares. It isn't the same alarm as on a Chaonian ship, but if this isn't a call to battle stations then I was just faking my bad scores in training so as not to upstage Sun and the others.

The first thing I do is use the head, just in case, because who wants to be stuck in a physical conflagration while having the desperate urge to pee.

It seems unlikely a Phene ship would call battle stations as a drill upon arriving in the heart of their own empire, so I decide this is a good time to figure out a way to get into the adjoining compartment while the crew is busy. There's a decent chance it's part of the same security compartment with shared life support.

Like all of Sun's Companions, I have a node hidden beneath the skin of my left forearm, sewn into the ulna. It's a secret place to store physical information. It's also a convenient place to hide a needle-like tool, flat at one end and round at the other and strong enough to take on rough duty. I double over to hide my hand and slip out the eight-centimeter-long tool with a grunt of discomfort and a bead of blood, then palm it. I kneel beside the door panel and probe.

Ah. An irregularity reveals a seam.

What would James do?

The flat plane of the tool slides smoothly in through a sliver of a gap. I wiggle and waggle it, trying to get purchase. What I wouldn't give for James's expertise right now. One of the things Sun understands is that it takes a skilled and disciplined team. Not a strutting gaggle of unco-operative individuals who think they are better than everyone else. We all saw what happened to the Yele League when Eirene slammed them down with a military force they hadn't respected up until the moment they had to sign a demeaning treaty at the point of a stinger. Anyone my age is old enough to remember her marriage to Baron Voy, who made the best of a bad situation.

Ha ha. We are the best. Collectively, I mean.

I'm going to get this panel off, get out of this compartment, and take over the ship. Any moment now. If only I weren't so lightheaded. What is up with that?

Dizziness sways me. The tool slips out of my grasp and falls to the deck. My legs give way. I fall to the deck as spots glimmer in my vision and I can't catch my breath. I am also a tool, aren't I? Clones are tools that can theoretically be manufactured in bulk. That is one of the reasons they were outlawed, if we can believe the historical accounts that survived. Because they were manufactured, they were not considered people and that led to abuse, and abuse led to declaring new subsets of people not being considered people even from among humans born by biological means, even though cloning is also biology. It's so complicated.

I don't have enough air. For a while I lie there panting as the view hazes in and out. Then, slowly, I can breathe again. Slowly my dizziness fades.

Eventually I push myself to hands and knees. Stand by leaning on the table. Drink something that tastes nasty. Coffee. Ugh. As the stimulant hits my system, I realize my captors reduced the ventilation flow into the compartment. Oxygen deprivation did the rest. I am truly a prisoner.

Fuck. Now what?

Just as I slip the tool back into my arm, the ship's engines change tune. Deceleration pushes. I strap myself in, just in case. They haven't left me a vac suit.

Forty-seven minutes later the engines go quiet. Twenty-three minutes after that, we dock with a solid thump.

I tidy up. No one comes to get me. After a while, I busy myself in cutting off a section of the sheet to create a face shield, something that might delay a murderous banner soldier from being triggered by a glimpse of my face. It lacks a screen for my eyes but is better than nothing, and it stays on when I do handstands and flips.

At the six-hour mark from the last food packet, no new packet arrives.

The food packets are all hermetically sealed. I have wisely not thrown all of the emptied packets into the recycling chute, which is too small for me to fit into or I would try to escape through that outlet. I set out eighteen packets unsealed, seal them, line them up beside the panel alongside my beacon badge, and set my implant to monitor oxygen levels. Then I go back to work.

Within two minutes the oxygen levels start to drop. It's tricky timing a suck of air out of a packet and holding my breath, but we did all kinds of drills at CeDCA, endlessly, over and over. The key is to keep your head.

I have five packets left when I finally get enough purchase to pry the panel up. It pops out with such force the panel claps my shoulder and clatters to the deck. The air flow in the compartment ceases entirely. Automatic shutdown.

Don't panic. I take another packet of air into my lungs. Then I pick up the beacon badge and its blade and, because I am not James to have the steadiness of hand to fuss with wiring, I say curse this to the hells and slice right through everything damn-the-torpedoes-full-speed-ahead.

There's a crackling like fireworks, a spray of sparks, the door hisses open, and the gravity on the whole damn ship cuts. A klaxon begins hooting with a repeated message in Phenish that I imagine means something like: *You have really fucked things up now, asshole.* The tone is sardonic, like your worst enemy and best closet squeeze mocking you. Not that I would know anything about that.

I grab the tool and the beacon badge as they float upward and tuck them away before I lose them. I twist the sheet around my waist to make a holding bag, then pull myself via handholds into a passageway lit by red emergency strips. There's air, and since all the doors and hatches are open I'm not concerned about asphyxiating immediately.

I propel myself into the adjoining room where the lifepods are fixed to the deck. The first thing I see is a clear bag holding my stinger baton, my boots, and my formal dress half cape, which is also secretly an emergency vac skin. I cut the bag open. Everything feels better once I'm armed and shod.

These are standard-issue universal lifepods. The closest is empty. The second contains a youth. It takes me a moment to recognize Metis as she would look in mid-adolescence, still some baby fat and not fully developed. This individual is at least ten years younger than the Metis twins who captured me. The next lifepod holds another young Metis.

I pull myself to the fourth lifepod.

The shock of seeing Tiana numbs my hands. I lose my grip and begin to drift upward. Catch a handle with a booted toe and drag myself back down.

She lies suspended in the lifepod in such ominous repose that if it were not for the green glow of the indicator panel I might believe her dead.

I have to make a decision. Decant her immediately or scout the ship first.

Prudence dictates I scout the ship first but that would mean leaving her here unguarded with all the doors open. Those open doors could mean anything under Phene protocol. The oxygen levels have dropped a tiny percentage, nothing worrying yet, but I have to wonder if this is how the Phene abandon ships through an automated procedure when they think they've lost control of a vessel but hope to be able to reclaim the ship later. Since the Phene left life support on, they didn't intend to kill me right away. But they might return at any moment. I can't take the chance of losing Ti again.

I unlock the seal manually and start the de-suspension process. Mist clouds the interior. A timer counts backward.

What about the Metises? They exist only as a means to dethrone Sun. I could push them out an airlock. I could tamper with the lifepod so it shuts off and kills them while they're still in stasis. Is that what Sun would want?

Even if it was, they never asked to be created. They aren't the schemers, just the pawns.

The light blinks and a chime beeps. The outer transparent plate rolls back to leave a wafer-thin barrier like a soap bubble. Air jets through. Ti's eyes stir beneath closed eyelids. Her lips part as might a drowsy lover recalling the pleasures of the bed.

I look away, throat tight. *The radiant glance of your face.*

What is wrong with me? She's not my beloved. She's my employee. It's safer to watch the panel, wait for the next chime. The brush of air like a kiss on my elbow as the last seal clears.

"Perse?"

Her voice is hoarse and so gloriously alive that I grasp her hands and help her as she sits up woozily. She rests a hand against her eyes, sagging trustfully against me. An incredible sense of well-being washes through me as her body is warmed by mine, slowly restored to full function.

The euphoria doesn't last. She coughs out a bit of sticky, clotted residue. "Ugh, that tastes nasty. What happened? No, wait. The triplets. Where are we?"

"We're prisoners of my father and the Phene. In Anchor System. Docked. Apparently everyone left the ship. We have to get out of here while we have a chance."

"All right. All right." She releases me, pats herself down as if checking to see if all her limbs are intact. Our captors stripped her out of the working tunic and loose trousers she'd had on, so she is wearing only leggings and undershirt. The fabric hugs her voluptuous curves like paint. I look away quickly. It doesn't seem right to stare, not now and not ever, because of who we are to each other. If she notices my twitch she does not say. I hope she is muzzy enough from awakening to miss the nuances.

"Coffee," I say, handing her the last unsealed packet.

She sucks it down.

"No nausea?" I ask.

"No. We trained for this."

"I have to admit I had a very different idea of the curriculum at Vogue Academy before I met you."

She tips a smile at me that cuts me to the heart. "Everyone does."

I step back to give her room. Or myself room. "We need to find Command."

She clambers out, stops to stare at the other two lifepods. "Who are these?"

"Metis clones."

"Princess Metis? These two are just children. Fourteen or fifteen at most."

"I'll explain as we go."

We set off, pulling ourselves along. At CeDCA we studied blueprints of captured Phene ships. We even had a couple of mockups built in a big warehouse where we practiced boarding exercises in which the boarding party needed to reach Command before the enemy blew up the ship. Solomon loved those drills but, then again, any cadet aiming for the marines couldn't get enough of the sheer adrenaline rush of attacking into a confined area under deadly fire with a ticking clock and imminent death. That's why they become marines.

This ship appears to be a corvette equivalent with the old-fashioned stylings of a vessel that was new when my grandparents were young. It will therefore likely have four decks, one hangar, and two command centers, one in the center-rear of the ship and the other, closer to us, at the stem set back from the beacon drive's housing. We sail into forward Command's cylinder-like space to find it empty, the consoles powered down, the air sluggish. No fans. No engine hum. No *tick tick tick* of ship systems whirring away.

People speak all kinds of languages, and Argosy fleets separated from each other for a thousand years obviously would experience language shift. That is why the Argosies all functioned with a standard written language for communications with other ships and fleets. Ideograms are an elegant and powerful technology that can be adapted at a basic level to any language and thus be understandable between populations no matter what spoken language people use. Pilots and navigators learn specific sets of trade-and travel-related characters, as do merchants, diplomats, and travelers. On Chaonia we use ideograms as our written language. Not everyone does.

On a Phene military ship, where labels and instructions are written in Phenish letters, there is always a secondary screen displaying the universal characters. I identify weapons, navigation, sensors, and life support. The hangar bay console shows a shuttle on a pad, powered down. The docking compartment includes a camera. A banner soldier is sealed into the airlock. To get in or out you have to get past him.

"You've got the leash," says Tiana, indicating the baton I carry. "We can get past him."

"He's programmed with the engineered hallucination. He's wearing a vac suit so we can't asphyxiate him, at least not quickly."

"Ah. Other options? How about the shuttle?"

"These corvettes usually have a viewing bubble. I'd like to see if we can figure out where we are in-system." I map the ship's blueprint in my mind, then point. "Let's try that hatch."

"That hatch" lets us onto a short passageway that decants us onto a terrace-like compartment whose ceiling is a clear half dome. The angle of view reveals a segment of a habitat in orbit around a rocky moon, itself in orbit around a medium-large ice planet. The planet's delicately patterned blue-white surface fades as a distant sun sets behind it. The habitat has a blocky, low-rent look, the kind of place set up to funnel resources toward microgravity industrial production and fabrication.

Ti's hand tugs on my elbow, her touch like a bolt of lightning through flesh too weak to sustain such power. I flinch so hard away my motion alters, sending me tumbling sideways.

"Perse?"

"I'm all right."

"I . . ."

I break off as I look at her. What do I expect to see? What do I hope to see? I shouldn't admit such things even to myself, and that's for the best, because what I do see is apprehension, even outright fear, on a face that has borne up so magnificently under such a wild ride as we have had in Sun's orbit.

She's not looking at me at all.

"Is that what I think it is?" she asks, voice trembling.

I had been tracing the lines of the habitat, the curve of the moon, the authority of the planet. She is looking away from all those anchoring things, into space. Far away, although not at all far in astronomical terms, a kaleidoscope of phantasmic light spills, sparks, undulates, flashes. Dies.

My lips part in an unvoiced prayer. What I saw inside the infinity moment within the beacons is real, not an artifact of the system. Sun launched her audacious plan. She sent Zàofù and Anas by separate routes to Anchor to distract the Phene while she breaks through the mines in Sleepless System, and Windworn if Angharad Black can reach it, so the reserve fleets in Karnos System can enter imperial space.

The titanic battle has begun.

The Valiant One Does His Job

Gushers of steam scalded everything they touched. Flames roared toward a rent in the compartment bulkhead. Makinde hauled an unconscious, steam-burned spacer across the debris-strewn deck toward the only remaining way out: a twisted ladder funneling upward to an emergency hatch.

The relentless fusillade had finally pierced the *Red Hare*'s shields and massive hull. Ordnance had torn through the secondary engineering compartment and its tubes and consoles. The spacer he was carrying had lost both legs, bleeding stemmed for now by the vac suit's automatic seal. Paint blown off the bulkhead had sprayed the spacer's exposed face with gray freckles. The atmosphere was venting fast.

"This way!" shouted a marine from the ladder. It was Oanh, always singing out in the right place at the right time.

Makinde stumbled over a spacer lying suit-less, only his boots and gloves still on him, gear blown out by the seams and scattered like signal flags. Not a face he knew. The eyes were open and staring. Was he breathing? But Makinde's arms were already full. He couldn't carry both.

"Hurry!" shouted Oanh. "We're losing integrity."

She flung a line at Makinde, who could not grab it lest he lose hold of the spacer, so Oanh scrambled down and across the debris. She fastened the tether to Makinde and another to the unconscious spacer.

Just in time.

The rip in the bulkhead gaped as the pressure became too much. Makinde lost hold of the spacer, who slammed into an intact portion of the bulkhead. Where Oanh had gone he didn't know, but for himself, he felt the grip of space. Was that a hiss in the right forearm of his vac suit? They were meant to self-seal. A severed leg swept past and out through the rent. The tether jerked hard, yanking him to a stop.

The flames died as the last of the air escaped and the atmosphere equalized. He grabbed a bench still bolted to the deck and sat himself down in the airless, breached compartment. Dozer clung to his arm, pale with worry.

"Oh fucking hells," he said, knowing he needed to move. No time to freeze up. Go. Go.

The hull shuddered as the shields threw off another round of attack. His comms squawked but his ears couldn't register the speech. A figure loomed up beside him. A hand slapped his back. He looked up at a marine whose weathered face could be seen through a vac suit's faceplate. Like every marine, Gen looked like she lived for this kind of fucked-up shit. But maybe she wasn't so bright-eyed and bushy-tailed. Actually, she looked bone weary. She tapped at his helmet.

Oh. Was there something wrong with him? Did he have a concussion?

He got to his feet, swaying, and began arduously reeling himself in along the safety line, all the way to the ladder, as a squad of damage control squirted into the compartment and headed for the rent, Lieutenant Commander Zahrah Yún Albalasagun in the lead. Somehow he got up the ladder and then somehow he was in a passageway next to the legless spacer. A medic flipped his vac suit helmet to the side. He inhaled smoke and began coughing.

The medic stuck a breather to his face. Sweet oxygen poured into his lungs. "Your valve got jammed. I can't believe you didn't pass out."

Boom. Boom. Boom.

The pounding did not stop although the enemy hadn't managed to follow up on the breach. Even so, and although his hearing still jangled, his body could feel the difference in resonance in the big ship with one of its torch drives down.

When the medic removed the breather, Makinde said, "I don't remember how I got down here. Last I remember, I was up on the bridge."

"You need to go to medical, Lieutenant. Follow the gurneys."

His boots took him back to the bridge. No one looked up when he staggered in. One person was slumped on the floor. Passed out? No, with their head stuck inside a whining console, the way James would. Someone had found a chair for the crane marshal. The battle had gone on so long that the venerable Zàofù was no longer standing at the strategos dais but seated, leaning on the railing, sipping at a stim bulb. He looked one hundred years old, exhausted and grim.

Makinde crossed the bridge at what felt like a crawl. The air had turned to sludge to impede his path.

Zàofù looked up. "Makinde! Report."

His mouth moved as if someone else were working it and he but a puppet conveying its thoughts. "Secondary engineering compartment breached. Now equalized. Unknown casualties. Off line for now. Breach being repaired."

"The secondary engineering compartment? I sent you to Hangar 3."

Hangar 3? He pressed a hand to his head and it came away sticky, not blood but a pink-gray viscous substance.

Hangar 3 boiling with smoke. A cloud of ash. A spacer burned at such heat that his vac suit had melted into his skin and bones. Then a gap. A blank. No memory except for pulling wounded crew out of the compartment as steam spattered everywhere. Smeared the ash into mud coated in droplets of blood.

Dozer sent him an image of carnage that showed him right in the middle of it. His legs wobbled. He groped for a console, steadied himself, and sat down on the edge of the strategos dais. Panting.

"Medic!" called the crane marshal. Then, to someone else, "Did the courier from Hangar 3 depart?"

"It was destroyed in the explosion," said comms.

Another voice: "*Peregrine* reporting all their torch drives crippled. Structural damage. They are abandoning ship."

More damage reports, 50 percent of the fleet reporting significant damage. Another ship hulked. A trio of Chaonian cruisers rescued from a Phene dreadnought and its escorts just in time by a decisive attack from the Larissan Centaur Division. But even the Larissan cruisers with their heavy armor and tight maneuvers could not hold out forever.

A medic knelt before him, rations pouch slung against a hip. "Lieutenant? I can escort you to medical."

The youth was younger than Makinde, a recruit fresh from Chaonia with the fleet the crane marshal had brought to Trinity. Their face was sweat-stained and streaked with smoky residue but their expression was focused. The baby hatchling wasn't rattled by this disaster.

Dammit, he was not here to be rattled. He was here to fight.

"Are there stim bulbs?" he asked hoarsely. "I'm dehydrated."

He drained two and felt the combined hit of liquid, sugars, and stimulants slam into his body. Dozer brightened as Makinde's vitals improved.

Once his mind cleared, he sent a forlorn ping via the ring network.

ANYONE IN-SYSTEM?

No answer. Zàofù's fleet had reached Anchor with only token resistance. That had been strategy on the part of the enemy as the Phene pulled back to entice them into a single pitched battle fought in the heart of the empire. Sun was counting on it. She had maneuvered the Phene into acting the way she wanted them to. But Chaonia's superior discipline and strength could not hold out forever when they were outnumbered four to one. Five to one. Ten to one. Whatever.

A massive shudder rocked the huge ship. Alarms rang across the bridge and were silenced as spacers bent over their consoles, tense and determined.

A breathless voice over comms: "We are being boarded through the breach in Hangar 3."

Boarded!

"Lieutenant Nazir is down. Reinforcements requested in the immediate area."

Makinde scrambled to his feet, pumped on stimulants and on the shocking idea that he could grapple with the enemy; win or lose, live or die, he was finally going to scrap. "Marshal, I can take this."

"Go on." Grim Zàofù might be, but he never sounded panicked. "Let me know when my son arrives with the Second Fleet."

He did not say *if*. No one in Sun's fleet said *if*.

Makinde hustled back the way he'd come, fastening on a new helmet, picking up a fresh stinger from a locker. He had to make two detours past damaged passageways choked with debris, smoke, heat. Spacers hustled to clear routes and to patch severed wires or leaking pipes. On the way he pinged Oanh—alive, still kicking—and told her squad to hustle up and meet him there. She let him know they were already there, together with survivors from the damage control unit that had gone in to try to seal the breach.

"Give me vulnerabilities, any routes or schemes we can use to get at them. I'll send Dozer in to get visuals. Be careful, Doze. Don't show yourself."

Dozer warmed to a determined orange-brown readiness. One of the damage control chiefs pinged charts into Dozer's comms node. With a burst of excitement, the little symbiont slipped out of sight into a maintenance conduit.

The sound of fierce stinger fire grew in volume as they made their way aft and down three decks. Soon the pops and rebounds and staccato impacts were all he could hear. The lieutenant commander's body had been dragged back from an emplacement made by piling up debris to form a defensive barrier blocking access to Hangar 3. Wounded were being pulled back by a medic, and two more corpses sprawled in a bloody mess. Oanh's squad were crouched behind the barrier, shooting into the shattered hangar, but the Phene boarding party knew how to shelter in place. Taking in the situation at a glance, the best Makinde could say was that the marines weren't retreating despite being hard-pressed, but that was a marine for you.

With a buzz, Dozer initiated contact. Shots from the hangar's dark interior dropped into Makinde's network, images patched into a panorama as Dozer's tentacles cautiously snapped a sweep of the space in hi-res and infrared.

Makinde found the lieutenant in charge, the Honorable Carla Samtarras. "Oi, Carla." They'd been friends at the royal academy. By now he knew everyone in her platoon. "The old man wants us to kill them, kick any survivors into space, then seal up the breach before they can get another boarding pod in."

"We tried a direct assault. Nazzie's whole platoon got taken out by those fuckers. We can't get purchase because we end up charging straight into their line of fire."

"Look here." He pinged over Dozer's visuals. "Thirty-two heat signatures."

"Whoa. We can work with this! I'm sending this to the squads on a three-D grid with every hostile pinpointed."

He set virtual flags on the grid. "The chiefs have traced two additional entry routes we can use. This one here is through a maintenance conduit the hostiles haven't found. The other one is through this hole in the bulkhead into an adjoining compartment. It's blocked from Phene view by debris. The hostiles are stuck in there until more boarding pods drop more boots. We have to move right now from three directions."

Carla flashed an affirmative. "Squad one, through the conduit. Squad two, through the hole. Squad three, shield up to max. Double-secure your lines. You're with me. Chief, on my command, pump atmosphere into the hangar to try to blow the hostiles out or at least dislodge them if they've secured themselves."

Makinde tapped back into CIC. "What's the ETA of any returning hostile landing craft?"

"Eight to ten minutes," Ops replied.

His ring buzzed as a ping dropped in.

It was Razin: SECOND FLEET IN-SYSTEM. WE HAVE TAKEN DAMAGE IN CUT STONE BUT SHOULD TAKE SOME OF THE HEAT OFF YOU. ARE YOU THERE, MAKINDE?

"I'll be scratched in the hell of itches," he said with a grin as he sent the news onward to the old man, then pinged back: NOT DEAD YET BUT TAKING A LEGENDARY BEATING. ETA FOR SUN?

It would take Razin minutes to reply and he didn't have time to wait. A blast of heat scorched the passageway bulkhead a meter away. Shrapnel spun out from an impact in the debris line, peppering Oanh, who fell back bleeding as Gen scrambled up to her place in the firing line.

He grinned, eager to take charge. "Squareheads, the Second Fleet is in-system and cocking around like they think they are going to rescue us. Let's get these hostiles off our ship and go rescue them."

He grabbed Oanh's impact shield, already dialed up to its highest setting, and waved Carla back. "I'll take the first wave."

The squad lined up behind him as he pushed to the edge of the barrier. Exhilaration filled him almost to bursting. This is what Sun would do: draw attention to herself while a second attack slammed into the enemy. The flanking units pinged in with green. They were in position. He was ready to go. Ready. Ready. The hells was he ready.

Go!

He lunged forward into the gap. Immediately he was slammed by impact after impact trying to shove him backward. Adrenaline surged. He was solid as he tucked behind the shield. *Bam bam bam. Bam bam bam.* Each. Fucking. Step. Forward. He reached a shattered console just as his shield cracked along multiple lines. Damn, the Phene were good.

He ducked behind the console and shook off the damaged shield. A second later Gen dropped in beside him. They caught their breath as pops burst around them. Air blasted past, tugging on their lines as it tried to drag them out the breach. He braced against the console, stinger ready.

"Doze?"

An image from Dozer dropped onto his viewscreen. Two helmets, him and Gen. Blinking red flags were the hostiles, well positioned, using fixed debris that hadn't been torn out in the original breach to lock themselves into place. They could not see him but he knew where they were. From a ventilation shaft in the hangar ceiling, Dozer had a view of twenty-six of the thirty-two hostiles.

He fed the image to the squad. Only Ngân did not respond. No time to look for the wounded, that was Carla's job with the second wave. Clearing out this nest of interlopers was his job. Grinning like a fool, he gave the order—maybe he screamed it over the squad band—and rolled sideways. Railgun fire punched after his movement. Something thudded into his leg. No matter. He had this. He stood up exactly where Dozer's calculation said he could get a clear shot from two meters up. The gusting air caught his body and lofted him out of the way of the startled initial fire of two hostiles as he shot one, then the next. He sent a burst into their tethers to sever them, then reeled himself back to the console like it was the only place left in the entire universe. Droplets of red trailed after him. Two, then three, then four, then five bodies whirled and bounced back toward the breach. One was a headless marine but the rest were hostiles. Done. Gone.

The instant he reached the console he clamped his boots to the deck. No sign of Gen. Dozer flashed him a new image: green flags for the marines now swarming in from three sides. Nineteen hostiles still active. No, seventeen.

"Forward!"

He ran to the barrier that the two he'd shot had been hiding behind. It was part of the courier's tail that had gotten wedged into a jagged rent in the deck. No sign of the courier's crew. Probably blasted into oblivion. Railgun fire hailed around him. The slab of debris started to heat up under the sheer volume.

BOSS GO LEFT NOW. NOW.

He rolled left just as a flash-bang dropped into where he'd been lying. Its force hit him in the midsection, and a lucky shot or a sharp edge of shrapnel severed his line. The airstream caught him and sent him whirling toward the breach. He grabbed for a pillar but his hands were numb and he couldn't keep a grip. Abruptly, something caught hold of his boot and wrapped tight, securing him to the pillar. Dozer had swarmed out of hiding, symbiont body strained to its limits as ou struggled to hold him in place as yet more debris and sundered flesh swept past or thumped against them like whacks from a shovel.

Fuck fuck fuck. Drops of blood beaded out of his suit's midsection, and his chest hurt like a motherfucker, and his leg wouldn't bend, but none of that mattered. Ahead he saw a marine. Surely that was rugby-playing Zǐmò, from first squad, grappling hand-to-hand with a Phene straggler, tangled in their tethers as if fate had bound them together until death do us part. He had to get up there to help his buddy.

Carla came onto comms, shouting. "Pull back! Pull back!"

What in the hells? Twenty-five red flags were crossed out, four had been vented, and that left only two who Dozer couldn't see because all ou's efforts were now fixed on holding Makinde inside the ship. Plus the wrestler.

Why call a retreat when they'd won?

Then he saw a shadow outside the breach, a big, dark destroyer so close that if it had had portholes he could have telescoped his vision and seen the enemy's faces. Two boarding pods detached with flashes of energy. Sixteen to a pod. Thirty-two incoming. There would be more. A destroyer carried hundreds of troops, and they had finally after days of relentless battle penetrated past all of the *Red Hare*'s defenses.

"Makinde?" Carla's voice. "Talk to me. I'm sending Gen and Ngân to pull you out."

"Thought Ngân got hit." His voice came out strangely wheezy, bubbling. The effort punched spikes of agony farther into his chest.

"Some sharpshooter tagged his helmet but not his hard head—"

"Oh fuck." Gaze still on the ragged breach, he wondered if pain was making him hallucinate.

Light bloomed like fireworks. The destroyer lit up all across its stern as it was tagged with a fusillade of incoming fire. One of the boarding pods exploded. The other got grappled back just in time as the destroyer veered away like a huge charybdis on a laborious sideways roll as it dove back into the deep.

"They're running." Speaking made him cough. Blood spattered his faceplate from the inside. What the fuck? The pain seized up his insides.

BOSS YOU ARE WOUNDED.

A new ship loomed into view. He thought, *We are dead,* and then he realized that the bold symbol painted in huge letters on its massive hull marked it as one of the Larissan Centaurs.

"Just in time," he whispered, or maybe he couldn't whisper, maybe his voice was gone. He sagged as the airstream slackened, and the atmosphere equalized, and he floated in a timeless void as Dozer stung him with a shot of painkiller.

BOSS? BOSS! STAY AWAKE!

As the world faded, he thought, *That was some fight.* Then Gen's concerned face loomed over him, and he let go.

The Wily Persephone Plows Onward like an Awkward, Blunt Beast

Since Sun can't possibly be here yet with reinforcements, we must be watching the Second Fleet getting pummeled by the numerically superior Phene. Her daring plan will succeed only if Anas, here, and Zàofù with the Sixth and Ninth at the Gardens Beacon don't break before the rest arrive. I can't control the sensors to magnify the view so it is impossible to see detail, only the furious heaven of battle. Comms has a monotone voice on repeat, something we need to know but can't understand.

"There's something I need to know because I don't understand," I say.

"What? You never did explain how we got here but I guess I have an idea."

"How so?"

"I thought I was helping the triplets find a new situation for themselves. But they blocked me in and told me if I didn't take off the ring you'd be killed. So I took off the ring."

Ti took off the ring for the same reason I took off the ring. It's all I can do to keep an impassive face as she goes on.

"They slapped a fast-acting sedative on me. I woke up here." She rubs her eyes as if to clear the last of the drug from her vision.

I say, "My father kidnapped us. The triplets are clones from Nona's lab, as we suspected. The thing is, he told me you work for the Oculi."

Her expression congeals like pudding left out in the sun. "Do you believe him?"

It's a good thing I have already been through this conversation in my own head. "No, I don't believe you work for the Oculi."

Her tight shoulders drop. Her tense jawline relaxes. But she keeps a wary gaze fixed on me. "I hear a but."

"I do think you work for someone."

"That's right!" she counters indignantly. "I work for Kaspar, for my parents. I've told you all this. You know them."

"Sure, that adds up. But there's got to be more."

"Why does there have to be more, Persephone?"

Oof. I've offended her. I plow onward like an awkward, blunt beast. "Because I just don't buy all your skills come from Vogue Academy."

She turns her back on me.

The battle rages on, too far away to threaten the habitat. Not yet. It's an erratic lightshow, eerily magnificent only because we aren't in the thick of being ripped apart, burned, frozen, and dead of oxygen loss. Even though Sun can't have arrived, Razin is here with the Second Fleet and Makinde with Zàofù. If we had our rings we could ping them, with or without local comms.

"At least you didn't believe your father," Ti remarks as if addressing the battle.

"Of course I didn't believe him."

Her body blends into the background of space, the fabric reflecting bits and pieces of light as if she is herself a half-hidden treasure chest filled to the brim with something more valuable than material wealth. Is the oxygen level dropping again? Am I drowning in hypoxic euphoria?

Minh would tell me that's not a thing, wouldn't she? Is Minh out there on one of those ships? Where are Ikenna and Ay? How is Solomon? What if he is dead, bleeding out against the bulkhead of a deserted passageway?

"You have no idea what Vogue Academy really is." Tiana is the most brilliant object in the star system, incandescent. "I have never lied to you. I was sponsored into Vogue Academy by the Campaspe Guild. I have a duty to the guild and to all its members who are my guild-folk and thus my responsibility too."

I blink about ten times as her anger washes over me. I know her face too well because I sneak too much time looking at it. She is the best thing that has ever happened to me. I value her too much to violate the terms of our contract. Her friendship is enough. It is more than I could have expected or demanded from a cee-cee, not that I ever expected to have a personal attendant, because I thought I had walked away from all that. Yet here we are.

In the horrible moment as I wonder what will become of us all, I have to admit I am in love.

I never wanted this. My bad crushes are safer. This will never ever do.

Let it go, asshole. Nothing to see here. Move on.

"I apologize," I say briskly as my backside bumps into a console. Reflexively I hook a foot into a handle and, like the jerk I am, I jerk to a halt. "I had to ask, because he said that to upset me. To make me doubt you. To make me doubt Sun. But I don't doubt either of you. I never have. I remember how you stood up for me at Port Panic when you had no reason to."

A silence follows this glaringly obvious statement. It lasts for fifty-eight seconds.

"All right," she says as she dons the bland mask worn by every graduate of Vogue Academy. "Now what? I presume the Phene disembarked onto the habitat."

Action is better than hopeless pining.

"So I assume. Otherwise why leave the banner soldier in the airlock. Either they're planning to come back or they're planning to send someone back."

"Why not take us with them?"

"They have a Rider. He must be the crew's priority."

"Why leave the Metis clones?"

"My father has two older Metis clones, closer to the princess's real age. They're the ones who grabbed me. It could be days or weeks before anyone checks a closed-up ship. Maybe we are hostages. Or sacrifices. Or trade goods. I don't want to hang around to find out."

"I'm still not sure what we can do."

"I'm trying to think like Sun. What's the most outrageous option?"

She laughs drily. "I feel you are about to tell me. You've got that look."

I blush, not wanting to ask what look. "Habitats go unarmed. That makes it a criminal act to fire on an unarmed habitat—which is why most habitats go unarmed."

"Circular reasoning. We don't know what the Phene do."

"The Phene fight outside their borders, which means inside their borders they've had peace for so long they've maybe stopped expecting war on home soil."

"And?"

"What if we take over the habitat and claim it for Chaonia?"

"Really, Perse? For one thing, how do we get past the banner soldier?"

"We take the shuttle to a different docking section on the habitat."

"We can't operate Phene equipment."

"We have a pair of clones whose handprints taken together may be close enough to work."

"If they are trained as pilots."

"I can direct them. Utility shuttles are pretty much automated with built-in fail-safes. No reason to think the Phene are different."

"If the girls will cooperate."

"I have a hunch about that."

"We'll be immediately identifiable as hostiles with our two arms."

"Not every subject of the empire is imperial Phene. We'll say we're refugees from, uh, Troia. Karnos, maybe. Or Kanesh."

"No, not refugees." She rubs a knuckle along her lower lip. I watch the movement of her finger, and I think about the husky attraction of her voice when she spoke to Angharad Black, but I need to concentrate, so I look away. "This seems like an industrial installation. If so, there are working people assigned here without their families. If so, there is likely to be a Campaspe Guild."

"There are Campaspe Guilds in the empire?"

She smiles slyly. "We're everywhere. The oldest guild known to humankind. There are guild annexes in any Repose District. Here's my idea. The girls and I are reassigned guild members arriving in this hapless backwater to take on new jobs, and you're our hired security escort."

"Why can't I be a guild member too?"

She rolls her eyes. "No one will believe you're a campaspe."

My cheeks flame at the same time as I dip my chin in embarrassment, wishing I could melt into the deck and vanish.

"I just meant you don't have the posture and the diction. You're a Core House asshole through and through. So, are we on?" She grins like a marine.

"After all this, it turns out you're an adrenaline junkie too?"

"I never said I wasn't."

"Okay. If . . ."

No one in Sun's fleet says *if*.

I slap Ti's shoulder a little too hard, the way marines do, the gesture both solidarity and challenge. Comrades in arms. Buddies. Nothing more. "Let's go decant those clones."

There isn't time to search for pockets of crew. As we skim aft back the way we came, we have to assume they all disembarked.

Ti says, "These murals on the walls are amazing art but kind of a crowded aesthetic with too much detail, don't you think?"

"What? I didn't notice." The paintings display a lot of color and shape, and I need to focus. But when we reenter the compartment with the lifepods I can't help but notice how muted its walls are compared to the rest of the ship.

We activate the lifepods. As the girls wake, their eyes flutter open. Their gazes dart around, confused and frightened. When they see my familiar face—familiar because they grew up with my clones—they relax. Ti and I help them to their feet. One Metis starts retching as low gravity unsettles her stomach.

The other Metis shoves away from the thin stream of bile as its globules spread outward. "Auntie, what's going on? We were ordered into the suspension modules. But this doesn't look like home."

"No, it isn't. I'm sorry to tell you that for reasons you were removed in a hurry from home. Events got a little wild. I'm here to get you to a safe haven." They can dig out the truth later. "But I need your help. First, what do I call you?"

"I'm Eight," says the one who didn't barf. "And she's Seven."

"Okay. We need to move fast, so we can talk later. Okay?"

"Who is she?" Eight whispers in awe, staring at Tiana as if at a blinding sun.

"She's my partner. Obey her." I drag the still-gagging Seven into the passageway.

She burps, then says, "I'm okay, I can manage."

"What is this place? Is this a ship?" asks Eight. "We've only been on a ship once. We passed through a beacon and came back, that's all. It was boring."

I guess Nona had to find out if they would succumb to beacon sickness. Imagine being that cold.

"Do we really have to go back?" Seven says to Eight. "I don't want to go back. I want to see the universe."

"Shhh." Eight elbows her and they exchange significant looks.

Ti and I glance at each other. She arches an inquisitive eyebrow. I shrug and offer her the half cape.

"Isn't this also an emergency vac suit?" she asks.

"Yes. Take it. No argument." I am the Companion. She has to obey me.

We enter the hangar. By the mercy of all the hells, the girls' handprints work. The shuttle isn't dependent on ship's life support. There's a dicey moment when I'm not sure how we are going to get the hangar doors open but I spot a chain of instructional ideograms streaming at the base of the console. The hangar doors grind open, which will vent the entire ship, but I don't see any way around that, and the banner soldier stuck in the airlock already has a vac suit. Klaxons hoot excitedly as I hang over the girls' shoulders and move their hands.

Somebody talks to me through comms but I don't understand so I don't reply. The shuttle's viewscreen shows us an exterior view of the corvette. Inside it is clearly a military ship. From out here it looks like an old-fashioned and battered independent merchant vessel crewed by a misfit collection of fuck-ups and ne'er-do-wells forced to cooperate on a noble quest, like in the historical drama *Journey to the West*. Disguised like this, it is merely one among many docked at the ramshackle station, nothing to see here, powered down, on its lowest level of life support. No one would think to search it. Did my father intend me to starve to death?

Fuck him and the ship he rode in on.

I start looking for docking options. After seventeen minutes two big robot drones appear and clamp on. After I figure out how to turn off the engine, they guide us to an open docking ring. We can no longer distinguish the corvette among the many docked merchant vessels.

The clamps clunk into place. Seals pop. The airlock begins cycling.

Ti speaks to the girls in a tone of calm command she would never use on me. "You are underage and therefore not required to give testimony. Best to stay quiet, if you please." It's not a request, but it's not bossy either.

They nod, clutching each other's hand.

She stands at the front in all her skin-tight-garment glory with the formal cape a flourish off her shoulders. The girls huddle behind her and I stand at the back like responsible hired security. I've turned my military jacket inside out in the hope it'll get a pass since the seams are barely visible. The two Phene workers who open the airlock and usher us onto the station don't spare me a second glance, because they can't keep their eyes off Ti as she cocks a hip and turns on the Vogue Academy aura.

The Phene blink like their eyes are going to fall out of their heads. Ti weeps soft, elegant tears, then wipes her beautiful face with a sigh. When she asks an imploring question in halting but serviceable Phenish, I think my head has exploded into a parallel dimension but I maintain a stolid expression.

The next thing I know we are being escorted through a utilitarian station that looks like it was built five hundred years ago and never updated with any new tech. The murals on the walls have a blockier style than what we saw on the ship, although that might be a local fashion.

What happened to my father and the Rider I have no idea, but I peer around anxiously. We reach the entrance into the habitat's local Repose District, a separate module attached to an inside spoke of the habitat. For some reason the ventilation system is sluggish here, leaving the area stuffy and warm. As on Tjeker, there's a barrier to control access into the district. A bored-looking clerk yawns on duty, chin resting on a lower hand as he fans himself with both uppers while with his opposite-side lower hand he scratches an ample belly. When he sees us he startles up, looks past us, and slaps a button on the counter.

Footsteps hurry up behind. A man in a uniform catches up to us. He's so tall. He blocks our path and gestures that we are to follow him; he's taking charge, and three more uniformed people wait a few meters away in support.

The Repose District gate opens. A two-armed person emerges, wearing the nondenominational tabard and gender of a Bel acolyte. In Yele they say, "What is this?"

The man speaks. The acolyte listens, then turns to us.

"You are accused of being illegal intruders, maybe spies. The supervisor is here to escort you to the security office."

Ti doesn't miss a beat. She sketches a gesture in the air that makes the Bel acolyte lean away in surprise. "I claim asylum with the Campaspe Guild."

The Bel acolyte taps the button and speaks through it. "We have an asylum request. Campaspe annex. Yes. I'll wait."

The official says something exasperated in Phenish.

The acolyte replies in Yele, so we can understand. "The charter covers Repose District. Do you intend to challenge it?"

I love a good fume, and the Phene official delivers.

The acolyte presses a finger to an ear, listening to a voice we can't hear, then turns to Tiana. "We can continue the discussion inside, if you agree to enter on the terms of Repose District."

"We do. I speak for all four of us. The girls are underage, and the security escort is under hire."

I don't ask what the terms are. I just follow as Ti goes up on her tiptoes and gives a cheeky kiss to the two workers who brought us this far and might even get in trouble for it. They're enchanted, and one blushes with the adorable intensity of a beet. When the official tries to ask them a question they gesture rudely and walk off. I guess authority isn't as big a deal here as it is in Chaonia.

We enter via a gate and an airlock. Repose District on Tjeker's moon was built under a transparent dome that gave it the feel of being outdoors, like a normal planet district. On a habitat everything is contained and each building compartmentalized in the case of hull breach, but the layout follows a similar pattern. We follow a path to a spacious rectangular central plaza with interior gates onto the sacred places: a colonnaded Bel temple, a holy theatron, a sealed labyrinth dedicated to Lady Chaos, a Hesjan henge, a Temple of Celestial Peace, a lion of Al-lat, a house of healing marked with twinned snakes. No basilica, because that will be in the main habitat. I miss a step when I see a sign pointing down a side passage that is marked by the mediation "Eye" of the seers of Iros. A hermitage.

I cough. Ti tips her head to indicate she's already seen it and walks without breaking stride or by any expression betraying there is something for us to worry about. The Metis twins stare fixedly at Ti's back as if they fear they'll disintegrate into ash if they fall out of step.

We cross the plaza. I feel exposed, but there's no one else out. The entire district looks locked down and under siege, deserted, on edge, and why wouldn't it be? War has come to the empire.

The acolyte says, "How did you get here, if I may ask. We don't see many stunts here."

"Stunts?" asks Ti.

"Excuse me. It's a Phene word for people with only two arms. Everyone uses it."

"I see," says Ti. "I didn't realize it was used for any two-armed person. Well. Our story is simple but complicated. We escaped the Chaonian fleet in Mishirru."

The acolyte glances back with a press of her lips. "Those girls look underage."

"Now you understand why we took the chance to get free."

I hiss through my teeth. What kind of slander is she allowing this foreigner to believe about Chaonians? Ti slides a hand behind her back and waggles it at me to shut me up, but the gesture causes me to notice her very fine ass and the appealing sway of her stride. This really is not what any of us need right now as we try to escape the clutch of the enemy and my treacherous father in the midst of a system-wide battle that might blow us out into space at any moment if an off-target missile launched from a hundred thousand klicks away hits the habitat. I raise my eyes to the ceiling six meters above. It's painted with a replica of a sky as seen from a planet. The heavens appear lucid and calm. Illusion is a blessing, or a curse.

"Here we are," says the acolyte. The main entrance into the Campaspe Guild is a clamshell gateway, currently shut. "The Phryne said for you to go right in. She couldn't come herself. Some emergency she's dealing with. So here's a word of advice." They tap a finger to pale lips. "She's in tight with one of the syndicates. I favor Tanarctus, myself. Anyway, scuttlebutt whispers her sponsor is about to go down."

"Go down?"

The acolyte draws a finger like a knife blade across their throat.

"Ah," says Ti, inviting further commentary without revealing ignorance.

"You'd think the syndicates would put their personal grudges and factional jockeying on hold until the war is over, wouldn't you? You must have seen the reports. They're fighting those belligerent Chaonians out there right now."

"Too close for comfort," Ti agrees.

"It's why everyone is battened down and waiting it out, no foot traffic, everything closed, airlocks on short seal, lifeboats ready."

"You don't seem too worried, Honorable."

"If you ask me, there's no way the upstarts can win. I admit it's troublesome to know there's a space battle raging in-system. But no one wants to damage a docking and repair platform. So keep praying."

"My thanks. I'm not sure what the word of advice is."

"Foreigners never understand the importance of the syndicates here. The Council runs the empire, but the syndicates run everything at the local level. Find a syndicate to sponsor you, and they'll protect you."

"My thanks. May I thank you by name, Honorable?"

"If we survive this, you may. Good fortune to you, campaspe." The acolyte leaves without giving a name.

"Typical acolyte," mutters Ti with an unexpected grimace of disapproval.

I test the door's extruding knob. "This gate is locked," I say perceptively.

"Yes, and as you should know, I have the key."

"Of course you do."

She lets us in via the service entrance to a nondescript delivery foyer. A closed door with a one-way window looks onto the reception room that's on the interior side of the clamshell gate. The reception room's lights are dimmed but I can make out divans arranged for waiting, and walls and ceilings painted with what might best be described as enthusiastic frolicking. The room is empty.

Ti and the girls have already moved on down the service corridor. The scent of baking bread wakes my slumbering stomach, but it's the sound of voices that attracts Ti. She signals to the girls to wait in the passage. I hasten to catch up, and follow her into a big circular room, fitted like a ready room where people receive briefings on the day's forthcoming assignments and debrief after their shift. A tall woman with four arms stands at the center of the space. She wears a silver jacket and slacks, elegantly cut to fit her frame.

As we enter she says, in accented Yele, "Please give to me a moment. I am finished, almost."

She is adjusting the drape of an ankle-length gauze shawl on the shoulders of another four-armed Phene, this individual shorter and slighter of build. There is something deeply arresting about the shawl-wearing person's face and form, the sculpted cut of their hair, the pleasing line of their smooth jaw, and the casually perfect posture that allows the shawl to fall like a shimmering veil of water over a deceptively simple pale copper-bronze-colored tunic suit whose hue is perhaps meant to suggest nudity. *He,* I think. He looks vaguely familiar.

Ti halts dead, looking him up and down. In an appreciative voice she murmurs for my ears only, "He'd have given me a run for graduating top of my cohort."

Up to now he has been watching the older woman. Hearing Ti's voice, he looks at us with eyes so green they shine like emeralds. Maybe they are an enhancement. He looks her up and down with the same assaying gaze she just spent on him. His answering smile is an onslaught of charm. He's not my bedroom type but wow do I want to go out clubbing with him.

"I bow to the presence of true beauty and peerless acumen," he says to Tiana in perfect Chaonian-court Yele. He assays a palace bow to the exactly correct degree and gesture appropriate to a respected graduate of Vogue Academy.

"Who the fuck are you?" I demand. He looks Phene but he sounds Argos.

His gaze skips, startled, over to me when he hears my voice. His kohl-lined eyes widen. His cherry lips part with shock first, succeeded by puzzlement.

"You look so like Lieutenant Ereshkigal Lee, but you can't be her. Didn't she die in Aspera System some years ago?"

I can't escape the comparisons even here in the empire.

He presses beautifully manicured hands to his cheeks in an exaggerated expression of surprise and delight. "Oh my stars, you must be Persephone. Perseus's twin. He always talked about you."

"Nothing good, I hope," I say in a hearty, jocular tone.

He gets a frozen look on his pretty face that makes me realize that maybe it *was* nothing good. But surely Percy didn't bad-mouth me. We loved each other. We were best friends, partners in mischief, even if I did manipulate the situation that one time—okay, twice—maybe three times—so he took the blame when we got caught.

"Persephone," says Ti, turning on me with an expression of accusation, "do you know this resplendent individual but haven't yet introduced us?"

"Uh," I say intelligently. I still haven't figured out who he is. My mind ticks over gears so slowly I fear I have turned snail-witted in my old age.

Ti turns her attention to the woman. "My thanks for receiving us. You must be the Phryne of this establishment."

The older woman inclines her head. "You may address me as such. Who are you, to request asylum?"

"I am Tiana. We seek asylum with the guild."

"Do you?" The Phryne's gaze roves skeptically over me and flicks toward the door into the passage. "Where are the other two? Youths, I am given to understand."

"By the hells," I break in as my mind finally catches up with my eyes. "You must be Bartholomew Manalon."

"Kr Manalon," he corrects. "We aren't related to the Os Manalons, the Sr Manalons, or the Hf Manalons. But if you are Persephone Lee, how are you come here? And what are you doing with a campaspe? Are you really a refugee from the Chaonians? Or are you a spy for their fleet?"

The Phryne checks a console displaying camera views onto the entry and foyer, both mercifully empty. Another camera view rests on a group of people gathered in the kitchen, huddled together as they watch a screen with a talking head, maybe the news. "Bartholomew, this is very bad for Angursa. You must not be discovered together with a Chaonian spy."

"I'm not a spy!" I protest.

"What is Angursa?" Ti asks.

Bartholomew touches a silver laurel wreath he wears on a ribbon around his neck. "It's the syndicate my clan belongs to. My father Paulo is high admiral but he was stripped of his command. We are in disgrace."

My mind perks up. "Your people were exiled before. Which is why you lived in Argos for three years."

"That's right."

"But you were received back into the empire?"

"Yes. It's how the syndicates operate. Angursa has a long and distinguished history so it's not easy just to expel them out an airlock."

"Except it sounds like your syndicate is in disgrace again. How'd that happen?"

"Bartholomew," says the Phryne in a warning tone. She adds more in Phenish.

"No, it's all right." He has a calculating look in his eye, like someone paging through a book of secrets that will give them the answer they need. Like someone who has found the key to a locked gate. Like someone who snuck Ti in to see her brother during a battle exercise to be kind but also so she could surreptitiously record images of a rare and ancient map of the pre-collapse beacon network that she can't get her hands on any other way.

He says, "Here's the short version: old grudges stemming from Council factionalism because Angursa backed the old Speaker who was forced out. Add a larger dispute over which syndicate should be granted the high admiralty positions. There aren't enough high-command positions for every syndicate that wishes to be represented, and competition can be cutthroat. That also earned Angursa some enmity. If you don't have enough backing from other syndicates, you lose standing. If rival syndicates gang up on you, you get shoved out the door of the Exchange into the wilderness to wander for forty days and forty nights. That's metaphorical, mind you. They can't erase Angursa's laurel wreath, because it was granted in the Exchange Charter. But they can kick us into oblivion, steal our ships, poach from our member rolls, and sequester our resources, leaving us an empty container with no cargo nor crew to load it."

"Seems a weird time to fight among yourselves."

His wry smile makes me want to laugh, and I don't even know why. "It's Phene tradition to fight the most among ourselves when we most need unity."

Ti says, "This is an odd backwater industrial habitat to find such a scion of a clearly important lineage."

"Not at all! Syndicates empower the residents of places like this. Orbital Habitat Itliong has been under Angursa patronage for generations. It's our first stop as we decide what to do next."

"Running for your lives?" I ask, intrigued.

"Not quite running for our lives, that's not our way, but we have certainly made an enemy of one of the most prominent Riders. So making ourselves scarce and headed for the hills, as Heavenly Knife says in *Golden Blossoms in the Outer Mountains*."

Ti presses a dramatic hand to her ample bosom. "I loved Lucky Yún in that drama."

"Yes! Especially his blood-soaked forty-eight-minute death oration. Who can really still speak with a knife jammed in their neck?"

"A rhetorical question," agrees Ti.

Bartholomew laughs.

An idea blazes like a supernova seen from an appropriately safe distance. "I know someone who would be happy to see you."

"Do you?" he says in a tone so layered I can't catch which nuance is meant to stab me in the neck.

Ti's lashes flicker as she catches my drift. She is the epitome of hot but I swear it is her razor-wire mind I admire the most.

I go on. "I hear you and Sun were tight, back in the day. Now would be the time to recall if you had some secret buddy signal you can alert her with."

"Why would I want to do that?"

"Why wouldn't you? Sun is *loyal* to her *friends*."

He cocks a glitter-brushed eyebrow at the Phryne. She closes all the doors, flips a switch on the console, and nods at him.

"What are you suggesting?" he asks.

"You know what I'm suggesting. If you and your syndicate want Sun's attention, and support, bring them something she lost and wants back."

"You and your illustrious companion?"

"That would be a good start."

Ti says, "Are you a Campaspe Guild member?"

"I'm guild adjacent," says Bartholomew. "This is a good place to go to ground."

"It is," I agree. "It's also a good place to shift directions unnoticed even if there is a big battle in your backyard. Do you know what happened to the people who were aboard the corvette we arrived on? It's disguised to look like a merchant ship. The crew disembarked and left us as prisoners on board."

"Prisoners?"

"We were kidnapped in Mishirru by one of the people on that ship. Sun has a particular interest in him." I almost mention the older Metis twins but an unexpected frisson of clone solidarity causes me to leave their existence unspoken.

Ti says to me, "Are you sure?"

"I'm sure." The presence of Bartholomew Kr Manalon with his disgraced syndicate ties changes our situation as from night to day. "Sun already knows you, Bartholomew. She mentions you occasionally. Fondly."

Does his face brighten? I think it does. Then he frowns. For all his suave charm I see in his nervous hands and the shifting of his feet that he is desperate, or his family is desperate, which for an honest and loyal child is the same thing. He exchanges a look with the Phryne. She taps a button on the central console, then goes over and unlocks one of the doors. I take two steps back to place myself between Tiana and the door, but Bartholomew's stance doesn't change. He doesn't brace himself for violence; he stays relaxed. I don't have that luxury.

Moments later a distinguished-looking older man enters who was clearly aware of our presence. I recognize him instantly from Channel Idol all those years ago.

"Admiral Kr Manalon, I presume," I say.

"Please, call me Paulo. Uncle would also be appropriate. Here in the empire we are not so in thrall to hierarchical status and divisions of rank as you Chaonians. No offense meant." He presses his upper hands together in a mimicry of a Yele greeting. Unlike his son he speaks with a pronounced accent, but his grammar is correct.

"I am honored to meet you. I am Persephone Lee. This is my companion—"

Ti steps forward. "I am Tiana Yáo Alaksu. Peace be upon you, Uncle."

"And upon you peace, niece. You have the look of a Vogue Academy–trained individual. And the ear clip of a graduate of that institution."

"Are you really?" says Bartholomew excitedly. "I went there on a tour once as a boy. I even wrote up an application but I wasn't old enough to send it in."

"Not now," says Paulo in the tone of a fond but authoritative father. "Persephone Lee, of Lee House? Perseus's twin, Moira's niece, Aisa and Kiran's daughter? Sister of Ereshkigal Lee? You look startlingly like her."

"I am she." I should have thought of this clever play on words earlier.

That is when the other shoe finally drops, a fleeting memory of the banner soldier as he tried to hammer his way through the transparent wall while the Rider watched. Every Rider in the empire knows I am a clone of Nona Lee. So what happens to me if they decide to undercut Sun by revealing to all of Chaonia that I am illegal? Oh shit.

Fortunately everyone else in the room is looking not at my aghast face but at Paulo as he clears his throat. "Let me cut to the chase. I apologize for the lack of the gentler courtesies with which we smooth life's path. There isn't time."

Ti glances curiously at me, reading my distress, and turns back to him. "You listened in to our exchange with your son," she says.

"I did. While I no longer have access to the classified military channels, I still have my means of following the battle. The Chaonians have entered Anchor System via two different beacons. Our high command knew they were coming and have been able to keep the enemy fleets contained within one hundred million miles of each of the two beacons. Your side is losing."

By his reaction, I'd guess he doesn't know about Sun's race to Sleepless System. It's time for me to get back into the battle. "*Are* they losing? Excuse me for sounding skeptical."

"Perhaps it would be more accurate to say, Chaonia will lose."

"So our fleets are holding their own?"

"For now. But they cannot hold out for more than two or three more days. Numbers and supply chain are against you. Attrition dooms you."

When I say nothing, he goes on.

"It is a puzzle to me how this strategy is meant to work. The queen-marshal isn't in-system as far as my sources know. It was a rash gambit on her part. Her forces are barely hanging on as we bring more ships from Auger and Axiom. Chaonian training and discipline are excellent, but it's just a matter of time."

"Yes, it's just a matter of time." My confident tone causes him to tense.

"What do you mean?"

I look him dead in the eye, hinting with my gaze the details, the strategy, the incoming fleets out of Karnos I can't speak of out loud. "I would never bet against Sun. You shouldn't either. That means opportunity for you."

He says nothing. He's listening.

"Do you know what happened to the crew of the ship we arrived on?" I ask.

"Ah. While I may have been stripped of my own access codes, I still have allies in traffic control. The Rider was transferred to a fast courier with an Incorruptibles destroyer escort to get him out of the battle zone. But I don't think the Rider is the person *you* are most interested in, is it?"

He's sharp. And he wouldn't have said that much if he wasn't leaning hard in my direction. Sun wants Kiran Seth, and I have more reason than most to make sure she gets him.

"Give me the means to capture the seer, and I'll give you the means to negotiate with Sun as her newest ally."

When

When the *Boukephalas* arrived back in Haymarket System, pockets of battle still raged amid the outer reaches of the system, but it was nothing Sun needed to concern herself with because she'd left Alika in charge. She hadn't even gone to the bridge for the beacon drop but was sitting in the flagship lounge with her feet up on the strategos table, sipping at tea while she spun through the battle plans for the hundredth time.

Ten seconds after she arrived, a packet from Alika pinged in. First thing, she checked for news of Zàofù.

Nothing.

For an instant a strange, twisting darkness rose in her heart. What if she failed?

No.

Failure wasn't allowed to be possible. This was frustration, not fear. *If* she had Riders, she'd have an up-to-the-minute ongoing report on the situation in Anchor System. As it was, the *Boukephalas* was already speeding for the beacon that would take her newly expanded forces into Cut Stone. The *Huma* at the head of a frigate formation ran tight on her tail, behind them the rest of her task force, behind them troop ships ready for a planetary drop, and behind them the Third Fleet under Crane Marshal Qìngzhī Bō in highest fighting trim. Seventh Fleet would swing back through Destiny to follow the Aila route Zàofù had taken, with the goal of cutting off Phene reinforcements arriving from Auger and protecting the old man's back. If he was still alive. That was out of her hands. Either he was up to the task, or he wasn't.

She bent her attention to the message received months ago in Tsurru System from Senior Captain the Honorable Abiye Bō of the light cruiser *Raijū* and thence sent on via Argosy to Hellion Terminus and thus to Karnos where it was waiting for her. She had listened through it three times so far. It confirmed that sabotage had dealt the cowardly blow. The Karsh's death could not provide true recompense for the loss of so many people and for the years the survivors would lose as they torched toward Tsurru. But Adele Karsh hadn't gotten away with it. All down the beacon routes and Argosy lanes, people would know that you defied Chaonia at your peril. She settled in to read through the casualty list ship by ship and name by name.

A courier's urgent message slotted to the front of her comms queue.

Kite Marshal Anas sends: Have arrived in Anchor. Heavy fighting. Radio contact with combined Sixth and Ninth Fleets achieved. Their situation is dire, but we are pinned down by superior numbers and can't reinforce. Crane Marshal Zàofù is alive and still holding according to his orders, as he of course would do, whatever those orders might be and how beyond the capacity of any other, and with the experience and capability that is the hallmark of his stalwart life in service to the republic. Your ETA?

What a typically arrogant message from Anas, she thought with a surge of temper. But she couldn't fault his and his father's resolute courage. The bold offensive would work as long as the beleaguered vanguard in Anchor could hold open the two beacons they'd breached. If anyone would hold due to sheer stubborn vanity, it would be Samtarras, father and son. Although they might already both be dead, since the message had originated ten hours ago, dropped via courier through beacon and radioed across a star system to a courier waiting by another beacon. She had to find a way to get Riders of her own besides the untrained and reluctant Kaspar.

A new message from Alika pinged in. A QUAD OF PHENE CIVILIAN SHIPS ARRIVED YESTERDAY UNDER THE COMMAND OF UNCLE PAULO. HE IS ASKING FOR ASYLUM.

The name electrified her. Uncle Paulo! What manifold possibilities! She opened voice comms on the ring. "Paulo Kr Manalon?"

Alika's reply would take a minute to return.

Kurash was standing guard at the door. At the sound of her voice, he looked toward her. She gestured for him to come over as she pulled up such maps as Chaonian intelligence had of Anchor Prime, inconsistent and incomplete. "Familiarize yourself with this material. The capital city is called Melo."

"What is that large blank surface?" he asked.

"It is labeled as an inland sea."

"And this straight line?"

"An artificial ridge, like a large dam. It separates the sea from the city. Their Exchange, grand basilica, and Unity Hall are on the ridge. We believe their Riders live in a heavily fortified zone inside the ridge, probably beneath Unity Hall."

"I see."

"Our incoming fleets will relieve pressure from the Sixth and the Second while at the same time engaging all Phene fleets in-system with an aggressive charge. Meanwhile, while the Phene are distracted by those battles, I will lead an attack directly at the headquarters of the Rider Council."

"Cut off the head, and the body will die," said Kurash.

"Something like that." She studied his profile as he examined the maps. He and the other ghost soldiers were a unit in need of purpose. Where could their particular skillset be best utilized? Instinct shifted a barrier in her mind. "I want as many Riders as possible captured alive. Especially the young ones. You and your banner soldiers will go into Unity Hall with Hetty."

"Are we not better suited to be your bodyguards?" he asked with a flash of concern.

"You still are my bodyguards. I need those Riders. I trust Hetty to get them and your soldiers to assist her. You will have learned things in training about Phene tactics that will prove useful in confined combat conditions."

"As you wish, Your Highness."

Alika's reply dropped in. "Yes. I spoke to him."

She shifted conversations without pause. "You spoke to Paulo by voice?"

"With my own mouth, over comms."

Ah, her question irritated him. She'd long ago learned how to handle his perfectionist tendencies. "I'm not doubting your report. I'm clarifying for myself."

His reply sounded more cheerful. "He asked for voice contact, said it would convince me it is truly him and that he wants to parlay. He says he brought a gift for you." He added the ring network images of a pomegranate and a torch, the icons used by Persephone and Tiana.

"I'll be boiled in the hell of brine."

"I already sent him over. He should reach you soon."

"Is Bar with him? Never mind. Leave a garrison to hold Haymarket alongside the battleship *Endurance*, which I'll leave here with her task group. Fall in with your squadron as my rear guard."

AFFIRMATIVE. Alika had his quirks and weaknesses, his airs and conceits. But she trusted him absolutely.

"Nisaba, contact the *Elegant Moth*."

The high secretary was working at a console. She looked up in surprise. "Isn't that Paulo Kr Manalon's personal vessel?"

"It is. I want him here as soon as possible."

"Good fortune, then," said Nisaba with a laugh. "Because we just this second received his request to come aboard."

Sun glanced around the room, seeking Isis, then recalled she'd returned her to James, who had his own suite of rooms where he and his team were preparing strategies to crack the Phene military ciphers and command codes. Not that any Chaonian knew much about how the Phene collated and stored information, except that they didn't share it through a linked centralized network as Chaonians did. They liked to physically separate everything to keep it more secure, which struck her as inefficient but which James called prudent. She did not like being unable to get into things that she wanted to get into. She did not like when she had to ask someone else's permission to open a gate that ought to simply open before her.

"Hetty."

Hetty was stretched out along the couch, still in the tight black shorts and red sports bra she wore for training. Her long legs always attracted Sun's attention, so lean and shapely, bare midriff an invitation. The physical book Hetty had been reading rested against her face. She'd fallen asleep. Sun shut her eyes, listening, but she was too far away to hear, much less feel, the respiration of her beloved like the spirit of the universe pouring in and out of a precious vessel.

The book thumped to the floor as Hetty sat up abruptly. "Was that my name?"

Sun mouthed *Always* and Hetty's quiet smile slid onto her face as she glanced around the lounge to see who else was there: Kurash and Sunshine at the door; Nisaba and an assistant, Esme, at a console.

From the door into the galley, Eleuterio said, "Honored Hestia, may I fetch you tea?"

"Coffee."

He winced at the mention of this foreign interloper but vanished into the galley.

"Paulo Kr Manalon is asking for asylum, which isn't surprising considering his contentious history with the other syndicates. It's potentially excellent news for us. I think he may have found Persephone and means to return her."

Kurash stiffened, looking up, then dropped his gaze back to the map, but the tension in his body had altered like a person making ready to leap.

"Kurash, wait in the galley."

He nodded and left.

"Does that mean Paulo has Tiana too?" Hetty asked eagerly.

"I don't want to count my maiasauruses before they are hatched."

"Let me go change." Hetty jumped to her feet, strode toward her cabin, paused to look back. "Or have you more to say?"

"I'd like to send Persephone with you."

"Tiana, too. She'll want to see the Hall. Perhaps there will be information on what's known of Rider physiology that might be useful to help train the boy. That is, if we reach Anchor Prime—" She broke off, flushing slightly.

"*When* we reach Anchor Prime," said Sun.

The door chime announced a visitor. Hetty darted into the passageway to change into formal clothing. Sun rose to greet the distinguished Phene man. His height marked him out, of course, and as a mark of good faith he came without soldiers, only with noncombatant members of his extended family, young and old.

"Sun." With pleasant informality he took her hands in his lowers.

"You look the same," she said with a smile. "You are welcome here, Uncle Paulo. I sense you have a story to tell me."

"That I do. I have a great deal to tell you that you'll be eager to learn."

She looked among the assembled family. "Is Bartholomew not with you?"

"That's part of the story."

Tiana waited with the others. She wore loose slacks and a four-sleeved blouse whose lower arms she'd cleverly tied around her midriff to make a fashionable bow.

Sun gave her a nod, relieved to see her apparently unharmed. No one else came through the door. "Where is Persephone?"

The Wily Persephone Alone in the Enemy Stronghold

Carrying a big box tall enough to conceal my face, I follow Bartholomew up a flight of steps into a bar. This bar is connected to another bar that is connected to another bar, all linked by ramps, stairs, and twisting paths as if they are one huge beacon route map enhanced by liquor, eats, dancing, and whatever else the Phene do for a good time. I'm mad we don't have anything as cool as Antikythera Terrace in Argos, but there's no time to stew because we're in the middle of a stealth-ops mission. If anyone figures out who I am, we'll be dead sooner than a person can say

"Who's *this* little scrap, Bartholomew?" A man wipes his hands on a towel as he comes out to meet us. He has two arms, not four, and he speaks Yele with a funky accent I don't recognize. I'd guess he's either a Yele expatriate or a child of the same.

Bartholomew walks in front of me, hauling two bags filled with emergency gas masks. "*This* is Reynaldo's fifth child. Just turned thirteen. A stunt, poor thing. Fortunately she's a hard worker. How many of these masks are you going to need?"

"We were told to close down and leave last night but I came by this morning to check on the contract workers. It's a good thing, because no one told anyone at the contractors' barracks. Isn't safety the responsibility of a syndicate?"

"That fell under Angursa's ambit."

"We're worse off for the loss of Angursa's oversight," remarks the man. "We weren't informed which syndicate was taking over labor relations for the terrace workers. And I sure as hells won't kick out people who have nowhere to go. Most of the contractors took off when I told them what was up, but I've got three newbies who don't know what to do. I also have a boarder in the hermitage and his staff who may need masks if there's trouble. So I'll take fifteen. Appreciate it."

A boarder in the hermitage. Keeping my cool, suave as all the hells, I set my box on a table. Bar slowly untangles masks to give me time to survey the room. Behind the bar, shelves display bottles of liquor arranged according to height, some with labels I can read and others in Phenish script. The establishment is a big space with a lot of tables, a small stage with a microphone, and soundproof seating pods for eight off to one side, all empty. Debate pods are a Yele institution, and our late-night discussions in Sun's courtyard owe a lot to the tradition. Way off to my right, half lost in shadow, a trio is eating from a shared platter. I can't see their faces, only that they have two arms, not four. None have the posture or robes of my father. No one else is in the bar because, like the man said, the planet has gone into lockdown. Battles are being fought in the skies above, invisible to us except for occasional flashes on high like ancient gods casting celestial bolts at their enemies.

A radio sits on the counter. An announcer speaks in a stream of urgent Phenish. I look past the terrace balcony onto the city of Melo. Its streets sprawl westward across a wide plain to the foot of distant hills still muddy with night. There's minimal traffic on the streets, and military vehicles and soldiers at every intersection. Everything's hushed, everyone holding their breath. What's going on off-planet? Did Sun arrive before Zàofù's fleet got pulverized? Is Sun's fleet getting pulverized by the massive numbers of Phene ships I observed on our cross-system journey? There were a lot. A lot of a lot. I hate not having my ring.

Bartholomew laughs at something the other man said, pulling my attention inside. The diners look up from their food. There's no telltale sheen to their eyes, so they must be the temp workers. As Bar heads over to me I do a final scan of the room. There are eleven marked exits, one for each beacon in Yele System, although three are "closed." Of Yele's eleven beacons, three are dead, which, curiously enough, is the same number of dead beacons in Anchor's eleven-beacon system. But I mustn't get sidetracked.

My stinger is tucked in a holster against my left side, concealed by the baggy jacket Bar dressed me in. An elongated backpack holds my baton and the half cape rolled up in one of Bar's decorative shawls to hide its distinctive red and gold. What the pack doesn't hold is a crucial item taken from the last of the five things I brought with me when I escaped Lee House at the age of sixteen, one I carry with me everywhere as a precaution.

Bar stops beside me and says something in Phenish. I grunt in reply. He murmurs in Yele, "Folks believe you're a stunt because you're more gracile, not as stocky as most Chaonians."

"*Thirteen?*"

"I could have said twelve."

His grin is so rascally that I adore him, but my hands are sweating. It is weird and disturbing to be on Anchor Prime, with its slightly lighter gravity and eye-poppingly gaudy architecture. Alone in the enemy stronghold. Except for Bar, who is the enemy, only maybe not the enemy.

"Like I said," he goes on, "I saw Kiran Seth here once. Apama met him over beyond the marble columns when she thought I wasn't watching, but I was."

"Who is Apama?"

"Just someone I know." He shrugs elegantly, but there's emotion in the lift of his shoulders.

"Ooo, someone you *like*?" I'm intrigued by Bartholomew Kr Manalon, who masterminded getting me and him off Orbital Habitat Itliong and via freighter to Anchor Prime and then, with his cousin Reynaldo's help, via service truck to Antikythera Terrace. This is extra spice added to his ineffable air of being *the* person you want to be seen with on the dance floor.

"This way," he says so smoothly that we cross the restaurant space and walk down a line of marble columns before I realize he refused to answer. Oh well. He can have a Phene girlfriend. Whatever. She must be cool, too, or he wouldn't like her.

What is Tiana doing? Is she safe with Sun? Will I ever see Kurash again? Why does my brain spin like this when I most need it to focus? I have to get my head in the game.

We halt by a door with a big staring eye painted on it.

Bar whispers, "He won't be allowed in Unity Hall, so this is the closest he can stay to the Riders. Jahi did say there is a boarder."

"And a staff. What does that mean?"

The door opens and a banner soldier stalks out. It happens so fast I don't have time to pull the baton from the backpack or avert my gaze. I look the soldier in the eye, and she looks full into my face.

Nothing happens.

Bar takes a step back as if he's just realized this isn't another rehearsal; this is curtains up. We are in it now, no turning back, no retreat. The soldier leans onto her toes, ready to lunge the instant she determines we are genuine threats.

Never say I can't take the triceratops by the horns in a crisis. I put on a bold face and a bold voice. "I am here to see my father, Kiran Seth. Take me to him at once."

Banner soldiers are trained to obedience. She settles back as if struck by my haughty air of command. Then she says in Yele, "You are Persephone Lee. He said you might be coming. Follow me."

I motion behind my back, signaling Bartholomew to stay behind as he and I had discussed beforehand. No reason for both of us to be killed if this goes wrong, and there are an awful lot of ways in which this can go wrong.

Past the door lies a dim entry foyer where two banner soldiers stand guard. They exchange words with my escort in a language neither Yele nor Phenish. We pass under an arch into a square room lit by four red-hued lamps. Another two soldiers lurk in the shadows here, which means another six are around somewhere if this is a full arrow. My hand twitches restlessly but I do not draw my baton. Unleashing them won't do me any good, because these soldiers serve the empire with the unexamined loyalty Kurash must have felt before he was pulled into Sun's orbit.

The soldier opens a door onto an unlit hallway. I blink on my infrared lenses, not as effective as an Iros seer's vision but good enough for dark closets. Strips along the floor and marks patched on the doors provide a means by which seers navigate their environs. Using the hermitage blueprint Hetty gave us, I track my route so I can leave quickly.

If I get the chance. I'd hoped I wouldn't also have to deal with banner soldiers, but here we are.

Using the darkness as cover, I ease the baton out of the backpack and hold it alongside my leg with a finger next to the pressure point that turns it on. Because it is currently inert, the soldier can't feel any betraying tremor of energy. As we turn one corner after the next, I nervously run my thumb over the fingernail that hides a node for physical pins. Sun had us all fitted with them, and I have a pin secured in the node, but not one filled with information. Because that's the fifth thing I took: a Lee House medical kit tailored for use by undercover agents of the Ministry of Security, Punishment, and Corrections, by which I mean the family tradition of spying, torture, and extrajudicial murder.

The soldier leads me to a room identified on the blueprint as the infirmary. An actual light shines here. Its pale glow seems awfully bright as I blink off the infrared. Four banner soldiers sleep on the hard floor. Four lifepods are lined up along the wall to my left, two glowing green and two empty. A banner soldier sits in a chair at a table, preparing some kind of concoction using vials, liquids, and powders. He doesn't look up and works with a disturbingly trancelike focus.

A man in seer's robes stands looking through the drawers of an apothecary's cabinet. Hearing our footsteps, he turns.

"Persephone." My father speaks without surprise, without disapproval, without joy.

"Did you leave me to die?"

"I respect your capabilities. I am proven correct, am I not?"

"That's not reassuring. How did you guess I might come after you?"

"I hoped you would. Perhaps I feared you would."

"What does that mean?" I ask as I edge sideways to get a look into the lifepods. They contain the two older Metises. Why did he leave the younger Metises with me? It had to have been deliberate. I can't figure out his game.

He doesn't answer, just stands there with one hand in a drawer and the other on the baton he carries to control the soldiers.

My escort takes up guard by the door. There's a door opposite, which according to the blueprint opens into a garden, although what kind of garden they've built inside the ridge I don't know. Bar couldn't get access to the structural plans for the Antikythera Terrace because maintenance wasn't part of the Angursa Syndicate's ambit.

I walk up to my father, halt one meter from him, and square my shoulders. "I thought over your offer and came to join you and your cause."

"That is a lie, Persephone."

Busted. But I knew I would be. I already prepared a set of possible replies.

"Sun won't trust me now. She'll always wonder if you suborned me."

"You don't believe that. Please remember I watched you grow up. I know every nuance of your voice."

"Watched me," I say bitterly, losing hold of my rehearsed speech. "Studied me, more like. Was I ever anything more than an experiment to you?"

"There is honesty, at last." Does his tone change? Does he care? Did he ever care? But if I ask, he'll tell me the truth. Even now, even given what I intend, I don't want to know because I fear the answer. What if he didn't? *What if he did?*

"Easy for you to dismiss my words," I retort, edging my feet closer as best I can without seeming to move. "You dedicated your life to the hermitage and whatever agenda the seers and the Oculi serve. But what future is there for me if I'm tossed out of Sun's inner circle? No one trusts a disgraced Companion. Moira proved that. Even as a lowly functionary in Lee House, I'll never be trusted by Marduk Lee. Anyway, I ran away from Lee House because it wasn't the life I wanted."

He sighs. "I took the opportunity to liberate you from Sun's orbit because I succumbed to the weakness of parental concern. But when I saw you speaking with Manishtusu, I realized that while Nona Lee did not succeed, not with the ones who remained at the lab, not with Ereshkigal, not with Manea, she came closest with you."

"What does that mean?" I ask indignantly. I don't like being compared to Nona Lee. Anger is an opening, allowing me to shift a third of a meter forward as if I can't control my clenched fists and tense jaw. "Most closely with *me*? Are you saying of all the clones I'm the most like that narcissistic psychopath?"

"I wouldn't use such strong words, but they aren't entirely inaccurate. You can make a clone who is a zombie, with no will of its own, but such clones don't survive. Or you can make a human, who will develop in its unique way. The question is how much a caretaker influences the blend of nature, nurture, and environment. Not even Nona Lee can make a copy of herself, however much she may have wished she could."

Grab the opening and attack. I drop my gaze to the floor, suck in a sharp, teary breath—not entirely unfeigned—and drop to my knees. "That really is all I ever was to you, isn't it? An experiment. Resh is the only one who ever cared for me. Did Resh know? Did she guess? Is that why she sacrificed herself? So none of you would have the satisfaction of manipulating her anymore?"

He speaks in his coldest tone. "Colonel Bradman, put her in the lifepod."

"Please! Did you never care?" I choke out the words as I fumble my hands along the floor and, while doing so, draw the pin out of the node with a snap of pain that feels like nothing compared to how his icy demeanor rejects me.

"You'd be dead if I had never cared." His words hit like a punch to the gut.

I don't have time to untangle his meaning or his gambit. He's wearing sandals beneath the long seer's robe. I grab his left ankle as if I am a desperate supplicant in an overwrought historical drama. With my left hand I twist flesh hard enough to pinch, while with my right I jab a three-centimeter pin through his skin. The pressure against the point releases a fast-acting sedative, useful for agents capturing fugitives.

He gives a grunt of surprise but whether at the pinch, the pin, or the touch of my bare hands, I cannot say. Then he tries to shake me off, stumbling back. I hold on for the first two steps, letting myself be dragged so I don't lose position. A soldier looms over me. A powerful grip takes hold of my shoulders. I let go of my father's leg.

"I'm sorry. I'm sorry." My fake sob sounds fake as I scramble to hands and knees. A boot to my back stamps me down. Barely catching myself before my nose hits the floor, I bite my lip instead. The pain steadies me as I keep my gaze on the floor, gathering my strength as the sleeping soldiers wake up. My father's silence blares so loud in my imagination that I daren't breathe, because this is my gamble. Blood smears in my mouth, tangy and metallic. Hands fasten on my ankles to pull me away from him. I start screaming nonsense words at the top of my lungs, anything to distract. No. Please. I promise. I'll be good.

Father drops to his knees, swaying unsteadily. His fingers lose hold of the baton and it clatters to the floor. I snag its tip as I'm dragged back and I let the other baton roll out from under me so it looks like it's the one he dropped. A soldier hauls me toward the lifepods as others run to support Father as his head sags. I cling to the baton. My lip is throbbing like a motherfucker but I grin with triumph as I grope my hand up the shaft and find the tuning point. The on switch.

I press it too hard, and again. The baton leaps to life against my palm, a vicious hum like the lick of a neurological poison. The hands on my ankles spasm, and let go. All the banner soldiers freeze up, sweat on their faces, hands twitching.

I've leashed them.

Father's eyes roll as he struggles to stay conscious. He paws at the ground, clumsy and slow, and finally grabs the baton and flicks it on. But of course an unleashing baton doesn't work the same way as a Phene leashing baton, and he doesn't know that. He doesn't even know what he has in his hand.

I struggle to my knees. Blood trickles down my chin.

"Fuck," I mutter under my breath as I wipe blood onto the sleeve of the work tunic I'm wearing. Red smears along the gray fabric.

"Persephone." He blinks multiple times, trying to focus on my face. His daughter. His betrayer. I have condemned him to death, and he knows it.

I stagger over and kneel beside him. With all my strength, I prise open his clenched hand. He's clutching two stoppered vials, each filled with an oleaginous substance. I recognize the characters: *Late bloomer.* His eyes flicker with anger or desperation, or maybe even regret for the bond we never had, but he no longer has the ability to resist as I take the vials and secrete them in my holster.

I say, to the soldiers, "Place Kiran Seth in the lifepod."

He struggles weakly but there is nothing he can do. They deposit him swiftly and efficiently into the lifepod, close it, and seal it with a green light.

Then they turn to look at me. Is that dull obedience or stolid hatred? What will Kurash say to me when he learns how I've coerced them? If he is even alive.

Needs must. I have a job to do.

I rummage through the apothecary's cabinet. Its drawers contain packets, powders, and vials of medicinal herbs and healing oils. How ironic.

"What were you making here?" I ask, indicating the table.

When no soldier replies I turn up the leash one notch. They all twitch, and one answers. "When distilled in the correct order and proportion, these ingredients create the toxin known as late bloomer. Shall I finish my task?"

"No. Incinerate the evidence."

The tiny earring I'm wearing buzzes and I hear Bar's voice like a distant whisper. "Status? Something big is happening and I'm not sure what—"

A massive explosion shakes the ground. I'm flung to the floor, hitting my elbow. The burst of agony makes my eyes swim. The baton slips out of my grasp and rolls away. The blast is so powerful that half of the banner soldiers have lost their footing too, the other half grabbing hold of nearby objects. Chairs tip over, the contents of the vials on the table splash onto my face, and the light flickers but holds.

I secure the baton because none of the soldiers try to grab it, even though they could. Any of them could crush me in a heartbeat. Gritting my teeth, I clamber to my feet, lick my wet upper lip, and realize I've just swallowed whatever was in the vials from the tables. Oh fuck. I hope they weren't completed. I count to ten, then to twenty. The only thing hammering is my agitated pulse. I guess I'm not dead yet.

Another explosion rumbles through the ridge, this one deeper or farther away. I suck in a breath to steady myself. I could run now. I could leave, grab Bartholomew, and trust his contacts to guide us to safety through whatever is going on out there. The lifepods gleam green, waiting. I know what's going to happen to my father if I turn him over to Sun, if we survive that long. I could tell Sun he and I got separated. I got hit on the head. My path got blocked by rubble. The banner soldiers whisked him away.

I could say all that, and there would be no seer to see heat and lies.

"Colonel Bradman." The soldier I first encountered faces me. "Is there a secure area here that is proof against bombing?"

"Yes. A ramp leads from the internal garden enclosure to a secure bunker in the bedrock below sea level."

"Very good. We will take refuge there. Send two soldiers to fetch my compatriot Bartholomew. Tell him 'Tiana rules.'" Our code phrase. "The rest of you, bring the lifepods, including the empty one. We will shelter in place."

"Do we not fight the enemy?" asks Colonel Bradman.

"We will shelter in place," I repeat, tuning the baton up slightly. Their neuronics pulse in time to the baton's leashing mechanism. They rock a little but no discomfort shows on their faces. They're used to this treatment. My stomach churns with uneasiness, but the truth is, we're all up to our necks in blood already.

I spot my baton rolled half under the apothecary's cabinet. After grabbing it, I stick it back in the holder on the backpack.

Another explosion, maybe a secondary chain reaction, cracks the ceiling above us. A hairline fissure splinters through the floor. The ridge groans like a vast beast whose body fights in vain to withstand an implacable force.

The earring buzzes again. It works only within a one-klick radius. Bar told me it is meant to coordinate processions, not war. "Status? Persephone?"

I say, "Tiana rules. Come now with the rest of the banner soldiers. Bring the workers and Jahi if they want. Unless you have a better place we can shelter close by."

"On my way."

He doesn't ask what's coming.

He knows I won't tell him. Can't tell him. Anyway, I've been cut off from the fleet for so long I can no longer possibly know except for one thing.

Whatever timetable the Phene assume, Sun will be faster. Or she'll be dead.

91

Their Staggering Bravado

A flash woke Apama. Her eyes opened, mind instantly alert as she sat up. It wasn't the rising sun. It was still night.

She pressed an upper hand against the transparent wall of her sleeping quarters as she peered into the darkness beyond. No wave action whitened the waters of Fair Water; its surface lay tranquil and opaque. Windless. Thready clouds cut trails along the stars. No, that star was moving. And that one. And that one. Then a flash: a craft exploding in a bloom of bright death.

She pressed a lower hand to her belly, sickened by the sight and what it meant. We are all destined for death. More flashes spiked in the distance like a storm dancing across the horizon, lightning-like streaks echoed in the high heavens. One of the Incorruptibles' main military bases lay about sixty klicks to the northeast across the inland sea. But last night's report to the war council had been filled only with dispatches from the Cut Stone and Gardens Beacons, where massive space battles were still being fought with tenacious resolve as the military brought in yet more ships from Auger and Axiom.

There had also been a Rider report from Fanciful System claiming the Chaonians had broken through the Windworn minefield. Which meant more enemy fleets incoming from Karnos. The syndicate admirals had spent an hour arguing about how many ships to detach from the main engagements to strengthen the modest defense group stationed at Pure Lake Beacon. That's where the attacks coming from Windworn would drop through.

Not a single admiral or Rider had raised the possibility of an attack on Anchor Prime itself. What a clusterfuck.

She was reluctantly impressed with the Chaonians' staggering bravado and resolute toughness. It was the lack of Phene coordination that angered her. Even with Anchor System under a shocking attack, the syndicates fought among themselves for status and control. What was wrong with them?

How could the Chaonians have gotten here so fast?

She touched clasped hands to her mouth and murmured a swift prayer. "Revered Arthas, give me the strength to do my duty. Give me the means to protect my honored mother and—"

She broke off as the door into the parlor opened, the one always locked except at breakfast. A figure appeared, instantly recognizable to Apama's relieved gaze.

"Mom?" She swung her feet out of bed and stood.

"Get dressed. Get your kit. You have two minutes or we'll be separated. I'm not supposed to be here."

Rana had three sides: the loving mother, the compassionate-but-nononsense medic, and the girl who had survived by eating garbage in the ruins of a major industrial accident. Apama knew this voice.

"Done," she said. Her mother vanished into the parlor, leaving the door ajar.

Like every lancer pilot, she had her kit ready to go. Every night before she went to bed she made sure a uniform and a flight suit lay folded, side by side, in easy reach. She stripped off her sleeping clothes, then took thirty precious seconds to pee and to wash her hands and face as she scanned the room in her mind. But she lived with a light footprint. What she treasured was intangible, the things she carried in her heart.

She quickly pulled on bra and absorbent panties, skin-tight thermals, and flight suit. Kit bag in hand, she hurried into the parlor. The view through the floor-to-ceiling windows that normally seemed luxurious now cast ominous patterns of jerkily shifting light and shadow across the breakfast table, Dara's cluttered desk, the shelf with its four vases. Zakurru hadn't added the vase she'd given him to the arrangement. The wall was soundproof, as thick as a fortress's outer shield, and it occurred to her that it was a lot like a Rider's view of the universe: muffled by not wanting to hear anything that might disturb them on their lofty perch.

Her mother grasped her hand and squeezed hard.

Two Incorruptible stewards carrying luggage entered from the private quarters beyond, lighting the way with red penlights. Her sire walked behind them. Dasa glanced at Apama. His face unseen from where she stood, Zakurru spoke.

"How comes she here, Rana?"

"She was already awake," said Rana as if the matter interested her

662 · KATE ELLIOTT

not at all. And it wasn't a lie, was it? "It's like a storm out there. Is that the military base?"

"Yes."

His tone was shocking in its curtness, not because he was being rude to the woman he so possessively loved but because he was telling the truth. There was probably a Rider at the base right now and, this close, radio was almost as fast.

The Chaonians were really here. Walking on the soil of Anchor Prime, one of the three Triple-As, the great capital planets of the empire. A shudder of shock rippled through Apama's thoughts. But there was no time for panic. No room for surprise. You had to spin through the battle as it unfolded.

"Take it as it comes" was Rana's favorite phrase. In this desperate moment Apama saw how her mother's philosophy had prepared her daughter for the path she'd chosen.

Rana did not let go of her hand as they left the suite. Dasa and Zakurru were distracted, and by their twinned expressions the news was very bad. But her sire said nothing. The signs of battle were explanation enough.

They reached the bank of elevators but took the stairs, another bad sign because it meant no one was taking any chance that a power shutdown might leave them stranded inside a lift. Groups of Incorruptibles hauling luggage and escorting adult Riders were on the stairs, headed down. An elderly Rider was fastened into a harness on the back of a powerfully built steward, while another steward followed with a folded-up wheelchair.

At the security checkpoint on Level 3 that allowed access to the secure stairwell to Level 4, they found the creche on the move. Apama had never seen the children, and here they were, two babies cradled in the arms of stern nursery attendants, a squirming toddler, a four-or five-year-old with two very serious faces: doubled frowns and the ordinary face close to collapsing into tears. Five older children came shepherded by teachers and stewards. The six teens followed, looking frightened. One was crying, and his companion had two comforting arms around him. The companion was Teegee. The girl looked up and saw them. She let go of the youth and tried to wiggle back through the creche escorts to join Apama and Rana.

Zakurru spoke and Dasa repeated the words more loudly. "All in the creche must proceed. Their departure is essential."

The stewards blocked Teegee. She cast a glance back as she started down the stairs. Once the children were past, Zakurru started down at the front of their small group. Rana did not let go of Apama's hand, holding as tightly as she'd done when Apama was a little girl and they'd had to stand for an hour every day in a ration line with people shoving and jostling because folks feared the local syndicate would run out before they got to the counter.

Footfalls echoed above as more Incorruptibles descended in a hurry, twelve husky soldiers carrying glossy cylinders. Solid-state information storage, Apama thought. Something like a black box on a ship, the kind that can survive anything except falling into the sun. How apropos.

Rana whispered, "Do you think—"

"Silence," hissed Zakurru.

Apama squeezed her mother's hand and adjusted her kit bag more securely over her opposite shoulder. They reached Level 4 and headed down the passageway painted with star systems, now lost in shadow. Red emergency lights stippled the floor. The hum she remembered from last time had changed pitch. Its new resonance troubled her as if she had walked into a tunnel filled with once-industrious bees starting to get agitated. When they came to the big windows looking onto the vast interior greenhouse, the procession did not turn outward toward the sea and a sky lightening toward dawn but inward toward the core of the ridge. Into the garden.

The air inside was thick with the scent of flourishing vegetation and the fragrance of flowers. Water rippled in hydroponics tanks. Troughs of soil anchored rows of dwarf fruit trees beneath red lights. As they passed a kumquat tree at the end of a row, she yanked four off the nearest branch and handed two to her mother.

"Take it as it comes," she muttered. Rana gave her a nod but not the smile Apama had hoped for.

At length they reached a far wall, where they turned left and walked to the end of the cavern into what appeared to be a machinist shop. Tanks and valves sat atop worktables to be cleaned and repaired. An alcove contained an altar dedicated to Saint Cid. A Rider stepped into the alcove and turned sideways. Their faces triggered the opening of a secret door. Beyond it, a ramp descended deeper into the ground. The creche party headed down. Zakurru signaled Rana to go forward but Apama to stay.

Rana halted and said, "I'll wait with my daughter."

"I told you to go on," said Zakurru.

"I'll wait with my daughter."

Stewards and soldiers glanced at each other. Apama could not read their expressions. Were they sympathetic, or shocked by Rana's refusal? Zakurru scowled. The hurried footfalls of an approaching party interrupted the standoff.

Four Riders flanked by a squad of armed Incorruptibles walked in, including a worried-looking Manishtusu and a stern Kubaba.

"Is this everyone?" asked Zakurru.

A steward tapped at a counter, then said, "All Riders known to be in residence accounted for, Your Eminence."

Manishtusu said, "I had given assurances to Kiran Seth that we would meet with him and discuss his plan—"

"A bit late for that," said Zakurru.

"He said he'd wait at the terrace hermitage. We can't just leave him."

"Of course we can," said Zakurru. "Had his schemes borne fruit, we would not be in this situation, would we?"

"But I gave my word of honor."

"For once I am in agreement with Zakurru," broke in Kubaba with an impatient gesture of her lower right hand, cutting off debate. "Engaging the seer was a roll of the dice, nothing more. If he couldn't deliver, then he can find his own way. Regardless, we have neither time nor personnel to go seeking a single Yele fugitive. The medical, creche, and administrative repositories are cleared and the charges are set. We must make haste. What a disaster for the Council's recent policies."

She looked pointedly at Zakurru. He did not deign to reply.

Rana stirred. "What about the people who work on the terrace and in the Exchange?"

After a startled pause, and grunt of anger from Zakurru, Kubaba nodded to the steward beside her, who answered.

"All cadres were told last night to close their establishments and offices for the next three days and shelter in their home districts. A standard precaution."

"That's good, then," said Rana.

"No one asked you to comment," said Zakurru curtly.

"How quaint, a petty domestic disagreement in a time of great upheaval," remarked Kubaba sardonically as she walked past the others, flicking her cane as if to clear a path. "Let's move, shall we?"

Rana fell in behind Kubaba, pulling Apama behind her. They passed under the gate's threshold and onto the ramp. It sloped downward past several open security gates. As they descended, the gates closed behind them with heavy clangs. After about half a klick, they reached a line of flatbed trucks. The stewards helped them up, splitting the remaining Riders and the heavy cylinders onto two different trucks. Rana tried to follow Kubaba but her path was blocked by Zakurru's stewards so they had to climb up beside him. He indicated the bench next to him, padded, with armsrests and a safety belt. Rana sat, keeping Apama beside her. Manishtusu sagged down next to Apama, dropping his ordinary face in his hands.

Apama said softly, "Where is your partner?"

"When I left for my mission to Mishirru he went to Orbital Habitat Dolores to finish up an engineering project and . . . I don't know. There's been no contact with Dolores since the battle started. Days ago, now. They're right by Cut Stone Beacon. Right in the path of the invasion." His breathing hitched.

Thinking of Teegee, Apama rested an upper hand on his upper arm. He tensed.

Watching, Zakurru said sharply, "Hands off, Apama!"

Rana stiffened.

Manishtusu abruptly set his other upper on Apama's hand, catching hers there. "No, no, I appreciate your kindly meant reassurance. Thank you."

The trucks hummed to life and started rolling along the tunnel, inland. Red markers were set every ten meters to mark the distance, flashing past as they gained speed. At each interval blast doors rolled out to block anyone trying to follow.

Manishtusu released her hand. She clenched it against her chest, thinking of all those she had left behind: her rack-mates Splash, Deadstick, and Cricket; Gail; the doctor on the *Virtuous Heart*; Gil's family; Greensleeves and Fry-baby; Gurak and the rest of the Se Xar security team; the crew of the *Overly Devoted*. Living means leaving behind that which you can no longer carry along with you. Maybe her entire life had grown from the act of leaving. The deaths of Rana's extended family rang continual changes through the unfolding pattern of her life. She would never be free of those who had been lost. Nor did she want to be.

They traveled on in silence.

After a while, as the tunnel leveled out and they drove on, she whispered, "Mom, my fingers are starting to go numb."

"I'm not letting go," said Rana hoarsely.

A muffled boom shook the earth. The truck veered, then settled back on track. Lights appeared ahead where the tunnel ended in a siding. The other trucks were lined up along the tunnel wall, receding into shadows. A high-speed train waited, its engine humming. Its armored cars were fitted with railguns and crammed with people. When the truck halted, they clambered down and hurried to the train.

Another shock rumbled through the ground, pitching her sideways.

"What is that?" Apama asked. But she knew what it had to be.

It wasn't possible for the Chaonians to strike Anchor System, to break past the empire's fleets, to launch a ground attack onto Anchor Prime itself. But they had. They were here. The Rider Council had chosen to destroy Unity Hall rather than take the chance it might fall into the hands of the invaders.

They Didn't Deserve to Inherit the Empire Their Ancestors Had Built

The skimmers raced a bare five meters above the water, closing in on the monumental ridge that that marked the most important political center of the empire. Sun stood behind the pilots in the skimmer running at the point of the wedge. Booms from unseen emplacements in the city were followed by vicious impacts that threw up water and dirt from the bed of the shallow sea. Down the line and thus farther back, a skimmer shuddered as it was hit in the stern, tipped sideways, and spun to slam into the water with a tremendous splash before it sank beneath the waves.

"Your Highness, we should pull back to the second line." Isis stood beside Sun with her usual resigned disapproval.

Sun raised a hand to let her know she didn't want to hear any more. "That was a lucky shot. They don't have our range yet. We're coming in too fast."

Cutters roared past overhead, firing at the emplacements that had revealed themselves. More flashes and one big explosion burst up from beyond the ridge. From down here next to the water she couldn't see the city past the barrier ridge.

Frowning, she leaned against the back of the copilot's crash couch. "That's the Exchange to the right, the basilica in the center on an island, and that should be the Rider hall to the left. I thought it had a dome. Why is the ridge slumped like that?"

"James is just getting telemetry now," said Isis. "Hold on."

"In five," said the pilot, whose eyes hadn't left the target landing point to the left of the Rider hall at the southernmost point of the artificial ridge.

"Very good, Sarra."

Sun left the cockpit, balancing as the skimmer hit a muddy patch of air when they sped the last klick across a reef. A ladder took her down to the hold, where her pick of elite marines waited, crammed together, silent, tense, and ready. As she made her way to the front to join her bodyguards, she tapped arms with brief greetings.

"Colonel. Minh."

"Your Highness, can I look at that brace?" Minh had put the brace on Sun's knee at the airfield when Sun's armored leg had been peppered by shrapnel and small-arms fire. "No leakage. Does it feel secure? Do I need to adjust it?"

"It's secure. Garcia. Kou. Solomon."

"We're hearing they blew up the Rider hall about twenty minutes ago," Solomon remarked.

"We should have gotten here faster," Sun said.

"I had a bet they would blast it rather than let us get in there. Garcia's gotta pay up."

"Anyone ever tell you you're an asshole, Solomon?" Garcia muttered.

Solomon grinned. "My rule is to always hang out with a bigger asshole so they take the heat. That's why I like you, Garcia."

Sun gave Solomon a look. "I miss Persephone too. If my sources are correct, she's on-planet somewhere."

He whistled. "If anyone can wiggle a way through this, it'll be her."

The skimmer dipped, rocking hard as an impact hit nearby. The vessel veered sharply to the left, braking so hard the marines tightened their grips on the overhead hold-bar as they swayed.

Sun took a place beside Kurash. His expression was calm, his neural patterns so faint it was only possible to discern them because of the dim red light inside the hold. All the ghost soldiers waited with a steady demeanor. This is what they were created for: to throw themselves into the fire. To burn.

Her mother had once called it a waste. It was why Eirene had supported João's initiative to unleash the banner soldiers. People die because death flies on the wings of battle. To be queen-marshal was to accept this responsibility. But Eirene believed in training people so they could win and live, not so they would burn and die in order that others might walk across their ashes. She was the most ruthless person Sun knew, and yet, to her mother, an honorable victory was created by the republic acting together for the common good, not by the few lifting themselves up atop the bone-heap of the many. The Phene claimed a humble and honest origin for their empire in a rebellion of scientists and laborers against a rigid hierocracy. Maybe so, but they had themselves become top-heavy and sluggish, their officials eager to enrich their syndicates at the expense of others. Their best soldiers and spacers were mishandled by selfish admirals who fled at the first sign of defeat. Even Paulo, who she liked, had abandoned his own people for a second time because he wasn't getting the accolades and influence he wanted. No wonder they couldn't stand against Chaonia's proud citizens, even with the advantage of superior numbers and resources.

They didn't deserve to inherit the empire their ancestors had built.

The engines heightened to a shrill pitch as the skimmer thumped down. It took two jolting bumps, skipping across a hard surface. The ramp popped. The skimmer's gunners let loose a hailstorm of fire toward the ridge.

"Go! Go! Go!"

Sun led the charge down the ramp into a rank mess of shallows, knee-deep in murky liquid. Rough footing tripped up several marines who crashed face-first into the water, hauled up by comrades as they splashed thunderously forward to the base of the southern point. A saddle-like slope connected the cliff face of the artificial ridge to a natural chain of rocky hills that walled off the sea from the plain.

Cutters screamed past overhead. A *boom-boom-boom* of enemy fire melded with bangs and the shrieking whistle of atmosphere javelins streaking toward targets. A phalanx of Striker Hummingbirds swooped low across the ridge top with their characteristic *chutter-chutter-chutter*. Waves slapped up against rubble that had tumbled down along the ridge's front face. Debris spread outward across the reef like the forward front of an avalanche. Water was being sucked into a glassy cavity along the lowest level of the ridge. A luxurious divan embroidered with flowers was caught amid rocks. Water sloshed over a pair of café chairs. Scraps of vegetation swirled in eddies. Incongruously, a pristine kumquat bobbed alongside her boots.

She started toward the cavity, which offered a possible entrance into the interior of the fortified ridge and the headquarters of the Rider Council.

Kurash stepped in front of her. "Your Highness, I advise you not to enter."

"Has Isis been giving you instructions?"

"She has, Your Highness. But I would have said this anyway. The structural integrity of the interior is compromised. No one should go in except engineers and ordnance. Besides the danger of collapse, it's probably also booby-trapped. My squad can investigate. It's something arrows are trained to do."

Her jaw tensed as she thought of the Phene sending leashed soldiers to use their bodies to trigger traps. "Not under my command. We'll find a different route in."

A big set of steps at the southern point descended from an outdoor viewing balcony above to the shoreline marina where they'd landed. Kurash insisted on taking point, Sun behind him, the ghosts flanking her and the marines at her back. They raced to the top without resistance, there to discover Unity Hall's dome had become a pile of shattered solar panels, broken roof tiles, and curved rows of intact seating. Here and there a hole gaped onto shafts of darkness.

Colonel Wallace trotted up beside her. "Your Highness, please get down. The Phene infantry has pulled back into the city but there are defensive emplacements."

She scanned the processional way. Some of its statues had been toppled by cannonade. The terraces along the western slope of the ridge were riddled with collapsed awnings, furniture chewed into splinters, and what looked like waterfalls spilling down level to level from burst water pipes. The basilica was miraculously untouched, while a thick column of smoke rose from the distant Exchange. To the west, in the city, drop-ships were landing in every plaza to fierce resistance. Phene defenders pulled back, street by street, while Guards swarmed outward from the landing craft.

Sun walked to the eastern edge of the ridge and peered down onto the debris that had avalanched into the sea. Hetty trotted up with a pair of combat engineers assigned to her unit, the group meant to crash the Rider information banks and take charge of valuable files as well as secure Rider prisoners.

"Captain Nazir, can you explore through that hole?" Sun pointed to the reef below, the way the water was flowing under the ridge as if into unseen cavities.

"We can start by sending in wasps and hornets to get a visual. I have some moles that can map the integrity of the structure, but it'll take a while."

"Where are the Riders? There have to be children with them, too. No airships took off from the main airfield and none have lifted from inside the city. James? Possible escape routes?" She pinged her voice through the ring network.

James pinged in from an offshore comms unit where he and his team were collating incoming information. ABOVEGROUND TRANSPORT ON THE MOVE TOWARD THE HILLS. SOME MILITARY VEHICLES BUT MOSTLY CIVILIAN WHEELS, MAYBE COMMANDEERED BY MILITARY. CAN'T KNOW. MAPS INDICATE RAIL LINES UNDERNEATH THE CITY IN NORMAL SUBWAY CONFIGURATIONS. WE ARE ZEROING IN ON MICRO LEVEL SEISMIC ACTIVITY THAT MAY INDICATE SUB-SUBWAY TRAIN ACTIVITY AT AN EVEN DEEPER LEVEL. NO MEASURABLE ACTIVITY ON OR UNDER THE SEA BESIDES OUR OWN ASSAULT VESSELS.

Evacuating all the Riders ahead of her lightning attack was a smart move on the part of the Council, one of the first truly smart moves they'd made since the ultimately unsuccessful but bold attack on Molossia. It made her think they had strict emergency protocols in place, or maybe a good tactician had finally taken charge. So be it. She would use the shifting battlefield itself to create advantage for her situation.

"Hetty, take a unit to seize the Exchange. I want it as intact as possible. Captain Nazir, investigate the entry below. Drill all the way through if you can, through multiple points of entry."

"Your Highness, drilling will destabilize this end of the ridge. If the interior is badly enough damaged, it could even cause the sea to break through the unstable rubble and flood the plain—in other words, the city—which according to our measurements is one meter lower in elevation than the seabed."

A starburst exploded overhead and everyone ducked except Sun, who recognized its distinctive whir and pop as a range-finder from their own forces. She shaded her eyes to look westward across the city. The sun had not yet reached zenith. Her network told her that the hills were about fifty klicks distant, and that beyond these foothills extended hundreds of klicks of rugged mountainous territory. Perfect country for concealed airbases and hidden refuges.

"Well, then, Captain. We'll make sure our ground forces are prepared if they have to evacuate quickly ahead of a flood. James?"

AFFIRMATIVE.

"Follow the trains. Solomon."

"Yes."

"Take a company according to James's direction. Garcia, likewise. Colonel Wallace, assign as many more companies as the Honorable James suggests. I don't know how many rail lines there are, or how far they go."

Persephone might know. Surely it would have been the first thing she'd have checked when arriving here. If she had arrived. If she was still alive.

She pinged Jade. "Situation?"

A set of coordinates in central Melo dropped into the network, followed by a message.

UNDER FIRE. HOLDING POSITION AS WE WAIT FOR
REINFORCEMENTS FROM THE HATCHETS. I MEAN,
TWELFTH BATTALION.

She smiled. "I know who you mean. Tell Grace hello from me when he gets there. Move as soon as you can. We're going to push outward at speed. The Twelfth Battalion will cordon off the city. Any hostile infantry caught behind the cordon will be left without access to further supply alongside a trapped civilian population. We'll circle back once we've secured all crucial military targets on-planet and in-system. If their local syndicates fight among themselves, as I suspect they will, we'll look like saviors to the civilians when we return. For now, I'll be joining the ground push with my Shields. We will find those fugitive Riders."

She paused to consider the ruins of Unity Hall. Plans had to move as fast as the attack did. "Kurash, change of orders. You'll stay with me."

Interlude on the Outskirts of the City of Melo

The big booms go on all day. Erratic. Shattering. Now and again Dante hears crying from elsewhere in the stricken district and once an ugly scream that fades into a cruel, agonized moan that drags on and on before mercifully cutting off. He wants to go outside to search for wounded neighbors but Xaista won't let him.

"We have to try to help! We can't do nothing!" he insists.

She keeps a tight hold on his lower wrist. "If you go outside you'll be shot. Then what if we need to move Lolo and the babies?"

She is the big sister, so he obeys even though he is sixteen and already on the infantry track at school because he is the fifth child of the house and can choose his own path. He wants to fight for truth and honor. He will volunteer for every thankless mission. We are all destined for death.

As night falls, booming rumbles shake the air, followed by emergency sirens waking up to scream. The littles all start to cry. The radio transmission cuts off in a crackle of static just as a frantic announcer starts saying something about flooding. The sirens go silent between one breath and the next.

A lull settles.

They're all so exhausted. Xaista falls asleep on the cot next to Lolo's recliner, her arms curled protectively around her pregnant belly. Their elder siblings' children huddle together on a blanket like a heap of disconnected limbs and heads. The thought shivers through him with a prickle of foreboding. His brain travels to places he can't confess to his family: harsh images, grotesque futures, blood and iron and tears. All his life he has kept his head down and his mouth closed over his terrible visions, and now he fears they are coming true.

Sleep eludes him, so he slips out of the basement and creeps up the stairs. The ground floor is dark and he doesn't dare turn on any lights as he feels his way down the main corridor and into the carpentry shop. Immediately his feet hit debris. He checks the shelf by the door and finds a head lamp, which mercifully still works. The yellow beam reveals that half the shop has fallen in. The back stairs in its corner are blocked by broken ceiling beams, crushed furniture, and an avalanche of roof tiles. The gap opens up all the way through the upper floor and roof to a sky so unexpectedly thick with stars that it means the city has gone dark.

The lights of an airship speed past. He snaps off the head lamp. Another three lights chase past. In a burst of brilliance, one of the vessels explodes.

Sweet Aveline! The power of movement drains from his body. He feels hung out to dry as he stares upward. Sparks shower. A rumble stirs the quiet, then fades. His hands sweat even though it isn't a hot night. He smells smoke.

Smoke!

Backtracking, he tries the corridor that leads past the storerooms. The doors feel intact although he can't see a thing and he's too rattled to use the head lamp in case the barbaric enemy waits out of sight, crouching in the night. The doors aren't warm to the touch, which would mean something was burning beyond them. Not that the family stores anything for the shop in a hazardous way.

As he works his way forward nothing moves. No light. No sound. Just an occasional far-off rattle of gunfire. He and Xaista were alone in the big house. Xaista, the fourth child, has accepted her role as hearth-keeper and caretaker. He is too young to leave home yet. Their grand-mothers are dead, grandfather Aquilino was called in to do medical work for a field hospital, Lolo is no longer able to care for himself, and all the other adults are off doing what adults do except for his eldest brother, Aweng, who died at Kanesh years ago on the infamous Espla-nade. Everyone else should be safe at work, but nothing is safe. Lolo says that in all his ninety-eight years there has never been an invasion of Anchor System, much less Anchor Prime. The history curriculum says it's never happened at all. Anchor has always been at peace.

Dante reaches the double-gated doors that should open onto the en-try patio. They're stuck. When he shoves, they hit an object too heavy for him to move. He finds a window, opens a shutter, and crawls out.

By now his eyes have adapted. Starlight and a crescent moon reveal the scatter of shadows across a street broken by fragments, houses tumbled as if they have gotten too tired to stand, a body sprawled like a starfish flung far from the nourishing sea.

He's afraid to go out there but has to go, doesn't he? Saint Aveline would go. A strange rhythmic thumping blends with a weird rising-and-falling whine. Beams of light swing back and forth above the district administrative center about three klicks away. A staccato jack-hammering makes him jump.

What if the person is bleeding, and he could save them? All of a sudden he starts sweating. If he thinks, he'll freeze. He dashes down the hillside stairs and stumbles out onto the street, not looking either way, straight to the body. Dropping to his knees, he risks turning on the head lamp. He has to know. But the face it illuminates is no one he recognizes. Not even a soldier. Just a random stranger, an older man wearing a look of surprise and a piece of metal like rebar stuck out crazily from the back of his head, something that flew through the air and hit him by chance.

We are all destined for death.

Fortunately Dante can't see the wound. From this angle, the man looks at peace.

Will any family ever collect the body? Gather for a funeral procession? Sing the proper songs and afterward eat and drink in a syndicate hall?

Shaking, he grabs the man by his ankles and drags the rigid body into the entry alcove of the neighborhood barber shop. He doesn't want a vehicle to run over it in the dark. He'll ask Xaista what they should do with the corpse. But then he'll have to admit he went against her direct orders.

What does that even matter now? he thinks bitterly as he stands over the body. The world has turned upside-down.

His hands are suddenly cold, as stiff as if he is going to turn into a corpse. He runs back to the house, sure death is reaching from the shadows to crush him. But he races up the hillside stairs and reaches the entry patio with nothing more than a bit of dust in his eyes.

Hugging the wall, he ascends the formal stairs to the upper level where his family lives. The west side of the house got hit by something he guesses wasn't a bomb but a huge piece of debris flung by fate in this direction. That's what collapsed half of the house into the shop below. The staircase up to the mirador is miraculously intact. He climbs, careful to test each stair to make sure it will hold his weight. An outdoor walkway surrounds the square parlor where the family gathers for games and coffee and pastries on so many long evenings, all together in raucous harmony. He crawls to the walkway's railing. Their compound is sited on the lower slopes of the first foothill, giving them a view across the plain all the way to Government Ridge, forty klicks away.

Their local district center is on fire, flames leaping and writhing, heat boiling upward. Wind throws foul smoke and stinging ash into his face. A line of vehicles rolls along the Avenue of the Righteous. Probably they are headed for the power stations. The great sprawl of the city is a patchwork of flames, smoke, shifting lights, and, in the farthest distance, slowly expanding stretches of an undulating darkness like inky tendrils working their way through the city. Like water, if the sea had found a way to breach the ridge. Surely that can't be possible. The ridge, like the empire, is indestructible because it was born from righteousness.

A thump sounds to his right, like feet hitting the roof of the next house. He glances that way but doesn't see anything moving. That family packed up and left for the countryside two days ago. Their house is untouched by the fighting but it's also silent and dark. No one is there. The walkway quivers beneath his knees. A click sounds by his ear as an object presses against his head. The blunt point of a weapon.

"Put up hands," says a voice in crude Phenish. Then, in Yele, "What do you think, Garcia?"

"I think he's just a kid, and this isn't the hidden launch pad we're looking for. That downstairs looks like my aunt's carpentry shop. I like this upper-deck lookout with couches. Fancy."

Dante raises his hands and, scarcely daring to breathe, glances to his left. Three squat, stocky shadows stand on the walkway like they own the place.

The one called Garcia goes on. Dante wishes his elder sibs were here to see why it wasn't a waste of time for him to learn Common Yele by watching all those shameful foreign melodramas. "Why would they place a secret launch zone less than fifty klicks from the seat of government? I'd make it a thousand klicks away."

"That's why you're not in charge," says the third soldier. "Closer is better."

Garcia retorts, "Closer is where we'd most likely shoot them down. Anyway, they've had all day to get away. We haven't heard a thing about captured Riders."

"Like command tells us that kind of classified shit," replies a third.

The first soldier says, "Take cover."

The weapon pokes him, and he crawls backward to get under the roof of the mirador. Once he's there he keeps his hands clasped to the back of his head. He has to stay alive to take care of the others. What will they do if something happens to him? Xaista is near her time, Lolo is too old, and the niblings are too young.

"The hells, those arms are creepy," says Garcia.

"Shut up, buzzmouth." The first soldier nudges Dante, who is still kneeling. "No talk. No talk! Eh?"

"Yes, I do not talk," he says in Yele. "Pardon me. With your favor, do not shoot. I have no weapon."

They gape at him in surprise, not that he can really see their faces except as gleaming ovals against the night. He has an instant to wonder if he should tell them about his family in the basement, or hope they leave without searching further into the house. They haven't shot him. Maybe they're not totally barbarians.

A storm of noise breaks over them out of nowhere. What starts as a frantic hail of flares explodes into the frenetic hammer of railguns, pops and shrieks, and a big *boom boom* like an industrial-grade piston suddenly turned on and rampant.

Garcia swears incomprehensibly as Phene infantry scramble into view along the street. They're retreating in good order, leapfrogging one group back as another group uses debris as shelter to lay down covering fire.

Can he warn them with a shout? Dare he try?

A blow to the back of the head lays him flat, head spinning, body slumped against the legs of Nanay's favorite divan. He sways on the edge of consciousness as a terrific staccato of weapons fire streams a nightmare around him. Bits of the wooden balcony decoration pepper his legs as railgun fire tears it apart. Woozy and muddled, he has fallen beneath the waves like the time he almost drowned in the great pool of the Auric Falls where they'd gone on a once-in-a-lifetime family vacation. He'd drifted downward toward a light gleaming in the abyss with such languorous promise it seemed easier to sink than to swim. If he could just reach it and discover the hidden lair rumored to lie beyond the central waterfall . . .

He is yanked roughly upward and dragged as he stumbles, trying to get his feet under him. A splintering crash blows up the whole world and he blacks out, then shakes his head to find himself sitting upright on Nanay's divan as if the family is about to take coffee and flan while Lolo holds forth about the good old days when the syndicates cooperated instead of competed.

How did he get here? Sparks dazzle his eyes. Smoke billows up from the street below as if its thick substance has consumed all life and churned it into gauzy particles. His hands are shaking. His ears ring.

Even when he blinks he can't see what happened to the enemy soldiers. He should get down, get on the floor, but he can't move. Does he even have all his limbs? Is he dead?

The dense ground layer of smoke starts to lift, teased apart by a salty wind rising off the sea. The street filters back into view and he wishes it hadn't because bodies lie strewn everywhere. The saints preserve their souls. His lips move but no sound comes out, or maybe it does and his ears are still ringing too loudly for him to hear his own voice.

In the haze beyond, a light rises like the dawn only it isn't even midnight. Feet tramp in crescendo as a monstrous regiment approaches, head lamps swaying. Out of the mist they come walking like legends from an ancient tale, weapons raised, alert, confident in victory. An unusually handsome person strides at the front like a saint who has emerged from the basilica to hearten and lead their prayerful followers.

Why would he even notice such a ridiculous and terrible thing except he loves the foreign dramas with their impossibly attractive casts; even with only two arms they're so much more emotional and gripping than local dramas, which always have to teach a lesson or embody a moralistic theme. Lolo says back when he was a boy, the dramas were more adventurous and there was a lot more skin.

Lolo.

Xaista.

The littles.

He whispers, hoarsely, "Can I go? Pardon me, ma'am. Can I go?"

No one answers, because they're looking outward. Low-flying skimmers race toward their position. Dante recognizes the Osprey-class attack ships from *Old Hands at the Youngest Shore*. Flowing down the Avenue of the Righteous, a thin skin of water glimmers beneath skimmer searchlights as it surges forward, a fringe of foam at the front pushed along by a thick swell behind. The flood!

A squad of stocky hostiles swarms up a ladder dropped from a skimmer, climbing out of the water. Garcia shouts, and the company on the street below break into a run and head for the house. Dante can hear them laughing as they reach safety and start up the stairs. Below, the water sweeps along the street, tossing and tumbling bodies, and reaches its limit in a cresting burst of spume and spray that brushes the entry porch two floors below and falls back. Which means it is deep enough to flood

"The basement," he says, louder, trying to stand. "The basement!"

"Who's this?" Suddenly the very handsome person is standing in front of him with a quizzical eye.

"A kid. Speaks Yele."

"Look for a basement, do a full perimeter check," says the captain, speaking to a soldier who hurries off down the stairs. No, the person is not a captain; they are wearing seven stripes. That insignia means something different but Dante's thoughts are too fractured because he can only think of his family trapped as water seeps in.

"Family in basement," he says. Let them shoot him for speaking without permission. Nothing matters except that he save them. "My family is in the basement. My grandfather. My sister. She is pregnant. The children. They are civilians. Please."

"Garcia, did you find a basement?"

"Uh. Just the carpentry shop. And a lot of collateral damage from debris."

"The queen-marshal expects better. But maybe Solomon is in charge of this company."

Garcia bristles. "He took his company inland, on a different route. This has nothing to do with him. No wonder he says you are—" He breaks off.

"Says I am what?" asks Seven Stripes with a gleam of *I doubt you dare to say it* in lambent eyes.

A shout from below. "Found it! Just civvies."

Seven Stripes makes a hand gesture. "Garcia, take a squad and deal with them. Grab a medic in case it's true about the pregnant sister." The gaze, weary, worn, and yet dazzling, drops to regard Dante. Grime-smeared lips part as a prelude to speech.

Shouts interrupt. Lights are winking all along the roofs of the houses that line the lower slope of this hillside district. More Chaonian soldiers drop in. There's a big commotion as a platoon splashes up from the flooded street. Whatever it is about the arriving platoon that's caught people's attention is eclipsed when streaks of light rise on a thunderous echo out of the hills five or ten klicks distant: ships streaking skyward.

By the saints! Was there a hidden base out there all along? Like most his age, Dante has hiked to Kissing Rock and Skinny Pool, but never past the canyon. Nobody goes past the canyon.

Swift fighters blaze past overhead but they don't shoot. They arc heavenward in a heady howl of engines as they chase after the ships that came out of the hills.

The enemy soldiers are jabbering too fast for him to understand what they're saying, but they are excited as they point upward, no longer interested in the flooded city and its victims. It's up to him to save his family. Sweet Aveline give him strength. He braces his feet to see if he can find enough balance to stand. Pushing up, he feels nauseated, so sinks back down, panting. Patience. He'll make it. He'll get to them.

A firm hand comes to rest on his shoulder.

He looks up into the face of a young woman, another officer by her gear, although she has eight stripes on her shoulder boards and he has no idea what that means. His brain is still scattered and muzzy.

She speaks in a clear, commanding voice. It's not an angry voice, but it is a voice no one can ignore. "You're the boy who speaks Yele?"

"Yes, ma'am." He uses the correct honorific for an officer. It's what Nanay would want him to do, even with an enemy. Manners are like gravity, she would say, they keep the world from flying apart.

The officer measures him with an extraordinary gaze that seems able to sum up his entire existence in five seconds. "Not a boy, are you? You're old enough to do an adult's work. We need translators. We pay well. How about it?"

There's only one thing he needs right now. "My family."

She nods. "They're being brought up from the basement. I met your grandfather. Always respect the elders. I'd like to know what he said in reply."

The words surprise a dizzy laugh from him. "No, you wouldn't. He doesn't like Chaonians."

"Was he calling me rude names?"

He's terrified she's going to charge down and murder Lolo for the crime of impertinence, but she laughs. It's as if she's giddy, or drunk, but he's pretty sure she's not drunk. She's just incredibly intense and wired, like she'd rather drink down the adrenaline rush of battle than Lolo's award-winning palm wine.

"That's why I need a translator. I'm told your sister may have gone into labor. I have a medic with her right now. We'll get you checked for a concussion. Then you can go down and see them. What's your name?"

"Dante Hg Bantay."

"All right, Dante. You work for us as a translator, and we'll pay you. We'll also give your family a secure shelter, food, and medical care."

"How do I know you keep your word and not kill them?"

"That's a fair question. What assurances do you want?"

"Can they stay with me?"

"Not while we're moving, but I tell you what. I have other high-profile guests, including Speaker Baragesi's family. Do you know about them?"

The conversation has become even more surreal. "Sure. We saw on the news, like, two or three years ago, was it? The Council elected Baragesi as Speaker. Lolo complained there was no need because Speaker Kubaba was doing a good job. The Council allowed Riders to claim families. Is that what you mean?"

"Yes. If you have more family, they can be collected and granted safe passage to join the other guests. They will live in good, safe, secure conditions. They won't be on-planet but you'll be able to communicate with them via courier. Once we establish order there will be more options. Or they can stay here in the house, but it might be for the best if they don't."

"Because our neighbors will call us traitors?"

She shrugs. "I don't know your neighbors. The city is going to be a mess for a while. It's what I can offer. I'll be moving on in a few minutes."

"You are not giving to me a choice, are you?"

"No. But I mean what I say. They'll be safe. You'll work for us."

His mind circles back to the most glaring indictment. "You are asking for me to be a traitor to my empire."

She captures his gaze with hers. "Not if I'm the empire."

"How can you be the empire?" A warning wobbles in his mind. His thoughts cohere as the ringing in his ears fades. Everyone else is standing around her the way plants open their blooms toward the star. It is the way she stands with such absolute conviction of her presence in the world that, in the midst of battle, she appears relaxed. At home. She is in the place she belongs because wherever she stands is that place.

"Who are you?" he whispers.

She tilts her head, as if she's been asked the question before and didn't have the right answer then and wants to make sure she has the right answer now.

"I am queen-marshal of Chaonia. Like my mother before me, I was elected strategos and military leader of the allied Yele League. I am the named heir to the dynasts of Karnos. By my own declaration, I rule the Trinity Coalition. The holy establishment of Mishirru has acknowledged me as the incarnation of their Great Mother Queen. With this victory I am Speaker for the Council of the Phene Empire. So in truth, Dante, it is those who fight against me who are the traitors to the empire."

Years ago when he was little, the family went to the seashore and Nanay drew a line in the sand around her five children and said, "This is the world we live in. We know its bounds, and the dangers that lie outside proper comportment. As long as we live and work with truth and honor, our world will hold."

A mournful ache afflicts his heart. It isn't grief, exactly. It isn't only pain. It is recognition. The world Nanay believed in is gone, swept away by the implacable flood.

She'd Been Here Before

The escape route was like a river delta, branching at intervals into new channels. At each split the train stopped and one of the carriages would unhitch and race away into the dark alone, taking a group of Riders and Incorruptibles with it. Apama caught glimpses of decoy cars and other tunnels, a confusing tangle to make it hard for the invaders to track them. It was a good plan. They had to separate lest they be captured or killed in a single group.

Besides the fifteen children, adult Riders who'd been in residence at Anchor's Unity Hall had fled on the train. Zakurru would not tell her how many, or if others had escaped via other routes. Manishtusu was too preoccupied to answer. Every time Apama woke up, he was tense and awake, although clearly exhausted. She felt for him, for his terror. Riders surely got used to having instant access to information, and now he was almost as in the dark as she was. The difference was that she had her loved one next to her. Rana only let go of her daughter's hand when she needed to drink, eat, or use the toilet.

Eighteen hours after their departure the last two conjoined carriages coasted to a halt. Soldiers leaped down to the tracks, clipping into a security system whose cameras ran the entire route, checking the rails for signs of vibration, and setting up explosive charges.

A colonel called up to Zakurru. "There is pursuit, about twenty klicks behind us and gaining. I recommend sending this carriage as a decoy to Mount Maelstrom while the last car takes the emergency tunnel to Wainwright Field."

Maelstrom and Wainwright. So that's where they had ended up. Apama straightened, sharply alert, ready to move.

Zakurru rose. There was a pause for communication between Riders.

Manishtusu nodded. "Yes, I'm prepared to go through with it. It's the best way."

"As you wish." Zakurru, or perhaps Dasa, extended an upper hand to shake Manishtusu's upper, a rare formal gesture between Riders. Then he turned. "Rana, with me. We are leaving in company with the four Riders in the forward carriage."

Rana did not stand. "What about Apama?"

He said in his chilliest tone, "You can rise of your own will or the stewards will carry you. It is up to you how you proceed from here. But

I will no longer tolerate this defiance. Apama is a soldier. She is being assigned to a different mission."

"What mission is that?" asked Rana.

Zakurru's eyes and mouth narrowed to slits. It was scary how much anger a body could convey without raising its voice or striking out.

Apama stood, gently pulling out of her grip. "Mom! It's okay."

"No, it isn't okay. I have the right to know why you are being separated from me when we are trying to escape. Lancers don't have atmosphere capability, so it's not like you're going to fly."

"I can fly other ships . . ." Apama trailed off as she realized she wasn't the bone of contention, not really. At long last Rana had reached the end of her rope, flung to the limit of her tether by the shocking events. Zakurru had taken the stance of an immovable object, so Apama turned to Manishtusu, anything to shift the ugly focus of Zakurru's anger. "What is the mission?"

"Enough." Zakurru signaled to the stewards to come forward.

Rana braced herself on the seat as if she intended to fight rather than go. The reaction shocked Apama, used to her mother's resigned persistence that had never, ever exploded into outright revolt. Her mother's lower right hand fluttered to rest protectively on her belly.

Blessed Arthas. She was pregnant.

Apama stepped in front of the approaching stewards. "I will not let my mother be mishandled."

The stewards looked to Zakurru. Manishtusu seemed unaware of the conflict, caught up in his own crisis. Tears welled in Rana's eyes, the sight a kick to Apama's gut. They were both trapped, weren't they, in a web not of their weaving?

The door into the other carriage opened. Teegee scrambled in, pursued by a frantic steward who wasn't willing to lay hands on the young Rider.

"Your Eminence," called the steward, "I couldn't stop her."

"I volunteer," said Teegee in Giolla's louder voice. "Manishtusu can't be captured alone. It's too obvious a ploy to get a spy into their fleet. But I'm young and they won't think the Council will risk me. They'll think he's trying to get me away."

Zakurru snapped, "Tadukhipa, return to the forward carriage at once."

She set all four arms akimbo, the authentic picture of an obstreperous adolescent. "You can't make me. I put it to a vote. I put it to a vote. I put it to a vote." She raised a hand to mark her statement. Giolla's eyes flickered with nystagmus.

"This is ridiculous. Unacceptable!" Zakurru was really beside himself now, if Riders could be beside themselves, if they weren't already, a conundrum that chased through Apama's mind like tracer fire and vanished as quickly. "The wrong time—"

"An emergency is the *right time* to make the boldest choices," retorted Tadukhipa with a cocky grin. "I win with a majority of votes in my favor. I'll stay with Manishtusu and the guards. Apama can go with her mother, in my place."

"Oh no, I do not give my permission for Apama. I am her sire and thus her sponsor and commander. If you are determined in this reckless course, Tadukhipa, then you need a trusted escort. After all, Apama has seen you safely through the fire before. She will stay with you and with Manishtusu, as I have intended all along. Rana. We leave now. The enemy approaches."

Apama grabbed her mother's hands. "Mom, will you be all right?"

"Of course I'll be all right. It's you I worry about."

"Then please go. This isn't over. I know Mount Maelstrom. We trained there for four months. I know where the concealed launch tunnels are."

Zakurru slapped her arm. "Your task is to create a plausible opportunity to be captured. Not to escape."

"Mom. *Please.*" A sob caught in Apama's throat. She couldn't bear thinking of what might happen to her mother if the Chaonians caught up with them. Her pregnant mother. She'd have a baby sibling. Someone else to protect. Someone else who would need love and shelter. "I'm trained for this. Let me know you'll be okay. Let me do my duty. We are all destined for death."

Rana crushed her with a hug, released her, paused to give Teegee an auntly kiss, then trudged forward into the adjoining carriage without waiting for Zakurru or Dasa. Incorruptibles vanished after her with bags and gear, leaving Apama, Teegee, the morosely silent Manishtusu, and four doughty Incorruptibles to serve them: two stewards and two soldiers. Sacrifices, she thought. But the Incorruptibles stood with stalwart expressions as their carriage lurched in the decoupling, then began rolling at an agonizingly slow pace onward along the main tunnel.

The stewards brought food and drink for the two Riders and, as an afterthought, for her. The soldiers set up additional physical shields around the carriage and adjusted weaponry at the windows and at the rear. Neither wore officer insignia. One was a senior chief technician and the other a specialist first class. They knew each other well enough to casually use nicknames: Rummy and Scramble.

Apama opened a window as the train car picked up speed. Air whooshed by, metallic with the scent of bedrock and overworked fans. The wheels had set back down, humming. The tunnel began to bank upward. She recalled a locked train siding deep in the bowels of Maelstrom's caldera base with a single carriage ready to go, but in the four months she'd been stationed at the base, no train had ever come or gone. Pilots snuck down via the maintenance shaft to drink hooch and have sex.

"This is the stupidest idea I've ever heard," she said, turning to face the two Riders. "We can get out via the base. That's why this train is running there. They'll be waiting for us."

Manishtusu said, "I will stay behind, according to the plan. We need to place a Rider inside the Chaonian command."

"Why are you so insistent on this?" Apama asked. "What good can possibly come from falling into Chaonian hands?"

"That's *Your Eminence* to you, Captain," said the older steward snippily.

Apama had no patience for precious niceties in an emergency so she ignored it. "By my reckoning, at the speed this train is moving, we will barely make it to Maelstrom before pursuit catches us. That's the point, right? We go slow, like we're broken, and they catch us and don't look for the other carriage. But Maelstrom doesn't know that. Can we speed up the carriage?"

"But I want to," said Manishtusu.

"I get it, you want to serve the empire and this seems like a noble way. Trust me, it's a half-cocked plan born of desperation. You think the Chaonians will bring you into their war meetings and you can convey all their plans to a Council-in-Exile?"

He dipped his chin. "It's the only way I can find out if Jacobo survived. They can track him down. I'm willing to trade myself for word of him. If it helps the Council as well, then all the better."

She caught Giolla's eye. The girl gave a warning shake of her head.

"Even if he's dead?" Apama said. This wasn't the time to avoid ugly truths.

"Yes. Even then." Determination lifted his shoulders. His mouths bore an identical line, taut, sure of themselves. "I can't bear to not know."

Teegee nudged Apama and said in a low voice, "In the creche we know everything about everyone. Some of us can't manage without that constant assurance."

"Not you."

The girls shrugged in the way they had that made it seem like a gesture shared between them.

The man's riding face glanced toward Tadukhipa as if in wordless speech, and of course it was. He added, in a weary tone, "If he's dead, I have nothing to live for."

"Manishtusu, what about your embodied person? What do they say? Do they agree? I don't even know their name."

The stewards hissed in displeasure. The soldiers looked startled, then offended that she would dare speak so bluntly to a Rider.

Manishtusu met her gaze calmly. "Unlike the others, I am not two people. I am Manishtusu, one person. Structurally mutated. That's all."

Heat flamed in Apama's cheeks. She had asked an intimate question and been given an intimate answer. "I apologize, Your Eminence. That was intrusive of me."

"It doesn't matter," he said, and she realized he spoke with either mouth, alternating back and forth in a way different from the other Riders. "I volunteered. I mean to be captured, but that doesn't mean the rest of you must."

"I stay with you, Your Eminence," said the older steward stoutly.

"Of course, Zeno. Tadukhipa, you and the others will escape with the captain. Zakurru can't interfere, as much as he wishes to complain in my head and yours."

His grin was wry, a bit sour, and Apama liked him for it. A quiet individual revealing unexpected depths.

"All right," said Teegee with twinned frowns.

"Don't sound so reluctant," said Apama. "Being captured by the Chaonians won't be the adventurous spy-at-the-picnic you think it will be."

"Not just a spy. If we can get close enough to her, we can kill her."

Alarm stung like an electric shock through her flesh. "That's a death sentence for the assassin."

"A fair trade though."

Apama rubbed her face, suddenly exhausted by the inability to *do something* while the emergency, the disaster, just ground on and on. "You're not wrong about it being a fair trade, for the empire's sake. But no one should bet the outcome on that kind of long shot. Anyway, you're coming with me."

The girls sighed but did not argue.

Ahead, a basso *thrum thrum thrum* welcomed them. Attuned to sound, she recognized it as the base's elaborate ventilation system still chugging along. The train slid through an archway into a chamber hewn out of rock. Blast doors rolled down behind them. Dull red emergency lights flickered on as they came to rest at a short siding behind an empty train car.

"There should be a crew here to receive us," said Zeno, looking at Apama as if she were responsible for the lapse.

Apama shared a glance with the soldiers. The senior chief—Rummy—cracked a door and stepped halfway out, sweeping up and down the dark siding with an infrared scope. He lifted a hand with an all clear. Apama stepped out onto the siding, pistol raised as she took in a breath to get her bearings. The air was a little stale but had good oxygen content and not too much nitrogen. She trotted over to the main door as Rummy covered her back. The panel gleamed red as the comms system clicked over with a repeated message.

"Maelstrom Base evacuated. Maelstrom Base evacuated. Code red to go. Code red to go. Do not resuscitate until code green received. Do not resuscitate until code green received. Maelstrom Base evacuated."

Revered Arthas. The truth crashed down as she checked the time stamp for message initiation. Ninety-one minutes ago, exactly when the trains had split.

Zakurru had stranded them, leaving nothing to chance.

A spike of emotion buzzed in her head, in her hands. Her vision smeared with absolute rage and helpless fury. But she'd been here before. She knew how to spin through chaos.

A body popped in beside her: Rummy. "Captain?"

"Give me thirty seconds." She placed a palm on the panel and received Rider-level access. It took her twenty long seconds to find the access ladder for the base surveillance cameras. She began clicking backward from the central control center through levels, quadrants, zones.

"You've been here before," he said.

"I trained here for four months. There's a pair of Blizzard-class strikers mothballed in an old lava tube, Level 4, Southwest Quadrant, Zone Smiles."

"Smiles?"

"Decorated with scenes from—"

"—Procession of Smiles, got it."

"It's an older atmosphere fighter, but it's maneuverable and fast. Most crucially, it can go short-range vacuum. It doesn't have a beacon drive but we can get to Auger or Axiom Beacons. There we go." Grainy, dark images revealed a lava tube turned into a hangar, the two strikers sleek blots against a faint background glow she couldn't identify. She blew out a breath to bleed off the adrenaline of relief. "Like I'd hoped. Not worth flying out in an evacuation. Any pilots besides me?"

"No. You sure these can fly?"

"I've flown both. Every ship not in a mechanics' bay is ready to go, even the old ones. Base standard for drills. But it can take only four."

"All right." The Incorruptibles were the best-trained soldiers in the empire. He didn't hesitate. "Scramble will stay with the Eminent Manishtusu. I'll accompany the Eminent Tadukhipa."

"What's wrong? What did you do?" called Zeno loudly, in complete contraindication of military procedure in a potentially hostile zone.

Apama ran back to the open door, where Scramble was covering the siding and Zeno was standing, arms akimbo, looking annoyed and bossy. The two Riders looked at Zeno, then at Apama. She had one chance to take charge of this operation.

"The base has been evacuated. We're on our own. Zeno, you'll stay with the Eminent Manishtusu and Specialist Sc Ramla on the siding. Get out in the open so the Chaonians won't think you are trying to ambush them. Administer a sedative to the Eminence and station yourself in an unthreatening position beside him so there will be less chance for twitchy fingers to shoot."

"But—"

"It's a risk, yes. But we are already gambling the Chaonians wish to capture Riders alive. If they're here to kill, no gambit will matter. The evidence of Rider Anchi suggests otherwise."

"The Eminent Anchi is dead," objected Zeno with a sneer.

Manishtusu silenced the steward with a gesture. "Anchi was killed by *our* operation, the Council's decision, not by her captors. What about Tadukhipa?"

"There's a Blizzard striker available. It's in a storage hangar. Nothing they'll look for at first. Four of us can get off-planet and make it to one of the open beacons."

Manishtusu clasped hands awkwardly with Teegee in farewell. Apama wondered how often Riders touched in their day-to-day lives. In these circumstances, such an ordinary gesture seemed so final.

A muffled thunk from the other side of the blast door startled them, followed by a barely audible rumble. The Chaonians had arrived sooner than she'd anticipated.

"Good luck." Apama grabbed a short-stock railgun from the carriage wall, looped an ammunition sash around her torso, and slung her kit bag over a shoulder.

Zeno said, pissily, "Those railguns only work for Incorruptibles and Riders."

Apama smiled. What people didn't know meant an advantage to her. The chief handed Apama an infantry helmet equipped with a targeting screen. She tugged its straps to fit as the younger steward started to gather up suitcases. "Toia, leave the luggage. Take only an emergency bag. Teegee, I hope you packed like I trained you."

"I did." Giolla held up a bag just big enough for a change of clothing and a few toiletries. Her teddy-rex was strapped on the back. Toia helped her fasten the specially constructed Rider helmet whose clear back allowed her riding face to see.

"This is it." Apama met each gaze, fixing their attention to her. "We are all destined for death."

The soldiers exchanged a fist bump. Toia offered a gesture of respect to Manishtusu. Apama led them down the siding into darkness past the parked train car.

"We're going to take the maintenance shaft," she said to the chief. "I don't like how fast that pursuit got here. Feels off to me."

"Like they could have caught up sooner if they'd wanted to?"

"Yeah." They reached the far wall, an apparent dead end with a bench set into an alcove. A memory flashed, funny and awkward. Not a position you would try unless you were really drunk. That very bench. But this was no time to drift into the past. The bench's right back leg had a manual lever hidden amid filigree decoration. With its click, the ceiling popped open. A rectangular platform glided down as the bench folded up beneath it.

"Clever," said Teegee.

The chief stepped on first, gun raised as he sighted up the shaft. He nodded, and they crowded onto the platform. Apama placed a finger on the button for Level 4 and then thought better of it and pressed Level 7 instead.

As the platform began to rise she caught a last glimpse in the hazy red light of Zeno hauling baggage up to the main door to create a scenario in which it might seem they'd been trying to escape. Manishtusu knelt like a worshipper at the basilica, offering a prayer to one of the saints. But of course, the saints weren't for the Riders; they were for the people. Yet weren't Riders also people? When had they become something else? Something so disconnected from the people and empire they ruled? Perhaps that was the inevitable result of an entrenched hierarchy, that in time it led to coagulation.

The view cut off as the platform continued to rise, mercifully quiet. Pale red strips marked horizontal cable and pipe access. An emergency ladder gripped one wall, a long climb but a plausible escape path should the platform lose power.

Teegee stared upward in awe. "How far does this go?" she whispered.

"No talking," murmured Apama.

The chief stirred, bringing his gun to bear as they came up to a square marked Level 1 with a dedicated landing and access tunnel. The tunnel was dark. Nothing moved. No sound, just a few pale emergency lights and the steady repeating message in a reassuring alto. "Maelstrom Base evacuated."

Teegee was still looking up. She nudged Apama, tapping her ear. *Listen.*

Just air, and the ventilation system . . . no, there was a high pitch as soft as the buzz of wings. The light from an emergency strip flashed on an almost infinitesimal curve about half a meter above Apama's head, and she saw it: a tiny flying object no bigger than her thumb. It dropped into their midst, swept a complete circle of Teegee as if confirming she was a Rider, and then, strangely, swerved back to hover at arm's length in front of Apama's face.

This wasn't any Phene construct she knew of. She was absolutely certain someone was studying her through the eyes of the miniature drone. Taunting her.

"Hornet," said the chief. "That's what they call them. Attack cameras."

Apama shot it. It sparked, spun, and dropped to the platform. The chief stamped on it with a satisfying crunch.

"That's torn it," said Apama as they passed the two squares marking Level 2. "All right. Everyone off."

She went first. The platform was slow enough that the transfer from platform to grasping a rung wasn't difficult. Teegee came after, panting harshly. Two more thunks, shudders felt on the ladder as Toia and the chief came over. Apama climbed down the Level 2 landing, waited for them to assemble.

"Southwest Quadrant. Zone Smiles. There'll be another maintenance shaft and ladder there. We're headed for Level 4."

"Why'd you hit the button for Level 7?" Teegee asked.

"Prudence. From now on, presume there are hornets we can't see. Shoot anything that moves."

She led them at a jog along the maintenance tunnel. Its walls were painted with a spectacular rendition of the Procession of Masks as if in promenade from Anchor's processional way onto Axiom's floating concourse and thence across the plain of triple-headed Cyclops on Auger, all bound together by a shared culture and history. Down here were barracks and living quarters, all abandoned. Had Maelstrom Base's crew made it to safety? Had they surrendered? Were they dead? She couldn't dwell on that. Her immediate responsibility was her companions.

It wasn't even the Chaonians who had betrayed her. They were just doing their job, as she was. It was her sire. He'd thrown her out the airlock. With another child on the way, he didn't need Apama to keep Rana in line. She was a nuisance. Expendable. It had never been her he had cared about. She'd been nothing more than his path to Rana.

The chief whirled, popped off a shot, and a hornet that had been following them cracked and tumbled to the floor, dead.

She shook her head. Pointless thoughts would kill you. Stay focused.

She led them through a darkened cafeteria with empty tables. Through a gym whose machines had the look of petrified monsters frozen in shadow. Through a barracks, along a row of toilets, then past a bank of showers into an old decon unit that their training officer had told them hadn't been used for a hundred years. All the bases were old, refurbished, rebuilt, repurposed. Old passageways were blocked. Forgotten.

Past the decon unit was a shaft with a ladder, a tube in full darkness. She didn't even know what it had been built for. But growing up in the ruins of Tranquility Harbor she'd learned early that it was best to know every meter of ground in case one day a gang tried to steal your week's ration and you had to get away by slipping into places they were too afraid to have explored.

As they climbed in silence, she was glad for her gloves on the rough, pitted surface of the rungs. Teegee and the chief did well but Toia was breathing hard and murmured once, under his breath, "Just leave me for the fucking vultures." But he didn't stop climbing. He was responsible for Teegee.

The next opening was Level 4, the lowest hangar level, with its machine shops, parts storehouses, and the old lava tube hangars, later replaced with modern hangars on Levels 5 and 6.

It was also the floor of the caldera. She tapped a *stay in place* on the chief's arm and crept forward through a matching decon unit, a bank of showers, a row of toilets, and up a flight of stairs into the oldest wardroom on the base. Once the haunt of the most swaggering of pilots, in her time it had been a backwater dive to grab a cup of cold coffee and yesterday's pastry while you were waiting for mechanics to certify your ride. The chamber boasted a viewing window onto the caldera floor, a balcony view. As she crossed the wardroom, the shadows of remembered comrades looked up from the tables at which she'd shared gossip and grievances. How many were still alive? How many would she ever see again? Or even know their fate? The universe was large and we are but sparks in the darkness that vanish as quickly as they shine.

No. The sparks were coming from the caldera. Its walls sloped steeply to the flat bowl of the caldera floor, a perfect training ground for difficult approaches and tightly conscribed takeoffs. Lights fell out of the sky and into the caldera like brilliantly shining rain, only it wasn't rain. The Chaonians were dropping marines by ropes from hovering skimmers, a full-on assault. Whoever was in charge of this strike team knew what they were doing. They'd triangulated the tunnel and the departure of at least sixty-four flying vehicles in a short span, however concealed the ships would have been once night had fallen. They'd figured out the caldera was a target of opportunity.

Maybe they hadn't found the lava tube hangars. There were a lot of tunnels and shafts for hornets, and cautious assault teams, to investigate.

She eased backward, listened at the stairs for the telltale whir of a hornet, but heard nothing. As she padded into the decon unit where the others waited, she blinked her helmet's head lamp four times to identify herself. The ammonia scent of urine hit her as she came up. Someone in the group had peed in their gear; she didn't ask—it didn't matter, not unless hornets were equipped with sensors to detect smells.

"They're here in force," she said in a low voice. "If they spot us before we get in the striker, it's all over. In that case, we surrender to save the Rider."

"Check," said the chief, echoed by Toia.

Teegee gave a watery sigh. Apama squeezed her hands, the only reassurance she could give.

They went out single file, turning right after the toilets along a corridor wide and tall enough to accommodate loaders. A few loaders had been abandoned in place, so they leapfrogged forward in the shadows of the hulks. Once the chief raised a hand to tap his ear. They all froze. Apama tossed a kumquat back the way they'd come. A glinting movement followed the rolling fruit. The chief shot it in one.

They went on.

Soon afterward they reached an intersection. Apama froze when a light flashed along the ceiling down the connecting passageway. The rustle of feet whispered perhaps a hundred meters away. A spear of light turned in their direction. She dropped to the ground. The light vanished away down the far passage. No one came shouting or shot at them. But she had the team crawl across the intersection in case the enemy had left sentries.

Rising, they ran to a machine shop where she'd sat and listened to the tales of an old salt who'd seen it all. He'd claimed—swear by Saint Mercy—that he'd once repaired a lancer that had been damaged at the Battle of Eel Gulf, salvaged after fifty years drifting. A ghost ship, its frozen crew still inside.

The blast doors onto the hangar were closed but there was a secondary door, locked and sealed. Unlocking it, she eased it open to let the chief do a preliminary sweep. He waved them in. She locked and sealed the door behind.

The narrow hangar had once been a lava tube, now smoothed and surfaced to provide a launching zone that extended exactly 123 meters to the tube's circular mouth. The view revealed a night sky that looked like a platter dusted with stars. The hangar lay in shadow except for the two strikers, each with a faint glow along their underbellies that indicated they were powered down but not off.

Had the commander of the base left them behind on purpose? Or had there simply not been time or pilots enough to evacuate the two oldest ships still in service, mere training vehicles. They didn't even have functioning weapons systems, but you did with what you had. And this was what she had.

They ran to the nearest striker. The belly ramp would be too loud, so she took them forward to a fold-down step that connected to the emergency cockpit airlock. The muted clunk of the airlock's pop resonated like a crash of thunder, but only because the hangar was so empty and silent. It was barely audible, and then only because they were right beside it.

They scrambled up a ladder into the tight interior with its clear cockpit shield. Apama engaged the power-up sequence as the others shoved their kit bags into the tiny overhead locker. She strapped Toia into the gunnery chair, pretending he didn't smell of piss, and installed Teegee in the navigator's seat behind the pilots, where she'd be less of a target. The Chaonians weren't likely to know the striker had no working guns. The chief took the copilot's seat. Apama secured the locker and slid into the pilot's seat.

Three. Two. One. The engines hummed to life.

"Ready," she said. "I'm going by feel, no lights. I know the terrain."

"You're cool," remarked the chief.

"I'm Ice."

Lights popped on at the mouth of the hangar. A skimmer lowered into view outside, spotlights glaring right into her eyes. She had to raise an upper hand to block the brilliance. Marines moved out from the deeper shadows of the hangar.

The striker was surrounded.

The chief swore. "Spawn of a bitch."

Toia gave a single sob, choked off into silence.

Teegee whispered, "What happened?"

Apama felt too sick to answer. Too angry, burning with frustration.

She'd been so sure this would work. They'd come so close. Had she gotten cocky? No. There could still be a way out as long as she stayed calm.

One marine strode forward, stinger raised to point not at the striker but at the ceiling. At five meters from the cockpit he halted, snapped on his head lamp, and flipped up his faceplate to look up at her. She stiffened, sure she recognized his face, and opened the comms so she could both hear and speak to the outside.

"I'll thank you to get out our way. Politely, of course," she said in Yele. "As strangers do."

"We're not strangers, we met before," he replied in Yele. "Maybe you don't recall. On the Phene command ship, in Karnos System. You played a trick in a galley and got out by a back route. The hells clever, if you ask me." Then he added, in badly accented Phenish, "I am Captain Solomon. I never got your name."

What a cheeky bastard. In Yele she said, "*Captain!* You were an ensign."

"So you do remember me."

Holy Arthas. Was she blushing?

"Do you really know the Handsome Alika?" she said in Phenish, to test him.

"I really know the Handsome Alika. He is now Marshal Alika." He used the Yele rank "marshal" instead of the Phenish rank "admiral." "I was an ensign, but I got promoted. Weren't you wearing lieutenant's insignia? You're a captain now, too. What a coincidence."

The chief murmured, "What's going on?"

She silenced the comms. "He's negotiating. I'm waiting to time our escape to cut below the skimmer hovering outside."

She saw the marine's lips move and flipped comms back on.

"—because you've got a Rider on the striker. I don't want to hurt anyone."

"I'm the one in the striker!" she retorted.

"My company arrived on ten skimmers. Can you outfly our squadron?"

"I can outfly twenty skimmers, Captain."

He grinned with easy humor. "I bet you can."

He gave a signal. The marines moved back to the walls, giving her a clear route to the hangar's mouth. The skimmer beyond drifted upward as if deliberately offering her an opening. But he didn't move. He stayed right where he was, relaxed, unflappable, directly in the path she would have to take.

One death for a chance at freedom.

In battle, she'd have taken the shot without hesitation.

He cocked to one side and remarked, in Yele, "I am betting there's no functional weapons systems in either striker. You have my word on a safe conduct. You will be taken prisoner with honor. Ask the Rider you've got on board. They'll confirm we have taken the other Rider and their attendants prisoner without harming them. They're being escorted up here now so you can see for yourself."

Behind her, Teegee murmured, "They are unharmed and being treated with restraint."

Apama didn't hate Chaonians as she might hate villains in a drama. She didn't love them either. She appreciated their toughness, and disliked and distrusted their aggressive ambition. They were on their side, and she was on hers. In battle, soldiers drew a line, and made their choice. Or they were Captain Solomon and deliberately blurred the line as a tactical move.

If she kept running, then she wouldn't just be a fugitive. She would still be Zakurru's pawn. He'd help or hinder, depending on how he felt he could use her to control her mother. Or maybe just because he was that kind of person. And if not him, then she would be a fugitive at loose ends in an empire undergoing a profound convulsion. An empire that was still fighting the last war, not the current war.

What if she altered vector? What if she spun onto a new flight plan? What if she stopped being Zakurru's pawn and charted her own strategy? What if she became the spy at the picnic?

To defeat the enemy, you have to know the enemy.

She powered down.

"What's wrong?" asked the chief.

"We don't have enough fuel to get off-world," she lied. "I guess that's why they left these strikers behind."

He sighed. "So be it. It's what the Eminent Zakurru wanted."

She unstrapped and ducked back to the emergency airlock. "Stay here," she said, mostly for Teegee's sake, giving the girls a reassuring nod. Teegee nodded back with determined bravado.

The seal popped open. Apama jumped down to the deck, walked past the nose of the striker, and halted two meters from Captain Solomon. He was tall for a Chaonian. It was strangely attractive to stand eye to eye with the enemy, or maybe it was the competent way he had roped them in. She respected a worthy opponent.

He met her challenging gaze with a tranquil one. Not gloating, more intrigued. "Why didn't you run over me? The way was clear."

"Why did you bet I wouldn't?"

"I had a hunch," he said with a startlingly mischievous grin. "You're a lancer pilot, which means you're as smart and as tough as they come. You know we won."

"For now. You lucked out. You haven't seen who we really are, not yet."

He gave an amused snort, the grin widening. "And you're going to show us all by yourself? You still haven't told me your name, Captain."

"Apama At Sabao. You won't forget it."

The Wily Persephone Has Always Felt One Step Too Close to Death

For fifty-four hours I hang on awake in the bunker, wired first on coffee and then stim until I'm woozy, shaking, and increasingly disoriented. Every hour I circle around to check on the lifepods, sure my father will jolt up out of suspension to condemn me as an unfilial child. For the hundredth time I wish Jahi or the workers had taken Bartholomew up on his offer of shelter, but they refused to enter the hermitage. I'm alone with the banner soldiers, who eye the baton and the lifepods. Wondering how soon I'll collapse and they can release my father and stuff me in.

Of course Bartholomew sleeps peacefully for hours at a time despite the rumbling and creaking that suggests the ridge is trying to crash down around us but never quite does. When he gets up, he washes, does his makeup, and restyles his hair with gel. By means of two scarves and a belt he transforms the stodgy laborer's garb into glamorous themed fashion.

He swans over to me. "You look terrible, Persephone."

"Thank you! I love hearing that I do!"

"No, seriously. I mean you need to sleep. Reynaldo knows where we went. When it's safe, he'll come looking. He has one of these comms earrings."

"If he survived."

He looks so morose that I feel bad for ruining his mood. "We just have to wait this out," he says with an attempt at patient fortitude.

I gesture with my chin toward the banner soldiers. They're sleeping in shifts, six stretched out on racks, five on duty.

"Really?" He raises all four hands, palms out, in a gesture of incredulity. "Even with you having the leash—"

"Shh!"

"What? You think they forgot you have it? That they aren't aware you don't trust them? That they don't know you can't stay awake indefinitely? That you're getting less competent and coordinated with each additional hour you stay awake?"

"Sure, why don't we just discuss the situation out loud in front of them?"

"Their hearing is far better than ours. Whispering won't cut it."

I think of Kurash as I look around the bunker. It has the appearance of the interior of a quonset hut, if such a hut had a ceramic superstructure that can withstand a direct hit from bombardment and was constructed inside a big barrier ridge for extra shielding. It officially holds thirty and, according to a manifest attached to its reinforced storeroom, can feed thirty people for thirty days on a strictly rationed schedule. The meals are dry and tasteless but filling. Fleet food is far superior. As Eirene always said in her yearly addresses praising the cooks and mess operators: An army marches on its stomach.

"They'll obey me because I'm imperial Phene." He extends a hand. "But if that isn't enough assurance, then give me the baton. Get some rest. If you don't trust me, it's too late now. You have another option?"

My eyelids are drooping. The racks sing with a siren's seductive lullaby. *Sleep.*

How many times in my life should I already have been dead? I hand the leashing baton to Bartholomew, although I keep the unleashing baton and wedge it in with the holster between me and the wall as I settle into a rack. Not that it will matter. They don't have to wake me up to kill me. How comforting!

Once I've lain down my thoughts spin back to the terrible secret my father revealed. Is beacon sickness a sickness or is it like drinking alcohol? Fine up to a point but poison when you drink too much too fast or too steadily for too long. Will it catch up to me some day when I least expect it? On that heartening thought, I drop straight into hard slumber.

A rattle and moan stir me into wakefulness. There's a lilt in the air, a humming of voices in harmonic intervals, although two of the threads keep drifting flat. What in the hells? I sit up, forgetting I'm in a rack, and bump my head. Pain jolts my memory. My bruised lip throbs.

Checking my watch, I'm stunned to see that ten hours have passed. I'm trapped in a sealed bunker with an arrow of savage banner soldiers, my murdering father, and two illegal clones of Princess Metis. I unsheathe my stinger as I wonder if I have given myself a concussion. The room is shifting and moving as I blink. The dimmed lights make it hard to see.

They've pushed the furniture to one side and Bartholomew is leading the soldiers in an arcane ritual. No, it's a complicated set of dance steps, if a dance was a parade conducted in an ever-moving circle. The dancers are humming softly, and all their movements are gracefully light, as if they are trying not to wake me. It's magical to watch, to hear the lift of a melody that swings up and down the way life does: joy tempered by grief, victory by defeat, connection severed by solitude as a single dancer spins into the middle of the circle alone and spins back out to join the others.

Bartholomew leads them with the skill of a person who knows and loves what they're doing. He sees me sitting up but lets the cadence complete before whistling the formation to a halt. Trotting over, he sits down sweaty beside me.

"What was that?" I ask.

"To pass the time I've been teaching them the Procession of Rings. It's the most complicated of the processions, takes years for most people to learn, but as you can imagine, they catch on fast."

"They're not the best singers though. There's a couple of voices that keep drifting flat."

Bartholomew gives me side-eye worthy of Tiana. "Is that so? You have a good ear for that kind of thing, do you?"

I shrug, as embarrassed as if my mother's most needlessly critical tone just emerged unchecked from my once-unsullied lips. But she's dead. She and Aunt Moira died two years ago, Resh and Percy were dead before them, Kadmos was never my ally, and I am handing my father over to die, burying him with my own bloody hands. Nona is not my future, and she can never return to the republic anyway. I have no kin to call my own now that my branch of the Lee House lineage has sunk into the dissolving lye of disgrace. Who will I be, adrift on the ocean of existence with no stabilizing anchor?

The banner soldiers line up in column, waiting for their orders. Their ability to move with speed and power is equaled by their ability to stand at rest like statues. None in this arrow has features as striking as Kurash, but they all have the same air of deadly beauty and threatening grace that draws my eye the same way I grabbed those two vials of late bloomer. It's not that I'm a thrill seeker. It's that I've always felt one step too close to death.

Bartholomew pats my arm like we're pals. "Are you all right?"

"Sure. Anything from outside?"

He goes over to a console that has both a radio and a comms unit. The comms unit is picking up only static. It can't be Phene military, not here in an expatriate Yele hermitage, so I don't know who it is meant to connect with. Every channel on the radio repeats an ominously monotone statement. En route from the habitat to here, I got Bartholomew to start teaching me Phenish. I use this opportunity to pick out words.

"Flood?"

"It's a recorded evacuation message. I think the entire city lost comms. The entire planet, maybe." He rubs his face wearily.

"Are you sorry you helped me?" I ask as I edge my hand toward the holster with its vials. "Do you think your father made a mistake by going to Sun?"

He straightens with a brave little smile. "What's happening out there is horrible, either way it goes. As for my father, I don't see that the other syndicates gave him any choice. It's one thing to lay down your life in battle for the empire and the people. It's quite another to be expected to roll over and die so some rival syndicate can use your corpse as a stepping-stone to expand their influence and resources."

"I'm not sure the metaphor quite works."

He waggles perfectly groomed eyebrows. "Everyone's a critic." But he offers me a pallid smile to show he doesn't mean it.

I'm about to punch him on the shoulder in cynical solidarity when he twitches. I hear it too: a buzz in the close-range-comms earring.

Bracing for action, the banner soldiers look our way. Their attention is hugely unsettling, as if we have disturbed an eleven-headed monster that we ought to have left behind to be crushed in the cataclysm of the Chaonian assault. But I think of Kurash and I'm glad I brought them with me, although I don't know if I've saved them, or if they want to be saved.

A voice crackles through static. "Bartholomew?"

"Tatay?" he whispers, voice catching on the word.

"Thank the saints, my dear child. Where are you?" It is his father, hoarse with relief.

"Bunker below the hermitage hostel on Yele Central on the Antikythera Terrace."

"There's a bunker?"

"It surprised me too. No injuries except for this appalling outfit I'm wearing."

"Now I'm doubly sure it's you. What news?"

"The Honorable Persephone and I hooked the fish. We also gathered up an arrow."

"Is there a clear exit? I'm at the Exchange now, negotiating with some surviving syndicate presidents. I will ask the commander for a skimmer. Be careful. The southern end of the ridge collapsed, taking Unity Hall with it."

Bartholomew gasps with such a stricken expression that all the banner soldiers look at me as if his shock is my fault.

Paulo is still talking in a rush. "Antikythera Terrace has taken massive damage. The core of the central ridge has so far remained stable but you must get out immediately. Do you hear me?" His tone has turned comically fussy but it is because he cares. He's worried about his beloved child.

"I hear you." Bar smiles wryly, as if accustomed to this tone from his parent. Envy bites me, but I'm used to its sting so I let it itch without scratching. And I don't look toward the lifepods. I definitely don't look toward the lifepods.

"Let me just pee first," I say as I stand. "In fact, everybody pee. Be quick about it! Grab your emergency bags. Colonel, assign two soldiers to handle each lifepod. Bring all four. We go in five minutes."

I don't leash them. They've accepted me as a person who has the right to command them. After all, they accepted my father. Why not me? Yet who are we really to them, who no longer have a home except the arrow? We are the ones who tell them to kill. Isn't that what Kurash said so very long ago? The graves of innocents mark our path.

This thought cycles in my head as we ascend the entry ramp, Bartholomew in front and me at the rear where my two batons and I can keep an eye on everyone as well as on the hover carts that convey the lifepods. Whatever Nona Lee intended for her clones, I am not her tool. I have made my final play for autonomy, and it's a lonely and vulnerable peak.

The main entrance doesn't open, blocked on the other side, but there is an emergency shaft whose ladder Bartholomew clambers up. With the assistance of the colonel he wedges open an airlock, cycles it out, and vanishes from my sight. Through the open hole a hot wind brings with it the nose-tickling scent of smoke and dust. I hear voices raised, a shout, then a sound I don't at first recognize until I poke my head up to find him laughing and crying in his father's embrace. So much for my cool-headed comrade of the last many days; he's sobbing like a little boy, and I like him for it. Everyone knows the Phene are an emotional people.

Then I see her, and my heart stops. She's dressed magnificently, not as for a party but as for a serious negotiation: the elegant attendant who pours tea in the proper way and at exactly the right moment brings forward the tray on which lie the brushes and ink and paper with which the frowning victors and the stern losers will sign their armistice. An indigo turban conceals her hair. A formal jacket in a lighter hue of the same blue falls to her knees over trousers. Her gaze meets mine, all the beauty of the universe distilled into those brown eyes. I stumble forward with my heart full and my body desperate for the embrace I yearn for.

She presses her hands in front of her and inclines her head in the formal palace manner. It's like slamming into a wall. I stagger to a halt, completely unmoored.

"Honored Persephone," she says. "It is a relief to know you are safe."

We are in a public space, surrounded by Chaonian soldiers. Many don't seem to recognize me without my uniform. I'm just a thirteen-year-old Phene stunt to them, so Tiana is making sure they all know and see who I am.

But there's more than that at work here. Something subtle has shifted in her posture. Did she realize what I tried not to reveal on the abandoned ship? Is she letting me know we can't be more than what we already are? Will I lose her friendship too, if I push where I'm not meant to go? There is no dramatic love story for me. I'm the tragic counterpoint whose sadder but wiser experience highlights the glowing happiness of the favored pair.

Get a grip, asshole.

From behind Tiana, Jade Kim strolls into view like the secondary hero of the tale, the one who gets a much-applauded happy ending with a wedding and a banquet. They wear a uniform scuffed with the marks of being worn under armor. A smudge of dried blood ornaments the chiseled chin. Jade measures me in my rumpled garb. For an instant I think Jade means to cross their arms with familiar contempt, but that would be too clichéd.

"I'll give you this, Perse, you did better than I thought you would. You captured an entire arrow. How about that? All my unit did was destroy the main military airbase, secure the city of Melo, and oversee the capture of syndicate presidents and assemble them here so they can officially surrender to Sun." A condescending smile boils off the last of my miserable confusion.

Ti's eyes widen in a warning flash. *Don't take the bait.*

"So we won?" I ask guilelessly. "Good fortune for us. You wouldn't know Bartholomew since you weren't raised with access to the palace. He is Admiral Kr Manalon's son, and was a great help to me."

Bar has good instincts. He hustles over with a sly smile, tears forgotten. "You must be the cadet Persephone spoke so much about. I feel I know you already."

"Who are you?" Jade stares down that famously well-shaped nose.

"No one of any importance to a fine Companion like yourself," says Bartholomew with an easy wink. He gives Tiana a clubby greeting kiss to either cheek before returning to his father.

Jade gives in to the cliché, crossing arms, and snaps, "Sun's incoming. We need to return to Airbase Capstone to meet her."

Ti flashes a hand to me so I can see she wears a ring from Sun's network. Once Razin, Makinde, and Jade hired cee-cees there were no extras, which means Sun recovered the ones my father took from us. My whole heart expands in relief.

I grin at Ti, and she flashes a reassuring smile. It feels effortless to slide back into our once-companionable relationship. It's better this way. I'm out of my depth with her and have transgressed even my own hazy limits. Friendship can also be love. She doesn't deserve to bear the burden of my long-unmet needs. Maybe that's all my yearning for her is anyway: transference. I have to get back to my usual bad crushes. They keep me at a safe remove.

It still hurts. I just pretend that it doesn't.

As Bartholomew escorts the arrow into the skimmer, I shade my eyes and look south along the ridge. What was once a monumental processional way with noble statues is strewn with broken stone heads, bits of shrapnel, and a fluttering green banner caught beneath the severed hover-blade of a Hummingbird, although there's no sign of the rest of the vessel. Most bizarrely, the beautiful glass basilica and the lacework pedestrian bridge that links it to the ridge look untouched, as if the saints themselves protected the sacred building. Not that I believe in saints.

The southern end of the ridge is indeed collapsed the way it might look if a jealous little girl had repeatedly slammed a tonfa down on her twin brother's mud-stick dam that their father had just praised him for building across a tiny streamlet at the back of the estate. Water flows where it finds opportunity, and a steady current runs out of the sea, beneath and through the rubble in multiple runnels and gushing cascades.

The city of Melo has become a lake. Thousands of rooftops create grim islands above murky, debris-filled water. At an intersection, a corpse has gotten stuck amid the antennas of a barely visible ground vehicle, legs and too many arms swaying like kelp as ripples tug on the lifeless body. The *clutter-clutter-clutter* of military Hummingbirds fills the air with a harsh rhythm as they drop supplies to stranded civilians. There's smoke on the western horizon. The splintering boom of a far-off explosion marks where a battle is still being fought in the hinterlands.

Ti glides up beside me. "They're waiting for us. The Honorable Jade will leave without you if you give them the slightest excuse."

We hustle to the skimmer. I send Ti forward to the crash seat Bar has saved for me, while I take a place with banner soldiers, who've been crammed into one of the troop compartments in the back. My jagged nerves need time to settle, but because of Tiana, not because of Jade.

Jade's attempt to get my gorgosaur has fallen flat. I understand Sun better than Jade does. Conquering the main planetary center of the empire is a big thing, definitely. But in Sun's eyes, seen through the prism of Sun's honor and pride, the capture of Kiran Seth matters more to her heart and her gut. My father killed Sun's cherished bodyguard. I watched it happen. I saw her face as Octavian died.

We lift off, flying east across the inland sea to what was once a Phene airbase and that Sun has renamed, in classic Sun style, Airbase Capstone. Bartholomew keeps exclaiming over what the sea looks like now that part of its waters have drained out, but from back here, I can't see. The banner soldiers endure the journey with the patience of people who have accepted they have no control over fate. The children of Lady Chaos blow where the winds take them. Has Kurash returned to Sun alongside the frigate captain she so values that she wanted him to command a squadron for the attack on Anchor? Not that Kurash's decisions have anything to do with me.

After about half an hour we circle, then land. I keep a hand on the leashed baton as we disembark. The Guards who accompany Jade eye the banner soldiers with suspicion, but they keep their cool. They're Chaonians, after all. Disciplined and victorious, they can afford to be magnanimous.

The airbase is buzzing with activity, cargo shuttles landing, cutters taking off, a construction battalion hard at work repaving the shattered tarmac. The base's control tower is a twisted ruin so I'm not sure where traffic control has relocated.

Jade starts walking toward the perimeter, heading for a big medical tent. I hurry up beside Ti. "Is Sun wounded again?"

She indicates her ring. "No. She's inbound on a medical evacuation shuttle." Then she laughs. "I mean, yes, she's wounded again, but nothing that wasn't patched up on the battlefield. You know how she is."

I do know how she is. We reach the tent as a shuttle lands in the designated medical zone. Jade strides out in front as the shuttle's ramp lowers. A familiar figure appears, shading her eyes. Is she looking for me?

I drop back beside Bartholomew and hand him the leashing baton and one vial.

"What's this?" He examines the vial's oleaginous contents.

"A horrible, deadly toxin. Don't unseal it. Give it to Sun. Tell her the prisoner was holding it when we captured him. You can present it with the arrow and the lifepods."

"I can't steal the credit from you, Persephone. Or not more than I deserve."

"Sun will know what I did. The point is what the people around us see. It will help your family's standing both with Sun and with the Chaonians. Trust me, you'll need it going forward."

Ti shades me an approving nod. My heart warms a thousand degrees, boiling away into ecstasy. It will have to be enough. Smoke and dust burn at my eyes, and I wipe away the sting of tears as we approach Sun, who has halted on the ramp to allow us to come to her.

There's another reason for relinquishing the prize: if Bartholomew does it, then the final betrayal of my father isn't mine. Or so I can lie to myself.

The bodyguards at her back are banner soldiers, not Chaonians. I don't see Kurash among them but he might be on the shuttle. I hang back as Paulo brings Bartholomew forward. Seeing him, Sun's eyes widen and she utterly loses her usual expression of confident command. It's rare to see her taken by surprise. Whatever she sees when Bartholomew walks up the ramp isn't what she expected to see.

She says in shock, "Bar? What in the hells happened to you?"

He presses his upper right hand to his chest. "I got beautiful," he says with his rascally charm, and she's smitten, everyone can see it. Let's be real. Half the hard-bitten marines stationed around us are staring at Bartholomew as if it never occurred to them that Phene could be so attractive. He's slighter, not as tall as most Phene, so maybe that makes his appearance less daunting. Sun doesn't hide her admiration as she looks him up and down and shakes her head. He walks right up to her as her bodyguards tense, but she gestures them to move back.

He brushes a cheek intimately against hers and whispers something in her ear.

She laughs. Is she blushing? *Sun* blushing?

I'm riveted. We are all riveted. Then I wonder if Hetty is around to see this, but have no ring to connect with the others, to discover where she is. I have only my eyes, and my network struggling to link up to the shuttle's comms, because the Phene don't connect via system-wide universal clouds the way Chaonia does.

Bartholomew steps back and makes a big deal of handing over the baton to Sun, his way of transferring possession of the captured banner soldiers to her. She takes the baton, gestures the banner soldiers forward. Their impassive expressions fracture briefly as they stare at a unit of banner soldiers stationed behind her: Disbelief? Dismay? Since when did Sun take banner soldiers as bodyguards?

The captured arrow kneels as one before her, who is the Royal. I've seen this ritual before.

"Where the heavens above did not exist, and the earth beneath had not come into being, there dwelled the cosmic waters, which are the substance of all. Out of this ocean rose Lady Chaos, who gave birth to the eleven exiles."

To each soldier she extends her hands. Each places theirs in hers, to place their service into her keeping. After they have pledged their loyalty to her, she uses a baton of her own to remove the leash. They will serve her now as do all in her fleet and army, out of loyalty, not through coercion.

After they step aside, she studies the vial with a grimace of anger she does not bother to stifle. She waves away everyone around her and clears the cloudy surface that obscures the features of the individuals lying in suspension. The occupants of the first two lifepods—the Metis clones—give her pause. She tilts her head to the left, intrigued, mind ticking over as she considers the implications. No one else is close enough to see their faces. She looks up at me, because she knew I was here all along. I shrug as if to say, *Your guess is as good as mine.* She nods and tunes the panels back to opacity.

Ti whispers, "She doesn't know about the younger ones. You promised."

I promised to let them go. The Phryne took custody of them. If Ti has her way, we will never see or hear of them again. Once they are old enough, they'll be released to make their own lives. I'm skeptical they can survive in anonymity without being hunted down, but I didn't have a better solution at the time and don't have one now. Those girls shouldn't have to bear the weight of a burden they never consented to.

Last, Sun halts by the lifepod containing Kiran Seth. Fingers still grasping the vial, she studies its readings, then lifts her chin and beckons me forward.

I have nowhere to go except to her side. I walk forward alone.

When I reach her, she speaks in a voice meant only for me. "You turned disaster into triumph. Well done."

Well done.

I try not to smile with an overwhelming sense of gratification, and I fail.

She hands me my lost ring without fanfare, merely with the expectation I will put it back on as one of her inner circle.

Let my past blow away with the ashes. I am here in the place I belong. The ring slides onto my finger as though it was made for me. And perhaps, if destiny has any power, it was.

A Vast Span of Time and Space Between Us

Keep your distance, Sun had told Kurash when she'd learned that Persephone had been found. Since she had not been more specific, he had decided to interpret the order in his own way. Thus, he trailed the dauntless Persephone from a safe distance with his gaze on his boots and some solid object between them, listening with his enhanced hearing as she accompanied the queen-marshal into the hospital tent.

Sun said, "Your rack-mate Ikenna was in charge of a platoon taking control of a communications center in northeastern Melo that had been booby-trapped. Lost his right arm below the elbow. Minh tells me he is already designing a prosthetic to allow him enhanced system access. Here he is. I see he has visitors."

"Perse? I heard they found you hiding in a hole in the ground!"

Kurash recognized Ay's voice, and he smiled to hear it, relieved his friend had survived the brutal vanguard action led by Captain Shi's frigate squadron into the thick of the battle raging around Cut Stone Beacon when Sun had arrived with her long-awaited reinforcements.

Friend. Was Ay his friend? He hoped so. Almost he looked up to call out a greeting as he would have on the *Huma.* Instead he stepped behind a screen. Temptation must not drag him into carrying out the terrible deed he wished above all things to avoid. He shouldn't be here at all—*keep your distance*—yet he could not stay away. He had lost so much. Maybe there was one precious thing he could salvage.

"Who are you?"

He turned to see a person sitting in a hospital bed, attended by an adjutant wearing the uniform of one of the allied forces, not Chaonian. A spotlessly clean officer's jacket hung from a hook on the partition.

"My apologies," he said. "I am Lieutenant Kurash. One of the queen-marshal's bodyguards."

A temporary tent facility like this lacked separate rooms, using only privacy partitions. Nearby, Sun laughed. She was always at her most expansive after a victory.

"I see," the patient said, who spoke Yele with a different accent than the Chaonians. "You're one of the ghost soldiers. That's what they're calling the decommissioned banner soldiers who fought for the Phene."

"Yes, Captain. And you are?"

"Captain Qulan Yeh, Larissan Centaur Division."

He pressed a hand to his heart, a gesture of respect on the wheelships. "The Centaur Division is much praised. They are said to have saved the beleaguered remnants of the Sixth and Ninth Fleets as well as arriving just in time to rescue Marshal Zàofù's flagship from a boarding action."

To deny the praise would have been false modesty. To affirm it, bad manners. The captain inclined her head to accept it without comment.

Footsteps approached their area. Sun appeared, glanced at Kurash as if surprised to see him, then went to the bedside.

"Captain Yeh, I have heard excellent reports about the conduct of the Centaur Division. But I expect no less."

"My thanks, Your Highness." The woman flushed under the pressure of Sun's gaze but she had enough pride to sustain it without flinching. "I wish to take this opportunity again to thank you for offering me a command of my own, back when I was stuck in the spatharioi." Her adjutant coughed, and the captain hurried on. "Not that it isn't an honor to serve in the palace guard."

"You need not apologize for wishing to fight. I would have done the same in your situation." She looked at Kurash, her gaze direct. "You shouldn't be here. Return to my tent and wait for me. Traps will accompany you."

Was it a rebuke?

Traps thought so, trotting beside him as they crossed the tarmac to a rank of tents set at the perimeter of the airfield. "What was that about?"

"Nothing."

"Fine then, Lieutenant, keep your troubles to yourself." The older man had started taking the tone of a world-weary uncle, from the vast height of his twenty-six years. Yet among the soldiers sent to the Phene, surviving to twenty-six was old age of a kind. "You know anything about those lifepods that got delivered to her tent?"

"The Royal will tell us what she wants us to know."

Traps thought this over before nodding. "She's all right. Doesn't act like she's better than others. Treats her people with respect. Fights the same as the rest of us. Gets the job done."

When they reached the tent, Traps set himself at the entrance as sentry: "To make sure you don't wander off where you're not meant to be."

Kurash nodded to the bodyguards on duty and went inside. The big tent's front half was set up with a portable strategos table and a set of couches. The back half was split with curtains into three smaller rooms: her personal attendant's staging room, her private office, and her sleeping quarters. The lifepods had been hauled into the office and sat there blocking access to the desk. Sunshine was the guard on duty with the lifepods, standing at attention.

"I'll take over," he told her. "See if Eleuterio has an assignment for you."

She nodded and left.

Kurash knew from traffic on the ring network that one of the life-pods contained the captured Yele seer Kiran Seth de Lee, father of Persephone Lee and Sun's most hated adversary. She had never in his hearing spoken of the Phene with as much barely repressed rage. Her displeasure with the Phene was an old grudge welded to a new am-bition and propelled into this heroic campaign by a fortuitous con-vergence of events and opportunity. The individuals concealed in the other two lifepods he did not know, nor had Sun revealed any hints in messages sent to the others.

He placed himself at attention and waited.

After about an hour, he heard Sun speaking as two people entered the outer chamber.

The curtained entry into the office stirred, and Sun stuck her head in. "Go into my sleeping quarters and don't come out until I give you permission."

"Yes, Your Highness." His nerves, already strung taut, stung hot as he realized what her command must mean. He shot a dampening spurt of calming meds down his neural network and retreated into the dim sleeping quarters. The space was furnished with a double wide cot, a travel chest, a wash stand, and a tiny, fully enclosed and sealed sanitary toilet unit, one of the few perks allowed the highest ranks in the Chao-nian military since everyone else used barracks-style communal toilets. The temporary shelters were enclosed in blackout curtains woven of a tough ceramic fabric that could repel minor shrapnel and allowed un-disturbed rest no matter the hour or brightness of the local star.

In the darkness, a lingering fragrance brushed at his senses. Honored Hestia had been here not so long ago while Sun had been off fighting in the hinterlands beyond the city. Maybe she had slept here, alone on the cot. It was a privilege Sun would have allowed no one else. Not every re-lationship is sanctioned. The Chaonians had their own peculiar customs, as he was learning. *What is love?* he had once asked his grandmother, but what she had replied he could no longer remember. Or maybe he could no longer bear to remember.

Sun spoke from the office, easy to hear past the curtain. "I need you to confirm these two are what they seem to be."

"Yes, clones of Princess Metis." Persephone's voice had the same molasses tone he recalled, smoother and sweeter than one would imagine from the defensive way she often stood, the frequent stab of her glare, the sense she was ready to bolt and could outrun anyone if the distance was far enough.

Maybe she couldn't outrun a banner soldier. But a wheelship-raised person would never pursue one who did not want to be caught. Not for love, anyway. War was another matter.

"So, the Metis clones are a potential replacement for me. Kiran's goals I understand. Nona Lee's are a bit more opaque. Did she tell you anything?"

"We barely spoke. But from things my father said I wonder if her goals had more to do with studying beacon sickness and less to do with creating a puppet queen-marshal with a Metis clone."

"Beacon sickness? You'll have to fill me in later, once Anchor is fully secured."

"Either way, they didn't ask to be cloned. No individual conceived in that lab did."

"Yet they obeyed Kiran Seth. Kidnapped you and Tiana, and might have killed you had he ordered them to."

"Maybe." Her tone suggested an accompanying shrug. "They know nothing other than what they've been told all their lives. I can't blame them for that."

"Mmm. Well. They are a complication."

"Please don't punish them for something they had no hand in."

"Strange to hear you, of all people, beg for mercy for them."

"Is it? How so? I'd think I'd be the first person to beg mercy for them." Was Persephone offended?

"Would you? You have a hard and pragmatic heart, Perse. But that's neither here nor there. For the time being, I will keep them in suspension. No need for a hasty decision."

"Will you send the lifepods back to Chaonia?"

"Into my father's keeping? That would indeed solve the problem, but in a more permanent way than I currently desire. No. For now, we need to keep their existence secret, as you can appreciate."

"I can."

"Very good. You have done me a signal service. I will never forget it."

"What about my father? Are you going to put him on trial?"

"Under Chaonian law? He'll claim it does not apply to him. And because Chaonian law requires him to be allowed to testify on his own behalf in a public setting, he'll tell tales neither of us can afford the court and the fleet to hear."

"What do you mean to do with him?"

The ring buzzed with an all-network message from Solomon.

MISSION ACCOMPLISHED. TWO RIDERS CAPTURED.
ESTIMATED TRAVEL TIME TO AIRBASE CAPSTONE IS
FOURTEEN HOURS.

"That's my Solomon!" Persephone laughed delightedly. Kurash
loved the way she relished her friends' successes. Yet the words she spoke
next cut through her levity like a razor. "Jade will take Solomon's success as a direct challenge."

"And strive more because of it," remarked Sun.

"That's a cold-blooded way to look at it."

"Is it? To set systems in place that bring out the best fighting edge
in people? To choose what will elevate Chaonia's power? Was it cold-
blooded of my great-great-grandfather Yǔ to negotiate peace with the
Phene Empire to spare the republic from a war they couldn't win in
those days? Was it cold-blooded of my great-grandmother Metis to
take advantage of imperial and league disorder in the wake of the war
between the Yele and the Phene to stake out Troia System as part of republic territory? When my grandfather made a treaty with the Hesjan
because he needed their support? When my mother sent her brother's
young son into internal exile because the fleet needed an adult queen-
marshal to lead it? We build on what she established to make our Fleet
and our Guards unbeatable. The person who commands all the worlds
can do great work to the benefit of the republic. To the betterment of
all of fractured humankind. Is that not so?"

"'To the betterment of all of fractured humankind'? Did you hear
that at the Gyre? You never told any of us exactly what the Oracle said
to you. Not even Hetty."

"Did you ask Hetty?" Sun's voice sharpened with an emotion Kurash could not quite identify, but it had a flavor like the most stringent
acid, something that might catch fire or even explode when exposed to
the wrong substance. The question was a warning.

Persephone snorted obliviously. "Of course I asked Hetty!"

A silence followed, thick with danger, an explosion primed to blow.

Persephone abruptly added, "It would have helped if you'd explained your situation after your encounter. You might have offered
some portentous proclamation like, 'The Oracle demanded I never
speak of what passed between us.' You just came back on board and we
returned to Destiny and that was that. If you're going to have Companions, you can't shut us out. Have any of us let you down? Have any of us
not supported and believed in you all the way when you went against
the establishment's advice and broke every single rule to lead the fleet
against the empire?"

In a tight voice, Sun said, "I can't speak of what passed between me and the Oracle."

"See, that wasn't so hard. Please tell James the same thing. He cried all night every night on the voyage back because he thinks you don't trust him."

The words seemed meant as a joke, but Sun jabbed back. "How would you know James cried all night every night on the voyage back? You were busy—"

"Yeah, yeah, I was busy collating and constructing as up-to-date a map of the imperial heartland as I could with the beacon route information you were able to pry out of the Oracle, so thanks for that. James takes these things hard, though. And you didn't answer my question about us Companions, did you?"

Sun laughed the way she did when a skilled player outmaneuvered her in a game: she respected their expertise and mastery, but even the tiniest defeats chafed her. "You are the ones who understand I need an inner circle who isn't too intimidated or mealy-mouthed to disagree with me. I'll talk to James. As for you, be ready an hour before dawn."

"Am I being dismissed?"

Another silence. What look passed between them Kurash could not guess.

"Oh, all right then," said Persephone, sounding exasperated. "I could use a decent night's rest for the first time in weeks."

Her footsteps receded. Papers rustled. Then Sun spoke.

"Attend me, Kurash."

He navigated the pitch-dark sleeping quarters without bumping into anything and emerged blinking into the office, lit by two shining globes like miniature stars. Standing at her desk, she looked at him with her usual gaze, a javelin cast at your soul.

"What of the new arrow?"

"They won't work with us, Your Highness. We are ghosts to them. Dishonored."

"Your recommendation? I removed the leash from them."

"Any banner soldiers you capture who pledge to you as Royal can be trusted."

"As you pledged."

"Yes. As I pledged. If you prefer honorable arrows as your bodyguards, then transfer us to another unit."

"I am keeping my ghosts under your command, Kurash. And you, with me."

"You honor me, who deserve no honor, Your Highness."

"Let me be the judge of that. Go on. I asked for your advice about the new arrow, and any such arrows that come into my keeping in the future."

He thought it over. "Choose a Chaonian commander for them and assign them to a place where their skills can be useful. Until they become accustomed to Chaonian ways I recommend using them for shock troops and targeted missions. That's what the Phene do, and what we are trained for, so make use of it. Make sure their commander is someone who will not mistreat them, as some might do because Chaonians often call us savages."

She nodded. "Yes, that's a good place to start. I'll assign them to Jade."

She set her hands on her desk and, for an interval, stared as into a distance only she could see, although really she was just staring at the tent wall. Then she came to a conclusion and straightened.

After using her palm print to unlock a drawer in the desk, she extracted a small vial filled with an oily gold liquid. With the vial carefully cradled in a hand, she walked over to the lifepod where Kiran Seth lay, visible because she'd cleared the viewplate. For several minutes she rolled the vial within her fingers as she studied the face fallen deep into a form of suspended animation that could potentially survive years drifting in space for the faint hope of being rescued.

By her severe expression, Kurash could see there would be no rescue for the man who had shot her previous bodyguard, the retired soldier Octavian who had guarded and trained her and, Kurash suspected, offered her a simple affection she could get nowhere else, not from her aggressive and powerful mother nor her protective and ruthless father.

Almost conversationally she said, "I could wake him up just enough to pour this vial of late bloomer down his throat and let him feel what Octavian felt in his last hour."

"You could, or you could save the vial for a time you will need it more."

"Need it more than to exact justice for his crime?" Her tone trembled on the edge of what Kurash felt as a rage so intense it could obliterate even a banner soldier were it to be turned up to full force. After an eternity, she blew out and spoke to herself in a tone thick with emotion. "Keep your temper in check. Stay focused on what lies ahead."

With an obvious effort of will she dialed herself down from the brink of the fiery furnace. After tucking the vial into a brush holder, she set a hand on the controls.

"He knew his fate when Persephone captured him. I don't know if that will be enough. For me, I mean. Octavian held a different view of these things."

"Of justice and forgiveness?"

"Of letting go of what cannot be changed."

"You have to let go," he said.

"Or you have to stop believing it can't be changed."

She coded in the decontamination cycle. The lifepod's panel beeped, objecting because there was still living organic tissue in suspension.

"Incinerate," she commanded, and overrode three attempts to convince her otherwise.

She did not look away from the faceplate as the lifepod increased its internal temperature stage by stage, as the atmosphere inside steamed, the flesh charred and lost its distinctive facial features as it broke down by stages into a sludgy mush, liquified, evaporated. Through it all Kurash thought of the pyre at Autumn West. By her seared and grieving expression and the tears on her face he assumed she was thinking of the same event, but he would never have asked such a private question.

In the end she said only, "It was more dignity than Kiran Seth deserved."

Afterward she ran the lifepod through a full decon cycle, taking about an hour, and wiped the record of its last three days.

"Kurash, deliver the empty lifepod to medical. Then you're off duty for the rest of the night. Join one of the celebrations, if you'd like. Or sleep, if you'd rather. Be here an hour before dawn."

Thus she released him. He maneuvered the lifepod out of the tent to find Traps had already been dismissed and a new trio at sentry stations. Anchor's star had recently set, drowning the tent city in a fading gloom enlivened by strains of music and revelry from various places around the huge encampment. A constant patrol of skimmers and Hummingbirds secured the perimeter, but inside the camp, the Chaonians were saluting their triumph with drink, food, and song.

He had started walking when the Honorable Hestia's familiar, musical laugh brought his head around. She was approaching Sun's tent in company with another individual, the two of them pressed close like intimates, or maybe they were a little drunk and leaning together to steady one another. It took him a moment to recognize the other person as the young Phene man named Bartholomew who had arrived at the airbase with dauntless Persephone.

The fellow raised an upper arm and waved the bottle he was holding. As if finishing an anecdote, Bartholomew said in a tone of great joviality and not a little flirtatiousness, "That's why four arms, not to mention four hands, are so useful."

They entered the tent, still laughing.

A squadron of cutters streaked past overhead, on their way to an unseen battleground. But Kurash thought the battle for Anchor System was as good as over, even if pockets of resistance would thrash on for a while. A star system was a big place. You could hide for years and not be found. He wondered if there were ghost soldiers to be discovered even here, in the heart of the empire that had bought, trained, and discarded those they had no further use for. He'd keep looking in the places where folk threw their rubbish. There would be more, he was sure of it.

He delivered the lifepod to the hospital tent, then stood at the edge of the tarmac as night settled over the airbase. Someone had lit a fire around which people were dancing. The mess tent was overflowing, brilliant with lights as people crowded inside, talking and eating. At one rubble-strewn edge of the tarmac an impromptu concert was taking place using a pair of damaged skimmers as stage and backdrop. A light illuminated Marshal Alika strumming his ukulele as the audience sang along.

Two moons had risen like children playing a game of tag, although the second, smaller moon was swifter, overtaking the first, larger one as they climbed heavenward out of the east. It remained quiet in the central area of the encampment. The Companions' tents had been pitched in a ring around the queen-marshal's shelter. All seven had arrived in order to stand at her side in the coming dawn. His uniform allowed him to walk where he wished as a prerogative of Sun's trusted bodyguard.

Persephone had not amassed a household unit by which he could identify her tent, or anyone really except her cee-cee and perhaps her old comrades from the citizens' academy who she gave a helping hand to as she could. So Ay had told him. He moved through the darkness until he identified shining Tiana's tuneful voice from inside one of the tents.

"Your uniform is laid out. The blackout walls are in place. The bedding is turned down. With your permission I'd like to ask for eight hours off duty. I would be back at oh four hundred."

A hesitation before the molasses voice replied. "Of course you know I don't mind, but . . . why? Are your parents here? I know Sun sent for your brother."

"They're in a secure location until tomorrow. That's not why." Tiana's tone never failed to be gracious and accommodating. "Captain Black has reached Anchor Prime. You might not have heard about this yet, but she and her task force pushed through to Windworn System and opened up its mined beacon into Karnos. They had quite a string of battles, I'm told, both going to Windworn and coming back. The

Fifth, Tenth, and Eleventh Fleets got here from Karnos just in time to secure the Axiom and Auger Beacons and turn back a Phene force that was massing to attack Sun's planetary assault task group."

A wind skated up through the lanes between the tents, rustling pennants marked with unit logos and Core House badges. The drawn-out trill of a passing bird dopplered across the camp. On the farther landing strips, ships were landing at precise intervals, heard, not seen except as lights winking downward before they vanished behind the scrum of tents.

Persephone had not replied.

Tiana said, almost anxiously, "I don't have to go."

Too fast an answer came. "No, no, you should go. You deserve a break. You . . . Ti . . . I . . ."

"Are you all right?" Tiana's voice rang rich with the concern of a person who knows their job is to take care of another's well-being and intends to do it exceptionally well.

"No, I'm not all right." The words cut with an edge of truth. "I'm tired. It's been a long haul. And . . . I guess I need time alone to absorb everything that's happened. What it means to me. Where I am now."

"I understand."

"Just go," snapped Persephone.

"Ugh, the head-biting-off voice," muttered Tiana to herself as she emerged from the tent.

Kurash waited unseen in the shadows as the cee-cee strode off, a spring in her step. She began whistling a saucy tune he recognized from a turgid old romantic drama the other ghost soldiers liked to watch when off duty. Distracted by the melody, he almost missed Persephone speaking again, more sour than sweet.

"I am pretty hells sure you do not understand. It's better this way. I was just making things up in my head like I do. Get a grip, asshole."

He eased through the front flaps and halted in a narrow entryway. No meeting room, this, just a space to shed shoes and gear before stepping up onto the portable floorboards of the tent's inner rooms. The world around him was swallowed by darkness. He had to move carefully lest he stumble.

Maybe he was already stumbling. Maybe this was a miscalculation. He had rejected her once, starkly, and she might not be willing to forget. But he meant to ask, and he would abide by her answer.

Sharply, from beyond the interior fabric wall, she said, "Who's there?"

He drew in a shuddering breath and all at once realized he had lost his voice.

"Kurash?" Her whisper was a blade plunged into his flesh.

He couldn't speak.

She said, "I'm picking up the very faint resonance of your neuronics. Did anyone ever tell you that your presence sounds the way I imagine the heavenly music of the spheres? It's a shifting harmony, barely audible. It reminds me of beacons."

Her tone had become reserved and distant. She had a way of holding herself out of reach, as if bound to other concerns, never to true intimacy. But the wistfulness was there, the vulnerability she worked so hard to conceal.

He said, "Are your blackout curtains in place?"

"What if they aren't, and I ask you to come in anyway?"

"Would you be so reckless?"

"Why not?" she asked bitterly. "What does it matter if I die? No, I'm sorry. That's unfair and unkind. If there's anything I hate, it's wallowing in self-pity, because I'm so good at it."

"I was also betrayed by those who loved me."

"But see, there's the difference. I only wished he loved me. In my heart I always knew he didn't, not really. Maybe I wouldn't have done it, if he'd loved me. Or maybe I would have anyway because I'm just that much of a hard and pragmatic bitch like . . . well, anyway. That's all."

"You did what you had to do, just as I did. Besides that, it is what Sun wished. She will sleep easier knowing Octavian's murderer is dead. Not that she sleeps much, but you know what I mean."

Beyond the inner wall she shifted. He heard the *click-click-click* of blackout fabric being locked into place.

She said, in a severe voice, "Step inside, if you wish."

He shed his boots, then shut his eyes as he pushed past a layered pair of heavy curtains into an enclosed space made fragrant with a drowsy incense. Her presence was the gravity drawing him in. She wasn't more than two meters from him. He could feel the heat and weight of her, so close at long last.

But first he turned his back and opened his eyes away from her. He had damped down his neural coils and could not even see his hand in front of his face.

She said, "I wondered if you would return from the wheelship. Did you find your honor there?"

"I found a path to follow and a place to stand and people to stand with. That is honor enough. Were you offended, when I asked you to leave that day on the *Huma*?"

"No." Her tone was wry, even self-mocking. "Not at all. I admired it, Kurash. I'm not honest and pure, not like you."

He cleared his throat, so self-conscious he wondered if he could get the words out. But he must. He would not shrink from this task. He owed it to himself and, more than that, he owed it to her. "Dauntless Persephone, do not underestimate yourself. That day on Tjeker you told me I have a choice. When I was Zizou, you were the first person ever to ask what I wanted, not just tell me what I was required to do. So I am come to you to say that I can honorably accept now what you offered on the *Huma*. But there has been a vast span of time and space between us. I do not know if it is still what you wish."

"Oh the hells," she murmured as if choked. She sniffed hard, and he smelled the salt of tears. But only a few.

Hoarsely she said, "Why were you one of the ones chosen to be forced away from your home and sent to the Phene?"

"Lady Chaos chose me. It was my destiny to die to the wheelship and be sent to the worlds beyond."

"'Do we live in harmony with fate or do we suffer powerless in life as fate's demands adhere to a set pattern?' Where is your destiny now, Kurash?"

"Lady Chaos unfolds as She wills. It is not up to us to know. On the wheelships we are taught that we choose in each moment we are alive. That's why those of us who are sent away have to die first. Beyond death, there is no choice."

She made a quiet noise, a soft laugh or a muffled sob. Her murmur might have been meant for her ears alone, or for the universe entire, or maybe it was her challenge to Lady Chaos. "What if I've been looking for answers in all the wrong places? What if all those dark closets were just fate's way of preparing me? Fuck it. I'm in."

He did not move as she walked up behind him. A hand touched his back, a pressure so light and yet as irresistible as the maul of time and chance as it crashes through lives unbidden, unexpected, foreboding, bewildering, miraculous.

97

Sun

She lit the funeral pyre at dawn. The light of the rising star shimmered across the murky, muddy shallows of the denuded sea as if reaching for the leaping flames.

"Behold the cost of victory," Sun proclaimed, a message broadcast to all on-planet, to all in-system, and eventually, by courier, to all the citizens of the republic here and elsewhere and at home. "In battle we kill, and we are killed. We lose both friends and enemies. Many who do not die are irrevocably altered, and none can go back to being what they were before. That is the pledge we make as citizens of the Republic of Chaonia: to offer our lives as our comrades, predecessors, and ancestors did before us. There is no limit to our courage and our strength. Let me tell you of Private Rose Makiadi Alkivu, fresh out of training camp, who died taking out a railgun emplacement that had pinned down her squad. Let me tell you of Lieutenant Commander Zahrah Yún Albalasagun who died in an explosion aboard the *Red Hare* while sealing a breach caused by a Phene boarding action. Let me tell you of Ensign the Honorable Felix Hope, now in command of the indomitable remnant on the *Seker* on its heroic journey across the ocean of space. Let us fulfill our vow to give them an honorable rite of passage."

In answer, the light of other pyres sprang to life across the city, more than anyone would wish, fewer than many had feared. Heat rose, lifting the scent of sandalwood into the heavens. Pumps thumped steadily as a rhythmic accompaniment to the Hymn of Leaving sung by spacers and Guards assembled along the ridge overlooking the drowned city. The line of Chaonian mourners reached all the way to the massive scaffolding being raised at the southern end as combat engineers worked to plug the gaps in the collapsed ruins of Unity Hall.

> *Crossing the ocean of stars we leave our home behind us.*
> *We are the spears cast at the furious heaven*
> *And we will burn one by one into ashes*
> *As with the last sparks we vanish.*
> *This memory we carry to our own death which awaits us*
> *And from which none of us will return.*
> *Do not forget. Goodbye forever.*

She turned toward the Exchange, where representatives of the empire and its syndicates waited. The big building had taken damage but was mostly intact. The Phene had burial customs centered on a funeral procession and involving the interment of a coffin in a family tomb rather than the cremation of a shrouded corpse. At Sun's request and Paulo Kr Manalon's urging, four of the flatbed burial vans had been conveyed to the Exchange's entrance portico. Here, Sun lit a candle and presented a wreath of flowers at each van in honor of the Phene combatants who had died. Subdued admirals, exhausted syndicate presidents, and anxious officials filed past under the alert gaze of the ghost soldiers and the Silver Shields to pay their respects to their new Speaker. Of course, many had fled with the Riders rather than surrender. At least half of the Phene fleets had escaped Anchor System. That was a problem for tomorrow, not for today.

The Shields opened a pathway for her along the processional way between rows of notables from the provinces, most of them lacking the four arms that would mark them as imperial Phene. Their situation was more complicated. Some would prefer Chaonian rule to that of the empire, but it wasn't always clear who was who. These notables she greeted with Nisaba at her shoulder, feeding her the necessary names.

One man pressed forward confidently from this section of the line, ignoring the way the ghost soldiers converged on him. "Sun!"

"Aloysius!" She gestured for her bodyguards to allow him to pass unmolested. "I wondered if I would run into you here."

Baron Voy took both of her hands in his, as would a family member. "I wanted to be the first of the Yele contingent to greet and congratulate you."

"Of course you did. I absolve you of any complicity in Eirene's death."

He feigned a look of startlement, but she could see he was pleased. "I held no personal grudge against Eirene."

"No, I think your grudges are all political. How Yele of you. What is it you want?"

He chuckled. "Direct and to the point, as always. I want negotiations."

"Of course you do. Although I'm not so certain you speak for the League, not anymore. Regardless, I would be delighted to host you for a dinner. Nisaba has my schedule."

"You are generous. You might have been angry."

She smiled, shading her eyes to consider the eastern horizon, then met his gaze again. "The day's not over yet."

He laughed in that equable way she had always admired. He was a diplomat who rarely allowed his feathers to get ruffled, who made the best of any bad situation he found himself in. He knew when to retire gracefully from the fray, as he did now, dropping back among the other Yele.

She continued along the processional way. Spacers and soldiers given commendations by their commanding officers had been brought from all over the system-wide battleground to await her recognition. She spoke to each one, learned their name, went on to the next. Many of the performers who had accompanied the fleet had been tasked with entertaining the wounded and brought here as thanks for their service. They stood by Beau's Fleet Idol contingent but remained silent out of respect for the solemnity of the occasion. Beau stood among his Idol crew with ill-concealed displeasure. He had wanted to film the whole ceremony but Sun had refused. The rest he could have. Not this day, as ephemeral as the wind.

As she neared the bridge that led to the basilica she acknowledged the members of the Chaonian court who had accompanied the fleet or joined it after the route through Karnos was opened. Paulo had found old friends among the chamberlains and officials who were willing to include him in in their midst, seeing he was newly approved of by the queen-marshal. So it ever was and would be in the palace. Bartholomew stood as meek as a lambeosaurus behind his father with an expression as bland as unflavored pudding. How he had gotten so attractive she could not fathom, but then again, she had conquered half the Phene Empire, and who had ever expected that? Perhaps her face got a little hot, glancing at him, but the wind was cool and he knew better than to give any indication of last night's unexpected but satisfying developments.

"Your Highness?" Nisaba broke into her thoughts.

"Is something amiss?" Sun asked, hearing the sharpness of concern in her high secretary's tone.

"You just had an odd expression, Your Highness. But it's gone now."

"The light in my eyes," said Sun easily, moving on.

After the palace officials were assembled officers and marshals, to represent those who remained in the field. At their head, Zàofù leaned on a cane, looking as stubborn as ever. Proud Anas stood beside his father as if ready to confront anyone who did not give the old marshal the respect he deserved.

"I wasn't sure you would make it here," she said, greeting them. "Without your intrepid and indomitable efforts, we would not be standing here today."

"That's right," said Anas. She bristled, but he went on. "The ships under my command never faltered, never gave up. True Chaonians, all of them."

"They were well commanded, Anas," she said, which was truthful enough and also the praise he needed to hear. "Zàofù, how fares the *Red Hare*? I know how you love that ship."

"She's like me, Sun. She may be old and battered, but she will still fight."

"No one but you could have held that beacon."

He accepted the praise without any evidence he desired it. "I do my duty to my beloved republic and to the memory of my comrade, Eirene."

Not to me? she wanted to ask, but her dislike of his phrasing faded against the light of this blessed day. She walked on to the pedestrian bridge that led to the basilica. Here her Companions waited.

James in his cap, rubbing fatigue-stained eyes, and Isis at attention behind him with Wing on her shoulder.

Alika carrying his ukulele case as if it were again part of his uniform and standing with his usual confidence in a job well done. Candace at his back.

Hestia neatly turned out and trying not to smile at a secret, pleasurable thought that certainly wasn't appropriate at such a solemn occasion, not that Sun hadn't just been thinking the same thing minutes ago. She did not wink but Sun could tell she wanted to.

Persephone easy to overlook beside resplendent Tiana.

Doughty Razin. Her cee-cee and Mèimei had remained on duty at the encampment.

Makinde grinning from a wheelchair where he was recovering from his wounds, Dozer draped over his shoulders and pulsing a warm, happy yellow. Sayre smiling like a proud aunt.

Jade Kim with a gaze that measured everything and everyone.

They followed at her heels as she started across the span toward the basilica on its artificial island. Sunlight winked on stretches of standing water separated by hillocks of reef and mounds of drying mud that had once been wholly submerged. The empire was something like the sea known as Fair Water: it had seemed powerful and vast when seen from on high but really the sheen of its surface had disguised the shallowness of its strength.

The Silver Shields and the bodyguards halted on the basilica's portico as the rest entered the vestibule, an enclosed porch whose glass doors let onto the lofty nave beyond. Here she left her Companions, even Hetty.

Alone she pushed through the doors and into the nave, its long vault bathed in an early-morning light that transformed each alcove into a shining tableau with a saint waiting to receive those who needed strength and purpose. But she walked past the saints. She did not need their guidance. From an early age, she had set her face to the heavens and never looked down. Today, this moment, was for her alone.

Kaspar and his parents waited at the far end of the nave. Here, the basilica ended in an empty space called the apse, a place no one could enter because it was shielded by a shimmering curtain of lethal energy. No one, that is, except Riders, who alone could unlock the circuit with their janus faces.

On Tjeker, they had discovered that apses contained hidden lifepods where a Rider might conceal themselves in suspension rather than be

an enemy. Sun did not believe that was the sole purpose of
e basilica was greater than its parts, even if official impe-
sdained belief in a supernatural being of omnipotent and
omnipresent power.

Kaspar was fifteen now, a stoutly built and tall boy who swung
between enthusiasm and guardedness. "It's all like I saw before," he
greeted her excitedly, then frowned, remembering that it wasn't *he* who
had seen. It was his Rider.

His cap was already off, held in his mother's hand. At Sun's nod,
Vontae and Nanea retreated to an alcove, although they kept their
gazes turned protectively toward the scene.

Kaspar sighed as Sun walked around him in order to greet Qíshì.
The Rider rarely spoke, and never to her. The bizarre sketch of a face
wore a suspicious, apprehensive expression, gaze darting from side to
side as if looking for the knitted cap that could be pulled down over its
face at any instant without warning or consent.

"Qíshì, I greet you. If any of the Rider Council can hear me, I offer
you amnesty. Any Rider who surrenders into my keeping will be given
a safe harbor."

She didn't expect an answer. None of the researchers were even sure
Qíshì could actively communicate with other Riders. How would the
youth ever have learned? Nor did they know if the other Riders could
see through Qíshì's eyes. But if they could, they would witness with her
now, her only audience beyond the boy and his anxious parents. Let
them witness. Let them understand her, if they thought they could keep
fighting her and win.

She walked back around to Kaspar. "Is it all just as you saw it in your
mind?"

"It is! So magnificent! Except for the battle damage, I mean. I feel
bad for the people in the city who got flooded out. Will they get their
homes back?"

"They will."

"That's good." He grinned, as if this news lightened his burden
enough that he could go back to being thrilled to be here. "I never
thought I'd get to see the processional way and all its statues!"

"You will have time to explore."

"We're going to stay here?"

"For now. And we have captured two Riders for you to meet."

His eyes got very big and his mouth dropped open. "Really?" he murmured in a tone of hopeful awe. "Do you think they'll be nice to me?"

"I hear one is a girl about your age."

The comment struck him speechless. Qíshì whispered but she

couldn't make out any words and she wasn't going to ask. She gestured toward the curtain. Kaspar had opened every other basilica apse they'd encountered on the campaign, but alas they had found no more hidden Riders. And why would they? The Riders now knew she had the means and the knowledge to look for them there.

He stepped sideways into the energy field, a face looking in each direction for the circuit to read. An unseen mechanism clicked. The curtain vanished. She walked into the apse. The floor beneath her feet took on a muted glow, as if in her honor. She waited for a cylinder to rise but nothing moved. Maybe it was more deeply hidden, or maybe the Grand Basilica on Anchor Prime held no secret safe room. Maybe it held something else she was looking for.

She turned and from the height of the apse looked down the nave as into history, what the figures of the saints meant for humankind, how people were led out of disaster and collapse. As a place of worship, a basilica was in its way a great ship that held millions of souls in a sheltering embrace.

From behind her, higher up in the spire that rose above the apse, sunlight refracted through the lower of a pair of eight-sided windows. A convex lens converged the light so it appeared to coalesce near the vestibule, like an entity venturing to enter the nave. The brilliance spun together until it resembled a pillar of flame. Was that an insubstantial form dancing in its center? She heard the Oracle's voice as if the churning of the Gyre had traveled with her all this way.

A person who commands all the worlds can do greater work yet.

How long she stared she did not know, only that the light rose yet higher and passed out of the lens, and the pillar of flame vanished. The nave still shone with different patterns of light, illuminated by the promise of morning, but she felt the Oracle's absence keenly. She turned to face east, where the day rose, and tilted her head back to look up the towering front wall of the basilica's spire, like a prow cutting through the ocean of space. The Celestial Emperor had embarked in just this way, had she not? Knowing she must lead where others feared to go.

Above the convex window was a second window, this one concave. The light that caught in it was scattered outward and, by some mechanism she could not perceive, it cast her vision into space. Perhaps the lens linked to a camera on an orbital habitat or to a satellite drifting at the heliopause. Perhaps it was the Oracle's doing, connected to an ancient Argosy technology woven into the basilica's structure whether the builders had known it or not.

For there, beyond the bright basilica, beyond the sea and the shore, beyond the atmosphere where ships patrolled and beyond the habitats and the prowling fleets, beyond the planets as they sped in their orbits as in a vast orrery, beyond even that. The beacons linking one system to another. The Argosy fleets on their slow, swift routes. The abandoned planets where a remnant survived however they might or vanished one by one into oblivion. The barque of history. The invisible wings of that which has not yet come to pass. Lives lived, lost, forgotten amid stars which themselves would live, die, and dissipate in the hall of eternity.

She had won something, it was true. But it wasn't enough. How could it be enough?

"Sun."

The sound of her name yanked her back to the mundane pavement, spoken by the only voice that could have reached her. Blinking as her vision shifted away from the lens, she turned. Hetty stood outside the apse, watching her not so much with caution as with the clear-sighted gaze of a person who does not pretend things are otherwise than they are.

"You have stood there so long, over an hour. Poor Kaspar's father came to ask my help. He feared you might be mesmerized."

"I'm not!"

Hetty's smile was balm. "Of course you aren't, dear Sun. But Kas must also stand there while you do, and I daresay the boy would like a break."

Sun had forgotten him. He stood rigid, afraid to move lest the curtain slam shut and kill her beneath a lethal blanket of energy. The strain was showing in his eyes.

"Of course." She let go of the vision and walked out of the apse.

With a sigh of relief he stepped away. The shimmering curtain sizzled back into place. He retreated into his parents' embrace, and they hustled him toward the vestibule and hurried out as if trying to escape Kaspar's inescapable destiny. Even so, was he truly bound to a set path or did people bind themselves by refusing to break through what they thought was expected of them or what they believed was attainable? Surely even the Riders had become what they were now because of myriad incremental choices made by those who came before.

Sun remained standing on the step poised between the nave and the apse, between the past and future, between that which she held and that which had not yet fallen into her grasp.

She spoke, although not precisely to Hetty, maybe to the Oracle whose presence she could no longer see but which she felt like fire in her flesh. "I cannot live in harmony with fate. I am the spear cast at the furious heaven."

"Of course you are, dear Sun. But even you . . ." Because they were alone, Hetty closed the gap between them to take Sun's hands in hers with the intimate touch of one who shares a soul with her beloved, palm to palm and fingers intertwined. To anchor Sun as if to keep her from spinning too fast until she burned away into ashes. "But even you must eat, must drink, must sleep. Must take a breath of this sweet air. Slow down. Tomorrow will come soon enough, I vow."

Sun kissed her as both promise and seal, then released her hand and started down the nave, picking up speed as she approached its doors onto a world that awaited her presence.

ACKNOWLEDGMENTS

Huge thanks to the amazing folks at Tor Books, because it takes a team to make a book: Miriam Weinberg, Tessa Villanueva, Jocelyn Bright, Jim Kapp, Christina MacDonald, Hayley Jozwiak, Ryan Jenkins, Natassja Haught, Lauren Levite, Peter Lutjen, Caroline Perny, Heather Saunders, Jamie Stafford-Hill, Renata Sweeney, and Devi Pillai.

My utmost thanks to my beta readers and expert consultants: Jeanne Reames, Petty Officer First Class Alexander M. Rasmussen-Silverstein, Tade Thompson, fashion advisor M. L. Brennan, Vida Cruz, and Ken Liu. Amanda Weinstein came up with the concept for the knnu drive bubble so naturally I named it after her; you're the best, Amanda. Big thank yous to Haviva Avirom and Josh Smolow for their respective contributions to Persephone's reading list. If I missed thanking you (yes, you!), my sincerest apologies; it's been a long haul and I didn't keep notes as well as I ought to have done. As always, all mistakes and infelicities are my own. So much gratitude to my Patreon patrons whose support has been crucial to my ability to work. Special shout-out to my friends and my writing group for having my back when I needed it (you know who you are and what you did), and of course to my wonderful children and their partners for always being there.